THE DARK LORD TRILOGY

STAR WARS

THE DARK LORD TRILOGY

LEGENDS

LABYRINTH OF EVIL
JAMES LUCENO

REVENGE OF THE SITH™
MATTHEW STOVER

BASED ON THE STORY AND SCREENPLAY BY GEORGE LUCAS

LEGENDS

DARK LORD
THE RISE OF DARTH VADER
JAMES LUCENO

DEL REY
NEW YORK

A Del Rey Books Trade Paperback Original

Star Wars: Labyrinth of Evil copyright © 2005
by Lucasfilm Ltd. & ® or ™ where indicated.

Star Wars: Episode III *Revenge of the Sith* copyright © 2005
by Lucasfilm Ltd. & ® or ™ where indicated.

Star Wars: Dark Lord: The Rise of Darth Vader copyright © 2005
by Lucasfilm Ltd. & ® or ™ where indicated.

All Rights Reserved. Used Under Authorization.

Published in the United States by Del Rey Books,
an imprint of The Random House Publishing Group,
a division of Random House, Inc., New York.

The stories contained in this work were
originally published separately as follows:

Star Wars: Labyrinth of Evil was originally published
in hardcover in the United States by Del Rey Books,
an imprint of The Random House Publishing Group,
a division of Random House, Inc., in 2005.

Star Wars: Episode III *Revenge of the Sith* was originally published
in hardcover in the United States by Del Rey Books,
an imprint of The Random House Publishing Group,
a division of Random House, Inc., in 2005.

Star Wars: Dark Lord: The Rise of Darth Vader was originally
published in hardcover in the United States by Del Rey Books,
an imprint of The Random House Publishing Group,
a division of Random House, Inc., in 2005.

DEL REY is a registered trademark and the Del Rey colophon
is a trademark of Random House, Inc.

ISBN 978-0-345-48538-0

Printed in the United States of America

www.starwars.com
www.delreybooks.com

11th Printing

A LONG TIME AGO IN A GALAXY FAR, FAR AWAY....

LABYRINTH OF EVIL

JAMES LUCENO

For my loving aunt and uncle
Rosemary and Joe Savoca
And for my earliest mentors,
Pat Mathison, who was forever urging me
to tell him stories,
and Richard Thomas, who introduced me
to science fiction,
Ian Fleming, and Thomas Pynchon

ACKNOWLEDGMENTS

Heartfelt thanks to Shelly Shapiro, Sue Rostoni, and Howard Roffman, for remaining in my corner throughout this project; to George Lucas, for responding to my many queries; to Matt Stover, for providing additional material and creative inspiration; to Dan Wallace, for sending me an early version of his Prequel Era chronology; to Haden Blackman, for graciously yielding some of the Big Moments; to the staff of the Hotel Casona, in Flores, Guatemala, for keeping the espressos coming; and to Karen-Ann and Jake, for granting me the time and space to daydream.

Darkness was encroaching on Cato Neimoidia's western hemisphere, though exchanges of coherent light high above the beleaguered world ripped looming night to shreds. Well under the fractured sky, in an orchard of manax trees that studded the lower ramparts of Viceroy Gunray's majestic redoubt, companies of clone troopers and battle droids were slaughtering one another with bloodless precision.

A flashing fan of blue energy lit the undersides of a cluster of trees: the lightsaber of Obi-Wan Kenobi.

Attacked by two sentry droids, Obi-Wan stood his ground, twisting his upraised blade right and left to swat blaster bolts back at his enemies. Caught midsection by their own salvos, both droids came apart, with a scattering of alloy limbs.

Obi-Wan moved again.

Tumbling under the segmented thorax of a Neimoidian harvester beetle, he sprang to his feet and raced forward. Explosive light shunted from the citadel's deflector shield dappled the loamy ground between the trees, casting long shadows of their buttressed trunks. Oblivious to the chaos occurring in their midst, columns of the five-meter-long harvesters continued their stal-

wart march toward a mound that supported the fortress. In their
cutting jaws or on their upsweeping backs they carried cargoes of
pruned foliage. The crushing sounds of their ceaseless gnawing
provided an eerie cadence to the rumbling detonations and the
hiss and whine of blaster bolts.

From off to Obi-Wan's left came a sudden click of servos; to
his right, a hushed cry of warning.

"Down, Master!"

He dropped into a crouch even before Anakin's lips formed
the final word, lightsaber aimed to the ground to keep from impaling his onrushing former Padawan. A blur of thrumming blue
energy sizzled through the humid air, followed by a sharp smell
of cauterized circuitry, the tang of ozone. A blaster discharged
into soft soil, then the stalked, elongated head of a battle droid
struck the ground not a meter from Obi-Wan's feet, sparking as
it bounced and rolled out of sight, repeating: *"Roger, roger . . .
Roger, roger . . ."*

In a tuck, Obi-Wan pivoted on his right foot in time to see
the droid's spindly body collapse. The fact that Anakin had saved
his life was nothing new, but Anakin's blade had passed a little
too close for comfort. Eyes somewhat wide with surprise, he came
to his feet.

"You nearly took my head off."

Anakin held his blade to one side. In the strobing light of
battle his blue eyes shone with wry amusement. "Sorry, Master,
but your head was where my lightsaber needed to go."

Master.

Anakin used the honorific not as learner to teacher, but as
Jedi Knight to Jedi Council member. The braid that had defined
his earlier status had been ritually severed after his audacious actions at Praesitlyn. His tunic, knee-high boots, and tight-fitting
trousers were as black as the night. His face scarred from a
contest with Dooku-trained Asajj Ventress. His mechanical right
hand sheathed in an elbow-length glove. He had let his hair grow

long the past few months, falling almost to his shoulders now. His face he kept clean-shaven, unlike Obi-Wan, whose strong jaw was defined by a short beard.

"I suppose I should be grateful your lightsaber *needed* to go there, rather than desired to."

Anakin's grin blossomed into a full-fledged smile. "Last time I checked we were on the same side, Master."

"Still, if I'd been a moment slower . . ."

Anakin booted the battle droid's blaster aside. "Your fears are only in your mind."

Obi-Wan scowled. "Without a head I wouldn't have much mind left, now, would I?" He swept his lightsaber in a flourishing pass, nodding up the alley of manax trees. "After you."

They resumed their charge, moving with the supernatural speed and grace afforded by the Force, Obi-Wan's brown cloak swirling behind him. Victims of the initial bombardment, scores of battle droids lay sprawled on the ground. Others dangled like broken marionettes from the branches of the trees into which they had been hurled.

Areas of the leafy canopy were in flames.

Two scorched droids little more than arms and torsos lifted their weapons as the Jedi approached, but Anakin only raised his left hand in a Force push that shoved the droids flat onto their backs.

They jinked right, somersaulting under the wide bodies of two harvester beetles, then hurdling a tangle of barbed underbrush that had managed to anchor itself in the otherwise meticulously tended orchard. They emerged from the tree line at the shore of a broad irrigation canal, fed by a lake that delimited the Neimoidians' citadel on three sides. In the west a trio of wedge-shaped *Venator*-class assault cruisers hung in scudding clouds. North and east the sky was in turmoil, crosshatched with ion trails, turbolaser beams, hyphens of scarlet light streaming upward from weapons emplacements outside the citadel's energy shield. Rising from high ground at the end of the peninsula, the tiered fastness was reminiscent of the command towers of the Trade Federation core ships, and indeed had been the inspiration for them.

Somewhere inside, trapped by Republic forces, were the Trade Federation elite.

With his homeworld threatened and the purse worlds of Deko and Koru Neimoidia devastated, Viceroy Gunray would have been wiser to retreat to the Outer Rim, as other members of the Separatist Council were thought to be doing. But rational thinking had never been a Neimoidian strong suit, especially when possessions remained on Cato Neimoidia the viceroy apparently couldn't live without. Backed by a battle group of Federation warships, he had slipped onto Cato Neimoidia, intent on looting the citadel before it fell. But Republic forces had been lying in wait, eager to capture him alive and bring him to justice—thirteen years late, in the judgment of many.

Cato Neimoidia was as close to Coruscant as Obi-Wan and Anakin had been in almost four standard months, and with the last remaining Separatist strongholds now cleared from the Core and Colonies, they expected to be back in the Outer Rim by week's end.

Obi-Wan heard movement on the far side of the irrigation canal.

An instant later, four clone troopers crept from the tree line on the opposite bank to take up firing positions amid the water-smoothed rocks that lined the ditch. Far behind them a crashed gunship was burning. Protruding from the canopy, the LAAT's blunt tail was stenciled with the eight-rayed battle standard of the Galactic Republic.

A gunboat glided into view from downstream, maneuvering to where the Jedi were waiting. Standing in the bow, a clone commander named Cody waved hand signals to the troopers on shore and to others in the gunboat, who immediately fanned out to create a safe perimeter.

Troopers could communicate with one another through the comlinks built into their T-visored helmets, but the Advanced Recon Commando teams had created an elaborate system of gestures meant to thwart enemy attempts at eavesdropping.

A few nimble leaps brought Cody face-to-face with Obi-Wan and Anakin.

"Sirs, I have the latest from airborne command."

"Show us," Anakin said.

Cody dropped to one knee, his right hand activating a device built into his left wrist gauntlet. A cone of blue light emanated from the device, and a hologram of task force commander Dodonna resolved.

"Generals Kenobi and Skywalker, provincial recon unit reports that Viceroy Gunray and his entourage are making their way to the north side of the redoubt. Our forces have been hammering at the shield from above and from points along the shore, but the shield generator is in a hardened site, and difficult to get at. Gunships are taking heavy fire from turbolaser cannons in the lower ramparts. If your team is still committed to taking Gunray alive, you're going to have to skirt those defenses and find an alternative way into the palace. At this point we cannot reinforce, repeat, cannot reinforce."

Obi-Wan looked at Cody when the hologram had faded. "Suggestions, Commander?"

Cody made an adjustment to the wrist projector, and a 3-D schematic of the redoubt formed in midair. "Assuming that Gunray's fortress is similar to what we found on Deko and Koru, the underground levels will contain fungus farms and processing and shipment areas. There will be access from the shipping areas into the midlevel grub hatcheries, and from the hatcheries we'll be able to infiltrate the upper reaches."

Cody carried a short-stocked DC-15 blaster rifle and wore the white armor and imaging system helmet that had come to symbolize the Grand Army of the Republic—grown, nurtured, and trained on the remote world of Kamino, three years earlier. Just now, though, areas of white showed only where there were no smears of mud or dried blood, no gouges, abrasions, or charred patches. Cody's position was designated by orange markings on his helmet crest and shoulder guards. His upper right arm bore stripes signifying campaigns in which he had participated: Aagonar, Praesitlyn, Paracelus Minor, Antar 4, Tibrin, Skor II, and dozens of other worlds from Core to Outer Rim.

Over the years Obi-Wan had formed battlefield partnerships with several Advanced Recon Commandos—Alpha, with whom he had been imprisoned on Rattatak, and Jangotat, on Ord Cestus. Early-generation ARCs had received training by the Mandalorian clone template, Jango Fett. While the Kaminoans had managed to breed some of Fett out of the regulars, they had been more selective in the case of the ARCs. As a consequence, ARCs displayed more individual initiative and leadership abilities. In short, they were more like the late bounty hunter himself, which was to say, more *human*. While Cody wasn't genetically an Advanced Recon Commando, he had ARC training and shared many ARC attributes.

In the initial stages of the war, clone troopers were treated no differently from the war machines they piloted or the weapons they fired. To many they had more in common with battle droids poured by the tens of thousands from Baktoid Armor Workshops on a host of Separatist-held worlds. But attitudes began to shift as more and more troopers died. The clones' unfaltering dedication to the Republic, and to the Jedi, showed them to be true comrades in arms, and deserving of all the respect and compassion they were now afforded. It was the Jedi themselves, in addition to other progressive thinking officials in the Republic, who had urged that second- and third-generation troopers be given names rather than numbers, to foster a growing fellowship.

"I agree that we can probably reach the upper levels, Commander," Obi-Wan said at last. "But how do you propose we reach the fungus farms to begin with?"

Cody stood to his full height and pointed toward the orchards. "We go in with the harvesters."

Obi-Wan glanced uncertainly at Anakin and motioned him off to one side.

"It's just the two of us. What do you think?"

"I think you worry too much, Master."

Obi-Wan folded his arms across his chest. "And who'll worry about you if I don't?"

Anakin canted his head and grinned. "There are others."

"You can only be referring to See-Threepio. And you had to *build* him."

"Think what you will."

Obi-Wan narrowed his eyes with purpose. "Oh, I see. But I would have thought Senator Amidala of greater interest to you than Supreme Chancellor Palpatine." Before Anakin could respond, he added: "Despite that she's a politician also."

"Don't think I haven't tried to attract her interest, Master."

Obi-Wan regarded Anakin for a moment. "What's more, if Chancellor Palpatine had genuine concern for your welfare, he would have kept you closer to Coruscant."

Anakin placed his artificial hand on Obi-Wan's left shoulder. "Perhaps, Master. But then, who would look after you?"

Despite their two pairs of powerful legs and the saw-toothed pincers that extended from their lower mandibles, the broad-bodied harvesters were single-minded creatures, complaisant except when threatened directly. From their flat heads sprouted looping antennae, which served not only as feelers, but also as organs of communication, by means of powerful phero-mones. Each beetle was capable of carrying five times its considerable weight in foliage and branches. Similar to the Neimoidians who had domesticated them, their society was hierarchical, and included laborers, harvesters, soldiers, and breeders, all of whom served a distant queen that rewarded effort with food.

Obi-Wan, Anakin, and the commandos who made up Squad Seven had to run to keep up with the beetles as they hurried their fresh-picked loads from the orchard to the cave-like entrance to a natural mound at the base of the redoubt. The beetles' cara-paces afforded them cover from surveillance sorties by battle droid STAP patrols. More important, the harvesters knew safe routes through mined stretches of cleared ground that separated the trees from the fortress itself.

The beetles' frequent habit of lowering their heads to exchange information with hivemates moving in the opposite direction demanded that the Jedi and troopers keep between the harvesters' rear legs. Hunched over, Obi-Wan ran with his lightsaber in hand but deactivated. As the shielded royal residence came into view, a certain uneasiness seemed to take hold of the creatures, disrupting the ordered nature of their columns. Obi-Wan suspected that outbound beetles were relaying accounts of potential perils to the nest posed by the Republic's unrelenting barrage. In response to the crisis, soldier beetles were joining the procession, quick to shepherd nervous strays back into line.

Anakin's greater height required him to remain farther back, almost directly under the beetle's pug tail. To Obi-Wan's right ran Cody, with his teammates trailing behind and flanking him.

Soldier beetles or no, discipline was breaking down fast.

A harvester providing cover for one of the commandos veered from the column before it could be guided back into line. Instead of hurrying under another beetle, the commando stuck with the stray, and quickly found himself out in open ground.

Obi-Wan felt a ripple in the Force an instant before the harvester's right foreleg tripped a land mine.

A potent explosion fountained from the rocky ground, blowing away half the creature's foreleg. The commando threw himself to one side, rolling out from under a trio now of pounding legs, only to have to bob and weave as the harvester began to run in frantic circles, seemingly determined to trample the commando underfoot. A glancing blow from the beetle's left rear leg tipped the commando off his feet. Confused, the harvester lowered its head and butted at the hard white object in its path, again and again, until there wasn't a smooth area left in the commando's armor.

The harvester's distress was having an impact on the rest of the beetles, as well.

While most were pressed tightly together, others were suddenly scurrying away from the main column, sending the soldier beetles to high alert. Tripping two mines in succession, a second harvester was lifted off the ground by the ensuing explosions. With that, the column dissolved into disorder, with harvesters and soldiers running every which way, and commandos and Jedi alike doing their best to protect themselves.

"Stay close to the ones who are still headed for the nest!" Anakin shouted.

Obi-Wan was doing just that when he noticed that the trampled commando was back on his feet and staggering toward him, tapping the side of his helmet with the palm of his gloved hand, and obviously indifferent to where he placed his booted feet. Barreling straight for the maw of the mound, a harvester bore down on the commando, clamping its pincers around his waist, then lifting him high into the air. Summoning the last of his reserves, the commando twisted his body back and forth, but was unable to break free.

All at once Anakin was out from under his protective harvester.

Lightsaber tight in his gloved hand, he bounded across the denuded landscape toward the captive commando, the Force guiding him to safe landings among the mines. The harvesters might have taken him for a demented turfjumper were they not so fixed on safeguarding their loads and reaching the security of the nest.

Anakin's final leap dropped him directly in front of the harvester that had seized the commando. With one upward stroke of his lightsaber he rid the beetle of its pincers, freeing the commando, but also sending the soldier beetles into a frenzy. Obi-Wan could almost smell the pheromone release, and decipher the information being exchanged: *The area is rife with predators!*

From the brood rose a shriek so high-pitched as to be barely audible, and a stampede was under way. Mines began to detonate to all sides, and out from billowing smoke above the orchard canopy swarmed more than a hundred STAPs.

A Neimoidian version of the agile repulsorlift airhook used as an observation vehicle throughout the galaxy, each Single Trooper Aerial Platform was equipped with twin blasters that delivered more firepower than the stubby-barreled models carried by infantry droids.

From maximum range the swarm rained energy bolts on everything in sight, dropping harvesters in their tracks and turning the rocky ground into a killing field. Explosions erupted in jagged lines as scores of mines were detonated. Supporting the commando trooper with his left arm, Anakin warded off blaster bolts on the run. The rest of Squad Seven supplied cover, blowing STAPs out the sky with uninterrupted fire.

Cody motioned everyone into a shallow irrigation trench just short of the mound. By the time Obi-Wan arrived, the troopers were deployed in a circle, and continuing to pour fire into the sky. Anakin slid into the trench a moment later, lowering the commando gently to the muddy slope. Squad Seven's medical specialist crawled over, removing the commando's ravaged utility belt and deeply dented helmet.

Obi-Wan gazed at the face of the injured clone.

A face he would never forget; now a face he *couldn't* forget.

All these years later, he could still recall his brief conversation with Jango Fett, on Kamino. He glanced at Cody and the rest. *An army of one man . . . But the right man for the job.*

The clones' rallying cry.

The injured commando had already prompted his armor to inject him with painkillers, so he remained pliant while his chest plastron was removed and the black bodyglove undergarment knifed open. The harvester's pincers had crushed the armor into the commando's abdomen. His skin was intact, but the bruising was severe.

With only half the original army of 1.2 million in fighting shape, the life of every clone was vital. Blood and replacement organs—what the regular troopers referred to as "spare parts"—

were readily available—"easily requisitioned"—but with the war reaching a crescendo, battlefield casualties were on the rise and treated as high priority.

"Not much I can do for him here," the medspec told Anakin. "Maybe if we can get an FX-Seven air-dropped—"

"We don't need a droid," Anakin interrupted. Kneeling, he placed his hands on the injured commando's abdomen and used a Jedi healing technique to keep the clone from going into deep shock.

A sudden noise from above caught everyone's attention.

Scores of boulder-sized objects were spewing from openings in the lower ramparts of the fortress. Cody pressed a pair of macrobinoculars to his eyes and gazed upward.

"That's no ordinary avalanche," he said, passing the glasses to Obi-Wan.

Obi-Wan raised the glasses and waited for the lens to autofocus.

Rolling toward the trench at better than eighty kilometers per hour were some of the most feared of the Separatists' infantry arsenal.

Droidekas.

Known also by the fearsome title *destroyer droids,* droidekas were rapid-deployment killing machines produced by an alien species that encouraged mayhem at every opportunity. A combination of sheer momentum and sequenced microrepulsors allowed the bronzium-armored droids to roll like balls then unfurl in a blink as tripoded gunfighters, shielded by individual deflectors and armed with paired, twin-barreled, high-output blasters.

Since the shields were powerful enough to resist lightsabers, blasters, even light artillery bolts, the proven strategy for dealing with droidekas was simply to run from them.

More so, because surrender was never an option.

But Anakin had another idea.

"Comm fire support for an artillery strike," he ordered Cody, loud enough to be heard above STAP and DC-15 fire. "Do it now."

Cody was more than willing to comply. After all, the order had come directly from "the Hero with no Fear," as Anakin was sometimes known. "The Warrior of the Infinite." There was, though, a chain of command to maintain, so Cody looked to Obi-Wan for confirmation.

Obi-Wan nodded. "Do as he says."

The commando called for his comm specialist, who splashed through the shallow water and flattened himself alongside Cody. When the spec had provided needed coordinates, Cody opened a frequency to the fire support base and spoke in a rush.

"To FSB from Squad Seven. We're taking continuous fire from STAPs in sector Jenth-Bacta-Ion, and are about to be buried under destroyer droids deployed from the redoubt. Request immediate artillery support at coordinates accompanying transmission. Recommend tactical electromagnetic pulse airburst, followed by SPHA-T barrage."

"Pulse weapons don't discriminate, Commander," Obi-Wan thought to point out.

Cody shrugged. "It's the only way, sir."

"Tell them we've got a wounded trooper for the Rimsoo," Anakin said. The term stood for "Republic Mobile Surgical Unit."

Cody relayed the message. "Warn the evac pilot that he'll be setting down in a hot area. We'll mark a safe landing zone with smoke, and leave two behind to assist."

The assistant squad leader moved his right hand through a series of gestures. When the gestures had been repeated down the line, the commandos removed their helmets and began to deactivate the electronic systems built into their armor.

To a clone, they hunkered down in the fetid water.

A screaming came from the south.

Then: a nova-bright flare of white light, followed two seconds later by a roar that turned Obi-Wan's eardrums to mush. A shock wave spread from the ramparts, down onto the clear ground at the foot of the mound and out over the already blazing orchards. Above the trench, half the droidekas deployed prematurely from ball position and began to tumble down the slope in a tangle of limbs and weapons. Behind the trench, STAPs fell like stones, plunging from the sky into the burning trees.

What harvesters remained alive ran in dizzying circles, spilling their precious loads.

Now from the south came an infernal wail as SPHA-Ts—the Republic's walking artillery—loosed lasers on those droidekas that had survived the pulse weapon. Deprived of shields and unable to fire, they melted like wax in the gushes of radiant energy that struck the slopes.

Still without helmet, Cody stood up, signaling with both hands.

Obi-Wan interpreted the gestures: *Sixty count, then suit up and break for the entrance to the nest.*

He prepared by calming himself.

For all their reliance on droids, for all their infatuation with high technology, for all their inborn cowardice, greed, and guile, Neimoidians had a soft spot for their youth—their seven formative years as grubs, struggling for limited food in communal hives, discovering early on the benefits of duplicity and self-regard. The fungus foodstuff of those early years was as dear to them as adults as it was to them as hatchlings, and no wonder, since it was that same fungus that had found favor with species galaxywide, and from which the Neimoidians had evolved into a wealthy, spacefaring society, with ships enough to attract the eye of the notorious Trade Federation and, ultimately, droids enough to equal an army.

It would have been natural to assume that the fungus—prized for its medicinal as well as nutritional value—was somehow concocted from manax foliage gathered by the harvesters. But in fact the leaves and branches provided little more than a growth medium. Enzymes produced by the beetles, coupled with the dank conditions within the burrows and grottoes of the nest mounds, encouraged the rapid growth of a product that required only a modicum of refinement to become palatable.

Elsewhere during the sieges of Deko and Koru Neimoidia,

Obi-Wan had never visited a fungus farm, but no sooner had he and Anakin dashed through the cavelike opening to the nest than the briefings he had received more than ten standard years earlier came back to him in a flash.

Here were the partly masticated leaves, carefully arranged in layers; the clumps of branches and other impurities; the laborer beetles; the droid overseers; the conveyors and similar contraptions devoted to sorting and transport . . . Not a Neimoidian in sight, but that was consistent with their doctrine that exertion of any sort was anathema. In the deep recesses of the mound, untouched by sunlight, the starter fungi—molds, mildews, and sickly-white mushrooms—would be undergoing treatments with natural and synthetic growth-acceleration agents. And higher up, in what constituted the basement of the citadel, the matured end product was probably being consumed by grubs, or packed and readied for shipment.

Cody ordered the squad to secure the area. Those in the rear were still taking sporadic fire from STAPs, but the droid pilots couldn't get close to the entrance because of the bodies of dead beetles piled outside.

Squad Seven's medspec hurried over to Obi-Wan and Anakin.

"Sirs, I recommend you keep your rebreathers close at hand. Odds are we won't have to penetrate any deeper into the nest, but there's always a chance of encountering free-floating spores in other areas."

Obi-Wan quirked his brows together. "Toxic, Sergeant?"

"No, sir. But the spores have been known to have an adverse effect on humans."

"Adverse how?" Anakin asked.

"The effect is most often described as 'dislocating,' sir."

Obi-Wan glanced at Anakin. "Then I suggest we do as he says."

The fingers of his left hand were prizing the small, twin-tanked rebreather from its pouch on his utility belt when a volley of blaster bolts streaked into the grotto. Caught in their upper chests, two troopers were knocked off their feet.

The source of the sudden fire was the mouth of a narrow side tunnel that could be sealed by an overhead door. Anakin was already racing for the tunnel, lightsaber gripped in both hands, deflecting most of the bolts back through the entrance.

Obi-Wan leapt to one side, raising his blade to deal with two bolts that got past Anakin. The first he returned toward its source; the second, he parried at a deliberately downward angle. Striking the grotto's hard-packed floor, the deflected bolt ricocheted to one wall, then to the ceiling, to the other wall, and back to the floor, from which it caromed squarely into the control panel that operated the tunnel door.

Showering sparks, the device shorted out, and a slab of thick alloy dropped from its pocket in the wall, sealing the tunnel with a loud *thud!*

Switching off his lightsaber, Anakin cast a complimentary glance over his shoulder.

"Nicely done, Master."

"The beauty of Form Three," Obi-Wan said with theatrical nonchalance. "You should try it sometime."

"You've always been better at evasion than I have," Anakin said. "I prefer more straightforward tactics."

Obi-Wan rolled his eyes. "Master of understatement."

"General Kenobi," the comm spec said from across the grotto. "Provincial recon reports that Viceroy Gunray and his entourage are heading for the launching bays. They're protected by super battle droids, a group of which are now closing on our position."

Anakin swung to Obi-Wan. "One of us has to divert the droids."

"One of us," Obi-Wan repeated. "Haven't we been through this before?"

"The beauty of our partnership, Master. You lure the body-guards away, I capture Gunray. It hasn't failed us yet, has it?"

Obi-Wan compressed his lips. "From a certain point of view, Anakin."

Anakin scowled. "Fine. Then I'll be the bait this time."

"That makes no sense," Obi-Wan said quickly, shaking his head. "We play to our separate strengths."

Anakin couldn't restrain a smile. "I knew you'd listen to reason, Master." He singled out four commandos. "You'll come with me."

"Sir!" they said in unison.

Obi-Wan, Cody, and the rest of Squad Seven set out for the turbolift shafts. Obi-Wan hadn't gone five meters when he stopped and swung around.

"Anakin, I know we've got a score to settle with Gunray, but don't make it personal. We want to take him *alive*!"

Oh, but it is personal, Anakin told himself while he watched Obi-Wan, Cody, and four troopers disappear into the turbolift.

It was personal because of what Nute Gunray had done to Naboo thirteen years ago.

It was personal because of Gunray's hiring of Jango Fett to assassinate Padmé three years ago—first with a bomb planted on her ship, then with the pair of kouhuns a changling had inserted into Padmé's Senatorial quarters on Coruscant.

The woman Anakin loved above all else. *His wife.* The deepest though brightest of his secrets. Even Obi-Wan didn't know, for that would have created problems.

Finally, it was personal because of all that had occurred on Geonosis: the mock trial, the sentencing, the executions that were to have taken place in the arena . . .

Even if he could put all that aside, as Obi-Wan plainly wanted him to do, it was personal because Gunray had aligned himself with Dooku and the Separatists, and the war they had planned from the start had brought ruin to a thousand worlds.

The deaths of the Separatist leaders was the only solution

now. It had always been the solution, despite objections by certain members of the Jedi Council, who still believed in peaceful resolutions. Despite the Senate's attempts to bind the hands of Supreme Chancellor Palpatine, so that corrupt politicians could continue to turn a profit. Line the pockets of their shimmersilk cloaks with kickbacks from the immoral corporations that funded the war machine. Supplying both sides with weapons, ships, whatever was needed to extend the conflict.

It made Anakin's blood boil.

Yes, just as Yoda had sensed after Qui-Gon Jinn and Obi-Wan had freed him from slavery on Tatooine and brought him to the Jedi Temple, he had a lot of anger in him. But what Yoda failed to realize was that anger could be a kind of fuel. In peaceful times Anakin might have been able to bridle his rage, but now he relied on it to drive him forward, to transform him into the person he needed to be.

Cut off the head.

Twice he might have been able to kill Dooku himself had Obi-Wan not held him back. But he didn't hold that against his former Master. For all his skills, Anakin still looked to Obi-Wan for guidance.

On occasion.

As he and the four troopers were exiting the grotto, the tip of his boot sent some object skittering across the floor. On the fly he used the Force to call the thing to his left hand and realized that it was Obi-Wan's rebreather, which must have fallen from its utility pouch during the brief exchange with the unseen battle droids. But no matter; Obi-Wan was probably already in the lower levels of the redoubt, where there would be little need for the device.

Opening one of the pouches on his belt, Anakin wedged the rebreather inside.

He urged the troopers on, and they stayed close on his heels. Upward: following burrows, ramps, and shafts used only by droids. Through processing and shipment areas, through hatcheries filled with squealing grubs. Upward: into the citadel's gleaming middle levels. Through rooms large as starship docking bays filled floor to ceiling with . . . *stuff*. A boundless collection of junk, ritual gifts, impulsive purchases. Thousands of faddish devices never to be used but too prized as possessions to be thrown out, donated, handed down, or destroyed. More technology than existed on entire worlds, hoarded, stacked, piled about, crammed into every available space.

Anakin could only shake his head in wonder. In Mos Espa, on Tatooine, he and his mother had lived simply, and never wanted for anything.

His grin was short-lived.

Anger and despair made him grit his teeth.

Upward: until they reached the citadel's semicircular projection of launching bays, which overlooked the surrounding lake and a ridge of forested mountains.

Anakin brought his team to a halt. One of the commandos held up his hand, palm outward, then tapped the side of his helmet to indicate an incoming transmission. The commando listened, then spoke to Anakin with hand signals.

Gunray's party is nearby.

"They're testing escape vectors for the shuttle by lowering the defensive shield and launching decoys," the commando said quietly. "Turbolaser fire has allowed several of the decoys to get past our blockade and reach orbiting core ships."

The muscles in Anakin's jaw bunched. "Then we have to act quickly."

No one contested when Anakin held point position. The commandos accepted without question that body armor and imaging systems were primitive compared to the power of the Force. They moved vigilantly through a maze of elegant corridors, abandoned in a rush, strewn with belongings dropped during flight.

Approaching an intersection, Anakin made a halting gesture with his left hand.

He listened for a moment; heard from around the corner the telltale heavy footfalls of super battle droids. The commando to Anakin's left nodded in confirmation, then extended a finger-thin holocam around the corner and activated his gauntlet holo-projector. Noisy images of Nute Gunray and his entourage of elite officers formed in midair. Hurrying down the corridor, tall headpieces bobbing, rich robes aswirl, safeguarded front and rear by burly battle droids.

Anakin motioned for silence, and was just about to step into the intersecting corridor when a banged-up silver protocol droid appeared from across the hall, raising its hands in delighted surprise.

"Welcome, sirs!" it said loudly. "I can't tell you how good it is to find guests in the palace! I am TeeCee-Sixteen and I am at your service. Nearly everyone has left—because of the invasion, of course—but I'm sure that we can make you comfortable, and that Viceroy Gunray will be most pleased—"

One hand clamped over TC-16's small rectangle of vocabulator, a commando yanked the droid to one side, but it was too late. Anakin leapt around the corner in time to see the Neimoidians set off at a run, red-eyed, flat-nosed Gunray casting a nervous glance over his shoulder.

As for the super battle droids, they had about-faced and were marching stiff-legged in Anakin's direction. Catching sight of him, their right arms elevated, twisted downward, locked into firing position.

And the corridor began to fill with blaster bolts.

Qui-Gon Jinn hadn't believed in baiting, Obi-Wan thought as he and the commandos rode the turbolift to the fortress's lowest level. Baiting implied a certain amount of advance planning, and Qui-Gon had no patience for that. He took situations as they came, throwing back his shoulders and striding boldly to the center of things, relying as much on his instincts as his lightsaber to deal with the consequences. It must have been difficult for him to have served under a methodical master such as Dooku, consummate planner, consummate duelist.

Now a *Sith*.

But that made sense, of a sort.

The desire to dominate and control.

For a time the same issues had stood at the center of Obi-Wan's conflicts with Anakin. Clearly Anakin was as strong in the Force as any Jedi who had ever sat on the Council. But as Obi-Wan had told him time and again, the essence of being a Jedi didn't hinge on attaining mastery of the Force, but on attaining mastery over oneself. Someday Anakin would come to accept that, and then he would be truly unstoppable. Qui-Gon had had the insight to recognize it more than a decade earlier, and Obi-

Wan felt duty-bound to his former Master to help Anakin fulfill his destiny.

His faith in Anakin had grown so strong that he had become Anakin's staunchest defender to those on the Council who had grown apprehensive about the young man's prowess, and uncomfortable with his confidential, almost familial relationship with Supreme Chancellor Palpatine. If Obi-Wan was, as Anakin sometimes said, the father he never had, then Palpatine was his wise uncle, adviser, mentor in the ways of life outside the Temple.

Obi-Wan understood that Anakin envied him for having been appointed to the Council. But how could he not, having been all but anointed "the Chosen One," continually bolstered by Palpatine's praise, driven to prove to *his* former Master that he could be the perfect Jedi Knight.

On countless occasions Anakin's bold actions had allowed them to prevail against seemingly impossible odds. But just as often it had been Obi-Wan's circumspection that had pulled them back from the brink. Whether foresight was something innate in Obi-Wan or the result of his continuing fascination with the unifying Force—the long view—Obi-Wan couldn't say. What he could say was that he had learned to trust Anakin's instincts.

On occasion.

He wouldn't have been able to go on playing the bait, otherwise.

"The next stop is ours, General," Cody said from behind him.

Obi-Wan turned, watched Cody slam a new blasterpack into his DC-15, heard the familiar whine of the weapon's repower mechanism.

Reflexively, he placed his thumb on the lightsaber's activator button.

"How do you want to handle this, sir?"

"You're the master of warcraft, Commander. I'll follow your lead."

Cody nodded, perhaps grinning beneath his helmet. "Well, sir, our mandate is a simple one: Kill as many of the enemy as possible."

Obi-Wan recalled a conversation he had had on Ord Cestus with a clone trooper named Nate, regarding analogies between the Jedi and the clones: the former ushered by midi-chlorians to serve the Force; the latter, grown and programmed to serve the Republic.

But the analogies ended there, because the troopers never paused to consider possible repercussions of their actions. Tasked, they executed their orders to the best of their abilities, whereas lately, even the most forceful Jedi knew moments of doubt. Qui-Gon had always criticized the Council for being too authoritative, and for cultivating inflexible methods of teaching. He saw the Temple as a place where candidates were *programmed* to become Jedi, instead of a place were beings were allowed to grow into Jedihood. Qui-Gon was no stranger to what the Jedi referred to as "aggressive negotiations," which typically involved lightsabers more than diplomacy. But Obi-Wan wondered what he would have had to say about the war. He recalled, as if yesterday, Dooku's taunt on Geonosis that Qui-Gon would have joined Dooku in championing the Separatist cause.

As soon as the turbolift came to rest, two commandos tossed concussion grenades into the corridor beyond. Right and left, battle droids were blown against the walls and ceiling. Obi-Wan knew, because the corridor quickly became a torrent of blaster bolts. He, Cody, and the others threw themselves into the horizontal hail. Repeating blasters roared to life. Staccato bursts made short work of the droids, but reinforcements were already appearing.

Two commandos fell to fire while Obi-Wan's team was making its way down the corridor in the direction of the citadel's packing and shipping rooms. Halfway there, they encountered the contingent of super battle droids the Neimoidians had sent to root out the infiltrators.

Comparing the spindly infantry droid to the black-bodied super battle droid was like comparing a Muun to a champion shock-ball player. Quick decapitations weren't possible because the droid's head was all but buried in and fused to its broad torso. Heavy-gauge armor protected long arms and legs. Mono-grip hands were suited only for gripping and firing high-energy dispersal blasters.

"Looks like they've taken the bait, General!" Cody said while he, Obi-Wan, and two commandos fought their way into a side room.

"Another successful action! Now we just have to survive it!"

Cody pointed to the entrance to a second room, opposite their present position.

"Through there," he said. "A second bank of turbolifts on the far side." He tapped Obi-Wan on the shoulder. "You first. We'll provide cover. Go!"

Obi-Wan shot for the room, deflecting bolts and mangling two super battle droids that stood in his way. The room beyond was stacked with coffin-sized repulsorlift shipping containers, constructed of some lightweight alloy. Treaded labor droids were moving additional containers into the room from an adjacent packaging area. Without warning, a battle droid appeared in the entrance. Obi-Wan glanced at the wall-mounted mechanism that operated the sliding doors. Adopting a defensive stance, he did just as he had done in the grotto, returning the first of the droid's blaster bolts, and sending the second caroming around the room in a path calculated to disable the door apparatus.

Things might have gone as planned had a labor droid not entered the room at an inopportune moment, guiding a levitated shipping container behind him. Ricocheting from the floor, the deflected bolt passed completely through the container before it struck the door mechanism. The pair of sliding doors attempted to close, but the crippled container was now in the way, so they began to cycle through attempts to repocket themselves, close, repocket themselves . . .

Each time they opened, a battle droid would squeeze into the room, firing away, forcing Obi-Wan back toward the entryway through which he had originally come, where a brutal firefight was still raging between commandos and super battle droids.

While all this was occurring, something else was afoot. Strands of some gauzy white substance were beginning to drift from the holed shipping container.

Obi-Wan realized instantly what the substance was.

Taking one hand from the hilt of lightsaber, he began to fumble for the rebreather pouched on his belt, only to find it empty.

"Stars' end," he cursed, more in disappointment than anger.

Already beginning to feel woozy.

Sirs, this a terrible mistake!" TC-16 inserted into a brief pause in the firefight.

"Keep him quiet," Anakin snapped at the commando closest to the droid.

"But, sirs—"

A second commando glanced at Anakin and motioned down the corridor behind them. "Six infantry droids advancing. We're going to be caught in a crossfire."

Anakin gave his head a quick shake. "Wrong. Follow me—and bring the droid."

A muffled sound of dismay escaped TC-16's vocabulator.

Fury clouded Anakin's eyes. Lightsaber held high in his crooked right arm, he whirled into the intersecting corridor. No need to *use* the Force, as many Jedi said, for he was never any-where but fully in the Force. He called instead on his anger, bringing images to mind to fuel his rage. It wasn't difficult, with so many to choose from: images of a Tusken Raider camp on Tatooine, Yavin 4, the defeat at Jabiim, Praesitlyn . . .

Blue blade flashing, he cut a swath through the super battle droids, opening their burnished carapaces with diagonal slashes, cutting off blaster arms, hobbling the droids by deflecting bolts into their hermetically sealed knees. Scarcely letting a shot get past him, so that the commandos following in his wake could concentrate their fire on the ones Anakin only wounded.

Their enemies fell aside, almost as if surrendering.

Focused on the route Gunray and his lackeys had taken, Anakin raced through corridors, rounding corners without slowing down, sprinting for the launching bay at the far end of the final corridor. Confronted with an iris-hatch blast door, he thrust his glowing blade into the metal as if it were living flesh. Lips drawn back over his teeth, he tried to force the lightsaber to burn a fast circle in the door. He brought his will to bear on the task, but the lightsaber could accomplish only so much, even in the hands of a powerful Jedi.

Withdrawing the blade, he stepped back from the door and moved his hands through a Force pass, willing the iris portal to open. The door shuddered but remained sealed. Screaming through gnashed teeth, he tried again.

When the commandos finally caught up with him, he spun to them.

"Blow the door!"

A commando hurried forward to place magnetic charges against the alloy. Anakin paced behind him, waiting. Another commando had to tug him to a safe distance.

The charges blew, and the portal yielded. Anakin charged through the irising seal even before it had opened fully.

The launching bay was littered with containers, articles of clothing, objects the Neimoidians hadn't had time or space to take with them.

The shuttle was gone.

Wisps of vapor swirled about, and the air smelled faintly of fuel. Anakin ran to the platform's forward-curving edge, eyes scanning Cato Neimoidia's light-riddled night sky for some sign of the fleeing ship. The palace's defensive shield had been deactivated. Thick packets of crimson light lanced from laser cannon batteries on the slopes below.

Anakin's teammates joined him at the brink, one with a hand vised on TC-16's upper left arm.

"What type of ship is it?" Anakin demanded of the droid.

TC-16 tipped his head to one side. "Ship, sir?"

"The shuttle—Gunray's shuttle. What model?"

"Why, I believe it was a *Sheathipede*-class, sir."

"Haor Chall Engineering *Sheathipede*-class transport shuttle," one of the commandos explained. "Design is based on the soldier beetles. Upraised stern, bow ramp, clawfoot landing gear. Gunray's named it the *Lapiz Cutter.*"

A second commando spoke up, signaling that he was receiving commo.

"General. From Commander Dodonna's flagship: more than sixty shuttles and landing craft launched from the redoubt. Thirteen destroyed, eighteen seized. An unknown quantity have managed to dock aboard Trade Federation core ships and open-ring Lucrehulk carriers. Additional shuttles are still in the envelope."

Anakin turned through a circle, gloved hand gripped on the lightsaber pommel, the other balled into a fist. A conduit nearby took the brunt of his anger. Cleaved by the blade, it fell in pieces to the landing platform's seamless floor. Anakin began to pace again, then stopped, yanking a commando around by his shoulder.

"Comm forward command. I want my ship and astromech droid flown here immediately. One of the ARC-one-seventy pilots can fly it."

The commando nodded, relayed the message, then said: "FCC will comply, sir. You'll have your starfighter soonest."

Anakin returned to the lip of the platform, blowing his breath into the night. The battle appeared to be winding down, except within him. Not until he had Gunray in his grip—

"General Skywalker," a commando said from behind him.

"Urgent from Commander Cody. He and General Kenobi are pinned down on level one."

Anakin shot him a questioning look. "By *droids*?"

"A lot of them, apparently."

Anakin glanced into the glowing sky, then back at the commando who had delivered Cody's message.

"General, forward command reports that your starfighter is on the way," another commando updated.

Again, Anakin glanced at the sky, only to turn back to the commando. "Where did you say Obi-Wan and Cody are?"

"Level one, sir. In the shipping area."

Anakin compressed his lips. "All right. Let's go rescue them."

7

In the shipping room, the sliding doors were still cycling—striking the punctured shipping container, retracting, attempting to close once more. Battle droids were still entering with each parting of the doors, and spores were still wafting through the air.

Not much had changed, except within Obi-Wan, who felt as if he had downed three bottles of Whyren's Reserve. Bleary-eyed but lucid, tipsy but sure-footed, weary but attentive, Obi-Wan seemed to be the sum of all contrasts.

More or less rooted in place, he swayed, wobbled, tottered, and reeled, evading or parrying an almost unremitting current of blaster bolts. His singed and burned cloak bore evidence of all the near hits, but the floor—heaped with droids, whole and in parts, bodies sparking and limbs twitching—spoke to the accuracy of his deflections.

He felt at times as if he were merely holding the lightsaber and letting it to do all the work. In one hand, in both, it made no difference. Other times he was able to anticipate the bolts, twist himself aside at the last instant, and allow the walls and floor to handle the ricochets.

Sometimes he actually took a moment to congratulate himself on the skill of his returns.

He was in the Force, to be sure, but deep in some other zone as well, giddy with astonishment, as the world unfolded in slow motion.

Alerted by the commandos that the air was saturated with spores, Anakin had his rebreather in his mouth as he approached the room in which Obi-Wan had held his own against better than fifty droids, all of which lay scattered about the room. A weaving, shuffling, staggering Obi-Wan was dealing with the last of them when Anakin entered.

When the final droid collapsed, Obi-Wan aimed the blade of his lightsaber casually toward the floor and stood swaying in place, breathing hard but almost grinning.

"Anakin," he said happily. "How are you?"

When Anakin went to him, Obi-Wan promptly collapsed in his arms.

Anakin deactivated Obi-Wan's blade and inserted a rebreather into his mouth—the same one that had ended up on the floor of the grotto. Then he carried him from the room to where Cody and several commandos were waiting, some with their helmets removed.

"Exactly what lightsaber form were you using back there, Master?" Anakin asked when Obi-Wan had come around and the rebreathers were no longer necessary.

"Form?"

"More the absence of it." Anakin laughed shortly. "If only Mace, Kit, or Shaak Ti could have seen you."

Obi-Wan blinked in confusion and glanced around at the carnage of droids in the shipping area. "We did this?" he said to Cody.

"You did most of it, General."

Obi-Wan regarded Anakin in confusion.

"I'll explain later," Anakin said.

Obi-Wan ran his hand through his hair, then, as if just re-membering, said: "Gunray! Did you get him?"

Anakin's shoulders dropped. "The entire entourage escaped the palace."

Obi-Wan mulled it over for a moment. "You could have gone after them."

Anakin shrugged. "And leave you?" He paused, then added: "Of course, if I'd known you'd become master of a new light-saber form . . ."

Obi-Wan's eyes brightened. "They'll be taken in orbit."

"Maybe."

"If not, there'll be other times, Anakin. We'll see to it."

Anakin nodded. "I know that, Master."

Obi-Wan was about to add something when a helmeted commando stepped from a nearby turbolift and hurried over to them.

"General Kenobi, General Skywalker, we've found some-thing of interest among the equipment the Neimoidians left be-hind."

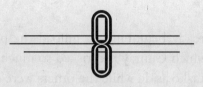

The fact that the Sheathipede shuttle had managed to thread its way through a storm of turbolaser bolts and dock in the core ship's port-side command tower was no guarantee of safety. Indeed, while everyone was filing down the shuttle's tongue-like boarding ramp, the core ship was still being pummeled by fire from Republic warships.

First to set foot on deck, Viceroy Nute Gunray, attired in blood-red robes and sporting a tall, helmet-like miter, asked for a situation report from one of the goggle-wearing technicians who was waiting in the docking bay.

"Even now coordinates for the jump to lightspeed are being calculated, Viceroy," the nearest one said. "A matter of moments and we will be well away from Cato Neimoidia. Your peers on the Council of Separatists await us in the Outer Rim."

"Let us hope so," Gunray said, as the vessel was rocked by a massive explosion.

Behind Gunray walked settlement officer Rune Haako, wearing a crested skullcap; and behind Haako, various financial, legal, and diplomatic officers, each wearing a distinctive headpiece.

Droids were already beginning to unload the possessions—the treasures—for which Gunray had risked so much.

He called Haako aside while the others were exiting the sterile docking bay. "Do you think there will be a chance to return and reclaim what we had to leave behind?"

"Not a chance," puckered Haako said flatly. "Our purse worlds now belong to the Republic. Our only hope is to find sanctuary in the Outer Rim. Otherwise, this ship will have to serve as our home—and perhaps our final resting place!"

Sadness crept into Gunray's red orbs. "But my collections, my keepsakes . . ."

"Your most cherished items accompany you," Haako said, gesturing to the containers already piled at the foot of the boarding ramp. "More important, we escaped with our *lives*. Another instant and the Jedi would have had us."

Gunray allowed a nod of agreement. "You warned me."

"I did."

"Count Dooku will help us find new worlds to settle when the war is won."

"*If* the war is won, you mean. The Republic seems keen on driving us from the galaxy."

Gunray made a dismissive gesture with his fat fingers. "Temporary setbacks. The Republic has yet to see the face of its real enemy."

Haako hunched slightly at the reference. "But is even *he* enough, Viceroy?" he asked quietly.

Gunray said nothing, although he had been asking himself the same question for the past several weeks.

One thing was clear: the glory days of the Trade Federation had come to an untimely end. Ironically, the individual most responsible for that bright burning—for the rise of Nute Gunray himself—was the same individual who had repeatedly betrayed him, and to whom Gunray and the other Separatists were now forced to look for salvation.

The Sith Lord, Darth Sidious.

There at Dorvalla and Eriadu, manipulating events to shunt power and influence to the Neimoidians; there at Naboo, ordering a blockade of the planet, the murder of Jedi, assassination of the Queen . . . a debacle for the Trade Federation. Years of attempts by the Republic to try to convict Gunray and his chief officers, to break the hold the Trade Federation enjoyed on galactic shipping. But not once during that time of public disgrace did Gunray mention the role Sidious had played.

Out of fear?

Certainly.

But also because he had sensed that Sidious had not abandoned him completely. Rather, the Dark Lord was somehow seeing to it that the trials never came to fruition, that no lasting verdicts were rendered or punishments handed down. As the Separatist movement gained strength, threatening the security of ships and shipments in the far sectors, the Trade Federation had actually been able to increase the size of its standing army of battle droids by dealing directly with foundry worlds, such as Geonosis and Hypori. Making the most of the Republic's sudden instability, lucrative deals had been arranged between the Trade Federation and the Corporate Alliance, the InterGalactic Banking Clan, the Techno Union, the Commerce Guild, and other corporate entities.

It was during the final trial that Gunray had been approached by Count Dooku, who had promised that all would ultimately turn out well for the Trade Federation. In a moment of weakness, Gunray had revealed the truth about his dealings with Darth Sidious. Dooku has listened attentively; had promised to bring the matter to the attention of the Jedi Council, though he himself had left the Order some years earlier. Gunray had mixed feelings about Dooku's purpose in creating a Separatist movement, chiefly because corruption in the Republic Senate had so often worked to the Trade Federation's advantage. But if

Dooku's Confederacy of Independent Systems could eliminate even some of the bribes and kickbacks commonplace in galactic trade, then so much the better.

By and by Dooku's real aims had been made clear: he was less interested in providing an alternative to the Republic than he was in bringing the Republic to its knees—through the use of force if necessary. In much the same way that the Trade Federation had amassed an army right under the nose of Supreme Chancellor Finis Valorum, Dooku—in plain sight—was seeing to it that Baktoid Armor Workshops was supplying weapons to any corporations that agreed to ally with him.

Regardless, Gunray had resisted offers to throw his full support to the Separatists—not when there were still profits to be made in countless Republic star systems. Playing a game of his own, teasing Dooku along, he had informed Dooku that a precondition to their entering into any exclusive arrangement was the death of former Naboo Queen Padmé Amidala, who had foiled Gunray on two occasions, and had been the loudest opposition voice at his trials.

Dooku had hired a bounty hunter to oversee the business, but two attempts at assassinating Senator Amidala had failed.

Then came Geonosis.

But just when Gunray finally had Amidala in his grasp—on trial, no less, for espionage—Dooku had equivocated, refusing to have Amidala killed outright, and not lifting a hand against the Jedi until some two hundred of them had showed up with a clone army the Republic had grown in secret!

That day had provided Gunray with the first in what would be a series of narrow escapes. Hurrying to the catacombs with Dooku at their side, Gunray and Haako had barely managed to flee the embattled surface and recall what core ships and droid carriers remained.

By then, though, it was too late for anyone to resign from Dooku's Confederacy.

The war was begun, and it was Dooku's turn for revelations: he, too, was Sith, and his Master was none other than Sidious! Whether a replacement for the fearsome Darth Maul, or a Sith even during his years in the Jedi Order, Gunray didn't care to know. What mattered was simply that Nute Gunray was right back where he had been so many years earlier: in service to forces over which he had no control whatsoever.

When the war had been going well, the issue of whom he served had been scarcely a problem. Trade had continued, and the Trade Federation had continued in the black. For a time it appeared that Sidious and Dooku's dreams of toppling the Republic might succeed after all. But they found themselves facing a worthy opponent in the person of Supreme Chancellor Palpatine—also from Naboo—who had never much impressed Gunray, but who had managed through a combination of charm and artfulness not only to remain in power long past his term of office, but also, in conjunction with the Jedi, to conduct the war. Slowly, the wheel began to turn, as one Separatist world after another was retaken by the Republic, and now Viceroy Nute Gunray himself had been driven from the Core.

A tragedy for the Trade Federation; a tragedy, he feared, for the entire Neimoidian species.

He gazed at the few possessions he had been able to gather: his costly robes and miters, resplendent jewelry, priceless works of art—

A sudden chill laddered up his spine. His bulging forehead and lower jaw tingled in dread. Eyes protruding from his mottled gray face, he swung to Rune Haako.

"The chair! Where is the chair?"

Haako stared at him.

"The mechno-chair!" Gunray said. "It's not here anywhere!"

Now Haako's eyes widened in apprehension. "Surely we couldn't have overlooked it."

Gunray paced worriedly, trying to recall when and where he

had last seen the device. "I'm certain that I had it moved to the launching bay. Yes, yes, I remember seeing it there! But in the rush to launch—"

"But you armed it to self-destruct," Haako said. "Tell me you armed it!"

Gunray stared at him. "I thought you had armed it."

Haako gestured to himself. "I don't even know the sequence codes!"

Gunray fell silent for a moment. "Haako, what if they should decide to tamper with it?"

Haako's broad slash of mouth twitched with worry. "Without the codes, what could they possibly gain from it?"

"You're right. Of course, you're right."

Gunray tried to convince himself. It was just a mechno-chair, after all; finely wrought, but just a walking chair. A walking chair equipped with a hyperwave transceiver. A hyperwave transceiver given to him fourteen years ago by—

"What if he should learn that we left it behind?" Gunray rasped.

"Sidious," Haako said softly.

"Not Sidious!"

"Count Dooku, you mean."

"Are you brain-dead?" Gunray fairly screeched. "Grievous! What if *Grievous* should find out?"

Supreme Commander of the droid armies, General Grievous had been San Hill and Poggle the Lesser's gift to Dooku. Once merely a barbaric living being; now a cyborg monstrosity, devoted to death and destruction. Already the butcher of entire populations; the devastator of countless worlds—

"It's not too late," Haako said suddenly. "We can communicate with the chair from here."

"Can we arm it to self-destruct?"

Haako shook his head negatively. "But we might be able to instruct it to arm itself."

A technician intercepted them while they were hurrying toward a communications console.

"Viceroy, we are prepared to make the jump to lightspeed."

"You will do no such thing!" Gunray cried. "Not until I give the order!"

"But, Viceroy, our vessel can only withstand so much bombardment."

"Bombardment is the least of our concerns!"

"Hurry," Haako insisted, "we haven't much time!"

Gunray rushed to join him at the console. "Say nothing of this to *anyone*," he warned.

Sickle-footed, humpbacked, incised with intricate designs, the mechno-chair sat in the launching bay of the now seized fortress, amid a heap of equally exquisite belongings left by the fleeing Neimoidians.

Obi-Wan was circling it, right hand caressing his bearded chin. "I think I've seen this chair before."

Squatting alongside it, Anakin looked up at him. "Where?"

Obi-Wan stopped. "On Naboo. Shortly after Viceroy Gunray and his entourage were taken into custody in Theed."

Anakin shook his head. "I don't remember seeing it."

Obi-Wan snorted. "I suspect you were too excited about having blown up the Droid Control Ship to take much notice of anything. What's more, I saw it only for a moment. But I do remember being struck by the design of the holoprojector plate. I'd never seen one quite like it—or since, for that matter."

On the far side of the spacious bay, up on its hardstand, sat Anakin's sleek yellow starfighter. R2-D2 stood nearby, communing with TC-16. Commander Cody and the rest of Squad Seven were elsewhere in the palace, "mopping up," as the clones liked to say.

Anakin examined the chair's holoprojector without touching it. An oval of ribbed alloy, it was equipped with a pair of dorsal sockets sized to accept data cells of some sort. "It is unusual. You know, Master, these cells could contain valuable messages in storage."

"All the more reason to leave it be until someone from Intelligence can have a look at it."

Anakin frowned. "That could take forever."

Obi-Wan folded his arms and regarded him. "Are you in a rush, Anakin?"

"For all we know, the cells could be programmed to erase themselves."

"Do you see any evidence of that?"

"No, but—"

"Then we're better off waiting until we can run a proper diagnostic."

Anakin grimaced. "What do you know about running diagnostics? Master."

"I'm not exactly a stranger to the Temple's cyberlabs, Anakin."

"I know that. But Artoo can run the diagnostic." He beckoned for the droid to join him at the mechno-chair.

"Anakin," Obi-Wan started to say.

"Really, sirs, I must protest," TC-16 interrupted, hurrying behind R2-D2. "These items remain the property of Viceroy Gunray and other members of his party."

"You don't have a say in the matter," Anakin said.

R2-D2 trilled and hooted at the battered protocol droid. The two had been bickering since R2-D2's arrival a short time earlier.

"I'm fully aware that my circuits are corroded," TC-16 said. "As for my posture, there's little I can do about that until my pelvic joint is serviced. You astromechs think very highly of yourselves, just because you can pilot starfighters."

"Don't pay Artoo any mind, TeeCee," Anakin said. "He's been spoiled by another protocol droid. Haven't you, Artoo?"

Artoo toodled a response, extended his computer interface arm, and inserted the magnetic tip into an output socket in the chair.

"Anakin!" Obi-Wan said sharply.

Anakin stood up and joined Obi-Wan on the launch platform. Obi-Wan was pointing to a blinking light that was growing larger by the second in the night sky.

"Do you see that? That is very likely the ship we're waiting for. And the Intelligence officers aboard are not going to take kindly to our sticking our noses in their business."

"Sirs," TC-16 said from behind them.

"Not now," Obi-Wan said.

R2-D2 began to loose a long series of whistles, chirps, and chitters.

"If and when they give the okay," Obi-Wan went on, "then feel free to dissect the entire chair, if that's your objective."

"That's not my objective, Master."

"Maybe Qui-Gon should have left you at Watto's junk shop."

"You don't mean that, Master."

"Of course not. But I know how you love to tinker with things."

"Sirs—"

"Keep quiet, TeeCee," Anakin said.

R2-D2 honked and razzed, though as if from a distance.

"And you, too, Artoo."

Obi-Wan glanced over his shoulder, and his jaw dropped. "Where's the mechno-chair?"

Anakin swung around and scanned the bay. "Where's Artoo?"

"I've been trying to tell you, sirs," TC-16 said, gesturing toward the launching bay's ruined iris hatch. "The chair walked away—taking your high-thinking little droid with it!"

Obi-Wan stared at Anakin in bewilderment.

"Well, it couldn't have gotten far on foot, Master."

They rushed into the corridor, saw that it was deserted in both directions, and began searching the rooms that adjoined the bay. A prolonged electronic squeal brought both of them back into the main corridor.

"That's Artoo," Anakin said.

"Either that, or TeeCee has developed a talent for mimicry."

The protocol droid following behind, they hurried into a compact data room, where they saw R2-D2 with his interface arm still jacked into the chair, and the gripper of his grasping arm clamped to the bar handle of a storage cabinet. Stretched to its full extent, a computer interface cable now connected the mechno-chair to a control console of some sort. The chair's talon-like feet were in constant motion, attempting to gain purchase on the smooth floor in an effort to propel the chair closer to the console.

"What's it doing?" Obi-Wan asked.

Anakin made his face long and shook his head. "Recharging itself?"

"Never seen such tenacity in a mechno-chair."

R2-D2 chattered and wheezed.

"What's Artoo saying?" Obi-Wan asked TC-16.

"He's saying, sir, that the mechno-chair has *just armed itself to self-destruct*!"

Anakin made a mad dash for the console.

"Artoo, unplug yourself!" Obi-Wan shouted. "Anakin, get away from that thing!"

Anakin's fingers were already busy undoing leads that linked the holoprojector unit to the chair.

"Can't, Master. Now we know there's something stored in this chair no one wants us to see."

Obi-Wan glanced worriedly at R2-D2. "How much time, Artoo?"

TC-16 translated the astromech's response. "Seconds, sir!"

Obi-Wan rushed to Anakin's side. "There isn't time, Anakin. Besides, it could be rigged to detonate if tampered with."

"Almost there, Master . . ."

"You'll deactivate us in the process!"

Obi-Wan sensed a disturbance in the Force.

Without thinking, he pulled Anakin to the floor an instant before the chair shot a stream of white vapor into the space Anakin had occupied.

Coughing, Obi-Wan covered his mouth and nose with the wide sleeve of his robe. "Poison gas! Good bet it's the same one Gunray tried to use on Qui-Gon and me at Naboo."

"Thank you, Master," Anakin said. "What's that make it, twenty-five to thirty-seven?"

"Thirty-*six*—if you've any interest in accuracy."

Anakin studied the chair for a moment. "We have to take the chance."

Before Obi-Wan could even think about stopping him, Anakin had leaned forward and wrenched the interface cable from the control console.

R2-D2 yowled, and TC-16 moaned in distress.

A web of blue energy gamboled around the chair and the console, knocking Anakin onto his backside.

At the same time, a high-resolution blue hologram projected from the chair's holoplate.

R2-D2 mewled in alarm.

And to the meter-high figure in the hooded cloak, the unmistakable voice of Viceroy Nute Gunray was saying:

"*Yes, yes, of course. Trust that I will see to it personally, my Lord Sidious.*"

These days, an appointment with Supreme Chancellor Palpatine was not something to be taken lightly—even for a member of the so-called Loyalist Committee.

Appointment?

More an *audience*.

Bail Organa had just arrived on Coruscant, and was still wearing the deep blue cloak, ruffle-collared shirt, and knee-high black boots his wife had laid out for him for the trip from Alderaan. He had been away from the galactic capital for only a standard month, and could scarcely believe the disturbing changes that had taken place during his short absence.

Alderaan never seemed more a paradise, a sanctuary. Just thinking about his beautiful blue-and-white homeworld made Bail yearn to be there, yearn for the company of his loving wife.

"I'm going to need to see further identification," the clone trooper stationed at the landing platform's Homeworld Security checkpoint told him.

Bail motioned to the identichip he had already slotted in the scanner. "It's all there, Sergeant. I'm a member in good standing of the Republic Senate."

The helmeted noncom glanced at the display screen, then looked down at Bail. "So it says. But I'm still going to need to see further identification."

Bail sighed in exasperation and fished into the breast pocket of his brocaded tunic for his credit chip.

The new Coruscant, he thought.

Faceless, blaster-wielding soldiers on the shuttle landing plat-forms, in the plazas, arrayed in front of banks, hotels, theaters, wherever beings gathered or mingled. Scanning the crowds, stop-ping anyone who fit the current possible terrorist profile, con-ducting searches of individuals, belongings, residences. Not on a whim, because the cloned troopers didn't operate like that. They answered merely to their training, and the duties they performed were for the good of the Republic.

One heard rumors about antiwar demonstrations being put down by force; of disappearances and seizures of private prop-erty. Proof of such abuses of power rarely surfaced, and was quickly discredited.

The omnipresence of the soldiers seemed to bother Bail more than it did his few friends on Coruscant or his peers in the Senate. He had tried to attribute his agitation to the fact that he hailed from pacific Alderaan, but that explained only some of it. What bothered him most was the ease with which the majority of Coruscanti had acclimated to the changes. Their willingness—almost an eagerness—to surrender personal freedoms in the name of security. And a false security, at that. For while Corus-cant seemed far from the war, it was also at the center of it.

Now, three years into a conflict that might have been ended as abruptly as it had begun, every new security measure was taken in stride. Except, of course, by members of those species most closely associated with the Separatist agenda—Geonosians, Muuns, Neimoidians, Gossams, and the rest—many of whom had been ostracized or forced to flee the capital. Having lived for so long in fear and ignorance, few Coruscanti stopped to question what was really going on. Least of all the Senate itself, which was so busy modifying the Constitution that it had completely abandoned its role as a balancing arm of the government.

Before the war, widespread corruption had stifled the legislative process. Bills languished, measures sat for years without being addressed, votes were protested and subjected to endless recounts . . . But one effect of the war had been to replace corruption and inertia with dereliction of duty. Reasoned discourse and debate had become so rare as to be archaic. In a political climate where representatives were afraid to speak their minds, it was easier—and thought to be safer—to cede power to those who at least appeared to have some grasp of the truth.

"You're free to go," the trooper said at last, apparently satisfied that Bail was in fact who his credentials claimed him to be.

Bail laughed to himself.

Free to go where? he wondered.

This high up on Coruscant, one couldn't be a pedestrian. Walking was an activity reserved for the bottom feeders who occupied Coruscant's reflectively lit sublevels. Bail hailed a free-travel air taxi and instructed the droid driver to take him to the Senate Building.

Even outside the normal skylanes, above the myriad and abysmal canyons that fissured the urbanscape, far from patrols of security soldiers or the prying eyes of Republic spies, Coruscant looked much as it had for as long as Bail had known it. Traffic was as dense as ever, with ships arriving perpetually from all points in the galaxy. New restaurants had opened; more art was being created. Paradoxically, there seemed to be more joviality in the air, and more opportunities than ever for vice. Even with trade disrupted to the Outer Rim, many Coruscanti were living the good life, and many Senators were continuing to avail themselves of the limitless privileges they had enjoyed in the prewar years.

From up here one had to look closely to observe the changes.

In the oval, twin-drive air taxi, for example.

Running in tiny print across the passenger's-seat display screen was a public service ad extolling the virtues of COMPOR—the Commission for the Protection of the Republic.

NONHUMANS NEED NOT APPLY.

And there, dazzling the sheer face of a towering office building, a piece of late-breaking HoloNet news detailing the Republic's victory at Cato Neimoidia. Lately it was triumph after triumph, praise for the Grand Army of the Republic, all glory to the clone troopers.

Rarely a mention of the Jedi, save for when one of them was commended by Palpatine in the Senate's Great Rotunda. Young Anakin Skywalker or some other. Otherwise one rarely saw an adult Jedi on Coruscant any longer. Spread thin throughout the galaxy, they led companies of troopers into battle. The holo-feeds were fond of using the phrase *aggressive peacekeeping* to describe their actions. To the extent that friendships could be forged with them, Bail had come to know a few: Jedi Masters Obi-Wan Kenobi, Yoda, Mace Windu, Saesee Tiin—the privileged few who also were allowed to meet personally with Palpatine.

Bail stirred in his seat.

Even Palpatine's harshest critics in the Senate or in the various media couldn't hold him fully accountable for what Coruscant had become. Though hardly the innocent he sometimes pretended to be, Palpatine was not to blame. His talent for being at once sincere and exacting was what had gotten him elected in the first place. According to Bail Antilles, at any rate, Bail's predecessor in the Senate.

Thirteen years ago the Senate was interested only in ridding itself of Finis Valorum, Antilles had once told Bail. Valorum, who had believed he could put honesty on the Senate agenda. Even in those days Palpatine had had his share of influential friends.

Still, Bail couldn't help but wonder who might have succeeded Palpatine as Supreme Chancellor if the Separatist crises
on Raxus Prime and Antar 4 had not occurred when they did,
just as Palpatine's term of office was ending. He remembered the
arguments that had raged over passage of the Emergency Powers
Act; that it was dangerous to "change dewbacks in the middle of
a sand dune." Back then, many Senators felt that the Republic
should bide its time and simply allow Count Dooku's movement
to play itself out.

But not after the full extent of the Separatist threat became
clear.

Not after some six thousand worlds, lured by the promise of
free and unrestricted trade, had seceded from the Republic. Not
after heavily armed corporations such as the Commerce Guild
and the Techno Union had partnered with Dooku. Not after the
entire Rimward leg of the Rimma Trade Route had become inaccessible to Republic shipping.

As a consequence—and by an overwhelming majority—the
Senate had voted to amend the Constitution, and to extend Palpatine's term indefinitely, with the understanding that he would
voluntarily step down from office when the crisis was resolved. In
short order, however, the likelihood of a quick resolution evaporated. Formerly gracious and unassuming Palpatine was suddenly
democracy's champion, vowing that he could not condone a Republic divided against itself.

Rumors of a Military Creation Act began to circulate. But
Palpatine himself had refused to come out in favor of building
an army for the Republic. He left that to others—the Senate's
nominal Sand Panthers. Finally he attempted to arrange a peace
summit, but Count Dooku had refused to attend.

Instead came war.

Bail could recall clearly the day he had stood with Palpatine,
Mas Amedda, Malastarian Senators, and others on a balcony of

the Senate Office Building, watching tens of thousands of clone troopers march into the enormous ships that would take the war to the Separatists. He could recall clearly his utter disconsolation. That after a thousand years of peace, war and evil had returned.

More accurately, been allowed to return.

Regardless, Bail had put his feelings aside and had played his part, endorsing bills he might have previously denounced, supporting Palpatine's "efficient streamlining of cumbersome bureaucracy." It wasn't until passage of the Reflex Amendment, some fourteen months back, that his fears had begun to resurface and intensify. The sudden disappearance of Senator Seti Ashgad after he had argued against installation of surveillance cams in the Senate Building; the suspicious explosion of a star freighter aboard which Finis Valorum was a passenger; the passage of a security bill that granted Palpatine wide-ranging powers over Coruscant . . .

The behavior of the Supreme Chancellor himself— frequently isolated by his covey of advisers and illegal cadre of red-robed personal bodyguards; his unbending resolve to continue fighting until the war was won. Gone was humble, self-deprecating Palpatine. And with him, tractable Bail Organa. Bail vowed to speak openly of his concerns, and he began to cultivate friendships with Senators who shared those concerns.

Some of them were waiting for him when the air taxi touched down in the broad plaza that fronted the mushroom-shaped Senate Building. Padmé Amidala, of Naboo; Mon Mothma of Chandrila; human Senators Terr Taneel, Bana Breemu, and Fang Zar; and alien Senator Chi Eekway.

Slender, short-haired Mon Mothma hurried to embrace Bail as he approached. "A momentous occasion, Bail," she said into his left ear. "An audience with Palpatine."

Bail laughed to himself. They did think alike.

Padmé hugged him, as well, though somewhat stiffly. She

looked radiant. A bit more full-faced than Bail remembered, but the very picture of classic beauty in her elegant robes and elaborate coiffure. A golden protocol droid stood behind her. She told him she had just returned from a wonderful week on Naboo, visiting with her family.

"An extraordinary world, Naboo," Bail said. "I'll never understand how it spawned someone as stubborn as our Supreme Chancellor."

Padmé scolded him with a frown. "He's not stubborn, Bail. You just don't know him as I do. He'll take our concerns to heart."

"For all the good it will do," Chi Eekway said, displeasure wrinkling her blue face.

"You underestimate Palpatine's acuity," Padmé said. "Besides, he appreciates frank speech."

"We've been nothing if not frank, Senator," dark-complected, bib-bearded Fang Zar said. "With scant success."

Padme glanced at everyone. "Surely, faced with all of us . . ."

"Had we a tenth of the Senate we would prove too few," Bana said, draped head-to-toe in shimmersilk. "But it is important that we hold to our intention."

Eekway nodded gravely.

"It can be hoped," Fang Zar said, "not counted on."

The conversation turned to personal matters as they entered the vast building. They were an animated group when they finally arrived at the holding office, directly beneath the Great Rotunda, where Palpatine's human appointments secretary asked them to wait in the receiving area.

After an hour of waiting, their spirits began to flag. But then the door to Palpatine's office slid open, and Sate Pestage, one of Palpatine's chief advisers, appeared.

"Senators, what a surprise," he said.

Bail came to his feet, speaking for everyone when he said: "It shouldn't be. The appointment was confirmed more than three weeks ago."

Pestage glanced at the appointments secretary. "Really? I wasn't informed."

"You mostly certainly were informed," Padmé said, "since the appointment was secured through your office."

"Several of us have risked much and traveled great distances," Eekway added.

Pestage spread his hands in a patronizing way. "Such times require sacrifices, Senator. Or perhaps you feel you've risked more than the Supreme Chancellor has."

Bail spoke up. "No one is implying that the Supreme Chancellor has been anything but tireless in his . . . devotion. But the fact remains that he agreed to see us, and we're not about to leave here until he honors his pledge."

"We're not asking for much of his time," Terr Taneel said, in a more placating tone.

"Maybe not, but you must realize how busy he is. What with new developments occurring daily." Pestage looked at Bail. "I understand you've become quite friendly with the Jedi Council. Why not visit with them while I attempt to reschedule you?"

Anger mottled Bail's bearded face. "We're not leaving until we see him, Sate."

Pestage forced a smile. "As is your prerogative, Senator."

The shuttle whose landing lights had caught Obi-Wan's attention on Cato Neimoidia carried more than Intelligence analysts and technicians. Yoda was aboard, eager to see for himself what Obi-Wan and Anakin had discovered.

The technicians had succeeded in inducing the mechno-chair's holoprojector to replay the image of Lord Sidious, and Republic cryptographers working with the Jedi were confident that the unique device would yield even greater secrets once it was relocated to Coruscant and examined thoroughly.

Refusing to let the mechno-chair out of his sight, Anakin had demanded to oversee its transfer to the waiting shuttle. Feeling unnecessary, Obi-Wan and Yoda decided to take a stroll down the corridor of Viceroy Gunray's now appropriated palace. The venerable Jedi Master was pensive as they walked, the silence broken only by the sounds of distant blasterfire and the *tick, tick* of Yoda's gimer stick as it struck the polished floor.

Yoda was unreadable.

Obi-Wan wasn't sure if Yoda was pondering the image of Sidious, or the fact that two Jedi had been killed during the fighting on Cato Neimoidia. Every day saw more Jedi die. Many were as shot up as the clone troopers. Wounded, blinded, scarred, deprived of arms or legs . . . patched up by bota and bacta. More than a thousand Padawans had lost their Masters; more than a thousand Masters, their Padawans. When Jedi gathered now they talked not about the Force, but about their military campaigns. New lightsabers were constructed not as a meditative exercise, but to handle the rigors of close combat.

Reaching the end of the long corridor, Obi-Wan and Yoda turned and started back. Without taking his eyes from the floor, Yoda said: "Found something important, you have, Obi-Wan. That Count Dooku is in league with someone, proof this is. That in this war a greater part the Sith play than we realize."

The name *Sidious* had come up only once since the war began—on Geonosis, when Dooku had told an imprisoned Obi-Wan that a Sith Lord by that name had hundreds of Republic Senators under his influence. At the time, Obi-Wan assumed that Dooku was lying, in order to persuade Obi-Wan that he was still aligned with the Jedi, although attempting to thwart the powers of the dark side by his own methods. And yet, even after Dooku had revealed himself to be Sith-trained, Yoda and others on the Council continued to believe that he had been lying about Sidious. Two Council members were convinced that Dooku *was* the Dark Lord, having somehow tutored himself—by Sith Holocron, perhaps—in the use of dark side powers.

Now that Sidious appeared to be real, Obi-Wan didn't know what to think.

A hunt for Dooku's Sith allies had been going on almost since the start of the war. Dooku was known to have trained Jedi in the dark arts—Jedi Knights who had lost faith in the ideals of the Republic, Padawans fascinated by the power of the dark side, misinformed novices such as Asajj Ventress, who had been mentored by a Jedi—but the question remained, who, if anyone, had been Dooku's teacher?

Thirteen years earlier, when Obi-Wan had fought and killed a Sith on Naboo, had he killed a Master or an apprentice? The question was rooted in the belief that the Sith, having essentially defeated themselves a millennium earlier, had learned that an army of Sith could never stand, and that there should be only two at any given time, lest a pair of apprentices conspire to combine their strengths to eliminate a Master.

More a doctrine than a rule; but a doctrine that had managed to keep the Sith order alive, if well concealed, for going on a thousand years.

But the horned and tattooed Sith whom Obi-Wan killed could not have trained Dooku, because Dooku had still been a member of the Jedi Order then. As clouded as the dark side made some things, there was simply no way Dooku could have been living a double life within the walls of the Temple itself.

"Master Yoda," Obi-Wan said, "is it possible that Dooku wasn't lying about the Senate being under the control of Sidious?"

Yoda gave his head a quick shake while they walked. "Looked hard at the Senate, we did. And risked much we did by doing so—questioning in secret those we serve. But no evidence we found." He glanced up at Obi-Wan. "If in control of the Senate Sidious was, would not defeated the Republic already be? Would not to the Confederacy the Core and Inner Rim belong?"

Yoda paused for a moment, then added: "Perhaps at Geonosis, an accident it was that Dooku revealed himself. Had he not, searched we would have for Sidious, leaving Dooku to escalate his war. What think you, Obi-Wan? Hmmm?"

Obi-Wan folded his arms. "I've thought long and hard about that day, Master, and I believe Dooku couldn't help revealing himself—even though he may have regretted it. When he was fleeing for his ship, it was almost as if he *allowed* himself to be seen; almost as if he was attempting to draw us into an engagement. My first thought was that he was trying to ensure the safe escape of Gunray and the other Separatist leaders. But my instincts tell me that he wanted desperately to demonstrate how powerful he had become. I think he was genuinely surprised to see you turn up. But instead of killing Anakin or me, he deliberately left us alive, to send a message to the Jedi."

"Right you are, Obi-Wan. *Pride* undid him. Forced him, it did, to show us his true face."

"Could he have been trained by this . . . Sidious?"

"Stands to reason, it does. *Accepted* by Sidious he was, following the death of the one you killed."

Obi-Wan considered it. "I've heard rumors about Dooku's early fascination with the dark side. Was there not an incident in the Temple involving a stolen Sith Holocron?"

Yoda squeezed his eyes shut and nodded. "True that rumor is. But understand, Obi-Wan, a *Jedi* Dooku was. For many, many years. Difficult the decision is to leave the Order. Influenced he was by many things. The death of your former Master, for one— even though avenged Qui-Gon was."

He glanced at Obi-Wan. "Complicated this is. Not merely by what we know, but by what we do not know; what we have to *assume.*"

Yoda stopped, then gestured to a carved bench.

"Sit for a while, we will. Enlighten you, I can."

Obi-Wan sat, his heart wanting to race.

"A stern Master Dooku was, to Qui-Gon and others," Yoda began. "Powerful he was; skilled, disdainful. More important, convinced that lowering the shroud of the dark side was. Signs there were, all about us, long before to the Temple you came; long before Qui-Gon came. Gross injustices, favoritism, corruption . . . More and more, called the Jedi were to enforce the peace. More and more deaths there were. Out of control events were becoming."

"Did the Council sense that the Sith had returned?"

"Never absent they were, Obi-Wan. But stronger suddenly. Closer to the surface. Spoke much of the prophecy, Dooku did."

"The prophecy of the Chosen One?"

"The larger prophecy: that *unfold* the dark times would. Born into their midst the Chosen One is, to return balance to the Force."

"Anakin," Obi-Wan said.

Yoda regarded him for a long moment. "Difficult to say," he said quickly. "Maybe, yes; maybe, no. More important the shroud of the dark side is. Many, many discussions Dooku had. With me, with other members of the Council. Most of all, with Master Sifo-Dyas."

Obi-Wan waited.

"Close friends they were. Bound together by the unifying Force. But worried about Master Dooku, Sifo-Dyas was. Worried about his disenchantment with the Republic; about self-absorption among the Jedi. Saw in Dooku the effect of Qui-Gon's death, Sifo-Dyas did. The effect that resurfaced the Sith had." Yoda shook his head mournfully. "Knew of Dooku's imminent departure, Master Sifo-Dyas did. Sensed, he may have, the birth of the Separatist movement."

"And yet the Council dismissed Dooku as an idealist," Obi-Wan said.

Yoda gazed at the floor. "Saw with my own eyes what he had become, and refused to believe it, I did."

"But how could Dooku have searched out Sidious? Or was it the other way around?"

"Impossible to know. But accept Sidious as a mentor Dooku did."

"Could Sifo-Dyas have foreseen that, as well?"

"Also impossible to know. Believed he might have, that Sidious Dooku would hunt down. To *destroy*."

"Could that have motivated Dooku to leave the Order?"

"Perhaps. But by the power of the dark side, even the most steadfast heart can be seduced."

Obi-Wan turned to face Yoda. "Master, did Sifo-Dyas order the clone army?"

Yoda nodded. "Contacted the Kaminoans, he did."

"Without your knowledge?"

"Without it, yes. But *exists*, a record of his initial contact."

Obi-Wan gave in to some of his frustration. "I should have questioned Lama Su more extensively."

"Questioned, the Kaminoans were. Furnished much they did."

"Did they?" Obi-Wan said in surprise. "When?"

"Reticent they were when first to Kamino I went. Only what already they had told you, I heard. That Sifo-Dyas the order placed; that Tyranus the donor clone furnished. That for the Republic the clones were. Seen by the Kaminoans, neither Sifo-Dyas nor Tyranus was. But later, after attacked Kamino was, *more* I learned from Taun We and Ko Sai. About the payments."

"From Sifo-Dyas?"

"From Tyranus."

"Could *Tyranus* have been an alias for Sifo-Dyas? Could he have adopted the name to provide deniability for the Jedi in case the clone army was discovered?"

"Wished for that I did. But killed Sifo-Dyas was, *before* on Kamino Jango Fett arrived."

"Murdered?"

Yoda compressed his thin lips. "Unsolved the crime remains, but, yes: murdered."

"Someone knew," Obi-Wan said, more to himself. "Dooku?" he asked Yoda.

"A theory I have—nothing more. *Murder,* Dooku committed. Then, from the Jedi archives erased Kamino, he did. Of that tampering, proof Master Jocasta Nu found—proof of Dooku's action, though well concealed it was."

Obi-Wan recalled his visit to the archives to search out the location of Kamino, only to be told by Jocasta Nu that the planetary system didn't exist. What had caused him that day three years earlier to stare so intently at the library's bronzium bust of Count Dooku?

"Nevertheless, the clone army continued to be financed and built," he said at last. "Could Sifo-Dyas and Tyranus have been partners?"

"Of our ignorance, another example this is. But playing both sides Jango Fett clearly was. By someone on the side of the Republic, chosen he was on Bogg Four to be the clone template. But serving Dooku he was, as a hired killer. With the changeling who targeted Amidala, an intermediary he was."

Obi-Wan pictured Fett in the execution arena on Geonosis, standing behind Dooku in a box reserved for dignitaries. "He had knowledge of both armies. Could he have killed Sifo-Dyas?"

"Perhaps."

"Were you able to trace the source of the payments—beyond Tyranus, I mean?"

"From Bogg Four into a maze of deception, they led."

"Did the Kaminoans say whether anyone had tried to persuade them *not* to build the army?"

"Intercede, none did. Reveal themselves too soon, our enemies would have."

"So Dooku had no choice but to create an army before the clones were trained and ready."

"Appears that way, it does."

Obi-Wan fell silent for a moment.

"When I was being held captive on Geonosis, Dooku told me that the Trade Federation had been allied with Sidious during the blockade of Naboo, but that they had later been betrayed by him. Dooku said that Gunray had gone to him for help, and that Dooku had tried to appeal to the Council. He claimed that, even after several warnings, the Council refused to believe him. Is any of that true, Master?"

"More lies," Yoda said. "Building a case to enlist you in his cause, Dooku was."

You must join me, Obi-Wan, Dooku had said, *and together we will destroy the Sith!*

"If Gunray hadn't been so keen on assassinating Padmé Amidala," Obi-Wan mused. "If I'd failed to trace the saberdart that killed the changeling . . ."

"Ignorant about the clone army, we might have remained."

"But surely the Kaminoans would have contacted us, Master."

"Eventually. But grown greater in numbers the Separatist army would have. Invincible, perhaps."

Obi-Wan's eyes narrowed. "Mine wasn't a case of blind luck."

Yoda shook his head. "Meant to learn of the clone army, we were. Destined to fight this war, we were."

"In the nick of time. The Council couldn't conceive of Dooku as anything but an idealist. Perhaps he never believed that the Jedi could become generals."

"Nonsense," Yoda said. "Warriors always have we been."

"But are we helping to return balance to the Force, or are our actions contributing to the growth of the dark side?"

Yoda grimaced. "Impatient with such talk I grow. Cryptic this conflict is—the way it began, the way it unfolds. But for the ideals of the Republic we fight. To prevail and restore peace our priorities must remain. *Then* to the dark heart of this matter will we burrow. Expose the truth, we will."

Yoda was correct, Obi-Wan told himself. If the Jedi hadn't learned of the clone army, Dooku's Separatists would have suddenly appeared on the scene with tens of millions of battle droids, fleets of warships, and seceded from the Republic without contest. But there would have been no coexisting with the Confederacy. Ultimately it would have bled the Republic dry. War would have been inevitable, and the Jedi would have been caught in the middle, as they were now.

But why hadn't Yoda told him sooner about Sifo-Dyas?

Or was this yet another lesson, as the search for Kamino had been? Yoda's way of telling him to search for the thing that didn't seem to be there by analyzing its effects on the world around it. *The difference between knowledge and wisdom,* Obi-Wan's friend Dex might have said, as he did on identifying the source of the saberdart that had killed Zam Wessel, when the Temple analysis droids couldn't.

Yoda was regarding him when he lifted his head.

"Reveal you, your thoughts do, Obi-Wan. Believe I should have told you sooner, you do."

"Yours is the wisdom of centuries, Master."

"Years matter not. Busy fighting a war, you have been. Mentoring your headstrong Padawan. In pursuit of Dooku and his minions . . . *Darker,* events became. Attempting to turn this war to their own uses, Dooku and Sidious are."

"We'll have Dooku soon enough."

"Lifted the veil of the dark side wasn't after your success on Naboo. Grown beyond Dooku this war has. Now to justice *both* must be brought. And to justice all those Sidious to the dark side has turned." Yoda looked hard at Obi-Wan. "Uncover Sidious's tracks, you must. A chance this war to conclude, you and Anakin have been given."

In the launching bay Anakin kept his eyes on the mechno-chair, while R2-D2 and TC-16 kept their photoreceptors on Anakin. Now that the analysts had run their diagnostic routines, the technicians were preparing to pack the device for safe shipment to Coruscant.

Just as Obi-Wan had said, they resented the fact that Anakin had tampered with the chair, despite the fact that, had he not, the chair would have blown itself to pieces, taking with it the holoimage of Sidious and whatever other communications memories it might contain.

Maybe Qui-Gon should have left you at Watto's junk shop.

Obi-Wan's little joke. But the words had stung, for some reason. Probably because of Anakin's own musings about what might have become of him had the Jedi not been forced to land on Tatooine to find a replacement part for Padmé's starship. It wasn't hard to imagine himself stuck in Mos Espa. With his mom; with C-3PO, without the bright shell he now wore—

No.

At nine years of age he had been an expert Podracer; by

twenty-one he would have been a galactic champion. With or without Qui-Gon's or Watto's help, he would eventually have won the Boonta Eve race, and his reputation would have been made. He would have bought freedom for himself, his mother, all the slaves in Mos Espa, gone on to win the Grand Races on Malastare, been hailed in the gambling casinos on Ord Mantell and Coruscant. He wouldn't have become a Jedi—he would have been too old to train—would never have learned to wield a lightsaber. But he would have been able to fly rings around the finest of Jedi pilots, including Saesee Tiin.

And he still would have been stronger in the Force than any of them.

He might never have met Padmé . . .

He had thought her an Angel, arrived on Tatooine from the Moons of Viago. A playful remark on his part, but not as entirely innocent as it had sounded. Even so, to her he was just a funny little boy. Padmé didn't know then that his precocity wasn't limited to a skill for building and fixing things. He had an uncanny sense for knowing what was going to happen; a certainty that he would become celebrated. He was different—chosen long before the Jedi Order had bestowed the title. Mythical beings came to him—Angels and Jedi—and he excelled in contests in which humans weren't even meant to participate. And yet, even with an Angel and Jedi for guests in his home, he hadn't divined the sudden departure from Tatooine, the Jedi training, his marriage.

He was no longer the funny little boy. But Padmé remained his Angel—

A vision of her broke his reverie.

Something . . . something had changed. His heart filled with longing for her. Even through the Force he couldn't clarify what he was feeling. He simply knew that he should be with her. That he should be there to protect her . . .

He flexed his artificial hand.

Remain in the living Force, he told himself. A Jedi didn't dwell in the past. A Jedi surrendered attachment to persons and things that passed out of his or her life. A Jedi didn't fantasize, or think: *What if—*

He cut his eyes to the three human technicians who were fitting the mechno-chair into a crash-foam safety harness. One of them was working too fast, and almost knocked the chair over.

Anakin shot to his feet and stormed across the bay.

"Be careful with that!" he shouted.

The oldest of the three gave him a scornful glance. "Relax, kid, we know our job."

Kid.

He waved his hand, calling on the Force to keep the mechno-chair fixed in place. The three techs strained to move it, baffled until they realized what Anakin had done. Then the same one straightened and glared.

"All right, let go of it."

"When I'm convinced you actually know what you're doing."

"Look, kid—"

Anakin beetled his brows in anger and advanced a step. The three techs began to back away from the chair.

They're afraid of me. They've heard about me.

For an instant, their fear empowered him; then he felt shame, and averted his glance.

The eldest was holding up his hands. "Take it easy, Jedi. I didn't mean to offend you."

"Pack it yourself if you want to," another said.

Anakin swallowed hard. "It's important, that's all. I don't want anything to happen to it." He let the mechno-chair settle to the floor.

"Carefully, this time," the eldest said, refusing to so much as glance at Anakin.

"General Skywalker!" a trooper called from behind him.

Anakin turned, saw the trooper motioning to the shuttle.

"Hyperwave commo for you—from the office of the Supreme Chancellor."

Now the three technicians looked at him again. *As well they should.*

Without a word, Anakin spun on his heel and ascended the shuttle's boarding ramp. Above a holoprojector plate in the ship's comm center, a flickering image of Supreme Chancellor Palpatine was resolving. When Anakin had positioned himself on the transmission grate, Palpatine smiled.

"Congratulations, Anakin, on your victory at Cato Neimoidia."

"Thank you, sir. But I'm sorry to report that Viceroy Gunray escaped, and that fighting continues in the rock-arch cities."

Palpatine's smile faltered. "Yes, I was informed as much."

It wasn't the first time Anakin had heard from Palpatine in the field. At Jabiim, Palpatine had ordered Anakin to retreat before the planet fell to the Separatists; at Praesitlyn he had praised Anakin for having saved the day. Still, the communications were often as awkward as they were flattering.

"What's wrong, my boy?" Palpatine asked. "I sense that you're troubled about something. If it involves Gunray, accept my word that he won't be able to hide from us forever. None of them will. One day you'll have your chance for complete victory."

Anakin wet his lips. "It's not about Gunray, sir. Just a small incident here that made me angry."

"What incident?"

Anakin was tempted to disclose the details of his and Obi-Wan's discovery, but Yoda had told him to remain silent about the mechno-chair. "Nothing important," he said. "But I always feel guilty when I become angry."

"That's a mistake," Palpatine said gently. "Anger is natural, Anakin. I thought we'd been through all this—regarding what took place on Tatooine?"

"Obi-Wan doesn't show anger—except, of course, at me. Even then, it's more like . . . aggravation."

"Anakin, you're a passionate young man. That's what separates you from your Jedi comrades. Unlike Obi-Wan and the others, you weren't raised in the Temple, where younglings are taught to conquer their anger by transcending it. You enjoyed a natural childhood. You can dream, you have imagination and vision. You're not some unthinking machine, some heartless piece of technology. Not that I'm suggesting that the Jedi are," Palpatine was quick to add. "But for someone like you, any threat to someone or something important to you is likely to evoke an emotional response. It happened with your mother; it will happen again. But you shouldn't fight those responses. Learn from them, but don't fight them."

Anakin suppressed an impulse to reveal his marriage to Padmé, as well.

"Do you think I'm immune to anger?" Palpatine said into the short silence.

"I've never seen you angry."

"Well, perhaps I've grown adept at reserving my anger for private moments. But it grows more difficult to do so, in the face of the frustrations I face with the Senate. With the way this war persists . . . Oh, I know that you and the other Jedi are doing everything you can . . . But the Jedi Council and I don't always see eye-to-eye on how this war should be waged. You know my love for the Republic knows no bounds. That's why I'm struggling so hard to keep it from falling to pieces."

Anakin forced a derisive breath. "The Senate should simply follow your lead. Instead, they block you. They tie your hands. It's as if they envy the power they gave you."

"Yes, my boy, many do. But many support me, as well. More

important, we must abide by the rules and regulations of the Constitution, or else we are no better than those who stand in the way of freedom."

"Some individuals should be above the rules," Anakin grumbled.

"A case can be made for it. And, indeed, you are one of those people, Anakin. But you must know when to act, and when not to."

Anakin nodded. "I understand." He paused, then said, "How is Coruscant, sir? I miss it."

"Coruscant is as ever, a shining example of what life could be. But I'm far too busy to indulge in its manifold pleasures."

Anakin searched for some way to frame the question he needed to ask. "I guess you've been meeting frequently with the Loyalist Committee."

"As a matter of fact, I have. A treasured group of Senators, who value the high standards of the Republic as much as you and I do." Palpatine smiled. "Senator Amidala, for example. So filled with vigor and compassion—the same qualities she brought to her term as Queen of Naboo. She causes a stir wherever she goes." He looked directly at Anakin. "I'm so glad that you and she have become such dear friends."

Anakin swallowed nervously. "Will you tell her . . . will you tell her hello from me?"

"Of course I will."

An ensuing silence lingered an instant too long.

"Anakin, I will somehow see to it that you return from the Outer Rim soon," Palpatine said. "But we cannot rest until those responsible for this war have been held accountable for their crimes and eliminated as a threat to lasting peace. Do you understand?"

"I'll do my part, sir."

"Yes, my boy. I know you will."

In the reception area of the holding office, Bail Organa paced restlessly. He was preparing to vent his exasperation on Palpatine's appointments secretary when the door to the Supreme Chancellor's office opened once again, and his advisers began to file out between the imposing, red-cowled guards that flanked the opening.

Advisers Sim Aloo and Janus Greejatus; director of Intelligence Armand Isard; senior member of the Security and Intelligence Council, Jannie Ha'Nook of Glithnos; Chagrian Speaker of the Senate Mas Amedda; and staff aide Sly Moore, tall and ethereal looking in her Umbaran shadowcloak. Last to exit was Pestage.

"Senators, you're still here, I see."

"We're nothing if not patient," Bail said.

"Good to know, since the Supreme Chancellor still has much to attend to."

Just then Palpatine himself appeared, glancing at Bail and the others, then at Pestage.

"Senator Organa, Senator Amidala—all of you. What a delight to find you here."

"Supreme Chancellor," Bail said, "we were under the impression we had an appointment with you."

Palpatine lifted an eyebrow. "Indeed? Why wasn't I informed of this?" he asked Pestage.

"Your schedule is so full, I didn't want to overburden you."

Palpatine frowned. "My day is never so full that I can't take time to confer with members of the Loyalist Committee. Leave us, Sate, and don't allow us to be disturbed. I'll call for you when you're needed."

Stepping aside, he gestured Bail and the others into the circular office. C-3PO was last to cross the threshold, twisting his head to regard both of the motionless guards.

Bail took a seat directly across from Palpatine's high-backed chair, which was said to house some sort of shield generator—necessary for his protection, as were the guards, though something that would have been unheard of three years earlier. Saturated in red, the windowless, carpeted office contained several singular pieces of statuary, as did Palpatine's chambers in the Senate Office Building, and his suite in the crown of 500 Republica. Rumored to work for days on end without sleeping, Palpatine seemed alert, curious, somewhat imperious.

"So, what matters have brought you here on such a glorious Coruscant afternoon?" he said from his chair. "I can't help but sense a certain urgency . . ."

"We'll come directly to the point, Supreme Chancellor," Bail said. "Now that the Confederacy has been chased from the Core and Inner Rim, we wish to discuss the abrogation of some of the measures that were enacted in the name of public safety."

Palpatine gazed at Bail over steepled fingers. "Our recent victories have made you feel so secure?"

"They have, Supreme Chancellor," Padmé said.

"The Enhanced Security and Enforcement Act in particular," Bail continued. "Specifically those measures that permit the unrestricted use of observation droids, and searches and seizures without the need for warrants or due process."

"I see," Palpatine said slowly. "Unfortunately, the fact of the matter is that the war is far from won, and I, for one, am not entirely satisfied that traitors and terrorists are not a continued threat to public safety. Oh, I realize that our victories give all appearances of a quick resolution to the war, but as of this morning I was informed that the Separatists still hold many key worlds in the Outer Rim, and that our sieges there could go on indefinitely."

"Indefinitely?" Eekway said.

"Why not consider ceding some of those worlds," Fang Zar suggested. "Trade in the Core and Inner Rim has resumed almost to prewar standards."

Palpatine shook his head. "Some of those Outer Rim worlds were Republic worlds, taken by force. And I fear we risk setting a dangerous precedent by allowing the Confederacy to retain them. I believe, furthermore, that now is the very time to press our attack, until the Separatists no longer present a threat to our way of life."

"Is there not some other way than continued warfare?" Bail asked. "Surely Dooku can be persuaded to listen to reason now."

"You misjudge his resolve, Senator. But even if I'm wrong, suppose we decide to cede some worlds, as a conciliatory gesture. Who will choose which worlds? Me? You? Shall we submit the matter to a Senate vote? And how might the denizens of those ceded worlds respond to our gesture? How would the good people of Alderaan feel about being a Confederacy world? Should loyalty to the Republic count for so little? Such decisions were what prompted many worlds to ally with Count Dooku in the first place."

"But can we even triumph in the Outer Rim," Eekway said, "with the army so reduced, the Jedi so dispersed? Might it not appear that the Jedi are deliberately perpetuating this war?"

Palpatine stood up and paced away from his huge chair, turning his back to everyone. "This has become a very regrettable situation—one we have attempted to correct, with limited success." He swung around. "We must consider how others view this war. A former Jedi at the helm of the Separatist movement; the clone army of the Republic led by Jedi . . . Many remote worlds see this war as an attempt by the Jedi to dominate the galaxy. To many, the Jedi were not to be trusted before the war—in part as a result of the aggressive negotiations they were constrained to undertake during the terms of my predecessors. Word reaches those same worlds that it was the Jedi who invaded Geonosis, all because two of the Order had been sentenced to death for espionage. We know better, of course, but how to amend the misinterpretation?"

Realizing that he had allowed the discussion to go off track, Bail said: "Returning to the matter of rescinding the Security Act—"

"I serve the Republic, Senator Organa," Palpatine said, cutting him off. "Introduce a measure to repeal in the Senate. I will accept whatever outcome ensues from a vote."

"Will you remain impartial during the debates?"

"You have my word."

"And these amendments to the Constitution," Mon Mothma started to say.

"I view the Constitution as a *living* document," Palpatine interrupted. "As such, it must be allowed to expand and contract according to circumstances. Otherwise, what do we have but stasis."

"If we can be assured of a certain . . . exhalation of power," Bana Breemu said.

Palpatine grinned faintly. "Of course."

"Then we've made a beginning," Padmé said. "Just as I knew we would."

Palpatine beamed at her. "Senator Amidala, is that not the droid Jedi Skywalker constructed?"

Padmé looked at C-3PO. "Yes, it is."

For a moment it appeared that C-3PO was speechless—but only for a moment.

"I am honored that you remember me, Your Majesty," he said.

Palpatine returned an abrupt laugh. "A title more fit for a king or emperor." He glanced at Padmé. "In fact, I have just spoken with him, Your Highness."

"Anakin?" Padmé said in surprise.

Palpatine held her gaze. "Why Senator Amidala, I do believe you're blushing."

Returning to the launching bay with Yoda, Obi-Wan observed Anakin and Yoda trade the briefest of looks, the meaning of which escaped him. Neither Jedi appeared to be bothered by the silent exchange, and yet Yoda doddered off without a word to speak with the Intelligence analysts huddled near the shuttle's boarding ramp.

"Jedi Council business?" Anakin asked when Obi-Wan joined him.

"Nothing of the sort. Yoda believes that the mechno-chair may yield clues to the whereabouts of Darth Sidious. He wants us to take up the search."

Anakin didn't respond immediately. "Master, aren't we obligated to notify the Supreme Chancellor of our find?"

"We are, Anakin, and we will."

"When the Council sees fit, you mean."

"No. After the matter has been discussed."

"But suppose one or two of you should disagree with the majority?"

"Decisions are not always unanimous. When we are truly divided, we defer to Yoda's counsel."

"Then the Force can sometimes be felt more strongly by one than by eleven."

Obi-Wan tried to discern Anakin's intent. "Even Yoda is not infallible, if that's what you're getting at."

"The Jedi should be." Anakin glanced furtively at Obi-Wan. "We *could* be."

"I'm listening."

"By going farther with the Force than we allow ourselves. By riding its crest."

"Master Sora Bulq and many others would agree, Anakin. But few Jedi have the stomach for such a ride. We're not all as self-composed as Yoda or Master Windu."

"But maybe we're wrong to attach ourselves to the Force at the expense of life as most beings know it, which includes lust, love, and a lot of other emotions that are forbidden to us. Devotion to a higher cause is fine and good, Master, but we shouldn't ignore what's going on in front of our own eyes. You said yourself that we're not infallible. Dooku understood that. He looked things squarely in the eye, and decided to do something about it."

"Dooku is a Sith, Anakin. He may have had his good reasons for leaving the Order, but he is nothing now but a master of deceit. He and Sidious prey on the weak-willed. They deceive themselves into *believing* that they are infallible."

"But I've seen instances where the Jedi lie to one another. Master Kolar lied about Quinlan Vos going to the dark side. We're lying now, by not sharing our information about Sidious with Chancellor Palpatine. What would Sidious or Dooku have to say about our lies?"

"Don't compare us to them," Obi-Wan said, more harshly than he meant. "The Jedi are not a cult, Anakin. We don't worship a leadership of elites. We're encouraged to find our paths; to validate through personal experience the value of what we have been taught. We don't offer facile justifications for exterminating a perceived enemy. We're guided by compassion, and the belief that the Force is greater than the sum of those who open themselves to it."

Anakin grew quiet. "I'm only asking, Master."

Obi-Wan took a calming breath. *Too sure of themselves, the Jedi have become,* Yoda had once told him. *Even the older, more experienced ones . . .*

How might Anakin have fared under Qui-Gon's guidance? he wondered. He was merely Anakin's adoptive mentor, and a flawed mentor in many ways. So eager to live up to the memory of Qui-Gon that he was continually overlooking Anakin's attempts to live up to him.

"Carries on his shoulders the weight of the galaxy, Obi-Wan does," Yoda said, approaching with one of the Intelligence analysts. "Ease your concerns, this news might," he added before Obi-Wan could respond.

The dark-haired, robust-looking analyst Captain Dyne perched himself on the edge of a shipping container. "While we still don't know whether the mechno-chair was left behind deliberately, as some kind of trap, the image of Sidious is authentic. The transmission appears to have been received two days ago, local, but we're going to have trouble tracking its source because it was routed through a system of hyperwave transceivers used by the Confederacy as a substitute for the HoloNet, and was encrypted using a code developed by the InterGalactic Banking Clan. We've been working on cracking that code for some time now, and when we do, we might be able to use the chair's hyperwave receiver to eavesdrop on enemy communications."

"Better you feel already, *ummm?*" Yoda said to Obi-Wan, motioning with his gimer stick.

"The chair bears the stamps of several of the manufacturers affiliated with Dooku," Dyne continued. "The hyperwave receiver is equipped with a type-summoning chip and transponding antenna that are similar to ones we discovered in a mine-laying chameleon droid Master Yoda brought back from Ilum."

"An image of *Dooku*, the droid contained."

"For the time being we're proceeding on the assumption that Dooku—or Sidious, for that matter—might have developed the chips, and had them installed in transceivers awarded to Gunray and other key members of the Council of Separatists."

"Is the mechno-chair the same one I saw on Naboo?" Obi-Wan asked.

"We think so," Dyne said. "But it has undergone some modifications in the years since. The self-destruct mechanism, for one, along with the self-defense gas." He looked at Obi-Wan. "Your hunch was right about it being the same one the Neimoidians have been using for years, and appears to have originally been developed by a Separatist researcher named Zan Arbor."

"Zan Arbor," Anakin said angrily. "The gas used on the Gungans at Ohma-D'un." He looked at Obi-Wan. "No wonder you were able to sense it!"

Dyne glanced from Anakin to Obi-Wan. "The gas-emitter mechanism is identical to what you find in some of the Techno Union's E-Five-Twenty-Two assassin droids."

Obi-Wan stroked his chin in thought. "If Gunray has had the chair for fourteen years, then he could have been using it to contact Sidious during the Naboo crisis. If we could learn who manufactured the chair . . ."

Yoda laughed. "Ahead of Obi-Wan, the experts are," he said to Anakin.

"We know who's responsible for the chair's Neimoidian engravings," Dyne explained. "A Xi Charrian whose name I'm not even going to attempt to pronounce."

"How do you know?" Anakin asked.

The analyst grinned. "Because he signed his work."

*   *   *

Padmé parted company with Bail and the others in the Senate Plaza. She spied Captain Typho waving to her from the landing platform, and hastened toward their waiting speeder. The towering statues that graced the plaza seemed to stare down at her; the building had never seemed so enormous.

The brief meeting with Palpatine had left her flustered—but for all the wrong reasons. Though her every other thought was of Anakin, she had resolved to put him from her mind for the meeting; to focus on what was expected of her both as a public servant and concerned citizen of the Republic. And yet, despite her best intentions, Palpatine had brought Anakin to the fore.

Had Anakin confessed to him? she wondered. Had the Supreme Chancellor learned of their secret ceremony on Naboo, from Anakin or others?

A feeling of light-headedness forced her to slow her pace. The heat of the afternoon. The glare. The enormity of recent events . . .

She could feel Anakin at a great remove. He was thinking of her; she was certain of it. Images of him riffled through her mind. She paused at one that made her smile: their first dinner together on Tatooine. Qui-Gon reprimanding Jar Jar Binks for his uncouth behavior. Anakin sitting beside her. Shmi . . . Was she sitting opposite her? Wasn't Shmi's gaze fixed on her when Shmi said, referring to Anakin: *He was meant to help you.*

The truth didn't matter.

That was the way she remembered it.

Protected by two squadrons of Trade Federation Vulture fighters, Nute Gunray's organic-looking shuttle cut a blazing trail through the void of deep space, plasma bolts from a dozen Republic V-wings nipping at its upraised tail. The droid fighters were matching the twists and slaloms of the faster enemy ships, and the blaster cannons buried deep in the clefts of their narrow wings were spewing continuous cover fire.

From the bridge of the Trade Federation cruiser the *Invisible Hand*—flagship of the Confederacy fleet—General Grievous observed the whole mad dance.

To any other spectator it might appear that the viceroy was risking his wattled neck, but Grievous knew better. Late to arrive at the rendezvous because of his decision to detour to Cato Neimoidia, Gunray was putting on a show for the general's benefit, attempting to make it seem that he had been *chased* to the Outer Rim when, in fact, he had undoubtedly allowed his hyperspace vectors to be plotted by Republic forces. Where common sense would have dictated using secret routes pioneered by and known only to members of the Trade Federation, the core ship

the shuttle had launched from had adhered to standard hyperlanes in jumping from the inner systems.

More to the point, Gunray's vessel was in no real peril. Outnumbered by better than two to one and flying headlong into
the vanguard vessels of the Confederacy fleet, it was the pilots of
the Republic starfighters who were risking their necks. At another time Grievous might have applauded their bravery by allowing them to escape with their lives, but Gunray's transparent
attempts at pretense had exposed the fleet to surveillance, and
now the Republic pilots would have to die.

But not immediately.

First, Gunray would have to be punished for his blunder;
given a foretaste of what awaited him the next time he disobeyed
a directive.

Grievous turned from the cruiser's forward viewports to the
weapons stations, where a pair of rangy droids were monitoring
the pursuit.

"Gunners, the Republic starfighters are not to leave this sector. Target and destroy their hyperdrive rings. Then you are to
target and destroy one squadron of the shuttle's escort Vulture
fighters."

"Acquiring targets," one of the droids said.

"Firing," the other said.

Grievous swung back to the viewport in time to see the half-
dozen hyperdrive rings come apart in short-lived explosions. An
instant later, clouds of billowing fire began to erupt to both sides
of Gunray's shuttle, and twelve droid fighters vanished from
sight. The unexpected explosions wreaked havoc on the rest of
the escort, leaving the shuttle vulnerable to strafing runs by the
starfighters. With the formation in tatters, the Vultures followed
protocol by attempting to regroup, but in so doing left themselves open to precisely placed bolts from the starfighters.

A consequence of the Neimoidians' reluctance to augment

the droid brains of the fighters with interface capabilities, Grievous noted. Although they functioned better now than they had five years earlier.

Three more Vulture fighters blew to pieces, this time due to Republic fire.

Now the Neimoidian pilots of the shuttle weren't sure what to do. Attempts to go evasive were sabotaged by the droid ships' attempts to keep the shuttle centered in their shield array.

Enemy laser bolts kept finding their marks.

The destruction of the hyperdrive rings had alerted the Republic pilots to the fact that they were well inside the range of the cruiser's weapons, and that they had to make their kill quickly if they hoped to escape. Jinking and weaving among the remaining escort droids, they pressed the attack on the shuttle.

Grievous wondered for a moment if any of the pilots might be Jedi, in which case he would opt to capture rather than kill. The more closely he studied the maneuvers, however, the more certain he grew that the pilots were clones. Skilled fliers nevertheless—as indeed their Mandalorian template had been—but they evinced none of the supernatural perception afforded to the Jedi by the Force.

Still, Gunray's shuttle was taking a beating. One of its landing appendages had been amputated, and vapor streamed from its pug tail. The vessel's primitive particle and ray shields were still holding, but they weakened steadily with each direct hit. The convergence of a few more plasma bolts would overwhelm them. Then the ship the shields protected could be sliced and diced or taken out by a well-placed proton torpedo.

Grievous pictured Gunray, Haako, and the others strapped into luxurious acceleration couches, shivering with dread, perhaps sorry for the brief detour to Cato Neimoidia, wondering how a handful of Republic pilots had so easily decimated their squadrons, certainly comlinking the core ship to dispatch reinforcements.

The general was almost of a mind to award the Republic pilots their kill, for he and Gunray had been at odds frequently over the past three years. One of the first spacefaring species to build a droid army, the Neimoidians had grown accustomed to thinking of their soldiers and workers as thoroughly expendable. Their extraordinary wealth had allowed them to replace whatever they lost, so they had never developed a sense of respect for the machines fashioned for them by Baktoid Armor Workshops, the Xi Char, Colicoids, or others.

From their first acquaintance, Gunray had made the mistake of treating Grievous as just another droid—even though he had been told that this was not the case.

Perhaps Gunray had thought of him as some mindless entity, like the reawakened Gen'Dai, Durge; or Dooku's misguided apprentice, Asajj Ventress; or the human bounty hunter called Aurra Sing—all three of whom had been so driven by personal hatred of the Jedi that they had proved worthless, mere distractions while Grievous went about the real business of war.

The attitude of the Neimoidians had changed quickly enough, though, in part because they had been witness to Grievous's capabilities, but more as a result of what had occurred on Geonosis. Had it not been for Grievous, Gunray and the rest might have suffered the same fate as Poggle the Lesser's lieutenant, Sun Fac. Grievous's actions in the catacombs that day—with the Geonosians retreating by the thousands from the arena and companies of clone commandos following them in—had allowed Gunray to escape the planet alive.

Sometimes he wondered just how many clones he had killed or wounded that day.

And Jedi, of course—though none had lived to speak of him.

The Jedi corpses that were retrieved bespoke something atrocious that resided in those dark underground passages. Perhaps the Jedi believed that a rancor or a reek had shredded the bodies of their Forceful comrades; or perhaps they thought the damage had been done by Geonosian sonic weapons set to maximum power.

Either way, they must have wondered what became of the victims' lightsabers.

Grievous regretted that he hadn't been able to see the reactions, but he, too, had been forced to flee as Geonosis fell.

The revelation of his existence had had to wait until a handful of hapless Jedi had arrived on the foundry world of Hypori. By then, Grievous had already amassed a sizable collection of lightsabers, but at Hypori he had been able to add several more, two of which he wore inside his command cloak even now.

As trophies they were superior to the pelts of hunted beings he knew some bounty hunters to affect. He admired the precision and care that had gone into the construction of the lightsabers; more, each seemed to retain a faint memory of its wielder. As a former swordmaster, he could appreciate that each had been handcrafted, rather than turned out in quantity like blasters or pike weapons.

He could respect the Jedi for that, though he had nothing but hatred for them as an Order.

Because of the remoteness of their homeworld, his species, the Kaleesh, had had few dealings with the Jedi. But then war had broken out between the Kaleesh and their planetary neighbors—a savage, insectile species known as the Huk. Grievous had become infamous during the long conflict: conquering worlds, defeating grand armies, exterminating entire colonies of Huk. But instead of surrendering, as would have been the honorable course, the Huk had appealed to the Republic to intercede, and the Jedi had arrived on Kalee. In what passed for negotiations—fifty Jedi Knights and Masters ready to loose their lightsabers on Grievous and his army—the Kaleesh were made to appear the aggressors. The reason was plain: where Kalee had little to offer in the way of trade, the Huk worlds were rich in ore and other resources lusted after by the Trade Federation and others. Chastised by the Republic, the Kaleesh foundered. Sanctions and reparations were imposed; traders avoided the planet; Grievous's people starved and perished by the hundreds of thousands.

Ultimately the InterGalactic Banking Clan had come to their rescue, helping with funds, reinstating trade, providing Grievous with a new direction.

Years later, the Muuns would come again . . .

Grievous's eyes tracked the course of the now imperiled shuttle.

Count Dooku and his Sith Master would never forgive him if he allowed anything untoward to happen to Gunray. Neimoidians were clever. Their knowledge of secret hyperlanes was unparalleled, and their immense army of infantry and super battle droids were rigged with devices that compelled them to respond principally to Gunray and his elite. Should the Neimoidian chiefs die, the Confederacy would lose a powerful ally.

It was time to spring Gunray from the trap he had fashioned for him.

"Launch tri-fighters to assist the shuttle," Grievous instructed the gunners. "Target and destroy the Republic starfighters outright."

Deployed from the cruiser, a wing of the new red-eyed droid fighters was soon visible from the bridge viewports.

Alerted to the approaching tri-droids, the Republic pilots had sense enough to realize that they were severely outnumbered. Disengaging from the last of the Vulture fighters, they began to make for free space, the nearest habitable planets, wherever their sublight ion drives could deliver them, since their means of jumping to lightspeed had already been destroyed.

Two of the starfighters were slower than the rest to disengage. Calling for magnification of the shuttle pursuit, Grievous saw that the stragglers were newly minted ARC-170s, copiloted crafts equipped with powerful laser cannons at the tips of their outstretched wings and multiple torpedo launchers. He was eager to see what they were capable of.

"Instruct three squadrons of the tri-fighter wing to shield the shuttle and escort it to our docking bay. Set the rest against the fleeing starfighters, except for the ARC-one-seventies. The ARC-one-seventies should be lured into engagement, without disintegration—even if some of the tri-droids are forced to succumb to enemy fire."

Grievous sharpened his gaze.

The tri-fighters had split into two groups, the larger forming up around Gunray's impaired shuttle and pouncing on the retreating V-wings, while the diverted squadron began to tease the pair of ARC-170s into duels and sallies.

What impressed Grievous was how quickly the pilots came to each other's assistance. Combat camaraderie hadn't been bred into them by the Kaminoan cloners, or been something they had learned from the Jedi. It had come from the Mandalorian bounty hunter. Fett would have denied it, of course, would have insisted that he was out only for himself. But that was not the way of his warrior brethren, and that was not the way of the clone pilots now. Exaggerating the value of each life, as if the clones were uncontrived humans.

Was the Republic so shorthanded it couldn't afford losses?

Something to bear in mind. Something that could be exploited at some point.

Without glancing at the bridge gunners, Grievous said: "Finish them off."

Then, turning to a droid at the communications suite, he added: "See to it that the Neimoidians are ushered directly to the briefing room. Inform the others that I am on my way."

Still shaken from the ordeal of transiting from the core ship to the *Invisible Hand*, Nute Gunray sat restively in the cabin space to which he and Haako been shown immediately on disembarking. He had expected that a few Republic starfighters might pursue the core ship from Cato Neimoidia—as they no doubt had other Trade Federation vessels launched to equally distant star systems in the Outer Rim. And he had hoped that the appearance of those starfighters would convey the impression that he had been chased from the Neimoidian purse world. But the scenario hadn't unfolded as planned. What should have been a quick, effortless crossing had ended up a flight for life, with the shuttle left seriously damaged and more than a squadron of Vulture fighters destroyed.

It was almost beyond explanation until the shuttle pilot confirmed that most of the Vultures had been atomized by fire from the cruiser's turbolaser batteries.

Grievous!

Castigating him for arriving late.

Gunray would have liked nothing more than to inform Dooku of the general's actions, but he feared that the Sith would stand with Grievous.

Every bit as shaken, Rune Haako sat alongside Gunray at the cabin's gleaming table. Other members of the Separatist Council occupied the choice seats: the almost two-dimensionally thin San Hill, Muun chairman of the InterGalactic Banking Clan; the Skakoan foreman of the Techno Union, Wat Tambor, encased in the cumbersome pressure suit that supplied him with methane; the vestigial-winged Geonosian Poggle the Lesser, Archduke of the Stalgasin Hive; the stalk-necked Gossam president of the Commerce Guild, Shu Mai; the cranial-horned Corporate Alliance Magistrate, Passel Argente; and former Republic Senators Po Nudo and Tikkes—Aqualish and Quarren, respectively.

Separate conversations were in progress when the sound of clanging footfalls echoed from the long corridor that led to the briefing room. Abruptly everyone fell silent, and a moment later General Grievous appeared in the hatchway, the rounded crown of his elongated death mask of a helmet grazing the top of the

opening, his high-backed collar of ceramic armorplast reminiscent of a neck brace. Sheathed in metal more suited to a starfighter, his skeletal upper limbs were spread wide, clawlike
duranium hands just touching the hatchway frame. His two feet,
which also resembled claws, were capable of increasing his height
by several centimeters. Legs of sleek alloy bones looked as if they
could propel him into orbit. His campaign cloak, slit down one
side from left shoulder to floor, was thrown back so that twin
pectorals of armor plating were exposed, along with the reverse
ribs that began at Grievous's hip girdle and extended upward to
his shielded sternum. Beneath it all, encased in a kind of fluid-
filled, forest-green gutsac, were the organs that nurtured the
living part of him.

Behind helmet holes that rendered his visage at once mournful and fearsome, sallow reptilian eyes fixed Gunray with a gimlet
stare. In a synthesized voice, deep and grating, he said: "Welcome aboard, Viceroy. For a moment we feared that you weren't
going to arrive."

Gunray felt the gazes of everyone in the cabin fall on him.
His distrust of the cyborg was no secret; nor was Grievous's en-
mity for him.

"And I can only assume that you were very troubled by the
prospect, General."

"You must know how important you are to our cause."

"I know it, General. Though I confess to wondering if you
do."

"I am your keeper, Viceroy. Your protector."

Striding into the cabin, he began to circle the table, stopping
directly behind Gunray, towering over him. Peripherally, Gunray
saw Haako slouch deeper into his chair, refusing to look either at
him or at Grievous, circling his hands in a nervous gesture.

"I have no favorite among you," the general said at last. "I
champion all of you. That is why I summoned you here: to ensure your continued protection."

No one said a word.

"The Republic fools itself believing that they have you on the run, but, in fact, Lord Sidious and Darth Tyranus have engineered this, for reasons that will be made clear soon enough. All is proceeding according to plan. However, with your homeworlds fallen to the Republic, your purse and colony worlds throughout the galaxy threatened, you are ordered to remain a group for the foreseeable future. I have been instructed to find a safe harbor for you here, in the Outer Rim."

"What world will accept us now?" equine-faced San Hill asked in a disconsolate voice.

"If none offers, Chairman, then I will take one."

Grievous walked to the hatchway, his talons screeching along the deck. "For now, return to your separate vessels. When a world has been selected, I will contact each of you in the usual manner, and provide you with new rendezvous coordinates."

Careful not to betray his sudden misgiving, Gunray traded covert glances with Haako.

The "usual manner" meant the mechno-chair inadvertently left behind on Cato Neimoidia.

16

A patchwork of dull red and pale brown, Charros IV filled the forward viewports of the Republic cruiser. The twin-piloted ship had been an antique twenty years earlier, but its sublight and hyperdrive engines were reliable, and with vessels deployed on so many fronts Obi-Wan and Anakin couldn't be choosy. The cruiser's once emblematic crimson color was obscured under fresh coats of white paint; as a result of the war, laser cannons were carefully tucked astern under the radiator panel wings, and forward, beneath the cockpit, in the space that had once functioned as a salon for passengers.

Obi-Wan had plotted the three jumps it had taken them to reach the Xi Char world from the Inner Rim, but Anakin had done all the piloting.

"Landing coordinates coming in," Anakin said, eyes fixed on a display screen set into the instrument panel.

Obi-Wan was pleasantly surprised. "That will teach me not to be skeptical. In the past when we've been informed that Intelligence has done the advance work, I've found that to be anything but the case."

Anakin looked at him and laughed.

"Something funny?"

"I was just thinking, *Here you are again* . . ."

Obi-Wan sat back in his chair, waiting for the rest of it.

"I only mean that, for someone with a reputation for hating space travel, you've certainly taken part in more than your share of exotic missions. Kamino, Geonosis, Ord Cestus . . ."

Obi-Wan plucked at his beard. "Let's just say that the war has prompted me to take a long view of things."

"Master Qui-Gon would have been proud of you."

"Don't be too sure."

Obi-Wan had argued against going to Charros IV. Dexter Jettster, his Besalisk friend on Coruscant, could probably have furnished the Intelligence analysts with everything they needed to know about Viceroy Gunray's mechno-chair. But Yoda had insisted that Obi-Wan and Anakin attempt to speak personally with the Xi Charrian whose sigil had been discovered on the walking chair.

Now Obi-Wan wondered why he had been so averse to making the trip. Compared to the past few months, the mission already felt like a furlough. Anakin was correct about Obi-Wan's having had more than his share of such assignments. But several other Jedi had also doubled as Intelligence operatives during the course of the war. Aayla Secura and the Caamasi Jedi Ylenic It'kla had taken a Techno Union defector into custody on Corellia; Quinlan Vos had gone undercover to infiltrate Dooku's circle of dark side apprentices . . .

And Supreme Chancellor Palpatine hadn't been told—or learned since—about any of the covert operations.

It wasn't that the Jedi Council didn't trust him; it was more a matter of no longer trusting *anyone*.

"Do you think the Xi Char will talk to us?" Anakin said.

Obi-Wan swiveled to face him. "They've every reason to be accommodating. After the Battle of Naboo, the Republic refused to do any business with them, for their having supplied the

Neimoidians with proscribed weapons. They've been eager to atone ever since, especially now that their signature designs are being mass-produced more cheaply by Baktoid Armor and other Confederacy suppliers."

The Xi Char's principal contribution to the Neimoidian arsenal had been the so-called Variable Geometry Self-Propelled Battle Droid starfighter, a meticulously engineered solid-fuel craft that was capable of configuring itself into three separate modes.

Anakin adopted a thin-lipped expression of wariness. "I hope they won't hold it against us that I destroyed so many of their fighters."

Obi-Wan laughed shortly. "Yes, let's hope your fame hasn't spread this far into the Outer Rim. But in fact, our success hinges almost entirely on whether TeeCee-Sixteen can speak Xi Char as fluently as he claims."

"Master Kenobi, I assure you that I can speak the tongue almost as well as an indigenous Xi Charrian," the protocol droid chimed in from one of the cockpit's rear seats. "My term of service to Viceroy Gunray demanded that I familiarize myself with the trader's tongues used by all the hive species, including the Xi Char, the Geonosians, the Colicoids, and many others. My fluency will ensure complete cooperation on the part of the Xi Char. Although I expect that they will be rather disgusted by my physical appearance."

"Why's that?" Anakin asked.

"Devotion to precision technology forms the basis of Xi Char religious beliefs. They accept as a matter of faith that meticulous work is no different from prayer; indeed, their workshops have more in common with temples than factories. When a Xi Charrian is injured, he goes into self-exile, so that others won't have to look upon his imperfections or deformities. A Xi Char adage has it that 'The deity is in the details.' "

"Wear your flaws proudly, TeeCee," Anakin said, raising and clenching his right hand. "I do, mine."

The cruiser was descending into Charros IV's ice-clouded atmosphere. Leaning toward the viewport, Obi-Wan gazed down on an arid, almost treeless world. The Xi Char lived on high plateaus, hemmed in by ranges of snowcapped mountains. Expansive black-water lakes dotted the landscape.

"A bleak planet," Obi-Wan said.

Anakin made adjustments to the controls to compensate for strong winds that were buffeting the ship. "I'll take it over Tatooine any day."

Obi-Wan shrugged. "I can think of far worse places to live than Tatooine."

Into view came the landing platform to which they had been directed. Oval in shape and perfectly sized to the cruiser, it looked newly built.

"I'm certain that it was constructed specifically for us," TC-16 said. "That's why the Xi Char were unremitting in their requests to know the cruiser's exact dimensions."

Anakin glanced at Obi-Wan. "The Republic could use the Xi Char right about now."

He set the cruiser down on its broad disks of landing gear and extended the vessel's starboard boarding ramp. At the top of the ramp, Obi-Wan raised the hood of his cloak against a frigid wind that howled down the slopes. Ahead, a gleaming alloy runner ran from the edge of the landing platform to a cathedral-like structure half a kilometer distant. To both sides of the runner stood hundreds of excited Xi Charrians.

"Guess they don't get many guests," Anakin said as he, Obi-Wan, and TC-16 started down the ramp.

As was often the case, the Xi Char's technological creations mirrored their own anatomy and physiology. With their short, chitinous bodies, quartets of pointed legs, scissor-action feet, and teardrop-shaped heads, they might have been living versions of the shapeshifting droid fighters they had helped produce for the Trade Federation—in walk/patrol mode, at any rate. The wild chitterings of the hundreds-strong mob of welcomers was so loud that Anakin had to raise his voice to be heard.

"Celebrity treatment! I think I'm going to enjoy this!"

"Just be sure to follow my lead, Anakin."

"I'll try, Master."

The closer the Jedi and the protocol droid drew to the edge of the landing platform, the louder the chitterings became. Obi-Wan didn't know what to make of the sheer eagerness he felt from the aliens. It was as if some sort of footrace were about to begin. Frequently, an individual Xi Charrian, carried away by enthusiasm, would leap onto the sleek runner, only to be yanked back into the crowd by others.

"TeeCee, are they normally so zealous?" Obi-Wan asked.

"Yes, Master Kenobi. But their zest has nothing to do with us. It's the ship!"

The meaning of the remark became clear the instant the three of them stepped from the landing platform. At once the Xi Charrians surged forward and swarmed the cruiser, covering it from flat-faced bow to barrel-thrustered stern. Obi-Wan and Anakin watched in awe as patches of carbon scoring disappeared, dents were straightened, pieces of superstructure were realigned, and transparisteel viewports were polished.

"Let's remember to tip them when we leave," Anakin said.

Occasionally a Xi Charrian would leap on TC-16 or make a grab for one of his limbs, but the droid was able to shake his assailants off.

"In their eagerness to perfect me, I'm afraid they'll wipe my memory!" the droid said.

"Would that be such a bad thing," Anakin said, "after what you claim to have been through?"

"How can I be expected to learn from my mistakes if I can no longer *remember* them?"

They were halfway down the runner when a pair of larger Xi

Charrians scurried out to meet them. TC-16 exchanged chitterings and stridulations with them, and explained.

"These two will take us to the Prelate."

"No weapons," Anakin said quietly. "That's a good sign."

"The Xi Char are a peaceful species," the droid explained.
"They care only about the engineering of a piece of technology,
not its intended use. That was why they felt unjustly accused and
harshly judged by the Republic for the part their droid fighters
played in the Battle of Naboo."

The enormous building TC-16 had called a workshop
topped two hundred meters in height and was crowned with
latticework spires and towers that evoked strains of eerie music
from the steady wind. Arrays of tall skylights lit the vast interior
space, in which thousands of Xi Charrians toiled. Arcades of
exquisitely engraved columns supported a vaulted ceiling of exposed roof trusses, among which roosted several thousand more
Xi Charrians, suspended by their scissor feet and humming con-
tentedly.

"The night shift?" Anakin wondered aloud.

Their pair of escorts led them into a kind of chancery, whose
tall doors opened on a spotless room that could have passed for
the captain's cabin of a luxury space yacht. Occupying a throne-
like chair in the center of the room was the largest Xi Charrian
the Jedi had yet seen, being attended to by a dozen smaller
ones. Elsewhere, groups of tool-wielding Xi Charrians were
going over every square millimeter of the chamber, scrubbing,
cleaning, polishing.

Without ceremony, TC-16 approached the Prelate and ten-
dered a greeting. The droid had tasked his vocoder to provide
Obi-Wan and Anakin with simultaneous translations of his utter-
ances.

"May I present Jedi Obi-Wan Kenobi, and Jedi Anakin Skywalker," he began.

Waving away his retinue, the Prelate pivoted his long head to regard Obi-Wan.

"TeeCee," Obi-Wan said, "tell him we're sorry to have disturbed him during his ablutions."

"You're not disturbing him, sir. The Prelate is attended to in similar fashion at all hours of the day."

The Prelate chittered.

"Excellency, I speak your language as a result of my former employment in the court of Viceroy Nute Gunray." The droid listened to the Prelate's response, then said: "Yes, I realize that does not endear me to you. But may I say in defense that my time among the Neimoidians was the most trying of my existence. To which my physical appearance surely attests, and is cause for my great shame."

Clearly mollified, the Prelate chittered again.

"These Jedi have come to seek permission from you to pose questions to a devotee in Workshop Xcan—a certain t'laalak-s'lalak-t'th'ak."

TC-16 supplied the glottal stops and clicking sounds necessary to pronounce the name.

"A virtuoso engraver, to be sure, Excellency. As to the Jedi's interest in him, it is hoped that a work of art to which he devoted himself will provide a clue as to the current whereabouts of an important Separatist leader." The droid listened, then added: "And may I add that anything that brings joy to the Xi Char brings contentment to the Republic."

The Prelate's eye grooves found the Jedi again.

"The lightsabers are not weapons, Excellency," TC-16 said after a brief exchange. "But if permission to speak with t'laalak-s'lalak-t'th'ak rests on their surrendering the lightsabers, then I'm certain they will comply."

Obi-Wan was already reaching for his lightsaber, but Anakin looked dubious.

"You did say you would follow my lead."

Anakin opened his cloak. "I said I'd try, Master."

They handed the lightsabers to TC-16, who presented them to the Prelate for inspection.

"It hardly surprises me that you see room for improvement, Excellency," the droid said after a moment. "But then, what tool could fail to benefit from the touch of a Xi Charrian?" He listened, then added: "I'm certain that the Jedi know you will honor your pledge to leave the imperfections intact."

"That went better than expected," Obi-Wan said as he, Anakin, and TC-16 were being escorted into the heart of Workshop Xcan.

Anakin wasn't convinced. "You're too trusting, Master. I sense much suspicion."

"We can thank Raith Sienar for some of that."

Almost two decades earlier, the wealthy and influential owner-president of Sienar Design Systems—a chief supplier of starfighters to the Republic—had spent time among the Xi Char, mastering ultraprecision engineering techniques he would later incorporate into his own designs. Revealed to be a "nonbeliever," Sienar had been exiled from Charros IV, and been made the target of bounty hunters, four of whom Sienar had managed to strand at a black hole known only to him and a handful of other hotshot hyperspace explorers. Sienar had engaged in similar acts of corporate espionage among the Trade Federation, Baktoid Armor, Corellian Engineering, and Incom Corporations, but the Xi Char had a long memory for what they considered sacrilege. Six years before the Battle of Naboo, a second attempt on Raith's life had resulted in the death of his father, Narro, at Dantooine. But once again the heretic had escaped.

Ten years back, Obi-Wan and Anakin had had their own brush with Sienar at the living world known as Zonama Sekot.

Because Sienar had been partly responsible for Zonama Sekot's *disappearance*, he was also the reason that the Xi Char no longer accepted human apprentices.

Workshop Xcan was a marvel to behold.

Xi Char artisans worked individually or in groups of three to three hundred, on devices ranging from high-end home appliances to starfighters, adding enhancements or adornments, tweaking, personalizing, customizing in a thousand different ways. Here were all the priceless devices Obi-Wan and Anakin had found crammed into storage rooms in Gunray's Cato Neimoidia citadel. The environment was the antithesis of the deafening freneticism that characterized a Baktoid Armor foundry, such as the one the Republic had commandeered on Geonosis. Xi Charrians rarely conversed with one another while working, preferring instead to amplify their concentration through the repetition of high-pitched stridulations, analogous to chants. The few who did take notice of the three visitors in their midst showed more interest in TC-16 than in the Jedi.

And yet, for all the fine work that was performed in Workshop Xcan, the cathedral-factory was little more than a stepping-stone for many Xi Charrians, who aspired to work for the Haor Chall Engineering conglomerate which had abandoned Charros IV for other worlds in the Outer Rim.

The same pair of outsized aliens who had escorted Obi-Wan and Anakin to the Prelate's chancery guided them to t'laalak-s'lalak-t'th'ak's altar, which was located in the workshop's western colonnade, the piers of which were decorated with mosaics of engraved tiles. High overhead, resting Xi Charrians hung inverted from the great curving rafters that supported the roof, like configurable droid fighters arrayed inside a Trade Federation carrier.

Obi-Wan could see how the sound of their ceaseless humming could be slightly unnerving.

t'laalak-s'lalak-t'th'ak was engrossed in engraving a corporate logo into a piece of starship console. Dozens of yet-to-be-completed pieces walled him in on one side; completed pieces were on the other. On hearing his name called, he glanced up from his work.

The escorts chittered to him briefly before TC-16 took over.

"t'laalak-s'lalak-t'th'ak, first allow me to say that your work is of such exceptional quality that the deities themselves must be covetous."

The Xi Charrian accepted the compliment in humility, and chittered a response.

"We appreciate the offer to watch you at work. But in fact, we are not unacquainted with some of your finer pieces, and it is because of one piece in particular that we have journeyed so far to speak with you. An example that recently came to light on Cato Neimoidia."

The Xi Charrian took a long moment to respond.

"A mechno-chair you adorned for Trade Federation viceroy, Nute Gunray, some fourteen standard years ago." TC-16 listened, then added: "But surely it was yours, for the inner portion of the rear leg bears your devotional symbol." Again he listened. "A Baktoid forgery? Are you suggesting that your work could so easily be imitated?"

Anakin nudged Obi-Wan in the upper arm: Xi Charrians working nearby were beginning to take a keen interest in the conversation.

"We understand your reluctance to discuss such matters," TC-16 was saying quietly. "Why, the very fact that you *autographed* a piece could be interpreted by the Prelate as a statement of pride."

t'laalak-s'lalak-t'th'ak's anger was apparent.

"Well, of course, you should be proud. But should the Prelate learn that the piece has for all these years resided with a personage such as Viceroy Gunray—"

Without another chitter, the Xi Charrian let go his tools and launched himself from his work pallet—not at TC-16 or either of the Jedi, but straight up into the web of overhead girders. Ignoring indignant squeals from rudely awakened Xi Charrians, he began to leap from one girder to the next, clearly determined to reach one of the tall skylights that perforated the roof.

Obi-Wan watched him for a moment, then turned to Anakin. "I don't think he wants to speak with us."

Anakin kept his eyes on t'laalak-s'lalak-t'th'ak. "Well, he has to."

And with that, he leapt in pursuit.

"Anakin, wait!" Obi-Wan said, then added, more to himself, "Oh, what's the use," and sprang up toward the ceiling.

Hurling himself from truss to truss like some circus performer, Anakin arrived quickly at the intricate tracery surrounding the partially opened roof window through which t'laalak-s'lalak-t'th'ak was desperately trying to squirm. The Xi Charrian's insectile forelegs were already outside the window when Anakin leapt again, clutching on to him in an effort to return him to the floor. But the alien was stronger than he looked. Chittering madly, he leapt for a higher window, this time taking Anakin with him.

Ten meters away, Obi-Wan paralleled the Xi Charrian's flight into the upper reaches of the vaulted ceiling, where the chase had now roused scores of roosting Xi Charrians, inciting more than a few to join in.

Anakin was still trying to drag his quarry down, but his weight was insufficient to the task. Fearing what might result should Anakin call too strongly on the Force—Obi-Wan had visions of the entire workshop crumbing to pieces!—he fairly flew after them, barely managing at the apex of his ascent to grab hold of t'laalak-s'lalak-t'th'ak's rear legs.

And down they came.

All three, entwined, and bringing with them more than thirty inverted Xi Charrians. Cascading onto the floor, Obi-Wan and Anakin lost their hold on t'laalak-s'lalak-t'th'ak, and suddenly couldn't tell one Xi Charrian from the next. Losing t'laalak-s'lalak-t'th'ak had ceased to be an immediate concern, in any case, because Xi Charrians throughout the workshop were rushing to the aid of those the two Jedi had caused to plummet from the rafters. Some were already attempting to zap the Jedi into submission by brandishing assorted soldering and engraving tools, while others were busy constructing a plasteel hemisphere under which the violence might be contained.

"No mayhem!" Obi-Wan shouted.

Anakin showed him a wide-eyed glance from beneath a three-meter-tall heap of irate Xi Charrians.

"Who exactly are you talking to?"

Obi-Wan glanced around the workshop. "Topple something—quickly! Before they complete the mound!"

With a shoving motion of his free hand, Obi-Wan over-turned a small table twenty meters away, spilling several stacks of freshly engraved comlinks and droid summoners. Chittering in panic, half the Xi Charrians who were holding him to the floor—and most of the ones rushing toward him—scampered off to re-pair the damaged devices.

"Quickly, Anakin!'

Even with his hands pinned under him, Anakin managed to upend a pallet of kitchen appliances, then knock over a carefully arranged collection of toys, then tear from the wall more than half a dozen sconces.

Chittering in dismay, more Xi Charrians raced off.

"Stop making it look like fun!" Obi-Wan cautioned.

Eyes riveted on a bin filled with musical instruments, he was about to rid himself of his remaining tormenters when blasterfire erupted in the workshop, and into the midst of the throng of in-furiated Xi Char appeared the Prelate himself, seated on a litter carried by six bearers and grasping a weapon in each foot.

Twenty Xi Charrians flattened themselves to the floor as the Prelate brought the blasters to bear on Obi-Wan and Anakin.

But before a bolt could be fired TC-16 emerged from a side gallery, his body realigned and polished to a dazzling luster, shouting: "Look what they've done to me!"

The droid's tone of voice combined anguish and wonder, but the change in him was so unexpected and remarkable that the Prelate and his bearers could only gape, as if a miracle had occurred in their midst. A babble of chitterings was exchanged, before the Prelate swung back to Obi-Wan and Anakin, raising the blasters once more.

"But they meant no harm, Excellency!" the droid intervened. "t'laalak-s'lalak-t'th'ak fled in response to their questions! Master Obi-Wan and Jedi Skywalker sought merely to ascertain the reason!"

The Prelate's gaze singled out t'laalak-s'lalak-t'th'ak.

TC-16 translated.

"Master Kenobi, the Prelate advises you to pose your questions, and to leave Charros Four before he has a change of heart."

Obi-Wan looked at t'laalak-s'lalak-t'th'ak, then at TC-16. "Ask him if he remembers the chair."

The droid relayed the question.

"He remembers it now."

"Was the engraving done here?"

"He answers, 'yes,' sir."

"Was the chair brought to Charros Four by the Neimoidians or by another?"

"He says, sir: 'By another.' "

Obi-Wan and Anakin traded eager looks.

"Was the hyperwave transceiver already affixed to it?" Anakin asked.

TC-16 listened. "Both the tranceiver and the holoprojector itself were already affixed to the chair. He says that he did little but inscribe the legs of the chair and tweak some of its motion systems." Lowering his voice, the droid added: "May I say, sirs, that t'laalak-s'lalak-t'th'ak's voice is . . . quavering. I suspect that he is hiding something."

"He's afraid," Anakin said. "And not of Nute Gunray."

Obi-Wan looked at TC-16. "Ask him who made the transceiver. Ask him where it shipped from."

t'laalak-s'lalak-t'th'ak's chitterings sounded contrite.

TC-16 said: "The transceiver unit arrived from a facility known as Escarte. He believes that the device's maker is still there."

"Escarte?" Anakin said.

"An asteroid mining facility," TC-16 explained, "belonging to the Commerce Guild."

17

"Ten years ago it would have had all the makings of a full-blown diplomatic incident," Intelligence officer Dyne was explaining to Yoda and Mace Windu in the data room of the Jedi Temple.

Filled with computers, holoprojector tables, and communications apparatus, the windowless chamber also housed an emergency beacon that transmitted on a frequency known only to the Jedi, allowing the Temple to send and receive encrypted messages without having to rely on the more public HoloNet.

"Since when are the Xi Char so forgiving?" Mace asked. Dressed in a brown belted tunic and beige trousers, he was poised on the edge of a desk, one booted foot planted on the shiny floor.

"Since they've been forced to make do with subcontracting work," Dyne said. "What they want is to get back in the game by landing a nice fat Republic contract for starfighters or combat droids. It has to be driving them mad, knowing that Sienar is getting even richer on techniques he basically stole from them."

Mace glanced at Yoda, who was standing off to one side,

both hands resting on the knob of his gimer stick. "Then the Xi Char Prelate isn't likely to report the incident to the Senate."

Dyne shook his head. "Not a chance. No real harm was done, anyway."

"Reach the ears of the Supreme Chancellor, it won't," Yoda said. "But surprised I was by Obi-Wan's report. Losing some of his better judgment, Obi-Wan is."

"We both know why," Mace said. "He's become Anakin's partisan."

"If the Chosen One Skywalker is, then a hundred such diplomatic incidents we should suffer without concern." Yoda shut his eyes for a moment, then looked at the Intelligence analyst. "But come to tell us of these things, Captain Dyne hasn't."

Dyne grinned. "We've succeeded in deciphering the code Dooku—and, we have to assume, Sidious—has been using to communicate with the Council of Separatists. Using the code, we were able to intercept a message sent to Viceroy Gunray, through the mechno-chair."

Mace came to his feet. "Your people have been working on cracking that code for years."

"The chair's hyperwave transceiver provided us with our first solid lead. We saw right away that the code embedded in the transceiver's memory was a variant on codes used by the InterGalactic Banking Clan. So we decided to offer a deal to one of the Muuns arrested after the Battle of Muunilinst. It took some convincing, but the Muun finally confirmed that the Confederacy code comes closest to a code used on Aargau, for transferring bank funds and such." Dyne paused, then added: "Remember the missing credits that became the basis for accusations leveled against Chancellor Valorum back in the day?"

Yoda nodded. "Remember the incident well, we do."

"The credits that allegedly disappeared into the pockets of Valorum's family members on Eriadu were routed through Aargau."

"Interesting, this is."

Dyne opened an alloy briefcase and removed a ribbed data cell. Moving to one of the holoprojector tables, he inserted the cell into a socket. A meter-high holoimage appeared in the table's cone of blue light.

"General *Grievous*," Yoda said, narrowing his eyes.

"You'll be pleased to learn that I've chosen a world for us, Viceroy," Grievous was saying. *"Belderone will be our temporary home."* The cyborg fell silent for a moment. *"Viceroy? Viceroy!"* Whirling to someone off cam, he barked: *"End transmission."*

Dyne paused the message before Grievous had faded from view.

"As high-resolution an image as I've ever seen," he said. "Technology of a different order than we're used to seeing— even from the Confederacy."

"About his image, Sidious cares, *ummm*?"

Mace's clean-shaven upper lip curled. "What was the source of the transmission?"

"Deep in the Outer Rim," Dyne said. "Six clone pilots pursued a core ship that jumped to the sector following the Battle of Cato Neimoidia. None returned."

"Rendezvous of the Confederacy fleet, it is," Yoda said.

Mace nodded. "And Belderone next." Again his gaze fell on Dyne. "Anything further on the source of the original Sidious transmission?"

Dyne shook his head. "Still working on it."

Mace paced away from the table. "Belderone is not a highly populated world, but it is friendly to the Republic. Grievous will kill millions just to make a point." He glanced at Yoda. "We can't let that happen."

Dyne looked from Mace to Yoda and back again. "If Republic forces are waiting when Grievous attacks, the Separatists will realize that we've managed to eavesdrop on their transmissions."

Yoda pressed his fingers to his lips in thought. "Act, we must. Lying in wait, Republic forces will be."

Dyne nodded. "You're right, of course. If no actions are taken, and word of this intelligence were to leak . . ." He regarded Yoda. "Do we inform the Supreme Chancellor?"

Yoda's ears twitched. "Difficult, this decision is."

"The information stays here," Mace said firmly.

Yoda sighed with purpose. "Agree I do. Use the beacon we will, to gather a force."

"Obi-Wan and Anakin aren't far from Belderone," Mace said. "But they're pursuing another lead to Sidious's whereabouts."

"Wait, the lead will. Needed Obi-Wan and Anakin will be." Yoda turned to the still image of General Grievous. "Prepare carefully for this battle, we must."

In dreams, Grievous remembered his life.

His mortal life.

On Kalee, and in the aftermath of the Huk War.

After all the close calls on battlefields on his home system worlds, on Huk worlds, sowing destruction, exterminating as many of them as he could . . . After all the times he had returned home wounded, bloodied to the bone, surrounded by his wives and offspring, basking in their support—relying on it to recall him to life.

After all the brushes with death . . . to be fatally injured in *a shuttle crash*.

The unfairness, the indignity had cost him more pain than the injuries themselves. To be denied a warrior's death—as was his due!

Floating suspended in bacta, keenly aware that no healing fluid or gamma blade wielded by living being or droid could repair his body. In moments of consciousness: seeing his wives and offspring gazing on his ravaged body from the far side of the permaglass. Offering words of encouragement; prayers for his return to health.

He had asked himself: could he be content to be a mind in a body without feeling? More, could he abandon a life of combat for a life in which the only battles he fought were with himself? The struggle to endure, to live another day . . .

No. It was beyond him.

By then, the Huk War had ended—more accurately had been ended by the Jedi, and the Kaleesh were still reaping the whirlwind. Their world in ruins, their appeals for justice and fair play ignored by the Republic.

Ever on the alert for investment opportunities, members of the InterGalactic Banking Clan had offered Kalee a dubious sort of rescue. They would support the planet financially, assume its staggering debt, if Grievous would agree to serve the clan as an enforcer. Their hailfire weapons were proficient at delivering "payment reminders" to delinquent clients, and their IG-series assassin droids took care of the wet work. But the hailfires had to be programmed, the IGs were dangerously unpredictable, and assassination was bad for business.

The clan wanted someone with a talent for intimidation.

Both to save his world and to provide himself with a touch of the life he had known as a warrior, a strategist, a leader of armies, Grievous had accepted the offer. IBC chairman San Hill himself had overseen the details of the arrangement. Still, Grievous wasn't entirely proud of his decision. Debt collection was a far cry from warcraft. An arena for beings without principles; for beings so attached to their possessions that they feared death. But Kalee had profited from his work for IBC. And Grievous's previous notoriety was such that it could not be eclipsed.

Then: the shuttle crash. The accident. The misfortune . . .

He told his would-be healers to fish him from the bacta tank. He could bear to die in atmosphere or the vacuum of deep space, but not in liquid. In the shadow of felled trees that would fuel his funeral pyre, he lapsed in and out of consciousness. That was when San Hill had paid him a second visit. Something consequential in mind. Obvious even to someone who could barely see straight.

"We can keep you alive," rail-thin Hill had whispered into Grievous's unimpaired ear.

Others had promised as much. He pictured breathing devices, a hover platform, a surround of life-sustaining machines.

But Hill had said: "None of that. You will walk, you will speak, you will retain your memories—your mind."

"I have my mind," Grievous had said. "What I *lack* is a body."

"Most of your internal organs are damaged beyond the repair of the finest surgeons," Hill had continued. "And you will have to surrender even more than you already have. You will no longer know the pleasures of the flesh."

"Flesh is weak. You need only gaze on me to see that."

Encouraged by the remark, Hill had talked in glowing terms of the Geonosians: how they had raised cyborg technology to an art form, and how the blending of living and machine technology was the future.

"Consider the battle droids of the Trade Federation," Hill had said. "They answer to a brain that is also nothing more than a droid. Protocol droids, astromechs, even assassin droids—all require programming and frequent maintenance."

Two words had caught Grievous's attention: *battle droids.*

"A war is brewing that will call many droids to the front," Hill had said just loudly enough to be heard. "I am not privy to when it will begin, but when that day comes, the entire galaxy will be involved."

His interest piqued, Grievous had said: "A war begun by whom? The Banking Clan? The Trade Federation?"

"Someone more powerful."

"Who?"

"In time, you will meet him. And you will be impressed."

"Then why does he need me?"

"In every war, there are leaders and there are commanders."

"A commander of *droids.*"

"More precisely, a *living* commander of droids."

So he had allowed the Geonosians to go to work on him, constructing a duranium and ceramic shell for what little of him remained. His recuperation had been long and difficult. Coming to terms with his new and in many ways improved self, even longer and more difficult. Only then had he been presented to Count Dooku, and only then had his real training begun. From the Geonosians and members of the Techno Union he had already come to understand the inner workings of droids. But from Dooku—Lord Tyranus—he came to understand the inner workings of the Sith.

Tyranus himself had trained him in lightsaber technique. In mere weeks he had surpassed any of Tyranus's previous students. It helped, of course, to have an indestructible body reminiscent of a Krath wardroid. The ability to tower over most sentient beings. Crystal circuitry. Four grasping appendages . . .

In dreams he remembered his past life.

But in fact, he was not dreaming, for dreams were a product of sleep, and General Grievous did not sleep. He endured instead brief periods of stasis in a pod-like chamber that had been created for him by his body's builders. While inside that chamber he could sometimes recall what it had felt like to live. And while inside, he was not to be disturbed—unless in the event of inimical circumstances.

The chamber was equipped with displays linked to devices that monitored the status of the *Invisible Hand.* But Grievous was aware of a problem even before the displays told him as much.

As he exited the chamber and hurried for the cruiser's bridge, a droid joined him, supplying updates.

No sooner had the Separatist fleet emerged from hyperspace at Belderone than it had come under attack—not by Belderone's meager planetary defense force, but by a Republic battle group.

"Wings of starfighters are converging on the fleet," the droid reported. "Assault cruisers, destroyers, and other capital vessels are arrayed in a screen formation above night-side Belderone."

Klaxons were blaring in the corridors, and gunner droids and Neimoidians were hastening to battle stations.

"Order our ships to raise shields and form up behind us. Vanguard pickets are to fall back in shield formation to protect the core vessels."

"Affirmative, General."

"Roll the ship starboard to minimize our profile, and reorient the deflector shields. Deploy all wings of droid tri-fighters and ready all port-side batteries for enfilade fire."

Grievous braced himself against a bulkhead as the cruiser was shaken by an explosion.

"Ranged fire from the Republic destroyers," the droid said. "No damage. Shields functioning at better than ninety percent."

Grievous quickened his pace.

On the bridge, a real-time hologram of the battle was running above the tactical console. Grievous took a moment to study the deployment of the Republic ships and starfighter squadrons. Made up of sixty capital vessels, the battle group wasn't large enough to overwhelm the Separatist fleet, but it packed enough combined firepower to defend trivial Belderone.

On the far side of the dun-colored planet, a convoy of transports was angling toward the lesser of Belderone's two inhabited moons, starfighters and corvettes flying escort.

"Evacuees, General," one of the droids explained.

Grievous was stunned. An organized evacuation could mean only one thing: the Republic had somehow learned that Belderone had been targeted! But how could that be, when only the Separatist leaders had been apprised?

He moved to the forward viewports to observe the strobing spectacle of battle.

He would learn how he had been foiled. But survival was the first order of business.

With its stubby wings and bulbous aft cockpit, Anakin's starfighter was closer in design to the Delta-7 Aethersprite he had flown at the start of the war than it was to the newer-generation V-wings and ARC-170s flown by clone pilots. But where the Delta-7 was triangular in shape, the silver-and-yellow starfighter had a blunt bow composed of two separate fuselages, each equipped with a missile launcher. Laser cannons occupied notches forward of the wings. As with the Delta-7, the astromech socket was located to one side of the humpbacked cockpit.

Plus, Anakin had made a few significant modifications.

Already a veteran of battles at Xagobah and other worlds, the craft looked as if it had been around for ten years. But it handled better than the modified Torpil he had flown at Praesitlyn, and was faster, as well.

Launched from the *Integrity*, Anakin poured on speed in an effort to catch up with the ARCs and V-wings that had been first to deploy from the assault cruiser's massive ventral bay. An instrument panel monitor indicated that the starfighter's ion drive was functioning at just under optimal.

"Artoo," he said toward the comlink, "run a diagnostic on the starboard thruster."

The starfighter's console display translated the droid's too-dled response into Basic characters.

"I thought so. Well, go ahead and make the adjustments. We don't want to be last to arrive."

R2-D2's plaintive mewl needed no translation.

The drive readout graph pulsed and climbed, and the starfighter surged forward.

"That's it, pal. Now we're moving!"

Settling back into the padded seat, he flexed his gloved hands and exhaled slowly through his mouth. Enough spying, he told himself. He wasn't any closer to Coruscant, but at least he was back where he belonged, wedded to a starfighter, and prepared to show the enemy a thing or two about space combat.

Ahead of him—spearhead to groups of needle-nosed pickets that were screening the capital ships—slued hundreds of enemy craft. Some were thirteen-year-old Vulture fighters with paired wings that resembled seedpods; others were compact tri-fighter droids; and still others were space-capable Geonosian twin-beaked Nantex starfighters. Just now the lead ARC-170s were weaving through permutations of close combat with the droid fighters, the glowing pulses of energy beams turning local space into a web of devastation.

Not since Praesitlyn had he soared into such an enemy-rich environment.

Target practice, he thought, allowing a grin.

He took his right hand from the control yoke to activate the long-range scanners. The threat-assessment screen displayed the signatures and deployment of the Separatist capital vessels: Trade Federation Lucrehulks and core ships; Techno Union Hardcells, with their columnar thruster packages and egg-shaped fuselages; Commerce Guild Diamond cruisers and Corporate Alliance Fantails; frigates, gunboats, and communications ships featuring huge circular transponders.

The whole Separatist parade.

Switching his comlink over to the battle net, Anakin hailed his wingmate.

"I say we leave the small stuff to Odd Ball and the other pilots, and go straight for the ones that matter."

Accustomed to Anakin's disregard for call signs, Obi-Wan answered in kind.

"Anakin, there are approximately five hundred droids positioned between Grievous and us. What's more, the capital ships are too heavily shielded."

"Just follow my lead, Master."

Obi-Wan sighed into the comlink microphone. "I'll try. *Master.*"

Anakin scanned the threat-assessment display, committing to memory vector lines of the closest enemy fighters. Then he reopened a channel to R2-D2.

"Battle speed, Artoo!"

Again, the starfighter shot forward. Indicators on the console redlined. Just short of the roiling fray, when he could sense the droid ships drawing a bead on him, he shoved the yoke into a corner for a pushover and streaked out of the maneuver with all weapons blazing.

Droids flared and flamed to all sides of him.

Wending through clouds of expanding fire, he locked down the trigger of the laser cannons and made a second pass through the enemy wave, destroying a dozen more fighters in a heartbeat. But the tri-fighters were onto him now, eager for payback. A sunburst of scarlet beams seared past the bubble canopy, and a fighter appeared to starboard. An instant later, a second volley sizzled down from overhead. R2-D2 loosed a series of urgent whistles and tweets as the starfighter was rocked to its shields.

Blue lightning coruscated across the console, and droid fighters appeared to port and starboard. More bolts found their mark, throwing Anakin hard against the safety harness.

"Just what I needed," he said, in appreciation.

Swerving hard to starboard, he caught the first ship with a sideslip shot. The second fighter sheared off as quickly as it could from the expanding fragmentation cloud. As it did, Anakin raced into its aft wash and triggered the lasers.

A ball of fire, the droid careened into a flak-dazzled tri-fighter and the two of them exploded.

Anakin checked the display to make certain that Obi-Wan was still with him.

"Are you all right?"

"A bit toasted, but okay."

"Stay with me."

"Do I have a choice?"

"Always, Master."

Deeper into the melee now, ARC-170s, V-wings, and droid fighters were joined in a great cloverleaf of combat, chasing one another, colliding into one another, twirling out of the fight with engines smoking or wings blown away. Weapons themselves, the droids were accurate with their bolts, but slower to recover, and easily confused by random maneuvers. While at times this made for effortless kills, there were just so many of them . . .

Anakin squared off with the enemy leader of the cloverleaf clash, and began to harass it with laser bolts. Adapting to his tactics, Obi-Wan fell back; then leapt his starfighter into kill position and opened up.

"Nice shot!" Anakin said when the wing leader vanished.

"Nice setup!"

Signaling Obi-Wan to follow, Anakin climbed out of the main battle, veering tangent to it, and rocketed toward the nearest of the Separatists' needle-nosed picket ships. Loosing two missiles to draw the picket's attention, he yawed to port, pushed over, then came back at the vessel with lasers.

"Run the hull! Target the shield generator!"

"Any closer and we'll be inside the thing!"

"That's the idea!"

Obi-Wan followed, unleashing with all cannons.

They were in the thick of the heaviest fighting now, where ranged fire from the Republic capital ships was breaking against the particle and ray shields of their targets. Blinding light pulsed behind the canopy blast tinting. The picket Anakin had piqued with missiles was under heavy bombardment. He grasped that a high-yield torpedo would be too much for it, and rushed to deliver it.

The torpedo tore from between the starfighter's cockpit-linked fuselages and burned its way toward the picket.

The picket's shield failed for an instant, and in that instant the huge incoming turbolaser bolts did their worst. Struck broadside, the picket burst like an overripe fruit, venting long plumes of incandescence and spilling light and guts into space.

Anakin jinked away, whooping into the comlink.

"We've got a clear shot at Grievous!" he told Obi-Wan.

With its tapered bow and large outrigger fins, the general's cruiser resembled a classic-era Coruscant skyscraper laid on its side.

"This hardly seems the time to bait him, Anakin. Have you had a look at those point-defense arrays?"

"When are you going to learn to trust me?"

"I do trust you! I just can't keep up with you!"

"Fine. Then I'll be right back."

Anakin pushed the starfighter to its limits, paying out plasma and missiles that exploded harmlessly against the great ship's deflector shield. He peeled away from the fiery wash, only to fall back at the ship in predatory banks, breaking ultimately for its 200-meter-tall conning tower.

The cruiser's in-close batteries came alive, chundering, gushing enormous gouts of spun plasma at the pest that was attempting to besiege it. Snap-rolling, Anakin slid the starfighter hard to port, belly-up, and continued to fire.

Again he tried to harry the invulnerable bridge with bursts of his lasers. And again the batteries of the colossal vessel tried but failed to get him in target lock.

Anakin pictured Grievous standing stalwart behind the transparisteel viewports.

"A taste of what's coming when we meet in the flesh," he growled.

Grievous's reptilian eyes tracked the audacious maneuvers of the yellow-and-green starfighter that was attempting to strafe the bridge. Firing with precision, anticipating the responses of the forward batteries, taking chances even a clone wouldn't take . . . the pilot could only be a Jedi.

But a Jedi unafraid to call on his rage.

Grievous could see that in the pilot's dauntless determination, his abandon. He could sense it, even through the *Invisible Hand*'s shimmering shields and the viewport's transparisteel. Oh, to have the lightsaber of that one dangling from his belt, he thought.

Anakin Skywalker.

Certainly it was him. And in the starfighter that was guarding Anakin's stern: Obi-Wan Kenobi.

Thorns in the Separatists' side.

Elsewhere in the battle arena Republic forces were demonstrating similar enthusiasm, atomizing droid fighters and punishing the capital ships with long-range cannon fire. Grievous was confident that, if pressed, he could turn the tide of battle, but that was not his present mandate. His Sith Masters had ordered him to safeguard the lives of the Council members—though, in fact, the Confederacy needed none other than Lords Sidious and Tyranus.

He turned to watch the simulation playing above the tactical console, then swung back to the viewports, recalling the ARC-170 pilots who had hounded Gunray's shuttle only days earlier. He waved for one of the droids.

"Alert our vessel commanders to stand by to receive revised battle orders."

"Yes, General," the droid acknowledged in monotone.

"Raise the ship. Prepare to fire all guns on my command."

There is no death; there is only the Force.

Obi-Wan wondered if he had ever witnessed a more lucid demonstration of the Jedi axiom than Anakin's Force-centered, death-defying harassment of Grievous's ship. His speck of a starfighter all but nose-to-nose with the mammoth cruiser, leaving Obi-Wan to deal with the vengeful droid fighters Anakin was either ignorant of or deliberately disregarding.

"He really is going to be the death of me," Obi-Wan mumbled.

But he was indifferent to his own fate, wondering instead: What if Anakin should be killed?

Could he even be killed?

As the Chosen One, was he destined to fulfill both the title and the prophecy? Was he immune to real harm, or—as someone born to restore balance to the Force—did he require defenders to guide him to that destiny? Was it Obi-Wan's duty— more, the duty of all the Jedi—to see to it that he survived at all costs?

Was that what Qui-Gon had intuited so many years earlier on Tatooine, and had motivated him to attack with such resolve the Sith who had revealed himself in that parched landscape?

Though the cruiser's shield was removing the sting of Anakin's laser bolts, he could not be deterred from persevering. Even

Obi-Wan's repeated attempts to hail him through the battle net had had no effect. But now the huge ship was beginning to climb and reorient itself.

Obi-Wan thought for a moment that Grievous was actually going to bring all forward guns to bear on Anakin. Instead, the cruiser continued to rise until it was well above the plane of the ecliptic, with its bow angled slightly Coreward.

Then it fired.

Not at the Republic battle group, nor at Belderone itself, but at the convoy of evacuees and its escort starfighters.

Obi-Wan felt a great disturbance in the Force, as ship after ship disintegrated or erupted in flames. Thousands of voices cried out, and the battle and command nets grew shrill with shouts of dismay and outrage.

The follow-up volley Obi-Wan waited for never arrived.

Tri-fighters and Vulture droids were suddenly slinking back to the ships from which they had been disgorged. At the same time, the entire Separatist fleet was turning tail. Of course Grievous realized that his barbaric act had caught the Republic forces by surprise, but he had nothing more in mind than escape into hyperspace. The general had obviously made up his mind that Belderone simply wasn't worth the risk—not with so many defenseless Outer Rim worlds still up for grabs.

"Anakin, the evacuees need our help!" Obi-Wan said.

"I'm coming, Master."

Obi-Wan watched Anakin's starfighter break off its futile pursuit of the cruiser. Farther out, Separatist ships were disappearing from sight as they made the jump to lightspeed.

"Vessels of the main fleet are safely away," a droid reported to Grievous as soon as the cruiser entered hyperspace. "Expected arrival at the alternate rally point: ten standard hours."

"Losses at Belderone?" Grievous said.

"Acceptable."

Beyond the forward viewports, the smoky vortices of out-raced light.

Grievous ran the fingers of his clawlike hand down the bulk-head.

"Instruct my elite to meet me in the shuttle launching bay on emergence from hyperspace," he said to no droid in particular. "When all ships have arrived at the rally point, advise Viceroy Gunray that I will be paying him a visit."

Trained well by Dooku, General Grievous was," Yoda said. He and Mace Windu were in Yoda's chambers in the Jedi Temple, each atop a meditation dais. "Entrapped, they strike at the weakest. Force us, they do, to choose between saving lives and continuing the fight."

Yoda recalled his duel with Dooku in the solar sailer's docking bay on Geonosis. Dooku bested, left with no alternative but to distract and flee . . .

"Representatives from Belderone have expressed their gratitude to the Senate," Mace said. "Despite the losses."

Yoda shook his head sadly. "More than ten thousand killed. *Twenty-seven* Jedi."

The muscles in Mace's jaw bunched. "Billions have died in this war. Belderone was saved, and, more importantly, we were able to keep Grievous on the run."

"Know where he jumped to, we do."

"We'll chase him to the ends of known space, if we have to."

Yoda fell silent for a moment, then said: "Speak with the Supreme Chancellor, we must."

"Without apology," Mace said bluntly. "Our deference to him has to end."

"With the war's end, it will." Yoda turned slightly to regard Mace. "A terrible warning, Belderone is. *Increasing*, the power of the dark side is. Rooted out, Sidious must be."

Mace nodded gravely. "Rooted out and eliminated."

General Grievous has left the docking bay," a Trade Federation lieutenant relayed to Gunray in his lavish quarters in the core ship's port-side command tower.

"Which docking bay?" Gunray said toward the comlink's audio pickup. "Below, or in the tower?"

"The general's shuttle availed itself of the tower docking ring, Viceroy."

Gunray swung around to face Rune Haako. "That means he will be here any moment!"

He turned to a large circular screen that displayed a real-time view of the antechamber outside his suite. The Neimoidian guards stationed there had also been alerted to Grievous's arrival. Armed with blaster rifles taller than they were, the four wore bulky torso and lower-leg armor, and pot-shaped helmets that left their red eyes and green faces exposed.

"It has to be the mechno-chair," Gunray said, striding back and forth in front of the screen.

"What did you tell him?" Haako asked.

Gunray came to a halt. "Immediately on being apprised by

Shu Mai of the Belderone rendezvous, I contacted Grievous, expressing anger that he hadn't informed me personally. I accused him of purposely leaving me out of the command loop."

Haako was horrified. "You said that to him?"

Gunray nodded. "He maintained that he had attempted to communicate through the mechno-chair hyperwave transceiver. I said that I had received no such transmission."

"They're coming!" Haako said, aiming a quivering finger at the display screen.

Gunray saw that Grievous was accompanied by four of his elite MagnaGuards. Fearsome bipedal battle droids built to exacting specifications, they stood as tall as the general and were armed with combat staffs tipped with electromagnetic pulse generators. Armorweave capes fell diagonally across their broad-shouldered bodies, swathing the crowns of their heads and lower faces. Benefiting from Grievous's own programming, as well as from the instruction Grievous had received from Dooku, the elite were trained in the Jedi arts, and more than a match for most.

The four Neimoidians stood their ground, bringing their rifles across their chests in a gesture of warning.

Grievous's elite didn't even slow down. Mirroring the Neimoidians, they raised their double-tipped electroshock batons, then swung them forward with such speed and precision that Gunray's sentinels were literally swept off their feet, as if they were children.

Grievous glared into the lens of the holocam mounted outside the hatch.

"Admit us, Viceroy. Or shall I instruct my elite to lay waste to everything that stands between me and you?"

Haako spun on his heel and hurried for the suite's rear hatch.

"Where are you going?" Gunray said. "Running will only make us appear guilty!"

"We are guilty!" Haako threw over his shoulder.

"He doesn't know that."

"Viceroy!" Grievous rasped.

Haako stood in the open hatch. "He will." And disappeared through it.

Gunray paced for a moment, wringing his hands, then, straightening robes and miter and pulling his shoulders back, he pressed a fat finger to the hatch release.

The general swept into the suite, the four MagnaGuards in his angry wake spreading out to both sides, ready for violence.

"What is the meaning of this intrusion?" Gunray said from the center of the main room. "Your Masters will not tolerate such ill treatment of me!"

Grievous glowered at him. "They will when they learn what you've done."

Gunray touched himself in the chest. "What are you talking about, you . . . *abomination*. When Lord Sidious hears that you promised us a world you could not deliver—"

Stepping forward, a MagnaGuard thrust his staff to within a millimeter of Gunray's face.

"Lord Sidious's alloy puppet," Gunray said, his voice quavering. "If not for the Trade Federation, you would have no army to command."

Grievous raised his right claw and pointed to Gunray. "The mechno-chair. I want to see it."

Gunray gulped. "In a fit of anger, I had it destroyed and purged from the ship."

"You're lying. There was no problem with my transmission to you. The chair relayed my message."

"What are you suggesting?"

"The chair is no longer in your possession. It has somehow fallen into enemy hands, and, through it, the Republic was able to learn of my plan to attack Belderone."

"You're brain-dead."

Grabbing Gunray by the neck, Grievous lifted him a meter off the floor.

"Before I leave here, you will tell me everything I wish to know."

Poor Gunray, Dooku thought. *Pitiful creature . . .*

But for having left the mechno-chair behind on Cato Neimoidia, he deserved all the fear Grievous had put into him.

Secluded in his castle on Kaon, Dooku had just spoken with the general and was pondering how best to handle the situation. While the incident at Belderone wasn't conclusive proof that the Republic had managed to decrypt the Separatist code and intercept Grievous's transmission to Gunray, it was prudent to assume that this was the case. Dooku had already ordered the general to refrain from using the code for the time being. But the matter of the expropriated hyperwave transceiver was cause for added concern. The very fact that the Republic had tipped its hand at Belderone, declaring the success of its eavesdropping, implied that the mechno-chair had furnished more than intelligence. Clues to secrets that would astonish even Grievous.

The general was not accustomed to losing in battle. Even when a general among his own species, he had suffered few defeats. That was orginally what had brought him to the attention of Sidious. After the Sith Lord had expressed interest in Grievous to Dooku, Dooku, in turn, had expressed interest in Grievous to Chairman San Hill, of the InterGalactic Banking Clan.

Poor Grievous, Dooku thought. *Pitiful creature . . .*

During the Huk War, and later, while in the employ of the IBC, Grievous had survived numerous attempts on his life, so an assassination attempt was ruled out almost immediately. Hill himself had come up with the idea of a shuttle crash, though that, too, presented risks.

What if Grievous should actually die in the crash?

Then the Separatists would simply have to look elsewhere for a commander, Dooku had told Hill. But Grievous had survived—and only too well. In fact, most of the life-threatening injuries he sustained had occurred *after* he had been pulled from the flaming shuttle wreck, and with great calculation.

When at last he had agreed to be rebuilt, promises were made that no critical alterations would be made to his mind. But the Geonosians had ways of modifying the mind without a patient ever being aware that he had been tampered with. Grievous certainly believed that he had always been the cold-blooded conqueror he was now, when in truth his cruelty and prowess owed much to his rebuilding.

Sidious and Dooku couldn't have been more pleased with the result. Dooku, especially, since he had no interest in commanding an army of droids, and already had his hands full nursemaiding the likes of Nute Gunray, Shu Mai, and the hive-minded others who eventually would form the Council of Separatists.

Grievous had been a delight to train, as well. No need to coax him to release his anger and rage, as Dooku had been forced to do during the training of his so-called Dark Jedi disciples. The Geonosians had arranged for Grievous to be nothing but anger and rage. And as to the general's combat skills, few, if any, Jedi would be capable of defeating him. There had been moments during the extensive combat sessions when even Dooku had been hard-pressed to outduel the cyborg.

But then, Dooku had kept some secrets to himself.

Just in case.

Manipulation of the sort that had gone into the transformation of Grievous went to the heart of what it meant to be a Sith—if, indeed, the words *heart* and *Sith* could be used together. The essence of the dark side lay in a willingness to use any means possible to arrive at a desired end—which, in the case of Lord Sidious, meant a galaxy brought under the dominion of a single, brilliant mind.

The current war had been the result of a thousand years of careful planning by the Sith—generations of bequeathing knowledge of the dark side from mentor to apprentice. Rarely more than two in each generation, from Darth Bane forward, Master and apprentice would devote themselves to harnessing the strength that flowed from the dark side, and to making the most of every opportunity to allow darkness to wax. Facilitating war, murder, corruption, injustice, and avarice when- and wherever possible.

Analogous to introducing a covert malignancy to the body politic of the Republic, then monitoring its spread from one organ to another until the mass reached such size that it began to disrupt vital systems . . .

The Sith had learned from their own internecine struggles that systems were often brought down from within when power became their reason for being. The greater the threat to that power, the tighter the threatened would cling.

That had been the case with the Jedi Order.

For two hundred years before the coming of Darth Sidious the power of the dark side had been gaining strength, and yet the Jedi had made only minimal efforts to thwart it. The Sith were pleased by the fact that the Jedi, too, had been allowed to grow so powerful, because, in the end, their sense of entitlement would blind them to what was occurring in their midst.

So, let them be placed on a pedestal. Let them grow soft and set in their ways. Let them forget that good and evil coexist. Let them look no farther than their vaunted Temple, so that they would fail to see the proverbial forest for the trees. And, by all means, let them grow possessive of the power they had gained, so that they might be that much easier to topple.

Not that *all* of them were blind, of course. Many Jedi were aware of the changes, the drift toward darkness. None, perhaps, more than aged Yoda. But the Masters who made up the Jedi Council were enslaved to the *inevitability* of that drift. Instead of attempting to get to the root of the coming darkness, they merely did their best to contain it. They waited for the Chosen One to be born, mistakenly believing that only he or she would be capable of restoring balance.

Such was the danger of prophecy.

It was into such times that Dooku had been born, placed because of a strong connection to the Force among an Order that had grown complacent, self-involved, arrogant about the power they wielded in the name of the Republic. Turning a blind eye to injustices the Republic had little interest in eradicating, because of profitable deals forged among those who held the reins of command.

While midi-chlorians determined to some degree a Jedi's ability to use the Force, other inherited characteristics also played a part—notwithstanding the Temple's best efforts to eradicate them. Having hailed from nobility and great wealth, Dooku yearned for prestige. Even as a youngster, he had been obsessed with learning all he could about the Sith and the dark side of the Force. He had toed the Jedi line; become the Temple's most agile swordmaster and instructor. And yet the makings of his eventual transformation had been there from the start. Without the Jedi ever realizing it, Dooku had been as disruptive to the Order as would be a young boy raised in slavery on Tatooine.

His discontent had continued to grow and fester; his frustration with the Republic Senate, with ineffectual Supreme Chancellor Valorum, with the shortsightedness of the Jedi Council members themselves. A Trade Federation blockade of Naboo, rumors of a Chosen One found on a desert world, the death of Qui-Gon Jinn at the hands of a Sith . . . How could the Council members not see what was happening? How could they continue to claim that the dark side obscured all?

Dooku had said as much to anyone who would listen. He wore his discontent on the sleeve of his robes. Though they hadn't enjoyed the smoothest of student–teacher relationships, he and Yoda had spoken openly of the portents. But Yoda was living proof of a conservatism that came with extended life. Dooku's true confidant had been Master Sifo-Dyas, who, while also disturbed by what was occurring, was too weak to take action.

The Battle of Naboo had revealed that the Sith were back in the open, and that a Sith Lord was at work somewhere.

The Sith Lord: the one born with the power needed to take the final step.

Dooku had given thought to seeking him out, perhaps killing him. But even what little faith he placed in the prophecy was enough to raise doubt that the death of a Sith could halt the advance of the dark side.

Another would come, and another.

As it happened, there had been no need to hunt for Sidious, for it was Sidious who had approached him. Sidious's boldness surprised him at first, but it hadn't taken long for Dooku to become fascinated by the Sith. Instead of a lightsaber duel to the death, there had been much discussion, and a gradual understanding that their separate visions for how the galaxy might be rescued from depravity were not so different after all.

But partnership with a Sith didn't make one a Sith.

As the Jedi arts had to be taught, so, too, did the power of the dark side. And so began his long apprenticeship. The Jedi warned that anger was the quickest path to the dark side, but anger was nothing more than raw emotion. To know the dark side one had to be willing to rise above all morality, to throw love and compassion aside, and to do whatever was necessary to bring about the vision of a world brought under control—even if that meant taking lives.

Dooku was an eager student, and yet Sidious had continued to hold him at arm's length. Perhaps he had been working with other potential replacements for his earlier apprentice, the savage Darth Maul, who, in fact, had been nothing more than a minion, like Asajj Ventress and General Grievous. Sidious had recognized in Dooku the makings of a true accomplice—an equal from the other camp, already trained in the Jedi arts, a master duelist, a political visionary. But he needed to gauge the depth of Dooku's commitment.

One of your former confidants at the Jedi Temple has perceived the coming change, Sidious had told him. *This one has contacted a group of cloners, regarding the creation of an army for the Republic. The order for the army can stand, for we will be able to make use of that army someday. But Master Sifo-Dyas cannot stand, for the Jedi cannot learn about the army until we are prepared to have them learn of it.*

And so with the murder of Sifo-Dyas, Dooku had embraced the dark side fully, and Sidious had conferred on him the title *Darth Tyranus*. His final act before leaving the Jedi Order was to erase all mentions of Kamino from the Jedi archives. Then, as Tyranus, he had found Fett on Bogg 4; had instructed the Mandalorian to deliver himself to Kamino; and had arranged for payments to be made to the cloners through circuitous routes . . .

Ten years passed.

Under its new Supreme Chancellor, the Republic recovered

somewhat, then grew more corrupt and beset with problems than before. As best they could, Sidious and Tyranus helped things along.

Sidious had the ability to see deep into the future, but there was always the unexpected. With the power of the dark side, however, came flexibility.

Having traced Fett to Kamino, Obi-Wan Kenobi had turned up on Geonosis. All at once, here was Qui-Gon Jinn's former Padawan, right under Dooku's nose. But when he had informed Sidious of Obi-Wan's presence, Sidious had only said, *Allow events to play out, Darth Tyranus. For our plans are unfolding exactly as I have foreseen. The Force is very much with us.*

And now, a new wrinkle: as a result of Nute Gunray's blunder at Cato Neimoidia, the Republic and the Jedi had chanced on a possible way to trace the whereabouts of Sidious and expose him.

The mechno-chair's exceptional transceiver—and others like it—had been created for Sidious by a host of beings, a few of whom were still alive. And if agents of the Republic—or the Jedi, for that matter—were clever and persistent enough, they could succeed in learning more about Sidious than he would want anyone to learn . . .

He had to be informed, Dooku thought.

Or did he?

For a heartbeat he hesitated, imagining the power that could be his.

Then he went directly to the hyperwave transmitter Sidious had given him, and began his transmission.

Mace Windu couldn't recall a visit to the Supreme Chancellor's chambers in the Senate Office Building when his attention hadn't been drawn to Palpatine's curious and somehow unsettling collection of quasi-religious statuary. On one occasion, picking up on Mace's interest, Palpatine had offered lengthy and enthusiastic accounts of when and how he had come by some of the pieces. Acquired at an auction on Commenor; procured after many years and at great expense from a Corellian dealer in antiquities; salvaged from an ancient temple discovered on a moon of the gas giant Yavin; a gift from the Theed Council of Naboo; another gift from that world's Gungans . . .

Just now Mace's eyes were on a small bronzium statue Palpatine had once identified as Wapoe, the mythical artisan demigod of disguise.

"I'm relieved that you contacted me, Master Jedi," the Supreme Chancellor was saying from the far side of his expansive desk. "As I was about to contact you on a matter of some gravity."

"Then speak of your matter first, we will," Yoda said.

He was seated for a change, atop a cushioned chair that made him appear even smaller than he was. Mace was at Yoda's left hand, sitting with legs widely spread, forearms resting on his knees.

Palpatine touched his steepled fingers to his lower lip, then inhaled and sat back in his throne of a chair. "This is rather awkward, Master Yoda, but I suspect that the matter I have in mind is the very one that brought you and Master Windu here. By that I mean Belderone."

Yoda compressed his lips. "Fail you, your intuition doesn't. About Belderone, much to say, we have."

Palpatine smiled without showing his teeth. "Well, then, suppose I begin by saying that I was most pleased to learn of our recent victory there. I only wish I had been informed of your plans before the fact."

"We had no time to corroborate the intelligence we received," Mace said without hesitation. "We thought it best to commit as few Republic ships as could be spared. It was essentially a Jedi operation."

"A Jedi operation," Palpatine said slowly. "And by all accounts you, that is, the Jedi, were successful in routing General Grievous's forces."

"A rout it was not," Yoda said. "To hyperspace Grievous fled. But protecting the Separatist leaders, he was."

"I see. And now?"

Mace leaned forward. "Wait for him to resurface, and strike again."

Palpatine regarded him. "Might I be informed of your intelligence next time? Didn't you and I have this discussion after Master Yoda was thought to have been killed at Ithor?" Before Mace could respond, he continued: "You see, the problem here is one of appearances. While I can appreciate the need to keep secret some intelligence, many in the Senate do not. In the instance of Belderone—and largely because it constituted a Republic victory—I was able to allay the fear of certain Senators that the Jedi are taking the war into their own hands, and are no longer accountable for their actions."

Mace's nostrils flared. "We can't allow the Senate to go on dictating the course of the war."

Yoda nodded, sagely. "Miring the Jedi in uncertainty, some of the Senate's decisions are." He looked askance at Palpatine. "A matter of *appearances,* this is."

Mace made it emphatic. "We're not rogues."

Palpatine spread his hands in a gesture of appeasement. "Of course you're not. Nothing could be farther from the truth. But, as I say . . . Well, if nothing else, the Senate at least needs to *believe* that it is being kept informed—particularly in light of the extraordinary powers it has granted this office." He sat straighter in the chair. "Not a day passes that I am not subjected to suspicion, accusations, suggestions of ulterior motive. And, I will tell you, the suspicions do not end here, in this office. They extend to the role of the Jedi in the war. Master Jedi, we cannot, under any circumstances, be perceived as being in collusion."

Yoda frowned. "In *collusion* we must be, if victory the goal remains."

Palpatine smiled tolerantly. "Master Yoda, far be it from me to lecture someone of your vast experience on the nature of politics. But the truth of the matter is that with the war now exiled to the Outer Rim, we must be judicious about the campaigns we undertake, and about the targets to which we assign our forces. If a lasting peace is ever to be achieved when this madness concludes, each and every act from this point forward must be handled with utmost delicacy." He shook his head. "Many worlds, loyal to the Republic, circumstance forced us to sacrifice. Others that joined the Separatists may wish to return to the Republic. These aren't matters with which I wish to burden the Jedi.

But they are the province of this office, and I need to place them first and foremost."

"The lessons learned from a thousand years of serving the Republic aren't entirely lost on us," Mace said strongly. "The Jedi Council is fully aware of such concerns."

Palpatine took the rebuke in stride. "Excellent. Then we can move on to other matters."

Mace and Yoda waited.

"May I inquire as to how the Jedi learned of Grievous's plan to attack Belderone?"

"A hyperwave transceiver that belonged to Viceroy Gunray was seized at Cato Neimoidia," Mace explained. "The device allowed Intelligence to decipher the Separatist code. A message transmitted by General Grievous to Viceroy Gunray regarding Belderone was monitored, and we acted on it."

Palpatine was staring at him in disbelief. "We have the ability to listen in on Separatist transmissions?"

"Unlikely," Yoda said. "After Belderone."

Palpatine considered it, then frowned. "For Belderone you forfeited the ability to continue monitoring the Separatists." He took a breath, and the frown ebbed. "Had I been included in this matter, I would have made the same choice. But I must add, Master Jedi, that I am greatly displeased about having been circumvented. Why wasn't I told? Am I to infer from this that you no longer trust me?"

"No," Yoda almost barked. "But into this office, come and go many. Our own counsel we kept."

Palpatine's face took on sudden color. "And yet you continue to place full trust in those around you? Do you realize how some might respond to that, when many of your Order have deliberately absented themselves from the war, and some have even gone over to the Separatist side?"

"A decade old, such reproaches are, Supreme Chancellor."

"I fear you delude yourself in this instance, Master Yoda, if you believe that the passage of time makes those 'reproaches' any less valid to your critics."

This is getting out of control, Mace thought. He calmed himself before speaking.

"There's a more important reason for your not being informed about the transceiver."

Now Palpatine waited.

"It contained a stored message—a message transmitted to Viceroy Gunray from Darth Sidious."

Palpatine's broad forehead wrinkled in uncertainty. "Sidious. I know the name . . ."

"Dooku's Sith Master, Sidious is. Learned of him on Geonosis, Master Kenobi did. But eluded us, proof of him has."

"Now I recall," Palpatine said. "Obi-Wan was told that this Sidious had somehow infiltrated the Senate."

"Dismissed that, we have. But lying about Sidious, Dooku wasn't."

Palpatine swiveled his chair toward the room's immense curved window, the panorama of Coruscant. "Another Sith." Turning back to Yoda, he said: "Forgive me, but why is this of such great concern?"

"Carefully balanced this war has been. Republic victories, Separatist victories . . . In prolonging it, a part the Sith may play."

Again, Palpatine paused to consider Yoda's words. "I think I begin to understand the reasons for your secrecy. The Jedi are attempting to expose Sidious."

"In pursuit of clues, we are."

"Might the capture of Sidious end the war?"

"Hasten the end," Mace said.

Palpatine nodded in finality. "Then I trust that you will accept my apologies. Do whatever you must to hunt Sidious down."

When the Xi Charrian said it was an asteroid mining operation, I wasn't picturing an actual asteroid," Obi-Wan said from the copilot's seat of the Republic cruiser.

"It was TeeCee-Sixteen who told us that," Anakin said. "Maybe something was lost in translation."

The protocol droid had been sent to Coruscant for further debriefing by Republic Intelligence; R2-D2 was on Belderone, where technicians were seeing to damages he had sustained during the battle there. Obi-Wan and Anakin had the old white ship to themselves, and had exchanged their Jedi robes for outfits more suitable to itinerant spacers.

Named for the asteroid belt in which it was prominent, the Escarte Commerce Guild facility orbited between massive, multi-mooned gas giants in an otherwise uninhabited star system two hyperspace jumps from Belderone, on the Rimward side of the Perlemian Trade Route. Oblate when mining operations had commenced twenty years earlier, Escarte was now a concave hemisphere, heavily cratered by the forces of nature and the gargantuan labor droids of the Commerce Guild. Satisfied that every bit of ore had been extracted from Escarte, the guild had converted the asteroid's consequent quarries, tunnels, and shafts into processing centers and field offices. State-of-the-art tractor beam technology allowed the guild to capture small asteroids and draw them directly into the facility, rather than have to use tugs or engage in on-site mining. In many ways Escarte was the ore-mining equivalent of the Tibanna-gas-mining facilities that floated in the dense atmosphere of Bespin, far across the stars.

Unfriendly space, the belt was defended by Commerce Guild corvettes and fleet patrol craft modeled on the Geonosian starfighter. Regardless, Republic Intelligence had managed to insert one of its agents onto Escarte. Obi-Wan and Anakin hadn't been told when or even if they were going to make contact with the agent, but moments before leaving Belderone they had been informed that Thal K'sar—the Bith artisan who allegedly had designed the hyperwave transceiver and holoprojector for Gunray's mechno-chair—had been arrested, on charges yet to be learned.

An alert chime sounded from the cruiser's instrument console.

"Escarte," Anakin said. "Demanding that we identify ourselves and state our intent."

"We're freelance merchants in search of work," Obi-Wan reminded him.

Anakin activated the comm and said as much into the microphone.

"Corellian cruiser," a husky voice returned, "negative on your request to dock. Escarte has no job openings. Suggest you try Ansion or Ord Mantell."

Obi-Wan's gaze drifted to the viewport. Off to starboard, a corvette was coming about.

"Intercept vector," Anakin said. "Any last-minute instructions, Master?"

"Yes: stick to the plan. Our best hope for getting close to K'sar is to get ourselves arrested."

Anakin grinned. "Shouldn't be a problem. Hang on."

Obi-Wan already was, and so was able to remain more or less upright in the chair as Anakin firewalled the thrusters and threw the cruiser into a hard turn—not away from the corvette, but aimed directly toward it.

The console chimed another alert.

"They're warning us away, Anakin."

Anakin kept the cruiser on course. "Quick flyby. Our way of saying we're not happy about being turned away."

"No lasers."

"Promise. We're just going to buzz them."

Obi-Wan watched the corvette grow larger in the viewport. The console continued to chime, in escalating alerts. An instant later, two turbolaser beams streaked across the cruiser's bow.

Obi-Wan clenched his hands on the chair armrests. "They're not amused."

"We'll just have to try harder."

Dropping the cruiser's nose, Anakin increased speed. He seemed bent on maneuvering directly under the corvette, but at the last moment he pulled back on the control yoke, taking the cruiser through a spiraling, high-boost climb. A fusillade from the corvette's forward batteries narrowly missed clipping the ship's tail.

"Enough plausibility," Obi-Wan said. "Level out and signal that we're complying."

"Master, you are not taking our assignment seriously enough. If we make it too easy for them, they'll suspect we're up to something."

Obi-Wan saw that two patrol craft were rushing in to join the pursuit. With flashes of scarlet light racing alongside, Anakin whipped the cruiser through a teeth-rattling bank and shot for the thick of the asteroid belt.

"The only thing worse than being your wingmate is being your passenger!"

Anakin had the ship tipped to one side, intent on weaving it

through a cluster of rocks, when a laser bolt struck the closest asteroid. Rubble from the explosion peppered the cruiser's shields,
but the console displays confirmed Obi-Wan's hunch that no
damage had been done.

Anakin took a firm grip on the control yoke and yanked the
cruiser into a turn. The patrol craft clung doggedly, angling to
outflank the larger ship, but Anakin kept cheating the turn tighter
and tighter, forcing the fighters to break off. The cruiser had no
sooner realigned itself than it gave a sudden lurch, snapping Obi-
Wan and Anakin back into their seats, then forward into the console. Anakin reached over his head to make adjustments, and the
cruiser raced forward once more, only to freeze, then tremble.

Obi-Wan scanned the displays. "Are we hit?"

"No."

"Asteroid?"

"Not that, either."

"Don't tell me you've come to your senses and decided to
surrender?"

Anakin showed him a long-suffering look. "Tractor beam."

"From Escarte? Impossible. We're much too far away."

"That's what I thought."

Anakin's hands flew across the instruments, shutting down
some systems and activating others.

"Don't try to fight it, Anakin. This ship won't hold together."

A deep shudder from the bowels of the cruiser reinforced his
words.

Anakin clenched his jaw, then let his hands fall to his sides.

"Look at it this way," Obi-Wan said, as the cruiser was being
drawn toward the distant facility. "At least you made them work
for it."

Gentle with the cruiser, the tractor beam had deposited it
in a guild-made crater that was now a docking bay. Ordered out

of the ship, Obi-Wan and Anakin stood at the foot of the boarding ramp with their hands clamped on top of their heads. Uniformed Neimoidians and Gossams surrounded the cruiser, and a security team comprising humans, Geonosians, and battle droids was marching toward them.

"Not exactly the warm welcome we received on Charros Four," Obi-Wan said.

Anakin nodded slightly. "Almost makes me nostalgic for the Xi Charrians."

"Keep your hands where we can see them!" the human chief of the security detail shouted as he stepped onto the landing platform. "Make no sudden moves!"

"Such drama," Anakin said.

"No mind tricks," Obi-Wan cautioned.

"Spoilsport."

The light-complected, blond security officer was as tall as Anakin and wider in the shoulders. A Commerce Guild badge affixed to the collar of his gray uniform showed him to be a captain in the Escarte Guard. He brought the security detail to a halt when everyone was still three meters from the boarding ramp. At his signal, the Geonosians spread out to both sides, brandishing wide-muzzled sonic blasters.

The captain looked Obi-Wan and Anakin up and down, then circled them once, hands clasped behind his back. Eyeing the ship, he said, "I haven't seen one of these in a while. But judging by the retrofitted cannons, I'd have to guess you're not ambassadors of goodwill."

"Let's just say we've been forced to adapt to the times," Obi-Wan said.

The captain scowled at him. "What's your business in this sector?"

"We were hoping to find freelance work," Anakin said.

"You were informed otherwise. Why create problems for yourselves by harassing one of our corvettes?"

"We felt that you'd been impolite—when all we wanted was to introduce ourselves."

The captain almost laughed. "Then this has all been a misunderstanding?"

"Exactly," Obi-Wan said.

The captain shook his head in amusement. "In that case we'd be glad to show you around—*starting with the detention level!*" He swung to two other humans in the detail. "Stun-cuff these comedians and search them for concealed weapons."

"Can't we simply pay a fine and be on our way?" Obi-Wan asked as the magnetic cuffs snapped into place around his wrists.

"Tell it to the judiciary."

Frisks completed, the two humans stepped away. "They're clean."

The captain nodded. "That's one thing in their favor. Search the ship and impound anything of value. And alert detention that I have two for containment." Drawing a blaster from his hip holster, he motioned Obi-Wan and Anakin toward the turbolifts.

The crater docking bay was accessed by several corridors, some unchanged since the days they had served as mining tunnels, others reinforced by plasteel girders and dressed up with ferrocrete panels. It was apparent also that some of the turbolifts were housed in former mine shafts.

The captain indicated an unoccupied lift and followed Obi-Wan and Anakin inside. When two Gossams hurried for the same lift, he waved them away. As soon as the door closed, he lowered his weapon and spoke with a sudden urgency.

"We have to make this quick."

"You're Travale," Obi-Wan said, using the code name he had been furnished.

"Things have gotten more complicated with the Bith. He's slated for execution."

Anakin's eyebrows met in a V. "What did he do, murder someone?"

"Some sort of accounting error."

"Execution seems a rather harsh penalty," Obi-Wan said.

"Escarte Judiciary claims it wants to make an example of him. But it's clear the charges were trumped up." Travale paused. "Could have something to do with your being here to see him."

Travale hadn't been given the reason, but Obi-Wan nodded in acknowledgment. "If he's expecting to die, he may not feel inclined to talk to us."

"My thought, too," Travale said. "But maybe if you could break him out . . ."

"You could arrange that?" Anakin said.

"I can try."

The turbolift car came to a rest and the door slid open.

"Welcome to the detention level," Travale said, back in character, and shoving Obi-Wan out into the anteroom beyond. Behind a semicircle of consoles stood five surly nonhumans—tusked and bald-domed Quara Aqualish—wearing Commerce Guild uniforms and sporting heavy sidearms.

"Show our two guests to cell four-eight-one-six," Travale told the sergeant among them.

"Already occupied by the Bith—K'sar."

"Misery loves company," Travale said.

Executing a crisp about-face, he returned to the turbolift. Emerged from the enclosure of display screens, a four-eyed Aqualish led Obi-Wan and Anakin into a narrow corridor lined with detention cells. Thirty meters along he stopped to enter a code into a wall-mounted touch pad, and the bloodstained door to 4816 slid open.

Square and squalid, it contained neither cots nor refresher.

The smell of waste was almost overpowering.

"Word of warning," the Aqualish said in Basic, "the quality

of the cuisine is surpassed only by the cleanliness of the accommodations."

"Then we'll hope to be released before lunch," Obi-Wan said.

Thal K'sar was slumped in a corner, his long-fingered hands cuffed in front of him. Slender even for a Bith, he was well dressed and seemingly unharmed. Obi-Wan recalled that he had been arrested only the previous day.

K'sar glanced up, but didn't return Obi-Wan's nod of greeting.

"Some fix," Anakin said loudly when the cell sealed. "Good job back there."

Obi-Wan played along. "You didn't help matters any by flooring that security guard."

"Ah, she had it coming."

Anakin ambled over to where K'sar was huddled.

"What landed you in here?" he asked.

Though surprised to hear his own language spoken by a human, K'sar kept silent. When Anakin made a second attempt, the Bith said in Basic, "It's none of your concern. Please leave me alone."

Anakin shrugged and joined Obi-Wan on the far side of the room.

"Patience," Obi-Wan said quietly.

Backs pressed to the filthy wall, the two of them sank down onto their haunches.

Less than a standard hour had passed when they heard voices in the corridor. The door grated open, revealing Travale and two Aqualish security officers. Without a word, the aliens standing to either side of Travale grabbed him by the arms and hurled him headlong into the cell.

Obi-Wan caught him before he hit the floor.

"Another unexpected development?"

Travale was cuffed, and rattled. "My cover's blown," he said quietly. "Don't know how, or by whom."

Anakin glanced at Obi-Wan. "No coincidence."

"Someone is onto us." Obi-Wan left it at that.

"Now what?"

"Where you able to arrange anything?" Obi-Wan asked Travale.

He nodded. "Power failure. Brief, but more than enough time for you to get out of here."

"*Us,*" Anakin amended. "You're coming along."

"I appreciate that." He frowned in uncertainty. "Hope I wasn't wrong in figuring that you two will be able open the door . . . manually, I mean."

"We can open the door," Obi-Wan assured him.

"How long before the power fails?" Anakin asked.

"An hour from now." Travale glanced at K'sar. "What about him?"

Anakin stood up and crossed the room. "I know you're not interested in small talk, but we think we may have a way out of here. Does that interest you?"

The Bith's lidless black eyes grew considerably larger. "Yes. Yes! Thank you."

"Just be ready."

"Take the tunnel to the left of the guard station," Travale was telling Obi-Wan when Anakin returned. "Keep taking lefts until you reach a stairway, then follow that to the docking level."

"You're going a different way?" Anakin said.

"Someone has to deactivate the tractor beam, or your ship's not leaving. Two levels below this one there's a power coupling station. I know just enough to disable it temporarily."

"You're not going alone," Obi-Wan said.

Anakin grinned at him. "I believe it's your turn . . ."

Obi-Wan didn't argue. "That means K'sar goes with you. Don't allow him out of your sight, Anakin."

Travale nodded toward the cell block corridor. "We'll still have the guards to deal with."

"Don't worry about them," Anakin said.

Spreading his hands, he snapped the cuffs from his wrists. Obi-Wan did the same, then snapped Travale's open.

Travale smiled broadly. "I love a good plan."

Anakin and Obi-Wan were standing by the door when the cell's grime-encrusted illuminator faltered and died. Obi-Wan shoved his hands sideways through the air, and the door retracted.

Travale shook his head in wonderment. "It never ceases to amaze me."

Anakin swung to K'sar. "Now! Hurry!"

The four of them moved into the unlit hall.

"Emergency power should come on shortly," Travale said.

Ahead of them they could hear the five guards toggling switches on the console and speaking in excited voices. Anakin wasn't halfway to the anteroom when one of the guards appeared at the end of the narrow corridor. The Aqualish's huge eyes allowed him to see in the dark, but not as well as the Bith, nor as well as the Jedi. Before the guard could realize what was happening, his raised blaster was soaring down the corridor into Anakin's hand. A Force push from Obi-Wan sent the Aqualish flailing back into the anteroom and slamming into the turbolift wall.

The rest of the guards hurried out from behind the darkened console to counterattack. By then Obi-Wan and Anakin were on them, dropping them with punches, side kicks, Force pushes. Bodies sailed across the anteroom, tumbled over one another, smashed into display screens. One Aqualish managed to get off a shot, but the blaster bolt missed anyone during its mad carom around the room.

The fracas was over almost before it began.

In the red glow of emergency lights, K'sar cast a dumb-founded look around.

"You're Jedi!"

"Two out of three," Travale said.

"But . . . what are you doing here—on Escarte?"

Anakin pressed his forefinger to his lips with elaborate seri-ousness. "Republic business." Then into K'sar's hands he pressed the blaster he had summoned from the guard.

K'sar stared at the weapon. "But—"

"I won't need it."

"Here's where we part company," Travale said to Anakin. "Remember: stay left until you reach the stairway."

"Where are you sending him?" K'sar asked.

"Docking Bay Thirty-Six."

The Bith nodded. "I know the way."

Travale chuckled. "This just gets keeps getting better and better." He swung back to Anakin. "K'sar will also know the way to Docking Bay Forty. That's where we'll be waiting for you. Es-carte Control won't be able to bring the tractor beam back on-line immediately, and judging by the way you fly, you shouldn't have much trouble dodging the patrol craft. But good luck, any-way."

"Thanks, but there's no such thing."

As Travale and Obi-Wan were running off, Anakin noticed that one of the turbolift cars was descending.

"Security detail coming to check on the guards," K'sar said.

Anakin nodded toward the dark corridor they were supposed to take. "Go!"

K'sar's long legs propelled him at a fast clip. But instead of going left as Travale had advised, he turned right at the first in-tersection.

Anakin grabbed him by the shoulder and spun him around. "This isn't the way we were told to go."

"The captain's a newcomer to Escarte," the Bith said, short

of breath. "I've been here for fifteen years. I know every route through this rock."

Anakin regarded him in silence.

"Trust me, Jedi, I have nothing to gain by lying to you and remaining here."

Anakin tapped him into motion. Several minutes of running brought them to a rickety stairway, which K'sar didn't hesitate to climb.

"I'd still like to know what you did to end up in detention," Anakin asked from behind K'sar.

"And I wish I could tell you," he said. "My superior—a Gossam—said I had made an accounting error that would cost the Commerce Guild a small fortune."

"You were always an exec?"

"I started out as a technician—design, installation, the whole gamut. Gradually, I worked my way up."

"Up, maybe. But you're on the wrong side in this war. Your entire species."

K'sar stopped to catch his breath. "Clak'dor Seven had little choice," he said. "The Separatists were offering unrestricted access to hyperspace routes, better deals on trade goods, no interference . . . As for me, I was already working for the guild. One day it was business as usual, the next—on the heels of what happened on Geonosis, at any rate—the guild was suddenly at war with the Republic." He raised his gaze. "We go left at the top of the stairs."

Anakin heard a note of indecision in his voice. "You don't sound as sure as you did."

"I haven't been in this area for a long while, but I'm certain we can reach the docking level."

The rock walls of the corridor into which they raced bore the scars of the giant drills that had hollowed Escarte. Light and oxygen were scant, and the uneven floor was slippery. Anakin clamped his right arm around the Bith's narrow waist to help him along.

"Wait, wait!" K'sar said suddenly.

"What's wrong?'

K'sar eyes filled with dread. "I made a mistake! We shouldn't have come this way!"

Anakin prevented him from moving. "Too late to turn back."

"We have to! You don't understand—"

K'sar words were swallowed by the sound of servomotors and hydraulics. Around a bend in the gloomy tunnel raced a dwarf spider droid, its long-barreled blaster cannon already sweeping side to side, in search of targets.

25

"**S**omeone's coming," Obi-Wan warned Travale.

They were standing on a narrow gantry that accessed the control panel for Escarte's number three tractor beam coupling station. Six meters high, the tower rose from a circular platform that projected from the wall of a deep air shaft. They'd had to wait for full power to return to the area before seeing to the task of disabling the tractor beam. Initially, Travale had made a few mistakes, but he had sorted through his confusion and was almost done.

Obi-Wan peered around the corner of the tower in the direction of the voices he had heard. Three Geonosian security guards were approaching the coupling station from a corridor on the far side of the shaft.

"Never a lightsaber when you need one," Travale whispered. "Can you divert them somehow?"

Obi-Wan considered his options, then made a flicking motion with the fingers of his right hand. An unidentifiable sound issued from deeper in the corridor the guards had taken. Whirling, the three Geonosians hurried off to investigate.

Travale shook his head back and forth in appreciation of Obi-Wan's skill. "It's a wonder the war isn't over yet."

"Too few of us."

Travale studied Obi-Wan for a moment. "Is that the reason?"

Obi-Wan touched Travale on the arm, and motioned with his bearded chin to the tower. "No time to waste."

The Jedi watched over Travale's shoulder as he dialed the coupling power feed to zero.

"These things are the future," Travale said. "Fill a ship with enough tractor beam arrays and you could prevent an enemy from jumping to hyperspace."

"There aren't ships large enough."

"There will be," Travale said. "To ensure that another war doesn't happen."

Mainstay of the Commerce Guild's mining operations, the dwarf spider droid was a hunter-killer. The spider didn't stand much taller than a Trade Federation battle droid, but it was agile and equipped with two powerful blaster cannons. Perched at the juncture of four splayed legs, the hemispherical body was dominated by two huge circular photoreceptors, which appeared to be fixed on Anakin and K'sar as the droid rushed in to make the kill.

Anakin threw K'sar to one side and rolled as the dwarf spider fired. Two glaring bolts gouged a trench in the hewn floor of the tunnel, and the report of the cannon resounded deafeningly from the walls. The head pivoted, photoreceptors finding Anakin, and the weapon discharged again.

Anakin flipped himself away. Calling on the Force, he swirled his hands in front of him to prevent the intense heat from engulfing him. Rolling once more, he tried to get underneath the droid's striding legs, but the spider anticipated him, skittered backward, and loosed another burst.

Anakin leapt.

Propelled by the Force, as well as the force of the explosion, he struck the arched ceiling and fell hard to the floor. Blacking out for a moment, he awoke to find the droid charging toward him, reorienting the smaller of its cannons to place him in the crosshairs. Catapulting to his feet, he flew forward, intent on ripping the power cells from beneath the droid's dome. No less determined, the droid countered by retreating and rearing up. Falling short of the mark, Anakin curled his body, counting on momentum to carry him forward.

The spider continued to retreat, then dropped back on all fours, traversing its cannon.

Feigning a sidestep, Anakin hurled himself completely under the droid, but still couldn't find cover. He heard the sound of the spider's dome rotating, then the sound of the muzzle of the long cannon hitting the scabrous wall. Realizing that it had entered a section of the tunnel too narrow to allow for a half turn, the droid stamped its legs in frustration, then began to back itself into the wider stretch.

Without a clear plan in mind, Anakin chased it, heard the dome begin to pivot once more, then the sound of a hand blaster set on full automatic.

Ten meters down the corridor, K'sar was on his feet, the heavy weapon held in front of him in a two-handed grip, firing directly into the spider's bulging red photoreceptors and power cells. Confused, the droid tried desperately to spin around, but there wasn't room. Loose rock calved from the walls as the barrel of the cannon struck again and again. All the while, the Bith continued to advance, emptying the blaster's power cell. An electronic shriek tore from somewhere inside the spider, and sparks began to geyser from its perforated dome. The four legs danced in anger for a moment longer, then stopped, and the tunnel began to fill with smoke. Finally the droid collapsed, the tip of its cannon slamming into the floor at K'sar's feet.

Anakin eased around the smoking machine and gently removed the blaster from the Bith's shaking grip. The droid's dome
pinged as it cooled; a steady susurration escaped the blaster's gas
chamber.

"How much farther?" Anakin asked after a moment.

"We're close," K'sar said in a daze. "Half a kilometer or so
past the bend."

"Can you make it?"

K'sar nodded, and they hurried through the final stretch,
emerging from a tunnel opening at the rear of the docking bay.
A hundred meters away the cruiser was sitting just where the
tractor beam had left it. Few guards were about, and most of
them were battle droids.

Anakin took a moment to study the disposition of the droids,
then turned to K'sar, who seemed to have recovered from the ordeal in the tunnel.

"No matter what I do, I want you to head straight for the
boarding ramp. Don't stop running until you're inside the ship,
understand?"

K'sar nodded.

Anakin leapt out of the corridor, deliberately calling attention to himself to distract the droids from firing at K'sar. Evading
blaster bolts with perfectly timed jumps and rolls, he got close
enough to the droids to wave some of them into others, toppling
them as if they had been picked up by a strong wind. From one,
he called a blaster rifle into his own hands, and mowed down
those that were still on their feet.

Following K'sar up the boarding ramp, he rushed into the
cockpit and began to power up the cruiser's defensive systems.
Bolts from the droids' blasters ricocheted from the fuselage and
transparisteel panels. Traversing the cruiser's fore and aft cannons, Anakin fired, burying the droids under huge chunks of ferrocrete blown from the walls and ceiling.

When the flight systems were online he left the cockpit to search for K'sar, who was sitting on the floor of the main hold, panting.

"Why aren't you raising the ship?" the Bith said. "Guild corvettes are probably already on the way."

Anakin stepped closer to him, his expression darkening visibly. "You and I need to talk first. And either you answer my questions, or I jettison you here, and let the Gossams do what they will with you."

The Bith's eyes expanded. "Talk? About what?"

"A hyperwave transceiver you designed fourteen years ago."

"Fourteen years ago? I can barely remember last *week*."

Anakin glared at him from beneath an angrily furrowed brow. "Think harder."

"Why are you doing this to me? I just saved your life!"

"Remind me to thank you later. Right now you're going to tell me about the transceiver. It would have been a special order. More than the usual secrecy. You would have been well paid. You installed it in a mechno-chair."

K'sar started. His wrinkled mouth puckered and he stared at Anakin in terror. "Now it all comes together—my arrest and imprisonment, the death sentence! The transceiver . . . that's what brought you here."

"Who placed the order?"

"I suspect you already know the answer."

"How did he contact you?"

"Through my personal comlink. He needed someone of great skill. Someone willing to follow his every instruction without question. The designs he sent were like nothing I had ever seen. The end result was almost . . . artistic."

"Why did he allow you to live—afterward?"

"I was never sure. I knew I'd been useful. I thought he might require additional devices, but I never heard from him again."

"If you're right about your arrest, that means he *has* been keeping an eye on you. Tell me the rest and we might be able to keep you from his long reach."

"That's everything!"

"You're holding something back," Anakin said in a flat, menacing tone. "I can feel it."

K'sar gulped, and clutched at his neck. "I built two of them!"

"Who received the second one? One of the Separatist leaders?"

Swallowing with difficulty, K'sar said: "It went to Sienar!"

Anakin blinked in surprise. "Raith Sienar?"

"To Sienar Advanced Projects. It was designed for some sort of experimental spacecraft they were building."

"Who was the craft meant for?"

"I don't know—I swear, Jedi, I don't." K'sar paused, then added: "But I knew the pilot Sienar hired to deliver the ship."

"Knew?"

"I don't know if she's still alive. But I know where you could begin to look."

Obi-Wan and Travale negotiated the cofferdam that linked Escarte's air lock to a docking ring just forward of the cruiser's tri-barreled thruster fantail.

Stepping into the main hold, Travale gave a shout of joy.

"Good to be alive!"

Obi-Wan glanced at Thal K'sar, thinking the Bith might feel the same. Instead, K'sar was curled up on the hold's worn acceleration couch. Obi-Wan hurried on to the cockpit and strapped into the copilot's seat.

"Any problems reaching the ship?"

"The usual close calls," Anakin said evasively. "Obviously you were successful at disabling the tractor beam."

"Not a skill I expect to draw on again, but, yes, thanks to Travale."

Anakin glanced at the console, waiting for the cofferdam telltale to go off, then called on the thrusters to move the cruiser away from Escarte. Off to port, Obi-Wan saw two Guild corvettes dead in space.

"And here I was certain we weren't out of this yet."

Anakin shrugged. "Anticlimactic."

Obi-Wan regarded him for a moment. "K'sar seemed rather . . . subdued. Were you able to question him?"

Anakin busied himself with the controls. "Briefly."

"And?"

"We have a new lead." Before Obi-Wan could reply, Anakin said: "Hyperspace coordinates coming in."

Banking widely, the cruiser left Escarte and sluggish light behind.

Coruscant had places one couldn't persuade a droid air taxi driver to take one, even with the promise of a free year of lubrication baths at Industrial Automaton.

The labyrinth of dark back streets south of Corusca Circus.

Daring Way, where it crossed Vos Gesal in upper Uscru.

Hazad's Skytunnel in the Manarai Uplift.

And just about anywhere in the sector known colloquially as "The Works."

Foot mat to the Senate District, with its New Architecture spires and domes, its blade-thin obelisks that resembled oft-used candles dipped in gleaming alloy, The Works had been a booming manufacturing area until escalating costs had driven the production of spacecraft parts, labor droids, and construction materials offworld.

Kilometer after cheerless kilometer of flat-roofed factories and assembly plants; towering cranes and enormous gantries; endless stretches of pitted mag-lev tracks that might have been overgrown with weeds if weeds grew on Coruscant; skyscraping clusters of vacant corporate buildings with rocket-fin buttresses . . . For standard centuries, the sector had been the destination for billions of hardworking immigrants from the Inner Rim and the Colonies, seeking employment and new lives in the Core. Now The Works was a destination for fugitives from Nar Shaddaa who needed a hole to crawl into. A Coruscanti might risk a visit to The Works if he had just been laid off by the Bank of Aargau and was looking for someone to disintegrate his former boss. Or perhaps when death sticks no longer satisfied and a capsule of Crude was in order . . .

It was the gritty, toxic smoke that still belched from the stacks of factories closed for generations that made for the crimson-and-gold splendor of Coruscant's sunsets, gawked at by the affluent habitués of the Senate District's Skysitter Restaurant.

The entire sector might have been demolished if it could be determined with any certainty just who owned what. Rumors persisted that hired assassins and crime syndicates had buried so many bodies in The Works that it should be considered a cemetery.

And yet Dooku loved the place.

The antithesis of his native Serenno, The Works was very much a home away from home for the human who had earned the title *Darth Tyranus.*

One structure in particular—columnar in shape, round-topped, propped by angular ramparts—rising from the defiled core of The Works like a stake driven into its heart. Strong in the dark side—made so by Darth Sidious—the building had been the place of Dooku's apprenticeship, just as it had served as a training ground for Darth Maul before Dooku, and who knew who or how many other Sith disciples before Maul.

During the ten years preceding the outbreak of the war—when Count Dooku of Serenno was believed to have been peddling his Separatist agenda to disenfranchised worlds in the Mid and Outer Rims—he had, in fact, spent long periods of time in The Works, coming and going at will, or as required of him by

Darth Sidious. Even in the three years since, he had been able to visit Coruscant without fear of detection, thanks in part to unique countermeasures the Geonosians had engineered into his interstellar sloop.

The modified Punworcca 116 rested on its slight landing gear in the building's vast docking space. With its needle-tipped bow carapaces and the spherical cockpit module they gripped, the sloop was typically Geonosian in design. Its signature sail, however, had been obtained with Sidious's help from a dealer in pre-Republic antiquities in the Gree Enclave. Furled into the ventral carapace now—seldom used any longer—it had been created by an ancient spacefaring race that had taken to the grave the secrets of supralight emission propulsion.

Having ordered the sloop's FA-4 pilot droid to remain in the ball cockpit, Dooku was walking some of the stiffness of the long voyage out of his legs. His black trousers were tucked into black dress boots, and his black tunic was cinched by a wide belt of costly leather. Thrown back over his shoulders, the Serenno armorweave-lined cape shimmered behind him. He made no efforts to disguise himself for such trips to Coruscant. The silver hair, mustache, beard, and flaring eyebrows that gave him the look of a stage magician were as meticulously groomed as ever.

Normally measured, Dooku's pace was rushed and somewhat haphazard—evidence to anyone who knew him that the Count was troubled. If asked, he might have admitted as much. Even so, in moments when he could put aside the reasons for his visit, he surveyed the docking bay with a certain fondness, recalling the years he had spent under Sidious's tutelage, learning the ways of the Sith, practicing the dark arts, perfecting himself.

Mastering evil, Yoda would have said.

The problem was partly semantic, in that the Jedi Order had seen to it that the dark side of the Force had become equated with evil. But was shade more evil than stark sunlight? Recognizing that the dark side was on the ascendant, the Jedi—in service to the Force—should have known enough to embrace it, to ally themselves with it. After all, it was all a matter of balance, and if the preservation of balance required the dark side to be on top, then so be it.

With Dooku, Sidious hadn't had to waste precious hours on lightsaber technique, nor on ridding Dooku of ill habits born of a lifetime spent in the Jedi Temple, for Dooku had long before rid himself of those. Instead, Sidious had focused on giving Dooku what had amounted to a crash course in tapping into the power of the dark side—a mere taste of which had proved intoxicating. Enough to convince Dooku that no course was left open to him but to abandon the Order; more, that his entire life had been preparation for his apprenticeship to Sidious.

That at long last he had found a true mentor.

The Sith saw no need to take on only young disciples, though they often did. Sometimes the training went smoother with disciples who had lived long enough to grow disillusioned or angry or vengeful. The Jedi, by contrast, were shackled by compassion. Their penchant for showing mercy, for granting forgiveness, for heeding the dictates of conscience, prevented them from giving themselves over to the dark side. From becoming as a force of nature itself, paranormally strong and quick, capable of conjuring Sith lightning, of exteriorizing rage, all without the need for the magic hand passes the Jedi were so fond of employing.

The Sith understood that the elitism and mobsterism of the Republic could be ended only by bringing the diverse beings of the galaxy under the control of a single hand. The galaxy could only be saved from itself by the imposition of order.

What fools the Jedi were not to see it. Blind to their own downfall, the coming of their endtime.

What fools—

The sound of soft footfalls made Dooku turn.

From off to one side of the docking bay a figure approached. Dressed in a hooded cloak of burgundy material, closed at the neck by a distinctive clasp, and so soft and voluminous that it covered everything but the lower portion of the figure's face and his hands. Rarely was that hood lowered, allowing the wearer to walk unnoticed through the byways and plazas of Coruscant's blurred underground, just another recluse or religious initiate arrived in the Core from some world beyond imagining.

Of his youth, Sidious had offered little these past thirteen years; of his Master, Darth Plagueis, even less.

More than once it had occurred to Dooku that Sidious and Yoda had certain qualities in common. Principally, that neither was entirely what he appeared to be—that is, made frail by age, or by the intensity required to master the Sith or Jedi arts.

On Geonosis, Yoda's easy parrying and, indeed, *handling* of the Sith lightning Dooku hurled at him had come as a surprise. Had made him wonder if, on some level during the course of Yoda's eight-hundred-odd years, the Jedi Master hadn't delved into the dark arts, if only as a means of familiarizing himself with his perceived enemy. And on Vjun, only months ago, Yoda himself had admitted as much. *Carry a darkness within me, I do,* he had said. Yoda probably believed that he had defeated Dooku on Geonosis. But in fact, Dooku had only fled the fight to safeguard the plans he had been carrying—the technical readouts to what would one day become the Ultimate Weapon . . .

"Welcome, Darth Tyranus," Sidious said as he drew nearer.

"Lord Sidious," Dooku said, bowing slightly at the waist. "I spared no haste in leaving Kaon."

"And took a great risk you did, my apprentice."

Whether by nature or design, Sidious's words came slowly, sibilantly.

"A calculated risk, my lord."

"Do you fear that the Republic has become so adept at eavesdropping that they can now listen in on our private transmissions?"

"No, my lord. As I told you, the Republic has probably deciphered the code we have been using to communicate with our . . . partners, shall we say. But I am confident that the Intelligence division knew nothing of our plans for dealing with the Bith at Escarte."

"Then my instructions were carried out?"

"They were."

"And still you have come here," Sidious said.

"Some matters are best discussed in real time."

Sidious nodded. "Then let us speak of these things in real time."

They walked in silence to a balcony that overlooked the desolate sprawl of The Works. In the far distance the glassy towers of the Senate District disappeared into clouds. One of Dooku's previous visits had followed the assassination of a faithless Senator by Jedi Knight Quinlan Vos. Duped by Dooku on several occasions, Vos had managed to track Dooku to The Works, though he apparently hadn't perceived just how deeply the dark side had taken root there.

"I suspect that the planned disappearance of Thal K'sar did not go according to plan," Sidious said finally.

"Regretfully, my lord. He *was* taken into custody, but our guild confederates at Escarte failed to act quickly enough. Hours from execution, K'sar was rescued and spirited from the facility by a Republic Intelligence agent, who had the help of two Jedi."

Dooku had been able to count on one hand the number of times he had seen Sidious angry.

Suddenly he needed two hands.

"I would hear more of this, Lord Tyranus," Sidious said with purposeful slowness.

"I have since learned that these same two Jedi recently visited the Xi Char world of Charros Four."

Well ahead of Dooku, Sidious said: "The engraver of the mechno-chair . . ."

"The same."

Sidious pondered it for a moment. "From Viceroy Gunray to the Xi Char engraver to the Bith who implemented my designs for the hyperwave transceiver and holoprojector . . ."

"The Jedi mean to expose you, my lord."

"And what if they should?" Sidious snapped. "Do you think that would bring an end to what I have set in motion?"

"No, my lord. But this is unexpected."

Sidious eyed Dooku from beneath the hood of his cloak. "Yes. Yes, it is, as you say, unexpected." He returned his gaze to the far-off towers. "Someday I may choose to reveal myself to the galaxy, but not now. This war must be made to continue a while longer. There are worlds and persons we still need to convert to our side."

"I understand."

"Tell me, who is conducting this . . . search?"

Dooku exhaled with purpose. "Skywalker and Kenobi."

Sidious took a long moment to respond. "The so-called Chosen One, and a Jedi with enough good fortune to almost make one believe in luck." Without turning from the view, he added: "I am displeased by this turn of events, Lord Tyranus. Greatly displeased."

Once Master and Padawan, Kenobi and Skywalker had become the scourge of Dooku's existence. On Geonosis he had deliberately allowed them to pursue him—just as Sidious had instructed him to do. Also as instructed, Dooku had made Kenobi aware of the existence of Darth Sidious, as a means of confusing the Jedi Order by telling them the truth. In the sloop's docking bay he had demonstrated his mastery to Kenobi and Skywalker—

although Skywalker hadn't been as easily defeated the second time they had dueled. Enraged, the young Jedi had proved a powerful opponent, and Dooku suspected that he had grown only more powerful since Geonosis.

Long have I watched young Skywalker, Sidious had once admitted.

And all the more so of late.

"My lord, the Jedi may search for others who contributed to fashioning the communications devices you distributed to Gunray, myself, and others. Also, there is the matter of Grievous's defeat at Belderone."

Sidious made a gesture accepting that defeat. "Do not trouble yourself about Belderone. It may suit our ultimate purpose to have the Republic believe that they have chased us from their precious Core. As regards your concern for keeping secret my whereabouts, I am moved. But here, too, I begin to see a way to engineer events in our favor." He paused to consider something, then said: "Yes, I begin to see the blazes along the trail Skywalker and Kenobi will follow."

Sidious turned to Dooku, grinning malevolently. "Their single-mindedness will deliver them into our hands, Lord Tyranus. We will set our trap for them on Naos Three."

Dooku allowed his skepticism to show. "As remote a world as can be found in known space, my lord."

"Nevertheless, Kenobi and young Skywalker will find their way to it."

Dooku decided to take it on faith. "What would you have me do?"

"Nothing more than make arrangements—for you are needed elsewhere. Employ outsiders."

Dooku nodded. "It is done."

"One small addendum. See to it that Obi-Wan Kenobi ceases to be an irritant." Sidious sneered the name.

"He represents so forceful a threat to our plans?"

Sidious shook his head. "But Skywalker does. And Kenobi . . . Kenobi has been as a father to him. Orphan Skywalker once and for all, and he will shift."

"Shift?"

"To the dark side."

"An apprentice?"

Sidious gazed at him. "In good time, Lord Tyranus. All in good time."

Having suffered through all four hours of Palpatine's State of the Republic address to the Senate, interrupted dozens of times by standing ovations—an archaic tradition not practiced since the era of Supreme Chancellor Valorum Eixes—Bail Organa watched from the backseat of the air taxi as a trio of assault cruisers lifted off into Coruscant's flame-orange sky, casting their wedge-shaped shadows on the spired roof of the Jedi Temple.

Bail's destination.

He instructed the droid pilot to set the taxi down on the Temple's northeast landing platform, where two Jedi younglings were waiting for him. The opulence of the Temple's wide corridors was lost on him as he followed his escort to the room the Order used for public meetings, rather than the circular chamber reserved for private conclaves in the summit of the High Council spire.

A holorecording of Palpatine's speech was running in the center of the room when Bail was admitted. Around the holoprojector table sat Council members Yoda, Mace Windu, Saesee Tiin, Ki-Adi-Mundi, Shaak Ti, Stass Allie, Plo Koon, and Kit Fisto.

"And so it is with a heavy heart that I commit two hundred thousand additional troopers to the Outer Rim sieges," the holoimage of the Supreme Chancellor was saying, "though in full confidence that the end of this brutal conflict is now in sight. Cast from the Core, expelled from the Inner Rim and Colonies, driven from the Mid Rim, and soon to be exiled in the spiral arms, the Confederacy will pay a dear price for what they have brought down on our fair house."

He paused for applause, which went on for far too long.

Droid cams buzzed around the Great Rotunda to highlight the more well-known of the Palpatine-friendly factions then, coming full circle, closed on Palpatine's thirty-meter-tall podium to linger on the two dozen human naval officers who were standing just below the summit, clapping enthusiastically.

"A show of force, this is," Yoda remarked.

Dressed in robes of magenta and forest green, Palpatine continued.

"Some of you may question why my heart is heavy when my tidings bring news of such long-awaited redress. The decision weighs on me because I would sooner say: *Enough is enough, let the Confederacy—the Separatists—wither and die on their own in the Outer Rim. Let us keep our best and brightest home; let us refrain from bringing bloodshed to any more worlds, harm to our noble soldiers, our trusted Jedi Knights.*"

Yoda harrumphed.

"Sadly, though, I cannot decide with my heart alone. Because we cannot allow the enemies of democracy to rest and recuperate. Like a life-threatening growth taken hold in the body, they must be excised. As a contagious disease, they must be eradicated. If not, our children's generation and generations to come will live under the threat that those who brought chaos to the galaxy will find the strength to regroup and attack anew."

"Applause break," Bail said—because he had been there.

The Jedi Masters stirred in their high-backed chairs but said nothing.

"Lest my statements convey an impression that the hardest decisions are behind us, let me hasten to add that much work remains to be done. So much rebuilding; so much reordering . . . To you, all of you, will I look for guidance in determining which worlds we should welcome back into the Republic's embrace, and which, if any, should be kept at arm's length, or shunned for the injuries they have heaped upon us. Similarly will I look to you for guidance in reshaping our Constitution to conform to the needs of the new epoch."

"What does he mean by that?" Mace Windu interjected.

"Finally will I look to you, all of you, to author a new spirit in Coruscant, in the Core, throughout the star systems where the light of democracy continues to shine, so that we can look forward to another thousand years of peace, and another thousand beyond that, and so on, until war itself is stamped from our just domain."

"Had enough?" Stass Allie asked while the Senate broke into extended applause. Tall, slender, and dark-complected, she wore a Tholoth headdress similar in design to that worn by her immediate predecessor on the Council, Adi Gallia. When no one objected, she deactivated the holoprojector.

Turning to Bail, Yoda said, "Appreciate your visit, we do, Senator Organa."

"I just wanted all of you to know that, despite what the HoloNet news might lead you believe, not all of us were on our feet."

"Aware of this, we are."

Bail gestured broadly to the room's triangular windows and shook his head in dismay. "Coruscant is already in a celebratory mood. You can practically taste it in the air."

"Premature, any celebration is," Yoda said ruefully.

Mace leaned forward in his chair. "What can Palpatine be

thinking—committing half of Coruscant's home force to the Outer Rim sieges?"

"Emboldened Palpatine is, by what we achieved at Belderone."

"The Supreme Chancellor singles out Mygeeto, Saleucami, and Felucia," Plo Koon said from beneath the mask that supplied him with life gases.

Ki-Adi-Mundi's elongated head made a subtle nod. "A 'triad of evil,' he labeled them."

"Separatist bastions, they are," Yoda said. "But so remote, so insignificant."

"A danger to the body of the Republic," Bail said.

Mace ridiculed the idea. "When the body is damaged, it prioritizes. It doesn't rally its defenses to deal with a pinprick when the chest has been holed by a blaster bolt."

Bail glanced around the room. "Some of us are concerned that the Supreme Chancellor has been persuaded to press these sieges as a means of acquiring worlds by force. There are bills before the Senate now that could grant him the authority to overrule local system governments."

Yoda compressed his lips in indignation. "A labyrinth of evil, this war has become. But protect ourselves, we must. Safeguard the traditions the Jedi have upheld for one thousand generations."

Mace ran a hand over his shaven head. "We can only hope that Obi-Wan and Anakin find their way to the source of this war before it's too late."

With a slurping sound, Anakin's right leg sank almost to the knee in the muck that passed for Naos III's main street. An equally onomatopoeic sound accompanied Anakin's reclaiming of the leg, and expletives flew from his lips as he hopped off on his left foot toward solid ground. Crossing his right leg over his left while standing, he tried to shake some of the filth from his boot, then pointed to a pinkish strand that refused to let go.

"What is that?" he asked in alarmed disgust, with breath clouds punctuating his every word.

Reluctantly, Obi-Wan leaned in to peer at the slick boot, not wanting to get too close.

"It could be something alive, or something that was once alive, or something that came from something alive."

"Well, whatever it is, it's going to have to catch a ride on someone else."

Obi-Wan straightened and shoved his hands deeper into the sleeves of his robe. "I warned you there are worse places than Tatooine."

Lining both sides of the puddled street were low-slung pre-fab buildings, their alloy roofs capped with crystalline snow and bearded with thick icicles. Pieces of a collapsed skyway had been moved to one side of the street, left to marinate in a puddle much like the one Anakin had inadvertently waded into, and fashioned by areas of radiant heating that still functioned beneath the mostly ruined ceramacrete paving.

Anakin began stomping his boot on the solid ice. Ultimately the clingy, unidentifiable pink thing decided that it had had enough and flew off into a snowdrift.

"Worse places than Tatooine," he mumbled. "And, what, you feel we need to visit every last one of them? When are we going to be allowed to return to Coruscant?"

"Blame Thal K'sar. He was the one who suggested we should start here."

Anakin gazed around. "I just can't help thinking the next place will be worse."

They both fell silent for a moment, then said in unison: "Almost makes me nostalgic for Escarte."

Anakin winced. "You know it's time to end the partnership when that happens. In fact, I could see you and Yoda teaming up. You share the same fondness for caution and lectures."

"Yes, we're two of a kind, old Yoda and me."

They continued their slog toward what seemed to be the heart of the place.

For most of its short year the moon known as Naos III was a frigid little orb with days that never seemed to end. Indigenous herbivores and carnivores had been hunted to extinction early on by colonists from Rodia and Ryloth, lured by the hope of discovering rich veins of ryll spice in Naos III's volcanically heated cave systems. The creatures one saw most often now were bovine rycrits and woollier-than-normal banthas.

The moon's continued habitation owed to a pink-fleshed delicacy fished from the ice-covered rivers that plunged turbulent and roaring from a surround of nearly sheer mountains. Known as the Naos sharptooth, the fish spawned only in the coldest months, was shipped offworld, flash-frozen, and sold at exorbitant prices in eateries from Mon Calamari to Corellia. Still, few locals banked enough credits to buy passage off Naos III, preferring instead to return their meager earnings to Naos III Mercantile, which oversaw the sharptooth industry and owned nearly every store, hotel, gambling parlor, and cantina.

The dispirited humanoids who had colonized the moon had never bothered to award a name to their principal population center, so it, too, was known as Naos III. Visitors expecting to find a typical spaceport found instead a cluster of fortified hilltops, interconnected by bridges that spanned a delta of waterways. As befitted a place with such a dearth of creativity, the moon had attracted nomads and spacers of dubious character, eager either to lose or reinvent themselves. While Rodians and Lethan Twi'leks comprised the majority, humans and other humanoids were well represented. A few wealthy sportfishers arrived each year, but Naos III was simply too remote and too lacking in infrastructure to support a tourist trade.

Despite the fact that the moon seemed a perfect place for a red-complected Twi'lek to hide, Obi-Wan doubted that Fa'ale Leh would be found here. To begin with, she would have certainly changed her name by now, possibly even the color of her complexion. More important, Naos III didn't offer much in the way of job opportunities for a former spicerunner—unless Leh was one of the death-defying few who piloted loads of flash-frozen sharptooths to the Tion or Coreward on the Perlemian.

According to K'sar, Leh had been in the business of transporting shipments of spice from Ryloth to worlds in Hutt space when Sienar had hired her to deliver the experimental spacecraft for which K'sar had constructed a transceiver identical to the one he had affixed to Gunray's mechno-chair.

To Obi-Wan's mind the ship in question could only be the modified star courier that had belonged to the Sith he had killed on Naboo, and had been confiscated by the Republic after the battle there. Flight, weapons, and communications systems had self-destructed when Republic Intelligence agents had bungled an attempt to enter the courier, but, unknown to many, its burned-out carcass still sat in a clandestine docking bay in Theed. It had long been assumed that the tattooed Zabrak Sith had performed the modifications, but information supplied by K'sar suggested that Raith Sienar's Advanced Projects Laboratory had been responsible not only for building the ship, but also for implementing Darth Sidious's designs.

Obi-Wan and Anakin might have gone directly to the source—to Raith Sienar—had Supreme Chancellor Palpatine not vetoed the idea.

The Republic's other major supplier of weapons, Kuat Drive Yards, was known to have contributed to both sides during the war. Under its subsidiary, Rothana Heavy Engineering—the builders of the *Acclamator*-class assault ships, as well as the AT-TE walkers—KDY had also supplied the Confederacy with the Storm Fleet, which had been "the Terror of the Perlemian" until retired from service with the help of Obi-Wan and Anakin.

With snow falling harder in Naos III, the two stopped to get their bearings. Obi-Wan gestured to a nearby cantina. "This has to be the fifteenth we've passed."

"On this street," Anakin said. "If we stop for a drink in each one, we'll be drunk before we reach the bridge."

"With any luck. Still, they're likely to be our best source of information."

"As opposed to just looking up her name in the local comm directory."

"And a lot more fun."

Anakin grinned. "Fine with me. Where do you want to start?"

Completing a circle, Obi-Wan pointed to a cantina diagonally across from them. The Desperate Pilot.

*　*　*

Four hours later, half drunk and near frozen, they entered the final cantina before the bridge. Brushing snow from the shoulders of their cloaks and lowering the hoods, they scanned the patrons crowding the bar and occupying nearly every table.

"Not a lot to do in Naos Three when you're not fishing," Anakin said.

"I've the distinct impression that some drinking goes on even during work hours."

Replacing two Rodians who stumbled away from the curved bar, they ordered drinks.

Anakin sipped from his glass. "Ten cantinas, as many Lethan females, and every one of them claims to have been born on-world. I'd say we're in for a long stay."

"K'sar didn't supply you with anything else to go on—scars, tattooed lekku, anything?"

Anakin shook his head. "Nothing." When Obi-Wan signaled for the human bartender, he added: "You order one more Twi'lek appetizer, I promise I'm going to cut your arm off."

Obi-Wan laughed. "I found the izzy-mold at the last place to be very flavorful."

Anakin took another sip. "And speaking of arms."

"Were we?"

"We were. At least I think we were. Anyway, remember in the Outlander Club when you went off to get a drink? Did you have an inkling that Zam Wessel would follow you?"

"On the contrary. I knew she would follow you."

"Implying that shapeshifters have a special fondness for me?"

"The way you were strutting around, what female could help herself?" Mimicking Anakin's voice, Obi-Wan said: " 'Jedi business.' "

"Then you admit it—you were using me as bait."

"A privilege that comes with being a Master. You have more than repaid me in kind, in any case."

Anakin raised his glass. "A toast to that."

Seeing the bartender approach, Obi-Wan placed a sizable credit chip under his empty glass and slid it forward. "Another drink. And the rest is for you."

An athletic man with red hair that fell almost to his waist, the bartender eyed the credit chip. "Rather large remuneration for such a rudimentary libation. Perhaps you'd permit me to concoct something a trifle more flavorsome."

"What I'd actually prefer is a bit of information."

"Now, how did I guess."

"We're looking for a Lethan female," Anakin said.

"Who isn't."

Obi-Wan shook his head. "Strictly business."

"That's what it often is with them. I suggest you try the Palace Hotel."

"You don't understand."

"Oh, I think I do."

"Look," Anakin said, "this one probably isn't a . . . masseuse."

"Or a dancer," Obi-Wan thought to add.

"Then what would she be doing on Naos Three?"

"She used to be a pilot—with a taste for spice."

Obi-Wan watched the bartender closely. "She would have arrived on Naos Three within the past ten or so years."

The bartender's eyes narrowed. "Why didn't you say so to begin with? You mean Genne."

"The name we know her by is Fa'ale Leh."

"My friends, on Naos Three a name is nothing more than a convenient handle."

"But you do know her," Obi-Wan said.

"I do."

"Then you know where she can be found."

The bartender jerked a thumb. "Upstairs. Room seven. She said you should go right up."

Anakin and Obi-Wan traded confused glances.

"She's expecting us?" Obi-Wan said.

The bartender heaved his massive shoulders in a shrug. "She didn't say who she was expecting. Just that if anyone came looking for her, I should send them up."

They canceled the drink order and walked to the foot of a long flight of stairs.

"Jedi mind trick?" Anakin asked.

"If it was, I wasn't aware of performing it."

"Ten drinks will do that to you."

"Yes, and maybe it was the Twi'lek izzy-mold. What seems infinitely more likely is that we're about to walk into a trap."

"So we should be on guard."

"Yes, Anakin, we should be on guard."

Obi-Wan led the way up the stairs and rapped his hand on room seven's green plastoid door.

"Door's unlocked," a voice said in Basic from within.

They made certain that their lightsabers were in easy reach, but left them affixed to their belts and concealed. Obi-Wan hit the door-release stud, then followed Anakin into the chill room.

Wearing trousers, boots, and an insulated jacket, Genne—perhaps Fa'ale Leh—was lounging on a narrow bed, her back and lekku against the headboard, long legs extended and crossed at the ankle. Beside her on a small table stood a half-full bottle of what Obi-Wan guessed was the local rocket-fuel homebrew.

Reaching for two clearly unwashed glasses, she said: "Fix you a drink?"

"We're already at the legal limit," Anakin said, vigilant.

The remark made her smile. "Naos Three doesn't have a legal limit, kid." She took a healthy swallow from her own glass, eyeing them over the rim. "I have to say, you're not what I expected."

"Was that surprise or disappointment?" Anakin asked Obi-Wan.

"Who were you expecting?" Obi-Wan said.

"Your classic rough-and-tumble types. Black Sun lackeys, bounty hunters. You two . . . You look more like lost Jedi." She paused, then said: "Maybe that's exactly what you are. Jedi have been known to outpunish even the punishers."

"Only when necessary," Anakin said.

She shrugged absently. "You want to do it here, or are you going to buy me a last meal?"

"Do what here?" Obi-Wan said.

"Kill me, of course."

Anakin took a forward step. "There's always that possibility."

She glanced from him to Obi-Wan. "Bad Jedi. Good Jedi."

"We want to talk to you about a star courier you piloted for Sienar Advanced Projects."

She nodded at Obi-Wan. "Of course you do. A round of questions and answers, then a blaster—no, a lightsaber to the side of the head."

"Then you are Fa'ale Leh."

"Who told you where to find me? Had to be Thal K'sar, am I right? He's the only one still alive. That betraying little Bith—"

"Tell us about the courier," Anakin said, cutting her off.

She smiled in apparent recollection. "An extraordinary ship—a work of genius. But I knew going in, it was a job that would come back to haunt me. And so it has."

Obi-Wan looked around the room. "You've been in hiding here for more than ten years."

"No, I came for the beaches." She motioned in dismissal. "You know, they killed the engineers, the mechanics, just about everyone who worked on that craft. But I knew. I made the delivery, grabbed what was due me, and I was away. Not far enough, though. They tracked me to Ryloth, Nar Shaddaa, half the starforsaken worlds in the Tingel Arm. I had my share of close calls. I could show you the scars."

"No need," Obi-Wan said as Fa'ale was bringing her left head-tail over her shoulder.

She threw back another drink. "So who sent you—Sienar? Or was it the one the courier was built for?"

"Who *was* it built for?" Anakin said.

She regarded him for a moment. "That's the funny thing. Sienar—Raith Sienar himself—told me it was for a Jedi. But the guy I handed the yoke over to—he was no Jedi. Oh, he had a lightsaber and all, but . . . I don't know, there was something off about him."

Obi-Wan nodded. "We've had dealings with him."

"Where did you deliver it?" Anakin pressed.

"Well, to Coruscant, of course."

Obi-Wan glanced at the ceiling.

An instant before it blew inward—raining plastoid rafters, ice-covered roof panels, ceiling tiles, and two heavily armed Trandoshans—he had rushed to the bed and overturned it, dumping Fa'ale Leh, foam mattresses, and bedcovers onto the cold floor.

In hand and activated, Anakin's lightsaber was already a streak of blue light, deflecting blaster bolts and parrying swings of a vibro-ax in the meaty hands of a red-skinned Falleen who had burst through the door. Behind the Falleen came two humans who, in their eagerness to race into the room, had wedged themselves in the door frame.

Whirling, Obi-Wan called his lightsaber from his belt and leapt to the doorway, his blade slicing both hands off one of the humans. An agonized howl pierced the frigid air as the man sank to his knees. Unstuck, the second one fell forward, directly onto Obi-Wan's blade. The smell of burned flesh filled the room, swirling about with smoke from the explosive that had taken out three square meters of roof, and big wet snowflakes that were drifting through the opening.

Off to Obi-Wan's left Anakin stood unmoving in the center of the room, holding his own against the two reptilian aliens and the wielder of the vibro-ax. Parried bolts flew directly through the thin walls, rousing shrieks from Fa'ale's neighbors to both sides. Doors opened and slammed, and footfalls pounded on the hallway floor.

Pivoting on his left foot, the Falleen swung the vibro-ax at Obi-Wan's head. Ducking the swing, Obi-Wan got underneath the blade and just managed to nick the Falleen in the left thigh.

The strike only fueled the humanoid's rage. Raising the ax over his head, he rushed forward, intent on splitting Obi-Wan down the middle. A backflip carried Obi-Wan out of the blade's path, but Fa'ale's bedside table wasn't as fortunate. Cleaved, each half table fell to the floor, launching the Twi'lek's bottle of firewater clear across the room and square into the face of the larger of the two Trandoshans. Screaming in anger, the alien raised a clawed hand to his bleeding brow ridge, even while his other hand continued to trigger bolts at Anakin. As the bolts began to go wide, Anakin raised his left hand, pushing it through the air in the Trandoshan's direction and blowing him backward through the room's only window.

Determined to make the most of Anakin's split attention, the reptiloid's partner risked a lunge forward.

Obi-Wan tracked the flight of the alien's head across the room, out the door, and into the hallway, where someone loosed a bloodcurdling screech. The Falleen, finding himself on his own with the two Jedi, extended the ax in front of him and began to whirl.

Anakin backed away from the circling blade, then dived forward, sliding across the wet floor on his belly with his lightsaber held out in front of him and amputating the Falleen's legs at the knees. Shorter by half a meter but no less enraged, the humanoid sent the vibro-ax flying straight for Obi-Wan, then drew from his hip holster a large blaster and began firing.

In midflight from the vibrating blade, Obi-Wan watched Anakin rid the Falleen of blaster and hand, and thrust his lightsaber directly into the Falleen's chest. Whatever torso armor the humanoid was wearing beneath his jacket gave the energy blade pause, but heat from the lightsaber set fire to the Falleen's bandolier of explosive rounds.

Backing away from the lightsaber on the cauterized stumps of his legs, the Falleen began swatting at the growing flames in mounting panic, then turned and executed a perfect front dive out the window—only to explode short of the snowdrift that might have been his destination.

The room fell suddenly silent, except for the sizzle of huge snowflakes hitting the lightsabers.

Obi-Wan shouted: "Get her out of here!"

Deactivating his blade, Anakin pulled Fa'ale out from under the mattresses and bedding, and yanked her to her feet.

Wobbling drunkenly, she took in the ruined room.

"You two seem like decent folk—even for Jedi. Sorry you have to get mixed up in this."

Catching sight of a bottle that had somehow survived the violence, she started for it. When Anakin tightened his hold on her, she balled her hands and hammered at his chest and upper arms.

"Stop trying to be a hero, kid! I'm tired of running. It's over—for all of us."

"Not till we say it is," Anakin said.

She sagged in his grip. "That's the problem. That's why we're in a war to begin with."

Anakin began to drag her toward the door.

"Right on time," Obi-Wan said from the window. "Six more that I can see." A blaster bolt destroyed what was left of the window frame.

Anakin hauled Fa'ale to her feet once more and planted himself face-to-face with her. "You've outwitted assassins for ten years. You have a way out of here." He shook her forcefully. "Where?"

She remained still for a moment, then shut her eyes and nodded.

Obi-Wan and Anakin followed her out the door to a utility closet at the end of the hall. Concealed behind a false rear wall, two shiny poles dropped into darkness. Fa'ale took hold of one of the poles and vanished from sight. Anakin went next. Through the closed door, Obi-Wan could hear a crowd of beings race past the closet, heading for the Twi'lek's room. Gripping the pole with hands and feet, he let gravity take over.

The descent was longer than expected. Instead of ending up in the basement of the cantina, the poles ran completely through the hill on which that portion of Naos III had been built, all the way to the river itself. The bottom of the poles disappeared into thick ice. In dim natural light Obi-Wan saw that he was in a cavern that had become an inlet for the river. Close to the base of the poles sat three surface-effect sleds of the sort the locals used for ice fishing, outfitted with powerful-looking engines and pairs of long skis.

"I'm too drunk to drive," Fa'ale was saying.

Anakin had already straddled the machine's narrow seat, and was studying the controls. "You leave that to me," he told her. With the flip of a switch, the speeder's engine coughed to life, then began to purr loudly in the hollow of the cave.

Obi-Wan mounted a second sled, while Fa'ale was positioning herself behind Anakin.

"That one, then that one," Anakin said, pointing out the ignition switch and the warmer. Demonstrating, he added: "Thrusters, pitch control, steer like this."

Obi-Wan was instantly confused.

"Like this?"

"Like this, like this!" Anakin emphasized, demonstrating again, then indicating another set of switches on the control panel of Obi-Wan's machine. "Repulsorlift. But strictly for handling small ice mounds, frozen debris, that sort of thing. This isn't a conventional speeder—or even a swoop."

"Do you remember where we parked the cruiser?"

"I don't even remember landing. But the field can't be far off."

"Downriver," Fa'ale said. "Swing south around the hillock, go under the bridge, then west around the next hillock. Under two more bridges, slalom south again, and we're there."

Obi-Wan stared at her. "I'll follow you two."

They roared from the mouth of the cavern and out onto the glacial river.

Blaster bolts began to sear into the ice around them before they made the first bridge. Glancing over his shoulder, Obi-Wan saw three sleds gaining on them from upriver.

On the bridge, two beings bundled up in cold-weather gear were drawing a bead on him with a pintle-mounted repeating blaster.

The star that warmed Naos III was a white blur, low on the horizon. Ominous clouds obscured the mountains to Obi-Wan's right.

Snow was falling harder.

Tearing into it as fast as the sled would carry him, he felt as if he had run smack into a blizzard. The lovely, crystalline flakes would have been like pellets against his face and hands if not for the Force. Even so, he could barely see, and the ice—gray, white, and sometimes blue—was nowhere near as smooth as he had thought it would be. Pebbly where surface water had thawed and refrozen countless times; mounded up over debris trapped during the freeze; pocked by fishing holes; heaped high with ice that had filled the holes . . .

Matters weren't helped any by the fact that he was being shot at.

Bolts from the repeating blaster on the bridge had him weaving all over the river, slaloming around ice dams and leaping small mounds. The repulsorlift would have allowed him to fly over the obstacles—as Anakin was doing, farther downriver—but Obi-Wan just couldn't get the hang of it. More to the point, engaging the repulsorlift required using two hands, and just now he had none to spare. His left was gripped on the control bar/throttle; his right, tight on the hilt of his ignited lightsaber, as he fended off bolts from above and behind.

For a moment he was back on Muunilinst, jousting with Durge's speeder-freak lancer droids.

Except for the snow.

A vacillating roar in his right ear told him that one of the pursuit sleds had caught up with him. Out of the corner of his streaming eye, Obi-Wan saw the sled's human pilot bend low over the control bars to provide his Rodian rider with the clearance he needed to send a blaster bolt through Obi-Wan's head. Braking, Obi-Wan allowed the sled to come alongside more quickly than the Rodian had planned. The rider's first shot raced past Obi-Wan's eyes; the second, he deflected slightly downward, straight into the sled's engine.

The machine exploded instantly, flinging pilot and rider head over heels in opposite directions.

Quickly, however, a second sled was catching up.

This one carried a pilot only, but a more skillful one. Twisting the throttle, the pilot drove his sled into Obi-Wan's, trying to send it spinning out of control or, better still, into the trunk of massive tree that was protruding acutely from the thick ice. Narrowly missing the latter, Obi-Wan went into a sideways skid. Overcorrecting, he added spin to his slide and couldn't resume his course until the sled had whipped through half a dozen counter rotations. By then his crash-helmeted pursuer was well positioned to ram him a second time, but Obi-Wan was ready for him. Turning sharply, he steered into the pursuit sled, hanging on through the jarring collision, then directing a Force push at the rebounding pilot.

The sled shot forward as if supercharged, with the pilot all but dangling from the control bars. Speeding up the face of a hummock, the craft went airborne, then ballistic, plummeting into a thinly iced-over fishing hole at an angle that took machine and rider both deep under solid ice.

Water geysered into the air, drenching Obi-Wan as he raced past. The third sled was still clinging to his tail, and blaster bolts were whizzing past his ears. Up ahead, he saw Anakin and Fa'ale lean their sled through a sweeping turn to the south, between two of Naos III's many hills. Lethal hyphens of light streaked down from the bridge that linked the hills, but not one found Anakin or Fa'ale.

Unable to replicate Anakin's deft turns, Obi-Wan was falling farther behind with each quarter kilometer, and was now making himself an easy target for the assassins on the bridge. With no hope of negotiating the hail of fire, he maneuvered the sled through a long turn away from the span. But no sooner did he emerge from his half circle than he found himself on a collision course with the last of the pursuit sleds.

The inevitability of a head-on crash left him no choice but to abandon his machine for what was going to be a very long slide on the ice. But just short of his leap, a bolt in the jagged line the bridge gunners were stitching along the river caught the pilot of the onrushing machine in the chest, hurling him into the air. Twisting the throttle, Obi-Wan swerved around the pilotless sled and continued to race upriver, out of range of the blasters.

To his right a clamor built over the hill, and the shadow of something large and swift fell over him. A repeating blaster clacked repeatedly, fracturing the ice directly in his path and opening a wide, surging breach of agitated water.

Uncertain he could leap the gap even if he wanted to try, Obi-Wan applied the brakes—hard!

The sled was ten meters from the ice-chunked fissure when a metal claw dropped over him, snapping shut and plucking him from the seat. Wrenched from his hand, his lightsaber flew onto the ice, and the sled sailed off into the frothing water.

"Stars' end," Obi-Wan muttered.

Suspended on a swaying cable, the claw began to ascend toward the open belly of a graceless snow skiff.

Red hands clamped around Anakin's waist, Fa'ale whooped and shouted, clearly enjoying herself. Even through the daze of too many drinks—or more likely because of them.

"You missed your calling, Jedi," she shouted into his right ear. "You could have been a champion Podracer!"

"Been there, done that," Anakin said over his shoulder.

It was then that he caught sight of Obi-Wan being lifted from his sled. Bringing brakes and thrusters to bear, Anakin powered the sled through a fast 180 and shot back upriver, under the bridge they had just left behind, dodging the unrelenting fire of hand blasters.

"Sharptooth collector," Fa'ale explained when she saw the snow skiff. "Gathers catch, so the fishers won't have to ferry their loads into the city. That's what I do here—my job, such as it is."

The claw that had Obi-Wan in its grip was halfway to the skiff.

"I don't see any way of reaching him in time," Fa'ale said.

"Get ready to take the control bars!" Anakin said.

Fa'ale's hands clutched his robe. "Where are you planning to go?"

"Up."

Pouring on all speed, Anakin steered the sled up the side of the hill that supported one half of the bridge. At the zenith of the climb, he engaged the repulsorlift. Then, leaping from the now rocketing sled, he called on the Force to propel himself toward the swaying cage.

The pilots of the skiff saw him coming, and banked hard to starboard, but not soon enough to prevent Anakin from latching onto the claw. A Rodian in the copilot's chair cracked open the door and began firing down at his moving target.

"I had a feeling you'd show up," Obi-Wan said from inside the claw.

A lucky shot from above hit the cage and ricocheted.

"Hang on, Master! This isn't going to be pretty."

Obi-Wan heard the *snap-hiss* of Anakin's lightsaber. Peering through the metal fingers of the claw, he saw what was coming.

"Anakin, wait—"

But there was no stopping him.

As the claw came within reach of the cargo hold, Anakin swung his lightsaber and sliced open the floor of the skiff's cockpit. Sparks and smoke poured from the rend, and almost immediately the craft slued to starboard. Passing within a meter of one of the bridge towers, it began to twirl toward the hillside.

An instant before the crash, Anakin severed the claw cable, and the cage plummeted, striking the slippery ground and racing down to the frozen river, out onto the ice, spinning crazily, with Obi-Wan bouncing around inside and Anakin Force-fastened to the outside through all the unpredictable pitches and tumbles. The skiff crashed into the hillside. By the time the claw came to a rest on the far side of the river, the two Jedi were so covered in snow they looked like wampas.

Anakin's lightsaber made short work of the fingers of the claw. Obi-Wan scrambled out, spitting snow, and shaking like a hound.

"That has to make it forty—"

"Stop," Obi-Wan said. "I concede." He paused to empty the sleeves and hood of his sodden cloak. "Where's Fa'ale?"

Anakin scanned the hillsides. The assassins on the bridge had packed up and fled. Ultimately, he pointed toward the opposite bank of the river, where a sled was wedged between two mounds of ice.

When they reached her, Fa'ale was laying facedown a few meters from the machine, which had been holed by blasterfire.

Gently turning her over, Anakin saw that one bolt had amputated the Twi'lek's right lekku. Her eyes blinked open, focusing on him as he cradled her in his arms.

"Don't tell me," she said weakly. "I'm going to live, right?"

"Sorry to be the bearer of bad news."

"A week in bacta and you'll be good as new," Obi-Wan said.

Fa'ale sighed. "I won't hold it against you. You did your best to get me killed." She gazed around. "Shouldn't we be looking for cover?"

"They're gone," Anakin said.

Fa'ale shook her head. "After all these years, they finally—"

"I don't think so," Obi-Wan interrupted. "Someone more important than Raith Sienar doesn't want us to learn too much about the star courier."

"Then I had better tell you the rest—about Coruscant, I mean."

Anakin raised her up. "Where did you deliver the ship?"

"To an old building in the industrial quarter, west of the Senate. An area called The Works."

Macrobinoculars pressed to his eyes, Mace studied the distant building top to bottom, his gaze lingering on broken windows, fissured ledges, canted balconies.

Central to a complex of half a dozen structures, the building was more than three centuries old and going to ruin. For two-thirds of its towering height it was an unadorned pillar with a rounded summit. Support for the superstructure was afforded by a circular base, reinforced by massive fins. Where the superstructure and the sloped tops of the buttresses met, the building was fenestrated by windows and antiquated gear-toothed docking gates. Many of the permaglass panels and skylights were intact, but time and corrosion had done their worst to the vertical hatches of the docking gates.

An investigation was under way to determine who had raised the building, and who owned it—although, judging by its location and prominence in The Works, it appeared to have served as corporate headquarters for the factories and assembly plants that surrounded it.

Mace and his team of Jedi, clone commandos, and Intelligence analysts were a kilometer east of the structure, in an area of squat, peak-roofed foundries, lorded over by smoke-belching permacrete stacks. A more dispiriting place this side of Eriadu or Korriban would have been hard to find, Mace told himself. Five hours spent here could take five years off someone's life. He could feel the damage with every breath he took, every grimy surface he touched, every vagrant-poisoned whiff that wafted his way. The acids in the air were fast digesting everything, but not quickly enough for some. Ambitious developers and urban renewalists had deliberately introduced stone mites, duracrete slugs, and conduit worms to aid and abet the caustic rain, without heed for the risk such vermin poised to the nearby skyscrapers of the Senate District.

All in all, the perfect environment for a Sith Lord.

"Probe remotes are away, General Windu," the ARC reported.

Mace trained the macrobinoculars on the flock of meter-wide spherical droids that were maneuvering with purposeful unevenness toward the building.

The Senate Intelligence Oversight Committee had attempted to interdict the use of commandos and probe droids. In the minds of the committee members, the idea that a Separatist stronghold could exist on Coruscant was absurd. Fortunately—and admittedly unexpectedly—Supreme Chancellor Palpatine had overruled the committee, and Mace had been allowed to compile a dream team that included not only ARC commander Valiant and Captain Dyne of Republic Intelligence, but also Jedi Master Shaak Ti and several capable Padawans.

"No indications that the probes are being targeted," the ARC updated.

Mace watched the black spheres begin to drift through shattered windows and into areas of the superstructure where the building's façade had disintegrated and the bones of its plasteel skeleton were exposed.

Moment of truth, he thought.

*   *   *

The Lothan pilot Obi-Wan and Anakin had searched out on Naos III hadn't been able to furnish anything more than a portrait of the building to which she had delivered the star courier. A product of Sienar Advanced Projects Laboratory, the craft had been modified—perhaps unwittingly by Sienar itself—for the Sith who had killed Qui-Gon Jinn. The pilot had been provided with landing coordinates on Coruscant, but, in fact, the courier itself had homed in on those. Paid in full for her services, she had been taxied to Westport, and had left for Ryloth soon after. The physical description of the courier's destination hadn't given the Jedi much to go on. Though more horizontal than most areas of equatorial Coruscant, The Works sprawled for hundreds of square kilometers and contained thousands of buildings that could have fit the description.

A break hadn't come until Jedi Master Tholme had recalled a detail from the debriefing of his former Padawan, Quinlan Vos. As part of Vos's covert mission to penetrate Count Dooku's inner circle of dark side apprentices, Vos had been tasked with assassinating a duplicitous Senator, named Viento. Immediately following the assassination—and a brutal duel with Master K'Kruhk—Vos had met briefly with Dooku in The Works. There, Dooku had informed his would-be protégé that Vos had been incorrect in assuming that Viento was a Sith, and had again denied that he himself answered to any Master.

At the time, no one had paid much attention to Vos's remarks, because Vos seemed to have been seduced by the dark side and lost to the Order. The rendezvous was considered to have been only that: an out-of-the-way meeting place. Of greater interest to the Jedi and Republic Intelligence was the fact that Dooku had managed to arrive at and depart Coruscant without detection.

"Holoimages of the interior coming in," Valiant said.

Mace lowered the macrobinoculars and shifted his gaze to the field holoprojector. Dazzled by diagonal lines of static, the

3-D images were of forlorn rooms, stretches of dark corridor, vast empty spaces.

"The building appears to be completely abandoned, General. No signs of droids or living beings—other than varieties common to similar manufacturing slums."

"Abandoned, perhaps, but not forgotten," Captain Dyne said from behind Valiant. "The building's *live*. It has power and illumination."

"Doesn't mean much," Mace said. "Many structures in this district were self-powered, often by dangerous, highly unstable fuels." He gestured broadly. "They're still belching smoke."

Dyne nodded. "But this one shows periodic and recent use of power."

Mace turned to Valiant. "All right, Commander. Give the go-ahead."

From behind and to both sides of the observation post, LAATs lifted off into the smoke-filled sky, doorway gunners traversing their repeating blasters and commandos standing ready to deploy from the gunship's troop bay. Elsewhere, AT-TEs and other mobile artillery vehicles began to lumber across the debris-filled urbanscape toward the target.

Valiant turned to the troopers who made up Aurek Team.

"The building is a free-strike zone. You are to consider anyone we find inside to be hostile." He slammed a fresh power pack into his short-stocked blaster. "Troopers: find, fix, finish!"

No matter how often he heard it, the grunting, communal response to the ARC's rallying cry continued to disturb Mace on some level. Although it was probably no different from what the clone troopers heard when the Jedi said to one another, *May the Force be with you.*

He swung and waved a signal to Shaak Ti.

"I'll ride with Aurek Team. You have Bacta."

As beautiful as a flower, as deadly as a viper, Shaak Ti was the Jedi Master one wanted by one's side in chaotic circumstances.

Graced with the ability to move quickly through crowds or tight spots, she was often the first to wade into close-quarter engagements, her striped montrals and lengthy head-tail alert to distances, her blue lightsaber quick to find its mark. She had proved instrumental in the defense of Kamino and Brentaal IV, and Mace was glad to have her with him now.

Aurek Team's gunship was already packed with commandos and Padawans by the time he clambered inside. Lifting off, the LAAT/i aimed straight for the summit of the building. The strategy was to work from the top down, in the hope of flushing hostiles out through the lowest levels, where infantry and artillery units were already taking up firing positions around the buttressed base. The entire area was undermined with tunnels that had been used for transporting workers, droids, and materials. While it wasn't possible to monitor every entrance and egress, many of the principal tunnels that opened on the building's subbasements had been outfitted with sensors capable of detecting droids or flesh-and-bloods.

No functioning docking bay large enough to accommodate a gunship had been discovered. The commandos had advocated blowing a gaping hole in the side of the superstructure, but engineers feared that an explosion of the strength required could very well collapse the entire structure. Instead the LAAT/i carried the team to the largest of the blown-out windows below the summit, and hovered there while everyone was inserted.

Leaping the gap, Mace activated his lightsaber and instructed the Padawans to follow suit.

Weapons raised to their chests, the commandos spread out in fire-and-maneuver squads and began to move deeper in the building, checking out each room and alcove before declaring any level secure. Mace's blade glowed amethyst in the gloom. Stretching out with the Force, he could feel the presence of the dark side. The only explanation for Quinlan Vos not having felt it was that he, too, had gone dark.

Yoda had warned Mace that the dark side might cloud his mind to certain rooms and passageways—places that the Sith Lords didn't want Mace to discover—but he felt alert in all ways. Besides, that was what the commandos were for.

They worked their way down and down, without encountering resistance or finding anything of interest.

"Quiet as a tomb, General," Valiant said when the top ten levels had been secured.

Mace studied the 3-D map displayed by the ARC's wrist gauntlet projector.

"Inform Bacta Team that we will rally with them in designated sector three."

Valiant was about to speak when his comlink toned.

"Commander, this is Bacta Team leader," a voice said. "We have a functioning docking gate on level six that shows evidence of recent use. And, sir, wait until you get a look at the landing zone."

The floor that served as a landing area was scarcely large enough for a gunship, but it gleamed as if scrubbed and polished daily by custodial droids. Parallel to the long sides of the rectangle were banks of slender blue illuminators.

"Everyone stay exactly where you are," Captain Dyne said when Mace and the rest of Aurek Team appeared at the mouth of a corridor that intersected the docking bay at its lengthwise centerpoint.

Deployed in a circle formation, Shaak Ti and the Padawans who had entered with Bacta were clustered in the middle of the floor.

Thirty meters to Mace's right, Dyne and two other Intelligence officers were interpreting the data being sent to them by several probe droids meandering with design throughout the room, some of them misting the floor with a highly volatile substance. The well-lubricated vertical docking gate was open, revealing an oval of blackened sky.

"A Huppla Pasa Tisc sloop occupied this docking bay less than two standard weeks ago," Dyne said, loud enough for everyone to hear. "The arrangement of its landing gear and aft boarding ramp match the footprint of the *Punworcca 116*-class that launched from Geonosis during the battle there."

"Dooku's ship," Mace said.

"A reasonable supposition, Master Windu," Dyne said loudly. After several moments of gazing at the monitor screens of his equipment and conferring with his associates, he added: "The floor reveals traces of two beings who were here contemporaneous with the sloop."

Green light from one of the drifting droids played across the alloy floor panels. Dyne directed the droid to concentrate on certain areas, and studied the data again.

"The first being exited the sloop and walked to this point." He indicated an area close to the open gate. "Taking into consideration trace impressions and the length of the being's stride, I would hazard that being one stands one hundred and ninety-five centimeters in height, and was wearing boots."

It was *Dooku!* Mace thought.

The droid focused its lights on another area, and Dyne continued.

"Here, being one met with being two, lighter in weight, perhaps shorter in stature, and wearing—" Dyne consulted what Mace assumed to be some sort of database. "—what can best be described as soft-soled footwear or slippers. This unknown being came from the direction of the building's east turbolifts, and accompanied . . . Dooku—for all intents and purposes—to a balconied niche above the docking gate. Following the same route, the pair returned to the docking bay and separated: Dooku to his ship; our unknown quarry, presumably to the turbolifts."

Tasking the probe droids to track the prints of the second being, Dyne began to trail them, waving for Mace, Shaak Ti, and the commandos to follow.

"Single file behind me," Dyne cautioned. "No straying out of line."

Mace and Shaak Ti took the point, with the Padawans and commandos strung out behind. By the time the two Jedi Masters caught up with Dyne and his droids, the Intelligence analyst was standing at the door to a dated turbolift.

"Verified," Dyne said, grinning in self-satisfaction. "Being two used the turbolift."

Turning to the wall, he pressed his gloved right hand to the call stud. When the summoned car appeared, he affixed a scanner to the control pad inside.

"The car's memory tells us that it arrived from sub-basement two. If we fail to discover evidence of our unknown quarry there, we'll have to work our way back up, one level at a time, until we do."

The turbolift was just roomy enough for Dyne, his associates, Mace, Shaak Ti, the two team commanders, and two probe droids. Comlinking troopers outside the building, Valiant ordered them to make their way to sub-basement two, but forewarned them to stay clear of the east turbolift and any nearby corridors or tunnels.

The probe droids were first to exit the car when it stopped, misting the corridor in both directions. One of the droids hadn't gone five meters before it stopped in midflight and began playing its detection lights across the floor.

"Footprints," Dyne said with enthusiasm. "We're still on track."

Stepping carefully from the car, he followed the probe droids to the entrance of a wide tunnel. After the droids had disappeared inside and returned, Dyne swung to Mace, who was waiting with everyone else at the base of the turbolift.

"The prints end here. From this point on the unknown used a vehicle—certainly a repulsorlift of some sort, although the droids aren't detecting any phantom emissions."

Mace and Shaak Ti joined Dyne and his teammates at the tunnel entrance.

Shaak Ti peered into the darkness. "Where does it lead?"

Dyne consulted a holomap. "If we can trust a map that's older than any of us, it connects to tunnels all over The Works—to adjacent buildings, to the foundries, to a onetime landing field . . . There must be a hundred branches."

"Forget the branches," Mace said. "What's at the far end of this one?"

Dyne called up a series of displays and studied them in silence. At last, he said: "The principal tunnel leads all the way to the western limit of the Senate District."

Mace walked two meters into the darkness, and ran his hand down the tunnel's tiled wall.

Hundreds of Senators are now under the influence of a Sith Lord called Darth Sidious, Dooku had told Obi-Wan on Geonosis.

Turning to face Shaak Ti and the clone commanders, Mace said: "We're going to need more troops."

In the Supreme Chancellor's Senate Office Building chambers, Yoda sat staring across the desk at Palpatine, silhouetted against the long window that overlooked western Coruscant. How many Supreme Chancellors had he sat with in this office and others like it? he asked himself. Half a hundred now. But why with this one did discussion so often skirt the edge of confrontation—especially when the topic turned to the Force. As ineffectual a leader as he was, Finis Valorum had tried to comport himself as if he placed the Force above all. With Palpatine, the Force was not placed last. It wasn't even on the agenda.

"I understand your concerns entirely, Master Yoda," he was saying. "More important, I am *sympathetic* to them. But the Outer Rim sieges must continue. Despite what you may think—and notwithstanding the extraordinary powers the Senate has deemed fit to bestow on me these past five years—I am one voice in a welter. At long last the Senate is galvanized to end this destructive conflict, and it will not permit me to stand in the way."

"Exhort me, you need not, Supreme Chancellor," Yoda said.

Palpatine smiled dryly. "I apologize if I sounded sermonizing."

"Galvanized by your State of the Republic address, the Senate was."

"My address was a reflection of the spirit of the times, Master Yoda. What's more, I spoke from my heart."

"Doubt you, I do not. But too soon, your encouragements came. Celebrates imminent victory, Coruscant does, when far from ended the war is."

Palpatine's frown contained a hint of warning, of malice. "After three years of fear, Coruscant craves relief."

"Agree with you, I do. But how from the seizure of Outer Rim worlds is relief sustained? Too many new fronts, the Senate urges us to open. Too dispersed the Jedi are, to serve effectively. A reasonable strategy, we lack."

"My military advisers would not be pleased to hear you categorize their strategy as irrational."

"Need to hear it, they do. *Say* it to them, I will."

Palpatine paused to consider the remark, then leveled a hard gaze. "Master Yoda, forgive my frankness, but if the Jedi are indeed too widely scattered to coordinate the sieges, then the burden will have to fall to my naval commanders."

Yoda compressed his lips and shook his head. "Answer foremost to the Jedi, our troopers do. Forged an alliance with them, we have. Forged in fire, this fidelity has been."

Palpatine sat upright, as if struck. "I'm certain I misconstrue your meaning, but you almost make it sound as if our army was created for the Jedi."

"Not true," Yoda snapped. "For the Republic, and none other."

Appeased, Palpatine said: "Then perhaps the clones can be trained to respond to others, as well as they respond to the Jedi."

Yoda made a glum face. "Trained the troopers can be. But wrong this strategy remains."

"May I ask that you think back to Geonosis? Do you not agree that we erred then by not pursuing the Separatists?"

"Unprepared, we were. New, the army was."

"Granted. But we are prepared now. We have the Confederacy on the run from the inner systems, and I will not allow us to repeat the mistake we made at Geonosis."

"No, a *different* mistake we make now."

Palpatine interlocked his fingers. "This is the wisdom of the Council?"

"It is."

"Then you will challenge the Senate's decision?"

Yoda shook his head. "Sworn by oath to uphold you, we are."

Palpatine spread his hands. "That does not instill confidence, Master Yoda. If it's nothing more than an oath, then you are duty-bound to reconsider."

"Reconsidered we *have*, Supreme Chancellor."

"You imply no threat, I trust."

"No threat."

Palpatine forced a fatigued exhale. "As I've told you on many occasions, I do not have the luxury of seeing this world through the Force. I see only the real world."

"No problem there would be, if the 'real world,' all there was."

"Unfortunately, we who are not attuned to the Force have that on Jedi authority only."

Yoda wagged his forefinger at Palpatine. "To end this war, *more* we will have to do than defeat Grievous and his army of war machines. More we will have to do than seize remote worlds."

"These Sith to whom you keep referring." Palpatine fell silent in thought, then said: "When you were believed killed at Ithor, Master Windu said as much to me."

"More attentive to his concerns, were you?"

Palpatine regarded him. "A skilled duelist you are."

"When need be, Supreme Chancellor."

"You never fully described what went on between you and

Count Dooku on Vjun. Was he at all inclined to return to the Order—to the side of the Republic?"

Yoda allowed his sadness to show. "From the dark path, no returning there is. Forever, the direction of your life it dominates."

"That may make Dooku difficult to rehabilitate."

Yoda raised his gaze. "Captured, he will never be. Die fighting, he will."

"This Darth Sidious, as well—should Dooku be found and killed?"

Yoda's eyes fidgeted. "Difficult to say. Deprived of an apprentice, Sidious may withdraw—to preserve the Sith."

"One person is all that's required to preserve the Sith traditions?"

"Traditions they are not. The *dark* side, it is."

"Then what if you should find Sidious first, and kill him? Would Dooku's power increase?"

"Only Dooku's determination. Different it will be, because a Sith late he has become." Yoda shook his head. "Hard to know if Dooku a true Sith is, or simply with the power of the dark side infatuated."

"And General Grievous?"

Yoda made a gesture of dismissal. "More machine than alive, Grievous is—though more dangerous for it. But without Dooku's or Sidious's leadership, collapse the Separatists will. Bound together by the Sith they are. Mortared by the dark side of the Force."

Palpatine leaned forward with interest. "Then the Council is of the opinion that we must kill the leadership—that this war is more a battle within the Force?"

"United we are in that matter."

"You are persuasive, Master Yoda. You have my word that I will bear this conversation in mind when I meet with the Senate to discuss our campaigns."

"Relieved, I am, Supreme Chancellor."

Palpatine reclined in his chair. "Tell me, how goes the hunt for Darth Sidious?"

Yoda leaned forward for emphasis. "Coming *closer* to him, are we."

In a forward hold of Grievous's flagship, Dooku watched the cyborg general duel with his elite MagnaGuards, three of his trophy lightsabers in constant motion, parrying thrusts of the guards' pulse-weaponed staffs, slicing the recycled air a hairbreadth from the expressionless faces of his opponents, incapacitating arm and leg servos when he could. Grievous was a force to be reckoned with, to be sure, but Dooku deplored his habit of collecting lightsabers. It had merely bothered him that Ventress and lesser combatants such as the bounty hunter Aurra Sing had adopted the foul practice. Grievous's habit struck Dooku as the worst kind of profanation. Even so, he was not about to discourage the practice. The more Jedi that could be dispatched, the better.

The only aspect of Grievous's technique that vexed him more was the general's penchant for using four blades. Two was bad enough—in the form they had been used by Darth Maul, or in Anakin Skywalker's sad attempt to employ the technique on Geonosis.

But *three?*

What was to become of elegance and gallantry if a duelist couldn't make do with one blade?

Well, what had become of elegance and gallantry, in any case?

Grievous was fast, and so were his IG 100-series sparring partners. They had the advantage of size and brute strength. They executed moves almost faster than the human eye could follow. Their thrusts and lunges demonstrated a singular lack of hesitancy. Once committed to a maneuver, they never faltered. They never stopped to recalculate their actions. Their weapons went exactly where they meant them to go. And they always aimed for points beyond their opponents in order to slice clear through.

Dooku had taught Grievous well, and Grievous had taught his elite well. Coupled with Dooku's coaching, their programming in the seven classic forms of lightsaber dueling—in the Jedi arts—made them lethal opponents. But they were not invincible, not even Grievous, because they could be confused by unpredictability, and they had no understanding of finesse. A player of dejarik could memorize all the classic openings and countermoves, and still not be a master of the game. Defeat often came at the hands of less experienced players who knew nothing about the traditional strategies. A professional fighter, a combat artist, could be defeated by a cantina brawler who knew nothing about form but everything about ending a conflict quickly, without a thought to winning gracefully or elegantly.

Enslavement to form opened one to defeat by the unforeseen.

This was often the failing of trained duelists, and it would be the failing of the Jedi Order.

Given that elegance, gallantry, and enchantment were gone from the galaxy, it was only fitting that the Order's days were numbered; that the fire that had been the Jedi was guttering and dying out. As with the corrupt Republic itself, the Order's time had come. The noble Jedi, bound to the Force, sworn to uphold peace and justice, were seldom seen as heroes or saviors any longer, but more often as bullies or mobsters.

Still, it was sad that it had fallen to Dooku to help usher them out.

The conversation he had had with Yoda on dreary Vjun was never far from his thoughts these days. For all his flair with words, all his Force-given personal power, Yoda was nothing more than an old one, unwilling to embrace anything new, indisposed to see any way but his own. Yet how terrible not simply to fade away but to expire in full knowledge that the galaxy had tipped inexorably and at long last to the dark side, to the Sith, and might remain so for as long as the Jedi themselves had ruled.

The unforeseen . . .

Grievous and his guards were dancing. Going through their programmed motions.

An Ataro attack answered by Shii-Cho; Soresu answered by Lus-ma . . .

Dooku couldn't suffer another moment of it.

"No, no, stop, stop," he yelled, coming to his feet and striding to the middle of the training circle, his arms extended to both sides. When he was certain that he had their attention, he swung to Grievous. "Power moves served you well on Hypori against Jedi such as Daakman Barrek and Tarr Seir. But I pity you should you have to face off against any of the Council Masters." He called into hand his courtly, curve-handled lightsaber and drew a rapid X in the air—a Makashi flourish. "Do I need to demonstrate what responses you can expect from Cin Drallig or Obi-Wan Kenobi? From Mace Windu or, stars help you, *Yoda*?"

He flicked his blade quickly, ridding two of the guards of their staffs, then placing the glowing tip a millimeter from Grievous's death-helmeted visage. "Finesse. Artfulness. Economy.

Otherwise, my friend, I fear that you will end up beyond the repair of even the Geonosians. Do you take my meaning?"

His vertically slit eyes unfathomable, Grievous nodded.

"I take your meaning, my lord."

Dooku withdrew his blade. "Again, then. With some measure of polish, if I'm not asking for too much."

Dooku seated himself and watched them go at it.

Hopeless, he thought.

But he knew that he was partly to blame. He had made the same mistake with Grievous that he had made with Ventress, by allowing her to fill herself with hate, as if hate could substitute for dispassion. Even the most hateful could be defeated. Even the most angry. There should be no emotion in killing, no self, only the act. When he should have been helping Ventress rid herself of *self,* he had instead permitted her to grow impassioned. Sidious had once confessed that he had erred similarly in his training of Darth Maul. Ventress and Maul had been driven by a desire to excel—to be the best—instead of merely allowing themselves to be pure instruments of the dark side.

The Jedi knew this about the Force: that the best of them were nothing more than instruments.

Dooku grew troubled.

Was Sidious thinking the same of him now? Thinking: *This is where I failed poor Dooku. Pitiful creature . . .*

It was entirely possible, considering how wrong things had gone on Naos III. Standard days earlier, Dooku had sent Sidious a coded transmission that was as much apology as explanation, and had yet to hear from him.

He watched Grievous disarm two of the MagnaGuards.

In fact, Grievous was *all* instrument.

And Dooku. What was Count Dooku of Serenno?

He glanced at the hold's holoprojector table a moment before a blue holoimage of Sidious appeared above it.

My time is at hand, he told himself as he centered himself proudly on the transmission grid, Grievous behind him, down on one knee, with head lowered.

"My lord," he said, bowing slightly at the waist. "I've been waiting."

"There have been matters that warranted my close attention, Lord Tyranus."

"Born, no doubt, of my failure at Naos Three. The ones I sent had every opportunity to kill Kenobi, Skywalker, and the Twi'lek pilot. Instead, they decided to attempt their capture, to extract additional funds from me, as well as to bolster their reputations."

Sidious was dismissive. "Such is the way of bounty hunters. I should have foreseen this."

Dooku blinked. Was this an admission of failure on Sidious's part? Was Sidious's upper lip twitching, or was it nothing more than noise in the transmission?

"The Force is strong in Skywalker," Sidious went on.

"Yes, my lord. Very strong. Next time I will deal with the Jedi personally."

"Yes, that time is drawing near, Lord Tyranus. But first we need to provide the Jedi with something that distracts them from hunting me."

Sidious's upper lip was definitely twitching. Was this worry? Worry from someone fond of saying that things were going precisely as planned?

"What has happened, my lord?"

"The Twi'lek's information led them to our rendezvous on Coruscant," Sidious said in a scurrilous voice.

Dooku was stunned. "Is there a greater danger?"

"They think they have my scent, Lord Tyranus, and perhaps they do."

"Can you leave Coruscant, my lord?"

From parsecs distant, Sidious stared at him. "Leave Coruscant?"

"For a time, my lord. Surely we can find some way."

Sidious fell silent for a long moment, then said: "Perhaps, Lord Tyranus. Perhaps."

"If not, then I will come to you."

Sidious shook his head. "That won't be necessary. I told you that their search for me would benefit us before too long, and thanks to you I begin to see a way."

"What is thy bidding, Master?" Grievous asked from behind Dooku.

Sidious turned slightly toward Grievous, but continued to speak to Dooku. "The Jedi have divided their forces. We must do the same. I will deal with the ones on Coruscant. I need you to deal with the rest."

"My fleet stands ready, Master," Grievous said, still without raising his gaze from the grid.

"The Republic is monitoring you?" Sidious asked the general.

"Yes, Master."

"Can you divide the fleet—judiciously?"

"It can be done, Master."

"Good, good. Then move however many ships are needed to crush and occupy Tythe."

Again Dooku was stunned. So, too, was Grievous.

"Is that wise, Master," the general asked carefully, "after what happened at Belderone?"

Sidious adopted a faint grin. "More than wise, General. *Inspired.*"

"But Tythe, my lord," Dooku said with equal care. "Less a world than a corpse."

"It has some strategic value, does it not, General?"

"As a jump point, Master. But a dubious prize, regardless, when far better targets exist."

"It may prove costly to us, my lord. The Republic will almost certainly flatten it," Dooku said.

"Not if the Jedi are convinced that it must be retaken rather than destroyed."

Confusion wrinkled Dooku's forehead. "How will we convince them?"

"We won't have to, Lord Tyranus. Their own investigations will lead them to that conclusion. Moreover, Kenobi and Skywalker will oversee the counterattack."

"Indeed, my lord?"

"They will not pass up an opportunity to capture Count Dooku."

Dooku saw Grievous's armorplast head elevate in surprise. "What leads you to believe that the Republic will not simply flatten me at this point?"

"The Jedi are predictable, Lord Tyranus. I needn't tell you this. Look what they risked on Cato Neimoidia in an effort to capture Viceroy Gunray. They are obsessed with bringing their enemies to justice, instead of merely administering justice themselves."

"It is their way."

"Then you don't mind serving as bait to lure them there?"

Dooku inclined his head. "As ever, I am at your disposal, my lord."

Sidious grinned once more. "Hold Kenobi and Skywalker, Lord Tyranus. Entertain them. Play to their weakness. Demonstrate your mastery, as you have on previous occasions."

Grievous made a meaningful sound. "I will do the same with their warships, Master."

"No, General," Sidious cut in. "I have something else in mind for you and the rest of the fleet. But tell me, can you tuck your charges somewhere safe for the time being?"

"The planet Utapau comes to mind, Lord Sidious."

"I will leave that to you."

"And when I have seen to that, Master?"

"General, I'm certain you recall the plans we discussed some time ago, regarding the final stage of the war."

"Regarding Coruscant."

"Regarding Coruscant, yes." Sidious paused, then said: "We must accelerate those plans. Prepare, General, for what will be your finest hour."

F a'ale is doing fine," Anakin said as he approached Obi-Wan
jauntily. "Two more days of bacta and she'll be on her feet. She
says she's through with Naos Three, though. She might even remain here on Belderone."

Obi-Wan looked at him askance. "Your relationship with females is an interesting one. The more jeopardy they're in, the
more you worry about them. And the more you worry about
them, the more they worry about *you*."

Anakin frowned. "You're basing this on, what, exactly?"

Obi-Wan looked away. "HoloNet gossip."

Anakin stepped deliberately into Obi-Wan's gaze. "Something's wrong. What is it?"

Obi-Wan sighed. "We won't be returning to Coruscant."

They were in a visitors' lounge in the largest of the MedStars
orbiting Belderone. For four standard days they had been awaiting instructions from the Jedi Council and visiting the medical
ward to check on Fa'ale's progress, and the strain of so much in-
activity was beginning to show.

Anakin was staring dumbfounded at Obi-Wan.

"Hear me out before you go critical. Mace and Shaak Ti were

able to locate the building in The Works. Not surprisingly, it turns out to have been the same one where Quinlan Vos met with Dooku last year. Once inside, Mace's team discovered more than we could have even hoped for—evidence of a more recent visit by Dooku, and of the person he apparently went to Coruscant to see."

"Sidious?"

"Possibly. Even if it wasn't, it's likely that Dooku has other confederates on Coruscant, and tracking them down could eventually lead us to Sidious. Other evidence has come to light, as well. Intelligence discovered that the building belonged to a corporation called LiMerge Power, which was believed to have been involved in the manufacture and distribution of prohibited weapons during Finis Valorum's term as Supreme Chancellor. It was rumored at the time that LiMerge was responsible for funding acts of piracy directed against Trade Federation vessels in the Outer Rim. And it was those acts of piracy that led ultimately to the Trade Federation being granted the right to defend their vessels with battle droids."

"Are you telling me that LiMerge might have been in league with the Sith?"

"Why not? At Naboo, the Trade Federation was in league with Sidious. The entire Confederacy is in league with him now."

Anakin shrugged impatiently. "I still don't understand how this keeps us from returning to Coruscant."

"I've just been informed that the Separatists have attacked a Republic garrison base on Tythe, and occupied the planet."

"Who cares? I mean, I'm sorry for any troopers we lost, but Tythe is a wasteland."

"Exactly," Obi-Wan said. "But before it became a wasteland, it was headquarters for LiMerge Power."

Anakin mulled it over for a moment. "Another attempt by Sidious to erase the trail we've been following?"

Obi-Wan ran his hand over his mouth. "The Council was able to convince Palpatine of the need to retake Tythe, and he has authorized a full battle group to divert there. It seems he is finally willing to follow Master Yoda's advice about concentrating on dismantling the Confederacy leadership."

"Grievous is on Tythe?"

Obi-Wan grinned. "Better: Dooku is there."

Anakin turned his back to Obi-Wan. His face was flushed when he finally swung around. "Not good enough."

Obi-Wan blinked. "Not good enough?"

"The search for Sidious began with us. We discovered the first clues. If he's thought to be on Coruscant, then we're the ones who should be there to capture him."

"Anakin, Mace and Shaak Ti are more than capable of seeing to that—*if* Sidious is even there."

Anakin was shaking his head. "Not as easily as . . . we could. Sidious is a Sith Lord!"

Obi-Wan took a moment to respond. "The way I remember it, we didn't fare all that well against Dooku."

"All that's changed!" Anakin said, becoming angrier as he spoke. "I'm stronger than I was. You're stronger. Together, we can defeat any Sith."

"Anakin, is this really about capturing Sidious?"

"Of course it is. We deserve the honor."

"Honor? Since when did this war become a contest for first place? If you're thinking that the capture of Sidious will earn you a place on the Council—"

"I don't care about the Council! I'm telling you we need to return to Coruscant. People are counting us."

"What people?"

"The . . . people of Coruscant."

Obi-Wan inhaled slowly. "Why don't I believe you?"

"I don't know, Master? Suppose you tell me?"

Obi-Wan narrowed his eyes. "Don't turn this into a game. There's something else at work here. Have you had a vision I should know about?"

Anakin started to reply, bit back whatever it was he had in mind to say, and began again. "The truth is . . . I want to be home. We've been out here longer than anyone—trooper or Jedi."

"That's what you get for being so good at what you do," Obi-Wan said, hoping to lighten the mood.

"I'm tired of it, Master. I want to be home."

Obi-Wan studied him. "You miss the Temple so much? The food? The lights of Coruscant?"

"Yes."

"Yes, to what?"

"All of it."

"Then your protests have nothing to do with capturing Sidious."

"No. They do."

"Well, which is it—home or Sidious?"

"Why can't it be both?"

Obi-Wan fell silent, as if struck by a sudden suspicion. "Anakin, is it Padmé?"

Anakin rolled his eyes. "Here you go again."

"Well, is it?"

Anakin compressed his lips, then said, "I won't lie to you and say that I don't miss her."

Obi-Wan frowned sympathetically. "You can't afford to miss her in that way."

"And exactly why is that, Master?"

"Because you cannot be married to both."

"Who said anything about *marriage*? She's a friend. I miss her as a friend!"

"You would forgo your destiny for Padmé?"

Anakin's brows beetled in anger. "I never claimed to be the

Chosen One. That was Qui-Gon. Even the Council doesn't believe it anymore, so why should you?"

"Because I think you believe it," Obi-Wan said calmly. "I think you know in your heart that you're meant for something extraordinary."

"And you, Master. What does your heart tell you you're meant for?"

"Infinite sadness," Obi-Wan said, even while smiling.

Anakin regarded him. "If you believe in destiny, then everything we do becomes part of that destiny—whether we go to Tythe or we return to Coruscant."

"You may be right. I don't have the answer. I wish I did."

"Then where does that leave us?"

Obi-Wan rested his hands on Anakin's shoulders. "Speak with Palpatine. Maybe he'll see something in this that I've missed."

Fifty meters ahead of Mace in the tunnel, Shaak Ti held up her hand, motioning for him to stop. Angling his purple blade to the floor, Mace turned to relay the signal to the commandos behind him.

Shaak Ti's whisper reached him through the Force: *Movement ahead*.

She gestured to the mouth of an intersecting tunnel just beyond where she stood, her profile limned blue by the glow of her raised lightsaber. Faint light spilled from the opening, as if someone with a handheld luma was approaching on foot.

Mace waved a signal to Commander Valiant, whose team moved forward stealthily, hugging the walls, their T-visor helmets allowing them to see in the dark.

Normally the probe droids would have the point, playing their lights and sensors across the dusty floor and tiled walls, sending data to Dyne and his team of analysts. Mace and Shaak Ti would ride in separate speeders behind the agents, intermingled with those of the commandos. Occasionally, however, the Jedi would assume the lead on foot for a couple of kilometers, usually in response to some anomaly discovered by the droids.

Ventilation, such as it was, came courtesy of ancient blowers that did little more than drag in the sooty air from above, and illumination was provided by what the team brought with them.

They were deep below an area of The Works called the Grungeon Block. Encompassing twenty square kilometers, the block had originally been a production center for Serv-O-Droid, Huvicko, and Nebula Manufacturing, but it had fallen on hard times when its three principal clients had declared bankruptcy. Unable to attract new businesses, the developers who owned the Grungeon had allowed stratts and other vermin to overrun the stamping plants, and cashed out.

In the days since the raid, Mace's team had searched nearly every nook and cranny of the confusion of tunnels and shafts that undermined the Grungeon and similar assembly areas. Ten kilometers into the tunnel that led to the LiMerge building's sub-basement, a shaft had been found, leading to a deeper, older tunnel that also ran east toward the Senate District. In appearance the parallel tunnels were similar, save for the fact that the floor of the older one hosted an ancient mag-lev rail. The probe droids had discovered places along the rail where the accumulated decades of dust and debris had been blown away by the rapid passage of a repulsorlift vehicle of some sort. With no other clues to go on, the team had made the mag-lev tunnel the focus of the investigation.

Still, Mace felt that the team was on the right track.

An extensive search of the LiMerge building had revealed the remains of several Trang Robotics Duelist Elite droids that had been reduced to durasteel pieces by a lightsaber. Only Sidious, Dooku, or Sidious's previous apprentice could have performed the amputations.

And there was more.

Shortly before Dooku had left the Jedi Order to return to his native Serenno—during the period when he had taken the title *Count* and had first gone public with his discontents about the

Republic—he had been known to frequent a tavern called the Golden Cuff, which had been a watering hole for Senators, lobbyists, and aides. Analysts at the Temple were going through files of security cam holoimages thirteen years old, hoping to find images of Dooku and anyone he may have met with repeatedly.

Thus far, no images of Dooku had surfaced in the recordings that had survived. Even if images of Dooku's tavern mates did surface, the Jedi had no means of identifying any of them as Darth Sidious, but the images could provide an additional starting point for further investigation.

By now Mace could hear movement and soft voices ahead.

Hardly a good tactic for hostiles intent on springing an ambush, but one never knew. He stretched out with his feelings, alert for diversions or clues he might have overlooked—obscured by the dark side, or owing to his own neglect.

Standing nearby, Valiant looked to Mace for the go signal.

When Mace nodded, Valiant said: "Light it up!"

Weapons raised, gas and fragmentation grenades enabled, the commandos sprinted into the intersecting tunnel, firing tracer bolts into the gloom.

Tight on their heels, Mace heard Valiant yell: "Down on the floor! Don't move! I said, don't move!"

More fire erupted, then several commando voices were shouting: "Stay still! Down on your faces! Hands up—all four of them!"

All four of them? Mace thought.

Edging through the commandos, he reached Valiant, whose BlasTech was aimed at a cowering crowd of thirty or so four-armed insectoid aliens, who were babbling in some language other than Basic, or speaking it with an accent so thick as to make their worlds unintelligible.

"Lower your weapons," Mace told the commandos. "And someone bring that interpreter droid forward!"

Mace's command was relayed down the line, and a moment later a highly polished silver protocol droid tottered into the tunnel, muttering to itself.

"I don't understand how I've gone from serving the Separatists to serving the Republic. Did I undergo a partial memory wipe?"

"Consider yourself lucky," one of the commandos said. "Now you're on the side of the good guys."

"Good guys, bad guys . . . who can tell anymore? What's more, you won't be so quick to say that should someone compel you to shift loyalties at a moment's notice."

"Droid!" Mace shouted.

"I do have a name, sir."

Mace glanced at Valiant.

"TeeCee something or other," the ARC said.

"Fine," Mace said, grabbing hold of TC-16 and pointing him in the direction of the terrified aliens. "See if you can make sense of what these folk are saying."

The droid listened to the babbling, responded in kind, and turned to face Mace. "They are Unets, General. Speaking their native language, which is called Une."

Mace regarded the huddled, shivering group. "What are they doing down here?"

TC-16 listened, then said: "They say that they haven't the slightest idea where they are, General. They arrived on Coruscant in a shipping container that was air-dropped at a decrepit landing platform some twenty kilometers from here. The personage who was to have guided them into the depths of the Uscru Sector stole all their credits and abandoned them in The Works."

"Undocumented refugees," Valiant said.

Mace frowned. The tunnels beneath the Grungeon Block held countless surprises.

"They almost got themselves killed."

"Apparently that's nothing new for them," TC-16 said. "Their planet fell to the Separatists, the freighter they originally took passage on was attacked by pirates, several of them—"

"That's enough," Mace said. "Assure them that they're not going to be harmed, and that we'll see to it they reach a refugee camp." He nodded to Valiant, who in turn told two of his troopers to carry out Mace's command.

"Talk about your corridor ghouls," Dyne said, eyeing the aliens as he approached Mace.

"Squatters, death stick runners, lost droids, now undocumented refugees . . ."

"Next it'll be Cthons," Dyne said, referring to the flesh-eating humanoids believed by many Coruscanti to inhabit the world's underground.

Shaak Ti joined them. "These corridors are highways for people who want to enter central Coruscant illegally."

Dyne sighed in disappointment. "Our chances for picking up Sidious's trail decrease with each person who passes."

"How far are we from the Senate District?" Shaak Ti asked.

"Within a couple of kilometers," Dyne said. "We might think about going directly to the buildings LiMerge Power once owned in the city core, and see if we can't work our way *toward* The Works from those."

Mace considered the idea, then shook his head.

"Not yet."

Mace waved everyone back into motion, then fell into step with Shaak Ti.

"Wild gundark chase?"

She nodded. "Only because our quarry is aware that we're closing in on him. He failed to silence the ones Obi-Wan and Anakin searched out, and by now he knows that we've discovered his and Dooku's den. It's unlikely he will wait around for us to surprise him."

"That's true. But there's much to gain from simply identifying him. If not here, then by means of something Obi-Wan and Anakin discover on Tythe."

"Assuming there's anything left after Dooku sterilizes the place. From everything we've seen, Sidious and Dooku don't make many mistakes."

The walked in silence for a long while. They were a kilometer closer to the outlying areas of the Senate District when Dyne called to them from behind.

Mace saw that the Intelligence analysts and commandos were gathered some twenty meters away. He and Shaak Ti had been so engrossed in their private thoughts that neither of them had noticed the probe droids stopping to investigate something. Joining the others, the Jedi watched the droids hover with clear purpose in front of a large niche in the tunnel wall.

Dyne's handheld sensor needed only a moment to discover a small control panel that operated the niche's sliding door.

The door concealed the entrance to a narrow, dimly lit corridor.

And all but hiding in plain sight: a repulsorlift speeder bike, semicircular in design, with an arc of concentric seat and a single steering handle.

Mace and Shaak Ti traded astonished looks.

"How did we miss seeing this?" she asked.

Mace's brow furrowed. "The answer is in the question."

As big as life, Palpatine's holoimage spoke from atop a projector table in a private comlink lounge aboard the medical frigate. With R2-D2 standing off to one side of the transmission grid, Anakin hung on the Supreme Chancellor's every word.

"Of course, the Council doesn't understand," Palpatine said. "Surely you don't find that surprising."

"They reject every suggestion I make—on principle, I'm beginning to think."

"It's obvious that you're upset, Anakin, but you must be patient. Your time will come."

"When, sir?"

Palpatine smiled lightly. "I can't see into the future, my boy."

Anakin's face contorted. "What if I told you that *I* could?"

"I would believe you," Palpatine said without pause. "Tell me what you see."

"Coruscant."

"Are we in danger?"

"I'm not certain. I just feel that I need to be there."

Palpatine gazed away from the holocam. "I suppose I could

invent some pretext . . ." His gaze returned to Anakin. "But is that wise?"

"I'm not the wise one. Ask anybody."

"What does Master Kenobi say?"

"He's the one who suggested I contact *you*," Anakin said sharply.

"Really? But what does he think you should do?"

Anakin blew out his breath. "Obi-Wan is under the illusion that I can't deny my destiny—no matter what I do."

"Your former Master is wiser than you think, Anakin."

"Yes, yes, and he is the only Jedi in a thousand years to have killed a Sith."

Palpatine spread his hands. "That alone has to count for something. Though I'm at a loss to know precisely what."

"Obi-Wan is wise. But he has no heart, sir. He sees everything in terms of the Force."

"If you want advice about the Force, you must look to him, because I'm of no help."

"That's exactly what I *don't* want. I live in the Force, but I also live in the real world. I came from . . . the real world. Just as you said, I had the advantage of a normal childhood. Well, sort of."

Palpatine waited until he was certain Anakin was finished. "My boy, I don't know that it's healthy to have a foot in each world. Soon you may have to make a choice."

Anakin nodded. "I'm ready."

Palpatine smiled again. "But back to the matter at hand. It sounds to me as if the recapture of Tythe could prove very important toward ending the war. I don't understand all of it. The Jedi Council is being very secretive with me."

Anakin fought the temptation to reveal everything about the search for Darth Sidious. He glanced at R2-D2, as if expecting commiseration, but the astromech only swiveled his dome, his processor status indicator flashing from blue to red.

Finally Anakin said: "I don't know what to do, sir."

Palpatine adopted a sympathetic expression. "It's decided. I shall prevail upon the Council to order you back to the Core. No one needs further proof of how intrepid you are, or how committed you are to defeating our enemies."

In time you will learn to trust your feelings; then you will be invincible.

Palpatine's advice to him, three years earlier.

"No," Anakin said in a rush. "No. Thank you, sir, but . . . I'm needed on Tythe. Dooku is there."

I'm sorry, Padmé. I'm so, so sorry. I miss you so much—

"Yes," Palpatine was saying. "Dooku is the key to everything just now. Despite all our victories in the inner systems . . . Do you suspect he and General Grievous may have some secret strategy?"

"If they do, Obi-Wan and I will defeat them before they can implement it."

"The Republic counts on it."

"Safeguard Coruscant, sir. Safeguard everyone there."

"I will, my boy. And rest assured that I will call on you if I need you."

Obi-Wan was in the MedStar's docking bay, waiting for the shuttle that would take him to the light cruiser *Integrity*. His arms were folded across his chest, and his small rucksack was sitting on the deck.

"Did you get through to him?" he asked as Anakin and R2-D2 approached.

"Well, I spoke to him."

"That's what I meant. And?"

Anakin averted his gaze. "We both decided that my place is here, Master." He sounded on the verge of tears.

Obi-Wan merely nodded. "For a moment I thought you were going to leave it to me to retake Tythe."

Anakin looked at him. "I know better than that."

"You don't think I'm capable?" Obi-Wan asked around a forming grin.

"I know you'd be willing to die trying."

"There is no trying—"

"Yes, there is," Anakin cut him off. "And you're living proof of it."

Obi-Wan smiled, then glanced out the hold's magcon transparency. "The shuttle's coming."

Anakin's eyes tracked the approaching light. "I'm as ready as I'll ever be." He still wasn't smiling.

Obi-Wan closed his hand around Anakin's upper right arm. "Anakin, let's get Dooku and end this."

Anakin swallowed and nodded. "If it's meant to be, Master."

With assistance from the probe droids, the discolored panels at the end of the corridor unlocked and parted. Brown robe swirling behind him and lightsaber in hand, Mace barreled through the doorway, with Shaak Ti and the commandos close behind.

By rote the troopers spread out, quickly and efficiently, but also unnecessarily.

"Surprise," Shaak Ti said flatly. "Another corridor."

"Another corridor closer," Mace said, determined to put a good spin on it.

The tunnel the team had followed from the hidden niche had led them through a maze of twists, turns, forks, steep climbs, and sudden drops. For stretches the dark corridor had been wide enough to contain a speeder; then it grew so narrow that everyone had had to edge through. For two kilometers, walls, ceiling, and floor were damp from water that had trickled down through Coruscant's layered surface. There, the prints of their prey had disappeared, but the probe droids had managed to pick up the trail farther along. Some of the prints were so recent and well preserved that Dyne had been able to calculate the human's slipper size.

Human.

That much the droids had determined from smudged fingerprints found on the speeder bike's steering grip and cushioned seat. The repulsorlift machine had also provided the droids with fibers, hairs, and other detritus. Slowly, a portrait of Dooku's unknown confederate was being compiled.

His eyes fixed on the display screen of his data processor, Captain Dyne ambled toward Mace and Shaak Ti.

"Master Jedi, our search is about to take us to a whole new level."

Mace looked around the tunnel for signs of a concealed turbolift or staircase.

"Up or down?" Shaak Ti asked, equally bewildered.

Dyne glanced up, blinking at her. "I didn't mean 'new level' in the literal sense." He indicated the hovering probe droids, which were eager to have the team follow them east. "If the prints lead us far enough, we're going to end up in the sub-basements of 500 Republica."

Mace tracked the droids as they moved deeper into the corridor.

Five Hundred Republica: home to thousands of Coruscant's wealthiest Senators, celebrities, shipping magnates, and media tycoons.

And one of them, very possibly a Sith Lord.

37

There was little the Confederacy or the Republic could add to the damage LiMerge Power had inflicted on Tythe generations earlier. From deep space, the surface—glimpsed through a pall of ash-gray clouds—looked as if it had been licked by a flare from its primary, or had had a brush with an enormous meteor. But Tythe's scars owed to none of that. The planet had been spared everything but LiMerge itself, whose attempts to exploit Tythe's abundant deposits of natural plasma had invoked a cataclysm of global proportions.

The three drifting hulks that had been Republic cruisers might have been caught up in the cataclysm but were, in fact, casualties of the Separatist attack, which had come swiftly and without quarter. Nimbused by what vacuum had drawn from their interiors, the scorched and lanced trio lazed midway between opposing battle groups of Separatist and Republic vessels.

"Just once I wish we could repay Dooku and Grievous in kind," Anakin said over the tactical net, as Red Squadron dropped from the belly of the *Integrity* and rocketed toward Tythe.

"The fact that we don't is what keeps us centered in the Force," Obi-Wan said.

Anakin grunted. "There'll come a time come when they'll have to answer to us personally, and it will be the Force that guides our blades."

The two starfighters were flying abreast, almost wingtip-to-wingtip, astromech droids R2-D2 and R4-P17 in their respective sockets. Tythe's rubicund star was at their backs, and the ships that made up the Separatist flotilla were strung menacingly above the planet's northern hemisphere.

With Tythe's brood of moons clustered in a two-hundred-degree arc, the Separatists had worked quickly to strew mines at several hyperspace jump points, leaving the Republic ships with only a narrow window in which to revert to realspace. Trade Federation, Techno Union, and Commerce Guild capital ships occupied the apex of that window, deployed from north pole to equator above Tythe's bright side, with wings of droid fighters boiling into space to the fore of the arrayed vessels.

To minimize their profiles, the Republic ships—widely dispositioned, like a group of predatory fish—had their triangular bows pointed toward the planet. Red and other squadrons were streaking forward, but well short of engaging the vanguard Vultures and tri-fighters.

"Prepare to break hard to starboard," Anakin said over the net to the entire squadron. "Watch your countdown displays. On my mark, ten seconds to break . . ."

Obi-Wan kept his eyes on the counter at the bottom of the instrument panel's tactical display screen. At the zero mark, he yanked the yoke to one side and peeled away for clear space.

Behind the squadrons of V-wings and Jedi and ARC-170 starfighters, the Republic battle group broke to port, drenching the distant Separatist ships with furious broadsides. Blinding payloads of spun plasma hurtled through space, detonating against the shields of the enemy vessels, atomizing any droid fighters unlucky enough to have been caught in the way.

The Separatist ships absorbed the first hits without flinching.

Vessels that sustained damage began to drift to the rear. Then the battle group responded with an equally ferocious barrage. Turbolasers silenced, the Republic ships had already broken formation. Small suns flared in their midst and blue energy capered over their shielded hulls. No sooner did the barrage end than the starfighter squadrons regrouped, accelerating in an effort to reach the big enemy ships before their cannons or shields could repower.

The droid fighters swooped in to meet them halfway, and the tight formations observed by both sides dissolved into dozens of separate skirmishes. Those Republic starfighters that managed to steal through the chaos drew into tight clusters and continued their fiery advance. The rest became embroiled in swift attacks and evasive maneuvers. Local space became a scrawl of scarlet lines and white spirals, punctuated by expanding explosions. Craft of both camps came apart, tumbling and spinning from the arena, wingless or in flames.

"They're being shot to pieces," Red Seven said over the net.

"They know their job," Anakin responded.

That job was to buy Red Squadron enough time to skirt the main action and race down Tythe's gravity well.

A burst-transmission from survivors of the assault on the Republic's small base had confirmed Dooku's presence on the surface. But on the possibility that Tythe was a calculated diversion, Palpatine's naval command staff had agreed to committing only a single battle group from the Outer Rim fleet. In the view of those same naval commanders, invasion was senseless; a Base Delta Zero attack, justified. In the end it was decided that saturation bombardment, augmented by limited starfighter engagement, would send Dooku fleeing, in keeping with the Republic's strategy to force the Separatists deeper into the galaxy's spiral arms.

The Jedi had insisted nevertheless that an attempt be made to take Dooku alive.

Obi-Wan and Anakin didn't need to be reminded of what had happened only weeks earlier on Cato Neimoidia when they had gone after Viceroy Gunray, but they were not about to forgo a chance to capture the Sith Lord.

Red Squadron's intended insertion point was twenty degrees south of Tythe's north pole, where the Separatist line was most dispersed. With droid fighters still pouring from the curving arms of Trade Federation Lucrehulks, and the recoiling barrels of Commerce Guild cannons filling local space with storms of un-leashed energy, Anakin led the starfighters on a weaving course through the heart of the enemy fleet.

"No signature for Grievous's cruiser," he said to Obi-Wan. "None of the ships of the Separatist leadership are here."

Obi-Wan glanced at the wire-frame display of his threat-assessment screen. "All the more reason to believe that Dooku was ordered here by Sidious."

"Then where's everyone else?"

Obi-Wan was troubled by the thought, but didn't admit to it. "Dooku will know," he started to say, when the starfighter's proximity scanners stammered a warning. "Techno Union star-ship is veering to intercept us."

"Droid fighters are away and locking on," Red Three added.

Obi-Wan acknowledged. "Angle shields. We can outfly them."

"We'll end up too far off course," Anakin said.

"We're almost at the insertion point," Obi-Wan said.

"That starship isn't just going to move aside. Form up on me. We'll show them how well we improvise."

There was no time to argue the point. Rolling to port, Obi-Wan fell in behind Anakin and fired his thrusters. Trailing behind, Red Squadron accelerated and banked for the narrow-waisted vessel.

"Ready proton torpedoes," Anakin said. "Sow them just above the fuel cells."

Point-defense turbolasers sought the starfighters as they fell on the ship, needling space with outpourings of gaudy energy. Corkscrewing missiles claimed Red Ten and Red Twelve, both of which disappeared in angry blossoms of fire. Sensing its sudden vulnerability, the huge vessel launched additional droid fighters. In the instant it lowered its shields to route power to the sublight drives, Red Squadron attacked.

Tight on Anakin, the ten remaining starfighters yawed for the waist of the ship, just forward of its cluster of cylindrical fuel cells. Dropping his craft to within one hundred meters of the pinched hull, Anakin began to hug the surface, surging onto a course that would whip Red Squadron through a tight circle around the forward ends of the fuel cells.

"Torpedoes away!" he said at the halfway mark.

Obi-Wan triggered the launchers and watched two torpedoes burn toward the target. Behind him, the rest of Red Squadron did the same. Hits began to score, fire and gas fountaining from breaches in the ship's dark hull.

The disabling run completed, Anakin boosted for Tythe. "She's finished!"

In single file, Red Squadron followed.

Almost instantly the punctured vessel exploded, stunning the fleeing starfighters with a wave of force. Red Nine disappeared at the edge of the roiling detonation zone, and Red Seven wheeled off into the void with both wings sheared away.

Obi-Wan regained control of his craft and once more attached himself to Anakin's six.

"Insertion point in fifteen seconds," Anakin updated. "Dial inertial compensators to maximum. All power to the ablative shields. Deceleration burn on my mark . . ."

Obi-Wan clamped his hands on the violently shaking yoke as Red Squadron ripped into Tythe's plundered atmosphere. He thought his teeth might rattle out of his jaws and drop into his lap; eyes and ears might implode from the pressure; chest might cave in and crush his heart.

Light flashed behind him; streaked past the cockpit.

Half a dozen droid fighters were chasing them down the well.

Not having to concern themselves with endangering living systems, the Vultures should have been able to descend even more rapidly and more acutely than the starfighters. But as the heat of entry built in the ships, survival protocols began to kick in, tasking the fighters to adjust the angle of their descents. For some of the droids it was already too late. Single contrails became particle showers as gravity summoned the broken fighters to their doom.

Punching through the blankets of clouds at suicidal velocity, Obi-Wan's starfighter went into a roll. Pinwheeling before his eyes, Tythe was a kaleidoscopic furor of white and brown, smeared occasionally with striations of blue-green.

Anakin's voice grew loud in his ears. "Nose up! Nose up!"

With effort, Obi-Wan leveled out of his plummet, his stomach lurching up into his throat. Reaching forward, he engaged the starfighter's topographic sensors. The ship was dropping toward ice floes and bergs. Then, far below, peninsulas of rocky islands came into view. The surging waves of a dead gray ocean. The denuded shelf of a continent. Barren land fissured by dry, sinuous riverbeds, and mounded by brown hills strewn with toppled trees.

A ruined world.

"Head count," he said into his helmet microphone.

Five voices responded. Reds Eight and Eleven were lost.

"Locking in target coordinates," Anakin said.

Red Squadron flew just above the contours of land that had once been as lush as the area surrounding Theed, on Naboo. Now a desert, save for areas where exotic species of vegetation thrived in lakes of red-brown water, their jagged shorelines crusted yellow and black.

Also like Naboo, Tythe had once mined plasma in sufficient quantities to ship offworld. But greed had driven LiMerge Power to experiment with dangerous methods for keeping the ionized gas under adequate heat. A chain reaction set in motion by nuclear fuels had destroyed facilities throughout Tythe's northern hemisphere and had left the planet uninhabitable for a generation.

"Target facility is ten kilometers west," Anakin said. "We should be hearing from artillery soon enough."

Soaring from the edge of a high plateau, the six starfighters dropped into a broad valley, disturbingly reminiscent of Geonosis, right down to the berthed starships and war machines spread across the floor.

Hailfire droids wheeled out to greet them with volleys of surface-to-air missiles. Turbolaser cannons affixed to Trade Federation landing ships cut the gray-yellow sky to ribbons. STAPs lifted into the air, and squads of infantry droids hurried for armed skimmers.

Unequipped to defend itself against the onslaught, tattered Red Squadron banked broadly to the north, evading plasma beams and flak from exploding heat seekers. Anakin and Obi-Wan paid out the last of their proton torpedoes in futile attempts to save Reds Three, Four, and Five. Bursts from their laser cannons crippled two enemy speeders and countless droid fighters, sending them crashing into the contaminated terrain. R4-P17 howled as Obi-Wan twisted the starfighter through violent airbursts and superheated clouds of billowing smoke.

Red Six vanished.

When they had juked their way through the worst of it, Anakin came alongside Obi-Wan.

It was just the two of them now.

"Point three-oh," Anakin said. "On the landing platform."

Obi-Wan gazed out the right side of the cockpit at what had been an enormous plasma-generating facility. Fractured containment domes and adjacent roofless structures revealed toppled extraction shafts, exploded activators, and tumbled walkways. In the center of the complex stood an elevated square of corroded ferrocrete, crowded with enemy fighter craft and bearing a single Geonosian fantail of distinctive design.

"Dooku's sloop."

The words had scarcely left Obi-Wan's mouth when battle droids began to gush from the facility and out onto the landing platform. Bolts from the droids' blasters clawed at the pair of prowling starfighters.

"I guess we're not going in through the front door," Obi-Wan said.

"There's another way," Anakin said, as they were emerging from their flyby. "We go in through the north dome."

Obi-Wan looked over his left shoulder at the partially collapsed hemisphere. The lid that had once topped the plasma containment structure was long gone, and the resultant circular opening was large enough for a starfighter to thread.

Obi-Wan had misgivings, nevertheless.

"What about residual radiation inside the dome?"

"Radiation?" Anakin laughed. "The maneuver alone will probably kill us!"

With its fifty-three skydocks, hundreds of private turbo-lifts, arrays of hidden security armaments, and towering atria, 500 Republica was a world unto itself. Containing more technology than many Outer Rim worlds and more residents than some, the sky-piercing structure was the unrivaled gem of the Senate District, and the elegant cynosure of the district's prestigious Ambassadorial Sector.

What had begun as a stately building in the classic style had, over the course of centuries, become a veritable mountain of steps and setbacks—some with flat roofs, others as gently rounded as shoulders, and still others as massive as any structure in the district. Up and up they climbed, profuse, organic, in seeming competition for Coruscant's sunlight, culminating in a graceful crown, banded with penthouses and topped by a lithe spire. Gilded by the rising sun, its head in the clouds, buttressed by the towers that had allowed it to outgrow all its neighbors, 500 Republica was the lofty vantage from which a privileged few could actually gaze *down* on Coruscant.

Which was precisely why the building had become the landmark the galaxy's disenfranchised pointed to when they spoke of

Coruscant's disproportionate wealth and elitism. Why 500 Republica was viewed by many as more emblematic of the bloated, indulgent Senate than the Senate's own squat mushroom of a home.

Mace could feel the oppressive weight of the structure bearing down on him as the team entered 500 Republica's level-one sub-basement—square kilometers of supportive ferrocrete and durasteel, crammed with whining, whirring machines that kept the tower stable, aloft, secure, climate-controlled, and supplied with water and power. As deep as it was, the sub-basement was still a hundred meters above Coruscant's true underground, and twice that above the original surface of the planet.

The team had had to wait hours for Republica security to grant them permission to enter and carry on with the investigation. For a time, Mace had considered appealing to Palpatine for permission, since the Supreme Chancellor had an upper-level suite in the building. For company, the probe droids had scores of custodial and maintenance droids, but the trail to Sidious had gone cold.

Lost among countless footprints that covered the floor.

"Unless we can find prints that say otherwise, there's no guarantee our quarry gained entrance to the sub-basement from Five Hundred Republica itself," Dyne pronounced, switching his handheld processor to standby mode. "He may have entered from the tunnels that connect to the east or west skydocks."

"In other words, he could have arrived here from just about anywhere on Coruscant," Shaak Ti said.

Dyne nodded. "Presumably."

Mace gazed down the tunnel the team had taken.

"Could we have missed something along the way?"

"The droids wouldn't."

Mace gestured to the smudged and stained ferrocrete floor. "Why would the prints suddenly end right here?"

Dyne compressed his lips and shook his head. "Maybe someone carried him here by repulsorlift. Unless you're suggesting he levitated across the floor." He thought about it for a long moment, then said: "All right, for the sake of argument, let's say that he *did* levitate here."

"There'll be prints at his starting point," Mace said.

Dyne scanned the sub-basement, pursed his lips, and blew out his breath. "We're going to need a lot more probe droids."

"How many more?" Mace said.

"A *lot*."

"How long to bring them here and search this entire level?"

"With all this machinery, the skydock access tunnels, the waste and supply turbolifts . . . I couldn't begin to guess. What's more, we're going to need additional security clearance to search the tunnels."

"You'll have whatever clearance you need," Shaak Ti promised.

Mace glanced around. "You'll have to run imaging scans of the partitions and the exterior walls."

"That could require several weeks," Dyne said cautiously.

"Then the sooner we begin, the better."

Dyne took a comlink from his belt and was about to activate it when the floor began to tremble.

"A quake?" Mace asked Shaak Ti.

She shook her head. "I'm not sure—"

A second jolt shook the sub-basement, strong enough to dust the team with loose ferrocrete from the high ceiling.

"Feels like something rammed the building," Dyne said.

It wouldn't be the first time an intoxicated or exhausted driver had veered from one of the free-travel skylanes and plowed into the side of a building, Mace told himself. And yet—

The next shudder was accompanied by the distant sound of a powerful explosion. Lights in the sub-basement faded momentarily, then returned to full illumination, sending the custodial and maintenance droids into frantic activity.

Also at a far remove, klaxons and sirens blared.

"My comlink isn't working," Dyne said, jabbing at the device's frequency search control with his forefinger.

"We're tiers below midlevel," Shaak Ti said.

Dyne shook his head. "That shouldn't matter. Not in here."

Stretching out with the Force, Mace sensed danger, frenzy, pain, and death. "Where's the nearest exit?"

Dyne pointed to his left. "The tunnel to the east skydock."

Mace's thoughts swirled. He turned to Valiant. "Commander, Shaak Ti and I will need half your squad. You and the rest of your team will assist Captain Dyne with the search. Keep me informed of your progress."

"What about me, sir?"

Mace looked at TC-16, then at Dyne. "The droid stays with you."

Flanked by commandos, Mace and Shaak Ti raced off. The tunnel to the east skydock shook as they hurried through mixed-species crowds of frightened pedestrians heading toward and away from 500 Republica. Ahead of them loomed a square of dim sunlight, almost aquatic in quality, typical of the lower reaches of Coruscant's urban canyons.

On the huge quadrangular skydock, humans, humanoids, and aliens were crouched behind parked limos, taxis, and private yachts, or hurrying for the entrance to the upper-level mag-lev platform. Shouts and screams punctuated the drone of overhead traffic. Panic gripped the free-travel skylanes. Taxis and transports were swerving in all directions, careening into one another and the sides of buildings, making desperate rooftop and plaza landings.

Higher, a plunging vehicle—a boxy cargo ship, engulfed in flames—came streaking through a horizontal autonavigation lane, surrendering some of its velocity to a violent collision with a public transport pod before continuing its fiery plunge toward the bottom of the canyon.

Mace tracked the ill-fated ship for a moment, then tilted his head back and put the edge of his hand to his brow. Distant buildings shimmered, as if miraged by heat.

The district's defensive shield had been raised!

Higher still, something was wrong with the flickering sky. Light flared behind stratified clouds, and thunder of a kind reverberated from the summits of the taller buildings. Far to the south, Coruscant's pale blue mantle was hashed into triangles and slivers by white contrails.

In their oblate pools of white skin, Shaak Ti's eyes were wide when she looked at Mace.

"An attack," she said in stunned disbelief.

Comlink already in hand, Mace activated the Jedi Temple frequency and held the device to his ear.

"Nothing but noise."

"The deflector shield," Shaak Ti said.

She craned her neck, striped montrals and head-tail quivering. "Or could they be jamming transmissions?"

Mace's nostrils flared. "Crowd control!" he told the commandos. To Shaak Ti, he said: "Find Palpatine. See to it he's conveyed to safety. I'll send backup."

In the ruined archive hall of LiMerge Power's plasma facility, Count Dooku waited for Kenobi and Skywalker to arrive. The room was enormous by any standard, thirty meters high and three times that in circumference. Dooku could imagine it when it had hummed with life and activity, before the catastrophe. Still, that it had remained intact was a testament to its builders. And with its curved walls of holobooks and data storage disks— irradiated beyond salvage—he accepted that some might believe that secrets of the most sinister sort were concealed here.

Jedi like Kenobi and Skywalker, who *wanted* to believe as much.

Despite their gullibility, they were nothing if not tenacious and—dare he admit it?—exceptional.

In the risks they undertook.

In how deluded they were—about so many things.

In their unabashed zeal to capture him they had actually piloted their starfighters straight through the roof of the largest of the facility's containment domes, and had managed to survive. Such superhuman feats were almost enough to convince Dooku that they still had the Force with them.

If only they weren't so naïve and easily manipulated.

Once again, Darth Sidious had divined the actions they would take well in advance of their own deciding. The talent had less to do with being able to peer into the future, than with having access to streams of possibilities. Sidious wasn't unerring. He could be surprised or taken off his guard—as at Geonosis, as in the case of Gunray's mechno-chair—but not for long. His mastery of the dark side of the Force endowed him with the power to decipher the currents that comprised the future, and to comprehend that while those currents were manifold, they were not boundless.

Such mastery was one of the skills that distinguished Sidious from Yoda, who believed the future was so much in motion it could not be read with any clarity—especially during times when the dark side was on the ascendant. But how could Yoda be expected to see the whole picture with one eye closed?

Deliberately closed.

The Jedi accepted as a matter of faith that embracing the dark side meant cutting themselves off from the light, when in fact the dark side opened one to the full range of the Force.

There was, after all, only the Force.

It was unfortunate for the Jedi that they believed the Force was theirs alone to use and honor. That sense of entitlement was evident in the way Kenobi and Skywalker called on the Force in their fervor to confront him: opening doors with waves of their hands, clearing obstacles from their path with similar gestures, moving with what appeared to be numinous speed and agility, flourishing their blue blades as if they were powered by the will of the Force itself . . .

While at the same time oblivious.

Dooku took a moment to set in place his compact welcoming device, then hurried through a series of decontamination chambers into the facility's control room, which overlooked the rear of the archive hall and the vast space enclosed by the containment dome itself. There he activated a second small holoprojector and positioned himself for the holocam. Owing to interference, images of the archive hall were nowhere near as clear as he might have wished, and the audio feed was worse. It was more important, though, that Kenobi and Skywalker be able to see him, than he them.

At long last the two Jedi rushed headlong into the hall, only to *stop* upon spying his life-sized holoimage emanating from the compact holoprojector he had left behind.

"Dooku!" young Skywalker said, as if his tone of voice should suffice to send shivers down the backbones of his opponents. "Show yourself!"

Rooms distant, Dooku merely spread his hands in a gesture of greeting, and aimed his words at the holoprojector's microphone. "Stand not amazed, young Jedi. Is this not the way you had your first glimpse of Lord Sidious?"

Instead of replying, Kenobi touched Skywalker on the arm, and the two of them began to scan the hall, no doubt in an attempt to locate him through the Force.

"You won't find me, Jedi—"

"We know you're here, Dooku," Kenobi said suddenly—and with irksome audio distortion. "We can sense you."

Dooku sighed in disappointment. They weren't hearing him. Worse, the video feed was also becoming hopelessly corrupted. More through the Force than the holocam feed he saw them moving toward the very doorway he had taken to reach the control room.

Exceptional, he thought.

Despite his mastery of the Quey'tek technique for hiding oneself in the Force, they had located him! Ah, well then, time to *entertain* them, in observance of Sidious's wishes.

Plucking his comlink from his belt, Dooku's right thumb leapt across the small touch pad.

Heralded by the sound of metallic footfalls, fifty infantry

droids crowded into the archive hall through two opposing doorways, perpendicular to the one through which the Jedi had entered.

"—beginning to . . . things almost as much . . . I hate sand," Skywalker was saying to his former mentor as he raised his lightsaber over one shoulder.

Kenobi spread his legs and brought his blade directly in front of him. "Then . . . sweep up."

Touched by their camaraderie, Dooku smiled to himself. Darth Sidious had his work cut out for him if he ever expected to turn Skywalker to the dark side.

He thumbed a final comlink key.

And with that, the droids leveled their blaster rifles at the Jedi and opened fire.

Yoda surrendered himself to the current of the Force. Sometimes, when the current was swift and steadfast, he could see through the eyes of his fellow Jedi, almost as if they were the Temple's remote sensors. And sometimes when the current was especially forceful, when it surged as if descending from great heights, he could hear the voice of Qui-Gon Jinn, as clearly as if he were still alive.

Master Yoda, he might say, *we still have much to learn. The Force remains a code only partially deciphered. But another key has been found. We will become stronger than we have ever been . . .*

Today was not one of those days. Today the current was interrupted by eddies and whirlpools, hydraulic traps whose roar overpowered the voices Yoda sought to hear. Today the current was not pellucid, but muddied by red soil eroded from distant shores, treacherous with obstacles, tainted.

Though he was scarcely aware of it, his eyelids were squeezed tight, his eyeballs dancing beneath as if incapable of focusing on any one thing. He had an image of himself drawing aside a veil only to find another, and another beyond that.

The dark side frustrated his every effort to see clearly.

The experience was still something new to him.

Even though he'd had centuries to grow accustomed to foreboding, he had lived far longer without it. The dark side never completely disappeared—it scratched at the surface like an insect crawling across a transparisteel panel—and he had been able to sense its incremental increases in strength when the Jedi erred, or when the Republic erred, and soon the two were hand in hand.

Drawn into the mistakes of the Republic, the Jedi had been. But knowingly, and sometimes with full complicity. Allowed the dark side to take root, the Jedi had. Allowed arrogance to infect the Order, the Jedi had. A priority, holding on to power had become. Inflated by their own conquests, the Jedi became.

Some Jedi believed that Yoda wasn't aware of these things, or that he hadn't done enough to stem the tide of the dark side. Some believed that the Council had acted improperly or, worse, ineptly. What they failed to understand was that, once rooted, the growth of the dark side was inexorable, and could only be reversed by the one born to restore balance.

Yoda was not that one.

Aged, experienced, diplomatic, informative, brilliant with a lightsaber . . . Yes, all of these things. And not unacquainted with the power of the dark side. For that reason he understood just how dangerous this new Sith Lord was. He hadn't had a sense of that danger until he had fought Dooku on Geonosis.

Then he understood.

In self-exile for a thousand years, the Sith had not merely been waiting for an appropriate time to reemerge and exact revenge, but for the birth of one strong enough to embrace the dark side fully and become its dedicated instrument. This was Sidious: powerful enough to hide in plain sight. Powerful enough to instruct his apprentice, Dooku, to expose him, and still remain hidden from the Jedi.

And as arrogant as the Jedi. Convinced that his way was the one and only way.

Did he know about Skywalker?

Surely he did. What better way to ensure total victory than by killing or corrupting the Chosen One? Even if not that One, someone so strong in midi-chlorians . . . *Someone birthed by the Force itself,* Qui-Gon would have said—never a doubt that Anakin's mother might have been lying.

The boy had no father.

None I choose to remember. None I would honor with that title.

The Sith were aware of Skywalker. How would he react when they tried finally to ensnare him?

Yoda's eyes snapped open. A disturbance in the Force—of such magnitude that he had been hurled from the current.

At his thought command, the window shutters in his quarters opened, and he gazed out on Coruscant, over the plain of The Works and beyond. Something was wrong with the sky. Behind gathered clouds turned red and gold by noxious smoke: a lightstorm. Pulsing light, brighter than the waning rays of Coruscant's sun. Movement, as well; outside Coruscant's busy envelope, not seen but sensed.

An attack.

The Sith Lord's response to his being chased? Was it possible?

He perceived Mace running down corridors in the Temple; then turned as Mace rushed through the doorway. At the same instant, a flaming Republic ship streaked past the Temple's crowning spires and crashed violently in the heart of The Works.

"Tiin, Koon, Ki-Adi-Mundi, and some of the others are on their way up the well," Mace said. "I sent Stass Allie to assist Shaak Ti in guarding Chancellor Palpatine."

Yoda nodded sagely. "Well trained the Supreme Chancellor's

Red Guards are. But display due concern for his safety, the Jedi must."

"Reports from naval command are garbled," Mace continued. "It's clear that the attack caught the home fleet by surprise. Groups of Separatist ships managed to penetrate the envelope before the fleet had time to engage. Now, by all accounts, our vessels are holding the line."

Yoda adopted an expression that mixed anger and bafflement. "Monitoring hyperspace reversion points, our commanders weren't?"

Mace's eyes narrowed. "The Separatist fleet jumped from the Deep Core."

"*Secret,* those routes were. Known to us and few others." Yoda looked at Mace. "Unrestricted access to the archives, Dooku had. Access enough to erase all mentions of Kamino. Access enough to learn of explorations in the Deep Core."

Mace went to the window wall and stared at the sky. "Dooku isn't leading this attack. Obi-Wan confirmed that he is on Tythe."

"Revealed, the importance of Tythe is. To draw into the Outer Rim additional Jedi."

"Maybe Palpatine will heed the Council's warnings next time."

"Improbable. But as you say: perhaps."

Mace swung back to Yoda. "It's Grievous. But he can't be planning to occupy Coruscant. There aren't enough battle droids in the entire galaxy for that."

"Desperate he is," Yoda said, more to himself.

"It's not in his programming."

Yoda looked up. "Not Grievous—*Sidious.*"

Mace took a moment to answer. "If that's true, then we're closer to finding him than we thought. Still, he can't believe we'd call off the search now."

"Demoralize Coruscant, Grievous will. Harry those who live

in the heights and who wield power. Send them fleeing for safer havens, the attack will. Disrupt the Senate."

Mace paced in front of the windows. "This will only encourage Palpatine to triple the size of the clone army, construct more and more starships and fighters, strike at more worlds. With the Senate crippled, no one will oppose him."

"*Modulate*, this war does. Recall every available Jedi, we must."

"The HoloNet is down," Mace said. "Surface communications are distorted by the defensive shields."

Yoda nodded. "Use the beacon, we will."

In the wake of the erratic and mostly unintelligible messages
that had reached 500 Republica regarding the Separatists' surprise attack, Dyne had considered the sub-basement to be the
safest place on Coruscant. But now that the team had discovered
a possible finish to the long trail they had followed from The
Works, the building's vast underground seemed the most dangerous place to be.

With a battle raging in space, and notwithstanding Mace
Windu's command to the contrary, Dyne had been tempted to
suspend the search for Sidious's lair and report back to the Intelligence division, as he had ordered the other analysts to do. But
as ARC commander Valiant had pointed out, the search team's
objective was as important to the war as the actions of the ships
that were protecting Coruscant.

So, while the team waited for Intelligence to deliver additional probe droids, a search of the sub-basement had begun—
admittedly superficial and somewhat desultory, but only in
response to the seeming impossibility of the task. Electronically
tethered to the probe droids, Dyne and the commandos had performed imagings of some of the partitions and walls, and investi-

gated numerous unlit hollows and recesses. The basement became a kind of microcosm for the entire war, with everyone on the team contributing separate skills.

Only the interpreter droid, TC-16, was at a loss for something to do.

Five Hundred Republica hadn't sustained any follow-up jolts. Dyne had learned that the initial jolts had owed not to bombardment, but to the fall of ships destroyed at the edge of space. With thousands of cargo and passenger vessels arriving at Coruscant at any given moment, he could scarcely imagine the chaos upside. Secondary shocks that had rocked the huge building had been traced to the firing of plasma weapons concealed in 500 Republica's cake of a crown.

Several hours into the cursory search, Dyne had been struck by the possibility that certain Coruscanti—perhaps the Sith Lord himself—could be helping to coordinate the attack. With HoloNet transmissions jammed and surface communications sabotaged by the defensive shields, he had theorized that the probe droids might be able to home in on exchanges occurring on eccentric frequencies.

He was as astonished as anyone when the hovering probe droids had led the team right back to where they had begun the search: where the footprints of their as-yet-unidentified quarry ended.

The source of the unusual frequency was determined to be directly beneath them. The droids had discovered further that the ferrocrete floor panel thought to have been the end of the trail was actually a movable platform, not unlike a turbolift, but powered hydraulically rather than by antigrav repulsor. The search for a hidden control panel, such as had been detected at the niche, hadn't come to anything. But by broadcasting sounds—both within and outside the range of human hearing— the probe droids had ultimately conjured a response from the platform.

Following what had sounded like a debate, the probe droids had chirped and bleated at the panel a second time. Issuing a resolved *click*, the panel had descended a couple of centimeters, then come to a halt.

Dyne recalled wondering where the platform's shaft could lead.

Unlike many of Coruscant's tallest buildings, 500 Republica did not rely on the support of earlier structures for its foundation, but was solid almost all the way down to bedrock. Or at least was thought to be. This far below Coruscant's civilized crust, there remained areas as unfamiliar as the surfaces of some distant worlds.

Dyne had decided to contact Mace Windu at the Jedi Temple for advice on how to proceed. But when his repeated attempts failed, he and Valiant had made a command decision to carry on without the Jedi.

Ground imaging scans had already shown the shaft to be fifty meters deep. Four meters in diameter, the panel was large enough to accommodate the entire team, including the interpreter droid.

Definitely the most dangerous place to be, Dyne thought as he wedged himself among the commandos.

The probe droids chirped instructions to the panel, and it began to drop.

Slower than would have been the case had it answered to a repulsorlift.

The wall of the circular shaft was ancient ceramacrete, cracked and stained in places.

"If anyone's down here," Dyne said to Valiant, "they're probably aware we're on the way."

The commandos didn't need to be told. Weapons enabled, they hurried to firing positions the moment the platform came to a rest.

Ribboned with conduits and crowded with ancient machinery, the dismal space bore some resemblance to the tunnels and rooms they had passed through and explored since leaving The Works. But this one, Dyne told himself, was an archaeologist's dream. Probably a maintenance node for buildings that had stood here in Coruscant's dim past.

Twenty meters ahead of them, flickering light lanced from around the edges of a large metal door.

Dyne sent the droids to investigate, then studied the processor's data screen.

"One flesh-and-blood behind the door," he whispered to Valiant. "Readings also indicate the presence of droids." He looked at the ARC. "It's your call, Commander."

Valiant regarded the door. "We've come this far. I say we go in like we own the place."

Dyne's heart began to race. "Find, fix, finish."

In what had served as the archive room for LiMerge Power's plasma facility, droid parts were piling up so fast and so high that Obi-Wan and Anakin could scarcely see Dooku's wavering holo-image any longer.

The business of destroying infantry droids—for that's precisely what the confrontation had come down to—was beginning to take a toll on Obi-Wan. The decapitations and amputations were no longer as surgical as they had been when Dooku had first unleashed the droids. The slices that halved his spindly opponents and the thrusts that pierced chest plastrons had lost some of their initial accuracy.

Neither he nor Anakin was relying on lightsabers only. Calling on the Force, they hurled whatever could be lifted from the floor or yanked from the walls. Force-pushing four droids to the floor, hewing half a dozen more with his flashing blade, Anakin leapt from Obi-Wan's side, landed on the head of a perplexed droid, and began to race toward the far side of the hall, using other heads as stepping-stones.

But for every droid either of them destroyed, five more would appear, creating an impenetrable barrier between them and the doorway through which Dooku had certainly disappeared moments before they had arrived.

"Dooku!" Anakin snarled through clenched teeth. "I will kill you!"

"Control your rage, Anakin," Obi-Wan managed to say between breaths. "Don't give him the satisfaction."

Anakin shot him a worrisome scowl. "Can't have me becoming *too* powerful, now, can we, Master?"

Before Obi-Wan could reply, twenty battle droids hurried into the room through the door behind him. Whirling, he deflected their first barrage, then fought his way to cover behind a heap of dismembered droids, where Anakin joined him.

In the hope that Dooku was listening from afar, he shouted: "Whatever happens here, Dooku, your Confederacy is finished! The Republic has all of you on the run—even your master, *Sidious.*"

More droids appeared.

To Dooku, this was nothing more than a *game,* Obi-Wan told himself. But if it was a demonstration of Force ability Dooku wanted, then Anakin was still more than willing to provide it.

"Dooku!" he howled.

With such force and wrath that the ceiling of the vast hall began to collapse.

"Hurry, Threepio," Padmé said over her shoulder. "Unless you want the Senate to be your final resting place."

The protocol droid hastened his pace. "I assure you, Mistress, I'm moving as quickly as my limbs permit. Oh, curse my metal body! I'll become entombed here!"

The broad, ornate hallways leading from the Great Rotunda were packed with Senators, their aides, staff members, and droids, many laden with armloads of documents and data disks, and in some cases expensive gifts received from appreciative lobbyists. Blue-robed Senate Guards and helmeted clone troopers were doing their best to oversee the evacuation, but, what with the warbling sirens and flying rumors, alarm was beginning to yield to panic.

"How could this happen?" a Sullustan was posing to the Gotal next to him. "How?"

To all sides of her—among Bith, Gran, Wookiees, Rodians—Padmé heard the same question being asked.

How could Coruscant be invaded?

She wondered, as well. But she had more to worry about than Coruscant.

Where is Anakin?

She reached for him in her thoughts, with her heart.

I need you. Come back to me—quickly!

Grievous's strike was impeccably timed. Many delegates who might not have been on Coruscant had come to hear Palpatine's State of the Republic address, and had remained onworld to attend the endless parties that followed. In light of the surprise attack, Palpatine's reassurances seemed even more woefully premature now than when he had uttered them. And despite the fact that the Supreme Chancellor's optimistic remarks had been echoed throughout the Great Rotunda, Padmé couldn't help notice that many of her peers were surrounded by cadres of bodyguards, or sporting body armor, jet packs, or other emergency escape devices.

Clearly Palpatine had failed to lull everyone into complacency.

Thirteen years earlier Padmé could have claimed to be one of the few dignitaries whose homeworld had succumbed to an invasion and occupation. Targeted by the Trade Federation, Naboo had fallen to the Neimoidians; her parents and advisers were arrested and jailed. Now she was just one of thousands of Senators whose worlds had been similarly invaded and ransacked. Regardless, she refused to accept that Coruscant could fall to the Confederacy—even with the home fleet reduced to half its former strength. Word of mouth had it that buildings in the Ambassadorial Sector had been toppled, that battle droids were surging through Loijin Plaza, that midlevel skylanes overflowed with Geonosian Fanblades and droid fighters . . . Even if the rumors proved true, Padmé was convinced that Palpatine would find some way to drive Grievous from the Core—*again*.

Perhaps he would recall battle groups participating in the Outer Rim sieges.

That meant that Anakin would be recalled.

She chided herself for being selfish. But didn't she have the right? Hadn't she *earned* the right?

Just this once?

Thus far, the Senate Building was unscathed. Nevertheless, Homeworld Security felt it prudent to move everyone to the shelters deep beneath the hemisphere and the enormous plaza that fronted it. With most of the autonavigation lanes congested, it wasn't as if anyone could flee Coruscant. And there was always the likelihood that Grievous would single out civilian targets, as he had done on countless occasions.

Jostled by the surging crowd, Padmé collided with a Gran delegate who fixed his trio of eyestalks on her.

"And you originally *opposed* the Military Creation Act," he barked. "What do you say now?"

There was really no answer. Besides, she had been on the receiving end of similar reproofs since the start of the war. Typically voiced by those who failed to grasp that her concern was for the Constitution, not for the ultimate fate of the free trade zones.

She heard her name called, and turned to see Bail Organa and Mon Mothma angling toward where she and C-3PO were momentarily hampered. With them were two female Jedi— Masters Shaak Ti and Stass Allie.

"Have you seen the Chancellor?" Bail asked when he could.

She shook her head. "He's probably in the holding office."

"We were just there," Shaak Ti said. "The office is empty. Even his guards are gone."

"They must have escorted him to the shelters," Padmé said.

Bail glanced at something over her shoulder and raised his hand over his head to call attention to himself. "Mas Amedda," he explained for Padmé's benefit. "He'll know where to find the Chancellor."

The tall, horned, gray-complected Chagrian fairly shouldered his way through the crowd.

"The Supreme Chancellor had no meetings scheduled until later today," he said in answer to Bail's question. "I assume he is in his residence."

"Five Hundred Republica," Shaak Ti muttered to herself in seeming frustration. "I was just there."

Amedda gazed down at her in sudden concern. "And the Chancellor wasn't?"

"I wasn't looking for him then," the Jedi started to say, then allowed her words to trail off. "Master Allie and I will check the Senate Office Building and Republica." She glanced at Padmé, Bail, and the others. "Where are you going?"

"Wherever we're directed to go," Bail said.

"The turbolifts to the shelters are overwhelmed," Stass Allie said. "It'll be hours before the Senate is evacuated. My skimmer is at the plaza's northwest landing platform. You can pilot that directly to the shelters."

"Won't you and Shaak Ti need it?" Padme asked.

"We'll use the speeder bike I arrived on," Shaak Ti said.

"We appreciate the gesture," Bail said. "But I heard that the front plaza is cordoned off."

Stass Allie took his arm. "We'll escort you."

Troopers stationed in the corridor opened a path for the group, and before long they reached the doorways to the main plaza. There, however, a commando blocked their path.

"You can't exit this way," the commando told Bail.

"They're with us," Shaak Ti said.

Waving signals to several of his white-armored comrades, the commando stood aside and allowed Padmé's group to pass. The sky above the statue-studded plaza was crowded with gunships and personnel carriers. AT-TEs and other mobile artillery pieces had already been deployed.

The Jedi led Padmé, C-3PO, Bail, and Mon Mothma to the open-roofed skimmer. The speeder bike was parked alongside. Shaak Ti swung one leg over the seat and started the engine. Stass Allie settled in behind her.

"Good luck," she said.

The Senators and the droid watched the two Jedi race off in the direction of the Senate Office Building; then, with Bail piloting, they boarded the oval-shaped Flash skimmer and dropped down into the wide canyon below the plaza.

Free-travel traffic was thick even there, but Bail's skill got them through the worst of it and on course for the shelter entrances, which were just below the main skydocks of the Senate Medcenter.

Without warning, two beams of scarlet light stabbed at them from somewhere above the dome of the Senate.

"Vulture droids!" Bail said.

Padmé clutched on to C-3PO as Bail veered away from the plasma bolts. The pod-winged droid fighter that had fired was one of several that were strafing vehicles, landing platforms, and buildings in the canyon. Republic gunships were in close pursuit, unleashing with powerful wingtip cannons.

Padmé's mouth fell open in astonishment. This was something she had never expected to witness on Coruscant.

Bail was doing everything he could to keep clear of blaster bolts, plasma, and flak, but so was every other driver, and collisions quickly became part of the obstacle course. Dropping the skimmer lower still, Bail began to head for the nearest shelter entrance, as friendly and unfriendly fire ranged closer.

A flash of intense light blinded Padmé momentarily. The skimmer tipped harshly, almost spilling its occupants into midair. Smoke poured from the starboard turbine nacelle, and the small craft went into a shallow dive.

"Hold tight!" Bail yelled.

"We're doomed!" C-3PO said.

Padmé understood that Bail was swerving for a landing plat-form that abutted a wide skybridge. Tears streaming from her eyes, stricken with a sudden nausea, she placed her right hand on her abdomen.

Anakin! she said to herself. *Anakin!*

43

Flagship of the Separatist flotilla, General Grievous's kilometers-long cruiser the *Invisible Hand* held to a stationary orbit above Coruscant's Senate District, just now in full sunlight, the most majestic of its forest of aeries standing tall above the clouds. Magnified holoimages of the buildings rose from the tactical table on the cruiser's bridge. Grievous studied the images for a moment before returning to his customary place at the forward viewscreens.

Glinting in daylight, the gargantuan wedge-shaped assault ships that were, for good reason, the pride of the Republic fleet were positioned to provide cover for the planet's most important centers. In the first moments of the sneak attack, Grievous had caught a few of the ships with their shields contracted, and those hapless few glided now like flaming torches above Coruscant's pearl-strung night side, fire-suppression tenders and rescue ships following in their wake, gobbling up escape pods and lifeboats. The surviving cruisers were managing to keep their Separatist counterparts at bay. Although that scarcely mattered, since neither aerial bombardment nor invasion was important to the plan.

From the point of view of Republic naval commanders, it

must have appeared that Grievous lacked a plan; that desperation resulting from his previous defeats in the Mid and Outer Rims had driven him to gather what remained of his fleet and hurl it into a battle he couldn't possibly hope to win. And indeed, Grievous was doing everything he could to encourage that misconception. The warships under his command were haphazardly dispersed, vulnerable to counterattack, concentrating fire on communications satellites and orbital mirrors, lobbing occasional and largely ineffectual volleys of plasma at the world they had come so far and risked so much to assail.

All this was crucial to the plan.

The tactics of terror had their place.

From hundreds of areas on Coruscant's bright and dark sides streamed columns of passenger and cargo ships, determined to reach the safety of deep space. Indeed, there were almost as many vessels attempting to depart as there were arriving, constrained to autonavigation lanes and easy prey because of that. Elsewhere in local space, inward-bound ships that had reverted to realspace outside the battle zone had diverted from their approach vectors and were either hanging well to the rear, close to Coruscant's small moons, or deviating for the star system's inner worlds at sublight speeds.

In the middle distance, droid fighters and clone-piloted starfighters were destroying one another with a vengeance. Perhaps a wing of Vulture fighters had penetrated Republic lines at the start of the battle, but many had since been destroyed by orbital platform cannons, flights of high-altitude patrol craft, or ground-based artillery. Others had dashed themselves against the defensive shields that provided additional safeguards for Coruscant's political districts. But that, too, was part of the plan to inspire panic, since the sight of plasma bolts or plummeting ships detonating against those transparent domes of energy could be terrifying. Smoke billowing from some of the capital world's deepest canyons told Grievous that a few of the spearhead droids had succeeded in evading both shields and antiaircraft fire.

Similarly, tentative maneuvers on the part of Coruscant's home fleet vessels told him how eager their commanders were to break formation and engage Grievous head-on. But they had a world to protect and, more important, were too meager in number to proceed with certainty. No doubt they were waiting for reinforcements to arrive from distant systems. Anticipating as much, Grievous had planted surprises for those Republic battle groups closest to the Core, surprises in the form of mass-shadow mines, and had station warships at reversion points along the hyperlanes. If he couldn't prevent reinforcements from arriving, he could at least delay them.

If everything went according to plan, the Separatist flotilla would be ready to jump to lightspeed long before reinforcements reverted in sufficient numbers to pose a serious threat.

Grievous took a long moment to absorb the silent battle that flared beyond the thick transparisteel of the bridge viewports. He loathed being so far from the action and bloodshed. But he knew that he had to be patient a while longer. Then all the waiting and frustration would be justified.

A Neimoidian addressed him from one of the duty stations.

"General: comlink transmissions are returning to normal in sectors of the planet. The enemy appears to have comprehended that we are using the jamming suite we employed to our advantage at Praesitlyn."

"This is not unexpected," Grievous said, without turning from the view. "Instruct Group One commanders that they should continue targeting orbital mirrors and communication satellites. Relocate the jamming platform to zero-one-zero ecliptic, and intensify the shields."

"Yes, General." The Neimoidian paused, then added: "I am

compelled to report that we are sustaining heavy losses in all groups."

Grievous glanced at the tactical table. Group One alone had lost two Trade Federation carriers. The Neimoidians had managed to jettison the spherical core of one of the carriers, but the other had been blown completely in half. In the holofield, the tiny dots spilling from the carrier's curved and now separated arms were droid fighters.

"Override the survival and engagement programs of those droid fighters," Grievous ordered. "Issue a command that they speed directly for Coruscant. They are to convert to explosive devices."

"Are any specific targets assigned?"

"The outskirts of the Senate District."

"General, some of our fighters have already infiltrated that sector."

"Excellent. Command those to target landing platforms, skyways, pedestrian plazas, and shelters. Wherever possible, they are to dedicate themselves to overwhelming Coruscant's civil defense forces."

"Affirmative."

"Have any Republic auxiliaries arrived?"

"A task force comprising four light cruisers is decanting from hyperspace and advancing from Coruscant's night side."

"Order our commanders there to engage them."

Sooner than expected, Grievous thought. Ordinarily he would have given thought to contingency plans, but he trusted that Lords Sidious and Tyranus would apprise him of any changes. Had it not been for the Deep Core hyperspace routes the flotilla had taken, the attack could not have been launched successfully. Those little-known routes had been furnished by Sidious, who was less concerned with battlefield tactics than with long-range strategies. It was warcraft of a sort Grievous had never practiced. Warcraft in which seeming defeats had resulted in victories;

seeming foes proved to be allies. Warcraft of a sort that left the losers with nothing, and the winners with everything.

The galaxy itself.

The Neimoidian communications officer had fallen silent, apparently in reception of an update from one of the duty stations. Now he said: "General, a group of Jedi starfighters has emerged from Coruscant's gravity well."

"How large a group?"

"Twenty-two craft."

"Deploy as many tri-fighters against them as are needed."

"Yes, sir."

Grievous turned from the viewports. "Is the strike force assembled?"

The gunnery officer took a moment to reply. "Your gunboat is ready, and your elites are standing by in the launching bay."

"Battle droids, as well?"

"Fifty, General."

Grievous nodded. "That should suffice." He glanced at the viewport a final time, then turned his gaze on the Neimoidian bridge crew. "Carry on. Consider every Republic vessel a target of opportunity."

"I'm sorry, Master, but the beacon still isn't transmitting."

Yoda continued to pace the floor of the Temple's computer room, then stopped and pointed the business end of his gimer stick at the Jedi seated at the beacon's control console.

"Nothing for which to be sorry," he said in reprimand. "The *Separatists'* fault this is. Jamming transmissions from this sector of Coruscant, Grievous is."

The Jedi—a brown-haired human female named Lari Oll—lifted her hands from the console and shook her head in confusion. "How could Grievous—"

"Dooku," Yoda cut her off. "Shares our secrets with his confederates, he does."

"If one of our starfighters could get past the Separatist block-ade, there might be a way of relaying a message through the HoloNet."

Yoda nodded. "Already considered that, Master Tiin has. At-tempt to recall Jedi from Belderone, Tythe, and other worlds, he will."

"Can they get back here in time?"

"*Hmph.* On Grievous's objective, that depends. Leave Cor-uscant soon and only slightly bruised, he might. Wait, we must, until he reveals his plan." Yoda paused to consider his own words, then leaned his weight on the gimer stick and looked hard at Lari Oll. "Enabled the comm is?"

"Intermittently, Master Yoda."

He nodded his chin to the communications console. "Call Master Windu."

Moments later, Windu's voice issued indistinctly from the console's annunciators.

". . . Fisto and I . . . Senate building. Shaak . . . Allie . . . to the Chancellor's quarters in Five Hundred Republica. We . . . with them—"

"Raised, the defense shields are. Among one another, dis-tricts are unable to communicate." Yoda grimaced, then nodded once more. "Master Ti, try."

Lari Oll tried several frequencies before giving up. "I'm sor—" She caught herself. "No response."

Yoda paced away from the console, deliberately turning his back to the glut of devices, screens, data displays, in a kind of countermeasure.

Shutting his eyes to distance himself farther, he stretched out with his feelings, placing in his mind's eye Mace and Kit Fisto skimming through the deranged sky; Shaak Ti and Stass Allie hurrying toward Palpatine's quarters in 500 Republica; Saesee Tiin, Agen Kolar, Bultar Swan, and other Jedi Masters and Jedi Knights streaking from Coruscant's envelope in their starfighters, local space flashing with energy bolts and globular explosions, ships too numerous to count embroiled in a monumental battle . . .

Grievous was loosing his war machines against both military and civilian targets, firing at anything and everything that wandered into his sights, commanding his droid fighters to dash themselves against Coruscant's defensive umbrellas or race down through traffic lanes, initiating chain reactions of collisions.

And yet, for all the diversion, disruption, and terror those stratagems incited, they had little to do with the real battle.

As was true of the war itself, the real battle was being fought in the Force.

Yoda stretched out farther, immersing himself fully in the Force—only to feel his breath catch in his throat.

Frigid, the current became.

Arctic.

And for the first time he could feel Sidious. *Feel him on Coruscant!*

Captain Dyne stepped cautiously from the platform that had dropped the team into the unexplored depths of 500 Republica. Here, at an intersection of spooky corridors made of permacrete and surfaced with panels of plasteel, no water dripped, no insects constructed hives, no conduit worms nursed on electrical current. Strangely, however, the air was stirred by a faint and fresh breeze.

Dyne took a breath to steady his nerves. He was trained for combat, but had spent so many of the past few years doing routine Intelligence work that his once sharp reflexes were shot. Commanding the hovering probe droids to go to stasis mode, he deactivated the handheld processor and hooked it on his belt.

Drawing his Merr-Sonn blaster from its holster, he hefted it, then thumbed off the stun setting switch.

Ahead of him, ghost-like in the dismal light, the commandos were moving toward the thick door at the end of the hall, keeping close to the walls, with weapons raised. Valiant had the point, with the squad's explosives expert close behind, a thermal detonator in hand.

Dyne stepped between the powered-down pair of probe droids, TC-16 following in his footsteps.

They hadn't advanced three meters down the corridor when Dyne's ears pricked up at the sound of gurgled voices.

He could sense TC-16 come to a sudden halt behind him.

"Why, someone is speaking Geonosian," the protocol droid started to say.

Whirling, Dyne found himself staring down the wide muzzles of two organic-looking sonic weapons, grasped in the thick-fingered hands of two Geonosian soldier drones, barely visible in the shadows, their wings angled down toward the corridor's grimy floor.

The next few moments unfurled in silent slow motion.

Dyne understood that it wasn't his life flashing before his eyes, but his death.

He saw the commandos drop in their tracks, as if blown over by a gale-force wind. He watched Valiant and the explosives expert leave the floor and hurtle headlong into the door. He observed a storm of probe droid parts whirl past him. He felt himself go airborne and crash into the wall, and his insides turn spongy.

It was possible, in that eternal moment of silence, that the troopers had reacted quickly enough to get off a few bolts, because when Dyne looked to his right, along the way he had come, there were no signs of the Geonosians or, for that matter, TC-16.

Then again, for all he knew he had lapsed into unconsciousness for an undetermined amount of time. He was vaguely aware of being slumped against the wall in a position that didn't come naturally to a human being. It was as if every bone in his body had been made pliant.

Soundlessly, the distant door opened inward, and light flooded into the corridor. The light was either red or tinted so by the blood that was filling his ruptured eyeballs.

Still set on slow motion, the immediate world came in and out of focus. What remained of his vision registered a room filled with blinking equipment, screens filled with scrolling data, a holo-projector table, above which drifted a Trade Federation battle-ship, halved and in flames. Two machine intelligences emerged from the room, their slender, tubular bodies identifying them as assassin droids. Behind them walked a human of medium height and build, who stepped nonchalantly over Valiant's grotesquely twisted body.

His liquefying brain notwithstanding, Dyne found a moment to be astonished, because he recognized the man instantly.

Incredible, he thought.

As the Jedi suspected, the Sith had managed to infiltrate the highest levels of the Republic government.

The fact that the man had made no attempt to mask himself assured and comforted Dyne that he was about to die, and shortly after the realization, he did.

Where is the Chancellor?" Shaak Ti demanded of the three Red Guards stationed outside the entrance to Palpatine's suite in 500 Republica.

Alongside her hurried Stass Allie, one hand on the hilt of her lightsaber. In their adamant wake followed four members of the building's small army of security personnel, who had escorted the Jedi women from a midlevel skydock to the penthouse level.

Despite having been notified of their arrival, the imposing Red Guards kept their force pikes raised in defensive postures.

"Where?" Stass Allie said, making it clear that she was going to get past them, one way or another.

Shaak Ti had her hand raised to part the doors with a Force wave when the guards lowered their pikes and stepped aside.

One punched a code into a wall panel, and the pair of burnished doors opened.

"This way," the same guard said, gesturing the Jedi inside.

A broad hallway lined with sculptures and holo-art images led into the suite itself, which, like Palpatine's chambers in the Senate Office Building, was predominantly red. There was no telling how large the suite was, but the exterior wall of the vast main room followed the curve of the building's crown and looked down on patchy clouds, typical of those that gathered around the building in late afternoon. Distant autonavigation lanes—transverse, and to and from orbit—were motionless with stalled traffic. Between them and 500 Republica hovered two LAAT gunships and a small flock of patrol skimmers.

A distinct disturbance at the crest of the Senate District's defensive umbrella meant that continued bombardment by Separatist forces had rendered the shield permeable. Beyond the superhot edge of the shield, light flashed within banks of gray clouds.

Lightning or plasma, Shaak Ti told herself.

Scarcely acknowledging her presence, Palpatine paced into the room like a caged animal, hands clasped behind his back, Senatorial robes trailing along the richly carpeted floor.

Additional Red Guards and several of Palpatine's advisers stood watching him, some with comlinks plugged into their ears, others with devices Shaak Ti understood to be vital to the continued operation of the Republic military. Should anything befall the Chancellor, authority to initiate battle campaigns and issue war codes would pass temporarily to Speaker of the Senate, Mas Amedda, who, Shaak Ti had learned, was already safely ensconced in a hardened bunker deep beneath the Great Rotunda.

She couldn't help noticing that Pestage and Isard—two of Palpatine's closest advisers—looked nervous.

"Why is he still here?" Stass Allie directed at Isard.

Isard made his lips a thin line. "Ask him yourself."

Shaak Ti practically had to plant herself in Palpatine's path to get his attention.

"Supreme Chancellor, we need to escort you to shelter."

They were not strangers. Palpatine had personally commended her for her actions at Geonosis, Kamino, Dagu, Brentaal IV, and Centares.

He stopped briefly to regard her, then swung around and

paced away from her. "Master Ti, while I appreciate your concern, I've no need of rescue. As I've made abundantly plain to my advisers and protectors, I feel that my place is here, where I can best communicate with our commanders. If I were to go anywhere, it would be to the holding office."

"Chancellor, communications will be clearer from the bunker," Pestage said.

Isard added: "All those familiarization drills you so despised were conducted for just this scenario, sir."

Palpatine sent him a skewered grin. "Practice and reality are different matters. The Supreme Chancellor of the Galactic Senate does not hide from enemies of the Republic. Can I be any clearer?"

The fact that Palpatine was flustered, confused, possibly frightened was obvious. But when Shaak Ti attempted to read him through the Force, she found it difficult to get a sense of what he was truly feeling.

"Chancellor, I'm sorry," Stass Allie chimed in, "but the Jedi are obliged to make this decision for you."

He swung to her. "I thought you answered to me!"

She remained unfazed. "We answer first to the Republic, and safeguarding you is tantamount to safeguarding the Republic."

Palpatine deployed his signature penetrating gaze. "And what will you do should I refuse? Use the Force to drag me from my quarters? Pit your lightsabers against the weapons of my guards, who are also sworn to safeguard me?"

Shaak Ti traded looks with one of the guards, wishing she could see through the face shield of his red cowl. The situation was becoming dangerous. A shiver born in the Force moved her to glance out the window.

"Supreme Chancellor," Pestage was saying. "You must listen to reason—"

"Reason?" Palpatine snapped. He aimed a finger toward the

window. "Have you gazed into our once tranquil skies? Is there anything *reasonable* about what's occurring there?"

"All the more reason to move you to safety as quickly as possible," Isard said. "So that you conduct Coruscant's defense from a hardened site."

Palpatine stared at him. "In other words, you agree with the Jedi."

"We do, sir," Isard said.

"And you?" Palpatine asked the captain of his guards.

The guard nodded.

"Then all of you are in error." Palpatine stormed to the window. "Perhaps you need to take a closer look—"

Before a further word could fly from his mouth, Shaak Ti and Stass Allie were in motion; Shaak Ti tackling Palpatine to the floor, while Allie ignited her blade and brought it vertically in front of her.

Without warning, the gunships closest to 500 Republica were lanced by plasma bolts. Their door gunners blown into midair, the two ships veered and began to fall through the clouds, trailing plumes of fire and thick black smoke.

"Unhand me!" Palpatine said. "How dare you?"

Shaak Ti kept him pinned to the floor and called her lightsaber into her hand.

A shrill sound overrode the window's noise cancellation feature, and a Separatist assault craft rose into view from somewhere below the suite. Crowded at the side hatches and ready to deploy stood a band of battle droids and others. As the craft hovered closer to the window Shaak Ti gaped in disbelief.

Grievous!

"Down!" Stass Allie shouted a moment before the entire window wall blew inward, filling the air with permaglass pebbles. Through the shattered window, droids leapt into the room, opening up with blaster rifles.

Stass Allie stood immobile in the rush of wind, noise, and blaster bolts. Six Red Guards raced to her side, their activated force pikes humming in concert with Allie's lightsaber. Droids fell armless, legless, headless before they made it two meters into the room. Blaster bolts deflected by Allie's flashing blue blade blazed out of the window opening, ripping into the other droids waiting to hurdle the gap between craft and building.

For a moment Shaak Ti was certain that Allie was going to throw herself aboard the hovering gunboat, but there were simply too many droids standing in the way. Keeping Palpatine in a crouch, she grabbed a handful of his robes and began to guide him deeper into the room, her upraised lightsaber parrying bolts that ricocheted from the walls and ceiling.

Beaten back, the battle droids broke off their attack. Outside the window, the gunboat was taking heavy fire from a surround of patrol skimmers. As Allie and the Red Guards were felling the final few droids, the Separatist craft dropped back into the clouds, with bolts from the skimmers chasing it.

Releasing Palpatine to the custody of two guards, Shaak Ti raced to the window and gazed down into the clouds. By then, there was little to see but angry exchanges of cyan and crimson light.

She turned to face Isard. "Alert Homeworld Security that General Grievous has broken through the perimeter."

Elsewhere in the room, Pestage was helping Palpatine to his feet.

"Ready now, sir?"

Palpatine returned a wide-eyed nod.

"These familiarization drills you've been conducting," Stass Allie started to say.

Isard gestured to one of the side rooms. "The suite is equipped with a secret turbolift that serves a secure, midlevel sky-dock. An armored gunship is standing by to transport the Chancellor to a bunker complex in the Sah'c District."

"Negative," Shaak Ti said, shaking her head. "Grievous knew enough to come here. We have to assume that the escape route has been compromised, as well."

"We can't just take him to a public shelter," Isard said.

"No," Shaak Ti agreed. "But there are other ways to reach the bunker complex."

"Why not use Republica's private turbolifts," one of the security guards suggested. "Ride them to the basement levels and you'll have access to any number of landing platforms."

Stass Allie nodded, then glanced at Palpatine. "Supreme Chancellor, your guards are going to encircle you. You are not to attempt to leave that circle under any circumstances. Do you understand?"

Palpatine nodded. "I'll do whatever you say."

Allie waited until the Red Guards had gathered around him. "Now—quickly!"

When everyone had moved into the hallway, Shaak Ti used her comlink to find Mace Windu.

"Mace, Grievous is onworld," she said the moment she heard his voice.

The response was noisy but intelligible. "I just heard."

"The Chancellor's escape route may be in jeopardy," she continued. "We're heading for Republica's sub-basements. Can you meet us there?"

"Kit and I are nearby."

Pressed into the turbolift with Stass Allie, Palpatine's guards and advisers, and Republica's security personnel, Shaak Ti watched the display tick off the floors.

No one spoke until the car had reached the first sublevel.

"Don't stop," Shaak Ti told the security man closest to the controls. "The deeper we go, the better."

"All the way to the bottom?" the man asked.

She nodded. "All the way to the bottom."

Again.

The turbolift deposited them not far from where she had been earlier, though on the opposite side of the tunnel leading to the east skydock. As they hurried for the tunnel, Shaak Ti took a moment to survey the huge space for some sign of Captain Dyne's team. Considering all that had happened since she left, it was likely that Dyne and Commander Valiant had curtailed the search for Sidious's hideaway. Or perhaps they were still at it, somewhere in the sub-basement. Just short of entering the tunnel, she caught a glance of a bright silver protocol droid that might have been TC-16 hastening toward the exit to the west skydock.

The tunnel was darker than it should have been at that time of day, and the lower reaches of the canyon were darker still.

"Wait here," Shaak Ti instructed the Red Guards and Palpatine when they had reached the mouth of the tunnel.

Stass Allie strode to the center of the platform and gazed up at the buildings that loomed on all sides. "Grievous's forces must have destroyed the orbital mirror that feeds this sector."

Shaak Ti looked straight up at the sliver of sky.

"The shield is down. They must have taken out the generator."

Allie blew out her breath. "I'll find an appropriate vehicle to confiscate."

Shaak Ti laid a hand on her upper arm. "Too risky. We should remain as close to ground as possible."

Allie indicated the stairway that led to the mag-lev platform. "The train won't take us to the bunker complex, but close enough."

Shaak Ti smiled at her and reactivated the comlink.

"Mace," she said when he answered. "Another change in plans . . ."

Dragging himself out from under plasteel girders and chunks of ferrocrete, Count Dooku came shakily to his feet and gazed in astonished disbelief at the shambles of the control room. Had the containment dome been so weak that it had succumbed to flurries of ricocheting blaster bolts, or had Skywalker's voiced rage actually called the ceiling down?

Had Dooku not leapt forcefully at the last moment, he might have been buried, as the two Jedi were, somewhere below, in the expanse of rubble that covered the archive room. He was certain that they had survived. But if nothing else they were trapped, which had been the intent from the start.

But Skywalker . . . Assuming that he had grown powerful enough to have collapsed the dome, the end result was simply further evidence that he would someday undo himself. Wasn't it? Because admitting to any alternative explanation meant accepting that Skywalker was potentially a greater threat to the Sith than anyone realized.

Initially, it had cheered him to observe that Skywalker and Kenobi had finally learned to fight together; to see how powerful they had become in partnership. Complementing each other's strengths, compensating for each other's weaknesses. Kenobi making full use of his inherent discretion to balance young Skywalker's inattentive rowdiness. He could have watched them until the light faded on fair Tythe. And he wished that General Grievous could have been there to witness the display for himself.

Now he wasn't so sure.

What if it should all *come crashing down?* he found himself thinking, as he dusted himself off and raced to exit the ruined facility.

What if Grievous was outwitted and destroyed at Coruscant? Sidious, apprehended and defeated? What if the Jedi should triumph, after all?

What would become of his dream of a galaxy brought under eminent stewardship?

On Vjun, Yoda had implied that the Jedi Temple would always be open to Dooku's return . . . But, no. There was no turning back from the dark side, especially from the depths in which he had swum. Was there, then, a life of retirement somewhere in the galaxy for the former Count Dooku of Serenno?

So much rested on what would take place over the next few standard days.

So much rested on whether Lord Sidious's plan could succeed on all fronts—even though forced to unfold hastily, because of a foolish oversight by Nute Gunray.

Outside, under Tythe's yellow-gray sky, his sloop was waiting, and standing alongside it the ship's pilot droid.

"A recorded message," the droid announced. "From General Grievous."

"Play it!" Dooku said as he hurried up the sloop's aft boarding ramp and into the instrument-filled main hold.

A paused holoimage of the cyborg floated in blue light.

Throwing off his dusty cape, Dooku paced while the FA-4 triggered the recording to replay.

"Lord Tyranus," Grievous said, in motion suddenly and genuflecting. *"Supreme Chancellor Palpatine will soon be ours."*

Dooku exhaled in satisfaction. "And just in time," he muttered.

As if recalled to life, he positioned himself on the transmission grid and sent a simple return message: "General, I will join you shortly."

Padmé's eyes fluttered open.

Into focus swam the faintly smiling face of Mon Mothma.

"No sleeping on the job, Senator," Mon Mothma said, as if from underwater. "We have to get you out of here."

Padmé took stock of herself; realized that she was reclined in the rear seat of Stass Allie's skimmer. Her head was pillowed on Mon Mothma's left arm, and her ears felt as if they were plugged with cotton.

"How long—"

"Just for a moment," Mon Mothma said in the same watery tone. "I don't think you struck your head. You were fine after the crash. Then you fainted. Can you move?"

Padmé sat up and saw that the skimmer's safety mechanisms had deployed. Light-headed but unhurt, she brushed her hair from her face. "I can barely hear you."

Mon Mothma regarded her in knowing silence, then extended a hand to help her climb from the craft. "Padmé, you have to be careful. Quickly, now."

She nodded. "Crashing wasn't exactly on my agenda."

Mon Mothma hurried her away from the skimmer, to where

Bail and C-3PO were hiding behind the blockish pedestal of a modernistic sculpture.

"Master Allie doesn't strike me as someone who will sue for damages," the droid was saying.

Still in a daze, Padmé grasped that they had skidded into the plaza that fronted the Embassy Mall, taking out a large holosign and three news kiosks along the way. Bail's skill had somehow kept them from mowing down pedestrians, who had apparently scattered on first sight of the nose-diving ship. Or perhaps at sight of the craft that had fallen to Separatist fire *ahead* of the skimmer—a military police vehicle, similar to a Naboo Gian speeder, tipped on its side against the façade of the mall and belching smoke. Sprawled on the plaza close to the vehicle were the charred corpses of three clone troopers.

Reality reasserted itself in a rush of deafening noise, flashing light, and acrid smells. From nearby came anguished moans and terrified screams; from the tiered heights above the plaza, distant discharges of artillery. Higher still, plasma bolts raked the sky; fire bloomed, detonations thundered.

Padmé saw a smear of blood on Bail's cheek. "You're hurt—"

"It's nothing," he said. "Besides, we have more to worry about."

She followed his grim gaze, and understood immediately why Coruscanti were fleeing the pedestrian skybridge that linked the mall to the midlevel entrances of the Senate Hospital. Five Vulture droids had alit on the far side of the span and reconfigured to patrol mode. Four-legged gargoyles, with heads deployed forward and sensor slits red as arterial blood, they were striding through Hospital Plaza, sowing destruction. Their four laser cannons were aimed downward, but from paired launchers in their semicircular fuselage flew torpedoes aimed at air taxis, craft attempting to dock at the hospital's emergency platforms, the tunnel entrances to the Senate shelters . . .

Republic LAATs had dropped from the Senate Plaza to engage the three-and-a-half-meter-tall droids but were maintaining a wary distance just now, pilots and gunners clearly worried about adding energy weapons or EMP missiles to the chaos.

"Xi Char monstrosities," Mon Mothma said.

Padmé remembered standing helplessly at the tall windows of Theed Palace, watching squadrons of Vulture fighters fill the sky, like cave creatures loosed on Naboo by darkness . . .

Caught in the crossfire, pedestrians had raced across the sky-bridge, hoping to find sanctuary in the Embassy Mall—midlevel in the dome-topped Nicandra Counterrevolutionary Signalmen's Memorial Building—but thick security grates had been lowered over the entrances, leaving crowds of Coruscanti to scramble for whatever cover could be found.

Padmé felt faint once more.

Huddled, frightened, panicked masses of Coruscanti were suddenly getting a taste of what the inhabitants of Jabiim, Brentaal, and countless other worlds had faced during the past three years. Caught up in a war of ideologies, often by dint of circumstance or location. Caught between the forces of a droid army led by a self-styled revolutionary and a cyborg butcher, and an army of vat-grown soldiers led by a monastic order of Jedi Knights who had once been the galaxy's peacekeepers.

Caught in the middle, with no allegiance to either side.

It was tragic and senseless, and she might have broken down and cried if her current circumstances had been different. She felt sick at heart, and in despair for the future of sentient life.

"Palpatine will never live this down, " Mon Mothma was saying. "Committing so many of our ships and troopers to the Outer Rim sieges. As if this war he is so intent on winning could never come to Coruscant."

Bail frowned in sympathy. "Not only will he live it down, he'll profit from it. The Senate will be blamed for voting to escalate the sieges, and while we're mired in accusations and counter-accusations of accountability, Palpatine will quietly accrue more and more power. Without realizing it, the Separatists have played right into his hands by launching this attack."

Padmé wanted to argue with him but didn't have the strength.

"They're all mad," Bail continued. "Dooku, Grievous, Gunray, Palpatine."

Mon Mothma nodded sadly. "The Jedi could have stopped this war. Now they're Palpatine's pawns."

Padmé squeezed her eyes shut. Even if she managed to summon the strength, how could she respond, when her own husband was one of them—a *general*? What had the Jedi gotten Anakin into—taking him from Tatooine, from his youth, his mother? And yet hadn't she done as much as anyone to encourage him to remain a Jedi; to heed the tutelage of Obi-Wan, Mace, and the others; to perpetuate the lie that was their secret life as husband and wife?

She hugged herself.

What had *she* gotten Anakin into? What had she gotten both of them into?

Bail's voice snapped her from self-pity.

"They're coming." He aimed a finger across the plaza. "They're coming across the bridge."

From somewhere in the Vultures' droid brains had come a revelation that the pedestrian skyway offered a better vantage for targeting buildings and craft to both sides of the kilometer-deep canyon. More important, the gunships were even less likely to fire on them there, lest they destroy the span and send it plummeting to the busy thoroughfares and mag-lev lines two hundred stories below.

"Perhaps if we throw ourselves on the mercy of the owners of the mall, they will raise the security grate," C-3PO started to say.

Bail looked at Padmé and Mon Mothma. "We have to keep those droids on the far side of the bridge, so the gunships can take them out."

Mon Mothma glanced at the overturned military craft. "I see a way to try."

The craft sat scarcely fifty meters from the base of the sculpture. Without further word, the three of them hurried for it.

"What could I have possibly been thinking?" C-3PO shouted as he watched them search the craft for weapons. "It can never be the easy answer!"

The three humans returned momentarily, carrying three blaster rifles.

"Not much power left," Bail said, checking one of them. "Yours?"

"Low on blaster gas," Padmé said.

Mon Mothma ejected the powerpack from hers. "Empty."

Bail nodded glumly. "We'll have to make do."

Hunkering down behind the pedestal, he and Padmé took careful aim on the closest of the walking droids.

By then three had started onto the skyway, firing at random. Exploding against the façades of buildings above and below, torpedoes sent slabs of durasteel-reinforced ferrocrete avalanching onto plazas, landing platforms, and balconies, burying scores of hapless Coruscanti.

"Be prepared to move as soon as we fire," Bail said. He indicated one of the kiosks that had survived the crashes of both speeders. "There's our first cover."

Padmé centered the lead droid in the blaster's targeting reticle and squeezed the trigger. Her initial bursts did little more than catch the droid's attention, but subsequent bolts from both blasters started to score hits on vital components. The droid actually retreated a couple of steps toward Hospital Plaza, only to launch a trio of torpedoes straight across the skyway.

Padmé and company were already in motion. One torpedo hit the pedestal, blowing it and the sculpture to fragments. A second slagged what was left of Stass Allie's skimmer. The third detonated against the lowered security grate, blowing a gaping hole into the mall. Pedestrians to both sides hastened for it, fighting with one another to be first through the smoking maw. Padmé thought that one of the Vultures would target them, but in their moment of inattention, the droids had left themselves open to strafing runs by the gunships. Converging beams of brilliant light streaked from the fire dishes of the LAATs' wing- and armature-mounted ball turrets, and staccato bursts erupted from the forward guns.

Two droids exploded.

One turned to answer the volleys, but not in time. Missiles from the gunships' mass-drive launchers took off the droid's left legs, then the head, then blew the rest clear across the plaza. The remaining two Vultures skittered onto the skyway to increase their odds of survival.

Bail and Padmé laid down steady lines of fire, but the droids were undeterred.

"And I thought the Senate was a battlefield!" Mon Mothma said.

The sight of smoke curling from holes in the lead droid's fuselage seemed to invigorate the one behind. Driving Padmé and the others in search of new cover with a single torpedo, the droid scurried forward, edging around its stricken comrade and stepping brazenly into the mall plaza, red sensors gleaming.

A gunship made a quick pass, but couldn't find a clear field of fire.

"I'm out," Bail said, dropping his rifle.

Padmé checked her weapon's display screen. "Same."

C-3PO shook his head. "How will I ever explain this to Artoo-Detoo?"

They broke for cover a final time, hoping to throw themselves through the ragged hole in the still-smoking security grate, but the droid hurried to intercept them; then, in seeming sadistic delight, began to back the four of them against the wall of the Nicandra Building.

A rage began to build in Padmé, born of instincts as old as life itself. She was on the verge of hurling herself against the towering machine, ripping the sensors from its teardrop-shaped head, when the droid came to a sudden halt, obviously in reception of some remote communication. Retracting its head and stiffening its scissor-like legs into wings, it turned and launched itself over the edge of the plaza into the canyon below.

The droid on the skyway did the same, even with two gunships in close pursuit.

Padmé was first to reach the skyway railing. Far below, the Senate District mag-lev was racing south toward the skytunnel that would take it through the kilometer-wide Heorem Complex and on into the wealthy Sah'c District. The two Vulture droids were swooping down to join ranks with a Separatist gunboat that was already chasing the train.

How had Grievous known to attack 500 Republica? Mace asked himself as the mag-lev rushed at three hundred kilometers per hour toward the skytunnel that would spirit the train from the Senate District.

Having boarded the mag-lev at its 500 Republica platform, he, Kit Fisto, Shaak Ti, and Stass Allie were in the car the Supreme Chancellor's Red Guards had commandeered—second in a train of some twenty cars. Through a gap in the protective circle the guards had forged, Mace caught a glimpse of Palpatine, his head of wavy gray hair lowered in what might have been anguish or deep concentration.

How had Grievous known? Mace asked himself.

Many Coruscanti knew that Palpatine resided in 500 Republica, but the location of his suite was a well-kept secret. More important, how had Grievous known that Palpatine wasn't to be found in either of his offices?

Not everything could be traced to Dooku.

It was conceivable that Dooku had furnished Grievous with data on hyperlanes that skimmed the outer limits of the Deep Core. That much, Dooku could have pilfered from the Jedi

archives before he left the Order, presumably when he was eras-
ing mentions of Kamino from the data banks. Similarly, Dooku
could have supplied Grievous with the orbital coordinates of specific communications satellites and mirrors, or with tactical information regarding the location of dedicated shield generators on
the surface. But Palpatine had only just been elected Supreme
Chancellor when Dooku left Coruscant to return to Serenno,
and back then, some thirteen years ago, Palpatine had been living in a high-rise tower close to the Senate Building.

So how had Grievous known to go to 500 Republica?

Sidious?

If it was true that hundreds of Senators had, for a time, been
under the Sith Lord's influence, then he may have had access to
the highest levels of confidential information. As many on the
Jedi Council feared, Sidious's network of agents and assets might
have infiltrated the Republic military command itself. Which
suggested that the sneak attack on Coruscant may have been
years in the planning!

Mace caught another glimpse of Palpatine, insulated by the
flowing red robes of his handpicked bodyguards.

This was hardly the time to question him about his closest
confidants.

But Mace would make it his business to find the time later.

Briefly, he wondered what had become of Captain Dyne's
team. Surmising that Dyne had called off the search for Sidious
shortly after the attack had commenced, Intelligence hadn't
dispatched a second search team—aimed at locating Dyne and
Valiant—until neither of them had been heard from, even after
communications had been restored to the Senate District.

Shaak Ti hadn't seen them when she and Palpatine's protectors had whisked the Supreme Chancellor through 500 Republica's sub-basement.

So had Dyne and the commandos fallen victim to Grievous's

attack? Were they trapped somewhere under a crashed cargo ship or tons of ferrocrete rubble?

Yet another ill-timed concern, Mace thought.

The mag-lev's other cars were packed cheek-to-jowl with Coruscanti attempting to flee the Senate and Financial Districts. Palpatine's guards would have commandeered the entire train if Palpatine hadn't intervened, refusing to allow it. Shaak Ti had told Mace and Kit about the Supreme Chancellor's earlier reluctance to leave his suite. Mace didn't know what to make of it. But now at least they were on the way to the bunker. The mag-lev line didn't run past the complex, but the first stop in Sah'c was close to a system of skyways and turbolifts that did.

Light filtering into the car through the tinted windows dimmed.

The mag-lev was entering the Heorem Skytunnel, a broad burrow that accommodated not only the speeding train, but also opposing lanes of autonavigation and free-travel traffic, passing through several of the Senate District's largest buildings. Lanes leading south—away from the district, and off to the right side of the mag-lev—were crawling with public transports and air taxis. By contrast, the northbound lanes were almost empty, the result of traffic having been rerouted well before it reached the Senate District.

A blur of light off to the left-hand side of the car caught Mace's eye, and he hurried to the closest window. Streaking southbound in the northbound free-travel lane, two droid fighters were trying to overtake the train. Before Mace could utter a word of warning, cannon fire from one of the twin-winged ships stitched a broken line of holes across the blunt nose of a transport in the autonavigation lane. Instantly the transport exploded, savaging nearby vehicles with shrapnel and nearly rocking the mag-lev from its elevated guide rails.

Screams issued from Coruscanti wedged into the cars to the front and rear of Palpatine's.

"Vulture fighters!" Mace told the Jedi and Red Guards.

Leaning low at the window, he saw one of the droids climb over the mag-lev, only to descend on the opposite side of the train in the midst of the free-travel lane, initiating a succession of collisions that flung speeders, taxis, and buses all over the sky-tunnel. Two vehicles careened into the train, only to rebound back into the travel lane, starting a second series of fatal crashes. Racing alongside Palpatine's car, the same droid responsible for the collisions surged into a steep climb and disappeared from view.

Not a moment later an earsplitting sound reached Mace from somewhere in the rear of the train and overhead. Behind the tinted glass, sparks showered down the rounded sides of the car, and the smell of molten metal wafted from the ventilation grilles. A tumult of terrified cries rose from the car directly behind Palpatine's, and hands and feet began to pound against the passage-way door.

Part of a group of mag-lev security personnel stationed there, a Weequay looked to Mace.

"We won't be able to hold them back!"

In turn, Mace whirled to Shaak Ti and Allie. "Move the Chancellor into the forward car!"

Shaak Ti regarded him as if he had lost his mind. "It's packed, Mace!"

"I know that. Find a way!"

He gestured for Kit Fisto, and the two of them shouldered through the cluster of security personnel at the rear of the car and activated their lightsabers. Faced with the purple and blue blades, passengers on the far side of the door's window began to retreat into the vestibule, battling with those behind them who were attempting to press into the forward car.

When there was space enough in the vestibule, Mace instructed the Weequay to unlock the door. Without hesitation he and Kit dashed through the vestibule and on into the rear car, where most of the mixed-species passengers were heaped atop seats to both sides of the wide aisle. Wind howled through the car from a jagged rend that had been opened in the roof, and through which had dropped half a dozen infantry droids.

Mace allowed himself a moment of bewilderment. Since the battle droids couldn't have been delivered by the droid fighters, there had to be a *third* Separatist craft racing alongside the train.

The battle droids opened fire.

To many of the passengers all but fused to the tinted windows, the situation must have seemed hopeless. Not because the two Jedi couldn't deflect the hail of blaster bolts aimed at them, but because they couldn't deflect them without sending some into or through people in the car. But those passengers failed to recognize that one of the Jedi was Mace Windu—rumored to have single-handedly destroyed a seismic tank on Dantooine—and that the other was Kit Fisto, Nautolan hero of the Battle of Mon Calamari.

Together they returned some of the sizzling bolts into the advancing droids. Others they sent whizzing through the opening in the roof, managing in the process to catch one of the Vultures in the belly and send it spiraling to its death somewhere below the mag-lev line. Sparks and smoke whirled through the car, and parts of spindly arms and legs flew about unavoidably, but Mace and Kit called on the Force to control even those. A few Coruscanti were struck, but, against all odds, the Jedi saw to it that none was critically injured.

No sooner had the final droid dropped than Mace leapt straight up through the rend, landing in a crouch on the roof of the next car down the line, holding himself in place by the Force with the wind whipping at the back of his shaved skull and coarse tunic. Senses on alert, he saw a Separatist craft drop down behind the final car in the line. Farther away, but quickly making up the distance, flew two Republic gunships.

Instinctively he glanced to the right just as the second Vulture droid was rocketing into view. Seeing him, the droid sprayed the roof of the car with cannon fire. Mace turned into the powerful wind and focused all his intention on a front flip that carried him back through the rend. The Vulture veered, positioning itself directly over the laceration its partner had opened, and reorienting its wing cannons.

In what would surely have been a futile act, Mace raised his lightsaber.

But the expected cannon blast never arrived. Wings clipped and repulsors damaged by missiles fired from the gunships, the Vulture slammed down onto the roof of the speeding train, then rolled out of sight.

Deactivating their blades, Mace and Kit rushed into the forward car, which was now filled with Palpatine's advisers and those passengers the Jedi women and Red Guards had relocated from the train's lead car. Mace and Kit continued to squirm forward, arriving in the Supreme Chancellor's car just as the mag-lev was emerging from the skytunnel. The sun was going down, and the tall buildings that rose to the west cast enormous shadows across the city canyon and the busy thoroughfares far below the cantilevered mag-lev line.

In the middle of the car, Palpatine stood at the center of the cordon the Red Guards had formed around him. And at a fixed-pane window they had deliberately shattered, Shaak Ti and Stass Allie were gazing toward the rear of the train.

"Those fighters could easily have derailed us with a torpedo," Shaak Ti said as Mace and Kit approached.

Mace leaned partway out the window, eyes searching the canyon. "And battle droids don't just drop from the sky. There's a third craft."

Kit's bulging black eyes indicated Palpatine. "They want to take him alive."

The words had scarcely left his mouth when something hit the train with sufficient force to whip everyone from one side of the car to the other, then back again. The Red Guards were just regaining their balance when the roof began to resound with the cadence of heavy, clanging footfalls, advancing from the rear of the train.

"Grievous," Mace grumbled.

Kit glanced at him. "Here we go again."

Hurrying into the vestibule between the two lead cars, they launched themselves to the roof. Three cars distant marched General Grievous and two of his elite droids, their capes snapping behind them in the wind, pulse-tipped batons angled across their barrel chests.

Farther back, clamped by animal-like claws to the roof of the train, was the gunboat from which the frightful trio had been released.

Without pausing, Grievous drew two lightsabers from inside his billowing cloak. By the time they were ignited, Mace was already on and all over the cyborg, batting away at the two blades, swinging low at Grievous's artificial legs, thrusting at his skeletal face.

The lightsabers thrummed and hissed, meeting one another in bursts of dazzling light. In a corner of Mace's mind he wondered to which Jedi Grievous's blades had belonged. Just as the Force was keeping Mace from being blown from the mag-lev's roof, magnetism of some sort was keeping the general fastened in place. For the cyborg, though, the coherence hindered as much as it helped, whereas Mace never remained in one place for very long. Again and again the three blades joined, in snarling attacks and parries.

As Mace already knew from Ki-Adi-Mundi and Shaak Ti, Grievous was well trained in the Jedi arts. He could recognize the hand of Dooku in the general's training and technique. His strikes were as forceful as any Mace had ever had to counter, and his speed was astonishing.

But he didn't know Vaapad—the technique of dark flirtation in which Mace excelled.

To the rear of the car, where Grievous's pair of MagnaGuards had made the mistake of pitting themselves against Kit Fisto, the Nautolan's blade was a cyclone of blazing blue light. Resistant to the energy outpourings of a lightsaber, the phrik alloy staffs were potent weapons, but like any weapon they needed to find their target, and Kit simply wasn't allowing that. In moves a Twi'lek dancer might envy, he spun around the guards, claiming a limb from both with each rotation: left legs, right arms, right legs . . .

The speed of the train saw to the rest, ultimately whisking the droids into the canyon like insects blown from the windscreen of a speeder bike.

The loss of his confederates was noted by whatever computers were slaved to Grievous's organic brain, but the loss neither distracted nor slowed him. His sole setting was *attack*. Successful at analyzing Mace's lightsaber style, those same computers suggested that Grievous alter his stance and posture, along with the angle of his parries, ripostes, and thrusts.

The result wasn't Vaapad, but it was close enough, and Mace wasn't interested in prolonging the contest any longer than necessary.

Crouching low, he angled the blade downward and slashed, guiding it through the roof of the car, perpendicular to Grievous's stalwart advance. Mace saw by the surprised look in the cyborg's reptilian eyes that, for all his strength, dexterity, and resolve, the living part of him wasn't always in perfect sync with his alloy servos. Clearly, Grievous—onetime courageous commander of sentient troops—realized what Mace had done and wanted to sidestep, where General Grievous—current commander of droids and other war machines—wanted nothing more than to impale Mace with lunging thrusts of the paired blades.

Slipping into the gap made by Mace's saber, Grievous's left talon lost magnetic purchase on the roof, and the general faltered. Mace came out of his crouch prepared to drive his sword into Grievous's guts, but some last-instant firing of the general's cybersynapses compelled the cyborg's torso through a swift half twist that would have sent Mace's head hurtling into the canyon had the maneuver prevailed. Instead Mace leapt backward, out of the range of the slicing blades, and Force-pushed outward, just at the instant of Grievous's single misstep.

Off the side of the car the general went, twisting and turning as he fell, Mace trying to track the general's contorted plunge, but unsuccessfully.

Had he fallen into the canyon? Had he managed to dig his duranium claws into the side of the car or grab hold of the mag-lev rail itself?

Mace couldn't take the time to puzzle it out. One hundred meters away, the gunboat retracted its landing gear and rose from the roof on repulsorlift power. Reckless shots from one of the pursuing gunships obliged the Separatist craft to skew, then dive, with the gunship following close behind.

Mace and Kit watched in awe as the two ships began to helix forward around the speeding mag-lev, exchanging constant fire. Climbing away from the train's sharp nose, within which the magnetic controls were housed, the gunboat made as if to bank west, only to bank east at the last instant.

By then, however, the gunship—leading its target west—had already fired.

Drilled by a swarm of deadly hyphens, the mag-lev's control system blew apart, and the entire train began to drop.

In the darkness, buried alive, Anakin stretched out with his feelings.

In his mind's eye he saw Padmé stalked by a dark, towering creature with a mechanical head, poised at the edge of a deep abyss, her world turned upside down. A surprise attack. Opponents locked in combat. Ground and sky filled with fire, smoke billowing in the air, clouding everything.

Death, destruction, deceit . . . A labyrinth of lies. *His* world turned upside down.

He shuddered, as if plunged into liquid gas. One touch would break him into a million shards.

His fear for Padmé expanded until he couldn't see past it. Yoda's voice in his ear: *Fear leads to anger; anger to hatred; hatred to the dark side . . .*

He was as afraid to lose her as he was to hold on to her, and the pain of that contradiction made him wish he had never been born. There was no solace, even in the Force. As Qui-Gon had told him, he needed to make his focus his reality. But how?

How?

Qui-Gon, who had died—even though, to his young mind, Jedi weren't supposed to . . .

Beside him, Obi-Wan stirred and coughed.

"You're getting awfully good at destroying things," he said. "On Vjun, you needed a grenade to do this much damage."

Anakin shook the vision from his mind. "I told you I was becoming more powerful."

"Then do us both a favor by getting us out from under all this."

They used the Force, their hands and backs to extricate themselves. Getting to their feet, they stood staring at each other, dusted white head-to-toe from the debris.

"Go ahead," Anakin said. "If you don't say it, I will."

"If you insist." Obi-Wan snorted dust from his nose. "Almost makes me nostalgic for Naos Three."

"Once more, with feeling."

"Some other time. Dooku, first."

Scampering over the remains of the dome, droid parts, buried pieces of furniture, overturned shelves of holodocuments, they raced for the landing platform, arriving in time to see Dooku's sloop, one among dozens of Separatist vessels, streaking for space.

"Coward," Obi-Wan said. "He flees."

Anakin watched the sloop for a moment longer, then looked at Obi-Wan. "That's not the reason, Master. We've been tricked. Tythe was never the target. *We* were."

Bleeding speed and loft, the mag-lev settled hard onto the guide rail that projected from the skyscraper-lined rim of Sah'c Canyon. Counterpoint to the sobs and moans of the passengers, the two dozen cars—two now with slashed-open roofs—pinged and creaked.

Balanced on the balls of their feet, Mace and Kit hooked their lightsabers to their belts and drifted back down into the vestibule, as gently as the Force allowed. As if buffeted by thermals, the train swayed lazily from side to side. But with traffic halted in both directions, the air at midlevel should have been unruffled.

A quick glance out the right side of the vestibule supplied Mace with the explanation.

The aged, cantilevered supports anchored to the sides of the buildings were beginning to bend under the weight of the train.

In the distance, sirens wailed and dopplered as emergency craft hurried to render aid. Left of the stricken mag-lev, two enormous repulsorlift platforms were making a careful approach. Waiting for the train to quiet, Mace and Kit stood like statues in the vestibule. When the rocking motion had subsided some-what, they pressed the release stud for the passageway door and eased themselves into the lead car.

The train continued to protest its peculiar circumstance with an assortment of stressful sounds, but the sagging supports held.

Held for a few seconds more.

Then, with explosive reports, the rail supports beneath the center of the train tore away from the canyon rim, taking a lengthy portion of the rail with them. The train V'ed into the sudden gap, and would have plunged completely but for the fact that enough forward and rear cars remained clasped to the rail to support the few that now formed an inverted triangle. Even so, Coruscanti in the rear were propelled forward by the collapse, while those in the lead cars were jerked violently backward.

Steps into Palpatine's car, Mace and Kit called on the Force to prevent everyone from flailing toward the vestibule door. Far-ther forward in the car, Shaak Ti and Stass Allie were keeping the Supreme Chancellor on his feet.

Strident sounds issued from the guide rail. The mag-lev lurched, and another two cars slipped into the V-notch, their motion adding a sudden twist to the train that turned some of the cars onto their sides, and sent passengers sliding and tum-bling toward the tinted windows. Coruscanti screamed in terror, bracing themselves as best they could, or clawing at one another for support.

Centered in the Force, Mace directed all his energy toward keeping the Red Guards and others rooted in place. He won-dered if he, Kit, Shaak Ti, and Allie—acting in concert—could support the entire train, but dismissed the idea immediately.

They would need Yoda.

Perhaps five Yodas.

Unexpectedly, a feeling of relief flowed through him.

"The emergency repulsorlifts," Kit said.

Once more the train lurched, but this time the cars began to level out as antigrav repulsors levitated those that had dropped into the notch.

By then, too, the pair of repulsorlift platforms had cozied up to the train's left side, and scores of emergency craft were rushing in from all sides. Mace could feel an increasing sense of desperation sweep through the cars as passengers grew frantic to exit. He knew that it was only going to get worse, since none of them would be allowed to leave until Palpatine had been moved to safety.

He and Kit did their best to make that happen as quickly as possible. Within moments, they had ushered everyone who had been in the lead car onto one of the platforms. Pressed in among his Red Guards, Palpatine couldn't even be seen. Disengaging from the mag-lev, the platform was moving away from the train before a single passenger—even any of Palpatine's advisers—could scramble out onto its twin.

The air was filled with escort craft and gunships, two of which put down on the platform as it was closing on the canyon's eastern rim. Leaping out of the craft, two platoons of commandos assumed firing positions along the platform's perimeter. Behind them came four Jedi Knights, who rushed to join Shaak Ti and Stass Allie in guarding Palpatine.

Mace recognized the more scorched of the pair of gunships as one of two that had been in pursuit of Grievous's gunboat. Hurrying over to it, he signaled the pilot to raise the bubble canopy.

Cupping his hands to his mouth, he said: "What became of the gunboat?"

"My wingmate is in pursuit, General," the pilot said. "We're awaiting word."

"Did Grievous fall from the mag-lev?"

"I was too far back to see much of anything, sir. But I didn't see him fall, and I didn't see anyone on the train."

Mace replayed the events in his mind. Saw himself Force-pushing Grievous from the roof of the car; saw Grievous plunging over the edge, down out of sight, toward the rail or the canyon floor. The cyborg's gunboat disengaging from the train, descending into the canyon before it and the second gunship had commenced their corkscrewing race around the mag-lev . . .

Mace clenched his hands, and swung to Kit. "The gunboat could have caught him—somehow." He gazed up at the pilot again. "Any word yet?"

"Coming in now, sir . . . Sector H-Fifty-Two. My wingmate is in close pursuit. I'd better get a move on."

"General Fisto and I are going with you." Mace turned to Shaak Ti, Allie, and the four newly arrived Jedi Knights.

Shaak Ti nodded at him. "We'll see the Chancellor the rest of the way to the bunker."

Shaak Ti was the last to board the gunship that would deliver Palpatine to shelter, somewhere deep in the narrow service chasms that fractured the exclusive Sah'c neighborhood. Encircled by the contingent of Red Guards, Palpatine stood silently in the rear of the troop bay. His hair and robes were mussed, and he looked pale and feeble among his striking protectors. Stass Allie and the four Jedi Knights Yoda had dispatched from the Temple stood just inside the door, shoulder-to-shoulder with commandos and government agents. Shaak Ti knew the human male Jedi and the female Twi'lek by sight, but she couldn't recall ever running into the other two—a male Talz and a male Ithorian. All four of them looked able enough, though she hoped there would be no call for them to demonstrate their skills.

Moments earlier, the gunship carrying Mace and Kit had banked north, back toward the Senate District, in apparent pursuit of Grievous's gunboat. Palpatine's gunship had taken off to the south, and had immediately begun to descend. Dusk had already fallen on the rim of the canyon. Bruised by the day's events, Coruscant's skies were a swirl of blood red, orange, and deep lavender. Down below, the buildings and thoroughfares were illuminated.

Halfway to the floor of the canyon, a gunship that had seen recent action fell in alongside the Supreme Chancellor's, and remained just off to starboard and slightly astern through the numerous twists and turns that led ultimately to the mountainous structure that served as the bunker complex.

A final turn to the north brought the two gunships to the mouth of a narrow urban ravine, where they hovered for the moment it took to lower the particle shield that safeguarded the shelters, tactical and communications centers, landing platforms, and the network of tunnels that linked them. The complex could be reached by alternative means—under normal circumstances, Palpatine would have been conveyed by repulsorlift speeder through deep tunnels that arrived from 500 Republica, the Great Rotunda, and the Senate Office Building—but the ravine was the best way of entering from anywhere west of the Senate or Financial Districts.

Shaak Ti didn't allow herself to relax until the gunships had been cleared through the shimmering screen and had been issued approach vectors for landing.

Her relieved exhale seemed to go on and on.

The escort gunship shot ahead and was already on the pad when Shaak Ti and the rest arrived moments later. The craft bearing the Supreme Chancellor had scarcely touched down when the side doors flew out and back, and the Red Guards hurried Palpatine off to a waiting speeder. The commandos leapt out to reinforce the bunker's contingent of troopers.

Shaak Ti instructed the four Jedi Knights to accompany the Red Guards, promising to join them after she and Stass Allie had apprised the Temple of their safe arrival.

The two Jedi women watched the speeder race off into the broad tunnel that accessed the bunker, then swung themselves down to the landing pad. Allie grabbed her comlink and depressed the SEND button. After several failed attempts to reach the Temple, she glanced at Shaak Ti.

"Too much interference. Let's move away from the ship."

It was the interference that saved them from the explosion that mangled and consumed the gunship. As it was, the blast set their robes on fire and hurled them ten meters through the air. Retaining consciousness, Shaak Ti used the momentum to propel herself through a tucked roll that carried her almost to the edge of the landing platform. Stass Allie lay facedown nearby. The missile that had destroyed the gunship had been launched by the craft that had preceded them into the ravine. That same craft's several cannons were firing now, laying waste to other vessels and making short work of the troopers.

Shaak Ti saw several soldiers jump from the gunship's doors and move with astounding speed into the mouth of the access tunnel. She raised herself to one knee, then sprinted to Stass Allie's side to put out the flames that had engulfed her cloak.

Allie stirred and raised herself on the palms of her hands.

"Stay down," Shaak Ti warned.

As the gunship was lifting off—no doubt to gain a better vantage on the landing platform—additional troopers appeared from somewhere below the landing pad. Rocket-propelled grenades swarmed after the rising craft, several of them infiltrating the vented nacelles of the repulsorlift engines. The ensuing detonation resounded in the ravine and cast fiery hunks of metal in all directions.

Shaak Ti curled her body and tucked her head to her chest. A wave of intense heat washed over her and Allie, and a hail of fragments clanged and clattered down around her.

One of the last pieces to land—not two meters from her face—was the charred head of a battle droid.

Mace and Kit stood in the open doorway of the Republic gunship as it threaded its way among the monads and skyscrapers of the Senate District. Grievous's gunboat raced ahead, darting left and right as it fired continuously at its pursuer.

Mace backed into the gunship as bolts sizzled past the doorway, nearly catching the underside of the starboard wing. The fact that it had taken so little effort to track and catch up with the Separatist craft gnawed at Mace. Neither he nor Kit could shake the feeling that the gunboat had practically been waiting for them above the squat Senate Building, and had only then attempted to go evasive. And yet it had obviously eluded the original gunship that had chased it through the Sah'c skytunnel.

Mace leaned into the hatch to the gunner's compartment and called up to him. "Where's your wingmate?"

"Lost him, sir," the gunner shouted. "He's not anywhere on the tactical screen."

"The ship could have gone down," Kit suggested.

Mace's brow furrowed. "I don't think so. Something's wrong about this."

Overhead, missiles roared from the launchers and an explosion boomed and echoed from the surround of buildings. Black smoke and debris swept past the doorway, and the gunner whooped.

"We got him, sir! He's trailing fire, and surface-bound!"

Mace and Kit leaned out the doorway in time to see the gunboat tip to one side, then begin a rapid downward spiral.

"Stay with him, pilot!" Mace yelled.

Coiling into a city chasm east of the Senate, the craft clipped the edge of a skydock and started to come apart. The pilot of the gunship jinked to avoid airborne wreckage, but managed to remain in the wake of the doomed ship. The collision with the skydock had added an end-over-end flip to the gunboat's spiral, and now the craft was simply falling like a stone, straight down toward brightly illuminated Uscru Boulevard, which was blessedly free of traffic. Fires sputtering out, it hit the surface nose-first, cratering the street and shattering windows in buildings to all sides.

Maintaining a safe distance from the crash site, the gunship pilot engaged the repulsorlift engines and hovered to a landing at the frayed edge of the impact crater. Mace, Kit, and a dozen commandos jumped to the hot ground to secure the area. Crowds of startled onlookers formed almost immediately, and the sirens of emergency vehicles began to wail in the distance.

Lightsabers ignited, Mace and Kit strode along the perimeter of the shallow well, alert to the slightest movements. The crumpled ship had been torn open from bow to stern along one side, and they had clear views into every cabin space. Neither Grievous nor any of his elite guards were anywhere to be found.

Only battle droids: slagged, mangled, twisted into peculiar shapes.

"I can accept that Grievous might have fallen from the maglev," Mace said, "but not that he would have included only *two* of his elite on a mission like this."

Kit gazed at the wedge of night sky. "There could be a second assault craft."

"Pilot!" Mace called toward the gunship. "Comlink the Supreme Chancellor's bunker, and arrange for us to be cleared through the shield."

Grievous and six MagnaGuards cut a bloody swath through the broad corridors that led ultimately to Palpatine's sanctuary. Republic soldiers—cloned and otherwise—fell to Grievous's lightsabers and the deadly staffs of his elite. Behind them, the firefight at the landing platform was raging. If nothing else, Grievous told himself, the clash would tie up two of the Jedi and dozens of troopers.

Thus far, things were still on target—if not proceeding according to plan.

At Palpatine's apartment, Grievous had managed to fool everyone by placing the gunboat on display, then clandestinely transferring himself and his combat droids into the Republic gunship Lord Tyranus had promised would be waiting for them. He had been forced to improvise when Palpatine's protectors had opted to follow an alternate route to the bunker, and he had enjoyed chasing the mag-lev—if not the brief duel on the roof of the train car.

Tyranus had warned him about Mace Windu's prowess with a blade, and now he understood. His literal "misstep" had shamed him, and he was grateful that the two MagnaGuards that had fought at his side had not survived to bear witness to it. Had he not managed at the last instant to grab hold of the mag-lev rail and be retrieved by the borrowed gunship, all the efforts the Banking Clan had undertaken to have him rebuilt would have been for nothing.

But as it happened he was now about to give the Separatists more than their credits' worth. Perhaps a means to proclaim themselves victors of the war.

Grievous and five remaining droids completed their march to the bunker, deflecting the fire of three troopers guarding the entrance, then decapitating them. Hexagonal, the sturdy portal was impervious to blaster bolts, radiation, or electromagnetic pulse. Grievous was well aware that his lightsabers were capable of burning through the door. While doing so would have heightened the drama of his entry, he did the next best thing.

He used the code Tyranus had provided.

"Under no circumstances are you to harm the Chancellor," he exhorted his elite, while layers of the thick hatch were retracting.

The astonishment registered by Palpatine and his quartet of Jedi Knights assured Grievous that he could not have made a more dramatic entry. A large desk dominated the circular room, and banks of communications consoles formed the circumference. Centered in the curved wall opposite the entrance was a second door. Posing for effect in the polygonal opening, Grievous granted his opponents a moment to activate their lightsabers, force pikes, and other weapons. Also for effect, he deflected the initial flurry of blaster bolts with his clawed hands, before drawing two of his lightsabers.

His brazenness summoned the Jedi to him in a flash, but he knew in the first moments of contest that he had nothing to worry about. Compared to Mace Windu, the four were mere novices, whose lightsaber techniques were some of the earliest Grievous had mastered.

Behind him rushed his elite droids, with a single purpose in mind: to tear into the guards and soldiers arrayed in a defensive semicircle in front of Palpatine. Tall, elegant looking, dramatic in their red robes and face-masked cowls, the Supreme Chancellor's protectors were well trained and fought with passion. Their fists and feet were fast and powerful, and their force pikes sliced and jabbed through the near-impervious armor of the droids. But they were no real match for fearless war machines, programmed to kill by any means possible. Perhaps if Palpatine had been intelligent enough to have surrounded himself with *real* Jedi—Jedi of the caliber of Windu and the tentacle-headed Kit Fisto—the engagement might have gone differently.

Fencing with his four adversaries—for that's all the fight amounted to—Grievous saw six of the soldiers and three of the Red Guards jolted to spasming deaths by the MagnaGuards' double-tipped scepters. One of his elite had gone down, as well, but even though blinded and savagely slashed by the guards' staffs, the droid was continuing to fight. And those elite still on their feet had altered their combat stances and offensive moves to adapt to the guards' defensive strategies.

Grievous enjoyed going against so many Jedi simultaneously. If time wasn't of the essence, he might have protracted the fight. Feinting with the blade in his right hand, he removed the head of one Jedi with the blade in his left. Distracted when his right foot inadvertently booted the rolling head of his comrade, the Ithorian dropped his guard momentarily, and received as penalty a thrust to the heart that dropped him to his knees before he pitched forward.

Stepping back to absorb what had happened, the two remaining Jedi came at Grievous in concert, twirling and leaping about as if putting on some sort of crowd-pleasing martial arts demonstration. For practice, Grievous called two more blades from his belt, grasping them in his feet even as the antigrav repulsors built into his legs were lifting him from the floor, making him every bit as agile as the Force did the Jedi.

With his four blades to the Jedi's two, the duel had come full circle.

Whirling, he severed the blade hand of the Talz, then his opposing foot, then took his life, as well. Mists of blood formed in the air, swirled about by the ventilators.

The fourth he intimidated into retreat by wheeling all four blades, transforming himself into a veritable chopping machine. Fear blossomed in the Twi'lek Jedi's dark eyes as she backed away. He had her on the run, poor thing. But he awarded her some measure of dignity by allowing her to land glancing blows on his forearms and shoulders. The burns did little more than add a new odor to the room. Emboldened, she pressed her attack, but was fast exhausting herself from the effort of trying to amputate one of his limbs—to *hurt* him in some fashion.

And all for what? Grievous asked himself. The timid old man backed to the bunker's rear wall? The would-be champion of democracy, who had loosed his clone army against the merchants and builders and traders who opposed his rule—his *Republic*?

Best to put the Jedi out of her misery, Grievous thought. Which he did with a single blade to the heart—for it would have been cruel to do otherwise.

Elsewhere his three surviving elites were doing well against five Red Guards. With time counting down, he waded into the thick of the action. Sensing him, one guard feinted a rotation to the left, then pivoted to the right with his force pike raised at face level. A move Grievous could appreciate, although he was no longer in the space through which the weapon sliced. Using two blades, he nipped the guard's cowled head from his torso. The next he speared from behind in both kidneys. Opening the backs of another's thighs, he moved on, disemboweling the fourth.

The last guard was already dead by the time he reached him.

With a gesture, Grievous instructed his elite to secure the bunker's hexagonal door. Then, deactivating his lightsabers, he turned to Palpatine.

"Now, Chancellor," he announced, "you're coming with us."

Palpatine neither cowered nor protested. He merely said: "You will be a true loss to the forces you represent."

The remark took Grievous by surprise. Was this praise?

"Four Jedi Knights, all these soldiers and guards," Palpatine went on, gesturing broadly. "Why not wait until Shaak Ti and Stass Allie arrive." He cocked his head to one side. "I think I hear them coming. They are *Masters*, after all."

Grievous didn't respond immediately. Was Palpatine trying to trick him? "I might at any other time," he said finally. "But a ship awaits us that will take you from Coruscant—and from your cherished Republic, as well."

Palpatine mocked him with a sneer. "Do you actually believe that this plan will succeed?"

Grievous returned the look. "You're more defiant than I was led to believe, Chancellor. But, yes, the plan will succeed—and to your deficit. I would gladly kill you now but for my orders."

"So you take orders," Palpatine said, moving with deliberate lethargy. "Which of us, then, is the lesser?" Before Grievous could reply, he added: "My death won't end this war, General."

Grievous had wondered about that. Understandably, Lord Sidious had his plan, but did he actually believe that Palpatine's death would prompt the Jedi to lay down their lightsabers? Thrown into turmoil by the Chancellor's death, could the Senate *order* the Jedi to stand down? After years of warfare, would the Republic suddenly capitulate?

The sound of rapid footfalls roused him, and he gestured to the bunker's rear door. "Move," he told Palpatine.

The MagnaGuards stepped forward to make certain that Palpatine obeyed.

Grievous hurried to the bunker's communication console. The stud switch and control pad for the emergency beacon were precisely where Tyranus said they would be. After entering the code Tyranus had provided, Grievous pressed his alloy hand to the switch.

Palpatine watched him from the doorway. "That will call many Jedi down on you, General—some of whom you may regret having summoned."

Grievous glared at him. "Only if they fail to challenge me."

Word of the firefight on the landing platform reached Mace and Kit in the gunship while they were returning to Sah'c. It hadn't taken long to piece together what had happened: the Separatists had managed to hijack a Republic gunship and infiltrate the bunker complex shield by timing their arrival to coincide with that of the ship carrying Palpatine, Shaak Ti, and the others. An ARC commander verified that the hijacked gunship had been piloted by droids, but the same ARC would neither confirm nor deny that Grievous had been aboard the destroyed ship.

That, alone, was cause for concern.

Mace and Kit thought they knew what had occurred, and hoped they were wrong.

In the white glare of spotlights, the gunship that had been brought down by RPGs was a flaming hulk, dangling from the edge of the landing pad. Even less remained of the gunship that had delivered Palpatine to the complex. Fatalities of the surprise attack—one in a series of terrible surprises now—had been removed from the scene, but the pad boasted a company of reinforcements, as well as two AT-STs that had been air-dropped by wide-winged LAAT carriers.

This time Mace and Kit didn't wait for the gunship to touch down. Jumping from five meters up, they raced across the brightly illuminated landing platform and directly into the access tunnel. Steps into the tunnel, their worst fears were realized when they saw three troopers hauling away a MagnaGuard, holed by more blaster bolts than would have been needed to demolish a police skimmer.

The hijacked gunship had rescued Grievous after his fall from the mag-lev, Mace told himself. But had the fall been deliberate—part of an increasingly elaborate ruse—or had Grievous originally planned to abduct Palpatine from the train?

Either way, how had the cyborg general known how many of his forces to commit to such a daring plan?

Unless, of course, he had received prior intelligence on the number of Red Guards in Palpatine's detail, and the number of troopers and other combatants stationed in the bunker complex.

Every meter of the tunnel presented Mace and Kit with fresh evidence of the ferocious fight that had taken place, in the form of slaughtered commandos and others. Without limbs, beheaded, shocked to death by EMP weapons . . .

Mace stopped counting after he reached forty.

The heavy, hexagonal entrance that was the terminus of the bloodstained tunnel was open. If the fight leading to the door had been fierce, the one inside the ravished bunker had been savage. Stass Allie, her face and hands blistered and her robes singed, was kneeling by the bodies of the four Jedi Knights with whom Mace had spoken briefly during the mag-lev evacuation. Only Grievous could be held accountable for what had been done to them. The same was true for those Red Guards whose corpses had been burned open by lightsaber.

Grievous had taken the blades with which the Jedi had fought.

Here, too, were the shells of two more MagnaGuards.

But Palpatine was missing.

"Sir, the Supreme Chancellor was gone by the time we arrived," a commando explained. "His captors exited the complex by way of the south tunnels."

Mace and Kit glanced at the door that led to those tunnels, then turned to Shaak Ti, who was standing by the bunker's holoprojector table as if lost. When Mace hurried over to her, she practically collapsed in his arms.

"I fought Grievous on Hypori," she said weakly. "I knew what he was capable of. But this . . . And taking Palpatine . . ."

Mace supported her. "There will be no negotiations. The Supreme Chancellor won't allow it."

"The Senate may not see it that way, Mace." Shaak Ti composed herself and gazed around. "Grievous had help. Help from someone close to the top."

Kit nodded. "We'll find out who. But our first priority is to rescue the Supreme Chancellor."

Mace looked at the commando. "How did they leave the complex?"

"I can show you," Shaak Ti said. Turning, she activated a security recording that had captured Grievous and several of his humanoid guards dragging Palpatine to the south landing pad, butchering the handful of troopers posted there, scrambling into a waiting tri-winged shuttle, lifting off into sunset clouds . . .

"How were they allowed through the shield?" Mace asked the commando.

"Same way they entered the bunker, General."

Mace hadn't even thought to ask. Had assumed they had burned their way in—

"They had the entry codes to the bunker, sir, as well as codes issued earlier today that permitted them to clear the screen."

Mace and Kit glanced at each other in angry bewilderment.

"What is the shuttle's location now?" Kit asked.

The commando conjured a 3-D image from the holo-projector.

"Sector I-Thirty-Three, sir. Outbound autonavigation trunk P-seventeen. Gunships are in pursuit."

Mace's eyes widened in alert. "Do your gunners know that the Supreme Chancellor is aboard? Do they realize they can't fire on the shuttle?"

"They have orders to disable if possible, sir. The shuttle is shielded and well armored, in any case."

"Who else knows of the abduction?" Kit thought to ask. "Has this been released or leaked to the media?"

"Yes, sir. Moments ago."

"On whose orders?" Mace fumed.

"The Supreme Chancellor's top advisers."

Shaak Ti forced an exhale. "All of Coruscant will panic."

Mace squared his shoulders. "Commander, scramble every available starfighter. That ship cannot be allowed to reach the Separatist fleet."

Dooku hadn't fled alone. The only indications of Tythe's invasion were the hulking remains of Separatist and Republic warships, tumbling indolently in starlight.

"We were all beginning to wonder if you were going to return," a human crew chief said by way of welcoming Obi-Wan and Anakin back to the assault cruiser's ventral landing bay.

Obi-Wan descended the ladder affixed to the starfighter's cockpit. "When did the Separatists jump?"

"Less than an hour, local. Guess they had enough of the pounding we were giving them."

Leaping to the deck, Anakin laughed nastily. "Believe whatever you want."

The crew chief furrowed his brow in uncertainty.

"Do we know where they're headed?" Obi-Wan asked quickly.

The crew chief turned to him. "Most of the capital ships jumped Rimward. A few appear to be headed for the Nelvaan system—thirteen parsecs from here."

"What are our orders?"

"We're still waiting to find out. The fact is, we haven't received any communications from Coruscant since the start of the battle."

Anakin took a sudden interest in the crew chief's remarks.

"Could be local interference," Obi-Wan said.

The crew chief looked dubious. "Several other battle groups reported that they have been unable to communicate with Coruscant."

Anakin shot Obi-Wan an embittered look and began to storm away.

"Anakin," Obi-Wan said, following in his footsteps.

Anakin whirled on him. "We were wrong to come here, Master. *I* was wrong to come here. It was all a feint, and we fell for it. We're being kept away from Coruscant. I can feel it."

Obi-Wan folded his arms across his chest. "You wouldn't be saying that if we'd captured Dooku."

"But we didn't, Master. That's what counts. And now no communication with Coruscant? You don't even see it, do you?"

Obi-Wan regarded him carefully. "See what, Anakin?"

Anakin started to speak, then cut himself off and began again. "You should keep me fighting. You shouldn't give me time to think."

Obi-Wan rested his hands on Anakin's shoulders. "Calm yourself."

Anakin shrugged him off, a new fire in his eyes. "You're my best friend. Tell me what I should do. Forget for a moment that you're wearing the robes of a Jedi and tell me what I should do!"

Stung by the gravity in Anakin's voice, Obi-Wan fell silent for a moment, then said: "The Force is our ally, Anakin. When we're mindful of the Force, our actions are in accord with the will of the Force. Tythe wasn't a wrong choice. It's simply that we're ignorant of its import in the greater scheme."

Anakin lowered his head in sadness. "You're right, Master.

My mind isn't as fast as my lightsaber." He stared at his artificial limb. "My heart isn't as impervious to pain as my right hand."

Obi-Wan felt as if someone had knotted his insides. He had failed his apprentice and closest friend. Anakin was suffering, and the only balm he offered were Jedi *platitudes.* His body heaved a stuttering breath. He had his mouth open to speak when the crew chief interrupted.

"General Skywalker, something has your astromech very flustered."

Obi-Wan and Anakin swung to Anakin's starfighter.

"Artoo?" Anakin said in a concerned tone.

The astromech tooted, shrilled, chittered.

"Does he understand droid?" the crew chief asked Obi-Wan as Anakin hurried past him.

"*That* droid," Obi-Wan said.

Anakin began to scale the cockpit ladder. "What is it, Artoo? What's wrong?"

The droid whistled and zithered.

Throwing himself into open cockpit, Anakin toggled switches. Obi-Wan had just reached the base of the ladder when he heard Palpatine's voice issuing through the cockpit annunciators.

"Anakin, if you are receiving this message, then I have urgent need of your help . . ."

The crew chief's comlink toned.

Obi-Wan glanced from the crew chief to Anakin and back again.

"What is it?" he asked in a rush.

"Tight-beam comm from Coruscant," the crew said. He listened for another moment, then added, in obvious disbelief: "Sir, the Separatists have invaded!"

Obi-Wan gaped at him.

Above him, Anakin lifted his face to the high ceiling and let out a sustained snarl. Glaring down at Obi-Wan, he said: "Why does fate target the people who are most important to me?"

"I—"

"Crew chief!" Anakin cut him off. "Refuel and rearm our starfighters at once!"

Grievous had a good lead on them.

Seated in the copilot's seat of a Republic cruiser, Mace accepted that the shuttle couldn't be intercepted before it left Coruscant's envelope. And perhaps not before it was in the protective embrace of the Separatist fleet.

Regardless, the hot scrambled starfighters were giving all they had to the chase.

Having access to high-clearance codes, Grievous could have plotted a proprietary launch vector for the shuttle. But by doing so he would have put the shuttle at risk of arrest by disabling fire or tractor beam. Instead, he had elected to avail himself of the protection afforded by starship traffic in one of the outbound autonavigation trunks.

Police, governmental, and emergency vessels were permitted to use free-travel lanes that paralleled the trunks, but even with that advantage, Mace and Kit's cruiser was still several kilometers behind the rising shuttle. Below, vast areas of darkness stained the usual circuit board perfection of night-side Coruscant.

That the vessels surrounding it were compelled by orbital tractor beam arrays to adhere to standard launch velocities benefited the shuttle. The tri-wing benefited even more from the fact that Grievous was almost as adept at handling a ship as he was a lightsaber. Each time flights of starfighters attempted to hem him in, Grievous would lead them on spiraling chases through the thick traffic, inserting the shuttle between ships, initiating collisions, resorting to firing the shuttle's meager weapons when necessary.

Recalled from the battle outside the well, Agen Kolar, Saesee Tiin, and Pablo-Jill had come closest to incapacitating the shuttle, but, twice now, Grievous had managed to evade them by bringing the shuttle's laser cannons to bear on cargo pods and strewing local space with debris. Even when the three Jedi had gotten near enough to launch disabling runs, the shuttle's shielding and armor had absorbed the bursts.

With the pursuit closing rapidly on the rim of the gravity well, the Jedi pilots were executing maneuvers they had been reluctant to employ deeper in the atmosphere. Weaving among the vessels, the starfighters fired on the shuttle at every opportunity, scorching its wings and tail, as the shield generator became overtaxed. Grievous was unable to match them maneuver for maneuver, but his response to the attacks was to target any innocent in his sights, ultimately forcing the Jedi to fall back once again.

Punching through Coruscant's sheath of gases, the autonavigation trunk branched like the crown of a shade tree. Thrusters flared as endangered ships slued and rolled onto vectors meant to distance them from the fray. With local space crosshatched with plasma trails and brilliant with explosions, escape was scarcely an option. Even so, many ships were attempting to follow the curve of the gravity well toward Coruscant's bright side, while others veered for the safety of Coruscant's moons, and still others sped for the nearest jump points.

Except for the shuttle, which accelerated straight for Grievous's flagship.

Calling full power from the cruiser, Kit Fisto joined the three

Jedi starfighters in a flat-out race for the shuttle. By then, too, several Republic frigates and corvettes were diverting from the principal battle to assist in the interception.

Despite his earlier misgivings, Mace thought for a moment that they might succeed.

Then he watched in disquiet as five hundred droid fighters—gushing from the great curving arms of a Trade Federation battleship—swarmed forward to safeguard the shuttle in its flight to freedom.

Three among a crowd several hundred strong standing in the Nicandra Plaza, Padmé, Bail, and Mon Mothma watched the late-breaking news report on the Embassy Mall's HoloNet monitor. When word of Supreme Chancellor Palpatine's capture had first been rumored, then verified, all anyone in the crowd could ask was, *How, in three short years, had it come to this?*

The armies of chaos were parked in stationary orbit above Coruscant, and the beloved leader of the Galactic Republic seized. For so many, what had been an abstraction was stark reality, playing out overhead, for all of Coruscant and half the galaxy to watch.

Now that time had passed, however, Padmé had begun to notice a change in the crowd. Though a climactic battle was raging as near as the night sky's frightening fireworks, most Coruscanti preferred to keep their gaze fixed on the real-time images of battle. That way, it was almost like watching an exciting HoloNet drama.

Would the starfighters be able to overtake the shuttle in which Palpatine was being held captive by a cyborg monster? Might the shuttle or the flagship that was its destination explode? What would become of the Republic should the Supreme Chancellor be killed, or Coruscant occupied by ten of thousands of battle droids? Would the Jedi and their clone army fly to the rescue?

When Padmé could take no more of the 3-D images or the remarks of the audience, she wended her way to the perimeter of the crowd to take hold of a handrail at the plaza's edge, and to lift her eyes to the strobing sky.

Anakin, she said to herself, as if she could reach him with a thought.

Anakin.

Tears coursed down her cheeks, and she wiped them away with the back of her hand. Her sadness was personal now, not for Palpatine, though his abduction hollowed her. She wept for a future she and Anakin might have had. For the family they might have been. More than ever she wished that she hadn't been a featured player in the events that had shaped the war, but merely one of the crowd.

Come home to me before it's too late.

Her gaze lowered, she caught sight of C-3PO, parting company with a silver protocol droid that disappeared into the crowd.

"What was that about, Threepio?" she asked as he approached.

"A most curious encounter, Mistress," C-3PO said. "I think that shiny droid fancies himself something of a seer."

Padmé looked at him askance. "In what way, Threepio?"

"In essence, he told me to *flee* while it was still possible. He said that dark times are coming, and that the line that separates good and bad will become blurred. That what seems good now will prove evil; and that what seems evil, will prove good."

Sensing there was more, Padmé waited.

C-3PO's photoreceptors locked on Padmé. "He said further that I should accept a memory wipe if it is ever offered to me, because the only alternative will be to live in fear and confusion for the rest of my days."

Slapped by fire, the tri-winged shuttle fairly crawled toward the docking bay of the *Invisible Hand*. Grievous held to his treacherous course, even while contingency plans formed in his mind. Wings of Trade Federation droid fighters had burned a path for the shuttle through areas of intense combat, but the vulnerable little ship was not yet in the clear. Many of Grievous's impassioned pursuers were so busy defending themselves that they no longer represented a threat, but three starfighters had managed to stay with the shuttle, and were continuing to harry it with surgical fire.

The spiraling chase up the gravity well and the twisting transit to the cruiser had left the ship battered. The sublight engine was whining in protest, the ray shield dangerously diminished, the minimal weapons depleted. Uncertain as to where Grievous had stashed Palpatine, the pilots of the trio of starfighters were being careful with their bolts, but every hit was inflicting further damage to the stabilizers and shield generator. Plasma fire from the *Invisible Hand*'s point-defense weapons had only prompted them to close ranks with the shuttle, using it in the same way Grievous was using Palpatine—as a kind of screen.

The mechanical voice of a control droid aboard the cruiser issued from the shuttle's cockpit speakers. *"General, do you wish us to deploy tri-fighters against the starfighters?"*

"Negative," Grievous said. "Save them for when we actually need them. Continue cannon fire."

"General, our computations suggest that continued close-range fire could subject the shuttle to fratricide."

Grievous didn't doubt it. As it was, the hull was blistering with each salvo from the cruiser.

"Ready the forward tractor beam," he said after a moment. "Fire a disabling burst at all four of us. Then utilize the beam to ensnare what remains of the shuttle and draw it into the docking bay—even if that means dragging a starfighter in, as well. Have battle droids standing by."

"Yes, General."

Grievous swiveled his seat toward Palpatine, who was strapped into an acceleration couch between two MagnaGuards. The Supreme Chancellor had been unexpectedly compliant since leaving the bunker, at times brazen enough to take Grievous to task for his less-than-perfect piloting skills.

You fool, you'll get us both killed! Palpatine had barked at him repeatedly.

What did Palpatine think was going to become of him after they reached the *Invisible Hand*? Grievous had asked himself. Was he under the delusion that Lords Sidious and Tyranus would simply hold him for ransom? Did it somehow escape him that he wasn't likely to see Coruscant again?

Once more, Grievous questioned the needless complexity of the Sith Lords' plan. Why not kill Palpatine sooner rather than later? If he hadn't been under orders . . .

You take orders? Palpatine had mocked him.

Which of them was the lesser, indeed?

"Strap in, Chancellor," Grievous said now. "This could get rough."

Palpatine sneered. "With you at the controls, I'm certain it will."

No sooner did Grievous swing back to the viewport than gouts of fire spewed from the *Invisible Hand*'s forward cannons. Two of the starfighter pilots must have sensed something coming, because they all but glued themselves to the shuttle. Rocked by the burst, the shuttle lost portions of itself to space, and all systems shut down. One of the starfighters was blown away, but the other two had lost little more than their wings.

The shuttle reeled as the tractor beam took hold of it.

With it came the pair of starfighters.

Grievous considered ordering that the docking bay be purged of atmosphere. Somewhere aboard the shuttle there would be extravehicular gear Palpatine could don. But with life support failing, Palpatine was already in enough trouble.

Grievous would just have to deal with the starfighter pilots when the ships were released from the beam.

The three were scarcely through the docking bay's containment field when explosive charges flung the canopies from the starfighters and two Jedi Knights leapt to the deck, lightsabers ablaze, deflecting blaster bolts from battle droids as they raced for the shuttle. Before the shuttle had even settled to the deck, one of the Jedi had plunged his glowing blue blade straight through the starboard hatch.

Hurrying aft through thickening smoke, Grievous caught sight of Palpatine's expression of derision.

"Surprise, surprise, General."

Grievous halted just long enough to say: "We'll see who's surprised."

He saw the lightsaber blade retract. By the time he had shouldered through the hatch onto the landing platform the Jedi had moved to either side. Even while continuing to parry blaster bolts, they surged at him, engaging the two lightsabers he drew from his cloak.

The duel raged through the hold. Battle droids lowered their weapons for fear of hitting Grievous. These Jedi were more proficient than the ones he had fought in the bunker, but not skilled enough to challenge him. The four blades seared through the recycled air, washing the burnished bulkheads with harsh light and outsized shadows.

Flanking him, the Jedi rushed in.

Grievous waited until the last instant to command his legs to raise him up several centimeters. Then he extended his lightsabers straight out from his sides, angled slightly downward. Slipping past the flashing strikes of his opponents, Grievous's blades pierced the chests of both. They fell away from him, faces contorted in surprise, of the sort only sudden death could bring.

Several battle droids hastened forward, almost prancing in eagerness.

"Jettison the bodies," Grievous instructed. "Choose a place where the Republic can have a good look at them."

Diminutive between two MagnaGuards, Palpatine was waiting at the foot of the shuttle boarding ramp.

"Take him," Grievous said.

Lifting Palpatine by his armpits, the combat droids followed Grievous through the cruiser, and at last through an oval of opalescent portal into a large cabin space containing a situation table surrounded by chairs. Grievous ordered the guards to set the Supreme Chancellor down in a swivel chair at the head of the table and to shackle his hands.

"Welcome to the general's quarters," he said while he did input at a console built into the table. Shortly the bulkhead behind the swivel chair became a hologrammic display, showing the battle of Coruscant. The flick of a final switch summoned a stalked, eyeball-shaped holocam from the tabletop.

"You're about to make an unscheduled appearance on the HoloNet, Chancellor," Grievous said. "I apologize for not providing a mirror, hairbrush, and cosmetics, so that you might at least camouflage some of your fear."

Palpatine's voice was sinister when he spoke. "You can display me, but I won't speak."

Grievous nodded at what seemed an obvious statement. "I'll display you, but you won't speak. Is that understood?"

"You will do all the talking."

"That's correct. I will do all the talking."

"Very good."

For no apparent reason, Grievous felt uncertain. "Lord Tyranus will soon be here to take charge of you."

Palpatine smiled without showing his teeth. "Then I am assured of being greatly entertained."

From aboard his cruiser, General Grievous addressed a captive audience of trillions of beings. His frightening visage dominating every frequency of the HoloNet, he delivered a message of gloom and doom, forecasting the end of Palpatine's reign, the long-delinquent downfall of the corrupt Republic, a bright new future for all the worlds and all the species that had been enslaved to it . . .

Crushed in among Nicandra Plaza's suddenly silent multitude, Bail touched Mon Mothma's arm in a gesture that promised his imminent return, and began to writhe his way to the edge of the crowd. Gazing around, he spied Padmé standing with C-3PO, arms cradled against her, elbows in the palms of her hands, her face raised to the light-splintered sky.

Hastening to her, he called her name, and she turned from the handrail into his comforting embrace, her tears wetting the front of his tunic.

"Padmé, listen to me," he said, stroking her hair. "The Separatists have nothing to gain by killing Palpatine. He'll be all right."

"What if you're wrong, Bail? What if they do kill him, and power falls into the hands of Mas Amedda and the rest of that gang? That doesn't worry you? What if Alderaan is next on Grievous's list of worlds to attack?"

"Of course it worries me. I fear for Alderaan. But I have faith that won't happen. This attack will put an end to the Outer Rim sieges. The Jedi will be back where they belong, here in the Core. And as for Mas Amedda, he won't last a week. There are thousands of Senators who think as we do, Padmé. We'll rally them into a force to be reckoned with. We'll put the Republic back on course, even if we have to fight tooth and nail to overcome anyone who opposes us." He put his hand under her chin to lift her face toward his. "We'll get through this, no matter what."

She sniffled; smiled lightly. "If I could keep my concerns focused only on the future of the Republic . . ."

Bail held her gaze, and nodded in understanding. "Padmé, if it's any comfort to you, please know that my wife and I would do anything to protect you and those close to you."

"Thank you, Bail," she said. "With all my heart, thank you."

On Utapau, an Outer Rim world of vast sinkholes and lizard mounts, Viceroy Nute Gunray watched a grainy HoloNet image of General Grievous lower the boom on Coruscant.

Had he been wrong to underestimate the cyborg? Might this war actually end with the Republic vanquished? It was almost too much to contemplate: unrestricted trade from Core to Outer Rim, undreamed of wealth, unlimited *possessions* . . .

Gunray glanced at Shu Mai, Passel Argente, San Hill, and the rest, a backslapping fellowship all of a sudden. Smiling broadly—for the first time in several years—he joined them in celebration.

In his quarters in the Temple, Yoda watched a HoloNet feed that showed the bodies of two Jedi drifting in space, close to the flagship of the Separatist fleet. The corners of his mouth pulled down in sadness, he turned to the comlink.

"See them, I do."

Mace's voice rumbled from the speaker. *"If we can ever break through this fighter screen, we'll storm the cruiser."*

"Kill the Supreme Chancellor, Grievous will."

"I don't think so. He's had plenty of chances already."

"Wait, then, to hear the Separatists' demands, we should."

"The Senate will give away Coruscant to effect Palpatine's release."

"Worse the situation will be if the Supreme Chancellor dies. Fall, the Republic will."

Mace fell silent for a moment. Yoda saw him in the cockpit of the cruiser he and Kit had piloted off Coruscant. *"What should we do?"*

"To the Force, look for guidance. Accept what fate has placed before us. For now, prevent Grievous's fleet from escaping to hyperspace, you must. Recalled, many Jedi and others have been. *Turn,* the battle will, when they arrive."

"Master Yoda, we were close to capturing Sidious. I could feel it."

"Knew this, Sidious did. Hiding, he is."

No longer on Coruscant, Yoda thought.

"We'll pin Grievous here, like the vermin he is."

Mace severed the transmission, and Yoda tottered to the windows. Western Coruscant was engulfed by darkness; the sky above, splintered by rabid light. Calling his lightsaber to his hand, he ignited the blade and waved it through the air.

Perilous the future will be. A cause for grave concern.

But the battle in local space wasn't the end.

Beginning, the final act was!

Dooku had ordered the droid pilot of the sloop to revert from hyperspace for a brief time at the planet Nelvaan. Should any ships among the Republic battle group at Tythe plot his escape course, it would appear that Nelvaan was his destination. The sloop's Geonosian technology would mask the fact that he had jumped almost immediately to Coruscant to join Grievous, and to play out the final act of the drama Sidious had composed.

The abduction of Palpatine had not only abbreviated the search for him, but also allowed Sidious to escape Coruscant undetected. But those events had been minor acts. Sidious would never have allowed the Jedi to expose him. And Palpatine was hardly the prize he appeared to be.

The greater prize, Sidious had told Dooku during their most recent communication, was Anakin Skywalker.

"Long have you watched him," Dooku had said, repeating words Sidious himself had spoken.

Longer than you know, Lord Tyranus. Longer than you know. And the time has come to test him again.

"His skills, my lord?"

The depth of his anger. His willingness to go beyond the Force,

as the Jedi know it, and to call on the power of the dark side. Gen-
eral Grievous will activate a special beacon that will call Skywalker
and Kenobi back to Coruscant, and onto the stage we will set for
them."

But not to capture them.

"You will duel them," Sidious had said. *"Kill Kenobi. His only*
purpose is to die and, in so doing, ignite young Skywalker to tap the
depths of his fear and rage. Should you defeat Skywalker easily, then
we will know that he is not prepared to serve us. Perhaps he never
will be prepared. Should he by some fluke best you, however, I will
control the outcome to spare you any unnecessary embarrassment,
and we will have gained a powerful ally. But above all you must
make the contest appear real, Lord Tyranus."

"I will treat it as if it were my crowning achievement,"
Dooku had promised.

Hyperspace awaited.

"To Coruscant," he told FA-4 from his comfortable chair in
the sloop's main hold.

And with that, the ship jumped.

The two starfighters sat side by side in the launching bay, only a few meters separating them, engines warming, droids in their sockets, cockpit canopies raised.

Neither pilot wore a helmet, so Anakin could hear Obi-Wan plainly when he shouted: "For all the jinks and jukes you've taken me through, there's no one else I'd rather fly with."

Anakin canted his head and smiled. "It's about time you admitted it. Can I take that to mean you'll follow my lead without question?"

"To the best of my ability," Obi-Wan said. "I may not always be able to remain at your wing, but I won't be far off, and I'll always have your back."

"When I call for help, you'll come speeding to the rescue."

"The day you call for help, I'll know that we're both in over our heads."

Anakin adopted a serious look. "Obi-Wan, you don't know how many times you've already rescued me."

Obi-Wan swallowed the lump that formed in his throat. "Then whatever lies ahead for us shouldn't be a problem."

Anakin laughed lightly. "Who'll restore peace to the galaxy if we don't?"

Obi-Wan returned a tight-lipped nod. "At least you said *we*."

They lowered the starfighters' canopies and engaged the re-pulsors, lifting off, rotating 180 degrees, and easing through the launching bay's transparent containment field.

Flying abreast, all but sharing a wing, they enabled their thrusters and banked away from the massive ship. Accelerating on columns of brilliant blue energy, sluing slightly to port, slightly sinister, they coupled with their hyperdrive rings and disappeared into the long night.

[TO BE CONCLUDED]

EPISODE III
REVENGE OF THE SITH

MATTHEW STOVER

BASED ON THE STORY AND SCREENPLAY BY
GEORGE LUCAS

the author respectfully dedicates this adaptation

To George Lucas

with gratitude for the dreams of a generation,
and of generations to come,
for twenty-eight years, and counting . . .

thank you, sir.

This story happened a long time ago in a galaxy far, far away. It is already over. Nothing can be done to change it.

It is a story of love and loss, brotherhood and betrayal, courage and sacrifice and the death of dreams. It is a story of the blurred line between our best and our worst.

It is the story of the end of an age.

A strange thing about stories—

Though this all happened so long ago and so far away that words cannot describe the time or the distance, it is also happening right now. Right here.

It is happening as you read these words.

This is how twenty-five millennia come to a close. Corruption and treachery have crushed a thousand years of peace. This is not just the end of a republic; night is falling on civilization itself.

This is the twilight of the Jedi.

The end starts now.

INTRODUCTION

THE AGE OF HEROES

The skies of Coruscant blaze with war.

The artificial daylight spread by the capital's orbital mirrors is sliced by intersecting flames of ion drives and punctuated by starburst explosions; contrails of debris raining into the atmosphere become tangled ribbons of cloud. The nightside sky is an infinite lattice of shining hairlines that interlock planetoids and track erratic spirals of glowing gnats. Beings watching from rooftops of Coruscant's endless cityscape can find it beautiful.

From the inside, it's different.

The gnats are drive-glows of starfighters. The shining hairlines are light-scatter from turbolaser bolts powerful enough to vaporize a small town. The planetoids are capital ships.

The battle from the inside is a storm of confusion and panic, of galvened particle beams flashing past your starfighter so close that your cockpit rings like a broken annunciator, of the boot-sole shock of concussion missiles that blast into your cruiser, killing beings you have trained with and eaten with and played and laughed and bickered with. From the inside, the battle is desperation and terror and the stomach-churning certainty that the whole galaxy is trying to kill you.

Across the remnants of the Republic, stunned beings watch in horror as the battle unfolds live on the HoloNet. Everyone knows the war has been going badly. Everyone knows that more Jedi are killed or captured every day, that the Grand Army of the Republic has been pushed out of system after system, but this—

A strike at the very heart of the Republic?

An *invasion* of *Coruscant itself*?

How can this *happen*?

It's a nightmare, and no one can wake up.

Live via HoloNet, beings watch the Separatist droid army flood the government district. The coverage is filled with images of overmatched clone troopers cut down by remorselessly powerful destroyer droids in the halls of the Galactic Senate itself.

A gasp of relief: the troopers seem to beat back the attack. There are hugs and even some quiet cheers in living rooms across the galaxy as the Separatist forces retreat to their landers and streak for orbit—

We won! beings tell each other. *We held them off!*

But then new reports trickle in—only rumors at first—that the attack wasn't an invasion at all. That the Separatists weren't trying to take the planet. That this was a lightning raid on the Senate itself.

The nightmare gets worse: the Supreme Chancellor is missing.

Palpatine of Naboo, the most admired man in the galaxy, whose unmatched political skills have held the Republic together. Whose personal integrity and courage prove that the Separatist propaganda of corruption in the Senate is nothing but lies. Whose charismatic leadership gives the whole Republic the will to fight on.

Palpatine is more than respected. He is loved.

Even the rumor of his disappearance strikes a dagger to the heart of every friend of the Republic. Every one of them knows it in her heart, in his gut, in its very bones—

Without Palpatine, the Republic will fall.

And now confirmation comes through, and the news is worse than anyone could have imagined. Supreme Chancellor Palpatine has been captured by the Separatists—and not just the Separatists.

He's in the hands of General Grievous.

Grievous is not like other leaders of the Separatists. Nute Gunray is treacherous and venal, but he's Neimoidian: venality and treachery are expected, and in the Chancellor of the Trade Federation they're even virtues. Poggle the Lesser is Archduke of the weapon masters of Geonosis, where the war began: he is analytical and pitiless, but also pragmatic. Reasonable. The political heart of the Separatist Confederacy, Count Dooku, is known for his integrity, his principled stand against what he sees as corruption in the Senate. Though they believe he's wrong, many respect him for the courage of his mistaken convictions.

These are hard beings. Dangerous beings. Ruthless and aggressive.

General Grievous, though—

Grievous is a *monster.*

The Separatist Supreme Commander is an abomination of nature, a fusion of flesh and droid—and his droid parts have more compassion than what remains of his alien flesh. This half-living creature is a slaughterer of billions. Whole planets have burned at his command. He is the evil genius of the Confederacy. The architect of their victories.

The author of their atrocities.

And his durasteel grip has closed upon Palpatine. He confirms the capture personally in a wideband transmission from his command cruiser in the midst of the orbital battle. Beings across the galaxy watch, and shudder, and pray that they might wake up from this awful dream.

Because they know that what they're watching, live on the HoloNet, is the death of the Republic.

Many among these beings break into tears; many more reach out to comfort their husbands or wives, their crèche-mates or kin-triads, and their younglings of all descriptions, from children to cubs to spawn-fry.

But here is a strange thing: few of the younglings *need* comfort. It is instead the younglings who offer comfort to their elders. Across the Republic—in words or pheromones, in magnetic pulses, tentacle-braids, or mental telepathy—the message from the younglings is the same: *Don't worry. It'll be all right.*

Anakin and Obi-Wan will be there any minute.

They say this as though these names can conjure miracles.

Anakin and Obi-Wan. Kenobi and Skywalker. From the beginning of the Clone Wars, the phrase *Kenobi and Skywalker* has become a single word. They are everywhere. HoloNet features of their operations against the Separatist enemy have made them the most famous Jedi in the galaxy.

Younglings across the galaxy know their names, know everything about them, follow their exploits as though they are sports heroes instead of warriors in a desperate battle to save civilization. Even grown-ups are not immune; it's not uncommon for an exasperated parent to ask, when faced with offspring who have just tried to pull off one of the spectacularly dangerous bits of foolishness that are the stock-in-trade of high-spirited younglings everywhere, *So which were you supposed to be, Kenobi or Skywalker?*

Kenobi would rather talk than fight, but when there is fighting to be done, few can match him. Skywalker is the master of audacity; his intensity, boldness, and sheer jaw-dropping luck are the perfect complement to Kenobi's deliberate, balanced steadiness. Together, they are a Jedi hammer that has crushed Separatist infestations on scores of worlds.

All the younglings watching the battle in Coruscant's sky know it: when Anakin and Obi-Wan get there, those dirty Seppers are going to wish they'd stayed in bed today.

The adults know better, of course. That's part of what being a grown-up is: understanding that heroes are created by the HoloNet, and that the real-life Kenobi and Skywalker are only human beings, after all.

Even if they really are everything the legends say they are, who's to say they'll show up in time? Who knows where they are right now? They might be trapped on some Separatist backwater. They might be captured, or wounded. Even dead.

Some of the adults even whisper to themselves, *They might have fallen.*

Because the stories are out there. Not on the HoloNet, of course—the HoloNet news is under the control of the Office of the Supreme Chancellor, and not even Palpatine's renowned candor would allow tales like these to be told—but people hear whispers. Whispers of names that the Jedi would like to pretend never existed.

Sora Bulq. Depa Billaba. Jedi who have fallen to the dark. Who have joined the Separatists, or worse: who have massacred civilians, or even murdered their comrades. The adults have a sickening suspicion that Jedi cannot be trusted. Not anymore. That even the greatest of them can suddenly just . . . snap.

The adults know that legendary heroes are merely legends, and not heroes at all.

These adults can take no comfort from their younglings. Palpatine is captured. Grievous will escape. The Republic will fall. No mere human beings can turn this tide. No mere human beings would even try. Not even Kenobi and Skywalker.

And so it is that these adults across the galaxy watch the HoloNet with ashes where their hearts should be.

Ashes because they can't see two prismatic bursts of realspace reversion, far out beyond the planet's gravity well; because they can't see a pair of starfighters crisply jettison hyperdrive rings and streak into the storm of Separatist vulture fighters with all guns blazing.

A pair of starfighters. Jedi starfighters. Only two.

Two is enough.

Two is enough because the adults are wrong, and their younglings are right.

Though this is the end of the age of heroes, it has saved its best for last.

PART ONE

VICTORY

The dark is generous.

Its first gift is concealment: our true faces lie in the dark beneath our skins, our true hearts remain shadowed deeper still. But the greatest concealment lies not in protecting our secret truths, but in hiding from us the truths of others.

The dark protects us from what we dare not know.

Its second gift is comforting illusion: the ease of gentle dreams in night's embrace, the beauty that imagination brings to what would repel in day's harsh light. But the greatest of its comforts is the illusion that the dark is temporary: that every night brings a new day. Because it is day that is temporary.

Day is the illusion.

Its third gift is the light itself: as days are defined by the nights that divide them, as stars are defined by the infinite black through which they wheel, the dark embraces the light, and brings it forth from the center of its own self.

With each victory of the light, it is the dark that wins.

ANAKIN AND OBI-WAN

Antifighter flak flashed on all sides. Even louder than the clatter of shrapnel and the snarl of his sublight drives, his cockpit hummed and rang with near hits from the turbolaser fire of the capital ships crowding space around him. Sometimes his whirling spinning dive through the cloud of battle skimmed bursts so closely that the energy-scatter would slam his starfighter hard enough to bounce his head off the supports of his pilot's chair.

Right now Obi-Wan Kenobi envied the clones: at least they had helmets.

"Arfour," he said on internal comm, "can't you do something with the inertials?"

The droid ganged into the socket on his starfighter's left wing whistled something that sounded suspiciously like a human apology. Obi-Wan's frown deepened. R4-P17 had been spending too much time with Anakin's eccentric astromech; it was picking up R2-D2's bad habits.

New bursts of flak bracketed his path. He reached into the Force, feeling for a safe channel through the swarms of shrapnel and sizzling nets of particle beams.

There wasn't one.

He locked a snarl behind his teeth, twisting his starfighter around another explosion that could have peeled its armor like an overripe Ithorian starfruit. He hated this part. *Hated* it.

Flying's for droids.

His cockpit speakers crackled. *"There isn't a droid made that can outfly you, Master."*

He could still be surprised by the new depth of that voice. The calm confidence. The maturity. It seemed that only last week Anakin had been a ten-year-old who wouldn't stop pestering him about Form I lightsaber combat.

"Sorry," he muttered, kicking into a dive that slipped a turbo-laser burst by no more than a meter. "Was that out loud?"

"Wouldn't matter if it wasn't. I know what you're thinking."

"Do you?" He looked up through the cockpit canopy to find his onetime Padawan flying inverted, mirroring him so closely that but for the transparisteel between them, they might have shaken hands. Obi-Wan smiled up at him. "Some new gift of the Force?"

"Not the Force, Master. Experience. That's what you're always thinking."

Obi-Wan kept hoping to hear some of Anakin's old cocky grin in his tone, but he never did. Not since Jabiim. Perhaps not since Geonosis.

The war had burned it out of him.

Obi-Wan still tried, now and again, to spark a real smile in his former Padawan. And Anakin still tried to answer.

They both still tried to pretend the war hadn't changed them.

"Ah." Obi-Wan took a hand from the starfighter's control yoke to direct his upside-down friend's attention forward. Dead ahead, a blue-white point of light splintered into four laser-straight trails of ion drives. "And what does experience tell you we should do about those incoming tri-fighters?"

"That we should break—right!"

Obi-Wan was already making that exact move as Anakin spoke. But they were inverted to each other: breaking right shot him one way while Anakin whipped the other. The tri-fighters' cannons ripped space between them, tracking faster than their starfighters could slip.

His onboard threat display chimed a warning: two of the droids had remote sensor locks on him. The others must have lit up his partner. "Anakin! Slip-jaws!"

"My thought exactly."

They blew past the tri-fighters, looping in evasive spirals. The droid ships wrenched themselves into pursuit maneuvers that would have killed any living pilot.

The slip-jaws maneuver was named for the scissorlike mandibles of the Kashyyyk slash-spider. Droids closing rapidly on their tails, cannonfire stitching space on all sides, the two Jedi pulled their ships through perfectly mirrored rolls that sent them streaking head-on for each other from opposite ends of a vast Republic cruiser.

For merely human pilots, this would be suicide. By the time you can see your partner's starfighter streaking toward you at a respectable fraction of lightspeed, it's already too late for your merely human reflexes to react.

But these particular pilots were far from merely human.

The Force nudged hands on control yokes and the Jedi starfighters twisted and flashed past each other belly-to-belly, close enough to scorch each other's paint. Tri-fighters were the Trade Federation's latest space-superiority droid. But even the electronic reflexes of the tri-fighters' droid brains were too slow for this: one of his pursuers met one of Anakin's head-on. Both vanished in a blossom of flame.

The shock wave of debris and expanding gas rocked Obi-Wan; he fought the control yoke, barely keeping his starfighter out of a tumble that would have smeared him across the cruiser's ventral hull. Before he could straighten out, his threat display chimed again.

"Oh, marvelous," he muttered under his breath. Anakin's surviving pursuer had switched targets. "Why is it always me?"

"Perfect." Through the cockpit speakers, Anakin's voice carried grim satisfaction. *"Both of them are on your tail."*

"Perfect is *not* the word I'd use." Obi-Wan twisted his yoke, juking madly as space around him flared scarlet. "We have to split them up!"

"Break left." Anakin sounded calm as a stone. *"The turbolaser tower off your port bow: thread its guns. I'll take things from there."*

"Easy for you to say." Obi-Wan whipped sideways along the cruiser's superstructure. Fire from the pursuing tri-fighters blasted burning chunks from the cruiser's armor. "Why am I always the bait?"

"I'm right behind you. Artoo, lock on."

Obi-Wan spun his starfighter between the recoiling turbocannons close enough that energy-scatter made his cockpit clang like a gong, but still cannonfire flashed past him from the tri-fighters behind. "Anakin, they're all over me!"

"Dead ahead. Move right to clear my shot. Now!"

Obi-Wan flared his port jets and the starfighter kicked to the right. One of the tri-fighters behind him decided it couldn't follow and went for a ventral slip that took it directly into the blasts from Anakin's cannons.

It vanished in a boil of superheated gas.

"Good shooting, Artoo." Anakin's dry chuckle in the cockpit's speakers vanished behind the clang of lasers blasting ablative shielding off Obi-Wan's left wing.

"I'm running out of *tricks* here—"

Clearing the vast Republic cruiser put him on course for the curving hull of one of the Trade Federation's battleships; space between the two capital ships blazed with turbolaser exchanges.

Some of those flashing energy blasts were as big around as his entire ship; the merest graze would blow him to atoms.

Obi-Wan dived right in.

He had the Force to guide him through, and the tri-fighter
had only its electronic reflexes—but those electronic reflexes operated at roughly the speed of light. It stayed on his tail as if he
were dragging it by a tow cable.

When Obi-Wan went left and Anakin right, the tri-fighter
would swing halfway through the difference. The same with up
and down. It was averaging his movements with Anakin's; somehow its droid brain had realized that as long as it stayed between
the two Jedi, Anakin couldn't fire on it without hitting his partner. The tri-fighter was under no similiar restraint: Obi-Wan flew
through a storm of scarlet needles.

"No wonder we're losing the war," he muttered. "They're
getting *smarter.*"

"What was that, Master? I didn't copy."

Obi-Wan kicked his starfighter into a tight spiral toward the
Federation cruiser. "I'm taking the deck!"

"Good idea. I need some room to maneuver."

Cannonfire tracked closer. Obi-Wan's cockpit speakers
buzzed. *"Cut right, Obi-Wan! Hard right! Don't let him get a
handle on you! Artoo, lock on!"*

Obi-Wan's starfighter streaked along the curve of the Separatist cruiser's dorsal hull. Antifighter flak burst on all sides as the
cruiser's guns tried to pick him up. He rolled a right wingover
into the service trench that stretched the length of the cruiser's
hull. This low and close to the deck, the cruiser's antifighter guns
couldn't depress their angle of fire enough to get a shot, but the
tri-fighter stayed right on his tail.

At the far end of the service trench, the massive support buttresses of the cruiser's towering bridge left no room for even
Obi-Wan's small craft. He kicked his starfighter into a half roll
that whipped him out of the trench and shot him straight up the

tower's angled leading edge. One burst of his underjets jerked him past the forward viewports of the bridge with only meters to spare—and the tri-fighter followed his path exactly.

"Of course," he muttered. "That would have been too easy. Anakin, where *are* you?"

One of the control surfaces on his left wing shattered in a burst of plasma. It felt like being shot in the arm. He toggled switches, fighting the yoke. R4-P17 shrilled at him. Obi-Wan keyed internal comm. "Don't try to fix it, Arfour. I've shut it down."

"I have the lock!" Anakin said. *"Go! Firing—now!"*

Obi-Wan hit maximum drag on his intact wing, and his starfighter shot into a barely controlled arc high and right as Anakin's cannons vaporized the last tri-fighter.

Obi-Wan fired retros to stall his starfighter in the blind spot behind the Separatist cruiser's bridge. He hung there for a few seconds to get his breathing and heart under control. "Thanks, Anakin. That was—thanks. That's all."

"Don't thank me. It was Artoo's shooting."

"Yes. I suppose, if you like, you can thank your droid for me as well. And, Anakin—?"

"Yes, Master?"

"Next time, *you're* the bait."

────────

This is Obi-Wan Kenobi:

A phenomenal pilot who doesn't like to fly. A devastating warrior who'd rather not fight. A negotiator without peer who frankly prefers to sit alone in a quiet cave and meditate.

Jedi Master. General in the Grand Army of the Republic. Member of the Jedi Council. And yet, inside, he feels like he's none of these things.

Inside, he still feels like a Padawan.

It is a truism of the Jedi Order that a Jedi Knight's education truly begins only when he becomes a Master: that everything important about being a Master is learned from one's student. Obi-Wan feels the truth of this every day.

He sometimes dreams of when he was a Padawan in fact as well as feeling; he dreams that his own Master, Qui-Gon Jinn, did not die at the plasma-fueled generator core in Theed. He dreams that his Master's wise guiding hand is still with him. But Qui-Gon's death is an old pain, one with which he long ago came to terms.

A Jedi does not cling to the past.

And Obi-Wan Kenobi knows, too, that to have lived his life without being Master to Anakin Skywalker would have left him a different man. A lesser man.

Anakin has taught him so much.

Obi-Wan sees so much of Qui-Gon in Anakin that sometimes it hurts his heart; at the very least, Anakin mirrors Qui-Gon's flair for the dramatic, and his casual disregard for rules. Training Anakin—and fighting beside him, all these years—has unlocked something inside Obi-Wan. It's as though Anakin has rubbed off on him a bit, and has loosened that clenched-jaw insistence on absolute correctness that Qui-Gon always said was his greatest flaw.

Obi-Wan Kenobi has learned to relax.

He smiles now, and sometimes even jokes, and has become known for the wisdom gentle humor can provide. Though he does not know it, his relationship with Anakin has molded him into the great Jedi Qui-Gon always said he might someday be.

It is characteristic of Obi-Wan that he is entirely unaware of this.

Being named to the Council came as a complete surprise; even now, he is sometimes astonished by the faith the Jedi Council has in his abilities, and the credit they give to his wisdom. Greatness was never his ambition. He wants only to perform whatever task he is given to the best of his ability.

He is respected throughout the Jedi Order for his insight as well as his warrior skill. He has become the hero of the next generation of Padawans; he is the Jedi their Masters hold up as a model. He is the being that the Council assigns to their most important missions. He is modest, centered, and always kind.

He is the ultimate Jedi.

And he is proud to be Anakin Skywalker's best friend.

"Artoo, where's that signal?"

From its socket beside the cockpit, R2-D2 whistled and beeped. A translation spidered across Anakin's console readout: SCANNING. LOTS OF ECM SIGNAL JAMMING.

"Keep on it." He glanced at Obi-Wan's starfighter limping through the battle, a hundred meters off his left wing. "I can feel his jitters from all the way over here."

A tootle: A JEDI IS ALWAYS CALM.

"He won't think it's funny. Neither do I. Less joking, more scanning."

For Anakin Skywalker, starfighter battles were usually as close to fun as he ever came.

This one wasn't.

Not because of the overwhelming odds, or the danger he was in; he didn't care about odds, and he didn't think of himself as being in any particular danger. A few wings of droid fighters didn't much scare a man who'd been a Podracer since he was six, and had won the Boonta Cup at nine. Who was, in fact, the only human to ever *finish* a Podrace, let alone win one.

In those days he had used the Force without knowing it; he'd thought the Force was something inside him, just a feeling, an

instinct, a string of lucky guesses that led him through maneuvers other pilots wouldn't dare attempt. Now, though . . .

Now—

Now he could reach into the Force and feel the engagement
throughout Coruscant space as though the whole battle were
happening inside his head.

His vehicle became his body. The pulses of its engines were
the beat of his own heart. Flying, he could forget about his slavery, about his mother, about Geonosis and Jabiim, Aargonar and
Muunilinst and all the catastrophes of this brutal war. About
everything that had been done to him.

And everything he had done.

He could even put aside, for as long as the battle roared
around him, the starfire of his love for the woman who waited for
him on the world below. The woman whose breath was his only
air, whose heartbeat was his only music, whose face was the only
beauty his eyes would ever see.

He could put all this aside because he was a Jedi. Because it
was time to do a Jedi's work.

But today was different.

Today wasn't about dodging lasers and blasting droids.
Today was about the life of the man who might as well have been
his father: a man who could die if the Jedi didn't reach him in
time.

Anakin had been late once before.

Obi-Wan's voice came over the cockpit speakers, flat and
tight. *"Does your droid have anything? Arfour's hopeless. I think
that last cannon hit cooked his motivator."*

Anakin could see exactly the look on his former Master's
face: a mask of calm belied by a jaw so tight that when he spoke
his mouth barely moved. "Don't worry, Master. If his beacon's
working, Artoo'll find it. Have you thought about how we'll find
the Chancellor if—"

"No." Obi-Wan sounded absolutely certain. *"There's no need*

to consider it. Until the possible becomes actual, it is only a distraction. Be mindful of what is, not what might be."

Anakin had to stop himself from reminding Obi-Wan that he wasn't a Padawan anymore. "I should have been here," he said through his teeth. "I *told* you. I should have *been* here."

"Anakin, he was defended by Stass Allie and Shaak Ti. If two Masters could not prevent this, do you think you could? Stass Allie is clever and valiant, and Shaak Ti is the most cunning Jedi I've ever met. She's even taught me *a few tricks."*

Anakin assumed he was supposed to be impressed. "But General Grievous—"

"Master Ti had faced him before, Anakin. After Muunilinst. She is not only subtle and experienced, but very capable indeed. Seats on the Jedi Council aren't handed out as party favors."

"I've noticed." He let it drop. The middle of a space battle was no place to get into this particular sore subject.

If only *he'd* been here, instead of Shaak Ti and Stass Allie, Council members or not. If he had been here, Chancellor Palpatine would be home and safe already. Instead, Anakin had been stuck running around the Outer Rim for months like some useless Padawan, and all Palpatine had for protectors were Jedi who were *clever* and *subtle*.

Clever and subtle. He could whip any ten *clever and subtle* Jedi with his lightsaber tied behind his back.

But he knew better than to say so.

"Put yourself in the moment, Anakin. Focus."

"Copy that, Master," Anakin said dryly. "Focusing now."

R2-D2 twittered, and Anakin checked his console readout. "We've got him, Master. The cruiser dead ahead. That's Grievous's flagship—*Invisible Hand.*"

"Anakin, there are dozens *of cruisers dead ahead!"*

"It's the one crawling with vulture fighters."

The vulture fighters clinging to the long curves of the Trade Federation cruiser indicated by Palpatine's beacon gave it eerily life-like ripples, like some metallic marine predator bristling with Alderaanian walking barnacles.

"*Oh. That one.*" He could practically hear Obi-Wan's stomach dropping. "*Oh,* this *should be easy . . .*"

Now some of them stripped themselves from the cruiser, ignited their drives, and came looping toward the two Jedi.

"Easy? No. But it might be fun." Sometimes a little teasing was the only way to get Obi-Wan to loosen up. "Lunch at Dex's says I'll blast two for each of yours. Artoo can keep score."

"*Anakin—*"

"All right, dinner. And I promise this time I won't let Artoo cheat."

"*No games, Anakin. There's too much at stake.*" There, that was the tone Anakin had been looking for: a slightly scolding, schoolmasterish edge. Obi-Wan was back on form. "*Have your droid tight-beam a report to the Temple. And send out a call for any Jedi in starfighters. We'll come at it from all sides.*"

"Way ahead of you." But when he checked his comm readout, he shook his head. "There's still too much ECM. Artoo can't raise the Temple. I think the only reason we can even talk to each other is that we're practically side by side."

"*And Jedi beacons?*"

"No joy, Master." Anakin's stomach clenched, but he fought the tension out of his voice. "We may be the only two Jedi out here."

"*Then we will have to be enough. Switching to clone fighter channel.*"

Anakin spun his comm dial to the new frequency in time to hear Obi-Wan say, "*Oddball, do you copy? We need help.*"

The clone captain's helmet speaker flattened the humanity out of his voice. "*Copy, Red Leader.*"

"*Mark my position and form your squad behind me. We're going in.*"

"*On our way.*"

The droid fighters had lost themselves against the back-ground of the battle, but R2-D2 was tracking them on scan. Anakin shifted his grip on his starfighter's control yoke. "Ten vultures inbound, high and left to my orientation. More on the way."

"I have them. Anakin, wait—the cruiser's bay shields have dropped! I'm reading four, no, six ships incoming." Obi-Wan's voice rose. *"Tri-fighters! Coming in fast!"*

Anakin's smile tightened. This was about to get interesting.

"Tri-fighters first, Master. The vultures can wait."

"Agreed. Slip back and right, swing behind me. We'll take them on the slant."

Let Obi-Wan go first? With a blown left control surface and a half-crippled R-unit? With Palpatine's *life* at stake?

Not likely.

"Negative," Anakin said. "I'm going head-to-head. See you on the far side."

"Take it easy. Wait for Oddball and Squad Seven. Anakin—"

He could hear the frustration in Obi-Wan's voice as he kicked his starfighter's sublights and surged past; his former Master still hadn't gotten used to not being able to order Anakin around.

Not that Anakin had ever been much for following orders. Obi-Wan's, or anyone else's.

"Sorry we're late." The digitized voice of the clone whose call sign was Oddball sounded as calm as if he were ordering dinner. *"We're on your right, Red Leader. Where's Red Five?"*

"Anakin, form up!"

But Anakin was already streaking to meet the Trade Federa-tion fighters. "Incoming!"

Obi-Wan's familiar sigh came clearly over the comm; Anakin knew exactly what the Jedi Master was thinking. The same thing he was *always* thinking.

He still has much to learn.

Anakin's smile thinned to a grim straight line as enemy

starfighters swarmed around him. And he thought the same thing *he* always thought.

We'll see about that.

He gave himself to the battle, and his starfighter whirled and his cannons hammered, and droids on all sides began to burst into clouds of debris and superheated gas.

This was how *he* relaxed.

———

This is Anakin Skywalker:

The most powerful Jedi of his generation. Perhaps of any generation. The fastest. The strongest. An unbeatable pilot. An unstoppable warrior. On the ground, in the air or sea or space, there is no one even close. He has not just power, not just skill, but *dash:* that rare, invaluable combination of boldness and grace.

He is the best there is at what he does. The best there has ever been. And he knows it.

HoloNet features call him the Hero With No Fear. And why not? What should he be afraid of?

Except—

Fear lives inside him anyway, chewing away the firewalls around his heart.

Anakin sometimes thinks of the dread that eats at his heart as a dragon. Children on Tatooine tell each other of the dragons that live inside the suns; smaller cousins of the sun-dragons are supposed to live inside the fusion furnaces that power everything from starships to Podracers.

But Anakin's fear is another kind of dragon. A cold kind. A dead kind.

Not nearly dead enough.

Not long after he became Obi-Wan's Padawan, all those years ago, a minor mission had brought them to a dead system: one so immeasurably old that its star had long ago turned to a frigid dwarf of hypercompacted trace metals, hovering a quantum fraction of a degree above absolute zero. Anakin couldn't even remember what the mission might have been, but he'd never forgotten that dead star.

It had scared him.

"*Stars* can *die*—?"

"It is the way of the universe, which is another manner of saying that it is the will of the Force," Obi-Wan had told him. "Everything dies. In time, even stars burn out. This is why Jedi form no attachments: all things pass. To hold on to something—or someone—beyond its time is to set your selfish desires against the Force. That is a path of misery, Anakin; the Jedi do not walk it."

That is the kind of fear that lives inside Anakin Skywalker: the dragon of that dead star. It is an ancient, cold dead voice within his heart that whispers *all things die* . . .

In bright day he can't hear it; battle, a mission, even a report before the Jedi Council, can make him forget it's even there. But at night—

At night, the walls he has built sometimes start to frost over. Sometimes they start to crack.

At night, the dead-star dragon sometimes sneaks through the cracks and crawls up into his brain and chews at the inside of his skull. The dragon whispers of what Anakin has lost. And what he will lose.

The dragon reminds him, every night, of how he held his dying mother in his arms, of how she had spent her last strength to say *I knew you would come for me, Anakin* . . .

The dragon reminds him, every night, that someday he will lose Obi-Wan. He will lose Padmé. Or they will lose him.

All things die, Anakin Skywalker. Even stars burn out . . .

And the only answers he ever has for these dead cold whispers are his memories of Obi-Wan's voice, or Yoda's.

But sometimes he can't quite remember them.

all things die . . .

He can barely even think about it.

But right now he doesn't have a choice: the man he flies to rescue is a closer friend than he'd ever hoped to have. That's what puts the edge in his voice when he tries to make a joke; that's what flattens his mouth and tightens the burn-scar high on his right cheek.

The Supreme Chancellor has been family to Anakin: always there, always caring, always free with advice and unstinting aid. A sympathetic ear and a kindly, loving, unconditional acceptance of Anakin exactly as he is—the sort of acceptance Anakin could never get from another Jedi. Not even from Obi-Wan. He can tell Palpatine things he could never share with his Master.

He can tell Palpatine things he can't even tell Padmé.

Now the Supreme Chancellor is in the worst kind of danger. And Anakin is on his way despite the dread boiling through his blood. That's what makes him a real hero. Not the way the HoloNet labels him; not without fear, but *stronger* than fear.

He looks the dragon in the eye and doesn't even slow down.

If anyone can save Palpatine, Anakin will. Because he's already the best, and he's still getting better. But locked away behind the walls of his heart, the dragon that is his fear coils and squirms and hisses.

Because his real fear, in a universe where even stars can die, is that being the best will never be quite good enough.

───

Obi-Wan's starfighter jolted sideways. Anakin whipped by him and used his forward attitude jets to kick himself into a skew-flip: facing backward to blast the last of the tri-fighters on his tail. Now there were only vulture droids left.

A *lot* of vulture droids.

"Did you like that one, Master?"

"Very pretty." Obi-Wan's cannons stitched plasma across the hull of a swooping vulture fighter until the droid exploded. "But we're not through yet."

"Watch this." Anakin flipped his starfighter again and dived, spinning, directly through the flock of vulture droids. Their drives blazed as they came around. He led them streaking for the upper deck of a laser-scarred Separatist cruiser. *"I'm going to lead them through the needle."*

"Don't lead them anywhere." Obi-Wan's threat display tallied the vultures on Anakin's tail. Twelve of them. *Twelve.* "First Jedi principle of combat: survive."

"No choice." Anakin slipped his starfighter through the storm of cannonfire. *"Come down and thin them out a little."*

Obi-Wan slammed his control yoke forward as though jamming it against its impact-rest would push his battered fighter faster in pursuit. "Nothing fancy, Arfour." As though the damaged droid were even capable of anything fancy. "Just hold me steady."

He reached into the Force and felt for his shot. "On my mark, break left—*now!*" The shutdown control surface of his left wing turned the left break into a tight overhead spiral that traversed Obi-Wan's guns across the paths of four vultures—

flash flash flash flash

—and all four were gone.

He flew on through the clouds of glowing plasma. He couldn't waste time going around; Anakin still had eight of them on his tail.

And what was this? Obi-Wan frowned.

The cruiser looked familiar.

The needle? he thought. *Oh, please say you're kidding.*

Anakin's starfighter skimmed only meters above the cruiser's dorsal hull. Cannon misses from the vulture fighters swooping toward him blasted chunks out of the cruiser's armor.

"Okay, Artoo. Where's that trench?"

His forward screen lit with a topograph of the cruiser's hull. Just ahead lay the trench that Obi-Wan had led the tri-fighter into. Anakin flipped his starfighter through a razor-sharp wingover down past the rim. The walls of the service trench flashed past him as he streaked for the bridge tower at the far end. From here, he couldn't even see the minuscule slit between its support struts.

With eight vulture droids in pursuit, he'd never pull off a slant up the tower's leading edge as Obi-Wan had. But that was all right.

He wasn't planning to.

His cockpit comm buzzed. *"Don't try it, Anakin. It's too tight."*

Too tight for you, maybe. "I'll get through."

R2-D2 whistled nervous agreement with Obi-Wan.

"Easy, Artoo," Anakin said. "We've done this before."

Cannonfire blazed past him, impacting on the support struts ahead. Too late to change his mind now: he was committed. He would bring his ship through, or he would die.

Right now, strangely, he didn't actually care which.

"Use the Force." Obi-Wan sounded worried. *"Think yourself through, and the ship will follow."*

"What do you expect me to do? Close my eyes and whistle?" Anakin muttered under his breath, then said aloud, "Copy that. Thinking now."

R2-D2's squeal was as close to terrified as a droid can sound. Glowing letters spidered across Anakin's readout: ABORT! ABORT ABORT!

Anakin smiled. "Wrong thought."

Obi-Wan could only stare openmouthed as Anakin's starfighter snapped onto its side and scraped through the slit with centimeters to spare. He fully expected one of the struts to knock R2's dome off.

The vulture droids tried to follow . . . but they were just a hair too big.

When the first two impacted, Obi-Wan triggered his cannons in a downward sweep. The evasion maneuvers preprogrammed into the vulture fighters' droid brains sent them diving away from Obi-Wan's lasers—straight into the fireball expanding from the front of the struts.

Obi-Wan looked up to find Anakin soaring straight out from the cruiser with a quick snap-roll of victory. Obi-Wan matched his course—without the flourish.

"I'll give you the first four," Anakin said over the comm, *"but the other eight are mine."*

"Anakin—"

"All right, we'll split them."

As they left the cruiser behind, their sensors showed Squad Seven dead ahead. The clone pilots were fully engaged, looping through a dogfight so tight that their ion trails looked like a glowing ball of string.

"Oddball's in trouble. I'm going to help him out."

"Don't. He's doing his job. We need to do ours."

"Master, they're getting eaten alive over—"

"Every one of them would gladly trade his life for Palpatine's. Will you trade Palpatine's life for theirs?"

"No—no, of course not, but—"

"Anakin, I understand: you want to save everyone. You always do. But you *can't.*"

Anakin's voice went tight. *"Don't remind me."*

"Head for the command ship." Without waiting for a reply, Obi-Wan targeted the command cruiser and shot away at maximum thrust.

The cross of burn-scar beside Anakin's eye went pale as he turned his starfighter in pursuit. Obi-Wan was right. He almost always was.

You can't save everyone

His mother's body, broken and bloody in his arms—

Her battered eyes struggling to open—

The touch of her smashed lips—

I knew you would come to me . . . I missed you so much . . .

That's what it was to be not quite good enough.

It could happen anytime. Anyplace. If he was a few minutes late. If he let his attention drift for a single second. If he was a whisker too weak.

Anyplace. Anytime.

But not here, and not now.

He forced his mother's face back down below the surface of his consciousness.

Time to get to work.

They flashed through the battle, dodging flak and turbolaser bolts, slipping around cruisers to eclipse themselves from the sensors of droid fighters. They were only a few dozen kilometers from the command cruiser when a pair of tri-fighters whipped across their path, firing on the deflection.

Anakin's sensor board lit up and R2-D2 shrilled a warning. "Missiles!"

He wasn't worried for himself: the two on his tail were coming at him in perfect tandem. Missiles lack the sophisticated brains of droid fighters; to keep them from colliding on their inbound vectors, one of them would lock onto his fighter's left drive, the other onto his right. A quick snap-roll would make those vectors intersect.

Which they did in a silent blossom of flame.

Obi-Wan wasn't so lucky. The pair of missiles locked onto his sublights weren't precisely side by side; a snap-roll would be worse than useless. Instead he fired retros and kicked his dorsal jets to halve his velocity and knock him a few meters planetward. The lead missile overshot and spiraled off into the orbital battle.

The trailing missile came close enough to trigger its proximity sensors, and detonated in a spray of glowing shrapnel. Obi-Wan's starfighter flew through the debris—and the shrapnel *tracked* him.

Little silver spheres flipped themselves into his path and latched onto the starfighter's skin, then split and sprouted spidery arrays of jointed arms that pried up hull plates, exposing the starfighter's internal works to multiple circular whirls of blade like ancient mechanical bone saws.

This was a problem.

"I'm hit." Obi-Wan sounded more irritated than concerned. *"I'm hit."*

"I have visual." Anakin swung his starfighter into closer pursuit. "Buzz droids. I count five."

"Get out of here, Anakin. There's nothing you can do."

"I'm not leaving you, Master."

Cascades of sparks fountained into space from the buzz droids' saws. *"Anakin, the mission! Get to the command ship! Get the Chancellor!"*

"Not without you," Anakin said through his teeth.

One of the buzz droids crouched beside the cockpit, silvery arms grappling with R4; another worked on the starfighter's nose, while a third skittered toward the ventral hydraulics. The last two of the aggressive little mechs had spidered to Obi-Wan's left wing, working on that damaged control surface.

"You can't help me." Obi-Wan still maintained his Jedi calm. *"They're shutting down the controls."*

"I can fix that . . ." Anakin brought his starfighter into line only a couple of meters off Obi-Wan's wing. "Steady . . . ," he muttered, "steady . . . ," and triggered a single burst of his right-side cannon that blasted the two buzz droids into gouts of molten metal.

Along with most of Obi-Wan's left wing.

Anakin said, "Whoops."

The starfighter bucked hard enough to knock Obi-Wan's skull against the transparisteel canopy. A gust of stinging smoke filled the cockpit. Obi-Wan fought the yoke to keep his starfighter out of an uncontrolled tumble. "Anakin, that's not *helping.*"

"You're right, bad idea. Here, let's try this—move left and swing under—easy . . ."

"Anakin, you're too close! Wait—" Obi-Wan stared in disbelief as Anakin's starfighter edged closer and with a dip of its wing physically slammed a buzz droid into a smear of metal. The impact jolted Obi-Wan again, pounded a deep streak of dent into his starfighter's hull, and shattered the forward control surface of Anakin's wing.

Anakin had forgotten the first principle of combat. Again. As usual.

"You're going to get us both killed!"

His atmospheric scrubbers drained smoke from the cockpit, but now the droid on the forward control surface of Obi-Wan's starfighter's right wing had peeled away enough of the hull plates that its jointed saw arms could get deep inside. Sparks flared into space, along with an expanding fountain of gas that instantly crystallized in the hard vacuum. Velocity identical to Obi-Wan's, the shimmering gas hung on his starfighter's nose like a cloud of fog. "Blast," Obi-Wan muttered. "I can't see. My controls are going."

"You're doing fine. Stay on my wing."

Easier said than done. "I have to accelerate out of this."

"I'm with you. Go."

Obi-Wan eased power to his thrusters, and his starfighter parted the cloud, but new vapor boiled out to replace it as he went. "Is that last one still on my nose? Arfour, can you do anything?"

The only response he got came from Anakin. *"That's a negative on Arfour. Buzz droid got him."*

"It," Obi-Wan corrected automatically. "Wait—they attacked *Arfour*?"

"*Not just Arfour. One of them jumped over when we hit.*"

Blast, Obi-Wan thought. *They* are *getting smarter.*

Through a gap torn in the cloud by the curve of his cockpit, Obi-Wan could see R2-D2 grappling with a buzz droid hand-to-hand. Well: saw-arm-to-saw-arm. Even flying blind and nearly out of control through the middle of a space battle, Obi-Wan could not avoid a second of disbelief at the bewildering variety of auxiliary tools and aftermarket behaviors Anakin had tinkered onto his starfighter's astromech, even beyond the sophisticated upgrades performed by the Royal Engineers of Naboo. The little device was virtually a partner in its own right.

R2's saw cut through one of the buzz droid's grapplers, sending the jointed arm flipping lazily off into space. Then it did the same to another. Then a panel opened in R2-D2's side and its datajack arm stabbed out and smacked the crippled buzz droid right off Anakin's hull. The buzz droid spun aft until it was caught in the blast wash of Anakin's sublights then blew away faster than even Obi-Wan's eye could follow.

Obi-Wan reflected that the Separatist droids weren't the only ones that were getting smarter.

The datajack retracted and a different panel opened, this time in R2-D2's dome. A claw-cable shot from it into the cloud of gas that still billowed from Obi-Wan's right forward wing, and pulled back out dragging a struggling buzz droid. The silver droid twisted and squirmed and its grapplers took hold of the cable, climbing back along it, saw arms waving, until Anakin popped the starfighter's underjets and R2 cut the cable and the buzz droid dropped away, tumbling helplessly through the battle.

"You know," Obi-Wan said, "I begin to understand why you speak of Artoo as though he's a living creature."

"*Do you?*" He could hear Anakin's smile. "*Don't you mean, it?*"

"Ah, yes." He frowned. "Yes, of course. It. Erm, thank it for me, will you?"

"Thank him yourself."

"Ah—yes. Thanks, Artoo."

The whistle that came back over the comm had a clear flavor of *you're welcome.*

Then the last of the fog finally dispersed, and the sky ahead was full of ship.

More than one kilometer from end to end, the vast command cruiser filled his visual field. At this range, all he could see were savannas of sand-colored hull studded with turbolaser mountains that lit up space with thunderbolts of disintegrating energy.

And that immense ship was getting bigger.

Fast.

"Anakin! We're going to collide!"

"That's the plan. Head for the hangar."

"That's not—"

"I know: first Jedi principle of—"

"No. It's not going to *work.* Not for me."

"What?"

"My controls are gone. I can't head for *anything.*"

"Oh. Well. All right, no problem."

"No *problem?*"

Then his starfighter clanged as if he'd crashed into a ship-sized gong.

Obi-Wan jerked and twisted his head around to find the other starfighter just above his tail. Literally just above: Anakin's left lead control surface was barely a hand span from Obi-Wan's sublight thrusters.

Anakin had *hit* him. On *purpose.*

Then he did it again.

CLANG

"What are you *doing?*"

"Just giving you . . ." Anakin's voice came slow, tight with concentration. *". . . a little help with your steering . . ."*

Obi-Wan shook his head. This was completely impossible. No other pilot would even attempt it. But for Anakin Skywalker, the completely impossible had an eerie way of being merely difficult.

He reflected that he should be used to it by now.

While these thoughts chased each other aimlessly through his mind, he had been staring bleakly at a blue shimmer of energy filling the yawning hangar bay ahead. Belatedly, he registered what he was looking at.

He thought, *Oh, this is bad.*

"Anakin—" Obi-Wan began. He tried rerouting control paths through his yoke. No luck.

Anakin drew up and tipped his forward surfaces down behind the sparking scrap that used to be Arfour.

"Anakin—!"

"Give me . . . just a second, Master." Anakin's voice had gone even tighter. A muffled thump, then another. Louder. And a scrape and a squeal of ripping metal. *"This isn't quite . . . as easy as it looks . . ."*

"Anakin!"

"What?"

"The hangar bay—"

"What about it?"

"Have you noticed that the *shield's still up?*"

"Really?"

"Really." Not to mention so close that Obi-Wan could practically *taste* it—

"Oh. Sorry. I've been busy."

Obi-Wan closed his eyes.

Reaching into the Force, his mind followed the starfighter's mangled circuitry to locate and activate the sublight engines' manual test board. With a slight push, he triggered a command normally used only in bench tests: full reverse.

The cometary tail of glowing debris shed by his disintegrating starfighter shot past him and evaporated in a cascade of miniature starbursts on contact with the hangar shield. Which was exactly what was about to happen to him.

The only effect of full reverse from his failing engines was to give him more time to see it coming.

Then Anakin's starfighter swooped in front of him, crossing left to right at a steep deflection. Energy flared from his cannons, and the shield emitters at the right side of the hangar door exploded into scrap. The blue shimmer of the bay shield flickered, faded, and vanished just as Obi-Wan came spinning across the threshold and slammed along the deck, trailing sparks and a scream of tortured metal.

His entire starfighter—what was left of it—vibrated with the roar of atmosphere howling out from the unshielded bay. Massive blast doors ground together like jaws. Another Force-touch on the manual test board cut power to his engines, but he couldn't trigger the explosive bolts on his cockpit canopy, and he had a bad feeling that those canopy bolts were the only thing on his craft that *weren't* about to explode.

His lightsaber found his hand and blue energy flared. One swipe and the canopy burst away, ripped into space by the hurricane of escaping air. Obi-Wan flipped himself up into the stunningly cold gale and let it blow him tumbling away as the remnants of his battered craft finally exploded.

He rode the shock wave while he let the Force right him in the air. He landed catfooted on the blackened streak—still hot enough to scorch his boots—that his landing had gouged into the deck.

The hangar was full of battle droids.

His shoulders dropped and his knees bent and his lightsaber

came up to angle in front of his face. There were far too many for him to fight alone, but he didn't mind.

At least he was out of that blasted starfighter.

Anakin slipped his craft toward the hangar through a fountain of junk and flash-frozen gas. One last touch of the yoke twisted his starfighter through the closing teeth of the blast doors just as Obi-Wan's canopy went the other way.

Obi-Wan's ship was a hunk of glowing scrap punctuating a long smoking skid mark. Obi-Wan himself, beard rimed with frost, lightsaber out and flaming, stood in a tightening ring of battle droids.

Anakin slewed his starfighter into a landing that scattered droids with the particle blast from his sublight thrusters and for one second he was nine years old again, behind the controls of a starfighter in the Theed royal hangar, his first touch of a real ship's real cannons blasting battle droids—

He'd have done the same right here, except that Palpatine was somewhere on this ship. They just might need one of the light shuttles in this hangar to get the Chancellor safely to the surface; a few dozen cannon blasts bouncing around in here could wreck them all.

This he'd have to do by hand.

One touch blew his canopy and he sprang from the cockpit, flipping upward to stand on the wing. Battle droids opened fire instantly, and Anakin's lightsaber flashed. "Artoo, locate a computer link."

The little droid whistled at him, and Anakin allowed himself a tight smile. Sometimes he thought he could almost understand the droid's electrosonic code. "Don't worry about us. Find Palpatine. Go on, I'll cover you."

R2 popped out of its socket and bounced to the deck. Anakin jumped ahead of it into a cascade of blasterfire and let the Force direct his blade. Battle droids began to spark and collapse.

"Get to that link!" Anakin had to shout above the whine of blasters and the roar of exploding droids. "I'm going for Obi-Wan!"

"No need."

Anakin whirled to find Obi-Wan right behind him in the act of slicing neatly through the braincase of a battle droid.

"I appreciate the thought, Anakin," the Jedi Master said with a gentle smile. "But I've already come for you."

This, then, is Obi-Wan and Anakin:

They are closer than friends. Closer than brothers. Though Obi-Wan is sixteen standard years Anakin's elder, they have become men together. Neither can imagine life without the other. The war has forged their two lives into one.

The war that has done this is not the Clone Wars; Obi-Wan and Anakin's war began on Naboo, when Qui-Gon Jinn died at the hand of a Sith Lord. Master and Padawan and Jedi Knights together, they have fought this war for thirteen years. Their war is their life.

And their life is a weapon.

Say what you will about the wisdom of ancient Master Yoda, or the deadly skill of grim Mace Windu, the courage of Ki-Adi-Mundi, or the subtle wiles of Shaak Ti; the greatness of all these Jedi is unquestioned, but it pales next to the legend that has grown around Kenobi and Skywalker.

They stand alone.

Together, they are unstoppable. Unbeatable. They are the ultimate go-to guys of the Jedi Order. When the Good Guys absolutely, positively have to *win,* the call goes out.

Obi-Wan and Anakin always answer.

Whether Obi-Wan's legendary cleverness might beat Anakin's raw power, straight up, no rules, is the subject of schoolyard fistfights, crèche-pool wriggle-matches, and pod-chamber stinkwars across the Republic. These struggles always end, somehow, with the combatants on both sides admitting that it doesn't matter.

Anakin and Obi-Wan would never fight each other.

They couldn't.

They're a team. They're *the* team.

And both of them are sure they always will be.

DOOKU

The storm of blasterfire ricocheting through the hangar bay suddenly ceased. Clusters of battle droids withdrew behind ships and slipped out hatchways.

Obi-Wan's familiar grimace showed past his blade as he let it shrink away. "I hate it when they do that."

Anakin's lightsaber was already back on his belt. "When they do what?"

"Disengage and fall back for no reason."

"There's always a reason, Master."

Obi-Wan nodded. "That's why I hate it."

Anakin looked at the litter of smoking droid parts scattered throughout the hangar bay, shrugged, and snugged his black glove. "Artoo, where's the Chancellor?"

The little droid's datajack rotated in the wall socket. Its holo-projector eye swiveled and the blue scanning laser built a ghostly image near Anakin's boot: Palpatine shackled into a large swivel chair. Even in the tiny translucent blur, he looked exhausted and in pain—but alive.

Anakin's heart thumped once, painfully, against his ribs. He wasn't too late. Not this time.

He dropped to one knee and squinted at the image. Palpatine looked as if he'd aged ten years since Anakin had last seen him. Muscle bulged along the young Jedi's jaw. If Grievous had hurt the Chancellor—had so much as *touched* him—

The hand of jointed durasteel inside his black glove clenched so hard that electronic feedback made his shoulder ache.

Obi-Wan spoke from over that shoulder. "Do you have a location?"

The image rippled and twisted into a schematic map of the cruiser. Far up at the top of the conning spire R2 showed a pulsar of brighter blue.

"In the General's Quarters." Obi-Wan scowled. "Any sign of Grievous himself?"

The pulsar shifted to the cruiser's bridge.

"Hmm. And guards?"

The holoimage rippled again, and transformed into an image of the cruiser's General's Quarters once more. Palpatine appeared to be alone: the chair sat in the center of an arc of empty floor, facing a huge curved viewing wall.

Anakin muttered, "That doesn't make *sense*."

"Of course it does. It's a trap."

Anakin barely heard him. He stared down at his black-gloved fist. He opened his fist, closed it, opened it again. The ache from his shoulder flowed down to the middle of his bicep—

And didn't stop.

His elbow sizzled, and his forearm; his wrist had been packed with red-hot gravel, and his hand—

His hand was on *fire*.

But it wasn't *his* hand. Or his wrist, or his forearm, or his elbow. It was a creation of jointed durasteel and electrodrivers.

"Anakin?"

Anakin's lips drew back from his teeth. "It hurts."

"What, your replacement arm? When did you have it equipped with pain sensors?"

"I *didn't*. That's the *point*."

"The pain is in your mind, Anakin—"

"No." Anakin's heart froze over. His voice went cold as space. "I can feel him."

"Him?"

"Dooku. He's here. Here on this ship."

"Ah." Obi-Wan nodded. "I'm sure he is."

"You *knew*?"

"I guessed. Do you think Grievous couldn't have found Palpatine's beacon? It can hardly be accident that through all the ECM, the Chancellor's homing signal was in the clear. This is a trap. A Jedi trap." Obi-Wan laid a warm hand upon Anakin's shoulder, and his face was as grim as Anakin had ever seen it. "Possibly a trap set for us. Personally."

Anakin's jaw tightened. "You're thinking of how he tried to recruit you on Geonosis. Before he sent you down for execution."

"It's not impossible that we will again face that choice."

"It's not a choice." Anakin rose. His durasteel hand clenched and stayed that way, a centimeter from his lightsaber. "Let him ask. My answer is right here on my belt."

"Be mindful, Anakin. The Chancellor's safety is our only priority."

"Yes—yes, of course." The ice in Anakin's chest thawed. "All right, it's a trap. Next move?"

Obi-Wan allowed himself a bit of a smile of his own as he headed for the nearest exit from the hangar bay. "Same as always, my young friend: we spring it."

"I can work with this plan." Anakin turned to his astromech. "You stay here, Artoo—"

The little droid interrupted him with a wheedling whirr.

"No arguments. Stay. I mean it."

R2-D2's whistling reply had a distinctly sulky tone.

"Listen, Artoo, someone has to maintain computer contact; do you see a datajack anywhere on *me*?"

The droid seemed to acquiesce, but not before wheeping what sounded like it might have been a suggestion where to look.

Waiting by the open hatchway, Obi-Wan shook his head. "Honestly, the way you talk to that thing."

Anakin started toward him. "Careful, Master, you'll hurt his feelings—" He stopped in his tracks, a curious look on his face as if he was trying to frown and to smile at the same time.

"Anakin?"

He didn't answer. He couldn't answer. He was looking at an image inside his head. Not an image. A reality.

A memory of something that hadn't happened yet.

He saw Count Dooku on his knees. He saw lightsabers crossed at the Count's throat.

Clouds lifted from his heart: clouds of Jabiim, of Aargonar, of Kamino, of even the Tusken camp. For the first time in too many years he felt young: as young as he really was.

Young, and free, and full of light.

"Master . . ." His voice seemed to be coming from someone else. Someone who hadn't seen what he'd seen. Hadn't done what he'd done. "Master, right here—right now—you and I . . ."

"Yes?"

He blinked. "I think we're about to win the war."

The vast semisphere of the view wall bloomed with battle. Sophisticated sensor algorithms compressed the combat that sprawled throughout the galactic capital's orbit to a view the naked eye could enjoy: cruisers hundreds of kilometers apart, exchanging fire at near lightspeed, appeared to be practically hull-to-hull, joined by pulsing cables of flame. Turbolaser blasts became swift shafts of light that shattered into prismatic splinters against shields, or bloomed into miniature supernovae that swallowed ships whole. The invisible gnat-clouds of starfighter dogfights became a gleaming dance of shadowmoths at the end of Coruscant's brief spring.

Within that immense curve of computer-filtered carnage, the only furnishing was one lone chair, centered in an expanse of empty floor. This was called the General's Chair, just as this apartment atop the flagship's conning spire was called the General's Quarters.

With his back to that chair and to the man shackled within it, hands folded behind him beneath his cloak of silken armor-weave, stood Count Dooku.

Stood Darth Tyranus, Lord of the Sith.

He looked upon his Master's handiwork, and it was good.

More than good. It was *magnificent*.

Even the occasional tremor of the deck beneath his boots, as the entire ship shuddered under enemy torpedo and turbolaser blasts, felt to him like applause.

Behind him sounded the initiating hum of the intraship holocomm, which crackled into a voice both electronic and oddly expressive: as though a man spoke through a droid's electrosonic vocabulator. *"Lord Tyranus, Kenobi and Skywalker have arrived."*

"Yes." Dooku had felt them both in the Force. "Drive them toward me."

"My lord, I must express once more my objections—"

Dooku turned. From his commanding height, he stared down at the blue-scanned holoimage of *Invisible Hand*'s commander. "Your objections have been noted already, General. Leave the Jedi to me."

"But driving them to you also sends them directly toward the Chancellor himself! Why does he remain on this ship at all? He should be hidden. He should be guarded. We should have had him outsystem hours ago!"

"Matters are so," Count Dooku said, "because Lord Sidious

wishes them so; should you desire to press your objections, please feel at liberty to take them up with *him*."

"I, ah, don't believe that will be necessary . . ."

"Very well, then. Confine your efforts to preventing support troops from boarding. Without their pet clones to back them up, no Jedi is a danger to me."

The deck shuddered again, more sharply, followed by a sudden shift in the vector of the cruiser's artificial gravity that would have sent a lesser man stumbling; with the Force to maintain the dignified solidity of his posture, the effect on Dooku was confined to the lift of one eyebrow. "And may I suggest that you devote some attention to protecting this ship? Having it destroyed with both you and me aboard might put something of a cramp in the war effort, don't you think?"

"It is already being done, my lord. Does my lord wish to observe the progress of the Jedi? I can feed the security monitors onto this channel."

"Thank you, General. That will be welcome."

"Gracious as ever, my lord. Grievous out."

Count Dooku allowed himself a near-invisible smile. His inviolable courtesy—the hallmark of a true aristocrat—was effortless, yet somehow it seemed always to impress the common rabble. As well as those with the intellect of common rabble, regardless of accomplishment or station: like, for example, that repulsive cyborg Grievous.

He sighed. Grievous had his uses; not only was he an able field commander, but he would soon make a marvelous scapegoat upon whom to hang every atrocity of this sadly necessary war. Someone had to take that particular fall, and Grievous was just the creature for the job. It certainly would not be Dooku.

This was, in fact, one purpose of the cataclysmic battle outside.

But not the only one.

The blue-scanned image before him now became miniatures

of Kenobi and Skywalker as he had seen them so many times before: shoulder-to-shoulder, lightsabers whirling as they enthusiastically dismantled droid after droid after droid. Feeling as if they were winning, while in truth they were being chivvied exactly where the Lords of the Sith wanted them to go.

Such children they were. Dooku shook his head.

It was almost too easy.

This is Dooku, Darth Tyranus, Count of Serenno:

Once a great Jedi Master, now an even greater Lord of the Sith, Dooku is a dark colossus bestriding the galaxy. Nemesis of the corrupt Republic, oriflamme of the principled Confederacy of Independent Systems, he is the very personification of shock and awe.

He was one of the most respected and powerful Jedi in the Order's twenty-five-thousand-year history, yet at the age of seventy Dooku's principles would no longer allow him to serve a Republic in which political power was for sale to the highest bidder. He'd said farewell to his close friends on the Jedi Council, Mace Windu and the ancient Master Yoda; he'd said farewell to the Jedi Order itself.

He is numbered among the Lost: the Jedi who renounced their fealty to the Order and resigned their commissions of Jedi Knighthood in service of ideals higher than even the Order itself professed. The Lost Twenty, as they have been known since Dooku joined their number, are remembered with both honor and regret among the Jedi; their images, sculpted from bronzium, stand enshrined in the Temple archives.

These bronzium images serve as melancholy reminders that some Jedi have needs the Order cannot satisfy.

Dooku had retired to his family estate, the planetary system of Serenno. Assuming his hereditary title as its Count made him one of the wealthiest beings in the galaxy. Amid the unabashed corruption endemic to the Republic, his immense wealth could have bought the allegiance of any given number of Senators; he could, perhaps, have bought control of the Republic itself.

But a man of such heritage, such principle, could never stoop to be lord of a garbage heap, chief of a horde of scavengers squabbling over scraps; the Republic, to him, was nothing more than this.

Instead, he used all the great power of his family fortune—and the vastly greater power of his unquestioned integrity—to begin the cleansing of the galaxy from the fester of this so-called democracy.

He is the icon of the Separatist movement, its public face. He is to the Confederacy of Independent Systems what Palpatine is to the Republic: the living symbol of the justice of its cause.

This is the public story.

This is the story that even Dooku, in his weaker moments, almost believes.

The truth is more complicated.

Dooku is . . . different.

He doesn't remember quite when he discovered this; it may have been when he was a young Padawan, betrayed by another learner who had claimed to be his friend. Lorian Nod had said it to his face: "You don't know what friendship is."

And he didn't.

He had been angry, certainly; furious that his reputation had been put at risk. And he had been angry at himself, for his error in judgment: trusting as an ally one who was in fact an enemy. The most astonishing part of the whole affair had been that even after turning on him before the Jedi, the other boy had expected him to participate in a lie, in the name of their "friendship."

It had been all so preposterous that he hadn't known how to reply.

In fact, he has never been entirely sure what beings mean when they speak of friendship. Love, hate, joy, anger—even when he can feel the energy of these emotions in others, they translate in his perception to other kinds of feelings.

The kinds that make sense.

Jealousy he understands, and possessiveness: he is fierce when any being encroaches on what is rightfully his.

Intolerance, at the intractability of the universe, and at the undisciplined lives of its inhabitants: this is his normal state.

Spite is a recreation: he takes considerable pleasure from the suffering of his enemies.

Pride is a virtue in an aristocrat, and indignation his inalienable right: when any dare to impugn his integrity, his honor, or his rightful place atop the natural hierarchy of authority.

And moral outrage makes perfect sense to him: when the incorrigibly untidy affairs of ordinary beings refuse to conform to the plainly obvious structure of How Society Ought To Be.

He is entirely incapable of caring what any given creature might feel for him. He cares only what that creature might do for him. Or to him.

Very possibly, he is what he is because other beings just aren't very . . . interesting.

Or even, in a sense, entirely real.

For Dooku, other beings are mostly abstractions, simple schematic sketches who fall into two essential categories. The first category is Assets: beings who can be used to serve his various interests. Such as—for most of his life, and to some extent even now—the Jedi, particularly Mace Windu and Yoda, both of whom had regarded him as their friend for so long that it had effectively blinded them to the truth of his activities. And of course—for now—the Trade Federation, and the InterGalactic

Banking Clan, the Techno Union, the Corporate Alliance, and the weapon lords of Geonosis. And even the common rabble of the galaxy, who exist largely to provide an audience of sufficient size to do justice to his grandeur.

The other category is Threats. In this second set, he numbers every sentient being he cannot include in the first.

There is no third category.

Someday there may be not even a second; being considered a Threat by Count Dooku is a death sentence. A death sentence he plans to pronounce, for example, on his current allies: the heads of the aforementioned Trade Federation, InterGalactic Banking Clan, Techno Union, and Corporate Alliance, and Geonosian weaponeers.

Treachery is the way of the Sith.

Count Dooku watched with clinical distaste as the blue-scanned images of Kenobi and Skywalker engaged in a preposterous farce-chase, pursued by destroyer droids into and out of turbolift pods that shot upward and downward and even sideways.

"It will be," he said slowly, meditatively, as though he spoke only to himself, "an embarrassment to be captured by him."

The voice that answered him was so familiar that sometimes his very thoughts spoke in it, instead of in his own. "An embarrassment you can survive, Lord Tyranus. After all, he is the greatest Jedi alive, is he not? And have we not ensured that all the galaxy shares this opinion?"

"Quite so, my Master. Quite so." Again, Dooku sighed. Today he felt every hour of his eighty-three years. "It is . . . fatiguing, to play the villain for so long, Master. I find myself looking forward to an honorable captivity."

A captivity that would allow him to sit out the rest of the war in comfort; a captivity that would allow him to forswear his former allegiances—when he would conveniently appear to finally discover the true extent of the Separatists' crimes against civilization—and bind himself to the *new* government with his reputation for integrity and idealism fully intact.

The new government . . .

This had been their star of destiny for lo, these many years.

A government clean, pure, direct: none of the messy scramble for the favor of ignorant rabble and subhuman creatures that made up the Republic he so despised. The government he would serve would be Authority personified.

Human authority.

It was no accident that the primary powers of the Confederacy of Independent Systems were Neimoidian, Skakoan, Quarren and Aqualish, Muun and Gossam, Sy Myrthian and Koorivar and Geonosian. At war's end the aliens would be crushed, stripped of all they possessed, and their systems and their wealth would be given into the hands of the only beings who could be trusted with them.

Human beings.

Dooku would serve an Empire of Man.

And he would serve it as only he could. As he was *born* to. He would smash the Jedi Order to create it anew: not shackled by the corrupt, narcissistic, shabby little beings who called themselves politicians, but free to bring true authority and true peace to a galaxy that so badly needed both.

An Order that would not negotiate. Would not mediate.

An Order that would *enforce*.

The survivors of the Jedi Order would become the Sith Army.

The Fist of the Empire.

And that Fist would become a power beyond any Jedi's darkest dreams. The Jedi were not the only users of the Force in the galaxy; from Hapes to Haruun Kal, from Kiffu to Dathomir, powerful Force-capable humans and near-humans had long refused to surrender their children to lifelong bound servitude in the Jedi Order. They would not so refuse the Sith Army.

They would not have the choice.

Dooku frowned down at the holoimage. Kenobi and Sky-walker were going through more low-comedy business with an-other balky turbolift—possibly Grievous having some fun with the shaft controls—while battle droids haplessly pursued.

Really, it was all so . . .

Undignified.

"May I suggest, Master, that we give Kenobi one last chance? The support of a Jedi of his integrity would be invaluable in es-tablishing the political legitimacy of our Empire."

"Ah, yes. Kenobi." His Master's voice went silken. "You have long been interested in Kenobi, haven't you?"

"Of course. His Master was my Padawan; in a sense, he's practically my grandson—"

"He is too old. Too indoctrinated. Irretrievably poisoned by Jedi fables. We established that on Geonosis, did we not? In his mind, he serves the Force itself; reality is nothing in the face of such conviction."

Dooku sighed. He should, he supposed, have no difficulty with this, having ordered the Jedi Master's death once already. "True enough, I suppose; how fortunate we are that I never la-bored under any such illusions."

"Kenobi must die. Today. At your hand. His death may be the code key of the final lock that will seal Skywalker to us for-ever."

Dooku understood: not only would the death of his mentor tip Skywalker's already unstable emotional balance down the darkest of slopes, but it would also remove the greatest obstacle to Skywalker's successful conversion. As long as Kenobi was alive, Skywalker would never be securely in the camp of the Sith; Kenobi's unshakable faith in the values of the Jedi would keep the Jedi blindfold on Skywalker's eyes and the Jedi shackles on the young man's true power.

Still, though, Dooku had some reservations. This had all come about too quickly; had Sidious thought through all the implications of this operation? "But I must ask, my Master: is Skywalker truly the man we want?"

"He is powerful. Potentially more powerful than even myself."

"Which is precisely," Dooku said meditatively, "why it might be best if I were to kill *him*, instead."

"Are you so certain that you can?"

"Please. Of what use is power unstructured by discipline? The boy is as much a danger to himself as he is to his enemies. And that mechanical arm—" Dooku's lip curled with cultivated distaste. "Revolting."

"Then perhaps you should have spared his real arm."

"Hmp. A gentleman would have learned to fight one-handed." Dooku flicked a dismissive wave. "He's no longer even entirely human. With Grievous, the use of these bio-droid devices is almost forgivable; he was such a disgusting creature already that his mechanical parts are clearly an improvement. But a blend of droid and *human*? Appalling. The depths of bad taste. How are we to justify associating with him?"

"How fortunate I am"—the silk in his Master's voice softened further—"to have an apprentice who feels it is appropriate to *lecture* me."

Dooku lifted an eyebrow. "I have overstepped, my Master," he said with his customary grace. "I am only observing, not arguing. Not at all."

"Skywalker's arm makes him, for our purposes, even better. It is the permanent symbol of the sacrifices he has made in the name of peace and justice. It is a badge of heroism that he must publicly wear for the rest of his life; no one can ever look at him and doubt his honor, his courage, his integrity. He is perfect, just as he is. *Perfect.* The only question that remains is whether he is capable of transcending the artificial limitations of his Jedi indoctrination. And that, my lord Count, is precisely what today's operation is designed to discover."

Dooku could not argue. Not only had the Dark Lord introduced Dooku to realms of power beyond his most spectacular fantasies, but Sidious was also a political manipulator so subtle that his abilities might be considered to dwarf even the power of the dark side itself. It was said that whenever the Force closes a hatch, it opens a viewport . . . and every viewport that had so much as cracked in this past thirteen standard years had found a Dark Lord of the Sith already at the rim, peering in, calculating how best to slip through.

Improving upon his Master's plan was near to impossible; his own idea, of substituting Kenobi for Skywalker, he had to admit was only the product of a certain misplaced sentimentality. Skywalker was almost certainly the man for the job.

He should be; Darth Sidious had spent a considerable number of years making him so.

Today's test would remove the *almost.*

He had no doubt that Skywalker would fall. Dooku understood that this was more than a test for Skywalker; though Sidious had never said so directly, Dooku was certain that he himself was being tested as well. Success today would show his Master that he was worthy of the mantle of Mastery himself: by the end of the coming battle, he would have initiated Skywalker into the manifold glories of the dark side, just as Sidious had initiated him.

He gave no thought to failure. Why should he?

"But—forgive me, Master. But Kenobi having fallen to my blade, are you certain Skywalker will ever accept my orders? You must admit that his biography offers little confidence that he is capable of obedience at all."

"Skywalker's power brings with it more than mere obedi-

ence. It brings creativity, and luck; we need never concern ourselves with the sort of instruction that Grievous, for example, requires. Even the blind fools on the Jedi Council see clearly
enough to understand this; even they no longer try to tell him
how, they merely tell him *what*. And he finds a way. He always
has."

Dooku nodded. For the first time since Sidious had revealed
the true subtlety of this masterpiece, Dooku allowed himself to
relax enough to imagine the outcome.

With his heroic capture of Count Dooku, Anakin Skywalker
will become the ultimate hero: the greatest hero in the history of
the Republic, perhaps of the Jedi Order itself. The loss of his
beloved partner will add just exactly the correct spice of tragedy
to give melancholy weight to his every word, when he gives his
HoloNet interviews denouncing the Senate's corruption as im-
peding the war effort, when he delicately—oh, so delicately, not
to mention *reluctantly*—insinuates that corruption in the Jedi
Order prolonged the war as well.

When he announces the creation of a new order of Force-
using warriors.

He will be the perfect commanding general for the Sith
Army.

Dooku could only shake his head in awe. And to think that
only days earlier, the Jedi had seemed so close to uncovering,
even destroying, all he and his Master had worked for. But he
should never have feared. His Master never lost. He would never
lose. He was the definition of unbeatable.

How can one defeat an enemy one thinks is a friend?

And now, with a single brilliant stroke, his Master would turn
the Jedi Order back upon itself like an Ethrani ourobouros de-
vouring its own tail.

This was the day. The hour.

The death of Obi-Wan Kenobi would be the death of the Republic.

Today would see the birth of the Empire.

"Tyranus? Are you well?"

"Am I . . ." Dooku realized that his eyes had misted. "Yes, my Master. I am beyond well. Today, the climax—the grand finale—the culmination of all your decades of work . . . I find myself somewhat overcome."

"Compose yourself, Tyranus. Kenobi and Skywalker are nearly at the door. Play your part, my apprentice, and the galaxy is ours."

Dooku straightened and for the first time looked his Master in the eyes.

Darth Sidious, Dark Lord of the Sith, sat in the General's Chair, shackled to it at the wrist and ankle.

Dooku bowed to him. "Thank you, Chancellor."

Palpatine of Naboo, Supreme Chancellor of the Republic, replied, "Withdraw. They are here."

THE WAY OF THE SITH

The turbolift's door whished open. Anakin pressed himself against the wall, a litter of saber-sliced droid parts around his feet. Beyond appeared to be a perfectly ordinary lift lobby: pale and bare and empty.

Made it. At last.

Anakin's whole body hummed to the tune of his blue-hot blade.

"Anakin."

Obi-Wan stood against the opposite wall. He looked calm in a way Anakin could barely understand. He gave a significant stare down at the lightsaber in Anakin's hand. "Anakin, rescue," he said softly. "Not mayhem."

Anakin kept his weapon right where it was. "And Dooku?"

"Once the Chancellor is safe," Obi-Wan said with a ghost of a smile, "we can blow up the ship."

Anakin's mechanical fingers tightened until the grip of his lightsaber creaked. "I'd rather do it by hand."

Obi-Wan slipped cautiously through the turbolift's door. Nothing shot at him. He beckoned. "I know this is difficult,

Anakin. I know it's personal for you on many levels. You must take extra care to be mindful of your training here—and not only your *combat* training."

Heat rose in Anakin's cheeks. "I am *not*—" *your Padawan anymore* snarled inside his head, but that was adrenaline talking; he bit back the words and said instead, "—going to let you down, Master. Or Chancellor Palpatine."

"I have no doubt of that. Just remember that Dooku is no mere Dark Jedi like that Ventress woman; he is a Lord of the Sith. The jaws of this trap are about to snap shut, and there may be danger here beyond the merely physical."

"Yes." Anakin let his blade shrink away and moved past Obi-Wan into the turbolift lobby. Distant concussions boomed throughout the ship, and the floor rocked like a raft on a river in flood; he barely noticed. "I just—there has been so much—what he's *done*—not just to the Jedi, but to the *galaxy*—"

"Anakin . . . ," Obi-Wan began warningly.

"Don't worry. I'm not angry, and I'm not looking for revenge. I'm just—" He lifted his lightsaber. "I'm just looking forward to ending it."

"Anticipation—"

"Is distraction. I know. And I know that hope is as hollow as fear." Anakin let himself smile, just a bit. "And I know everything else you're dying to tell me right now."

Obi-Wan's slightly rueful bow of acknowledgment was as affectionate as a hug. "I suppose at some point I will eventually have to stop trying to train you."

Anakin's smile broadened toward a soft chuckle. "I think that's the first time you've ever admitted it."

They stopped at the door to the General's Quarters: a huge oval of opalescent iridiite chased with gold. Anakin stared at his ghostly almost-reflection while he reached into the room beyond with the Force, and let the Force reach into him. "I'm ready, Master."

"I know you are."

They stood a moment, side by side.

Anakin didn't look at him; he stared into the door, through the door, searching in its shimmering depths for a hint of an unguessable future.

He couldn't imagine not being at war.

"Anakin." Obi-Wan's voice had gone soft, and his hand was warm on Anakin's arm. "There is no other Jedi I would rather have at my side right now. No other man."

Anakin turned, and found within Obi-Wan's eyes a depth of feeling he had only rarely glimpsed in all their years together; and the pure uncomplicated love that rose up within him then felt like a promise from the Force itself.

"I . . . wouldn't have it any other way, Master."

"I believe," his onetime Master said with a gently humorous look of astonishment at the words coming out of his mouth, "that you should get used to calling me Obi-Wan."

"Obi-Wan," Anakin said, "let's go get the Chancellor."

"Yes," Obi-Wan said. "Let's."

Inside a turbolift pod, Dooku watched hologrammic images of Kenobi and Skywalker cautiously pick their way down the curving stairs from the entrance balcony to the main level of the General's Quarters, moving slowly to stay braced against the pitching of the cruiser. The ship shuddered and bucked with multiple torpedo bursts, and the lights went out again; lighting was always the first to fail as power was diverted from life support to damage control.

My lord. On the intraship comm, Grievous sounded actively concerned. *Damage to this ship is becoming severe. Thirty percent of automated weapons systems are down, and we may soon lose hyperspace capability.*

Dooku nodded judiciously to himself, frowning down at the translucent blue ghosts slinking toward Palpatine. "Sound the retreat for the entire strike force, General, and prepare the ship for jump. Once the Jedi are dead, I will join you on the bridge."

"As my lord commands. Grievous out."

"Indeed you are, you vile creature," Dooku muttered to the dead comlink. "Out of luck, and out of time."

He cast the comlink aside and ignored its clatter across the deck. He had no further use for it. Let it be destroyed along with Grievous, those repulsive bodyguards of his, and the rest of the cruiser, once he was safely captured and away.

He nodded to the two hulking super battle droids that flanked him. One opened the lift door and they marched through, pivoting to take positions on either side.

Dooku straightened his cloak of shimmering armorweave and strode grandly into the half-dark lift lobby. In the pale emergency lighting, the door to the General's Quarters still smoldered where those two idiotic peasants had lightsabered it; to pick his way through the hole would risk getting his trousers scorched. Dooku sighed and gestured, and the opalescent wreckage of the door silently slid itself out of his way.

He certainly did not intend to fight two Jedi with his pants on fire.

Anakin slid along the bank of chairs on one side of the immense situation table that dominated the center of the General's Quarters' main room; Obi-Wan mirrored him on the opposite side. Silent lightning flashed and flared: the room's sole illumination came from the huge curving view wall at its far end, a storm of turbolaser blasts and flak bursts and the miniature supernovae that were the deaths of entire ships.

A stark shadow against that backdrop of carnage: the silhouette of one tall chair.

Anakin caught Obi-Wan's eye across the table and nodded toward the dark shape ahead. Obi-Wan replied with the Jedi hand signal for *approach with caution,* and added the signal for *be ready for action.*

Anakin's mouth compressed. Like he needed to be told. After all the trouble they'd had with the turbolifts, anything could be up here by now. The place could be full of droidekas, for all they knew.

The lights came back on.

Anakin froze.

The dark figure in the chair—it *was* Chancellor Palpatine, it was, and there were no droids to be seen, and his heart should have leapt within his chest, but—

Palpatine looked bad.

The Chancellor looked beyond old, looked ancient like Yoda was ancient: possessed of incomprehensible age. And exhausted, and in pain. And worse—

Anakin saw in the Chancellor's face something he'd never dreamed he'd find there, and it squeezed breath from his lungs and wiped words from his brain.

Palpatine looked *frightened.*

Anakin didn't know what to say. He couldn't *imagine* what to say. All he could imagine was what Grievous and Dooku must have done to put fear on the face of this brave good man—

And that imagining ignited a sizzle in his blood that drew his face tight and clouded his heart and started again the low roll of thunder in his ears: thunder from Aargonar. From Jabiim.

Thunder from the Tusken camp.

If Obi-Wan was struck by any similar distress, it was invisible. With his customary grave courtesy, the Jedi Master inclined his head. "Chancellor," he said, a calmly respectful greeting as though they had met by chance on the Grand Concourse of the Galactic Senate.

Palpatine's only response was a tight murmur. "Anakin, *behind* you—!"

Anakin didn't turn. He didn't have to. It wasn't just the clack of boot heels and clank of magnapeds crossing the threshold of the entrance balcony; the Force gathered within him and around him in a sudden clench like the fists of a startled man.

In the Force, he could feel the focus of Palpatine's eyes: the source of the fear that rolled off him in billows like vapor down a block of frozen air. And he could feel the even colder wave of power, colder than the frost on a mynock's mouth, that slid into the room behind him like an ice dagger into his back.

Funny, he thought. *After Ventress, somehow I always expect the dark side to be hot . . .*

Something unlocked in his chest. The thunder in his ears dissolved into red smoke that coiled at the base of his spine. His lightsaber found his hand, and his lips peeled off his teeth in a smile that a krayt dragon would have recognized.

That trouble he was having with talking went away.

"This," he murmured to Palpatine, and to himself, "is not a problem."

The voice that spoke from the entrance balcony was an elegant basso with undernotes of oily resonance like a kriin-oak cavernhorn.

Count Dooku's voice.

"General Kenobi. Anakin Skywalker. Gentlemen—a term I use in its loosest possible sense—you are my prisoners."

Now Anakin didn't have any troubles at all.

The entrance balcony provided an appropriate angle—far above the Jedi, looking down upon them—for Dooku to make final assessments before beginning the farce.

Like all true farce, the coming denouement would proceed with remorseless logic from its ridiculous premise: that Dooku could ever be overcome by mere Jedi. Any Jedi. What a pity his old friend Mace couldn't have joined them today; he had no doubt the Korun Master would have enjoyed the coming show.

Dooku had always preferred an educated audience.

At least Palpatine was here, shackled within the great chair at the far end of the room, the space battle whirling upon the view wall behind him as though his stark silhouette spread great wings of war. But Palpatine was less audience than he was author.

Not at all the same thing.

Skywalker gave Dooku only his back, but his blade was already out and his tall, lean frame stood frozen with anticipation: so motionless he almost seemed to shiver. Pathetic. It was an insult to call this boy a Jedi at all.

Kenobi, now—he was something else entirely: a classic of his obsolete kind. He simply stood gazing calmly up at Dooku and the super battle droids that flanked him, hands open, utterly relaxed, on his face only an expression of mild interest.

Dooku derived a certain melancholy satisfaction—a pleasurably lonely contemplation of his own unrecognized greatness— from a brief reflection that Skywalker would never understand how much thought and planning, how much *work*, Lord Sidious had invested in so hastily orchestrating his sham victory. Nor would he ever understand the artistry, the true mastery, that Dooku would wield in his own defeat.

But thus was life. Sacrifices must be made, for the greater good.

There was a war on, after all.

He called upon the Force, gathering it to himself and wrapping himself within it. He breathed it in and held it whirling inside his heart, clenching down upon it until he could feel the spin of the galaxy around him.

Until he became the axis of the Universe.

This was the real power of the dark side, the power he had suspected even as a boy, had sought through his long life until Darth Sidious had shown him that it had been his all along. The dark side didn't bring him to the center of the universe. It *made* him the center.

He drew power into his innermost being until the Force itself existed only to serve his will.

Now the scene below subtly altered, though to the physical eye there was no change. Powered by the dark side, Dooku's perception took the measure of those below him with exhilarating precision.

Kenobi was luminous, a transparent being, a window onto a sunlit meadow of the Force.

Skywalker was a storm cloud, flickering with dangerous lightning, building the rotation that threatens a tornado.

And then there was Palpatine, of course: he was beyond power. He showed nothing of what might be within. Though seen with the eyes of the dark side itself, Palpatine was an event horizon. Beneath his entirely ordinary surface was absolute, perfect nothingness. Darkness beyond darkness.

A black hole of the Force.

And he played his helpless-hostage role perfectly.

"Get help!" The edge of panic in his hoarse half whisper sounded real even to Dooku. "You *must* get help. Neither of you is any match for a Sith Lord!"

Now Skywalker turned, meeting Dooku's direct gaze for the first time since the abandoned hangar on Geonosis. His reply was clearly intended as much for Dooku as for Palpatine. "Tell that to the one Obi-Wan left in pieces on Naboo."

Hmp. Empty bravado. Maul had been an animal. A skilled animal, but a beast nonetheless.

"Anakin—" In the Force, Dooku could feel Kenobi's disapproval of Skywalker's boasting; and he could also feel Kenobi's effortless self-restraint in focusing on the matter at hand. "This time, we do it *together*."

Dooku's sharp eye picked up the tightening of Skywalker's droid hand on his lightsaber's grip. "I was about to say exactly that."

Fine, then. Time to move this little comedy along.

Dooku leaned forward, and his cloak of armorweave spread like wings; he lifted gently into the air and descended to the main level in a slow, dignified Force-glide. Touching down at the head of the situation table, he regarded the two Jedi from under a lifted brow.

"Your weapons, please, gentlemen. Let's not make a mess of this in front of the Chancellor."

Obi-Wan lifted his lightsaber into the balanced two-handed guard of Ataro: Qui-Gon's style, and Yoda's. His blade crackled into existence, and the air smelled of lightning. "You won't escape us this time, Dooku."

"Escape you? Please." Dooku allowed his customary mild smile to spread. "Do you think I orchestrated this entire operation with the intent to *escape*? I could have taken the Chancellor outsystem hours ago. But I have better things to do with my life than to babysit him while I wait for the pair of you to attempt a rescue."

Skywalker brought his lightsaber to a Shien ready: hand of black-gloved durasteel cocked high at his shoulder, blade angling upward and away. "This is a little more than an attempt."

"And a little less than a rescue."

With a flourish, Dooku cast his cloak back from his right shoulder, clearing his sword arm—which he used to gesture idly at the pair of super battle droids still on the entrance balcony above. "Now please, gentlemen. Must I order the droids to open fire? That becomes so untidy, what with blaster bolts bouncing about at random. Little danger to the three of us, of course, but I should certainly hate for any harm to come to the Chancellor."

Kenobi moved toward him with a slow, hypnotic grace, as though he floated on an invisible repulsor plate. "Why do I find that difficult to believe?"

Skywalker mirrored him, swinging wide toward Dooku's flank. "You weren't so particular about bloodshed on Geonosis."

"Ah." Dooku's smile spread even farther. "And how *is* Senator Amidala?"

"Don't—" The thunderstorm that was Skywalker in the Force boiled with sudden power. "Don't even speak her name."

Dooku waved this aside. The lad's personal issues were too tiresome to pursue; he knew far too much already about Skywalker's messy private life. "I bear Chancellor Palpatine no ill will, foolish boy. He is neither soldier nor spy, whereas you and your friend here are both. It is only an unfortunate accident of history that he has chosen to defend a corrupt Republic against my endeavor to reform it."

"You mean *destroy* it."

"The Chancellor is a civilian. You and General Kenobi, on the other hand, are legitimate military targets. It is up to you whether you will accompany me as captives—" A twitch of the Force brought his lightsaber to his hand with invisible speed, its brilliant scarlet blade angled downward at his side. "—or as *corpses.*"

"Now, there's a coincidence," Kenobi replied dryly as he swung around Dooku to place the Count precisely between Skywalker and himself. "You face the identical choice."

Dooku regarded each of them in turn with impregnable calm. He lifted his blade in the Makashi salute and swept it again to a low guard. "Just because there are two of you, do not presume you have the advantage."

"Oh, we know," Skywalker said. "Because there are two of *you.*"

Dooku barely managed to restrain a jolt of surprise.

"Or maybe I should say, *were* two of you," the young Jedi went on. "We're on to your partner *Sidious;* we tracked him all over the galaxy. He's probably in Jedi custody right now."

"Is he?" Dooku relaxed. He was terribly, terribly tempted to wink at Palpatine, but of course that would never do. "How fortunate for you."

Quite simple, in the end, he thought. *Isolate Skywalker, slaughter Kenobi.* Beyond that, it would be merely a matter of spinning Skywalker up into enough of a frenzy to break through his Jedi restraint and reveal the infinite vista of Sith power.

Lord Sidious would take it from there.

"Surrender." Kenobi's voice deepened into finality. "You will be given no further chance."

Dooku lifted an eyebrow. "Unless one of you happens to be carrying Yoda in his pocket, I hardly think I shall need one."

The Force crackled between them, and the ship pitched and bucked under a new turbolaser barrage, and Dooku decided that the time had come. He flicked a false glance over his shoulder— a hint of distraction to draw the attack—

And all three of them moved at once.

The ship shuddered and the red smoke surged from Anakin's spine into his arms and legs and head and when Dooku gave the slightest glance of concern over his shoulder, distracted for half an instant, Anakin just couldn't wait anymore.

He sprang, lightsaber angled for the kill.

Obi-Wan leapt from Dooku's far side in perfect coordination—and they met in midair, for the Sith Lord was no longer between them.

Anakin looked up just in time to glimpse the bottom of Dooku's rancor-leather boot as it came down on his face and smacked him tumbling toward the floor; he reached into the Force to effortlessly right himself and touched down in perfect balance to spring again toward the lightning flares, scarlet against sky blue, that sprayed from clashing lightsabers as Dooku pressed Obi-Wan away with a succession of weaving, flourishing thrusts that drove the Jedi's blade out of line while they reached for his heart.

Anakin launched himself at Dooku's back—and the Count half turned, gesturing casually while holding Obi-Wan at bay with an elegant one-handed bind. Chairs leapt up from the situation table and whirled toward Anakin's head. He slashed the first one in half contemptuously, but the second caught him across the knees and the third battered his shoulder and knocked him down.

He snarled to himself and reached through the Force to pick up some chairs of his own—and the situation table itself slammed into him and drove him back to crush him against the wall. His lightsaber came loose from his slackening fingers and clattered across the tabletop to drop to the floor on the far side.

And Dooku barely even seemed to be paying attention to him.

Pinned, breathless, half stunned, Anakin thought, *If this keeps up, I am going to get mad.*

While effortlessly deflecting a rain of blue-streaking cuts from Kenobi, Dooku felt the Force shove the situation table away from the wall and send it hurtling toward his back with astonishing speed; he barely managed to lift himself enough that he could backroll over it instead of having it shatter his spine.

"My my," he said, chuckling. "The boy has some power after all."

His backroll brought him to his feet directly in front of the lad, who was charging, headlong and unarmed, after the table he had tossed, and was already thoroughly red in the face.

"I'm *twice* the Jedi I was last time!"

Ah, Dooku thought. *Such a fragile little ego. Sidious will have to help him with that. But until then—*

The grip of Skywalker's blade whistled through the air to meet his hand in perfect synchrony with a sweeping slash. "My powers have *doubled* since we last met—"

"How lovely for you." Dooku neatly sidestepped, cutting at the boy's leg, yet Skywalker's blade met the cut as he passed and he managed to sweep his blade behind his head to slap aside the casual thrust Dooku aimed at the back of his neck—but his clumsy charge had put him in Kenobi's path, so that the Jedi Master had to Force-roll over his partner's head.

Directly at Dooku's upraised blade.

Kenobi drove a slash at the scarlet blade while he pivoted in the air, and again Dooku sidestepped so that now it was Kenobi in Skywalker's way.

"Really," Dooku said, "this is pathetic."

Oh, they were certainly energetic enough, leaping and whirling, raining blows almost at random, cutting chairs to pieces and Force-hurling them in every conceivable direction, while Dooku continued, in his gracefully methodical way, to out-maneuver them so thoroughly it was all he could do to keep from laughing out loud.

It was a simple matter of countering their tactics, which were depressingly straightforward; Skywalker was the swift one, whooshing here and there like a spastic hawk-bat—attempting a Jedi variant of neek-in-the-middle so they could come at him from both sides—while Kenobi came on in a measured Shii-Cho cadence, deliberate as a lumberdroid, moving step by step, cut-ting off the angles, clumsy but relentlessly dogged as he tried to chivvy Dooku into a corner.

Whereas all Dooku need do was to slip from one side to another—and occasionally flip over a head here and there—so that he could fight each of them in turn, rather than both of them at the same time. He supposed that in their own milieu, they might actually prove reasonably effective; it was clear that their style had been developed by fighting as a team against large numbers of opponents. They were not prepared to fight together against a single Force-user, certainly not one of Dooku's power; he, on the other hand, had always fought alone. It was laughably easy to keep the Jedi tripping and stumbling and getting in each other's way.

They didn't even comprehend how utterly he dominated the

combat. Because they fought as they had been trained, by releasing all desire and allowing the Force to flow through them, they had no hope of countering Dooku's mastery of Sith techniques. They had learned nothing since he had bested them on Geonosis.

They allowed the Force to direct them; Dooku directed the Force.

He drew their strikes to his parries, and drove his own ripostes with thrusts of dark power that subtly altered the Jedi's balance and disrupted their timing. He could have slaughtered both of them as casually as that creature Maul had destroyed the vigos of the Black Sun.

However, only one death was in his plan, and this dumbshow was becoming tiresome. Not to mention tiring. The dark power that served him went only so far, and he was, after all, not a young man.

He leaned into a thrust at Kenobi's gut that the Jedi Master deflected with a rising parry, bringing them chest-to-chest, blades flaring, locked together a handbreadth from each other's throats. "Your moves are too slow, Kenobi. Too predictable. You'll have to do better."

Kenobi's response to this friendly word was to regard him with a twinkle of gentle amusement in his eye.

"Very well, then," the Jedi said, and shot straight upward over Dooku's head so fast it seemed he'd vanished.

And in the space where Kenobi's chest had been was now only the blue lightning of Skywalker's blade driving straight for Dooku's heart.

Only a desperate whirl to one side made what would have been a smoking hole in his chest into a line of scorch through his armorweave cloak.

Dooku thought, *What?*

He threw himself spinning up and away from the two Jedi to land on the situation table, disengaging for a moment to recover his composure—that had been *entirely* too close—but by the time his boots touched down Kenobi was there to meet him, blade weaving through a defensive velocity so bewilderingly fast that Dooku dared not even try a strike; he threw a feint toward Kenobi's face, then dropped and spun in a reverse ankle-sweep—

But not only did Kenobi easily overleap this attack, Dooku nearly lost his *own* foot to a slash from *Skywalker* who had again come out of *nowhere* and now carved through the table so that it collapsed under Dooku's weight and dumped the Sith Lord unceremoniously to the floor.

This was *not* in the plan.

Skywalker slammed his following strike down so hard that the shock of deflecting it buckled Dooku's elbows. Dooku threw himself into a backroll that brought him to his feet—and Kenobi's blade was there to meet his neck. Only a desperate whirling slash-block, coupled with a wheel kick that caught Kenobi on the thigh, bought him enough time to leap away again, and when he touched down—

Skywalker was already there.

The first overhand chop of Skywalker's blade slid off Dooku's instinctive guard. The second bent Dooku's wrist. The third flash of blue forced Dooku's scarlet blade so far to the inside that his own lightsaber scorched his shoulder, and Dooku was forced to give ground.

Dooku felt himself blanch. Where had *this* come from?

Skywalker came on, mechanically inexorable, impossibly powerful, a destroyer droid with a lightsaber: each step a blow and each blow a step. Dooku backed away as fast as he dared; Skywalker stayed right on top of him. Dooku's breath went short and hard. He no longer tried to block Skywalker's strikes but only to guide them slanting away; he could not meet Skywalker strength-to-strength—not only did the boy wield tremendous reserves of Force energy, but his sheer physical power was astonishing—

And only then did Dooku understand that he'd been suckered.

Skywalker's Shien ready-stance had been a ruse, as had his Ataro gymmnastics; the boy was a Djem So stylist, and as fine a one as Dooku had ever seen. His own elegant Makashi simply did not generate the kinetic power to meet Djem So head-to-head. Especially not while also defending against a second attacker.

It was time to alter his own tactics.

He dropped low and spun into another reverse ankle-sweep—the weakness of Djem So was its lack of mobility—that slapped Skywalker's boot sharply enough to throw the young Jedi off balance, giving Dooku the opportunity to leap away—

Only to find himself again facing the wheel of blue lightning that was Kenobi's blade.

Dooku decided that the comedy had ended.

Now it was time to kill.

Kenobi's Master had been Qui-Gon Jinn, Dooku's own Padawan; Dooku had fenced Qui-Gon thousands of times, and he knew every weakness of the Ataro form, with its ridiculous acrobatics. He drove a series of flashing thrusts toward Kenobi's legs to draw the Jedi Master into a flipping overhead leap so that Dooku could burn through his spine from kidneys to shoulder blades—and this image, this plan, was so clear in Dooku's mind that he almost failed to notice that Kenobi met every one of his thrusts without so much as moving his feet, staying perfectly centered, perfectly balanced, blade never moving a millimeter more than was necessary, deflecting without effort, riposting with flickering strikes and stabs swifter than the tongue of a Garollian ghost viper, and when Dooku felt Skywalker regain his feet and stride once more toward his back, he finally registered the source of that blinding defensive velocity Kenobi had used a moment ago, and only then, belatedly, did he understand that Kenobi's Ataro and Shii-Cho had been ploys, as well.

Kenobi had become a master of Soresu.

Dooku found himself having a sudden, unexpected, over-powering, and entirely distressing *bad feeling* about this . . .

His farce had suddenly, inexplicably, spun from humorous to deadly serious and was tumbling rapidly toward terrifying. Realization burst through Dooku's consciousness like the blossoming fireballs of dying ships outside: this pair of Jedi fools had somehow managed to become entirely dangerous.

These clowns might—just possibly—actually be able to *beat* him.

No sense taking chances; even his Master would agree with that. Lord Sidious could come up with a new plan more easily than a new apprentice.

He gathered the Force once more in a single indrawn breath that summoned power from throughout the universe; the slightest whipcrack of that power, negligent as a flick of his wrist, sent Kenobi flying backward to crash hard against the wall, but Dooku didn't have time to enjoy it.

Skywalker was all over him.

The shining blue lightsaber whirled and spat and every overhand chop crashed against Dooku's defense with the unstoppable power of a meteor strike; the Sith Lord spent lavishly of his reserve of the Force merely to meet these attacks without being cut in half, and Skywalker—

Skywalker was getting *stronger.*

Each parry cost Dooku more power than he'd used to throw Kenobi across the room; each block aged him a decade.

He decided he'd best revise his strategy once again.

He no longer even tried to strike back. Force exhaustion began to close down his perceptions, drawing his consciousness back down to his physical form, trapping him within his own skull until he could barely even feel the contours of the room around him; he dimly sensed stairs at his back, stairs that led up to the entrance balcony. He retreated up them, using the higher ground for leverage, but Skywalker just kept on coming, tire-lessly ferocious.

That blue blade was everywhere, flashing and whirling faster and faster until Dooku saw the room through an electric haze, and now *Kenobi* was back in the picture: with a shout of the Force, he shot like a torpedo up the stairs behind Skywalker, and Dooku decided that under these rather extreme circumstances, it was at least arguably permissible for a gentleman to cheat.

"Guards!" he said to the pair of super battle droids that still stood at attention to either side of the entrance. "Open fire!"

Instantly the two droids sprang forward and lifted their hands. Energy hammered out from the heavy blasters built into their arms; Skywalker whirled and his blade batted every blast back at the droids, whose mirror-polished carapace armor de-flected the bolts again. Galvened particle beams screeched through the room in blinding ricochets.

Kenobi reached the top of the stairs and a single slash of his lightsaber dismantled both droids. Before their pieces could even hit the floor Dooku was in motion, landing a spinning side-stamp that folded Skywalker in half; he used his last burst of dark power to continue his spin into a blindingly fast wheel-kick that brought his heel against the point of Kenobi's chin with a *crack* like the report of a huge-bore slugthrower, knocking the Jedi Master back down the stairs. Sounded like he'd broken his neck.

Wouldn't that be lovely?

There was no sense in taking chances, however.

While Kenobi's bonelessly limp body was still tumbling toward the floor far below, Dooku sent a surge of energy through the Force. Kenobi's fall suddenly accelerated like a mis-sile burning the last of its drives before impact. The Jedi Master struck the floor at a steep angle, skidded along it, and slammed into the wall so hard the hydrofoamed permacrete buckled and collapsed onto him.

This Dooku found exceedingly gratifying.

Now, as for Skywalker—

Which was as far as Dooku got, because by the time his attention returned to the younger Jedi, his vision was rather completely obstructed by the sole of a boot approaching his face with something resembling terminal velocity.

The impact was a blast of white fire, and there was a second impact against his back that was the balcony rail, and then the room turned upside down and he fell toward the ceiling, but not really, of course: it only felt that way because he had flipped over the rail and he was falling headfirst toward the floor, and neither his arms nor his legs were paying any attention to what he was trying to make them do. The Force seemed to be busy elsewhere, and really, the whole process was entirely mortifying.

He was barely able to summon a last surge of dark power before what would have been a disabling impact. The Force cradled him, cushioning his fall and setting him on his feet.

He dusted himself off and fixed a supercilious gaze on Skywalker, who now stood upon the balcony looking down at him—and Dooku couldn't hold the stare; he found this reversal of their original positions oddly unsettling.

There was something troublingly *appropriate* about it.

Seeing Skywalker standing where Dooku himself had stood only moments ago . . . it was as though he was trying to remember a dream he'd never actually had . . .

He pushed this aside, drawing once more upon the certain knowledge of his personal invincibility to open a channel to the Force. Power flowed into him, and the weight of his years dropped away.

He lifted his blade, and beckoned.

Skywalker leapt from the balcony. Even as the boy hurtled downward, Dooku felt a new twist in the currents of the Force between them, and he finally understood.

He understood how Skywalker was getting stronger. Why he no longer spoke. How he had become a machine of battle. He understood why Sidious had been so interested in him for so long.

Skywalker was a natural.

There was a thermonuclear furnace where his heart should be, and it was burning through the firewalls of his Jedi training. He held the Force in the clench of a white-hot fist. He was half Sith already, and he didn't even know it.

This boy had the gift of fury.

And even now, he was holding himself back; even now, as he landed at Dooku's flank and rained blows upon the Sith Lord's defenses, even as he drove Dooku backward step after step, Dooku could feel how Skywalker kept his fury banked behind walls of will: walls that were hardened by some uncontrollable dread.

Dread, Dooku surmised, of himself. Of what might happen if he should ever allow that furnace he used for a heart to go supercritical.

Dooku slipped aside from an overhand chop and sprang backward. "I sense great fear in you. You are consumed by it. Hero With No Fear, indeed. You're a *fraud*, Skywalker. You are nothing but a posturing child."

He pointed his lightsaber at the young Jedi like an accusing finger. "Aren't you a little old to be afraid of the dark?"

Skywalker leapt for him again, and this time Dooku met the boy's charge easily. They stood nearly toe-to-toe, blades flashing faster than the eye could see, but Skywalker had lost his edge: a simple taunt was all that had been required to shift the focus of his attention from winning the fight to controlling his own emotions. The angrier he got, the more afraid he became, and the fear fed his anger in turn; like the proverbial Corellian multipede, now that he had started *thinking* about what he was doing, he could no longer walk.

Dooku allowed himself to relax; he felt that spirit of playfulness coming over him again as he and Skywalker spun 'round each other in their lethal dance. Whatever fun was to be had, he should enjoy while he could.

Then Sidious, for some reason, decided to intervene.

"Don't fear what you're feeling, Anakin, *use* it!" he barked in Palpatine's voice. "Call upon your fury. Focus it, and he cannot stand against you. *Rage* is your weapon. Strike now! *Strike! Kill* him!"

Dooku thought blankly, *Kill me?*

He and Skywalker paused for one single, final instant, blades locked together, staring at each other past a sizzling cross of scarlet against blue, and in that instant Dooku found himself wondering in bewildered astonishment if Sidious had suddenly lost his mind. Didn't he understand the advice he'd just given?

Whose side was he on, anyway?

And through the cross of their blades he saw in Skywalker's eyes the promise of hell, and he felt a sickening presentiment that he already knew the answer to that question.

Treachery is the way of the Sith.

JEDI TRAP

This is the death of Count Dooku:

A starburst of clarity blossoms within Anakin Skywalker's mind, when he says to himself *Oh. I get it, now* and discovers that the fear within his heart can be a weapon, too.

It is that simple, and that complex.

And it is final.

Dooku is dead already. The rest is mere detail.

The play is still on; the comedy of lightsabers flashes and snaps and hisses. Dooku & Skywalker, a one-time-only command performance, for an audience of one. Jedi and Sith and Sith and Jedi, spinning, whirling, crashing together, slashing and chopping, parrying, binding, slipping and whipping and ripping the air around them with snarls of power.

And all for nothing, because a nuclear flame has consumed Anakin Skywalker's Jedi restraint, and fear becomes fury without effort, and fury is a blade that makes his lightsaber into a toy.

The play goes on, but the suspense is over. It has become mere pantomime, as intricate and as meaningless as the space–time curves that guide galactic clusters through a measureless cosmos.

Dooku's decades of combat experience are irrelevant. His mastery of swordplay is useless. His vast wealth, his political influence, impeccable breeding, immaculate manners, exquisite taste—all the pursuits and points of pride to which he has devoted so much of his time and attention over the long, long years of his life—are now chains hung upon his spirit, bending his neck before the ax.

Even his knowledge of the Force has become a joke.

It is this knowledge that shows him his death, makes him handle it, turn it this way and that in his mind, examine it in detail like a black gemstone so cold it burns. Dooku's elegant farce has degenerated into bathetic melodrama, and not one shed tear will mark the passing of its hero.

But for Anakin, in the fight there is only terror, and rage.

Only he stands between death and the two men he loves best in all the world, and he can no longer afford to hold anything back. That imaginary dead-star dragon tries its best to freeze away his strength, to whisper him that Dooku has beaten him before, that Dooku has all the power of the darkness, to remind him how Dooku took his hand, how Dooku could strike down even Obi-Wan himself seemingly without effort and now Anakin is all alone and he will never be a match for any Lord of the Sith—

But Palpatine's words *rage is your weapon* have given Anakin permission to unseal the shielding around his furnace heart, and all his fears and all his doubts shrivel in its flame.

When Count Dooku flies at him, blade flashing, Watto's fist cracks out from Anakin's childhood to knock the Sith Lord tumbling back.

When with all the power that the dark side can draw from throughout the universe, Dooku hurls a jagged fragment of the durasteel table, Shmi Skywalker's gentle murmur *I knew you would come for me, Anakin* smashes it aside.

His head has been filled with the smoke from his smothered

heart for far too long; it has been the thunder that darkens his mind. On Aargonar, on Jabiim, in the Tusken camp on Tatooine, that smoke had clouded his mind, had blinded him and left him flailing in the dark, a mindless machine of slaughter; but here, now, within this ship, this microscopic cell of life in the infinite sterile desert of space, his firewalls have opened so that the terror and the rage are *out there,* in the fight instead of in his head, and Anakin's mind is clear as a crystal bell.

In that pristine clarity, there is only one thing he must do.

Decide.

So he does.

He decides to *win.*

He decides that Dooku should lose the same hand he took. Decision is reality, here: his blade moves simultaneously with his will and blue fire vaporizes black Corellian nanosilk and disintegrates flesh and shears bone, and away falls a Sith Lord's lightsaber hand, trailing smoke that tastes of charred meat and burned hair. The hand falls with a bar of scarlet blaze still extending from its spastic death grip, and Anakin's heart sings for the fall of that red blade.

He reaches out and the Force catches it for him.

And then Anakin takes Dooku's other hand as well.

Dooku crumples to his knees, face blank, mouth slack, and his weapon whirs through the air to the victor's hand, and Anakin finds his vision of the future happening before his eyes: two blades at Count Dooku's throat.

But here, now, the truth belies the dream. Both lightsabers are in *his* hands, and the one in his hand of flesh flares with the synthetic bloodshine of a Sith blade.

Dooku, cringing, shrinking with dread, still finds some hope in his heart that he is wrong, that Palpatine has not betrayed him, that this has all been proceeding according to plan—

Until he hears "Good, Anakin! Good! I *knew* you could do it!" and registers this is Palpatine's voice and feels within the

darkest depths of all he is the approach of the words that are to
come next.

"Kill him," Palpatine says. "Kill him now."

In Skywalker's eyes he sees only flames.

"Chancellor, please!" he gasps, desperate and helpless, his
aristocratic demeanor invisible, his courage only a bitter memory.
He is reduced to begging for his life, as so many of his victims
have. "Please, you promised me *immunity*! We had a *deal*! *Help*
me!"

And his begging gains him a share of mercy equal to that
which he has dispensed.

"A deal only if you released me," Palpatine replies, cold as intergalactic space. "Not if you used me as bait to kill my friends."

And he knows, then, that all has indeed been going according to plan. Sidious's plan, not his own. This had been a Jedi trap
indeed, but Jedi were not the quarry.

They were the bait.

"Anakin," Palpatine says quietly. "Finish him."

Years of Jedi training make Anakin hesitate; he looks down
upon Dooku and sees not a Lord of the Sith but a beaten, broken, cringing old man.

"I shouldn't—"

But when Palpatine barks, "Do it! Now!" Anakin realizes
that this isn't actually an order. That it is, in fact, nothing more
than what he's been waiting for his whole life.

Permission.

And Dooku—

As he looks up into the eyes of Anakin Skywalker for the final
time, Count Dooku knows that he has been deceived not just
today, but for many, many years. That he has never been the true
apprentice. That he has never been the heir to the power of the
Sith. He has been only a tool.

His whole life—all his victories, all his struggles, all his heritage, all his principles and his sacrifices, everything he's done,

everything he owns, everything he's been, all his dreams and grand vision for the future Empire and the Army of Sith—have been only a pathetic sham, because all of them, all of *him,* add up only to this.

He has existed only for this.

This.

To be the victim of Anakin Skywalker's first cold-blooded murder.

First but not, he knows, the last.

Then the blades crossed at his throat uncross like scissors.

Snip.

And all of him becomes nothing at all.

Murderer and murdered each stared blindly.

But only the murderer blinked.

I did that.

The severed head's stare was fixed on something beyond living sight. The desperate plea frozen in place on its lips echoed silence. The headless torso collapsed with a slowly fading sigh from the cauterized gape of its trachea, folding forward at the waist as though making obeisance before the power that had ripped away its life.

The murderer blinked again.

Who am *I?*

Was he the slave boy on a desert planet, valued for his astonishing gift with machines? Was he the legendary Podracer, the only human to survive that deadly sport? Was he the unruly, high-spirited, trouble-prone student of a great Jedi Master? The star pilot? The hero? The lover? The Jedi?

Could he be all these things—could he be *any* of them—and still have done what he has done?

He was already discovering the answer at the same time that he finally realized that he needed to ask the question.

The deck bucked as the cruiser absorbed a new barrage of torpedoes and turbolaser fire. Dooku's severed staring head bounced along the deck and rolled away, and Anakin woke up.

"What—?"

He'd been having a dream. He'd been flying, and fighting, and fighting again, and somehow, in the dream, he could do whatever he wanted. In the dream, whatever he did was the right thing to do simply because he wanted to do it. In the dream there were no rules, there was only power.

And the power was his.

Now he stood over a headless corpse that he couldn't bear to see but he couldn't make himself look away, and he knew it hadn't been a dream at all, that he'd really *done* this, the blades were still in his hands and the ocean of wrong he'd dived into had closed over his head.

And he was drowning.

The dead man's lightsaber tumbled from his loosening fingers. "I—I couldn't stop myself . . ."

And before the words left his lips he heard how hollow and obvious was the lie.

"You did well, Anakin." Palpatine's voice was warm as an arm around Anakin's shoulders. "You did not only well, but *right*. He was too dangerous to leave alive."

From the Chancellor this sounded true, but when Anakin repeated it inside his head he knew that Palpatine's truth would be one he could never make himself believe. A tremor that began between his shoulder blades threatened to expand into a full case of the shakes. "He was an unarmed *prisoner* . . ."

That, now—that simple unbearable fact—*that* was truth. Though it burned him like his own lightsaber, truth was something he could hang on to. And somehow it made him feel a little better. A little stronger. He tried another truth: not that he couldn't have stopped himself, but—

"I shouldn't have done that," he said, and now his voice came out solid, and simple, and final. Now he could look down at the corpse at his feet. He could look at the severed head.

He could see them for what they were.

A crime.

He'd become a war criminal.

Guilt hit him like a fist. He *felt* it—a punch to his heart that smacked breath from his lungs and buckled his knees. It hung on his shoulders like a yoke of collapsium: an invisible weight beyond his mortal strength, crushing his life.

There were no words in him for this. All he could say was, "It was wrong."

And that was the sum of it, right there.

It was wrong.

"Nonsense. Disarming him was nothing; he had powers beyond your imagination."

Anakin shook his head. "That doesn't matter. It's not the Jedi way."

The ship shuddered again, and the lights went out.

"Have you never noticed that the Jedi way," Palpatine said, invisible now within the stark shadow of the General's Chair, "is not always the *right* way?"

Anakin looked toward the shadow. "You don't understand. You're not a Jedi. You *can't* understand."

"Anakin, listen to me. How many lives have you just saved with this stroke of a lightsaber? Can you count them?"

"But—"

"It wasn't wrong, Anakin. It may be *not the Jedi way,* but it was *right.* Perfectly natural—he took your hand; you wanted revenge. And your revenge was *justice.*"

"Revenge is never just. It *can't* be—"

"Don't be childish, Anakin. Revenge is the *foundation* of justice. Justice began with revenge, and revenge is still the only justice some beings can ever hope for. After all, this is hardly your first time, is it? Did Dooku deserve mercy more than did the Sand People who tortured your mother to death?"

"That was *different*."

In the Tusken camp he had lost his mind; he had become a force of nature, indiscriminate, killing with no more thought or intention than a sand gale. The Tuskens had been killed, slaughtered, massacred—but that had been beyond his control, and now it seemed to him as if it had been done by someone else: like a story he had heard that had little to do with him at all.

But Dooku—

Dooku had been murdered.

By him.

On purpose.

Here in the General's Quarters, he had looked into the eyes of a living being and coldly decided to end that life. He could have chosen the right way. He could have chosen the Jedi way.

But instead—

He stared down at Dooku's severed head.

He could never unchoose this choice. He could never take it back. As Master Windu liked to say, there is no such thing as a second chance.

And he wasn't even sure he wanted one.

He couldn't let himself think about this. Just as he didn't let himself think about the dead on Tatooine. He put his hand to his eyes, trying to rub away the memory. "You promised we would never talk about that again."

"And we won't. Just as we need never speak of what has happened here today." It was as though the shadow itself spoke kindly. "I have always kept your secrets, have I not?"

"Yes—yes, of course, Chancellor, but—" Anakin wanted to crawl away into a corner somewhere; he felt sure that if things would just *stop* for a while—an hour, a minute—he could pull himself together and find some way to keep moving forward. He had to keep moving forward. Moving forward was all he could do.

Especially when he couldn't stand to look back.

The view wall behind the General's Chair blossomed with looping ion spirals of inbound missiles. The shuddering of the ship built itself into a continuous quake, gathering magnitude with each hit.

"Anakin, my restraints, please," the shadow said. "I'm afraid this ship is breaking up. I don't think we should be aboard when it does."

In the Force, the field-signatures of the magnetic locks on the Chancellor's shackles were as clear as text saying UNLOCK ME LIKE THIS; a simple twist of Anakin's mind popped them open. The shadow grew a head, then shoulders, then underwent a sudden mitosis that left the General's Chair standing behind and turned its other half into the Supreme Chancellor.

Palpatine picked his way through the debris that littered the gloom-shrouded room, moving surprisingly quickly toward the stairs. "Come along, Anakin. There is very little time."

The view wall flared white with the missiles' impacts, and one of them must have damaged the gravity generators: the ship seemed to heel over, forcing Palpatine to clutch desperately at the banister and sending Anakin skidding down a floor that had suddenly become a forty-five-degree ramp.

He rolled hard into a pile of rubble: shattered permacrete, hydrofoamed to reduce weight. "Obi-Wan—!"

He sprang to his feet and waved away the debris that had buried the body of his friend. Obi-Wan lay entirely still, eyes closed, dust-caked blood matting his hair where his scalp had split.

Bad as Obi-Wan looked, Anakin had stood over the bodies of too many friends on too many battlefields to be panicked by a little blood. One touch to Obi-Wan's throat confirmed the strength of his pulse, and that touch also let Anakin's Force perception flow through the whole body of his friend. His breathing was strong and regular, and no bones were broken: this was a concussion, no more.

Apparently Obi-Wan's head was somewhat harder than the cruiser's interior walls.

"Leave him, Anakin. There is no time." Palpatine was half hanging from the banister, both arms wrapped around a stanchion. "This whole spire may be about to break free—"

"Then we'll all be adrift together." Anakin glanced up at the Supreme Chancellor and for that instant he didn't like the man at all—but then he reminded himself that brave as Palpatine was, his was the courage of conviction; the man was no soldier. He had no way of truly comprehending what he was asking Anakin to do.

"His fate," he said in case Palpatine had not understood, "will be the same as ours."

With Obi-Wan unconscious and Palpatine waiting above, with responsibility for the lives of his two closest friends squarely upon him, Anakin found that he had recovered his inner balance. Under pressure, in crisis, with no one to call upon for help, he could focus again. He had to.

This was what he'd been born for: saving people.

The Force brought Obi-Wan's lightsaber to his hand and he clipped it to his friend's belt, then hoisted the limp body over his shoulder and let the Force help him run lightly up the steeply canted floor to Palpatine's side.

"Impressive," Palpatine said, but then he cast a significant gaze up the staircase, which the vector of the artificial gravity had made into a vertical cliff. "But what now?"

Before Anakin could answer, the erratic gravity swung like a pendulum; while they both clung to the railing, the room seemed to roll around them. All the broken chairs and table fragments and hunks of rubble slid toward the opposite side, and now instead of a cliff the staircase had become merely a corrugated stretch of floor.

"People say"—Anakin nodded toward the door to the turbolift lobby—"when the Force closes a hatch, it opens a viewport. After you?"

GRIEVOUS

The ARC-170s of Squad Seven had joined the V-wings of Squad Four in swarming the remaining vulture fighters that had screened the immense Trade Federation flagship, *Invisible Hand*. Clone pilots destroyed droid after droid with machine-like precision of their own. When the last of the vultures had been converted to an expanding globe of superheated gas, the clone fighters peeled away, leaving *Invisible Hand* exposed to the full fire of Home Fleet Strike Group Five: three *Carrack*-class light cruisers—*Integrity, Indomitable,* and *Perseverance*—in support of the Dreadnaught *Mas Ramdar*.

Strike Group Five had deployed in a triangle around *Mas Ramdar,* maintaining a higher orbit to pin *Invisible Hand* deep in Coruscant's gravity well. Turbolasers blasted against *Invisible Hand*'s faltering shields, but the flagship was giving as good as it got: *Mas Ramdar* had sustained so much damage already that it was little more than a target to absorb the *Hand*'s return fire, and *Indomitable* was only a shell, most of its crew dead or evacuated, being run remotely by its commander and bridge crew; it swung unsteadily through the *Hand*'s vector cone of escape routes to block any attempt to run up toward jump.

As its shields finally failed, *Invisible Hand* began to roll, whirling like a bullet from a rifled slugthrower, trailing spiral jets of crystallizing gas that gushed from multiple hull ruptures. The rolling picked up speed, breaking the targeting locks of the ship's Republic adversaries. Unable to pound the same point again and again, their turbolasers weren't powerful enough to breach the *Hand*'s heavy armor directly; their tracking points became rings that circled the ship, chewing gradually into the hull in tightening garrotes of fire.

On the *Hand*'s bridge, overheated Neimoidians were strapped into their battle stations in full crash webbing. The air reeked of burning metal and the funk of reptilian stress hormones, and the erratically shifting gravity threatened to add a sharper stench: the faces of several of the bridge officers had already paled from healthy gray-green to nauseated pink.

The sole being on the bridge who was not strapped into a chair stalked from one side to the other, floor-length cape draped over shoulders angular as exposed bone. He ignored the jolts of impact and was unaffected by the swirl of unpredictable gravity as he paced the deck with metal-on-metal clanks; he walked on taloned creations of magnetized duranium, jointed to grab and crush like the feet of a Vratixan blood eagle.

His expression could not be read—his face was a mask of bleached ceramic armorplast stylized to evoke a humanoid skull—but the pure venom in the voice that hissed through the mask's electrosonic vocabulator made up for it.

"Either get the gravity generators calibrated or disable them altogether," he snarled at a blue-scanned image of a cringing Neimoidian engineer. "If this continues, you won't live long enough to be killed by the Republic."

"But, but, but sir—it's really up to the repair droids—"

"And because they *are* droids, it's useless to threaten them. So I am threatening *you*. Understand?"

He turned away before the stammering engineer could summon a reply. The hand he extended toward the forward viewscreen wore a jointed gauntlet of armorplast fused to its bones of duranium alloy. "Concentrate fire on *Indomitable*," he told the senior gunnery officer. "All batteries at maximum. Fire for effect. Blast that hulk out of space, and we'll make a hyperspace jump through its wreckage."

"But—the forward towers are already *overloading*, sir." The officer's voice trembled on the edge of panic. "They'll be at critical failure in less than a *minute*—"

"Burn them out."

"But sir, once they're gone—"

The rest of the senior gunnery officer's objection was lost in the wetly final crunching sound his face made under the impact of an armorplast fist. That same fist opened, seized the collar of the officer's uniform, and yanked his corpse out of the chair, ripping the crash webbing free along with it.

An expressionless skull-face turned toward the junior gunnery officer. "Congratulations on your promotion. Take your post."

"Y-y-yes, sir." The newly promoted senior gunnery officer's hands shook so badly he could barely unbuckle his crash web, and his face had gone deathly pink.

"Do you understand your orders?"

"Y-y-y—"

"Do you have any objections?"

"N-n-n—"

"Very well, then," General Grievous said with flat, impenetrable calm. "Carry on."

This is General Grievous:

Durasteel. Ceramic armorplast-plated duranium. Electro-drivers and crystal circuitry.

Within them: the remnants of a living being.

He doesn't breathe. He doesn't eat. He cannot laugh, and he does not cry.

A lifetime ago he was an organic sentient being. A lifetime ago he had friends, a family, an occupation; a lifetime ago he had things to love, and things to fear. Now he has none of these.

Instead, he has *purpose*.

It's built into him.

He is built to intimidate. The resemblance to a human skeleton melded with limbs styled after the legendary Krath war droids is entirely intentional. It is a face and form born of childhood's infinite nightmares.

He is built to dominate. The ceramic armorplast plates protecting limbs and torso and face can stop a burst from a starfighter's laser cannon. Those indestructible arms are ten times stronger than human, and move with the blurring speed of electronic reflexes.

He is built to eradicate. Those human-sized hands have human-sized fingers for exactly one reason: to hold a lightsaber.

Four of them hang inside his cloak.

He has never constructed a lightsaber. He has never bought one, nor has he recovered one that was lost. Each and all, he has taken from the dead hands of Jedi he has killed.

Personally.

He has many, many such trophies; the four he carries with him are his particular favorites. One belonged to the interminable K'Kruhk, whom he had bested at Hypori; another to the Viraanntesse Jedi Jmmaar, who'd fallen at Vandos; the other two had been created by Puroth and Nystammall, whom Grievous had slaughtered together on the flame-grass plains of Tovarskl so that each would know the other's death, as well as their own;

these are murders he recalls with so much pleasure that touching these souvenirs with his hands of armorplast and durasteel brings him something resembling joy.

But only resembling.

He remembers joy. He remembers anger, and frustration. He remembers grief and sorrow.

He doesn't actually feel any of them. Not anymore.

He's not designed for it.

———

White-hot sparks zipped and crackled through the smoke that billowed across the turbolift lobby. Over Anakin's shoulder, the unconscious Jedi Master wheezed faintly. Beside his other shoulder, Palpatine coughed harshly into the sleeve of his robe, held over his face for protection from caustic combustion products of the overloading circuitry.

"Artoo?" Anakin shook his comlink sharply. The blasted thing had been on the blink ever since Obi-Wan had stepped on it during one of the turbolift fights.

"Artoo, do you copy? I need you to activate—" The smoke was so thick he could barely make out the numerals on the code plate. "—elevator three-two-two-four. *Three-two-two-four,* do you copy?"

The comlink emitted a fading *fwheep* that might have been an acknowledgment, and the doors slid apart, but before Anakin could carry Obi-Wan through, the turbolift pod shot upward and the artificial gravity vector shifted again, throwing him and his partner into a heap next to Palpatine in the lobby's opposite corner.

Palpatine was struggling to rise, still coughing, sounding weak. Anakin let the Force lift Obi-Wan back to his shoulder, then picked himself up. "Perhaps you should stay down, sir," he said to the Chancellor. "The gravity swings are getting worse."

Palpatine nodded. "But, Anakin—"

Anakin looked up. The turbolift doors still stood open. "Wait here, sir."

He opened himself more fully to the Force and in his mind placed himself and Obi-Wan balanced on the edge of the open doorway above. Holding this image, he leapt, and the Force made his intention into reality: his leap carried him and the unconscious Jedi Master precisely to the rim.

The altered gravitic vector had made the turbolift shaft into a horizontal hallway of unlit durasteel, laser-straight, shrinking into darkness. Anakin was familiar with the specs for Trade Federation command cruisers; the angled conning spire was some three hundred meters long. As it stood, they could walk it in two or three minutes. But if the wrong gravity shift were to catch them inside the shaft . . .

He shook his head, grimly calculating the odds. "We'll have to be fast."

He glanced back over his shoulder, down at Palpatine, who still huddled below. "Are you all right, Chancellor? Are you well enough to run?"

The Supreme Chancellor finally rose, patting his robes in a futile attempt to dust them off. "I haven't run since I was a boy on Naboo."

"It's never too late to start getting into shape." Anakin reached through the Force to give Palpatine a little help in clambering up to the open doorway. "There are light shuttles on the hangar deck. We can be there in five minutes."

Once Palpatine was safely within the shaft-hall, Anakin said, "Follow me," and turned to go, but the Chancellor stopped him with a hand on his arm.

"Anakin, wait. We need to get to the bridge."

Through an entire shipful of combat droids? Not likely. "The hangar deck's right below—well, *beside* us, now. It's our best chance."

"But the bridge—*Grievous* is there."

Now Anakin did stop. Grievous. The most prolific slaughterer of Jedi since Durge. In all the excitement, Anakin had entirely forgotten that the bio-droid general was aboard.

"You've defeated Dooku," Palpatine said. "Capture Grievous, and you will have dealt a wound from which the Separatists may never recover."

Anakin thought blankly: *I could do it*.

He had dreamed of capturing Grievous ever since Muunilinst—and now the general was close. So close Anakin could practically *smell* him . . . and Anakin had never felt so powerful. The Force was with him today in ways more potent than he had ever experienced.

"Think of it, Anakin." Palpatine stood close by his shoulder, opposite to Obi-Wan, so close he needed only to whisper. "You have destroyed their political head. Take their military commander, and you will have practically won the war. *Single-handed*. Who else could do that, Anakin? Yoda? Mace Windu? They couldn't even capture Dooku. Who would have a chance against Grievous, if not Anakin Skywalker? The Jedi have never faced a crisis like the Clone Wars—but also they have never had a hero like *you*. You can save them. You can save *everyone*."

Anakin jerked, startled. He turned a sharp glance toward Palpatine. The way he had said that . . .

Like a voice out of his dreams.

"That's—" Anakin tried to laugh; it came out a little shaky. "That's not what Obi-Wan keeps telling me."

"Forget Obi-Wan," Palpatine said. "He has no idea how powerful you truly are. *Use* your power, Anakin. Save the Republic."

Anakin could see it, vivid as a HoloNet feature: arriving at the Senate with Grievous in electrobonds, standing modestly aside as Palpatine announced the end of the war, returning to the Temple, to the Council Chamber, where finally, after all this time, there would be a chair waiting, just for him.

They could hardly refuse him Mastership now, after he had won the war for them . . .

But then Obi-Wan shifted on his shoulder, moaning faintly, and Anakin snapped back to reality.

"No," he said. "Sorry, Chancellor. My orders are clear. This is a rescue mission; your safety is my only priority."

"I will never be safe while Grievous lives," Palpatine countered. "Master Kenobi will recover at any moment. Leave him here with me; he can see me safely to the hangar deck. Go for the general."

"I—I *would* like to, sir, but—"

"I can make it an order, Anakin."

"With respect, sir: no. You can't. My orders come from the Jedi Council, and the Council's orders come from the Senate. You have no direct authority."

The Chancellor's face darkened. "That may change."

Anakin nodded. "And perhaps it should, sir. But until it does, we'll do things my way. Let's go."

"Sir?" The thin voice of the comm officer interrupted Grievous's pacing. "We are being hailed by *Integrity*, sir. They propose a cease-fire."

Dark yellow eyes squinted through the skull-mask at the tactical displays. A pause in the combat would allow *Invisible Hand*'s turbolaser batteries to cool, and give the engineers a chance to get the gravity generators under control. "Acknowledge receipt of transmission. Stand by to cease fire."

"Standing by, sir." The gunnery officer was still shaking.

"Cease fire."

The lances of energy that had joined the *Hand* to the Home Fleet Strike Force melted away.

"Further transmission, sir. It's *Integrity*'s commander."

Grievous nodded. "Initiate."

A ghostly image built itself above the bridge's ship-to-ship hologenerator: a young human male of distinctly average height and build, wearing the uniform of a lieutenant commander. The only thing distinctive about his otherwise rather bland features was the calm confidence in his eyes.

"General Grievous," the young man said briskly, *"I am Lieutenant Commander Lorth Needa of RSS* Integrity. *At my request, my superiors have consented to offer you the chance to surrender your ship, sir."*

"Surrender?" Grievous's vocabulator produced a very credible reproduction of a snort. "Preposterous."

"Please give this offer careful deliberation, General, as it will not be repeated. Consider the lives of your crew."

Grievous cast an icy glance around his bridge full of craven Neimoidians. "Why should I?"

The young man did not look surprised, though he did show a trace of sadness. *"Is this your reply, then?"*

"Not at all." Grievous drew himself up; by straightening the angles of his levered joints, he could add half a meter to his already imposing height. "I have a counteroffer. Maintain your cease-fire, move that hulk *Indomitable* out of my way, and withdraw to a minimum range of fifty kilometers until this ship achieves hyperspace jump."

"If I may use your word, sir: preposterous."

"Tell these superiors of yours that if my demands are not met within ten minutes, I will personally disembowel Supreme Chancellor Palpatine, live on the HoloNet. Am I understood?"

The young officer took this without a blink. *"Ah. The Chancellor is aboard your ship, then."*

"He is. Your pathetic Jedi so-called heroes have failed. They are dead, and Palpatine remains in my hands."

"Ah," the young officer repeated. *"So you will, of course, allow me to speak with him. To, ah, reassure my superiors that you are not simply—well, to put it charitably—bluffing?"*

"I would not lower myself to lie to the likes of you." Grievous turned to the comm officer. "Patch in Count Dooku."

The comm officer stroked his screen, then shook his head. "He's not responding, sir."

Grievous shook his head disgustedly. "Just *show* the Chancellor, then. Bring up my quarters on the security screen."

The security officer stroked his own screen, and made a choking sound. "Hrm, sir?"

"What are you *waiting* for? Bring it up!"

He'd gone as pink as the gunner. "Perhaps you should have a look *first,* sir?"

The plain urgency in his tone brought Grievous to his side without another word. The general bent over the screen that showed the view inside his quarters and found himself looking at jumbled piles of energy-sheared wreckage surrounding the empty shape of the General's Chair.

And that—that there—that looked like it could have been a body . . .

Draped in a cape of armorweave.

Grievous turned back toward the intership holocomm. "The Chancellor is—indisposed."

"Ah. I see."

Grievous suspected that the young officer saw entirely too well. "I *assure* you—"

"I do not require your assurance, General. You have the same amount of time you offered us. Ten minutes from now, I will have either your surrender, or confirmation that Supreme Chancellor Palpatine is alive, unharmed—and present—or Invisible Hand will be destroyed."

"Wait—you can't simply—"

"Ten minutes, General. Needa out."

When Grievous turned to the bridge security officer, his mask was blankly expressionless as ever, but he made up for it with the open murder in his voice.

"Dooku is dead and the Jedi are loose. They have the Chancellor. Find them and bring them to me."

His armorplast fingers curled into a fist that crashed down on the security console so hard the entire thing collapsed into a sparking, smoking ruin.

"*Find* them!"

RESCUE

Anakin counted paces as he trotted along the turbolift shaft, Obi-Wan over his shoulder and Palpatine at his side. He'd reached 102—only a third of the way along the conning spire—when he felt the gravity begin to shift.

Exactly the wrong way: changing the rest of the long, long shaft from *ahead* to *down*.

He put out his free arm to stop the Chancellor. "This is a problem. Find something to hang on to while I get us out of here."

One of the turbolift doors was nearby, seemingly lying on its side. Anakin's lightsaber found his hand and its sizzling blade burned open the door controls, but before he could even move aside the sparking wires, the gravitic vector lurched toward vertical and he fell, skidding along the wall, free hand grabbing desperately at a loop of cable, catching it, hanging from it—

And the turbolift doors opened.

Inviting. Safe. And mockingly out of reach: a meter above his outstretched arm—

And his other arm was the only thing holding Obi-Wan above a two-hundred-meter drop down which his lightsaber's handgrip now clanked and clattered, fading toward infinity. For half a second Anakin was actually glad Obi-Wan was unconscious, because he wasn't in the mood for another lecture about hanging on to his lightsaber right now, and that thought blew away and vanished because something *had grabbed on to his leg*—

He looked down.

It was Palpatine.

The Chancellor hugged Anakin's ankle with improbable strength, peering fearfully into the darkness below. "Anakin, do something! You have to *do* something!"

I'm open to suggestions, he thought, but he said, "Don't panic. Just hang on."

"I don't think I can . . ." The Chancellor turned his anguished face upward imploringly. "Anakin, I'm slipping. Give me your hand—you have to *give* me your *hand*!"

And drop Obi-Wan? Not in this millennium.

"Don't *panic*," Anakin repeated. The Chancellor had clearly lost his head. "I can get us out of this."

He wished he were as confident as he sounded. He had been counting on the artificial gravity to continue to swing until the shaft turned back into a hallway, but instead it seemed to have stopped where it was.

This would be an especially lousy time for the generators to start working right.

He fixed a measuring glance on the open lift doorway above; perhaps the Force could give him enough of a boost to carry all three of them to safety.

But that was an exceedingly large *perhaps.*

Obi-Wan, old buddy old pal, he thought, *this would be a really good time to wake up.*

Obi-Wan Kenobi opened his eyes to find himself staring at what he strongly suspected was Anakin's butt.

It *looked* like Anakin's butt—well, his pants, anyway—though it was thoroughly impossible for Obi-Wan to be certain, since he had never before had occasion to examine Anakin's butt upside down, which it currently appeared to be, nor from this rather uncomfortably close range.

And how he might have arrived at this angle and this range was entirely baffling.

He said, "Um, have I missed something?"

"Hang on," he heard Anakin say. "We're in a bit of a situation here."

So it *was* Anakin's butt after all. He supposed he might take a modicum of comfort from that. Looking up, he discovered Anakin's legs, and his boots—and a somewhat astonishing close-up view of the Supreme Chancellor, as Palpatine seemingly balanced overhead, supported only by a white-knuckled death-grip on Anakin's ankle.

"Oh, hello, Chancellor," he said mildly. "Are you well?"

The Chancellor cast a distressed glance over his shoulder. "I *hope* so . . ."

Obi-Wan followed the Chancellor's gaze; above Palpatine rose a long, long vertical shaft—

Which was when he finally realized that he wasn't looking *up* at all.

This must be what Anakin had meant by *a bit of a situation*.

"Ah," Obi-Wan said. At least he was finally coming to understand where he stood.

Well, lay. Hung. Whatever.

"And Count Dooku?"

Anakin said, "Dead."

"Pity." Obi-Wan sighed. "Alive, he might have been a help to us."

"Obi-Wan—"

"Not in this particular situation, granted, but nonetheless—"

"Can we discuss this *later*? The ship's breaking apart."

"Ah."

A familiar electrosonic *feroo-wheep* came thinly through some-one's comlink. "Was that Artoo? What does he want?"

"I asked him to activate the elevator," Anakin said.

From the distant darkness above came a *clank,* and a *shirr,* and a *clonk,* all of which evoked in Obi-Wan's still-somewhat-addled brain the image of turbolift brakes unlocking. The ac-curacy of his imagination was swiftly confirmed by a sudden downdraft that smelled strongly of burning oil, followed closely by the bottom of a turbolift pod hurtling down the shaft like a meteorite down a well.

Obi-Wan said, "Oh."

"It seemed like a good idea at the time—"

"No need to get defensive."

"Artoo!" Anakin shouted. "Shut it down!"

"No time for that," Obi-Wan said. "Jump."

"Jump?" Palpatine asked with a shaky laugh. "Don't you mean, *fall?*"

"Um, actually, yes. Anakin—?"

Anakin let go.

They fell.

And fell. The sides of the turboshaft blurred.

And fell some more, until the gravitic vector finally eased a couple of degrees and they found themselves sliding along the side of the shaft, which was quickly turning into the bottom of the shaft, and the lift pod was still shrieking toward them faster than they could possibly run until Anakin finally got the comlink work-ing and shouted, "Artoo, open the doors! All of them! All floors!"

One door opened just as they skidded onto it and all three of them tumbled through. They landed in a heap on a turbolift lobby's opposite wall as the pod shot past overhead.

They gradually managed to untangle themselves. "Are . . . all of your rescues so . . ." Palpatine gasped breathlessly. ". . . *enter-taining?*"

Obi-Wan gave Anakin a thoughtful frown.

Anakin returned it with a shrug.

"Actually, now that you mention it," Obi-Wan said, "yes."

Anakin stared into the tangled masses of wreckage that littered the hangar bay, trying to pick out anything that still even resembled a ship. This place looked as if it had taken a direct hit; wind howled against his back through the open hatchway where Obi-Wan stood with Chancellor Palpatine, and scraps of debris whirled into the air, blown toward space through gaps in the scorched and buckled blast doors.

"None of those ships will get us anywhere!" Palpatine shouted above the wind, and Anakin had to agree. "What are we going to do?"

Anakin shook his head. He didn't know, and the Force wasn't offering any clues. "Obi-Wan?"

"How should I know?" Obi-Wan said, bracing himself in the doorway, robe whipping in the wind. "You're the hero, I'm just a Master!"

Past Obi-Wan's shoulder Anakin saw a cadre of super battle droids marching around a corner into the corridor. "Master! Behind you!"

Obi-Wan whirled, lightsaber flaring to meet a barrage of blaster bolts. "Protect the Chancellor!"

And let you have all the fun? Anakin pulled the Chancellor into the hangar bay and pressed him against the wall beside the hatch. "Stay under cover until we handle the droids!"

He was about to jump out beside Obi-Wan when he remembered that he had dropped his lightsaber down the turboshaft; fighting super battle droids without it would be a bit tricky. Not to mention that Obi-Wan would never let him hear the end of it.

"Droids are not our only problem!" Palpatine pointed across the hangar bay. "Look!"

On the far side of the bay, masses of wreckage were shifting, sliding toward the wall against which Anakin and Palpatine stood. Then debris closer to them began to slide, followed by piles closer still. An invisible wave-front was passing through the hangar bay; behind it, the gravitic vector was rotated a full ninety degrees.

Gravity shear.

Anakin's jaw clenched. This just kept getting better and better.

He unspooled a length of his utility belt's safety cable and passed the end to Palpatine. The wind made it sing. "Cinch this around your waist. Things are about to get a little wild!"

"What's *happening*?"

"The gravity generators have desynchronized—they'll tear the ship apart!" Anakin grabbed one of the zero-g handles beside the hatchway, then leaned out into the firestorm of blaster bolts and saber flares and touched Obi-Wan's shoulder. "Time to go!"

"What?"

Explanation was obviated as the shear-front moved past them and the wall became the floor. Anakin grabbed the back of Obi-Wan's collar, but not to save him from falling; the torque of the gravity shear had buckled the blast doors—which were now overhead—and the hurricane of escaping air blasting from the corridor shaft blew the Jedi Master up through the hatch. Anakin dragged him out of the gale just as pieces of super battle droids began hurtling upward into the hangar bay like misfiring torpedoes.

Some of the super battle droids were still intact enough to open fire as they flew past. "Hang on to my belt!" Obi-Wan shouted and spun his lightsaber through an intricate flurry to deflect bolt after bolt. Anakin could do nothing but hold him braced against the gale; his grip on the zero-g handle was the only thing keeping him and Obi-Wan from being blown out into space and taking Palpatine with them.

"This is not the best plan we've ever had!" he shouted.

"This was a *plan*?" Palpatine sounded appalled.

"We'll make our way forward!" Obi-Wan shouted. "There are only droids back here! Once we hit live-crew areas, there will be escape pods!"

Only droids back here echoed inside Anakin's head. "Obi-Wan, *wait*!" he cried. "Artoo's still here somewhere! We can't leave him!"

"He's probably been destroyed, or blown into space!" Obi-Wan deflected blaster bursts from the last two gale-blown droids. They tumbled up to the gap in the blast doors and vanished into the infinite void. Obi-Wan put away his lightsaber and fought his way back to a grip beside Anakin's. "We can't afford the time to search for him. I'm sorry, Anakin. I know how much he meant to you."

Anakin desperately fished out his comlink. "Artoo! Artoo, come in!" He shook it, and shook it again. Artoo couldn't have been destroyed. He just *couldn't*. "Artoo, do you copy? Where are you?"

"Anakin—" Obi-Wan's hand was on his arm, and the Jedi Master leaned so close that his low tone could be heard over the rising gale. "We must go. Being a Jedi means allowing things— even things we love—to pass out of our lives."

Anakin shook the comlink again. "Artoo!" He couldn't just leave him. He couldn't. And he didn't exactly have an explanation.

Not one he could ever give Obi-Wan, anyway.

There are so few things a Jedi ever owns; even his lightsaber is less a possession than an expression of his identity. To be a Jedi is to renounce possessions. And Anakin had tried so hard, tried for so long, to do just that.

Even on their wedding day, Anakin had had no devotion-gift for his new wife; he didn't actually *own* anything.

But love will find a way.

He had brought something like a gift to her apartments in Theed, still a little shy with her, still overwhelmed by finding the feelings in her he'd felt so long himself, not knowing quite how to give her a gift which wasn't really a gift. Nor was it his to give.

Without anything of his own to give except his love, all he could bring her was a friend.

"I didn't have many friends when I was a kid," he'd told her, "so I built one."

And C-3PO had shuffled in behind him, gleaming as though he'd been plated with solid gold.

Padmé had lit up, her eyes gleaming, but she had at first tried to protest. "I can't accept him," she'd said. "I know how much he means to you."

Anakin had only laughed. What use is a protocol droid to a Jedi? Even one as upgraded as 3PO—Anakin had packed his creation with so many extra circuits and subprograms and heuristic algorithms that the droid was practically human.

"I'm not giving him to you," he'd told her. "He's not even really mine to give; when I built him, I was a slave, and everything I did belonged to Watto. Cliegg Lars bought him along with my mother; Owen gave him back to me, but I'm a Jedi. I have renounced possessions. I guess that means he's free now. What I'm really doing is asking you to look after him for me."

"Look after him?"

"Yes. Maybe even give him a job. He's a little fussy," he'd admitted, "and maybe I shouldn't have given him quite so much self-consciousness—he's a worrier—but he's very smart, and he might be a real help to a big-time diplomat . . . like, say, a Senator from Naboo?"

Padmé then had extended her hand and graciously invited C-3PO to join her staff, because on Naboo, high-functioning droids were respected as thinking beings, and 3PO had been so flustered at being treated like a sentient creature that he'd been barely able to speak, beyond muttering something about hoping he might make himself useful, because after all he was "fluent in over six million forms of communication." Then she had turned to Anakin and laid her soft, soft hand along his jawline to draw him down to kiss her, and that was all he had needed, all he had hoped for; he would give her everything he had, everything he was—

And there had come another day, two years later, a day that had meant nearly as much to him as the day they had wed: the day he had finally passed his trials.

The day he had become a Jedi Knight.

As soon as circumstances allowed he had slipped away, on his own now, no Master over his shoulder, no one to monitor his comings and his goings and so he could take himself to the vast Coruscant complex at 500 Republica where Naboo's senior Senator kept her spacious apartments.

And he had then, finally, two years late, a devotion-gift for her.

He had then one thing that he truly owned, that he had earned, that he was not required to renounce. One gift he could give her to celebrate their love.

The culmination of the Ceremony of Jedi Knighthood is the severing of the new Jedi Knight's Padawan braid. And it was this that he laid into Padmé's trembling hand.

One long, thin braid of his glossy hair: such a little thing, of no value at all.

Such a little thing, that meant the galaxy to him.

And she had kissed him then, and laid her soft cheek against his jaw, and she had whispered in his ear that she had something for him as well.

Out from her closet had whirred R2-D2.

Of course Anakin knew him; he had known him for years— the little droid was a decorated war hero himself, having saved

Padmé's life back when she had been Queen of Naboo, not to mention helping the nine-year-old Anakin destroy the Trade Federation's Droid Control Ship, breaking the blockade and saving the planet. The Royal Engineers of Naboo's aftermarket wizardry made their modified R-units the most sought after in the galaxy; he'd tried to protest, but she had silenced him with a soft finger against his lips and a gentle smile and a whisper of "After all, what does a politician need with an astromech?"

"But I'm a Jedi—"

"That's why I'm not giving him to you," she'd said with a smile. "I'm asking you to look after him. He's not really a gift. He's a friend."

All this flashed though Anakin's mind in the stretching second before his comlink finally crackled to life with a familiar *fwee-wheoo,* and his heart unclenched.

"Artoo, where are you? Come on, we have to get out of here!"

High above, on the wall that was supposed to be the floor, the lid of a battered durasteel storage locker shifted, pushed aside by a dome of silver and blue. The lid swung fully open and R2-D2 righted itself, deployed its booster rockets, and floated out from the locker, heading for the far exit.

Anakin gave Obi-Wan a fierce grin. Let someone he loves pass out of his life? Not likely. "What are we waiting for?" he said. "Let's go!"

From *Invisible Hand*'s bridge, the ship's spin made the vast curve of Coruscant's horizon appear to orbit the ship in a dizzying whirl. Each rotation also brought a view of the lazily tumbling wreckage of the conning spire, ripped from the ship and cast out of orbit by centripetal force, as it made the long burning fall toward the planetary city's surface.

General Grievous watched them both while his droid circuitry ticked off the seconds remaining in the life of his ship.

He had no fear for his own life; his specially designed escape module was preprogrammed to take him directly to a ship already primed for jump. Mere seconds after he sealed himself and the Chancellor within the module's heavily armored hull, they would be taken aboard the fleeing ship, which would then make a series of randomized microjumps to prevent being tracked before entering the final jump to the secret base on Utapau.

But he was not willing to go without the Chancellor. This operation had cost the Confederacy dearly in ships and personnel; to leave empty-handed would be an even graver cost in prestige. Winning this war was more than half a matter of propaganda: much of the weakness of the Republic grew from its citizens' superstitious dread of the Separatists' seemingly inevitable victory— a dread cultivated and nourished by the CIS shadowfeed that poisoned government propaganda on the HoloNet. The common masses of the Republic believed that the Republic was losing; to see the legendary Grievous himself beaten back and fleeing a battle would give them hope that the war might be won.

And hope was simply not to be allowed.

His built-in comlink buzzed in his left ear. He touched the sensor implant in the jaw of his mask. "Yes."

"The Jedi almost certainly escaped the conning spire, sir." The voice was that of one of his precious, custom-built IG 100-series MagnaGuards: prototype self-motivating humaniform combat droids designed, programmed, and armed specifically to fight Jedi. *"We recovered a lightsaber from the base of the turbolift shaft before the spire tore free."*

"Copy that. Stand by for instructions." One long stride put

Grievous next to the Neimoidian security officer. "Have you located them, or are you about to die?"

"I, ah, I ah—" The security officer's trembling finger pointed to a schematic of *Invisible Hand*'s hangar deck, where a bright blip slid slowly through Bay One.

"What is that?"

"It's, it's, it's the Chancellor's *beacon*, sir."

"What? The Jedi never deactivated it? Why not?"

"I, well, I can't actually—"

"Idiots." He looked down at the cringing security officer, considering killing the fool just for taking so long to figure this out.

The Neimoidian might as well have read Grievous's thought spelled out across his bone-colored mask. "If, if, if you hadn't—er, I mean, please recall my security console has been destroyed, and so I have been forced to reroute—"

"Silence." Grievous gave a mental shrug. The fool would be dead or captured soon enough regardless. "Order all combat droids to terminate their search algorithms and converge on the bridge. Wait, strike that: leave the battle droids. Useless things," he muttered into his mask. "A greater danger to us than to Jedi. Super battle droids and droidekas *only*, do you understand? We will take no chances."

As the security officer turned to his screens, Grievous again touched the sensor implant along the jaw of his mask. "IG-One-oh-one."

"*Sir.*"

"Assemble a team of super battle droids and droidekas—as many as you can gather—and report to the hangar deck. I'll give you the exact coordinates as soon as they are available."

"*Yes, sir.*"

"You will find at least one Jedi, possibly two, in the company of Chancellor Palpatine, imprisoned in a ray shield. They are to be considered extremely dangerous. Disarm them and deliver them to the bridge."

"If they are so dangerous, perhaps we should execute them on the spot."

"No. My orders are clear that the Chancellor is not to be harmed. And the Jedi—"

The general's right hand slipped beneath his cape to stroke the array of lightsabers clipped there.

"The Jedi, I will execute *personally*."

A sheet of shimmering energy suddenly flared in front of them, blocking the corridor on the far side of the intersection they were trotting across, and Obi-Wan stopped so short that Anakin almost slammed into his back. He reached over and caught Palpatine by the arm. "Careful, sir," he said, low. "Better not touch it till we know what it is."

Obi-Wan unclipped his lightsaber, activated it, and cautiously extended its tip to touch the energy field; an explosive burst of power flared sparks and streaks in all directions, nearly knocking the weapon from his hands. "Ray shield," he said, more to himself than to the others. "We'll have to find a way around—"

But even as he spoke another sheet shimmered into existence across the mouth of the corridor they'd just left, and two more sizzled into place to seal the corridors to either side.

They were boxed in.

Caught.

Obi-Wan stood there for a second or two, blinking, then looked at Anakin and shook his head in disbelief. "I thought we were smarter than this."

"Apparently not. The oldest trap in the book, and we walked right into it." Anakin felt as embarrassed as Obi-Wan looked. "Well, *you* walked right into it. I was just trying to keep up."

"Oh, so now this is *my* fault?"

Anakin gave him a slightly wicked smile. "Hey, you're the Master. I'm just a hero."

"Joke some other time," Obi-Wan muttered. "It's the dark side—the shadow on the Force. Our instincts still can't be trusted. Don't you feel it?"

The dark side was the last thing Anakin wanted to think about right now. "Or, you know, it could be that knock on the head," he offered.

Obi-Wan didn't even smile. "No. All our choices keep going awry. How could they even locate us so precisely? Something is definitely wrong, here. Dooku's death should have lifted the shadow—"

"If you've a taste for mysteries, Master Kenobi," Palpatine interrupted pointedly, "perhaps you could solve the mystery of how we're going to *escape*."

Obi-Wan nodded, scowling darkly at the ray shield box as though seeing it for the first time; after a moment, he took out his lightsaber again, ignited it, and sank its tip into the deck at his feet. The blade burned through the durasteel plate almost without resistance—and then flared and bucked and spat lightning as it hit a shield in place in a gap below the plate, and almost threw Obi-Wan into the annihilating energy of the ray shield behind him.

"No doubt in the ceiling as well." He looked at the others and sighed. "Ideas?"

"Perhaps," Palpatine said thoughtfully, as though the idea had only just occurred to him, "we should simply surrender to General Grievous. With the death of Count Dooku, I'm sure that the two of you can . . ." He cast a significant sidelong glance at Anakin. ". . . *negotiate* our release."

He's persistent, I'll give him that, Anakin thought. He caught himself smiling as he recalled discussing "negotiation" with Padmé, on Naboo before the war; he came back to the present when he realized that undertaking "aggressive negotiations" could prove embarrassing under his current lightsaber-challenged circumstances.

"*I* say . . . ," he put in slowly, "patience."

"Patience?" Obi-Wan lifted an eyebrow. "That's a plan?"

"You know what Master Yoda says: *Patience you must have, until the mud settles and the water becomes clear.* So let's wait."

Obi-Wan looked skeptical. "Wait."

"For the security patrol. A couple of droids will be along in a moment or two; they'll have to drop the ray shield to take us into custody."

"And then?"

Anakin shrugged cheerfully. "And then we'll wipe them out."

"Brilliant as usual," Obi-Wan said dryly. "What if they turn out to be destroyer droids? Or something worse?"

"Oh, come on, Master. Worse than destroyers? Besides, security patrols are always those skinny useless little battle droids."

At that moment, four of those skinny useless battle droids came marching toward them, one along each corridor, clanking along with blaster rifles leveled. One of them triggered one of its preprogrammed security commands: *"Hand over your weapons!"* The other three chimed in with enthusiastic barks of *"Roger, roger!"* and a round of spastic head-bobbing.

"See?" Anakin said. "No problem."

Before Obi-Wan could reply, concealed doors in the corridor walls zipped suddenly aside. Through them rolled the massive bronzium wheels of destroyer droids, two into each corridor. The eight destroyers unrolled themselves behind the battle droids, haloed by sparkling energy shields, twin blaster cannons targeting the two Jedi's chests.

Obi-Wan sighed. "You were saying?"

"Okay, fine. It's the dark side. Or something." Anakin rolled his eyes. "I guess you're off the hook for the ray shield trap."

Through those same doorways marched sixteen super battle

droids to back up the destroyers, their arm cannons raised to fire over the destroyers' shields.

Behind the super battle droids came two droids of a type Anakin had never seen. He had an idea what they were, though.

And he was not happy about it.

Obi-Wan scowled at them as they approached. "You're the expert, Anakin. What are those things?"

"Remember what you were saying about *worse than destroyers?*" Anakin said grimly. "I think we're looking at them."

They walked side by side, their gait easy and straightforward, almost as smooth as a human's. In fact, they could have *been* human—humans who were two meters tall and made out of metal. They wore long swirling cloaks that had once been white, but now were stained with smoke and what Anakin strongly suspected was blood. They walked with the cloaks thrown back over one shoulder, to clear their left arms, where they held some unfamiliar staff-like weapon about two meters long—something like the force-pike of a Senate Guard, but shorter, and with an odd-looking discharge blade at each end.

They walked like they were made to fight, and they had clearly seen some battle. The chest plate of one bore a round shallow crater surrounded by a corona of scorch, a direct blaster hit that hadn't come close to penetrating; the other bore a scar from its cranial dome down through one dead photoreceptor—a scar that looked like it might have come from a lightsaber.

This droid looked like it had fought a Jedi, and survived.

The Jedi, he guessed, hadn't.

These two droids threaded between the super battle droids and destroyers and casually shoved aside one battle droid hard enough that it slammed into the wall and collapsed into a sparking heap of metal.

The one with the damaged photoreceptor pointed its staff at them, and the ray shields around them dropped. "He *said,* hand over your *weapons,* Jedi!"

This definitely wasn't a preprogrammed security command.

Anakin said softly, "I saw an Intel report on this; I think those are Grievous's personal bodyguard droids. Prototypes built to his specifications." He looked from Obi-Wan to Palpatine and back again. "To fight Jedi."

"Ah," Obi-Wan said. "Then under the circumstances, I suppose we need a Plan B."

Anakin nodded at Palpatine. "The Chancellor's idea is sounding pretty good right now."

Obi-Wan nodded thoughtfully.

When the Jedi Master turned away to offer his lightsaber to the bodyguard droid, Anakin leaned close to the Supreme Chancellor and murmured, "So you get your way, after all."

Palpatine answered with a slight, unreadable smile. "I frequently do."

As super battle droids came forward with electrobinders for their wrists and a restraining bolt for R2-D2, Obi-Wan cast one frowning look back over his shoulder.

"Oh, Anakin," he said, with the sort of quiet, pained resignation that would be recognized instantly by any parent exhausted by a trouble-prone child. *Where* is your *lightsaber?*"

Anakin couldn't look at him. "It's not lost, if that's what you're thinking." This was the truth: Anakin could feel it in the Force, and he knew exactly where it was.

"No?"

"No."

"Where is it, then?"

"Can we talk about this later?"

"Without your lightsaber, you may not *have* a 'later.' "

"I don't need a lecture, okay? How many times have we had this talk?"

"Apparently, one time less than we needed to."

Anakin sighed. Obi-Wan could still make him feel about nine

years old. He gave a sullen nod toward one of the droid body-guards. "He's got it."

"He does? And how did this happen?"

"I don't want to talk about it."

"Anakin—"

"Hey, he's got yours, too!"

"That's different—"

"This weapon is your *life*, Obi-Wan!" He did a credible-enough Kenobi impression that Palpatine had to smother a snort. "You must take *care* of it!"

"Perhaps," Obi-Wan said, as the droids clicked the binders onto their wrists and led them all away, "we should talk about this later."

Anakin intoned severely, "Without your *lightsaber*, you may not *have* a—"

"All right, all right." The Jedi Master surrendered with a rueful smile. "You win."

Anakin grinned at him. "I'm sorry? What was that?" He couldn't remember the last time he'd won an argument with Obi-Wan. "Could you speak up a little?"

"It's not very Jedi to gloat, Anakin."

"I'm not gloating, Master," he said with a sidelong glance at Palpatine. "I'm just . . . savoring the moment."

This is how it feels to be Anakin Skywalker, for now:

The Supreme Chancellor returns your look with a hint of smile and a sliver of an approving nod, and for you, this tiny, trivial, comradely victory sparks a warmth and ease that relaxes the dragon-grip of dread on your heart.

Forget that you are captured; you and Obi-Wan have been captured before. Forget the deteriorating ship, forget the Jedi-killing droids; you've faced worse. Forget General Grievous. What is he compared with Dooku? He can't even use the Force.

So now, here, for you, the situation comes down to this: you are walking between the two best friends you have ever had, with your precious droid friend faithfully whirring after your heels—

On your way to win the Clone Wars.

What you have done—what happened in the General's Quarters and, more important, *why* it happened—is all burning away in Coruscant's atmosphere along with Dooku's decapitated corpse. Already it seems as if it happened to somebody else, as if *you* were somebody else when you did it, and it seems as if that man—the dragon-haunted man with a furnace for a heart and a mind as cold as the surface of that dead star—had really only been an image reflected in Dooku's open staring eyes.

And by the time what's left of the conning spire crashes into the kilometers-thick crust of city that is the surface of Coruscant, those dead eyes will have burned away, and the dragon will burn with them.

And you, for the first time in your life, will truly be free.

This is how it feels to be Anakin Skywalker.

For now.

OBI-WAN AND ANAKIN 2

This is Obi-Wan Kenobi in the light:

As he is prodded onto the bridge along with Anakin and Chancellor Palpatine, he has no need to look around to see the banks of control consoles tended by terrified Neimoidians. He doesn't have to turn his head to count the droidekas and super battle droids, or to gauge the positions of the brutal droid bodyguards. He doesn't bother to raise his eyes to meet the cold yellow stare fixed on him through a skull-mask of armorplast.

He doesn't even need to reach into the Force.

He has already let the Force reach into him.

The Force flows over him and around him as though he has stepped into a crystal-pure waterfall lost in the green coils of a forgotten rain forest; when he opens himself to that sparkling stream it flows into him and through him and out again without the slightest interference from his conscious will. The part of him that calls itself Obi-Wan Kenobi is no more than a ripple, an eddy in the pool into which he endlessly pours.

There are other parts of him here, as well; there is nothing here that is *not* a part of him, from the scuff mark on R2-D2's dome to the tattered hem of Palpatine's robe, from the spidering crack in one transparisteel panel of the curving view wall above to the great starships that still battle beyond it.

Because this is all part of the Force.

Somehow, mysteriously, the cloud that has darkened the Force for near to a decade and a half has lightened around him now, and he finds within himself the limpid clarity he recalls from his schooldays at the Jedi Temple, when the Force was pure, and clean, and perfect. It is as though the darkness has withdrawn, has coiled back upon itself, to allow him this moment of clarity, to return to him the full power of the light, if only for the moment; he does not know why, but he is incapable of even wondering. In the Force, he is beyond questions.

Why is meaningless; it is an echo of the past, or a whisper from the future. All that matters, for this infinite now, is *what,* and *where,* and *who.*

He is all sixteen of the super battle droids, gleaming in laser-reflective chrome, arms loaded with heavy blasters. He is those blasters and he is their targets. He is all eight destroyer droids waiting with electronic patience within their energy shields, and both bodyguards, and every single one of the shivering Neimoidians. He is their clothes, their boots, even each drop of reptile-scented moisture that rolls off them from the misting sprays they use to keep their internal temperatures down. He is the binders that cuff his hands, and he is the electrostaff in the hands of the bodyguard at his back.

He is both of the lightsabers that the other droid bodyguard marches forward to offer to General Grievous.

And he is the general himself.

He is the general's duranium ribs. He is the beating of Grievous's alien heart, and is the silent pulse of oxygen pumped through his alien veins. He is the weight of four lightsabers at the general's belt, and is the greedy anticipation the captured weapons sparked behind the general's eyes. He is even the plan for his own execution simmering within the general's brain.

He is all these things, but most importantly, he is still Obi-Wan Kenobi.

This is why he can simply stand. Why he can simply wait. He has no need to attack, or to defend. There will be battle here, but he is perfectly at ease, perfectly content to let the battle start when it will start, and let it end when it will end.

Just as he will let himself live, or let himself die.

This is how a great Jedi makes war.

General Grievous lifted the two lightsabers, one in each duranium hand, to admire them by the light of turbolaser blasts outside, and said, "Rare trophies, these: the weapon of Anakin Skywalker, and the weapon of General Kenobi. I look forward to adding them to my collection."

"That will not happen. I am in control here."

The reply came through Obi-Wan's lips, but it was not truly Obi-Wan who spoke. Obi-Wan was not in control; he had no need for control. He had the Force.

It was the Force that spoke through him.

Grievous stalked forward. Obi-Wan saw death in the cold yellow stare through the skull-mask's eyeholes, and it meant nothing to him at all.

There was no death. There was only the Force.

He didn't have to tell Anakin to subtly nudge Chancellor Palpatine out of the line of fire; part of him *was* Anakin, and was doing this already. He didn't have to tell R2-D2 to access its combat subprograms and divert power to its booster rockets, claw-arm, and cable-gun; the part of him that was the little astromech had seen to all these things before they had even entered the bridge.

Grievous towered over him. "So confident you are, Kenobi."

"Not confident, merely calm." From so close, Obi-Wan

could see the hairline cracks and pitting in the bone-pale mask, and could feel the resonance of the general's electrosonic voice humming in his chest. He remembered the Question of Master Jrul: *What is the good, if not the teacher of the bad? What is the bad, if not the task of the good?*

He said, "We can resolve this situation without further violence. I am willing to accept your surrender."

"I'm sure you are." The skull-mask tilted inquisitively. "Does this preposterous *I-will-accept-your-surrender* line of yours ever actually *work?*"

"Sometimes. When it doesn't, people get hurt. Sometimes they die." Obi-Wan's blue-gray eyes met squarely those of yellow behind the mask. "By *people,* in this case, you should understand that I mean *you.*"

"I understand enough. I understand that I will kill you." Grievous threw back his cloak and ignited both lightsabers. "Here. Now. With your own blade."

The Force replied through Obi-Wan's lips, "I don't think so."

The electrodrivers that powered Grievous's limbs could move them faster than the human eye can see; when he swung his arm, it and his fist and the lightsaber within it would literally vanish: wiped from existence by sheer mind-numbing speed, an imitation quantum event. No human being could move remotely as fast as Grievous, not even Obi-Wan—but he didn't have to.

In the Force, part of him was Grievous's intent to slaughter, and the surge from intent to action translated to Obi-Wan's response without thought. He had no need for a plan, no use for tactics.

He had the Force.

That sparkling waterfall coursed through him, washing away any thought of danger, or safety, of winning or losing. The Force, like water, takes on the shape of its container without effort, without thought. The water that was Obi-Wan poured itself into the container that was Grievous's attack, and while some materials might be water-tight, Obi-Wan had yet to encounter any that were entirely, as it were, *Force*-tight . . .

While the intent to swing was still forming in Grievous's mind, the part of the Force that was Obi-Wan was also the part of the Force that was R2-D2, as well as an internal fusion-welder Anakin had retrofitted into R2-D2's primary grappling arm, and so there was no need for actual communication between them; it was only Obi-Wan's personal sense of style that brought his customary gentle smile to his face and his customary gentle murmur to his lips.

"Artoo?"

Even as he opened his mouth, a panel was sliding aside in the little droid's fuselage; by the time the droid's nickname had left his lips, the fusion-welder had deployed and fired a blinding spray of sparks hot enough to melt duranium, and in the quarter of a second while even Grievous's electronically enhanced reflexes had him startled and distracted, the part of the Force that was Obi-Wan tried a little trick, a secret one that it had been saving up for just such an occasion as this.

Because all there on the bridge was one in the Force, from the gross structure of the ship itself to the quantum dance of the electron shells of individual atoms—and because, after all, the nerves and muscles of the bio-droid general were creations of electronics and duranium, not living tissue with will of its own— it was just barely possible that with exactly the right twist of his mind, in that one vulnerable quarter of a second while Grievous was distracted, flinching backward from a spray of flame hot enough to burn even his armored body, Obi-Wan might be able to temporarily reverse the polarity of the electrodrivers in the general's mechanical hands.

Which is exactly what he did.

Durasteel fingers sprang open, and two lightsabers fell free.

He reached through the Force and the Force reached through him; his blade flared to life while still in the air; it flipped toward him, and as he lifted his hands to meet it, its blue flame flashed between his wrists and severed the binders before the handgrip smacked solidly into his palm.

Obi-Wan was so deep in the Force that he wasn't even suprised it had worked.

He made a quarter turn to face Anakin, who was already in the air, having leapt simultaneously with Obi-Wan's gentle murmur because Obi-Wan and Anakin were, after all, two parts of the same thing; Anakin's flip carried him over Obi-Wan's head at the perfect range for Obi-Wan's blade to flick out and burn through his partner's binders, and while Grievous was still flinching away from the fountain of fusion fire, Anakin landed with his own hand extended; Obi-Wan felt a liquid surge in the waterfall that he was, and Anakin's lightsaber sang through the air and Anakin caught it, and so, one single second after Grievous had begun to summon the intent to swing, Obi-Wan Kenobi and Anakin Skywalker stood back-to-back in the center of the bridge, expressionlessly staring past the snarling blue energy of their lightsabers.

Obi-Wan regarded the general without emotion. "Perhaps you should reconsider my offer."

Grievous braced himself against a control console, its durasteel housing buckling under his grip. "This is my answer!"

He ripped the console wholly into the air, right out from under the hands of the astonished Neimoidian operator, raised it over his head, and hurled it at the Jedi. They split, rolling out of the console's way as it crashed to the deck, spitting smoke and sparks.

"Open *fire!*" Grievous shook his fists as though each held a Jedi's neck. "Kill them! *Kill them all!*"

For one more second there was only the scuttle of priming levers on dozens of blasters.

One second after that, the bridge exploded into a firestorm.

Grievous hung back, crouching, watching for a moment as his two MagnaGuards waded into the Jedi, electrostaffs whirling through the blinding hail of blasterfire that ricocheted around the bridge. Grievous had fought Jedi before, sometimes even in open battle, and he had found that fighting any one Jedi was much like fighting any other.

Kenobi, though—

The ease with which Kenobi had taken command of the situation was frightening. More frightening was the fact that of the two, Skywalker was reportedly the greater warrior. And even their *R2* unit could fight: the little astromech had some kind of aftermarket cable-gun it had used to entangle the legs of a super droid and yank it off its feet, and now was jerking the droid this way and that so that its arm cannons were blasting chunks off its squadmates instead of the Jedi.

Grievous was starting to think less about winning this particular encounter than about surviving it.

Let his MagnaGuards fight the Jedi; that's what they were designed for—and they were doing their jobs well. IG-101 had pressed Kenobi back against a console, lightning blazing from his electrostaff's energy shield where it pushed on Kenobi's blade; the Jedi general might have died then and there, except that one of the simple-minded super battle droids turned both arm cannons on his back, giving Kenobi the chance to duck and allow the hammering blaster bolts to slam 101 stumbling backward. Skywalker had stashed the Chancellor somewhere—that sniveling coward Palpatine was probably trembling under one of the control consoles—and had managed to sever both of 102's legs below the knee, which for some reason he apparently expected to end the fight; he seemed completely astonished when 102 whirled nimbly on one end of his electrostaff and used the stumps of his legs to thump Skywalker so soundly the Jedi went down skidding.

On the other hand, Grievous thought, *this might be salvageable after all.*

He tapped his internal comlink's jaw sensor to the general droid command frequency. "The Chancellor is hiding under one of the consoles. Squad Sixteen, find him, and deliver him to my escape pod immediately. Squad Eight, stay on mission. Kill the Jedi."

Then the ship bucked, sharper than it ever had, and the view wall panels whited out as radiation-scatter sleeted through the bridge. Alarm klaxons blared. The nav console flared sparks into the face of a Neimoidian pilot, setting his uniform on fire and adding his screams to the din, and another console exploded, ripping the newly promoted senior gunnery officer into a pile of shredded meat.

Ah, Grievous thought. In all the excitement, he had entirely forgotten about Lieutenant Commander Needa and *Integrity.*

The other pilot—the one who wasn't shrieking and slapping at the flames on his uniform until his own hands caught fire— leaned as far away from his screaming partner as his crash webbing would allow and shouted, "General, that shot destroyed the last of the aft control cells! The ship is *deorbiting!* We're going to burn!"

"Very well," Grievous said calmly. "Stay on course." Now it no longer mattered whether his bodyguards could overpower the Jedi or not: they would all burn together.

He tapped his jaw sensor to the control frequency for the escape pods; one coded order ensured that his personal pod would be waiting for him with engines hot and systems checks complete.

When he looked back to the fight, all he could see of IG-102 was one arm, the saber-cut joint still white hot. Skywalker was pursuing two super battle droids that had Palpatine by the arms. While Skywalker dismantled the droids with swift cuts, Kenobi was in the process of doing the same to IG-101—the MagnaGuard was hopping on its one remaining leg, whirling its electrostaff with its one remaining arm, and screeching some improbable threat regarding its staff and Kenobi's body cavities—and after Kenobi cut off the arm, 101 went hopping after him, still screeching. The droid actually managed to land one glancing kick before the Jedi casually severed its other leg, after which 101's limbless torso continued to writhe on the deck, howling.

With both MagnaGuards down, all eight destroyers opened up, dual cannons erupting gouts of galvened particle beams. The two Jedi leapt together to screen the Chancellor, and before Grievous could command the destroyers to cease fire, the Jedi had deflected enough of the bolts to blow apart three-quarters of the remaining super battle droids and send the survivors scurrying for cover beside what was left of the cringing Neimoidians.

The destroyers began to close in, hosing down the Jedi with heavy fire, advancing step by step, cannons against lightsabers; the Jedi caught every blast and sent them back against the destroyers' shields that flared in spherical haloes as they absorbed the reflected bolts. The destroyers might very well have prevailed over the Jedi, except for one unexpected difficulty—

Gravity shear.

All eight of them suddenly seemed, inexplicably, to leap into the air, followed by Skywalker, and Palpatine, and chairs and pieces of MagnaGuards and everything else on the bridge that was not bolted to the deck, except for Kenobi, who managed to grab a control console and now was hanging by one hand, upside down, still effortlessly deflecting blaster bolts.

The surviving Neimoidian pilot was screaming orders for the droids to magnetize, then started howling that the ship was breaking up, and managed to make so much annoying noise that

Grievous smashed his skull out of simple irritation. Then he looked around and realized he'd just killed the last of his crew: all the bridge crew he hadn't slain personally had sucked up the bulk of the random blaster ricochets.

Grievous shook the pilot's brains off his fist. Disgusting creatures, Neimoidians.

The invisible plane of altered gravity passed over the bio-droid general without effect—his talons of magnetized duranium kept him right where he was—and as one of the MagnaGuards' electrostaffs fell past him, his invisibly fast hand snatched it from the air. When another plane of gravity shear swept through the bridge, droids, Chancellor, and Jedi all fell back to the floor.

Though the droideka, also known as the destroyer droid, was the most powerful infantry combat droid in general production, it had one major design flaw. The energy shield that was so effective in stopping blasters, slugs, shrapnel, and even lightsabers was precisely tuned to englobe the droid in a standing position; if the droid was no longer standing—say, if it was knocked down, or thrown into a wall—the shield generator could not distinguish a floor or a wall from a weapon, and would keep ramping up power to disintegrate this perceived threat until the generator shorted itself out.

Between falling to the ceiling, bouncing off it, and falling back to the floor, the sum total output of all the shield generators of Squad Eight was, currently, one large cloud of black smoke.

It was impossible to say which one of them opened fire on the Jedi, and it didn't matter; inside of two seconds, eight droidekas had become eight piles of smoking scrap, and two Jedi, entirely unscathed, walked out of the smoke side by side.

Without a word, they parted to bracket the general.

Grievous clicked the electrostaff's power setting to overload; it spat lightning around him as he lifted it to combat ready. "I am sorry I don't have time to fight you—it would have been an interesting match—but I have an appointment with an escape pod. And you . . ."

He pointed at the transparisteel view wall and triggered his own concealed cable-gun, not unlike the one that fancy astromech of theirs had; the cable shot out and its grappling claw buried itself in one of the panel supports.

"You," he said, "have appointments with death."

The Jedi leapt, and Grievous hurled the overloading electrostaff—but not at the Jedi.

He threw it at a window.

One of the transparisteel panels of the view wall had cracked under a glancing hit from a starfighter's cannon; when the sparking electrostaff hit it squarely and exploded like a proton grenade, the whole panel blew out into space.

A hurricane roared to life, raging through the bridge, seizing Neimoidian corpses and pieces of droids and wreckage and hurling them out through the gap along with a white fountain of flash-frozen air. Grievous sprang straight up into the instant hurricane, narrowly avoiding the two Jedi, whose leaps had become frantic tumbles as they tried to avoid being sucked through along with him. Grievous, though, had no need to breathe, nor had he any fear of his body fluids boiling in the vacuum—the pressurized synthflesh that enclosed the living parts within his droid exoskeleton saw to that—so he simply rode the storm right out into space until he reached the end of the cable and it snapped tight and swung him whipping back toward *Invisible Hand*'s hull.

He cast off the cable. His hands and feet of magnetized duranium let him scramble along the hull without difficulty, the light-spidered curve of Coruscant's nightside whirling around him. He clambered over to the external locks of the bridge escape pods and punched in a command code. Looking back over his shoulder, he experienced a certain chilly satisfaction as he watched empty escape pods blast free of the *Hand*'s bridge and streak away.

All of them.

Well: all but one.

No trick of the Force would spring Kenobi and Skywalker out of this one. It was a shame he didn't have a spy probe handy to leave on the bridge; he would have enjoyed watching the Republic's greatest heroes burn.

The ion streaks of the escape pods spiraled through the battle that still flashed and flared silently in the void, pursued by starfighters and armed retrieval ships. Grievous nodded to himself; that should occupy them long enough for his command pod to make the run to his escape ship.

As he entered his customized pod, he reflected that he was, for the first time in his career, violating orders: though he was under strict orders to leave the Chancellor unharmed, Palpatine was about to die alongside his precious Jedi.

Then Grievous shrugged, and sighed. What more could he have done? There was a war on, after all.

He was sure Lord Sidious would forgive him.

On the bridge, a blast shield had closed over the destroyed transparisteel window, and every last surviving combat-model droid had been cut to pieces even before the atmosphere had had a chance to stabilize.

But there was a more serious problem.

The bucking of the ship had become continuous. White-hot sparks outside streamed backward past the view wall windows. Those sparks, according to the three different kinds of alarms that were all screaming through the bridge at once, were what was left of the ablative shielding on the nose of the disabled cruiser.

Anakin stared grimly down at a console readout. "All the escape pods are gone. Not one left on the whole ship." He looked up at Obi-Wan. "We're trapped."

Obi-Wan appeared more interested than actually concerned. "Well. Here's a chance to display your legendary piloting skills, my young friend. You can fly this cruiser, can't you?"

"Flying's no problem. The trick is *landing,* which, ah . . ." Anakin gave a slightly shaky laugh. "Which, you know, this cruiser is not exactly designed to do. Even when it's in *one* piece."

Obi-Wan looked unimpressed. "And so?"

Anakin unsnapped the crash webbing that held the pilot's corpse and pulled the body from its chair. "And so you'd better strap in," he said, settling into the chair, his fingers sliding over the unfamiliar controls.

The cruiser bounced even harder, and its attitude began to skew as a new klaxon joined the blare of the other alarms. "That wasn't me!" Anakin jerked his hands away from the board. "I haven't even *done* anything yet!"

"It certainly wasn't." Palpatine's voice was unnaturally calm. "It seems someone is shooting at us."

"Wonderful," Anakin muttered. "Could this day get any better?"

"Perhaps we can talk with them." Obi-Wan moved over to the comm station and began working the screen. "Let them know we've captured the ship."

"All right, take the comm," Anakin said. He pointed at the copilot's station. "Artoo: second chair. Chancellor?"

"Yes?"

"Strap in. Now. We're going in hot." Anakin grimaced at the scraps of burning hull flashing past the view wall. "In more ways than one."

The vast space battle that had ripped and battered Coruscant space all this long, long day, finally began to flicker out.

The shimmering canopy of ion trails and turbolaser bursts was fading into streaks of ships achieving jump as the Separatist strike force fled in full retreat. The light of Coruscant's distant star splintered through iridescent clouds of gas crystals that were the remains of starfighters, and of pilots. Damaged cruisers limped toward spaceyards, passing shattered hulks that hung dead in the infinite day that is interplanetary space. Prize crews took command of surrendered ships, imprisoning the living among their crews and affixing restraining bolts to the droids.

The dayside surface of the capital planet was shrouded in smoke from a million fires touched off by meteorite impacts of ship fragments; far too many had fallen to be tracked and destroyed by the planet's surface-defense umbrella. The nightside's sheet of artificial lights faded behind the red-white glow from craters of burning steel; each impact left a caldera of unimaginable death. In the skies of Coruscant now, the important vessels were no longer warships, but were instead the fire-suppression and rescue craft that crisscrossed the planet.

Now one last fragmentary ship screamed into the atmosphere, coming in too fast, too steep, pieces breaking off to spread apart and stream their own contrails of superheated vapor; banks of turbolasers on the surface-defense towers isolated their signature, and starfighters whipped onto interception courses to thin out whatever fragments the SD towers might miss, and far above, beyond the atmosphere, on the bridge of RSS *Integrity,* Lieutenant Commander Lorth Needa spoke urgently to a knee-high blue ghost scanned into existence by the phased-array lasers in a holocomm: an alien in Jedi robes, with bulging eyes set in a wrinkled face and long, pointed, oddly flexible ears.

"You have to stand down the surface-defense system, sir! It's General Kenobi!" Needa insisted. "His code verifies, Skywalker is with him—and *they have Chancellor Palpatine!*"

"Heard and understood this is," the Jedi responded calmly. *"Tell me what they require."*

Needa glanced down at the boil of hull plating that was burning off the falling cruiser, and even as he looked, the ship broke in half at the hangar deck; the rear half tumbled, exploding in sections, but whoever was flying the front half must have been one of the greatest pilots Needa had ever even *heard* of: the front half wobbled and slewed but somehow righted itself using nothing but a bank of thrusters and its atmospheric drag fins.

"First, a flight of fireships," Needa said, more calmly now. "If they don't get the burnoff under control, there won't be enough hull left to make the surface. And a hardened docking platform, the strongest available; they won't be able to set it down. This won't be a landing, it will be a controlled crash. Repeat: a controlled crash."

"Heard and understood this is," the hologrammic Jedi repeated. *"Crossload their transponder signature."* When this was done, the Jedi nodded grave approval. *"Thank you, Lieutenant Commander. Valiant service for the Republic you have done today—and the gratitude of the Jedi Order you have earned. Yoda out."*

On the bridge of *Integrity*, Lorth Needa now could only stand, and watch, hands clasped behind his back. Military discipline kept him expressionless, but pale bands began at his knuckles and spread whiteness nearly to his wrists.

Every bone in his body ached with helplessness.

Because he knew: that fragment of a ship was a death trap. No one could land such a hulk, not even Skywalker. Each second that passed before its final breakup and burn was a miracle in itself, a testament to the gifts of a pilot who was justly legendary— but when each second is a miracle, how many of them can be strung together in a row?

Lorth Needa was not religious, nor was he a philosopher or

metaphysician; he knew of the Force only by reputation, but nonetheless now he found himself asking the Force, in his heart, that when the fiery end came for the men in that scrap of a ship, it might as least come quickly.

His eyes stung. The irony of it burned the back of his throat. The Home Fleet had fought brilliantly, and the Jedi had done their superhuman part; against all odds, the Republic had won the day.

Yet this battle had been fought to save Supreme Chancellor Palpatine.

They had won the battle, but now, as Needa stood watching helplessly, he couldn't help feeling that they were about to lose the war.

This is Anakin Skywalker's masterpiece:

Many people say he is the best star pilot in the galaxy, but that's merely talk, born of the constant HoloNet references to his unmatched string of kills in starfighter combat. Blowing up vulture droids and tri-fighters is simply a matter of superior reflexes and trust in the Force; he has spent so many hours in the cockpit that he wears a Jedi starfighter like clothes. It's his own body, with thrusters for legs and cannons for fists.

What he is doing right now transcends mere flying the way Jedi combat transcends a schoolyard scuffle.

He sits in a blood-spattered, blaster-chopped chair behind a console he's never seen before, a console with controls designed for alien fingers. The ship he's in is not only bucking like a maddened dewback through brutal coils of clear-air turbulence, it's on fire and breaking up like a comet ripping apart as it crashes into a gas giant. He has only seconds to learn how to maneuver an alien craft that not only has no aft control cells, but has no *aft* at all.

This is, put simply, impossible. It can't be done.

He's going to do it anyway.

Because he is Anakin Skywalker, and he doesn't believe in *impossible*.

He extends his hands and for one long, long moment he merely strokes controls, feeling their shape under his fingers, listening to the shivers his soft touch brings to each remaining control surface of the disintegrating ship, allowing their resonances to join inside his head until they resolve into harmony like a Ferroan joy-harp virtuoso checking the tuning of his instrument.

And at the same time, he draws power from the Force. He gathers perception, and luck, and sucks into himself the instinctive, preconscious *what-will-happen-in-the-next-ten-seconds* intuition that has always been the core of his talent.

And then he begins.

On the downbeat, atmospheric drag fins deploy; as he tweaks their angles and cycles them in and out to slow the ship's descent without burning them off altogether, their contrabass roar takes on a punctuated rhythm like a heart that skips an occasional beat. The forward attitude thrusters, damaged in the ship-to-ship battle, now fire in random directions, but he can feel where they're taking him and he strokes them in sequence, making their song the theme of his impromptu concerto.

And the true inspiration, the sparkling grace note of genius that brings his masterpiece to life, is the soprano counterpoint: a syncopated sequence of exterior hatches in the outer hull sliding open and closed and open again, subtly altering the aerodynamics of the ship to give it just exactly the amount of sideslip or lift or yaw to bring the huge half cruiser into the approach cone of a pinpoint target an eighth of the planet away.

It is the Force that makes this possible, and more than the Force. Anakin has no interest in serene acceptance of what the Force will bring. Not here. Not now. Not with the lives of Palpatine and Obi-Wan at stake. It's just the opposite: he seizes upon the Force with a stark refusal to fail.

He *will* land this ship.

He *will* save his friends.

Between his will and the will of the Force, there is no contest.

PART TWO

SEDUCTION

The dark is generous, and it is patient.

It is the dark that seeds cruelty into justice, that drips contempt into compassion, that poisons love with grains of doubt.

The dark can be patient, because the slightest drop of rain will cause those seeds to sprout.

The rain will come, and the seeds will sprout, for the dark is the soil in which they grow, and it is the clouds above them, and it waits behind the star that gives them light.

The dark's patience is infinite.

Eventually, even stars burn out.

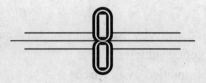

FAULT LINES

Mace Windu hung on to the corrugated hatch grip beside the gunship's open troop bay with one hand, squinting into the wind that whipped his overcloak behind him. His other hand shaded his eyes against the glare from one of the orbital mirrors that concentrated the capital planet's daylight. The mirror was slowly turning aside now, allowing a band of twilight to approach the gunship's destination.

That destination, a kilometer-thick landing platform in the planet's vast industrial zone, was marked with a steeply slanting tower of smoke and vapor that stretched from the planet's surface to the uppermost reaches of the atmosphere, a tower that only now was beginning to spread and coil from its tiny source point to a horizon-spanning smear across the stratospheric winds.

The gunship roared over the bottomless canyons of durasteel and permacrete that formed the landscape of Coruscant, arrowing straight for the industrial zone without regard for the rigid traffic laws that governed flight on the galactic planet; until martial law was officially lifted by the Senate, the darkening skies would be traveled only by Republic military craft, Jedi transports, and emergency vehicles.

The gunship qualified as all three.

Mace could see the ship now—what was left of it—resting on the scorched platform far ahead: a piece of a ship, a fragment, less than a third of what once had been the Trade Federation flagship, still burning despite the gouts of fire-suppression foam raining down on it from five different ships and the emergency-support clone troops who surrounded it on the platform.

Mace shook his head. Skywalker again. The chosen one.

Who else could have brought in this hulk? Who else could have even come close?

The gunship swung into a hot landing, repulsors howling; Mace hopped out before it could settle, and gave the pilot an open-palm gesture to signal him to wait. The pilot, faceless within his helmet, responded with a closed fist.

Though, of course, the pilot wasn't faceless at all. Under his armored helmet, that clone pilot had a face that Mace Windu remembered all too well.

That face would always remind him that he had once held Dooku within his grasp, and had let him slip away.

Across the platform, an escape pod hatch cycled open. Emergency crews scrambled with an escape slide, and a moment later the Supreme Chancellor, Obi-Wan Kenobi, and Anakin Skywalker were all on the deck beside the burning ship, closely followed by a somewhat battered R2 unit that lifted itself down on customized maneuvering rockets.

Mace strode swiftly out to meet them.

Palpatine's robes were scorched and tattered at the hem, and he seemed weak; he leaned a bit on Skywalker's shoulder as they moved away from the ship. On Skywalker's other side, Master Kenobi seemed a touch the worse for wear himself: caked with dust and leaking a trickle of blood from a scalp wound.

Skywalker, by contrast, looked every bit the HoloNet hero he was supposed to be. He seemed to tower over his companions, as though he had somehow gotten even taller in the months since Mace had seen him last. His hair was tousled, his color was high, and his walk still had the grounded grace of a natural fighter, but there was something new in his physicality: in the way he moved his head, perhaps, or the way the weight of Palpatine's arm on his shoulder seemed somehow to belong there . . . or something less definable. Some new ease, new confidence. An aura of inner power.

Presence.

Skywalker was not the same young man the Council had sent off to the Outer Rim five standard months ago.

"Chancellor," Mace said as he met them. "Are you well? Do you need medical attention?" He gestured over his shoulder at the waiting gunship. "I have a fully equipped field surgery—"

"No, no, no need," Palpatine said, rather faintly. "Thank you, Master Windu, but I am well. Quite well, thanks to these two."

Mace nodded. "Master Kenobi? Anakin?"

"Never better," Skywalker replied, looking as if he meant it, and Kenobi only shrugged, with a slight wince as he touched his scalp wound.

"Only a bump on the head. That field surgery must be needed elsewhere."

"It is." Mace looked grim. "We don't have even a preliminary estimate of civilian casualties."

He waved off the gunship, and it roared away toward the countless fires that painted red the approach of night.

"A shuttle is on its way. Chancellor, we'll have you on the Senate floor within the hour. The HoloNet has already been notified that you will want to make a statement."

"I will. I will, indeed." Palpatine touched Mace on the arm.

"You have always been of great value to me, Master Windu. Thank you."

"The Jedi are honored to serve the Senate, sir." There might have been the slightest emphasis on the word *Senate*. Mace remained expressionless as he subtly moved his arm away from the Chancellor's hand. He looked at Obi-Wan. "Is there anything else to report, Master Kenobi? What of General Grievous?"

"Count Dooku was there," Skywalker interjected. He had a look on his face that Mace couldn't decipher, proud yet wary—even unhappy. "He's dead now."

"Dead?" He looked from Anakin to Obi-Wan and back again. "Is this true? You killed Count *Dooku*?"

"My young friend is too modest; *he* killed Count Dooku." Smiling, Kenobi touched the lump on his head. "I was . . . taking a nap."

"But . . ." Mace blinked. Dooku was to the Separatists what Palpatine was to the Republic: the center of gravity binding together a spiral galaxy of special interests. With Dooku gone, the Confederacy of Independent Systems would no longer really be a confederacy at all. They'd fly to pieces within weeks.

Within *days*.

Mace said again, "But . . ."

And, in the end, he couldn't think of a *but*.

This was all so astonishing that he very nearly—almost, but not quite—cracked a smile.

"That is," he said, "the best news I've heard since . . ." He shook his head. "Since I can't remember. Anakin—how did you *do* it?"

Inexplicably, young Skywalker looked distinctly uncomfortable; that newly confident presence of his collapsed as suddenly as an overloaded deflector, and instead of meeting Mace's eyes, his gaze flicked to Palpatine. Somehow Mace didn't think this was modesty. He looked to the Chancellor as well, his elation sinking, becoming puzzlement tinged with suspicion.

"It was . . . entirely extraordinary," Palpatine said blandly, oblivious to Mace's narrowing stare. "I know next to nothing of swordplay, of course; to my amateur's eye, it seemed that Count Dooku may have been . . . a trace overconfident. Especially after having disposed of Master Kenobi so neatly."

Obi-Wan flushed, just a bit—and Anakin flushed considerably more deeply.

"Perhaps young Anakin was simply more . . . highly *motivated*," Palpatine said, turning a fond smile upon him. "After all, Dooku was fighting only to slay an enemy; Anakin was fighting to save—if I may presume the honor—a friend."

Mace's scowl darkened. Fine words. Perhaps even true words, but he still didn't like them.

No one on the Jedi Council had ever been comfortable with Skywalker's close relationship with the Chancellor—they'd had more than one conversation about it with Obi-Wan while Skywalker had still been his Padawan—and Mace was less than happy to hear Palpatine speaking for a young Jedi who seemed unprepared to speak for himself. He said, "I'm sure the Council will be very interested in your full report, Anakin," with just enough emphasis on *full* to get his point across.

Skywalker swallowed, and then, just as suddenly as it had collapsed, that aura of calm, centered confidence rebuilt itself around him. "Yes. Yes of course, Master Windu."

"And we must report that Grievous escaped," Obi-Wan said. "He is as cowardly as ever."

Mace accepted this news with a nod. "But he is only a military commander. Without Dooku to hold the coalition together, these so-called independent systems will splinter, and they know it." He looked straight into the Supreme Chancellor's eyes. "This is our best chance to sue for peace. We can end this war right now."

And while Palpatine answered, Mace Windu reached into the Force.

To Mace's Force perception, the world crystallized around them, becoming a gem of reality shot through with flaws and fault lines of possibility. This was Mace's particular gift: to see how people and situations fit together in the Force, to find the shear planes that can cause them to break in useful ways, and to intuit what sort of strike would best make the cut. Though he could not consistently determine the significance of the structures he perceived—the darkening cloud upon the Force that had risen with the rebirth of the Sith made that harder and harder with each passing day—the presence of shatterpoints was always clear.

Mace had supported the training of Anakin Skywalker, though it ran counter to millennia of Jedi tradition, because from the structure of fault lines in the Force around him, he had been able to intuit the truth of Qui-Gon Jinn's guess: that the young slave boy from Tatooine was in fact the prophesied chosen one, born to bring balance to the Force. He had argued for the elevation of Obi-Wan Kenobi to Mastership, and to give the training of the chosen one into the hands of this new, untested Master, because his unique perception had shown him powerful lines of destiny that bound their lives together, for good or ill. On the day of Palpatine's election to the Chancellorship, he had seen that Palpatine was himself a shatterpoint of unimaginable significance: a man upon whom might depend the fate of the Republic itself.

Now he saw the three men together, and the intricate lattice of fault lines and stress fractures that bound them each to the other was so staggeringly powerful that its structure was beyond calculation.

Anakin was somehow a pivot point, the fulcrum of a lever with Obi-Wan on one side, Palpatine on the other, and the galaxy in the balance, but the dark cloud on the Force prevented his perception from reaching into the future for so much as a hint of where this might lead. The balance was already so delicate that he could not guess the outcome of any given shift: the slightest tip in any direction would generate chaotic oscillation. Anything could happen.

Anything at all.

And the lattice of fault lines that bound all three of them to each other stank of the dark side.

He lifted his head and looked to the sky, picking out the dropping star of the Jedi shuttle as it swung toward them through the darkening afternoon.

"I'm afraid peace is out of the question while Grievous is at large," the Chancellor was saying sadly. "Dooku was the only check on Grievous's monstrous lust for slaughter; with Dooku gone, the general has been unleashed to rampage across the galaxy. I'm afraid that, far from being over, this war is about to get a very great deal *worse*."

"And what of the Sith?" Obi-Wan said. "Dooku's death should have at least begun the weakening of the darkness, but instead it feels stronger than ever. I fear Master Yoda's intuition is correct: that Dooku was merely the apprentice to the Sith Lord, not the Master."

Mace started walking toward the small-craft dock where the Jedi shuttle would land, and the others fell in with him.

"The Sith Lord, if one still exists, will reveal himself in time. They always do." He hoped Obi-Wan would take the hint and shut up about it; Mace had no desire to speak openly of the investigation in front of the Supreme Chancellor.

The less Palpatine knew, the better.

"A more interesting puzzle is Grievous," he said. "He had you at his mercy, Chancellor, and mercy is not numbered among his virtues. Though we all rejoice that he spared you, I cannot help but wonder why."

Palpatine spread his hands. "I can only assume the Separatists preferred to have me as a hostage rather than as a martyr. Though it is of course impossible to say; it may merely have been a whim of the general. He is notoriously erratic."

"Perhaps the Separatist leadership can restrain him, in exchange for certain . . ." Mace let his gaze drift casually to a point somewhere above the Chancellor's head. ". . . considerations."

"Absolutely not." Palpatine drew himself up, straightening his robes. "A negotiated peace would be a recognition of the CIS as the legitimate government of the rebellious systems— tantamount to losing the war! No, Master Windu, this war can end only one way. Unconditional surrender. And while Grievous lives, that will never happen."

"Very well," Mace said. "Then the Jedi will make the capture of General Grievous our particular task." He glanced at Anakin and Obi-Wan, then back to Palpatine. He leaned close to the Chancellor and his voice went low and final, with a buried intensity that hinted—just the slightest bit—of suspicion, and warning. "This war has gone on far too long already. We will find him, and this war *will* end."

"I have no doubt of it." Palpatine strolled along, seemingly oblivious. "But we should never underestimate the deviousness of the Separatists. It is possible that even the war itself has been only one further move," he said with elegant, understated precision, "in some greater game."

As the Jedi shuttle swung toward the Chancellor's private landing platform at the Senate Offices, Obi-Wan watched Anakin pretending not to stare out the window. On the platform was a small welcome-contingent of Senators, and Anakin was trying desperately to look as if he wasn't searching that little crowd hungrily for a particular face. The pretense was a waste of time; Anakin radiated excitement so powerfully in the Force that Obi-Wan could practically hear the thunder of his heartbeat.

Obi-Wan gave a silent sigh. He had entirely too good an idea whose face his former Padawan was so hoping to see.

When the shuttle touched down, Master Windu caught his eye from beyond Anakin's shoulder. The Korun Master made a nearly invisible gesture, to which Obi-Wan did not visibly respond; but when Palpatine and Anakin and R2 all debarked toward the crowd of well-wishers, Obi-Wan stayed behind.

Anakin stopped on the landing deck, looking back at Obi-Wan. "You coming?"

"I haven't the courage for politics," Obi-Wan said, showing his usual trace of a smile. "I'll brief the Council."

"Shouldn't I be there, too?"

"No need. This isn't the formal report. Besides—" Obi-Wan nodded toward the clot of HoloNet crews clogging the pedestrian gangway. "—someone has to be the poster boy."

Anakin looked pained. "Poster *man*."

"Quite right, quite right," Obi-Wan said with a gentle chuckle. "Go meet your public, Poster Man."

"Wait a minute—this whole operation was *your* idea. You planned it. You led the rescue. It's your turn to take the bows."

"You won't get out of it that easily, my young friend. Without you, I wouldn't even have made it to the flagship. You killed Count Dooku, and single-handedly rescued the Chancellor . . . all while, I might be forgiven for adding, carrying some old broken-down Jedi Master unconscious on your back. Not to mention making a landing that will be the standard of Impossible in every flight manual for the next thousand years."

"Only because of your training, Master—"

"That's just an excuse. You're the hero. Go spend your glorious day surrounded by—" Obi-Wan allowed himself a slightly disparaging cough. "—politicians."

"Come on, Master—you *owe* me. And not just for saving your skin for the tenth time—"

"*Ninth* time. Cato Neimoidia doesn't count; it was your fault in the first place." Obi-Wan waved him off. "See you at the Outer Rim briefing in the morning."

"Well . . . all right. Just this once." Anakin laughed and waved, and then headed briskly off to catch up with Palpatine as the Chancellor waded into the Senators with the smooth-as-oiled-transparisteel ease of the lifelong politician.

The hatch cycled shut, the shuttle lifted off, and Obi-Wan's smile faded as he turned to Mace Windu. "You wanted to speak with me."

Windu moved close to Obi-Wan's position by the window, nodding out at the scene on the landing platform. "It's Anakin. I don't like his relationship with Palpatine."

"We've had this conversation before."

"There is something between them. Something new. I could see it in the Force." Mace's voice was flat and grim. "It felt powerful. And incredibly dangerous."

Obi-Wan spread his hands. "I trust Anakin with my life."

"I know you do. I only wish we could trust the Chancellor with Anakin's."

"Yes," Obi-Wan said, frowning. "Palpatine's policies are . . . sometimes questionable. But he dotes on Anakin like a kindly old uncle on his favorite nephew."

Mace stared out the window. "The Chancellor loves power. If he has any other passion, I have not seen it."

Obi-Wan shook his head with a trace of disbelief. "I recall that not so long ago, you were something of an admirer of his."

"Things," Mace Windu said grimly, "change."

Flying over a landscape pocked with smoldering wreckage where once tall buildings filled with living beings had gleamed in the sun, toward a Temple filled with memories of so many, many Jedi who would never return from this war, Obi-Wan could not disagree.

After a moment, he said, "What would you have me do?"

"I am not certain. You know my power; I cannot always interpret what I've seen. Be alert. Be mindful of Anakin, and be careful of Palpatine. He is not to be trusted, and his influence on Anakin is dangerous."

"But Anakin is the chosen one—"

"All the more reason to fear an outsider's influence. We have circumstantial evidence that traces Sidious to Palpatine's inner circle."

Suddenly Obi-Wan had difficulty breathing. "Are you certain?"

Mace shook his head. "Nothing is certain. But this raid—the capture of Palpatine had to be an inside job. And the timing . . . we were closing *in* on him, Master Kenobi! The information you and Anakin discovered—we had traced the Sith Lord to an abandoned factory in The Works, not far from where Anakin landed the cruiser. When the attack began, we were tracking him through the downlevel tunnels." Mace stared out the viewport at a vast residential complex that dominated the skyline to the west. "The trail led to the sub-basement of Five Hundred Republica."

Five Hundred Republica was the most exclusive address on the planet. Its inhabitants included only the incredibly wealthy or the incredibly powerful, from Raith Sienar of the Sienar Systems conglomerate to Palpatine himself. Obi-Wan could only say, "Oh."

"We have to face the possibility—the probability—that what Dooku told you on Geonosis was actually *true*. That the Senate is under the influence—under the control—of Darth Sidious. That it has been for *years*."

"Do you—" Obi-Wan had to swallow before he could go on. "Do you have any suspects?"

"Too many. All we know of Sidious is that he's bipedal, of roughly human conformation. Sate Pestage springs to mind. I wouldn't rule out Mas Amedda, either. The Sith Lord might even be hiding among the Red Guards. There's no way to know."

"Who's handling the questioning?" Obi-Wan asked. "I'd be happy to sit in; my perceptions are not so refined as some, but—"

Mace shook his head. "Interrogate the Supreme Chancellor's personal aides and advisors? Impossible."

"But—"

"Palpatine will never allow it. Though he hasn't said so . . ." Mace stared out the window. ". . . I'm not sure he even believes the Sith exist."

Obi-Wan blinked. "But—how can he—"

"Look at it from his point of view: the only real evidence we have is Dooku's word. And he's dead now."

"The Sith Lord on Naboo—the Zabrak who killed Qui-Gon—"

Mace shrugged. "Destroyed. As you know." He shook his head. "Relations with the Chancellor's Office are . . . difficult. I feel he has lost his trust in the Jedi; I have certainly lost my trust in him."

"But he doesn't have the authority to interfere with a Jedi investigation . . ." Obi-Wan frowned, suddenly uncertain. "Does he?"

"The Senate has surrendered so much power, it's hard to say where his authority stops."

"It's that bad?"

Mace's jaw locked. "The only reason Palpatine's not a suspect is because he *already* rules the galaxy."

"But we are closer than we have ever been to rooting out the Sith," Obi-Wan said slowly. "That can only be good news. I would think that Anakin's friendship with Palpatine could be of use to us in this—he has the kind of access to Palpatine that other Jedi might only dream of. Their friendship is an asset, not a danger."

"You can't tell him."

"I beg your pardon?"

"Of the whole Council, only Yoda and myself know how deep this actually goes. And now you. I have decided to share this with you because you are in the best situation to watch Anakin. Watch him. Nothing more."

"We—" Obi-Wan shook his head helplessly. "We don't keep secrets from each other."

"You must keep this one." Mace laced his fingers together and squeezed until his knuckles crackled like blasterfire. "Skywalker is arguably the most powerful Jedi alive, and he is still getting stronger. But he is not *stable*. You know it. We all do. It is why he cannot be given Mastership. We must keep him off the Council, despite his extraordinary gifts. And Jedi prophecy . . . is not absolute. The less he has to do with Palpatine, the better."

"But surely—" Obi-Wan stopped himself. He thought of how many times Anakin had violated orders. He thought of how unflinchingly loyal Anakin was to anyone he considered a friend. He thought of the danger Palpatine faced unknowingly, with a Sith Lord among his advisers . . .

Master Windu was right. This was a secret Anakin could not be trusted to keep.

"What *can* I tell him?"

"Tell him nothing. I sense the dark side around him. Around them both."

"As it is around us all," Obi-Wan reminded him. "The dark side touches all of us, Master Windu. Even you."

"I know that too well, Obi-Wan." For one second Obi-Wan saw something raw and haunted in the Korun Master's eyes. Mace turned away. "It is possible that we may have to . . . move against Palpatine."

"Move *against*—?"

"If he is truly under the control of a Sith Lord, it may be the only way."

Obi-Wan's whole body had gone numb. This didn't seem real. It was not possible that he was actually having this conversation.

"You haven't *been* here, Obi-Wan." Mace stared bleakly down at his hands. "You've been off fighting the war in the Outer Rim. You don't know what it's been like, dealing with all the petty squabbles and special interests and greedy, grasping fools in the Senate, and Palpatine's constant, cynical, ruthless maneuvering for power—he carves away chunks of our freedom and bandages the wounds with tiny scraps of security. And for what? Look at this planet, Obi-Wan! We have given up so much freedom—how secure do we *look*?"

Obi-Wan's heart clenched. This was not the Mace Windu he knew and admired; it was as though the darkness in the Force was so much thicker here on Coruscant that it had breathed poison into Mace's spirit—and perhaps was even breeding suspicion and dissension among the members of the Jedi Council.

The greatest danger from the darkness outside came when Jedi fed it with the darkness within.

He had feared he might find matters had deteriorated when he returned to Coruscant and the Temple; not even in his darkest dreams had he thought it would get this bad.

"Master Windu—Mace. We'll go to Yoda together," he said firmly. "And among the three of us we'll work something out. We will. You'll see."

"It may be too late already."

"It may be. And it may not be. We can only do what we can do, Mace. A very, very wise Jedi once said to me, *We don't have to win. All we have to do is fight.*"

Some of the lines erased themselves from the Korun Master's face then, and when he met Obi-Wan's eye there was a quirk at the corner of his mouth that might someday develop into a smile—a tired, sad smile, but a smile nonetheless. "I seem," he said slowly, "to have forgotten that particular Jedi. Thank you for reminding me."

"It was the least I could do," Obi-Wan said lightly, but a sad weight had gathered on his chest.

Things change, indeed.

Anakin's heart pounded in his throat, but he kept smiling, and nodding, and shaking hands—and trying desperately to work his way toward a familiar golden-domed protocol droid who hung back beyond the crowd of Senators, right arm lifted in a small, tentative wave at R2-D2.

She wasn't here. Why wasn't she here?

Something must have happened.

He *knew*, deep in his guts, that something had happened to her. An accident, or she was sick, or she'd been caught in one of the vast number of buildings hit by debris from the battle today . . . She might be trapped somewhere *right now*, might be wounded, might be *smothering*, calling out his name, might be feeling the approach of *flames*—

Stop it, he told himself. *She's not hurt.* If anything had happened to her, he would know. Even from the far side of the Outer Rim, he would know.

So why wasn't she here?

Had something . . .

He could barely breathe. He couldn't make himself even think it. He couldn't stop himself from thinking it.

Had something *changed*? For her?

In how she felt?

He managed to disengage himself from Tundra Dowmeia's clammy grip and insistent invitations to visit his family's deepwater estate on Mon Calamari; he slid past the Malastarian Senator Ask Aak with an apologetic shrug.

He had a different Senator on his mind.

R2 was wheeping and beeping and whistling intensely when Anakin finally struggled free of the mass of sweaty, grasping politicians; C-3PO had turned away dismissively. "It couldn't have been that bad. Don't exaggerate! You're hardly even dented."

R2's answering *feroo* sounded a little defensive. C-3PO sent a wisp of static through his vocabulator that sounded distinctly like a disapproving sniff. "On that point I agree; you're long overdue for a tune-up. And, if I may say so, a *bath*."

"Threepio—"

Anakin came up close beside the droid he had built in the back room of his mother's slave hovel on Tatooine: the droid who had been both project and friend through his painful childhood: the droid who now served the woman he loved . . .

Threepio had been with her all these months, had seen her every day, had *touched* her, perhaps even *today*—he could feel echoes of her resonating outward from his electroplated shell, and they left him breathless.

"Oh, Master Anakin!" Threepio exclaimed. "I am *very* glad to find you well! One does worry, when friends fall out of touch! Why, I was saying to the Senator, just the other day—or was it last week? Time seems to run together so; do you think you might have the opportunity to adjust my internal calendar settings while you're—"

"Threepio, have you *seen* her?" Anakin was trying so hard not to shout that his voice came out a strangled croak. "Where *is* she? Why isn't she *here*?"

"Oh, well, certainly, certainly. Officially, Senator Amidala is *extremely* busy," C-3PO said imperturbably. "She has been sequestered all day in the Naboo embassy, reviewing the new Security Act, preparing for tomorrow's debate—"

Anakin couldn't breathe. She wasn't *here,* hadn't come to meet him, over some *debate*?

The Senate. He *hated* the Senate. Hated everything about it.

A red haze gathered inside his head. Those self-righteous, narrow-minded, grubby little *squabblers* . . . He'd be doing the galaxy a *favor* if he were to go over there right *now* and just—

"Wait," he murmured, blinking. "Did you say, *officially?*"

"Oh, yes, Master Anakin." Threepio sounded entirely virtuous. "That is my *official* answer to all queries regarding the Senator's whereabouts. All afternoon."

The red haze evaporated, leaving only sunlight and dizzyingly fresh air.

Anakin smiled.

"And *un*officially?"

The protocol droid leaned close with an exaggeratedly conspiratorial whisper: "Unofficially, she's waiting in the hallway."

It felt like being struck by lightning. But in a good way. In the best way any man has ever felt since, roughly, the birth of the universe.

Threepio gave a slight nod at the other Senators and the HoloNet crews on the gangway. "She thought it best to avoid a, ah, *public* scene. And she wished for me to relate to you that she believes the *both* of you might . . . *avoid* a public *scene* . . . all *afternoon*. And perhaps all night, as well."

"Threepio!" Anakin blinked at him. He felt an irrational desire to giggle. "What exactly are you suggesting?"

"I'm sure I couldn't say, sir. I am only performing as per the Senator's instructions."

"You—" Anakin shook his head in wonder while his smile grew to a grin he thought might split open his cheeks. "You are amazing."

"Thank you, Master Anakin, though credit for that is due largely—" C-3PO made an elegantly gracious bow. "—to my creator."

Anakin could only go on grinning.

With that, the golden protocol droid laid an affectionate hand on R2's dome. "Come along, Artoo. I have found the most delightful body shop down in the Lipartian Way."

They moved away, whirring and clanking after the Senators who were already off among the HoloNet crews. Anakin's smile faded as he watched them go.

He felt a presence at his shoulder and turned to find Palpatine beside him with a warm smile and a soft word, as he always seemed to be when Anakin was troubled.

"What is it, Anakin?" the Chancellor asked kindly. "Something is disturbing you. I can tell."

Anakin shrugged and gave his head a dismissive shake, embarrassed. "It's nothing."

"Anakin, anything that might upset a man such as yourself is certainly *some*thing. Let me help."

"There's nothing you can do. It's just—" Anakin nodded after 3PO and R2. "I was just thinking that even after all I've done, See-Threepio is still the only person I know who calls me *Master*."

"Ah. The Jedi Council." Palpatine slid an arm around Anakin's shoulders and gave him a comradely squeeze. "I believe I can be of some use to you in this problem after all."

"You can?"

"I should be very much surprised if I couldn't."

Palpatine's smile was still warm, but his eyes had gone distant.

"You may have noticed that I have a certain gift," he murmured, "for getting my way."

PADMÉ

From the shadow of a great pillar stretching up into the reddening afternoon that leaked through the vaulted roof of transparisteel over the Atrium of the Senate Office Building, she watched Senators clustering in through the archway from the Chancellor's landing platform, and then she saw the Chancellor himself and C-3PO and yes, that was *R2-D2*!—and so *he* could not be far behind . . . and only then did she finally find him among them, tall and straight, his hair radiation-bleached to golden streaks and on his lips a lively smile that opened her chest and unlocked her heart.

And she could breathe again.

Through the swirl of HoloNet reporters and the chatter of Senators and the gently comforting tones of Palpatine's most polished, reassuringly paternal voice, she did not move, not so much as to lift a hand or turn her head. She was silent, and still, only letting herself breathe, feeling the beat of her heart, and she could have stood there forever, in the shadows, and had her fondest dreams all fulfilled, simply by watching him be alive . . .

But when he moved away from the group, pacing in soft conversation with Bail Organa of Alderaan, and she heard Bail saying something about *the end of Count Dooku* and *the end of the war* and *finally an end to Palpatine's police-state tactics,* her breath caught again and she held it, because she knew the next thing she heard would be *his* voice.

"I wish that were so," he said, "but the fighting will continue until General Grievous is spare parts. The Chancellor is very clear on this, and I believe the Senate and the Jedi Council will both agree."

And beyond that, there was no hope she could be happier—until his eye found her silent, still shadow, and he straightened, and a new light broke over his golden face and he said, "Excuse me," to the Senator from Alderaan, and a moment later he came to her in the shadows and they were in each other's arms.

Their lips met, and the universe became, one last time, perfect.

This is Padmé Amidala:

She is an astonishingly accomplished young woman, who in her short life has been already the youngest-ever elected Queen of her planet, a daring partisan guerrilla, and a measured, articulate, and persuasive voice of reason in the Republic Senate.

But she is, at this moment, none of these things.

She can still play at them—she pretends to be a Senator, she still wields the moral authority of a former Queen, and she is not shy about using her reputation for fierce physical courage to her advantage in political debate—but her inmost reality, the most fundamental, unbreakable core of her being, is something entirely different.

She is Anakin Skywalker's wife.

Yet *wife* is a word too weak to carry the truth of her; *wife* is such a small word, such a common word, a word that can come from a downturned mouth with so many petty, unpleasant echoes. For Padmé Amidala, saying *I am Anakin Skywalker's wife* is saying neither more nor less than *I am alive.*

Her life before Anakin belonged to someone else, some lesser being to be pitied, some poor impoverished spirit who could never suspect how profoundly life should be lived.

Her real life began the first time she looked into Anakin Sky-walker's eyes and found in there not the uncritical worship of lit-tle Annie from Tatooine, but the direct, unashamed, smoldering passion of a powerful Jedi: a *young* man, to be sure, but every centimeter a *man*—a man whose legend was already growing within the Jedi Order and beyond. A man who knew exactly what he wanted and was honest enough to simply *ask* for it; a man strong enough to unroll his deepest feelings before her without fear and without shame. A man who had loved her for a decade, with faithful and patient heart, while he waited for the act of destiny he was sure would someday open her own heart to the fire in his.

But though she loves her husband without reservation, love does not blind her to his faults. She is older than he, and wise enough to understand him better than he does himself. He is not a perfect man: he is prideful, and moody, and quick to anger— but these faults only make her love him the more, for his every flaw is more than balanced by the greatness within him, his ca-pacity for joy and cleansing laughter, his extraordinary generosity of spirit, his passionate devotion not only to her but also in the service of every living being.

He is a wild creature who has come gently to her hand, a vine tiger purring against her cheek. Every softness of his touch, every kind glance or loving word is a small miracle in itself. How can she not be grateful for such gifts?

This is why she will not allow their marriage to become pub-lic knowledge. Her husband *needs* to be a Jedi. Saving people is what he was born for; to take that away from him would cripple every good thing in his troubled heart.

Now she holds him in their infinite kiss with both arms tight around his neck, because there is a cold dread in the center of her heart that whispers this kiss is not infinite at all, that it's only a pause in the headlong rush of the universe, and when it ends, she will have to face the future.

And she is terrified.

Because while he has been away, everything has changed.

Today, here in the hallway of the Senate Office Building, she brings him news of a gift they have given each other—a gift of joy, and of terror. This gift is the edge of a knife that has already cut their past from their future.

For these long years they have held each other only in secret, only in moments stolen from the business of the Republic and the war; their love has been the perfect refuge, a long quiet afternoon, warm and sunny, sealed away from fear and doubt, from duty and from danger. But now she carries within her a planetary terminator that will end their warm afternoon forever and leave them blind in the oncoming night.

She is more, now, than Anakin Skywalker's wife.

She is the mother of Anakin Skywalker's unborn child.

After an all-too-brief eternity, the kiss finally ended.

She clung to him, just breathing in the presence of him after so long, murmuring love against his broad strong chest while he murmured love into the coils of her softly scented hair.

Some time later, she found words again. "Anakin, Anakin, oh my Anakin, I—I can't believe you're *home*. They told me . . ." She almost choked on the memory. "There were whispers . . . that you'd been *killed*. I couldn't—every day—"

"Never believe stories like that," he whispered. "Never. I will always come back to you, Padmé."

"I've lived a year for every hour you were away—"

"It's been a lifetime. Two."

She reached up to the burn-scar high on his cheek. "You were hurt . . ."

"Nothing serious," he said with half a smile. "Just an unfriendly reminder to keep up with my lightsaber practice."

"Five *months*." It was almost a moan. "Five months—how could they *do* that to us?"

He rested his cheek lightly on the crown of her head. "If the Chancellor hadn't been kidnapped, I'd still be out there. I'm almost—it's terrible to say it, but I'm *grateful*. I'm glad he was kidnapped. It's like it was all arranged just to bring me home again . . ."

His arms were so strong, and so warm, and his hand touched her hair in the softest caress, as though he was afraid she were as fragile as a dream, and he bent down for another kiss, a new kiss, a kiss that would wipe away every dark dream and all the days and hours and minutes of unbearable dread—

But only steps away, the main vault of the Atrium still held Senators and HoloNet crews, and the knowledge of the price Anakin would pay when their love became known made her turn her face aside, and put her hands on his chest to hold him away. "Anakin, not here. It's too risky."

"No, *here*! *Exactly* here." He drew her against him again, effortlessly overpowering her halfhearted resistance. "I'm tired of the deception. Of the sneaking and the lying. We have *nothing* to be ashamed of! We love each other, and we are married. Just like trillions of beings across the galaxy. This is something we should *shout*, not whisper—"

"No, Anakin. *Not* like all those others. They are not Jedi. We can't let our love force you out of the Order—"

"Force me out of the Order?" He smiled down at her fondly. "Was that a pun?"

"Anakin—" He could still make her angry without even trying. "*Listen* to me. We have a duty to the Republic. Both of us— but yours is now so much more important. You are the face of the Jedi, Anakin. Even after these years of war, many people still love the Jedi, and it's mostly because they love *you,* do you understand that? They love the *story* of you. You're like something out of a bedtime tale, the secret prince, hidden among the peasants, growing up without ever a clue of his special destiny— except for you it's all *true.* Sometimes I think that the only reason the people of the Republic still believe we can win the war is because *you're* fighting it for them—"

"And it always comes back to politics for you," Anakin said. His smile had gone now. "I'm barely even home, and you're already trying to talk me into going back to the war—"

"This isn't about politics, Anakin, it's about *you.*"

"Something has changed, hasn't it?" Thunder gathered in his voice. "I felt it, even outside. Something has changed."

She lowered her head. "Everything has changed."

"What is it? What?" He took her by the shoulders now, his hands hard and irresistibly powerful. "There's someone else. I can *feel* it in the Force! There is someone coming *between* us—"

"Not the way you think," she said. "Anakin, listen—"

"Who is it? *Who?*"

"*Stop* it. Anakin, *stop.* You'll hurt us."

His hands sprang open as though she had burned them. He took an unsteady step backward, his face suddenly ashen. "Padmé—I would never—I'm so sorry, I just—"

He leaned on the pillar and brought a hand weakly to his eyes. "The Hero With No Fear. What a joke . . . Padmé, I can't *lose* you. I *can't.* You're all I *live* for. Wait . . ." He lifted his head, frowning quizzically. "Did you say, *us?*"

She reached for him, and he came to meet her hand. Rising

tears burned her eyes, and her lip trembled. "I'm . . . Annie, I'm *pregnant* . . ."

She watched him as everything their child would mean cycled through his mind, and her heart caught when she saw first of all the wild, almost explosive joy that dawned over his face, because that meant that whatever he had gone through on the Outer Rim, he was still her Annie.

It meant that the war that had scarred his face had not scarred his spirit.

And she watched that joy fade as he began to understand that their marriage could not stay hidden much longer; that even the voluminous robes she wore could not conceal a pregnancy forever. That he would be cast out in disgrace from the Jedi Order. That she would be relieved of her post and recalled to Naboo. That the very celebrity that had made him so important to the war would turn against them both, making them the freshest possible meat for an entire galaxy full of scandalmongers.

And she watched him decide that he didn't care.

"That is," he said slowly, that wild spark returning to his eyes, ". . . *wonderful* . . . Padmé—that's *wonderful.* How long have you known?"

She shook her head. "What are we going to *do?*"

"We're going to be happy, that's what we're going to do. And we're going to be *together.* All *three* of us."

"But—"

"No." He laid a gentle finger on her lips, smiling down at her. "No buts. No worries. You worry too much as it is."

"I have to," she said, smiling through the tears in her eyes. "Because you never worry at all."

Anakin lurched upright in bed, gasping, staring blindly into alien darkness.

How she had *screamed* for him—how she had begged for him, how her strength had failed on that alien table, how at the last she could only whimper, *Anakin, I'm sorry. I love you. I love you*—thundered inside his head, blinding him to the contours of the night-shrouded room, deafening him to every sound save the turbohammer of his heart.

His hand of flesh found unfamiliar coils of sweat-damp silken sheets around his waist. Finally he remembered where he was.

He half turned, and she was with him, lying on her side, her glorious fall of hair fanned across her pillow, eyes closed, half a smile on her precious lips, and when he saw the long, slow rise and fall of her chest with the cycle of her breathing, he turned away and buried his face in his hands and sobbed.

The tears that ran between his fingers then were tears of gratitude.

She was alive, and she was with him.

In silence so deep he could hear the whirring of the electro-drivers in his mechanical hand, he disentangled himself from the sheets and got up.

Through the closet, a long curving sweep of stairs led to the veranda that overlooked Padmé's private landing deck. Leaning on the night-chilled rail, Anakin stared out upon the endless nightscape of Coruscant.

It was still burning.

Coruscant at night had always been an endless galaxy of light, shining from trillions of windows in billions of buildings that reached kilometers into the sky, with navigation lights and advertising and the infinite streams of speeders' running lights coursing the rivers of traffic lanes overhead. But tonight, local power outages had swallowed ragged swaths of the city into vast nebulae of darkness, broken only by the malignant red-dwarf glares of innumerable fires.

Anakin didn't know how long he stood there, staring. The city looked like he felt. Damaged. Broken in battle.

Stained with darkness.

And he'd rather look at the city than think about why he was out here looking at it in the first place.

She moved more quietly than the smoky breeze, but he felt her approach.

She took a place beside him at the railing and laid her soft human hand along the back of his hard mechanical one. And she simply stood with him, staring silently out across the city that had become her second home. Waiting patiently for him to tell her what was wrong. Trusting that he would.

He could feel her patience, and her trust, and he was so grateful for both that tears welled once more. He had to blink out at the burning night, and blink again, to keep those fresh tears from spilling over onto his cheeks. He put his flesh hand on top of hers and held it gently until he could let himself speak.

"It was a dream," he said finally.

She accepted this with a slow, serious nod. "Bad?"

"It was—like the ones I used to have." He couldn't look at her. "About my mother."

Again, a nod, but even slower, and more serious. "And?"

"And—" He looked down at her small, slim fingers, and he slipped his between them, clasping their two hands into a knot of prayer. "It was about you."

Now she turned aside, leaning once more upon the rail, staring out into the night, and in the slowly pulsing rose-glow of the distant fires she was more beautiful than he had ever seen her. "All right," she said softly. "It was about me."

Then she simply waited, still trusting.

When Anakin could finally make himself tell her, his voice was raw and hoarse as though he'd been shouting all day. "It was . . . about you *dying*," he said. "I couldn't stand it. I can't stand it."

He couldn't look at her. He looked at the city, at the deck, at the stars, and he found no place he could bear to see.

All he could do was close his eyes.

"You're going to die in childbirth."

"Oh," she said.

That was all.

She had only a few months left to live. They had only a few months left to love each other. She would never see their child. And all she said was, "Oh."

After a moment, the touch of her hand to his cheek brought his eyes open again, and he found her gazing up at him calmly. "And the baby?"

He shook his head. "I don't know."

She nodded and pulled away, drifting toward one of the veranda chairs. She lowered herself into it and stared down at her hands, clasped together in her lap.

He couldn't take it. He couldn't watch her be calm and accepting about her own death. He came to her side and knelt.

"It won't happen, Padmé. I won't let it. I could have saved my mother—a day earlier, an hour—I . . ." He bit down on the rising pain inside him, and spoke through clenched teeth. "This dream will *not* become real."

She nodded. "I didn't think it would."

He blinked. "You didn't?"

"This is Coruscant, Annie, not Tatooine. Women don't die in childbirth on *Coruscant*—not even the twilighters in the downlevels. And I have a top-flight medical droid, who assures me I am in perfect health. Your dream must have been . . . some kind of metaphor, or something."

"I—my dreams are *literal*, Padmé. I wouldn't know a metaphor if it *bit* me. And I couldn't see the place you were in— you might not even *be* on Coruscant . . ."

She looked away. "I had been thinking—about going somewhere . . . somewhere else. Having the baby in secret, to protect you. So you can stay in the Order."

"I don't *want* to stay in the Order!" He took her face between his palms so that she had to look into his eyes, so that she had to see how much he meant every word he said. "Don't protect me. I don't need it. We have to start thinking, right now, about how we can protect *you*. Because all I want is for us to be together."

"And we will be," she said. "But there must be more to your dream than death in childbirth. That doesn't make any sense."

"I know. But I can't begin to guess what it might be. It's too—I can't even think about it, Padmé. I'll go crazy. What are we going to do?"

She kissed the palm of his hand of flesh. "We're going to do what you told me, when I asked you the same question this afternoon. We're going to be happy together."

"But we—we can't just . . . *wait. I* can't. I have to *do* something."

"Of course you do." She smiled fondly. "That's who you are. That's what being a hero is. What about Obi-Wan?"

He frowned. "What about him?"

"You told me once that he is as wise as Yoda and as powerful as Mace Windu. Couldn't he help us?"

"No." Anakin's chest clenched like a fist squeezing his heart. "I can't—I'd have to *tell* him . . ."

"He's your best friend, Annie. He must suspect already."

"It's one thing to have him suspect. It's something else to shove it in his face. He's still on the Council. He'd *have* to report me. And . . ."

"And what? Is there something you haven't told me?"

He turned away. "I'm not sure he's on my side."

"*Your* side? Anakin, what are you saying?"

"He's on the Jedi Council, Padmé. I *know* my name has come up for Mastery—I'm more powerful than any Jedi Master alive. But someone is blocking me. Obi-Wan could tell me who, and why . . . but he *doesn't*. I'm not sure he even stands up for me with them."

"I can't believe that."

"It has nothing to do with believing," he murmured, softly bitter. "It's the truth."

"There must be some *reason*, then. Anakin, he's your best friend. He loves you."

"Maybe he does. But I don't think he trusts me." His eyes went as bleak as the empty night. "And I'm not sure we can trust him."

"Anakin!" She clutched at his arm. "What would make you *say* that?"

"*None* of them trust me, Padmé. None of them. You know what I feel, when they look at me?"

"Anakin—"

He turned to her, and everything in him ached. He wanted to cry and he wanted to rage and he wanted to make his rage a weapon that would cut himself free forever. "Fear," he said. "I feel their *fear*. And for *nothing*."

He could show them something, though. He could show them a *reason* for their fear.

He could show them what he'd discovered within himself in the General's Quarters on *Invisible Hand*.

Something of it must have risen on his face, because he saw a flicker of doubt shadow her eyes, just for a second, just a flash, but still it burned into him like a lightsaber and he shuddered, and his shudder turned into a shiver that became shaking, and he gathered her to his chest and buried his face in her hair, and the strong sweet warmth of her cooled him, just enough.

"Padmé," he murmured, "oh, Padmé, I'm so sorry. Forget I said anything. None of that matters now. I'll be gone from the Order soon—because I will not let you go away to have our baby in some alien place. I will not let you face my dream alone. I *will* be there for you, Padmé. Always. No matter what."

"I know it, Annie. I know." She pulled gently away and looked up at him. Tears sparkled like red gems in the firelight.

Red as the synthetic bloodshine of Dooku's lightsaber.

He closed his eyes.

She said, "Come upstairs, Anakin. The night's getting cold. Come up to our bed."

"All right. All right." He found that he could breathe again, and his shaking had stilled. "Just—"

He put his arm around her shoulders so that he didn't have to meet her eyes. "Just don't say anything to Obi-Wan, all right?"

MASTERS

Obi-Wan sat beside Mace Windu while they watched Yoda scan the report. Here in Yoda's simple living space within the Jedi Temple, every softly curving pod chair and knurled organiform table hummed with gentle, comforting power: the same warm strength that Obi-Wan remembered enfolding him even as an infant. These chambers had been Yoda's home for more than eight hundred years. Everything within them echoed with the harmonic resonance of Yoda's calm wisdom, tuned through centuries of his touch. To sit within Yoda's chambers was to inhale serenity; to Obi-Wan, this was a great gift in these troubled times.

But when Yoda looked at them through the translucent shimmer of the holoprojected report on the contents of the latest amendment to the Security Act, his eyes were anything but calm: they had gone narrow and cold, and his ears had flattened back along his skull.

"This report—from where does it come?"

"The Jedi still have friends in the Senate," Mace Windu replied in his grim monotone, "for now."

"When presented this amendment is, passed it will be?"

Mace nodded. "My source expects passage by acclamation. Overwhelming passage. Perhaps as early as this afternoon."

"The Chancellor's goal in this—unclear to me it is," Yoda said slowly. "Though nominally in command of the Council, the Senate may place him, the Jedi he cannot control. Moral, our authority has always been; much more than merely *legal*. Simply follow orders, Jedi do not!"

"I don't think he intends to control the Jedi," Mace said. "By placing the Jedi Council under the control of the Office of the Supreme Chancellor, this amendment will give him the constitutional authority to disband the Order itself."

"Surely you cannot believe this is his intention."

"*His* intention?" Mace said darkly. "Perhaps not. But *his* intentions are irrelevant; all that matters now is the intent of the Sith Lord who has our government in his grip. And the Jedi Order may be all that stands between him and galactic domination. What do you *think* he will do?"

"Authority to disband the Jedi, the Senate would never grant."

"The Senate will vote to grant exactly that. This afternoon."

"The implications of this, they must not comprehend!"

"It no longer matters what they comprehend," Mace said. "They know where the power is."

"But even disbanded, even without legal authority, still Jedi we would be. Jedi Knights served the Force long before there was a Galactic Republic, and serve it we will when this Republic is but dust."

"Master Yoda, that day may be coming sooner than any of us think. That day may be *today*." Mace shot a frustrated look at Obi-Wan, who picked up his cue smoothly.

"We don't know what the Sith Lord's plans may be," Obi-Wan said, "but we can be certain that Palpatine is not to be trusted. Not anymore. This draft resolution is not the product of some overzealous Senator; we may be sure Palpatine wrote it himself and passed it along to someone he controls—to make it look like the Senate is once more 'forcing him to reluctantly accept extra powers in the name of security.' We are afraid that they will continue to do so until one day he's 'forced to reluctantly accept' dictatorship for *life*."

"I am convinced this is the next step in a plot aimed directly at the heart of the Jedi," Mace said. "This is a move toward our destruction. The dark side of the Force surrounds the Chancellor."

Obi-Wan added, "As it has surrounded and cloaked the Separatists since even before the war began. If the Chancellor is being influenced through the dark side, this whole war may have been, from the beginning, a plot by the Sith to destroy the Jedi Order."

"Speculation!" Yoda thumped the floor with his gimer stick, making his hoverchair bob gently. "On theories such as these we cannot rely. *Proof* we need. Proof!"

"Proof may be a luxury we cannot afford." A dangerous light had entered Mace Windu's eyes. "We must be ready to *act*."

"Act?" Obi-Wan asked mildly.

"He cannot be allowed to move against the Order. He cannot be allowed to prolong the war needlessly. Too many Jedi have died already. He is dismantling the Republic itself! I have *seen* life outside the Republic; so have you, Obi-Wan. Slavery. Torture. Endless war."

Mace's face darkened with the same distant, haunted shadow Obi-Wan had seen him wear the day before. "I have seen it in Nar Shaddaa, and I saw it on Haruun Kal. I saw what it did to Depa, and to Sora Bulq. Whatever its flaws, the Republic is our sole hope for justice, and for peace. It is our only defense against the dark. Palpatine may be about to do what the Separatists cannot: bring down the Republic. If he tries, he must be removed from office."

"Removed?" Obi-Wan said. "You mean, *arrested*?"

Yoda shook his head. "To a dark place, this line of thought will lead us. Great care, we must take."

"The Republic *is* civilization. It's the only one we have." Mace looked deeply into Yoda's eyes, and into Obi-Wan's, and Obi-Wan could feel the heat in the Korun Master's gaze. "We must be prepared for radical action. It is our duty."

"But," Obi-Wan protested numbly, "you're talking about *treason* . . ."

"I'm not afraid of words, Obi-Wan! If it's treason, then so be it. I would do this right now, if I had the Council's support. The *real* treason," Mace said, "would be failure to *act*."

"Such an act, destroy the Jedi Order it could," Yoda said. "Lost the trust of the public, we have already—"

"No disrespect, Master Yoda," Mace interrupted, "but that's a politician's argument. We can't let public opinion stop us from doing what's *right*."

"*Convinced* it is right, I am *not*," Yoda said severely. "Working behind the scenes we should be, to uncover Lord Sidious! To move against Palpatine while the Sith still exist—this may be part of the Sith plan *itself*, to turn the Senate and the public against the Jedi! So that we are not only disbanded, but *outlawed*."

Mace was half out of his pod. "To *wait* gives the Sith the advantage—"

"Have the advantage *already*, they do!" Yoda jabbed at him with his gimer stick. "*Increase* their advantage we will, if in haste we act!"

"Masters, Masters, please," Obi-Wan said. He looked from one to the other and inclined his head respectfully. "Perhaps there is a middle way."

"Ah, of course: Kenobi the Negotiator." Mace Windu settled back into his seating pod. "I should have guessed. That is why you asked for this meeting, isn't it? To mediate our differences. If you can."

"So sure of your skills you are?" Yoda folded his fists around the head of his stick. "Easy to negotiate, this matter is not!"

Obi-Wan kept his head down. "It seems to me," he said carefully, "that Palpatine himself has given us an opening. He has said—both to you, Master Windu, and in the HoloNet address he gave following his rescue—that General Grievous is the true obstacle to peace. Let us forget about the rest of the Separatist leadership, for now. Let Nute Gunray and San Hill and the rest run wherever they like, while we put every available Jedi and all of our agents—the whole of Republic Intelligence, if we can—to work on locating Grievous himself. This will force the hand of the Sith Lord; he will know that Grievous cannot elude our full efforts for long, once we devote ourselves exclusively to his capture. It will draw Sidious out; he will have to make some sort of move, if he wishes the war to continue."

"If?" Mace said. "The war has been a Sith operation from the beginning, with Dooku on one side and Sidious on the other—it has always been a plot aimed at *us*. At the Jedi. To bleed us dry of our youngest and best. To make us into something we were never intended to be."

He shook his head bitterly. "I had the truth in my hands years ago—back on Haruun Kal, in the first months of the war. I had it, but I did not understand how right I was."

"Seen glimpses of this truth, we all have," Yoda said sadly. "Our arrogance it is, which has stopped us from fully opening our eyes."

"Until now," Obi-Wan put in gently. "We understand now the goal of the Sith Lord, we know his tactics, and we know where to look for him. His actions will reveal him. He cannot escape us. He *will* not escape us."

Yoda and Mace frowned at each other for one long moment, then both of them turned to Obi-Wan and inclined their heads in mirrors of his respectful bow.

"Seen to the heart of the matter, young Kenobi has."

Mace nodded. "Yoda and I will remain on Coruscant, monitoring Palpatine's advisers and lackeys; we'll move against Sidious the instant he is revealed. But who will capture Grievous? I have fought him blade-to-blade. He is more than a match for most Jedi."

"We'll worry about that once we find him," Obi-Wan said. A slight, wistful smile crept over his face. "If I listen hard enough, I can almost hear Qui-Gon reminding me that *until the possible becomes actual, it is only a distraction.*"

General Grievous stood wide-legged, hands folded behind him, as he stared out through the reinforced viewport at the towering sphere of the Geonosian Dreadnaught. The immense ship looked small, though, against the scale of the vast sinkhole that rose around it.

This was Utapau, a remote backworld on the fringe of the Outer Rim. At ground level—far above where Grievous stood now—the planet appeared to be a featureless ball of barren rock, scoured flat by endless hyperwinds. From orbit, though, its cities and factories and spaceports could be seen as the planet's rotation brought its cavernous sinkholes one at a time into view. These sinkholes were the size of inverted mountains, and every available square meter of their interior walls was packed with city. And every square meter of every city was under the guns of Separatist war droids, making sure that the Utapauns behaved themselves.

Utapau had no interest in the Clone Wars; it had never been a member of the Republic, and had carefully maintained a stance of quiet neutrality.

Right up until Grievous had conquered it.

Neutrality, in these times, was a joke; a planet was neutral only so long as neither the Republic nor the Confederacy wanted it. If Grievous could laugh, he would have.

The members of the Separatist leadership scurried across

the permacrete landing platform like the alley rats they were— scampering for the ship that would take them to the safety of the newly constructed base on Mustafar.

But one alley rat was missing from the scuttle.

Grievous shifted his gaze fractionally and found the reflection of Nute Gunray in the transparisteel. The Neimoidian viceroy stood dithering in the control center's doorway. Grievous regarded the reflection of the bulbous, cold-blooded eyes below the tall peaked miter.

"Gunray." He made no other motion. "Why are you still here?"

"Some things should be said privately, General." The viceroy's reflection cast glances either way along the hallway beyond the door. "I am disturbed by this new move. You told us that Utapau would be safe for us. Why is the Leadership Council being moved now to Mustafar?"

Grievous sighed. He had no time for lengthy explanations; he was expecting a secret transmission from Sidious himself. He could not take the transmission with Gunray in the room, nor could he follow his natural inclinations and boot the Neimoidian viceroy so high he'd burn up on reentry. Grievous still hoped, every day, that Lord Sidious would give him leave to smash the skulls of Gunray and his toady, Rune Haako. Repulsive sniveling grub-greedy scum, both of them. And the rest of the Separatist leadership was every bit as vile.

But for now, a pretense of cordiality had to be maintained.

"Utapau," Grievous said slowly, as though explaining to a child, "is a hostile planet under military occupation. It was never intended to be more than a stopgap, while the defenses of the base on Mustafar were completed. Now that they are, Mustafar is the most secure planet in the galaxy. The stronghold prepared for you can withstand the entire Republic Navy."

"It should," Gunray muttered. "Construction nearly bankrupted the Trade Federation!"

"Don't whine to me about money, Viceroy. I have no interest in it."

"You had better, General. It's my *money* that finances this entire war! It's my money that pays for that *body* you wear, and for those insanely expensive MagnaGuards of yours! It's my *money*—"

Grievous moved so swiftly that he seemed to teleport from the window to half a meter in front of Gunray. "How much use is your money," he said, flexing his hand of jointed duranium in the Neimoidian's face, "against *this*?"

Gunray flinched and backed away. "I was only—I have some concerns about your ability to keep us *safe*, General, that's all. I—we—the Trade Federation cannot work in a climate of fear. What about the *Jedi*?"

"Forget the Jedi. They do not enter into this equation."

"They will be entering into that *base* soon enough!"

"The base is secure. It can stand against a thousand Jedi. *Ten* thousand."

"Do you *hear* yourself? Are you *mad*?"

"What I am," Grievous replied evenly, "is unaccustomed to having my orders challenged."

"We are the Leadership Council! You cannot give *us* orders! *We* give the orders here!"

"Are you certain of that? Would you care to wager?" Grievous leaned close enough that he could see the reflection of his mask in Gunray's rose-colored eyes. "Shall we, say, bet your life on it?"

Gunray kept on backing away. "You tell us we'll be safe on Mustafar—but you *also* told us you would deliver Palpatine as a *hostage,* and *he* managed to escape your grip!"

"Be thankful, Viceroy," Grievous said, admiring the smooth flexion of his finger joints as though his hand were some species of exotic predator, "that you have not found *yourself* in my grip."

He went back to the viewport and reassumed his original po-

sition, legs wide, hands clasped behind his back. To look on the
sickly pink in Gunray's pale green cheeks for one second longer
was to risk forgetting his orders and splattering the viceroy's
brains from here to Ord Mantell.

"Your ship is waiting."

His auditory sensors clearly picked up the slither of Gunray's
sandals retreating along the corridor, and not a second too soon:
his sensors were also registering the whine of the control center's
holocomm warming up. He turned to face the disk, and when
the enunciator chimed to indicate the incoming transmission, he
pressed the ACCEPT key and knelt.

Head down, he could see only the scanned image of the hem
of the great Lord's robes, but that was all he needed to see.

"Yes, Lord Sidious."

"Have you moved the Separatist Council to Mustafar?"

"Yes, Master." He risked a glance out the viewport. Most of
the council had reached the starship. Gunray should be joining
them any second; Grievous had seen firsthand how fast the
viceroy could run, given proper motivation. "The ship will lift off
within moments."

*"Well done, my general. Now you must turn your hand to
preparing our trap there on Utapau. The Jedi hunt you personally
at last; you must be ready for their attack."*

"Yes, Master."

*"I am arranging matters to give you a second chance to do my
bidding, Grievous. Expect that the Jedi sent to capture you will be
Obi-Wan Kenobi."*

"Kenobi?" Grievous's fists clenched hard enough that his
carpal electrodrivers whined in protest. "And Skywalker?"

"I believe Skywalker will be . . . otherwise engaged."

Grievous dropped his head even lower. "I will not fail you
again, my Master. Kenobi will die."

"See to it."

"Master? If I may trouble you with boldness—why did you

not let me kill Chancellor Palpatine? We may never get a better chance."

"The time was not yet ripe. Patience, my general. The end of the war is near, and victory is certain."

"Even with the loss of Count Dooku?"

"Dooku was not lost, he was sacrificed—a strategic sacrifice, as one offers up a piece in dejarik: to draw the opponent into a fatal blunder."

"I was never much the dejarik player, my Master. I prefer *real* war."

"And you shall have your fill, I promise you."

"This fatal blunder you speak of—if I may once again trouble you with boldness . . ."

"You will come to understand soon enough."

Grievous could hear the smile in his Master's voice.

"All will be clear, once you meet my new *apprentice."*

Anakin finger-combed his hair as he trotted out across the restricted landing deck atop the Temple ziggurat near the base of the High Council Tower. Far across the expanse of deck stood the Supreme Chancellor's shuttle. Anakin squinted at it, and at the two tall red-robed guards that stood flanking its open access ramp.

And coming toward him from the direction of the shuttle, shielding his eyes and leaning against the morning wind that whipped across the unprotected field—was that Obi-Wan?

"Finally," Anakin muttered. He'd scoured the Temple for his former Master; he'd nearly giving up hope of finding him when a passing Padawan had mentioned that he'd seen Obi-Wan on his way out to the landing deck to meet Palpatine's shuttle. He hoped Obi-Wan wouldn't notice he hadn't changed his clothes.

It wasn't like he could explain.

Though his secret couldn't last, he wasn't ready for it to come out just yet. He and Padmé had agreed last night that they would keep it as long as they could. He wasn't ready to leave the Jedi Order. Not while she was still in danger.

Padmé had said that his nightmare must be only a metaphor, but he knew better. He knew that Force prophecy was not absolute—but his had never been wrong. Not in the slightest detail. He had known as a boy that he would be chosen by the Jedi. He had known his adventures would span the galaxy. As a mere nine-year-old, long before he even understood what love was, he had looked upon Padmé Amidala's flawless face and seen there that she would love him, and that they would someday marry.

There had been no metaphor in his dreams of his mother. Screaming in pain. Tortured to death.

I knew you would come to me, Annie . . . I missed you so much.

He could have saved her.

Maybe.

It had always seemed so obvious to him—that if he had only returned to Tatooine a day earlier, an hour, he could have found his mother and she would still be alive. And yet—

And yet the great prophets of the Jedi had always taught that the gravest danger in trying to prevent a vision of the future from coming to pass is that in doing so, a Jedi can actually *bring* it to pass—as though if he'd run away in time to save his mother, he might have made himself somehow responsible for her death.

As though if he tried to save Padmé, he could end up— blankly impossible though it was—killing her *himself* . . .

But to do nothing . . . to simply wait for Padmé to die . . .

Could something be *more* than impossible?

When a Jedi had a question about the deepest subtleties of the Force, there was one source to whom he could always turn; and so, first thing that morning, without even taking time to stop by his own quarters for a change of clothing, Anakin had gone to Yoda for advice.

He'd been surprised by how graciously the ancient Jedi Master had invited him into his quarters, and by how patiently Yoda had listened to his stumbling attempts to explain his question without giving away his secret; Yoda had never made any attempt to conceal what had always seemed to Anakin to be a gruff disapproval of Anakin's very existence.

But this morning, despite clearly having other things on his mind—even Anakin's Force perceptions, far from the most subtle, had detected echoes of conflict and worry within the Master's chamber—Yoda had simply offered Anakin a place on one of the softly rounded pod seats and suggested that they meditate together.

He hadn't even asked for details.

Anakin had been so grateful—and so relieved, and so unexpectedly hopeful—that he'd found tears welling into his eyes, and some few minutes had been required for him to compose himself into proper Jedi serenity.

After a time, Yoda's eyes had slowly opened and the deep furrows on his ancient brow had deepened further. "Premonitions . . . premonitions . . . deep questions they are. Sense the future, once all Jedi could; now few alone have this skill. Visions . . . gifts from the Force, and curses. Signposts and snares. These visions of yours . . ."

"They are of pain," Anakin had said. "Of suffering."

He had barely been able to make himself add: "And death."

"In these troubled times, no surprise this is. Yourself you see, or someone you know?"

Anakin had not trusted himself to answer.

"Someone close to you?" Yoda had prompted gently.

"Yes," Anakin had replied, eyes turned away from Yoda's too-wise stare. Let him think he was talking about Obi-Wan. It was close enough.

Yoda's voice was still gentle, and understanding. "The fear of loss is a path to the dark side, young one."

"I won't let my visions come true, Master. I *won't*."

"Rejoice for those who transform into the Force. Mourn them not. Miss them not."

"Then why do we fight at all, Master? Why save *anybody*?"

"Speaking of *anybody,* we are not," Yoda had said sternly. "Speaking of you, and your vision, and your *fear,* we are. The shadow of greed, attachment is. What you fear to lose, train yourself to release. Let go of fear, and loss cannot harm you."

Which was when Anakin had realized Yoda wasn't going to be any help at all. The greatest sage of the Jedi Order had nothing better to offer him than more pious babble about Letting Things Pass Out Of His Life.

Like he hadn't heard that a million times already.

Easy for *him*—who had *Yoda* ever cared about? *Really* cared about? Of one thing Anakin was certain: the ancient Master had never been in love.

Or he would have known better than to expect Anakin to just fold his hands and close his eyes and settle in to *meditate* while what was left of Padmé's life evaporated like the ghost-mist of dew in a Tatooine winter dawn . . .

So all that had been left for him was to find some way to respectfully extricate himself.

And then go find Obi-Wan.

Because he wasn't about to give up. Not in this millennium.

The Jedi Temple was the greatest nexus of Force energy in the Republic; its ziggurat design focused the Force the way a lightsaber's gemstone focused its energy stream. With the thousands of Jedi and Padawans within it every day contemplating peace, seeking knowledge, and meditating on justice and surrender to the will of the Force, the Temple was a fountain of the light.

Just being on its rooftop landing deck sent a surge of power through Anakin's whole body; if the Force was ever to show him a way to change the dark future of his nightmares, it would do so here.

The Jedi Temple also contained the archives, the vast library that encompassed the Order's entire twenty-five millennia of existence: everything from the widest-ranging cosmographical surveys to the intimate journals of a billion Jedi Knights. It was there Anakin hoped to find everything that was known about prophetic dreams—and everything that was known about preventing these prophecies from coming to pass.

His only problem was that the deepest secrets of the greatest Masters of the Force were stored in restricted holocrons; since the Lorian Nod affair, some seventy standard years before, access to these holocrons was denied to all but Jedi Masters.

And he couldn't exactly explain to the archives Master why he wanted them.

But now here was Obi-Wan—Obi-Wan would help him, Anakin *knew* he would—if only Anakin could figure out the right way to ask . . .

While he was still hunting for words, Obi-Wan reached him. "You missed the report on the Outer Rim sieges."

"I—was held up," Anakin said. "I have no excuse."

That, at least, was true.

"Is Palpatine here?" Anakin asked. It was a convenient-enough way to change the subject. "Has something happened?"

"Quite the opposite," Obi-Wan said. "That shuttle did not bring the Chancellor. It is waiting to bring *you* to *him*."

"Waiting? For *me*?" Anakin frowned. Worries and lack of sleep had his head full of fog; he couldn't make this make sense. He patted his robes vacantly. "But—my beacon hasn't gone off. If the Council wanted me, why didn't they—"

"The Council," Obi-Wan said, "has not been consulted."

"I don't understand."

"Nor do I." Obi-Wan stepped close, nodding minutely back

toward the shuttle. "They simply arrived, some time ago. When the deck-duty Padawans questioned them, they said the Chancellor has requested your presence."

"Why wouldn't he go through the Council?"

"Perhaps he has some reason to believe," Obi-Wan said carefully, "that the Council might have resisted sending you. Perhaps he did not wish to reveal his reason for this summons. Relations between the Council and the Chancellor are . . . stressed."

A queasy knot began to tie itself behind Anakin's ribs. "Obi-Wan, what's going on? Something's wrong, isn't it? You know something, I can tell."

"Know? No: only suspect. Which is not at all the same thing."

Anakin remembered what he'd said to Padmé about exactly that last night. The queasy knot tightened. "And?"

"And that's why I am out here, Anakin. So I can talk to you. Privately. *Not* as a member of the Jedi Council—in fact, if the Council were to find out about this conversation . . . well, let's say, I'd rather they didn't."

"*What* conversation? I still don't know what's going on!"

"None of us does. Not really." Obi-Wan put a hand on Anakin's shoulder and frowned deeply into his eyes. "Anakin, you know I am your friend."

"Of course you are—"

"No. No *of course*s, Anakin. Nothing is *of course* anymore. I am your friend, and *as* your friend, I am asking you: be wary of Palpatine."

"What do you mean?"

"I know you are *his* friend. I am concerned that he may not be yours. Be careful of him, Anakin. And be careful of your own feelings."

"Careful? Don't you mean, *mindful*?"

Obi-Wan's frown deepened. "No. I don't. The Force grows ever darker around us, and we are all affected by it, even as we affect it. This is a dangerous time to be a Jedi. Please, Anakin—please be *careful*."

Anakin tried for his old rakish smile. "You worry too much."

"I *have* to—"

"—because I don't worry at all, right?" Anakin finished for him.

Obi-Wan's frown softened toward a smile. "How did you know I was going to say that?"

"You're wrong, you know." Anakin stared off through the morning haze toward the shuttle, past the shuttle—

Toward 500 Republica, and Padmé's apartment.

He said, "I worry plenty."

The ride to Palpatine's office was quietly tense. Anakin had tried making conversation with the two tall helmet-masked figures in the red robes, but they weren't exactly chatty.

Anakin's discomfort only increased when he arrived at Palpatine's office. He had been here so often that he didn't even really see it, most times: the deep red runner that matched the softly curving walls, the long comfortable couches, the huge arc of window behind Palpatine's desk—these were all so familiar that they were usually almost invisible, but today—

Today, with Obi-Wan's voice whispering *be wary of Palpatine* in the back of his head, everything looked different. New. And not in a good way.

Some indefinable gloom shrouded everything, as though the orbital mirrors that focused the light of Coruscant's distant sun into bright daylight had somehow been damaged, or smudged with the brown haze of smoke that still shrouded the cityscape. The light of the Chancellor's lampdisks seemed brighter than usual, almost harsh, but somehow that only deepened the gloom. He discovered now an odd, accidental echo of memory, a new harmonic resonance inside his head, when he looked at the curving view wall that threw into silhouette the Chancellor's single large chair.

Palpatine's office reminded him of the General's Quarters on *Invisible Hand*.

And it struck him as unaccountably sinister that the robes worn by the Chancellor's cadre of bodyguards were the exact color of Palpatine's carpet.

Palpatine himself stood at the view wall, hands clasped behind him, gazing out upon the smoke-hazed morning.

"Anakin." He must have seen Anakin's reflection in the curve of transparisteel; he had not moved. "Join me."

Anakin came up beside him, mirroring his stance. Endless cityscape stretched away before them. Here and there, the remains of shattered buildings still smoldered. Space lane traffic was beginning to return to normal, and rivers of gnat-like speeders and air taxis and repulsor buses crisscrossed the city. In the near distance, the vast dome of the Galactic Senate squatted like a gigantic gray mushroom sprung from the duracrete plain that was Republic Plaza. Farther, dim in the brown haze, he could pick out the quintuple spires that topped the ziggurat of the Jedi Temple.

"Do you see, Anakin?" Palpatine's voice was soft, hoarse with emotion. "Do you see what they have done to our magnificent city? This war *must* end. We cannot allow such . . . such . . ."

His voice trailed away, and he shook his head. Gently, Anakin laid a hand on Palpatine's shoulder, and a hint of frown fleeted over his face at how frail seemed the flesh and bone beneath the robe. "You know you have my best efforts, and those of every Jedi," he said.

Palpatine nodded, lowering his head. "I know I have yours, Anakin. The rest of the Jedi . . ." He sighed. He looked even more exhausted than he had yesterday. Perhaps he had passed a sleepless night as well.

"I have asked you here," he said slowly, "because I need your help on a matter of extreme delicacy. I hope I can depend upon your discretion, Anakin."

Anakin went still for a moment, then he very slowly lifted his hand from the Chancellor's shoulder.

Be wary of Palpatine

"As a Jedi, there are . . . limits . . . to my discretion, Chancellor."

"Oh, of course. Don't worry, my boy." A flash of his familiar fatherly smile forced its way into his eyes. "Anakin, in all the years we have been friends, have I ever asked you to do anything even the slightest bit against your conscience?"

"Well—"

"And I never will. I am very proud of your accomplishments as a Jedi, Anakin. You have won many battles the Jedi Council insisted to me were already lost—and you saved my *life*. It's frankly appalling that they still keep you off the Council yourself."

"My time will come . . . when I am older. And, I suppose, wiser." He didn't want to get into this with Palpatine; talking with the Chancellor like this—seriously, man-to-man—made him feel good, feel strong, despite Obi-Wan's warning. He certainly didn't want to start whining about being passed over for Mastery like some preadolescent Padawan who hadn't been chosen for a scramball team.

"Nonsense. Age is no measure of wisdom. They keep you off the Council because it is the last hold they have on you, Anakin; it is how they control you. Once you're a Master, as you deserve, how will they make you do their bidding?"

"Well . . ." Anakin gave him a half-sheepish smile. "They can't exactly *make* me, even now."

"I know, my boy. I know. That is precisely the point. You are not like them. You are younger. Stronger. *Better*. If they cannot control you now, what will happen once you are a Master in your own right? How will they keep your toes on their political line? You may become more powerful than all of them together. That is why they keep you down. They fear your power. They fear *you*."

Anakin looked down. This had struck a little close to the bone. "I have sensed . . . something like that."

"I have asked you here today, Anakin, because I have fears of my own." He turned, waiting, until Anakin met his eye, and on Palpatine's face was something approaching bleak despair. "I am coming to fear the Jedi themselves."

"Oh, Chancellor—" Anakin broke into a smile of disbelief. "There is no one more loyal than the Jedi, sir—surely, after all this time—"

But Palpatine had already turned away. He lowered himself into the chair behind his desk and kept his head down as though he was ashamed to say this directly to Anakin's face. "The Council keeps pushing for more control. More autonomy. They have lost all respect for the rule of law. They have become more concerned with avoiding the oversight of the Senate than with winning the war."

"With respect, sir, many on the Council would say the same of *you*." He thought of Obi-Wan, and he had to stop himself from wincing. Had he betrayed a confidence just now?

Or had Obi-Wan been doing the Council's bidding after all? . . . *Be wary of Palpatine,* he'd said, and *be careful of your feelings . . .*

Were these honest warnings, out of concern for him? Or had they been *calculated:* seeds of doubt planted to hedge Anakin away from the one man who really understood him?

The one man he could really trust . . .

"Oh, I have no doubt of it," Palpatine was saying. "Many of the Jedi on your Council would prefer I was out of office altogether—because they know I'm on to them, now. They're shrouded in secrecy, obsessed with covert action against mysteriously faceless enemies—"

"Well, the Sith are hardly faceless, are they? I mean, Dooku himself—"

"Was he truly a Lord of the Sith? Or was he just another in your string of fallen Jedi, posturing with a red lightsaber to intimidate you?"

"I . . ." Anakin frowned. How could he be sure? "But *Sidious* . . ."

"Ah, yes, the mysterious Lord Sidious. 'The *Sith infiltrator* in the *highest* levels of *government*.' Doesn't that sound a little overly familiar to you, Anakin? A little overly *convenient*? How do you know this Sidious even exists? How do you know he is not a *fiction*, a fiction created by the Jedi Council, to give them an excuse to harass their political enemies?"

"The Jedi are not political—"

"In a democracy, *everything* is political, Anakin. And everyone. This imaginary Sith Lord of theirs—even if he does exist, is he anyone to be feared? To be hunted down and exterminated without trial?"

"The Sith are the definition of evil—"

"Or so you have been trained to believe. I have been reading about the history of the Sith for some years now, Anakin. Ever since the Council saw fit to finally reveal to me their . . . *assertion* . . . that these millennium-dead sorcerers had supposedly sprung back to life. Not every tale about them is sequestered in your conveniently secret Temple archives. From what I have read, they were not so different from Jedi; seeking power, to be sure, but so does your Council."

"The dark side—"

"Oh, yes, yes, certainly, the dark side. Listen to me: if this 'Darth Sidious' of yours were to walk through *that* door right *now*—and I could somehow stop you from killing him on the spot—do you know what I would do?"

Palpatine rose, and his voice rose with him. "I would ask him to *sit down,* and I would ask him if he has any power he could use to *end this war*!"

"You—you would—" Anakin couldn't quite make himself believe what he was hearing. The blood-red rug beneath his feet seemed to shift under him, and his head was starting to spin.

"And if he said he *did,* I'd bloody well offer him a *brandy* and *talk it out*!"

"You—Chancellor, you can't be *serious*—"

"Well, not entirely." Palpatine sighed, and shrugged, and lowered himself once more into his chair. "It's only an example, Anakin. I would do anything to return peace to the galaxy, do you understand? That's all I mean. After all—" He offered a tired, sadly ironic smile. "—what are the chances of an actual Sith Lord ever walking through that door?"

"I wouldn't know," Anakin said feelingly, "but I do know that you probably shouldn't use that . . . *example* . . . in front of the Jedi Council."

"Oh, yes." Palpatine chuckled. "Yes, quite right. They might take it as an excuse to accuse *me*."

"I'm sure they'd never do *that*—"

"I am not. I am no longer sure they'll stop at anything, Anakin. That's actually the reason I asked you here today." He leaned forward intently, resting his elbows on the desk. "You may have heard that this afternoon, the Senate will call upon this office to assume direct control of the Jedi Council."

Anakin's frown deepened. "The Jedi will no longer report to the Senate?"

"They will report to me. Personally. The Senate is too unfocused to conduct this war; we've seen this for years. Now that this office will be the single authority to direct the prosecution of the war, we'll bring a quick end to things."

Anakin nodded. "I can see how that will help, sir, but the

Council probably won't. I can tell you that they are in no mood for further constitutional amendments."

"Yes, thank you, my friend. But in this case, I have no choice. This war must be won."

"Everyone agrees on that."

"I hope they do, my boy. I hope they do."

Inside his head, he heard the echo of Obi-Wan, murmuring *relations between the Council and the Chancellor are . . . stressed.* What had been going on, here in the capital?

Weren't they all on the same side?

"I can assure you," he said firmly, "that the Jedi are absolutely dedicated to the core values of the Republic."

One of Palpatine's eyebrows arched. "Their actions will speak more loudly than their words—as long as someone keeps an eye on them. And that, my boy, is exactly the favor I must ask of you."

"I don't understand."

"Anakin, I am asking you—as a personal favor to me, in respect for our long friendship—to accept a post as my personal representative on the Jedi Council."

Anakin blinked.

He blinked again.

He said, "Me?"

"Who else?" Palpatine spread his hands in a melancholy shrug. "You are the only Jedi I know, truly *know,* that I can trust. I *need* you, my boy. There is no one else who can do this job: to be the eyes and ears—and the voice—of the Republic on the Jedi Council."

"On the Council . . . ," Anakin murmured.

He could see himself seated in one of the low, curving chairs, opposite Mace Windu. Opposite *Yoda.* He might sit next to Ki-Adi-Mundi, or Plo Koon—or even beside Obi-Wan! And he could not quite ignore the quiet whisper, from down within the furnace doors that sealed his heart, that he was about to become the youngest Master in the twenty-five-thousand-year history of the Jedi Order . . .

But none of that really mattered.

Palpatine had somehow seen into his secret heart, and had chosen to offer him the one thing he most desired in all the galaxy. He didn't care about the Council, not really—that was a childish dream. He didn't need the Council. He didn't need recognition, and he didn't need respect. What he needed was the rank itself.

All that mattered was Mastery.

All that mattered was Padmé.

This was a gift beyond gifts: as a Master, he could access those forbidden holocrons in the restricted vault.

He could find a way to save her from his dream . . .

He shook himself back to the present. "I . . . am overwhelmed, sir. But the Council elects its own members. They will never accept this."

"I promise you they will," Palpatine murmured imperturbably. He swung his chair around to gaze out the window toward the distant spires of the Temple. "They need you more than they realize. All it will take is for someone to properly . . ."

He waved a hand expressively.

". . . *explain* it to them."

POLITICS

Orbital mirrors rotated, resolving the faint light of Coruscant's sun to erase the stars; fireships crosshatched the sky with contrails of chemical air scrubber, bleaching away the last reminders of the fires of days past; chill remnants of night slid down the High Council Tower of the Jedi Temple; and within the cloistered chamber itself, Obi-Wan was still trying to talk them out of it.

"Yes, of course I trust him," he said patiently. "We can always trust Anakin to do what he thinks is right. But we *can't* trust him to do what he's *told*. He can't be made to simply *obey*. Believe me: I've been trying for many years."

Conflicting currents of energy swirled and clashed in the Council Chamber. Traditionally, decisions of the Council were reached by quiet, mutual contemplation of the flow of the Force, until all the Council was of a single mind on the matter. But Obi-Wan knew of this tradition only by reputation, from tales in the archives and stories told by Masters whose tenure on the Council predated the return of the Sith. In the all-too-short years since Obi-Wan's own elevation, argument in this Chamber was more the rule than the exception.

"An unintentional opportunity, the Chancellor has given us," Yoda said gravely. "A window he has opened into the operations of his office. Fools we would be, to close our eyes."

"Then we should use someone else's eyes," Obi-Wan said. "Forgive me, Master Yoda, but you just don't know him the way I do. None of you does. He is *fiercely* loyal, and there is not a gram of deception in him. You've all seen it; it's one of the arguments that some of you, here in this room, have used against elevating him to Master: he *lacks true Jedi reserve,* that's what you've said. And by that we all mean that he wears his emotions like a HoloNet banner. How can you ask him to lie to a friend—to *spy* upon him?"

"That is why we must call upon a friend to ask him," said Agen Kolar in his gentle Zabrak baritone.

"You don't understand. Don't make him choose between me and Palpatine—"

"Why not?" asked the holopresence of Plo Koon from the bridge of *Courageous,* where he directed the Republic Navy strike force against the Separatist choke point in the Ywllandr system. *"Do you fear you would lose such a contest?"*

"You don't know how much Palpatine's friendship has meant to him over the years. You're asking him to use that friendship as a weapon! To stab his friend in the back. Don't you understand what this will cost him, even if Palpatine is entirely innocent? *Especially* if he's innocent. Their relationship will never be the same—"

"And that," Mace Windu said, "may be the best argument in favor of this plan. I have told you all what I have seen of the energy between Skywalker and the Supreme Chancellor. Anything that might distance young Skywalker from Palpatine's influence is worth the attempt."

Obi-Wan didn't need to reach into the Force to know that he would lose this argument. He inclined his head. "I will, of course, abide by the ruling of this Council."

"Doubt of that, none of us has." Yoda turned his green gaze on the other councilors. "But if to be done this is, decide we must how best to use him."

The holopresence of Ki-Adi-Mundi flickered in and out of focus as the Cerean Master leaned forward, folding his hands. *"I, too, have reservations on this matter, but it seems that in these desperate times, only desperate plans have hope of success. We have seen that young Skywalker has the power to battle a Sith Lord alone, if need be; he has proven that with Dooku. If he is indeed the chosen one, we must keep him in play against the Sith—keep him in a position to fulfill his destiny."*

"And even if the prophecy has been misread," Agen Kolar added, "Anakin is the one Jedi we can best hope would survive an encounter with a Sith Lord. So let us also use him to help us set our trap. In Council, let us emphasize that we are intensifying our search for Grievous. Anakin will certainly report this to the Chancellor's Office. Perhaps, as you say, that will draw Sidious into action."

"It may not be enough," Mace Windu said. "Let us take this one step farther—we should appear shorthanded, and weak, giving Sidious an opening to make a move he thinks will go unobserved. I'm thinking that perhaps we should let the Chancellor's Office know that Yoda and I have both been forced to take the field—"

"Too risky that is," Yoda said. "And too convenient. One of us only should go."

"Then it should be you, Master Yoda," Agen Kolar said. "It is your sensitivity to the broader currents of the Force that a Sith Lord has most reason to fear."

Obi-Wan felt the ripple of agreement flow through the Chamber, and Yoda nodded solemnly. "The Separatist attack on Kashyyyk, a compelling excuse will make. And good relations with the Wookiees I have; destroy the droid armies I can, and still be available to Coruscant, should Sidious take our bait."

"Agreed." Mace Windu looked around the half-empty Council Chamber with a deepening frown. "And one last touch. Let's let the Chancellor know, through Anakin, that our most cunning and insightful Master—and our most tenacious—is to lead the hunt for Grievous."

"So Sidious will need to act, and act fast, if the war is to be maintained," Plo Koon added approvingly.

Yoda nodded judiciously. "Agreed." Agen Kolar assented as well, and Ki-Adi-Mundi.

"This sounds like a good plan," Obi-Wan said. "But what Master do you have in mind?"

For a moment no one spoke, as though astonished he would ask such a question.

Only after a few seconds in which Obi-Wan looked from the faces of one Master to the next, puzzled by the expressions of gentle amusement each and every one of them wore, did it finally register that all of them were looking at *him*.

Bail Organa stopped cold in the middle of the Grand Concourse that ringed the Senate's Convocation Chamber. The torrent of multispecies foot traffic that streamed along the huge curving hall broke around him like a river around a boulder. He stared up in disbelief at one of the huge holoprojected Proclamation Boards; these had recently been installed above the concourse to keep the thousands of Senators up to the moment on news of the war, and on the Chancellor's latest executive orders.

His heart tripped, and he couldn't seem to make his eyes focus. He pushed his way through the press to a hardcopy stand and punched a quick code. When he had the flimsies in his hands, they still said the same thing.

He'd been expecting this day. Since yesterday, when the Senate had voted to give Palpatine control of the Jedi, he'd known it would come soon. He'd even started planning for it.

But that didn't make it any easier to bear.

He found his way to a public comm booth and keyed a privacy code. The transparisteel booth went opaque as stone, and a moment later a hand-sized image shimmered into existence above the small holodisk: a slender woman in floor-length white, with short, neatly clipped auburn hair and a clear, steadily intelligent gaze from her aquamarine eyes. *"Bail,"* she said. *"What's happened?"*

Bail's elegantly thin goatee pulled downward around his mouth. "Have you seen this morning's decree?"

"The Sector Governance Decree? Yes, I have—"

"It's time, Mon," he said grimly. "It's time to stop talking, and start *doing*. We have to bring in the Senate."

"I agree, but we must tread carefully. Have you thought about whom we should consult? Whom we can trust?"

"Not in detail. Giddean Danu springs to mind. I'm sure we can trust Fang Zar, too."

"Agreed. What about Iridik'k-stallu? Her hearts are in the right place. Or Chi Eekway."

Bail shook his head. "Maybe later. It'll take a few hours at least to figure out exactly where they stand. We need to start with Senators we *know* we can trust."

"All right. Then Terr Taneel would be my next choice. And, I think, Amidala of Naboo."

"Padmé?" Bail frowned. "I'm not sure."

"You know her better than I do, Bail, but to my mind she is exactly the type of Senator we need. She is intelligent, principled, extremely articulate, and she has the heart of a warrior."

"She is also a longtime associate of Palpatine," he reminded her. "He was her ambassador during her term as Queen of Naboo. How sure can you be that she will stand with us, and not with him?"

Senator Mon Mothma replied serenely, *"There's only one way to find out."*

By the time the doors to the Jedi Council Chamber finally swung open, Anakin was already angry.

If asked, he would have denied it, and would have thought he was telling the truth . . . but they had left him out here for so *long,* with nothing to do but stare through the soot-smudged curve of the High Council Tower's window ring at the scarred skyline of Galactic City—damaged in a battle *he* had won, by the way, *personally.* Almost *single-handedly*—and with nothing to think about except why it was taking them so long to reach such a simple decision . . .

Angry? Not at all. He was sure he wasn't angry. He kept telling himself he wasn't angry, and he made himself believe it.

Anakin walked into the Council Chamber, head lowered in a show of humility and respect. But down inside him, down around the nuclear shielding that banked his heart, he was hiding.

It wasn't anger he was hiding. His anger was only camouflage.

Behind his anger hid the dragon.

He remembered too well the first time he had entered this Chamber, the first time he had stood within a ring of Jedi Masters gathered to sit in judgment upon his fate. He remembered how Yoda's green stare had seen into his heart, had seen the cold worm of dread eating away at him, no matter how hard he'd tried to deny it: the awful fear he'd felt that he might never see his mother again.

He couldn't let them see what that worm had grown into.

He moved slowly into the center of the circle of brown-toned carpet, and turned toward the Senior Members.

Yoda was unreadable as always, his rumpled features composed in a mask of serene contemplation.

Mace Windu could have been carved from stone.

Ghost-images of Ki-Adi-Mundi and Plo Koon hovered a centimeter above their Council seats, maintained by the seats' internal holoprojectors. Agen Kolar sat alone, between the empty chairs belonging to Shaak Ti and Stass Allie.

Obi-Wan sat in the chair that once had belonged to Oppo Rancisis, looking pensive. Even worried.

"Anakin Skywalker." Master Windu's tone was so severe that the dragon inside Anakin coiled instinctively. "The Council has decided to comply with Chancellor Palpatine's directive, and with the instructions of the Senate that give him the unprecedented authority to command this Council. You are hereby granted a seat at the High Council of the Jedi, as the Chancellor's personal representative."

Anakin stood very still for a long moment, until he could be absolutely sure he had heard what he thought he'd heard.

Palpatine had been right. He seemed to be right about a lot of things, these days. In fact—now that Anakin came to think of it—he couldn't remember a single instance when the Supreme Chancellor had been wrong.

Finally, as it began to sink in upon him, as he gradually allowed himself to understand that the Council had finally decided to grant him his heart's desire, that they finally had recognized his accomplishments, his dedication, his *power*, he took a slow, deep breath.

"Thank you, Masters. You have my pledge that I will uphold the highest principles of the Jedi Order."

"Allow this appointment lightly, the Council does not." Yoda's ears curled forward at Anakin like accusing fingers. "Disturbing is this move by Chancellor Palpatine. On many levels."

They have become more concerned with avoiding the oversight of the Senate than they are with winning the war . . .

Anakin inclined his head. "I understand."

"I'm not sure you do." Mace Windu leaned forward, staring into Anakin's eyes with a measuring squint.

Anakin was barely paying attention; in his mind, he was already leaving the Council Chamber, riding the turbolift to the archives, demanding access to the restricted vault by authority of his new rank—

"You will attend the meetings of this Council," the Korun Master said, "but you will not be granted the rank and privileges of a Jedi Master."

"What?"

It was a small word, a simple word, an instinctive recoil from words that felt like punches, like stun blasts exploding inside his brain that left his head ringing and the room spinning around him—but even to his own ears, the voice that came from his lips didn't sound like his own. It was deeper, darker, clipped and oiled, resonating from the depths of his heart.

It didn't sound like him at all, and it smoked with fury.

"How dare you? How *dare* you?"

Anakin stood welded to the floor, motionless. He wasn't even truly aware of speaking. It was as if someone else were using his mouth—and now, finally, he recognized the voice.

It sounded like Dooku. But it was not Dooku's voice.

It was the voice of Dooku's destroyer.

"No Jedi in this room can match my power—no Jedi in the *galaxy*! You think you can deny Mastery to *me*?"

"The Chancellor's representative you are," Yoda said. "And it is as his representative you shall attend the Council. Sit in this Chamber you will, but no vote will you have. The Chancellor's views you shall present. His wishes. His ideas and directives. Not your own."

Up from the depths of his furnace heart came an answer so far transcending fury that it sounded cold as interstellar space. "This is an insult to me, and to the Chancellor. Do not imagine that it will be tolerated."

Mace Windu's eyes were as cold as the voice from Anakin's mouth. "Take your seat, young Skywalker."

Anakin matched his stare. *Perhaps I'll take yours.* His own voice, inside his head, had a hot black fire that smoked from the depths of his furnace heart. *You think you can stop me from saving my love? You think you can make me watch her die? Go ahead and Vaapad this, you—*

"Anakin," Obi-Wan said softly. He gestured to an empty seat beside him. "Please."

And something in Obi-Wan's gentle voice, in his simple, straightforward request, sent his anger slinking off ashamed, and Anakin found himself alone on the carpet in the middle of the Jedi Council, blinking.

He suddenly felt very young, and very foolish.

"Forgive me, Masters." His bow of contrition couldn't hide the blaze of embarrassment that climbed his cheeks.

The rest of the session passed in a haze; Ki-Adi-Mundi said something about no Republic world reporting any sign of Grievous, and Anakin felt a dull shock when the Council assigned the task of coordinating the search to Obi-Wan *alone*.

On top of everything else, now they were splitting up the *team?*

He was so numbly astonished by it all that he barely registered what they were saying about a droid landing on Kashyyyk—but he had to say *something,* he couldn't just *sit* here for his whole first meeting of the Council, Master or not—and he knew the Kashyyyk system almost as well as he knew the back alleys of Mos Espa. "I can handle it," he offered, suddenly brightening. "I could clear that planet in a day or two—"

"Skywalker, your assignment is *here.*" Mace Windu's stare was hard as durasteel, and only a scrape short of openly hostile.

Then Yoda volunteered, and for some reason, the Council didn't even bother to vote.

"It is settled then," Mace said. "May the Force be with us all."

And as the holopresences of Plo Koon and Ki-Adi-Mundi winked out, as Obi-Wan and Agen Kolar rose and spoke together in tones softly grave, as Yoda and Mace Windu walked from the room, Anakin could only sit, sick at heart, stunned with helplessness.

Padmé—oh, Padmé, what are we going to do?

He didn't know. He didn't have a clue. But he knew one thing he *wasn't* going to do.

He wasn't going to give up.

Even with the Council against him—even with the whole *Order* against him—he would find a way.

He would save her.

Somehow.

"I am no happier than the rest of you about this," Padmé said, gesturing at the flimsiplast of the Sector Governance Decree on Bail Organa's desk. "But I've known Palpatine for years; he was my most trusted adviser. I'm not prepared to believe his intent is to dismantle the Senate."

"Why should he bother?" Mon Mothma countered. "As a practical matter—as of this morning—the Senate no longer exists."

Padmé looked from one grim face to another. Giddean Danu nodded his agreement. Terr Taneel kept her eyes down, pretending to be adjusting her robes. Fang Zar ran a hand over his unruly gray-streaked topknot.

Bail leaned forward. His eyes were hard as chips of stone. "Palpatine no longer has to worry about controlling the Senate. By placing his own lackeys as governors over every planet in the Republic, he controls our systems *directly.*" He folded his hands, and squeezed them together until his knuckles hurt. "He's become a dictator. We *made* him a dictator."

And he's my husband's friend, and mentor, Padmé thought. *I shouldn't even be listening to this.*

"But what can we *do* about it?" Terr Taneel asked, still gazing down at her robe with a worried frown.

"That's what we asked you here to discuss," Mon Mothma told her calmly. "What we're going to do about it."

Fang Zar shifted uncomfortably. "I'm not sure I like where this is going."

"None of us likes where *anything* is going," Bail said, half rising. "That's exactly the point. We can't let a thousand years of democracy disappear without a fight!"

"A *fight?*" Padmé said. "I can't believe what I'm hearing— Bail, you sound like a Separatist!"

"I—" Bail sank back into his seat. "I apologize. That was not my intent. I asked you all here because of all the Senators in the galaxy, you four have been the most consistent—and *influential*— voices of reason and restraint, doing all you could to preserve our poor, tattered Constitution. We don't want to hurt the Republic. With your help, we hope to *save* it."

"It has become increasingly clear," Mon Mothma said, "that Palpatine has become an enemy of democracy. He must be stopped."

"The Senate gave him these powers," Padmé said. "The Senate can rein him in."

Giddean Danu sat forward. "I fear you underestimate just how deeply the Senate's corruption has taken hold. Who will vote against Palpatine now?"

"*I* will," Padmé said. She discovered that she meant it. "And I'll find others, too."

She'd have to. No matter how much it hurt Anakin. *Oh, my love, will you ever find a way to forgive me?*

"You do that," Bail said. "Make as much noise as you can— keep Palpatine watching what you're doing in the Senate. That should provide some cover while Mon Mothma and I begin building our organization—"

"Stop." Padmé rose. "It's better to leave some things unsaid. Right now, it's better I don't know anything about . . . anything."

Don't make me lie to my husband was her unspoken plea. She tried to convey it with her eyes. *Please, Bail. Don't make me lie to him. It will break his heart.*

Perhaps he saw something there; after a moment's indecision, he nodded. "Very well. Other matters can be left for other times. Until then, this meeting must remain absolutely secret. Even hinting at an effective opposition to Palpatine can be, as we've all seen, very dangerous. We must agree never to speak of these matters except among the people who are now in this room. We must bring no one into this secret without the agreement of each and every one of us."

"That includes even those closest to you," Mon Mothma added. "Even your families—to share anything of this will expose them to the same danger we all face. No one can be told. No one."

Padmé watched them all nod, and what could she do? What could she say? *You can keep your own secrets, but I'll have to tell my Jedi husband, who is Palpatine's beloved protégé . . .*

She sighed. "Yes. Yes: agreed."

And all she could think as the little group dispersed to their own offices was *Oh, Anakin—Anakin, I'm sorry . . .*

I'm so sorry.

Anakin was glad the vast vaulted Temple hallway was deserted save for him and Obi-Wan; he didn't have to keep his voice down.

"This is *outrageous*. How can they *do* this?"

"How can they not?" Obi-Wan countered. "It's your friendship with the Chancellor—the same friendship that got you a seat at the Council—that makes it impossible to grant you Mastery. In the Council's eyes, that would be the same as giving a vote to Palpatine himself!"

He waved this off. He didn't have time for the Council's political maneuvering—*Padmé* didn't have time. "I didn't ask for this. I don't *need* this. So if I wasn't friends with Palpatine I'd be a Master already, is that what you're saying?"

Obi-Wan looked pained. "I don't know."

"I have the power of any five Masters. Any *ten*. You know it, and so do they."

"Power alone is no credit to you—"

Anakin flung an arm back toward the Council Tower. "*They're* the ones who call me the chosen one! Chosen for what? To be a dupe in some slimy political game?"

Obi-Wan winced as if he'd been stung. "Didn't I warn you, Anakin? I told you of the . . . tension . . . between the Council and the Chancellor. I was very clear. Why didn't you *listen*? You walked right into it!"

"Like that ray shield trap." Anakin snorted. "Should I blame *this* on the dark side, too?"

"However it happened," Obi-Wan said, "you are in a very . . . delicate situation."

"*What* situation? Who cares about *me*? I'm no Master, I'm just a *kid*, right? Is that what it's about? Is Master Windu turning everyone against me because until I came along, he was the youngest Jedi ever named to the Council?"

"No one cares about that—"

"Sure they don't. Let me tell you something a smart *old* man said to me not so long ago: *Age is no measure of wisdom*. If it were, Yoda would be twenty times as wise as *you* are—"

"This has nothing to do with Master Yoda."

"That's right. It has to do with *me*. It has to do with them all being *against* me. They always *have* been—most of them didn't even want me to *be* a Jedi. And if they'd won out, where would they be right now? Who would have done the things I've done? Who would have saved Naboo? Who would have saved Kamino? Who would have killed Dooku, and rescued the Chancellor? Who would have come for you and Alpha after Ventress—"

"Yes, Anakin, yes. Of course. No one questions your accomplishments. It's your relationship to Palpatine that is the problem. And it is a very *serious* problem."

"I'm too close to him? Maybe I am. Maybe I should alienate a man who's been nothing but kind and generous to me ever since I first *came* to this planet! Maybe I should reject the only man who gives me the respect I *deserve*—"

"Anakin, stop. *Listen* to yourself. Your thoughts are of jealousy, and pride. These are dark thoughts, Anakin. Dangerous thoughts, in these dark times—you are focused on yourself when you need to focus on your service. Your outburst in the Council was an eloquent argument *against* granting you Mastery. How can you be a Jedi Master when you have not mastered yourself?"

Anakin passed his flesh hand over his eyes and drew a long, heavy breath. In a much lower, calmer, quieter tone, he said, "What do I have to do?"

Obi-Wan frowned. "I'm sorry?"

"They want something from me, don't they? That's what this is really about. That's what it's been about from the beginning. They won't give me my rank until I give them what they want."

"The Council does not operate that way, Anakin, and you know it."

Once you're a Master, as you deserve, how will they make you do their bidding?

"Yes, I know it. Sure I do," Anakin said. Suddenly he was tired. So incredibly tired. It hurt to talk. It hurt even to stand here. He was sick of the whole business. Why couldn't it just be *over*? "Tell me what they want."

Obi-Wan's eyes shifted, and the sick fatigue in Anakin's guts turned darker. How bad did it have to be to make Obi-Wan unable to look him in the eye?

"Anakin, look, I'm on your side," Obi-Wan said softly. He looked tired, too: he looked as tired and sick as Anakin felt. "I never wanted to see you put in this situation."

"What situation?"

Still Obi-Wan hesitated.

Anakin said, "Look, whatever it is, it's not getting any better while you're standing here working up the nerve to tell me. Come on, Obi-Wan. Let's have it."

Obi-Wan glanced around the empty hall as if he wanted to make sure they were still alone; Anakin had a feeling it was just an excuse to avoid facing him when he spoke.

"The Council," Obi-Wan said slowly, "approved your appointment because Palpatine trusts you. They want you to report on all his dealings. They have to know what he's up to."

"They want me to *spy* on the *Supreme Chancellor of the Republic*?" Anakin blinked numbly. No wonder Obi-Wan couldn't look him in the face. "Obi-Wan, that's *treason*!"

"We are at war, Anakin." Obi-Wan looked thoroughly miserable. "The Council is sworn to uphold the principles of the Republic through any means necessary. We *have* to. Especially when the greatest enemy of those principles seems to be the Chancellor himself!"

Anakin's eyes narrowed and turned hard. "Why didn't the Council give me this assignment while we were in session?"

"Because it's not for the record, Anakin. You must be able to understand why."

"What I understand," Anakin said grimly, "is that you are trying to turn me against Palpatine. You're trying to make me keep *secrets* from him—you want to make me *lie* to him. That's what this is *really* about."

"It *isn't*," Obi-Wan insisted. He looked wounded. "It's about keeping an eye on who he deals with, and who deals with him."

"He's not a bad man, Obi-Wan—he's a *great* man, who's holding this Republic together with his bare *hands*—"

"By staying in office long after his term has expired. By gathering dictatorial powers—"

"The Senate *demanded* that he stay! They *pushed* those powers on him—"

"Don't be naïve. The Senate is so intimidated they give him anything he wants!"

"Then it's *their* fault, not his! They should have the guts to stand up to him!"

"That is what we're asking *you* to do, Anakin."

Anakin had no answer. Silence fell between them like a hammer.

He shook his head and looked down at the fist he had made of his mechanical hand.

Finally, he said, "He's my *friend,* Obi-Wan."

"Yes," Obi-Wan said softly. Sadly. "I know."

"If *he* asked me to spy on *you,* do you think I would do it?"

Now it was Obi-Wan's turn to fall silent.

"You know how kind he has been to me." Anakin's voice was hushed. "You know how he's looked after me, how he's done everything he could to help me. He's like *family.*"

"The *Jedi* are your family—"

"No." Anakin turned on his former Master. "No, the Jedi are *your* family. The only one you've ever known. But I'm not *like* you—I had a mother who *loved* me—"

And a wife who loves me, he thought. *And soon a child who will love me, too.*

"Do you *remember* my mother? Do you remember what *happened* to her—?"

—because you didn't let me go to save her? he finished silently. *And the same will happen to Padmé, and the same will happen to our child.*

Within him, the dragon's cold whisper chewed at his strength. *All things die, Anakin Skywalker. Even stars burn out.*

"Anakin, yes. Of course. You know how sorry I am for your mother. Listen: we're not asking you to act against Palpatine. We're only asking you to . . . monitor his activities. You must believe me."

Obi-Wan stepped closer and put a hand on Anakin's arm. With a long, slowly indrawn breath, he seemed to reach some difficult decision. "Palpatine himself may be in danger," he said. "This may be the only way you can help him."

"What are you talking about?"

"I am not supposed to be telling you this. Please do not reveal we have had this conversation. To *anyone,* do you understand?"

Anakin said, "I can keep a secret."

"All right." Obi-Wan took another deep breath. "Master Windu traced Darth Sidious to Five Hundred Republica before Grievous's attack—we think that the Sith Lord is someone within Palpatine's closest circle of advisers. *That* is who we want you to spy on, do you understand?"

A fiction created by the Jedi Council . . . an excuse to harass their political enemies . . .

"If Palpatine is under the influence of a Sith Lord, he may be in the gravest danger. The only way we can help him is to find Sidious, and to stop him. What we are asking of you is *not* treason, Anakin—it may be the only way to save the Republic!"

If this Darth Sidious of yours were to walk through that door right now . . . I would ask him to sit down, and I would ask him if he has any power he could use to end this war

"So all you're really asking," Anakin said slowly, "is for me to help the Council find Darth Sidious."

"Yes." Obi-Wan looked relieved, incredibly relieved, as though some horrible chronic pain had suddenly and inexplicably eased. "Yes, that's it exactly."

Locked within the furnace of his heart, Anakin whispered an

echo—not quite an echo—slightly altered, just at the end: *I would ask him to sit down, and I would ask him if he has any power he could use—*

—*to save Padmé.*

The gunship streaked through the capital's sky.

Obi-Wan stared past Yoda and Mace Windu, out through the gunship's window at the vast deployment platform and the swarm of clones who were loading the assault cruiser at the far end.

"You weren't there," he said. "You didn't see his face. I think we have done a terrible thing."

"We don't always have the right answer," Mace Windu said. "Sometimes there *isn't* a right answer."

"Know how important your friendship with young Anakin is to you, I do." Yoda, too, stared out toward the stark angles of the assault cruiser being loaded for the counterinvasion of Kashyyyk; he stood leaning on his gimer stick as though he did not trust his legs. "Allow such attachments to pass out of one's life, a Jedi must."

Another man—even another Jedi—might have resented the rebuke, but Obi-Wan only sighed. "I suppose—he is the chosen one, after all. The prophecy says he was born to bring balance to the Force, but . . ."

The words trailed off. He couldn't remember what he'd been about to say. All he could remember was the look on Anakin's face.

"Yes. Always in motion, the future is." Yoda lifted his head and his eyes narrowed to thoughtful slits. "And the prophecy, misread it could have been."

Mace looked even grimmer than usual. "Since the fall of Darth Bane more than a millennium ago, there have been hundreds of thousands of Jedi—hundreds of thousands of Jedi feeding the light with each work of their hands, with each breath, with every beat of their hearts, bringing justice, building civil society, radiating peace, acting out of selfless love for all living things—and in all these thousand years, there have been only two Sith at any time. Only two. Jedi create light, but the Sith do not create darkness. They merely use the darkness that is always there. That has always been there. Greed and jealousy, aggression and lust and fear—these are all natural to sentient beings. The legacy of the jungle. Our inheritance from the dark."

"I'm sorry, Master Windu, but I'm not sure I follow you. Are you saying—to follow your metaphor—that the Jedi have cast too much light? From what I have seen these past years, the galaxy has not become all that bright a place."

"All I am saying is that we don't *know*. We don't even truly understand what it *means* to *bring balance to the Force*. We have no way of anticipating what this may involve."

"An infinite mystery is the Force," Yoda said softly. "The more we learn, the more we discover how much we do not know."

"So you both feel it, too," Obi-Wan said. The words hurt him. "You both can feel that we have turned some invisible corner."

"In motion, are the events of our time. Approach, the crisis does."

"Yes." Mace interlaced his fingers and squeezed until his knuckles popped. "But we're in a spice mine without a glow rod. If we stop walking, we'll never reach the light."

"And what if the light just isn't there?" Obi-Wan asked. "What if we get to the end of this tunnel and find only night?"

"Faith must we have. Trust in the will of the Force. What other choice is there?"

Obi-Wan accepted this with a nod, but still when he thought of Anakin, dread began to curdle below his heart. "I should have argued more strongly in Council today."

"You think Skywalker won't be able to handle this?" Mace Windu said. "I thought you had more confidence in his abilities."

"I trust him with my life," Obi-Wan said simply. "And that is precisely the problem."

The other two Jedi Masters watched him silently while he tried to summon the proper words.

"For Anakin," Obi-Wan said at length, "there is nothing more important than friendship. He is the most loyal man I have ever met—loyal beyond reason, in fact. Despite all I have tried to teach him about the sacrifices that are the heart of being a Jedi, he—he will never, I think, truly understand."

He looked over at Yoda. "Master Yoda, you and I have been close since I was a boy. An infant. Yet if ending this war one week sooner—one *day* sooner—were to require that I sacrifice your life, you know I would."

"As you should," Yoda said. "As I would yours, young Obi-Wan. As any Jedi would any other, in the cause of peace."

"Any Jedi," Obi-Wan said, "except Anakin."

Yoda and Mace exchanged glances, both thoughtfully grim. Obi-Wan guessed they were remembering the times Anakin had violated orders—the times he had put at risk entire operations, the lives of thousands, the control of whole planetary systems—to save a friend.

More than once, in fact, to save Obi-Wan.

"I think," Obi-Wan said carefully, "that abstractions like *peace* don't mean much to him. He's loyal to *people*, not to principles. And he expects loyalty in return. He will stop at nothing to save me, for example, because he thinks I would do the same for him."

Mace and Yoda gazed at him steadily, and Obi-Wan had to lower his head.

"Because," he admitted reluctantly, "he *knows* I would do the same for him."

"Understand exactly where your concern lies, I do not." Yoda's green eyes had gone softly sympathetic. "*Named* must your fear be, before banish it you can. Do you fear that perform his task, he cannot?"

"Oh, no. That's not it at all. I am firmly convinced that Anakin can do anything. Except betray a friend. What we have done to him today . . ."

"But that is what Jedi *are*," Mace Windu said. "That is what we have pledged ourselves to: selfless service—"

Obi-Wan turned to stare once more toward the assault ship that would carry Yoda and the clone battalions to Kashyyyk, but he could see only Anakin's face.

If he *asked me to spy on* you, *do you think I would do it?*

"Yes," he said slowly. "That's why I don't think he will ever trust us again."

He found his eyes turning unaccountably hot, and his vision swam with unshed tears.

"And I'm not entirely sure he should."

NOT FROM A JEDI

The sunset over Galactic City was stunning tonight: enough particulates from the fires remained in the capital planet's atmosphere to splinter the light of its distant blue-white sun into a prismatic smear across multilayered clouds.

Anakin barely noticed.

On the broad curving veranda that doubled as the landing deck for Padmé's apartment, he watched from the shadows as Padmé stepped out of her speeder and graciously accepted Captain Typho's good night. As Typho flew the vehicle off toward the immense residential tower's speeder park, she dismissed her two handmaidens and sent C-3PO on some busywork errand, then turned to lean on the veranda's balcony right where Anakin had leaned last night.

She gazed out on the sunset, but he gazed only at her.

This was all he needed. To be here, to be with her. To watch the sunset bring a blush to her ivory skin.

If not for his dreams, he'd withdraw from the Order today. Now. The Lost Twenty would be the Lost Twenty-One. Let the scandal come; it wouldn't destroy their lives. Not their real lives.

It would destroy only the lives they'd had before each other: those separate years that now meant nothing at all.

He said softly, "Beautiful, isn't it?"

She jumped as if he'd pricked her with a needle. "Anakin!"

"I'm sorry." He smiled fondly as he moved out from the shadows. "I didn't mean to startle you."

She held one hand pressed to her chest as though to keep her heart from leaping out. "No—no, it's all right. I just—Anakin, you shouldn't be out here. It's still *daylight*—"

"I couldn't wait, Padmé. I had to see you." He took her in his arms. "Tonight is *forever* from now—how am I supposed to live that long without you?"

Her hand went from her chest to his. "But we're in full view of a million people, and you're a very famous man. Let's go inside."

He drew her back from the edge of the veranda, but made no move to enter the apartment. "How are you feeling?"

Her smile was radiant as Tatooine's primary as she took his flesh hand and pressed it to the soft fullness of her belly. "He keeps kicking."

"He?" Anakin asked mildly. "I thought you'd ordered your medical droid not to spoil the surprise."

"Oh, I didn't get this from the Emdee. It's my . . ." Her smile went softly sly. ". . . motherly intuition."

He felt a sudden pulse against his palm and laughed. "Motherly intuition, huh? With a kick that hard? Definitely a girl."

She laid her head against his chest. "Anakin, let's go inside."

He nuzzled her gleaming coils of hair. "I can't stay. I'm on my way to meet with the Chancellor."

"Yes, I heard about your appointment to the Council. Anakin, I'm so proud of you."

He lifted his head, an instant scowl gathering on his forehead. Why did she have to bring that up?

"There's nothing to be proud of," he said. "This is just political maneuvering between the Council and the Chancellor. I got caught in the middle, that's all."

"But to be on the Council, at your age—"

"They put me on the Council because they *had* to. Because he told them to, once the Senate gave him control of the Jedi." His voice lowered toward a growl. "And because they think they can use me against him."

Padmé's eyes went oddly remote, and thoughtful. "*Against* him," she echoed. "The Jedi don't trust him?"

"That doesn't mean much. They don't trust me, either." Anakin's mouth compressed to a thin bitter line. "They'll give me a chair in the Council Chamber, but that's as far as it will go. They won't accept me as a Master."

Her gaze returned from that thoughtful distance, and she smiled up at him. "Patience, my love. In time, they will recognize your ability."

"They already recognize my abilities. They *fear* my abilities," he said bitterly. "But this isn't even about that. Like I said: it's a political game."

"Anakin—"

"I don't know what's happening to the Order, but whatever it is, I don't like it." He shook his head. "This war is destroying everything the Republic is supposed to stand for. I mean, what are we fighting for, anyway? What about all this is worth saving?"

Padmé nodded sadly, disengaging from Anakin's arms and drifting away. "Sometimes I wonder if we're on the wrong side."

"The wrong side?"

You think everything I've accomplished has been for nothing—?

He frowned at her. "You can't mean that."

She turned from him, speaking to the vast airway beyond the veranda's edge. "What if the democracy we're fighting for no longer *exists*? What if the Republic itself has become the very evil we've been fighting to destroy?"

"Oh, this again." Anakin irritably waved off her words. "I've been hearing that garbage ever since Geonosis. I never thought I'd hear it from you."

"A few seconds ago you were saying almost the same thing!"

"Where would the Republic be without Palpatine?"

"I don't know," she said. "But I'm not sure it would be worse than where we are."

All the danger, all the suffering, all the killing, all my friends who gave their lives—?

All for nothing—?

He bit down on his temper. "Everybody complains about Palpatine having too much power, but nobody offers a better alternative. Who *should* be running the war? The *Senate*? You're in the Senate, you know those people—how many of them do *you* trust?"

"All I know is that things are going wrong here. Our government is headed in exactly the wrong direction. You know it, too—you just *said* so!"

"I didn't mean that. I just—I'm tired of this, that's all. This political garbage. Sometimes I'd rather just be back out on the front lines. At least out there, I know who the bad guys are."

"I'm becoming afraid," she replied in a bitter undertone, "that I might know who the bad guys are *here*, too."

His eyes narrowed. "You're starting to sound like a Separatist."

"Anakin, the whole galaxy knows now that Count Dooku is dead. This is the time we should be pursing a *diplomatic* resolution to the war—but instead the fighting is intensifying! Palpatine's your friend, he might listen to you. When you see him tonight, ask him, in the name of simple *decency*, to offer a ceasefire—"

His face went hard. "Is that an order?"

She blinked. "What?"

"Do *I* get any say in this?" He stalked toward her. "Does *my* opinion matter? What if I don't agree with you? What if I think Palpatine's way is the *right* way?"

"Anakin, hundreds of thousands of beings are dying every day!"

"It's a *war,* Padmé. We didn't *ask* for it, remember? You were *there*—maybe we should have 'pursued a diplomatic resolution' in that *beast* arena!"

"I was—" She shrank away from what she saw on his face, blinking harder, brows drawn together. "I was only *asking . . .*"

"Everyone is *only asking.* Everyone *wants* something from me. And *I'm* the bad guy if they don't *get* it!" He spun away from her, cloak whirling, and found himself at the veranda's edge, leaning on the rail. The durasteel piping groaned in his mechanical grip.

"I'm sick of this," he muttered. "I'm sick of all of it."

He didn't hear her come to him; the rush of aircars through the lanes below the veranda drowned her footsteps. He didn't see the hurt on her face, or the hint of tears in her eyes, but he could feel them, in the tentative softness of her touch when she stroked his arm, and he could hear them in her hesitant voice. "Anakin, what is it? What is it really?"

He shook his head. He couldn't look at her.

"Nothing that's your fault," he said. "Nothing you can help."

"Don't shut me out, Anakin. Let me try."

"You can't help me." He stared down through dozens of crisscross lanes of traffic, down toward the invisible bedrock of the planet. "I'm trying to help *you.*"

He'd seen something in her eyes, when he'd mentioned the Council and Palpatine.

He'd seen it.

"What aren't you telling me?"

Her hand went still, and she did not answer.

"I can feel it, Padmé. I sense you're keeping a secret."

"Oh?" she said softly. Lightly. "That's funny, I was thinking the same about *you*."

He just kept staring down over the rail into the invisible distance below. She moved close to him, moved against him, her arm sliding around his shoulders, her cheek leaning lightly on his arm. "Why does it have to be like this? Why does there have to even be such a thing as war? Can't we just . . . go *back*? Even just to pretend. Let's pretend we're back at the lake on Naboo, just the two of us. When there was no war, no politics. No plotting. Just us. You and me, and love. That's all we need. You and me, and love."

Right now Anakin couldn't remember what that had been like.

"I have to go," he said. "The Chancellor is waiting."

Two masked, robed, silent Red Guards flanked the door to the Chancellor's private box at the Galaxies Opera. Anakin didn't need to speak; as he approached, one of them said, "You are expected," and opened the door.

The small round box had only a handful of seats, overlooking the spread of overdressed beings who filled every seat in the orchestra; on this opening night, it seemed everyone had forgotten there was a war on. Anakin barely gave a glance toward the immense sphere of shimmering water that rippled gently in the stage's artificial zero-g; he had no interest in ballet, Mon Calamari or otherwise.

In the dim semi-gloom, Palpatine sat with the speaker of the Senate, Mas Amedda, and his administrative aide, Sly Moore. Anakin stopped at the back of the box.

If I were the spy the Council wants me to be, I suppose I should be creeping up behind them so that I can listen in.

A spasm of distaste passed over his face; he took care to wipe it off before he spoke. "Chancellor. Sorry I'm late."

Palpatine turned toward him, and his face lit up. "Yes, Anakin! Don't worry. Come in, my boy, come in. Thank you for your report on the Council meeting this afternoon—it made most interesting reading. And now I have good news for you— Clone Intelligence has located General Grievous!"

"That's tremendous!" Anakin shook his head, wondering if Obi-Wan would be embarrassed to have been scooped by the clones. "He won't escape us again."

"I'm going to—Moore, take a note—I will direct the Council to give *you* this assignment, Anakin. Your gifts are wasted on Coruscant—you should be out in the field. You can attend Council meetings by holoconference."

Anakin frowned. "Thank you, sir, but the Council coordinates Jedi assignments."

"Of course, of course. Mustn't step on any Jedi toes, must we? They are so jealous of their political prerogatives. Still, I shall wonder at their collective wisdom if they choose someone else."

"As I said in my report, they've already assigned Obi-Wan to find Grievous." *Because they want to keep me here, where I am supposed to spy on you.*

"To find him, yes. But you are the best man to *apprehend* him—though of course the Jedi Council cannot always be trusted to do the right thing."

"They try. I—believe they try, sir."

"Do you still? Sit down." Palpatine looked at the other two beings in the box. "Leave us."

They rose and withdrew. Anakin took Mas Amedda's seat.

Palpatine gazed distractedly down at the graceful undulations of the Mon Calamari principal soloist for a long moment, frowning as though there was so much he wanted to say, he was unsure where to begin. Finally he sighed heavily and leaned close to Anakin.

"Anakin, I think you know by now that I cannot rely upon the Jedi Council. That is why I put you on it. If they have not yet tried to use you in their plot, they soon will."

Anakin kept his face carefully blank. "I'm not sure I understand."

"You must sense what I have come to suspect," Palpatine said grimly. "The Jedi Council is after more than independence from Senate oversight; I believe they intend to control the Republic itself."

"Chancellor—"

"I believe they are planning treason. They hope to overthrow my government, and replace me with someone weak enough that Jedi mind tricks can control his every word."

"I can't believe the Council—"

"Anakin, search your feelings. You do know, don't you?"

Anakin looked away. "I know they don't trust you . . ."

"Or the Senate. Or the Republic. Or democracy itself, for that matter. The Jedi Council is not *elected*. It selects its own members according to its own rules—a less generous man than I might say *whim*—and gives them authority backed by power. They rule the Jedi as they hope to rule the Republic: by fiat."

"I admit . . ." Anakin looked down at his hands. ". . . my faith in them has been . . . shaken."

"How? Have they approached you already? Have they ordered you to do something dishonest?" Palpatine's frown cleared into a gently wise smile that was oddly reminiscent of Yoda's. "They want you to spy on me, don't they?"

"I—"

"It's all right, Anakin. I have nothing to hide."

"I—don't know what to say . . ."

"Do you remember," Palpatine said, drawing away from Anakin so that he could lean back comfortably in his seat, "how as a young boy, when you first came to this planet, I tried to teach you the ins and outs of politics?"

Anakin smiled faintly. "I remember that I didn't much care for the lessons."

"For *any* lessons, as I recall. But it's a pity; you should have paid more attention. To understand politics is to understand the fundamental nature of thinking beings. Right now, you should remember one of my first teachings: all those who gain power are afraid to lose it."

"The Jedi use their power for *good*," Anakin said, a little too firmly.

"Good is a point of view, Anakin. And the Jedi concept of *good* is not the only valid one. Take your Dark Lords of the Sith, for example. From my reading, I have gathered that the Sith believed in justice and security every bit as much as the Jedi—"

"Jedi believe in justice and *peace*."

"In these troubled times, is there a difference?" Palpatine asked mildly. "The Jedi have not done a stellar job of bringing peace to the galaxy, you must agree. Who's to say the Sith might not have done better?"

"This is another of those arguments you probably shouldn't bring up in front of the Council, if you know what I mean," Anakin replied with a disbelieving smile.

"Oh, yes. Because the Sith would be a threat to the Jedi Order's *power*. Lesson one."

Anakin shook his head. "Because the Sith are *evil*."

"From a Jedi's point of view," Palpatine allowed. "*Evil* is a label we all put on those who threaten us, isn't it? Yet the Sith and the Jedi are similar in almost every way, including their quest for greater power."

"The Jedi's quest is for greater *understanding*," Anakin countered. "For greater knowledge of the Force—"

"Which brings with it greater power, does it not?"

"Well . . . yes." Anakin had to laugh. "I should know better than to argue with a politician."

"We're not arguing, Anakin. We're just talking." Palpatine shifted his weight, settling in comfortably. "Perhaps the real difference between the Jedi and the Sith lies only in their orientation; a Jedi gains power through understanding, and a Sith gains understanding through power. This is the true reason the Sith have always been more powerful than the Jedi. The Jedi fear the dark side so much they cut themselves off from the most important aspect of life: passion. Of any kind. They don't even allow themselves to love."

Except for me, Anakin thought. *But then, I've never been exactly the perfect Jedi.*

"The Sith do not fear the dark side. The Sith *have* no fear. They embrace the whole spectrum of experience, from the heights of transcendent joy to the depths of hatred and despair. Beings have these emotions for a reason, Anakin. That is why the Sith are more powerful: they are not afraid to *feel*."

"The Sith rely on passion for strength," Anakin said, "but when that passion runs dry, what's left?"

"Perhaps nothing. Perhaps a great deal. Perhaps it never runs dry at all. Who can say?"

"They think inward, only about themselves."

"And the Jedi don't?"

"The Jedi are selfless—we *erase* the self, to join with the flow of the Force. We care only about *others* . . ."

Palpatine again gave him that smile of gentle wisdom. "Or so you've been trained to believe. I hear the voice of Obi-Wan Kenobi in your answers, Anakin. What do you *really* think?"

Anakin suddenly found the ballet a great deal more interesting than Palpatine's face. "I . . . don't know anymore."

"It is said that if one could ever entirely comprehend a single grain of sand—really, truly understand *everything* about it—one would, at the same time, entirely comprehend the universe. Who's to say that a Sith, by looking inward, sees less than a Jedi does by looking out?"

"The Jedi—Jedi are *good*. That's the difference. I don't care *who* sees *what*."

"What the Jedi are," Palpatine said gently, "is a group of very powerful beings you consider to be your comrades. And you are loyal to your friends; I have known that for as long as I have known you, and I admire you for it. But are your friends loyal to *you*?"

Anakin shot him a sudden frown. "What do you mean?"

"Would a true friend ask you to do something that's wrong?"

"I'm not sure it's wrong," Anakin said. Obi-Wan might have been telling the truth. It was possible. They might only want to catch Sidious. They might really be trying to protect Palpatine.

They might.

Maybe.

"Have they asked you to break the Jedi Code? To violate the Constitution? To betray a friendship? To betray your own *values*?"

"Chancellor—"

"*Think*, Anakin! I have always tried to teach you to think— yes, yes, Jedi do not think, they *know*, but those stale answers aren't good enough now, in these changing times. Consider their motives. Keep your mind clear of assumptions. The fear of losing power is a weakness of both the Jedi and the Sith."

Anakin sank lower in his seat. Too much had happened in too short a time. Everything jumbled together in his head, and none of it seemed to make complete sense.

Except for what Palpatine said.

That made too *much* sense.

"This puts me in mind of an old legend," Palpatine murmured idly. "Anakin—are you familiar with *The Tragedy of Darth Plagueis the Wise*?"

Anakin shook his head.

"Ah, I thought not. It is not a story the Jedi would tell you.

It's a Sith legend, of a Dark Lord who had turned his sight inward so deeply that he had come to comprehend, and master, life itself. And—because the two are one, when seen clearly enough—death itself."

Anakin sat up. Was he actually hearing this? "He could keep someone safe from death?"

"According to the legend," Palpatine said, "he could directly influence the midi-chlorians to create life; with such knowledge, to maintain life in someone already living would seem a small matter, don't you agree?"

A universe of possibility blossomed inside Anakin's head. He murmured, "Stronger than *death* . . ."

"The dark side seems to be—from my reading—the pathway to many abilities some would consider unnatural."

Anakin couldn't seem to get his breath. "What happened to him?"

"Oh, well, it *is* a tragedy, after all, you know. Once he has gained this ultimate power, he has nothing to fear save losing it— that's why the Jedi Council brought him to mind, you know."

"But what *happened*?"

"Well, to safeguard his power's existence, he teaches the path toward it to his apprentice."

"And?"

"And his apprentice kills him in his sleep," Palpatine said with a careless shrug. "Plageuis never sees it coming. That's the tragic irony, you see: he can save anyone in the galaxy from death—except himself."

"What about the apprentice? What happens to *him*?"

"Oh, him. *He* goes on to become the greatest Dark Lord the Sith have ever known . . ."

"So," Anakin murmured, "it's only a tragedy for *Plagueis*— for the apprentice, the legend has a *happy* ending . . ."

"Oh, well, yes. Quite right. I'd never really thought of it that way—rather like what we were talking about earlier, isn't it?"

"What if," Anakin said slowly, almost not daring to speak the words, "it's not just a legend?"

"I'm sorry?"

"What if Darth Plagueis really *lived*—what if someone really *had* this power?"

"Oh, I am . . . rather certain . . . that Plagueis did indeed exist. And if someone actually had this power—well, he would indeed be one of the most powerful men in the galaxy, not to mention virtually immortal . . ."

"How would I *find* him?"

"I'm sure I couldn't say. You could ask your friends on the Jedi Council, I suppose—but of course, if they ever found him they'd kill him on the spot. Not as punishment for any crime, you understand. Innocence is irrelevant to the Jedi. They would kill him simply for being Sith, and his knowledge would die with him."

"I just—I have to—" Anakin found himself half out of his seat, fists clenched and trembling. He forced himself to relax and sit back down, and he took a deep breath. "You seem to know so much about this, I need you to tell me: would it be possible, possible at all, to learn this power?"

Palpatine shrugged, regarding him with that smile of gentle wisdom.

"Well, clearly," he said, "not from a Jedi."

For a long, long time after leaving the opera house, Anakin sat motionless in his idling speeder, eyes closed, resting his head against the edge of his mechanical hand. The speeder bobbed gently in the air-wakes of the passing traffic; he didn't feel it. Klaxons blared, rising and fading as angry pilots swerved around him; he didn't hear them.

Finally he sighed and lifted his head. He stroked a private code into the speeder's comm screen. After a moment the screen lit up with an image of Padmé's half-asleep face.

"Anakin—?" She rubbed her eyes, blinking. *"Where are you? What time is it?"*

"Padmé, I can't—" He stopped himself, huffing a sigh out through his nose. "Listen, Padmé, something's come up. I have to spend the night at the Temple."

"Oh . . . well, all right, Anakin. I'll miss you."

"I'll miss you, too." He swallowed. "I miss you already."

"We'll be together tomorrow?"

"Yes. And soon, for the rest of our lives. We'll never have to be apart again."

She nodded sleepily. *"Rest well, my love."*

"I'll do my best. You, too."

She blew him a kiss, and the screen went blank.

Anakin fired thrusters and slid the speeder expertly into traffic, angling toward the Jedi Temple, because that part—the part about spending the night at the Temple—was the part that wasn't a lie.

The lie was that he was going to rest. That he was going to even try. How could he rest when every time he closed his eyes he could see her screaming on the birthing table?

Now the Council's insult burned hotter than ever; he even had a name, a story, a place to start—but how could he explain to the archives Master why he needed to research a Sith legend of immortality?

Yet maybe he didn't need the archives after all.

The Temple was still the greatest nexus of Force energy on the planet, perhaps even the galaxy, and it was unquestionably the best place in the galaxy for intense, focused meditation. He had much he needed the Force to teach him, and a very short time to learn.

He would start by thinking inward.

Thinking about *himself* . . .

THE WILL OF THE FORCE

When her handmaiden Moteé awakened her with the word that C-3PO had announced a Jedi was waiting to see her, Padmé flew out of bed, threw on a robe, and hurried out to her living room, a smile breaking through her sleepiness like the dawn outside—

But it was Obi-Wan.

The Jedi Master had his back to her, hands clasped behind him as he drifted restlessly about the room, gazing with abstracted lack of interest at her collection of rare sculpture.

"Obi-Wan," she said breathlessly, "has—" She bit off the following *something happened to Anakin?* How would she explain why this was the first thing out of her mouth?

"—has See-Threepio offered you anything to drink?"

He turned to her, a frown clearing from his brow. "Senator," he said warmly. "So good to see you again. I apologize for the early hour, and yes, your protocol droid has been quite insistent on offering me refreshment." His frown began to regather. "But as you may guess, this is not a social call. I've come to speak with you about Anakin."

Her years in politics had trained her well; even as her heart lurched and a shrill *How much does he* know? echoed inside her head, her face remained only attentively blank.

A primary rule of Republic politics: tell as much truth as you can. Especially to a Jedi. "I was very happy to learn of his appointment to the Council."

"Yes. It is perhaps less than he deserves—though I'm afraid it may be more than he can handle. Has he been to see you?"

"Several times," she said evenly. "Something is wrong, isn't it?"

Obi-Wan tilted his head, and a hint of rueful smile showed through his beard. "You should have been a Jedi."

She managed a light laugh. "And you should never go into politics. You're not very good at hiding your feelings. What is it?"

"It's Anakin." With his pretense of cheer fading away, he seemed to age before her eyes. He looked very tired, and profoundly troubled. "May I sit?"

"Please." She waved him to the couch and lowered herself onto its edge beside him. "Is he in trouble again?"

"I certainly hope not. This is more . . . a personal matter." He shifted his weight uncomfortably. "He's been put in a difficult position as the Chancellor's representative, but I think there's more to it than that. We—had words, yesterday, and we parted badly."

Her heart shrank; he *must* know, and he'd come to confront her—to bring their whole lives crashing down around their ears. She ached for Anakin, but her face showed only polite curiosity.

"What were these words about?" she asked delicately.

"I'm afraid I can't tell you," he said with a vaguely apologetic frown. "Jedi business. You understand."

She inclined her head. "Of course."

"It's only that—well, I've been a bit worried about him. I was hoping he may have talked to you."

"Why would he talk to *me* about—" She favored him with her best friendly-but-skeptical smile. "—Jedi business?"

"Senator—Padmé. Please." He gazed into her eyes with nothing on his face but compassion and fatigued anxiety. "I am not blind, Padmé. Though I have tried to be, for Anakin's sake. And for yours."

"What do you mean?"

"Neither of you is very good at hiding feelings, either."

"Obi-Wan—"

"Anakin has loved you since the day you met, in that horrible junk shop on Tatooine. He's never even tried to hide it, though we do not speak of it. We . . . pretend that I don't know. And I was happy to, because it made him happy. *You* made him happy, when nothing else ever truly could." He sighed, his brows drawing together. "And you, Padmé, skilled as you are on the Senate floor, cannot hide the light that comes to your eyes when anyone so much as mentions his name."

"I—" She lurched to her feet. "I can't—Obi-Wan, don't make me talk about this . . ."

"I don't mean to hurt you, Padmé. Nor even to make you uncomfortable. I'm not here to interrogate you; I have no interest in the details of your relationship."

She turned away, walking just to be moving, barely conscious of passing through the door out onto the dawn-painted veranda. "Then why *are* you here?"

He followed her respectfully. "Anakin is under a great deal of pressure. He carries tremendous responsibilities for a man so young; when I was his age I still had some years to go as a Padawan. He is—changing. Quickly. And I have some anxiety about what he is changing into. It would be a . . . very great mistake . . . were he to leave the Jedi Order."

She blinked as though he'd slapped her. "Why—that seems . . . *unlikely,* doesn't it? What about this prophecy the Jedi put so much faith in? Isn't he the chosen one?"

"Very probably. But I have scanned this prophecy; it says

only that a chosen one will be born and bring balance to the Force; nowhere does it say he has to be a Jedi."

She blinked harder, fighting down a surge of desperate hope that left her breathless. "He doesn't *have* to—?"

"My Master, Qui-Gon Jinn, believed that it was the will of the Force that Anakin should be trained as a Jedi—and we all have a certain, oh, I suppose you could call it a Jedi-centric bias. It is a Jedi prophecy, after all."

"But the will of the Force—isn't that what Jedi follow?"

"Well, yes. But you must understand that not even the Jedi know all there is to be known about the Force; no mortal mind can. We speak of the *will of the Force* as someone ignorant of gravity might say it is the will of a river to flow to the ocean: it is a metaphor that describes our ignorance. The simple truth—if any truth is ever simple—is that we do not truly know what the will of the Force may be. We can *never* know. It is so far beyond our limited understanding that we can only surrender to its mystery."

"What does this have to do with Anakin?" She swallowed, but her voice stayed tight and thin. "And with me?"

"I fear that some of his current . . . difficulty . . . has to do with your relationship."

If you only knew how much, she thought. "What do you want me to do?"

He looked down. "I cannot tell you what to do, Padmé. I can only ask you to consider Anakin's best interests. You know the two of you can never be together while he remains in the Order."

A bleak chill settled into her chest. "Obi-Wan, I can't talk about this."

"Very well. But remember that the Jedi are his family. The Order gives his life *structure*. It gives him a direction. You know how . . . undisciplined he can be."

And that's why he is the only Jedi I could ever love . . . "Yes. Yes, of course."

"If his true path leads him away from the Jedi, so be it. But please, for both of your sakes, tread carefully. Be sure. Some decisions can never be reversed."

"Yes," she said slowly. Feelingly. "I know that too well."

He nodded as though he understood, though of course he did not understand at all. "We all do, these days."

A soft chiming came from within his robe. "Excuse me," he said, and turned aside, producing a comlink from an inner pocket. "Yes . . . ?"

A man's voice came thinly through the comlink, deep and clipped: *"We are calling the Council into special session. We've located General Grievous!"*

"Thank you, Master Windu," Obi-Wan said. "I'm on my way."

General Grievous? Her eyes went hot, and stung with sudden tears. And so they would take her Anakin away from her again.

She felt a stirring below her ribs. Away from *us,* she amended, and there was so much love and fear and joy and loss all swirling and clashing within her that she dared not speak. She only stared blindly out across the smog-shrouded cityscape as Obi-Wan came close to her shoulder.

"Padmé," he said softly. Gently. Almost regretfully. "I will not tell the Council of this. Any of it. I'm very sorry to burden you with this, and I—I hope I haven't upset you too much. We have all been friends for so long . . . and I hope we always will be."

"Thank you, Obi-Wan," she said faintly. She couldn't look at him. From the corner of her eye she saw him incline his head respectfully and turn to go.

For a moment she said nothing, but as his footsteps receded she said, "Obi-Wan?"

She heard him stop.

"You love him, too, don't you?"

When he didn't answer, she turned to look. He stood motionless, frowning, in the middle of the expanse of buff carpeting.

"You do. You love him."

He lowered his head. He looked very alone.

"Please do what you can to help him," he said, and left.

The holoscan of Utapau rotated silently in the center of the Jedi Council Chamber. Anakin had brought the holoprojector from the Chancellor's office; Obi-Wan wondered idly if the projector had been scanned for recording devices planted by the Chancellor to spy on their meeting, then dismissed the thought. In a sense, Anakin *was* the Chancellor's recording device.

And that's our fault, he thought.

The only Council members physically present, other than Obi-Wan and Anakin, were Mace Windu and Agen Kolar. The Council reached a quorum by the projected holopresences of Ki-Adi-Mundi, en route to Mygeeto, Plo Koon on Cato Neimoidia, and Yoda, who was about to make planetfall on Kashyyyk.

"Why Utapau?" Mace Windu was saying. "A neutral system, of little strategic significance, and virtually no planetary defense force—"

"Perhaps that is itself the reason," Agen Kolar offered. "Easily taken, and their sinkhole-based culture can hide a tremendous number of droids from long-range scans."

Ki-Adi-Mundi's frown wrinkled the whole length of his forehead. *"Our agents on Utapau have made no report of this."*

"They may be detained, or dead," Obi-Wan said.

Mace Windu leaned toward Anakin, scowling. "How could the Chancellor have come by this information when we know nothing about it?"

"Clone Intelligence intercepted a partial message in a diplomatic packet from the Chairman of Utapau," Anakin told him.

"We've only managed to verify its authenticity within the past hour."

Obi-Wan felt a frown crawl onto his forehead at the way Anakin now referred to the Chancellor's Office as *we* . . .

"Clone Intelligence," Mace said heavily, "reports to *us*."

"I beg your pardon, Master Windu, but that is no longer the case." Though Anakin's expression was perfectly solemn, Obi-Wan thought he could detect a hint of satisfaction in his young friend's voice. "I thought it had been already made clear. The constitutional amendment bringing the Jedi under the Chancellor's Office naturally includes troops commanded by Jedi. Palpatine is now Supreme Commander of the Grand Army of the Republic."

"Pointless it is, to squabble over jurisdiction," the image of Yoda said. *"Act on this, we must."*

"I believe we all agree on that," Anakin said briskly. "Let's move to the operational planning. The Chancellor has requested that I lead this mission, and so I—"

"The *Council* will decide this," Mace said sternly. "Not the Chancellor."

"Dangerous, Grievous is. To face him, steady minds are needed. Masters, we should send."

Perhaps of all the Council, only Obi-Wan could detect the shadow of disappointment and hurt that crept into Anakin's eyes. Obi-Wan understood perfectly, and could even sympathize: to take the field would have slipped Anakin out from under the pressures of what he saw as his conflicting duties.

"Given the strain on our current resources," Mace Windu said, "I recommend we send only one Jedi—Master Kenobi."

Which would leave Mace and Agen Kolar—both among the greatest bladesbeings the Jedi Order had ever produced—here on Coruscant in case Sidious did indeed take this opportunity to make a dramatic move. Not to mention Anakin, who was a brigade's worth of firepower in his own right.

Obi-Wan nodded. Perfectly logical. Everyone would agree.

Except Anakin. He leaned forward, red climbing his cheeks. "He wasn't so successful the *last* time he met Grievous!"

"Anakin—" Obi-Wan began.

"No offense, my Master. I am only stating a fact."

"Oh no, not at all. You're quite right. But I have a feel for how he fights now—and for how he runs away. I am certain I can catch him."

"Master—"

"And you, my young friend, have duties here on Coruscant. Extremely *important* duties, that require your *full attention*," Obi-Wan reminded him. "Am I being clear?"

Anakin didn't answer. He sank back into his chair and turned away.

"Obi-Wan, my choice is," Yoda said.

Ki-Adi-Mundi's image nodded. *"I concur. Let's put it to a vote."*

Mace Windu counted nods. "Six in favor."

He waited, looking at Anakin. "Further comment?"

Anakin only stared at the wall.

After a moment, Mace shrugged.

"It is unanimous."

Senator Chi Eekway accepted a tube of Aqualish hoi-broth from C-3PO's refreshment tray. "I am very grateful to be included here," she said, her dewlaps jiggling as she tilted her blue head in a gesture around Padmé's living room at the gathering of Senators. "I speak directly only for my own sector, of course, but I can tell you that many Senators are becoming very nervous indeed. You may not know that the new governors are arriving with full regiments of clone troops—what they call *security forces*. We all have begun to wonder if these regiments are intended to protect us from the Separatists . . . or to protect the governors from *us*."

Padmé looked up from the document reader in her hand. "I have . . . reliable information . . . that General Grievous has been located, and that the Jedi are already moving against his position. The war may be over in a matter of days."

"But what then?" Bail Organa leaned forward, elbows to knees, fingers laced together. "How do we make Palpatine withdraw his governors? How do we stop him from garrisoning troops in *all* our systems?"

"We don't have to *make* him do anything," Padmé said reasonably. "The Senate granted him executive powers only for the duration of the emergency—"

"Yet it is only Palpatine himself who has the authority to declare when the emergency is over," Bail countered. "How do we make him surrender power back to the Senate?"

Chi Eekway shifted backward. "There are many who are willing to do just that," she said. "Not just my own people. Many Senators. We are ready to *make* him surrender power."

Padmé snapped the document reader closed. She looked from Senator to Senator expressionlessly. "Would anyone care for further refreshment?"

"Senator Amidala," Eekway said, "I fear you don't understand—"

"Senator Eekway. Another hoi-broth?"

"No, that's—"

"Very well, then." She looked up at C-3PO. "Threepio, that will be all. Please tell Moteé and Ellé that they are dismissed for the day, then you are free to power down for a while."

"Thank you, Mistress," Threepio replied. "Though I must say, this discussion has been *most* stimu—"

"Threepio." Padmé's tone went a trace extra firm. "That will be *all*."

"Yes, Mistress. Of course. I quite understand." The droid turned stiffly and shuffled out of the room.

As soon as 3PO was safely out of earshot, Padmé brandished

the document reader as though it were a weapon. "This is a very dangerous step. We cannot let this turn into another war."

"That's the last thing any of us wants," Bail said with a disapproving look at Senator Eekway. "Alderaan has no armed forces; we don't even have a planetary defense system. A political solution is our only option."

"Which is the purpose of this petition," Mon Mothma said, laying her soft hand over Padmé's. "We're hoping that a show of solidarity within the Senate might stop Palpatine from further subverting the Constitution, that's all. With the signatures of a full two thousand Senators—"

"—we still have less than we need to stop his supermajority from amending the Constitution any way he happens to want," Padmé finished for her. She weighed the reader in her hand. "I am willing to present this to Palpatine, but I am losing faith in the Senate's readiness, or even ability, to rein him in. I think we should consult the Jedi."

Because I really think they can help, or because I just can't stand to lie to my husband? She couldn't say. She hoped that both were true, though she was sure only of the second.

Bana Breemu examined her long, elegantly manicured fingertips. "That," she said remotely, "would be dangerous."

Mon Mothma nodded. "We don't know where the Jedi stand in all this."

Padmé sat forward. "The Jedi aren't any happier with the situation than we are."

Senator Breemu's high-arched cheekbones made the look she gave Padmé appear even more distant and skeptical. "You seem . . . remarkably well informed about Jedi business, Senator Amidala."

Padmé felt herself flush, and she didn't trust herself to answer.

Giddean Danu shook his head, doubt plainly written across his dark face. "If we are to openly oppose the Chancellor, we need the support of the Jedi. We need their moral authority. Otherwise, what do we have?"

"The *moral authority* of the Jedi, such as it is," Bana Breemu said, "has been spent lavishly upon war; I fear they have none left for politics."

"*One* Jedi, then," Padmé offered to the others. *At least let me speak the truth to my love. At least. Please,* she pleaded with them silently. "There is one Jedi—one whom I truly know all of us can trust absolutely . . ."

Her voice trailed off into appalled silence when she realized that she wasn't talking about Anakin.

This had been all about him when she'd started—all about her love, her need to be open with him, the pain that keeping this secret stabbed her heart at each and every beat—but when the thought had turned to *trust,* when it became a question of someone she knew, truly and absolutely *knew,* she could trust—

She discovered that she was talking about Obi-Wan.

Anakin . . . Something was breaking inside her. *Oh, my love, what are they doing to us?*

Chi Eekway shook her head. "Patience, Senator."

Fang Zar unknotted his fingers from his raggedly bushy beard and shrugged. "Yes, we cannot block the Chancellor's supermajority—but we can show him that opposition to his methods is growing. Perhaps that alone might persuade him to moderate his tactics."

Bana Breemu went back to examining her fingertips. "When you present the Petition of the Two Thousand, many things may change."

"But," Giddean Danu said, "will they change for the better?"

Bail Organa and Mon Mothma exchanged glances that whispered of some shared secret. Bail said slowly, "Let us see what we can accomplish in the Senate before we involve the Jedi."

And as one after another of the Senators agreed, Padmé could only sit in silence. In mourning.

Grieving for the sudden death of an illusion.

Anakin—Anakin, I love you. If only—

But that *if only* would take her to a place she could not bear to go. In the end, she could only return to the thought she feared would echo within her for the rest of her life.

Anakin, I'm sorry.

The last of the hovertanks whirred up the ramp into the sky-shrouding wedge of the assault cruiser. It was followed by rank upon immaculately regimented rank of clone troopers, marshaled by battalions, marching in perfect synchrony.

Standing alongside Obi-Wan on the landing deck, Anakin watched them go.

He couldn't quite make himself believe he wasn't going along.

It wasn't that he really *wanted* to go with Obi-Wan to Utapau—even though it'd be a relief to pull out of the political quagmire that was sucking him down. But how could he leave Padmé now? He didn't even care anymore about being the Jedi to capture Grievous, though such a feat would almost certainly bring him his Mastery. He was no longer certain he needed to be a Master at all.

Through the long, black hours of meditation last night—meditation that was often indistinguishable from brooding—he had begun to sense a deeper truth within the Force: a submerged reality, lurking like a Sarlacc beneath the sunlit sands of Jedi training.

Somewhere down there was all the power he would ever need.

So no, it wasn't that he wanted to go. It was more, inexplicably, that he wanted Obi-Wan to *stay*.

There was a cold void in his chest that he was afraid would soon fill with regret, and grief.

Of course there was no chance at all that Obi-Wan wouldn't go; he'd be the last Jedi in the galaxy to defy an order of the

Council. Not for the first time, Anakin found himself wishing that Obi-Wan could be a little more like the late Qui-Gon. Though he'd known Qui-Gon for mere days, Anakin could almost see him right now, brow furrowing as he gently inclined his head over his shorter Padawan; he could almost hear his gentle baritone instructing Obi-Wan to *be mindful of the currents of the living Force: to do one's duty is not always to do right. Concern yourself with right action. Let duty take care of itself.*

But he couldn't say that. Though he'd passed his trials many months ago, to Obi-Wan he was still the learner, not the Master.

All he could say was, "I have a bad feeling about this."

Obi-Wan was frowning as he watched a clone deck crew load his blue-and-white starfighter onto the assault cruiser's flight deck. "I'm sorry, Anakin. Did you say something?"

"You're going to need me on this one, Master." And he could feel an unexpected truth there, too—if he *were* to go along, if he could somehow bring himself to forget about Padmé for a few days, if he could somehow get himself away from Palpatine and the Council and his meditations and politics and everything here on Coruscant that was dragging him this way and that way and sucking him under, if he could just tag along and play the *Kenobi and Skywalker* game for a few days, everything might still be all right.

If only.

"It may be nothing but a wild bantha chase," Obi-Wan said. "Your job here is much more important, Anakin."

"I know: the Sith." The word left a bitter taste in Anakin's mouth. The Council's manipulation had a rank stench of politics on it. "I just—" Anakin shrugged helplessly, looking away. "I don't like you going off without me like this. It's a bad idea to split up the team. I mean, look what happened *last* time."

"Don't remind me."

"You want to go spend another few months with somebody like Ventress? Or worse?"

"Anakin." Anakin could hear a gentle smile in Obi-Wan's voice. "Don't worry. I have enough clones to take three systems the size of Utapau's. I believe I should be able to handle the situation, even without your help."

Anakin had to answer his smile. "Well, there's always a first time."

Obi-Wan said, "We're not really splitting up, Anakin. We've worked on our own many times—like when you took Padmé to Naboo while I went to Kamino and Geonosis."

"And look how *that* turned out."

"All right, bad example," Obi-Wan admitted, his smile shading toward rueful. "Yet years later, here we all are: still alive, and still friends. My point, Anakin, is that even when we work separately, we work together. We have the same goals: end the war, and save the Republic from the Sith. As long as we're on the same side, everything will come out well in the end. I'm certain of it."

"Well . . ." Anakin sighed. "I suppose you could be right. You are, once in a while. Occasionally."

Obi-Wan chuckled and clapped him on the shoulder. "Farewell, old friend."

"Master, wait." Anakin turned to face him fully. He couldn't just stand here and let him walk away. Not now. He had to say *something* . . .

He had a sinking feeling he might not get another chance.

"Master . . . ," he said hesitantly, "I know I've . . . disappointed you in these past few days. I have been arrogant. I have . . . not been very appreciative of your training, and what's worse, of your friendship. I offer no excuse, Master. My frustration with the Council . . . I know that none of it is your fault, and I apologize. For all of it. Your friendship means everything to me."

Obi-Wan gripped Anakin's mechanical hand, and with his other he squeezed Anakin's arm above the joining of flesh and metal. "You are wise and strong, Anakin. You are a credit to the Jedi Order, and you have far surpassed my humble efforts at instruction."

Anakin felt his own smile turn melancholy. "Just the other day, you were saying that my power is no credit to me."

"I'm not speaking of your power, Anakin, but of your heart. The greatness in you is a greatness of spirit. Courage and generosity, compassion and commitment. These are your virtues," Obi-Wan said gently. "You have done great things, and I am very proud of you."

Anakin found he had nothing to say.

"Well." Obi-Wan looked down, chuckling, releasing Anakin's hand and arm. "I believe I hear General Grievous calling my name. Good-bye, old friend. May the Force be with you."

All Anakin could offer in return was a reflexive echo.

"May the Force be with you."

He stood, still and silent, and watched Obi-Wan walk away. Then he turned and slowly, head hanging, moved toward his speeder.

The Chancellor was waiting.

FREE FALL IN THE DARK

A chill wind scoured the Chancellor's private landing deck at the Senate Office Building. Anakin stood wrapped in his cloak, chin to his chest, staring down at the deck below his feet. He didn't feel the chill, or the wind. He didn't hear the whine of the Chancellor's private shuttle angling in for a landing, or smell the swirls of brown smog coiling along the wind.

What he saw were the faces of Senators who had stood on this deck to cheer for him; what he heard were exclamations of joy and congratulations when he returned their Supreme Chancellor to them unharmed. What he felt was a memory of hot pride at being the focus of so many eager HoloNet crews, anxious to get even the slightest glimpse of the man who had conquered Count Dooku.

How many days ago had that been? He couldn't remember. Not many. When you don't sleep, days smear together into a haze of fatigue so deep it becomes a physical pain. The Force could keep him upright, keep him moving, keep him thinking, but it could not give him rest. Not that he wanted rest. Rest might bring sleep.

What sleep might bring, he could not bear to know.

He remembered Obi-Wan telling him about some poet he'd once read—he couldn't remember the name, or the exact quote, but it was something about how there is no greater misery than to remember, with bitter regret, a day when you were happy . . .

How had everything gone so fast from so right to so wrong?

He couldn't even imagine.

Greasy dust swirled under the shuttle's repulsors as it settled to the deck. The hatch cycled open, and four of Palpatine's personal guards glided out, long robes catching the breeze in silken blood-colored ripples. They split into two pairs to flank the doors as the Chancellor emerged beside the tall, bulky form of Mas Amedda, the Speaker of the Senate. The Chagrian's horns tilted over Palpatine as they walked together, seemingly deep in conversation.

Anakin moved forward to meet them. "Chancellor," he said, bowing a greeting. "Lord Speaker."

Mas Amedda looked at Anakin with a curl to his blue lips that, on a human, would have signaled disgust; it was a Chagrian smile. "Greetings, Your Grace. I trust the day finds you well?"

Anakin's eyes felt as if they'd been dusted with sand. "Very well, Lord Speaker, thank you for asking."

Amedda turned back to Palpatine, and Anakin's polite smile faded to a twist of contempt. Maybe he was just overtired, but somehow, looking at the curlings of the Chagrian's naked head-tentacles as they twisted across his chest, he found himself hoping that Obi-Wan hadn't been lying to him about Sidious. He rather hoped that Mas Amedda might be a secret Sith, because something about the Speaker of the Senate was so revolting that Anakin could easily imagine just slicing his head in half . . .

It gradually dawned on Anakin that Palpatine was giving Mas Amedda the brush-off, and was sending the Redrobes with him.

Good. He wasn't in the mood to play games. By themselves, they could talk straight with each other. A little straight talk might be just what he needed. A little straight talk might burn through the fog of half-truths and subtle confusions that the Jedi Council had poured into his head.

"So, Anakin," Palpatine said as the others moved away, "did you see your friend off?"

Anakin nodded. "If I didn't hate Grievous so much, I'd almost feel sorry for him."

"Oh?" Palpatine appeared mildly interested. "Are Jedi allowed to hate?"

"Figure of speech," Anakin said, waving this off. "It doesn't matter how I feel about Grievous. Obi-Wan will soon have his head."

"Provided, of course," Palpatine murmured as he took Anakin's arm to guide him toward the entryway, "that the Council didn't make a mistake. I still believe Master Kenobi is not the Jedi for this job."

Anakin shrugged irritably. Why did everyone keep bringing up things he didn't want to talk about? "The Council was . . . very sure in its decision."

"Certainty is a fine thing," the Chancellor allowed. "Though it too often happens that those who are the most entirely certain are also the most entirely wrong. What will the Council do if Kenobi proves unable to apprehend Grievous without your help?"

"I'm sure I cannot say, sir. I imagine they will deal with that if and when it happens. The Jedi teach that anticipation is distraction."

"I am no philosopher, Anakin; in my work, anticipation is often my sole hope of success. I must anticipate the actions of my adversaries—and even those of my allies. Even—" He opened a hand toward Anakin, smiling. "—my friends. It is the only way I can be prepared to take advantage of opportunity . . . and conversely, to avoid disaster."

"But if a disaster comes about by the will of the Force—"

"I'm afraid I don't believe in the will of the Force," Palpatine said, his smile turning apologetic. "I believe it is *our* will that matters. I believe that everything good in our civilization has come about not by the blind action of some mystical field of energy, but by the focused will of *people:* lawmakers and warriors, inventors and engineers, struggling with every breath of their bodies to shape galactic culture. To improve the lives of all."

They stood now before the vaulted door to Palpatine's office. "Please come in, Anakin. Much as I enjoy a philosophical chat, that was not the reason I asked you to meet me. We have business to discuss, and I fear it may be very serious business indeed."

Anakin followed him through the outer chambers to Palpatine's intimate private office. He took up a respectful standing position opposite Palpatine's desk, but the Chancellor waved him to a chair. "Please, Anakin, make yourself comfortable. Some of this may be difficult for you to hear."

"Everything is, these days," Anakin muttered as he took a seat.

Palpatine didn't seem to hear. "It concerns Master Kenobi. My friends among the Senators have picked up some . . . disturbing rumors about him. Many in the Senate believe that Kenobi is not fit for this assignment."

Anakin frowned. "Are you serious?"

"I'm most serious, I'm afraid. It is a . . . complicated situation, Anakin. It seems there are some in the Senate who now regret having granted me emergency powers."

"There have been dissenters and naysayers since before Geonosis, sir. Why should it be cause for concern now? And how does it affect Obi-Wan?"

"I'm getting to that." Palpatine took a deep breath and swung his chair around so that he could gaze through his window of armored transparisteel onto the cityscape beyond. "The difference is that now, some of these Senators—actually a large number of them—seem to have given up on democracy. Unable to achieve their ends in the Senate, they are organizing into a cabal, preparing to remove me by . . . other means."

"You mean treason?" Anakin had enough Jedi discipline to force away his memory of using that word with Obi-Wan.

"I'm afraid so. The rumor is that the ringleaders of this group may have fallen victim to the . . . persuasive powers . . . of the Jedi Council, and are on their way to becoming accomplices in the Council's plot against the Republic."

"Sir, I—" Anakin shook his head. "This just seems . . . ridiculous."

"And it may be entirely false. Remember that these are only rumors. Entirely unconfirmed. Senate gossip is rarely accurate, but if this *is* true . . . we must be *prepared*, Anakin. I still have friends enough in the Senate to catch the scent of whatever this disloyal cabal is cooking up. And I have a very good idea of who the leaders are; in fact, my final meeting this afternoon is with a delegation representing the cabal. I would like you to be present for that as well."

"Me?" Couldn't everyone leave him alone for day? For even a few *hours*? "What for?"

"Your Jedi senses, Anakin. Your ability to read evil intent. I have no doubt these Senators will put some virtuous façade on their plotting; with your help, we will pierce that veil and discover the truth."

Anakin sighed, rubbing his stinging eyes. How could he let Palaptine down? "I'm willing to try, sir."

"We won't try, Anakin. We will *do*. After all, they are only Senators. Most of them couldn't hide what they're thinking from a brain-damaged blindworm, let alone the most powerful Jedi in the galaxy."

He leaned back in his chair and steepled his fingers pensively. "The Jedi Council, however, is another matter entirely. A secret society of antidemocratic beings who wield tremendous power, individually as well as collectively—how am I to trace the labyrinth of *their* plots? That's why I put you on the Council. If these rumors are true, you may be democracy's last hope."

Anakin let his chin sink once more to his chest, and his eyelids scraped shut. It seemed like he was always *somebody's* last hope.

Why did everyone always have to make their problems into *his* problems? Why couldn't people just let him be?

How was he supposed to deal with all this when Padmé could *die*?

He said slowly, eyes still closed, "You still haven't told me what this has to do with Obi-Wan."

"Ah, that—well, that is the difficult part. The *disturbing* part. It seems that Master Kenobi has been in contact with a certain Senator who is known to be among the leaders of this cabal. Apparently, very *close* contact. The rumor is that he was seen leaving this Senator's residence this very morning, at an . . . unseemly hour."

"Who?" Anakin opened his eyes and sat forward. "Who is this Senator? Let's go question *him*."

"I'm sorry, Anakin. But the Senator in question is, in fact, a *her*. A woman you know quite well, in fact."

"You—" He wasn't hearing this. He couldn't be. "You mean—"

Anakin choked on her name.

Palpatine gave him a look of melancholy sympathy. "I'm afraid so."

Anakin coughed his voice back to life. "That's *impossible*! I would *know*—she doesn't . . . she couldn't—"

"Sometimes the closest," Palpatine said sadly, "are those who cannot see."

Anakin sat back, stunned. He felt like he'd been punched in

the chest by a Gamorrean. By a *rancor*. His ears rang, and the room whirled around him.

"I would know," he repeated numbly. "I would know . . ."

"Don't take it too hard," Palpatine said. "It may be only idle gossip. All this may be only a figment of my overheated imagination; after all these years of war, I find myself inspecting every shadow that might hide an enemy. That is what I need from *you*, Anakin: I need you to find the truth. To set my mind at rest."

A distant smolder kindled under Anakin's breastbone, so faint as to be barely there at all, but even a hint of that fire gave Anakin the strength to throw himself to his feet.

"I can do that," he said.

The flame grew stronger now. Hotter. The numb fatigue that had dragged at his limbs began to burn away.

"Good, Anakin. I knew I could count on you."

"Always, sir. Always."

He turned to go. He would go to her. He would see her. He would get the truth. He would do it *now*. Right now. In the middle of the day. It didn't matter who might see him.

This was business.

"I know who my friends are," he said, and left.

He moved through Padmé's apartment like a shadow, like a ghost at a banquet. He touched nothing. He looked at everything.

He felt as if he'd never seen it before.

How could she do this to him?

Sometimes the closest are those who cannot see.

How *could* she?

How could *he*?

In the Force, the whole apartment stank of Obi-Wan.

His finger traced the curving back of her couch.

Here. Obi-Wan had sat here.

Anakin rounded the couch and settled into that same spot. His hand fell naturally to the seat beside him . . . and there he felt an echo of Padmé.

The dragon whispered, *That's a little close for casual conversation.*

This was a different kind of fear. Even colder. Even uglier.

Fear that Palpatine might be *right* . . .

The apartment's air still hummed with discord and worry, and there was a smell of oxidized spices and boiled seaweed—hoi-broth, that was it. Someone in the past few hours had been drinking hoi-broth in this room.

Padmé hated hoi-broth.

And Obi-Wan was allergic to it—once on a diplomatic mission to Ando, his violent reaction to a ceremonial toast had nearly triggered an intersystem incident.

So Padmé had been entertaining other visitors, too.

From a pocket on his equipment belt he pulled a flimsi of Palpatine's list of suspect Senators. He scanned down the list, looking for names of Senators he knew well enough that he might recognize the Force-echoes of their presence here. Many he'd never heard of; there were thousands of Senators, after all. But those he knew by reputation were the cream of the Senate: people like Terr Taneel, Fang Zar, Bail Organa, Garm Bel Iblis—

He began to think Palpatine *was* just imagining things after all. These beings were known to be incorruptible.

He frowned down at the flimsi. It was *possible* . . .

A Senator might carefully construct a reputation, appearing to all the galaxy as honest and upright and honorable, all the while holding the rotten truth of himself so absolutely secret that no one would sense his evil until he had so much power that it was too late to stop him . . .

It *was* possible.

But so many? Could they *all* have accomplished that?

Could Padmé?

Suspicion leaked back into his mind and gathered itself into so thick a cloud that he didn't sense her approach until she was already in the room.

"Anakin? What are you doing here? It's still the middle of the afternoon . . ."

He looked up to find her standing in the archway in full Senatorial regalia: heavy folds of burgundy robes and a coif like a starfighter's hyperdrive ring. Instead of a smile, instead of sunlight in her eyes, instead of the bell-clear joy with which she had always greeted him, her face was nearly expressionless: attentively blank.

Anakin called it her Politician Look, and he hated it.

"Waiting for you," he replied, a little unsteadily. "What are *you* doing here in the middle of the afternoon?"

"I have a very important meeting in two hours," she said stiffly. "I left a document reader here this morning—"

"This meeting—is it with the *Chancellor*?" Anakin's voice came out low and harsh. "Is it his *last meeting of the afternoon*?"

"Y-yes, yes it is." She frowned, blinking. "Anakin, what's—"

"I have to be there, too." He crumpled the flimsi and stuffed it back into his equipment belt. "I'm starting to look forward to it."

"Anakin, what is it?" She came toward him, one hand reaching for him. "What's wrong?"

He lurched to his feet. "Obi-Wan's been here, hasn't he?"

"He came by this morning." She stopped. Her hand slowly lowered back to her side. "Why?"

"What did you talk about?"

"Anakin, why are you acting like this?"

One long stride brought him to her. He towered over her. For one stretching second she looked very small, very insignificant, very much like some kind of bug that he could crush beneath his heel and just keep on walking.

"What did you *talk* about?"

She gazed steadily up at him, and on her face was only concern, shaded with growing hurt. "We talked about you."

"What *about* me?"

"He's worried about you, Anakin. He says you're under a lot of stress."

"And he's *not?*"

"The way you've been acting, since you got back—"

"*I'm* not the one doing the *acting*. I'm not the one doing the pretending! I'm not the one sneaking *in* here in the *morning!*"

"No," she said with a smile. She reached up to lay the palm of her hand along the line of his jaw. "That's usually when you're sneaking *out*."

Her touch unclenched his heart.

He half fell into a chair and pressed the edge of his flesh hand against his eyes.

When he could overcome his embarrassment enough to speak, he said softly, "I'm sorry, Padmé. I'm sorry. I know I've been . . . difficult to deal with. I just—I feel like I'm in free fall. Free fall in the dark. I don't know which way is up. I don't know where I'll be when I land. Or crash."

He frowned against his fingers, squeezing his eyes more tightly shut to make sure no tears leaked out. "I think it's going to be a crash."

She sat on the wide-rolled arm of his chair and laid her slim arm along his shoulders. "What has happened, my love? You've always been so sure of yourself. What's changed?"

"Nothing," he said. "Everything. I don't know. It's all so screwed up, I can't even tell you. The Council doesn't trust me, Palpatine doesn't trust the Council. They're plotting against each other and both sides are pressuring *me,* and—"

"Surely that's only your imagination, Anakin. The Jedi Council is the bedrock of the Republic."

"The bedrock of the Republic is *democracy*, Padmé—

something the Council doesn't much like when votes don't go their way. *All those who gain power are afraid to lose it*—that's something you should remember." He looked up at her. "You and your *friends* in the *Senate*."

She took this without a blink. "But Obi-Wan is on the Council; *he'd* never participate in anything the least bit underhanded—"

"You think so?"

Because it's not for the record, Anakin. You must be able to understand why.

He shook the memory away. "It doesn't matter. Obi-Wan's on his way to Utapau."

"What is this really about?"

"I don't *know*," he said helplessly. "I don't know *anything* anymore. All I know is, I'm not the Jedi I should be. I'm not the *man* I should be."

"You're the man for me," she said, leaning toward him to kiss his cheek, but he pulled away.

"You don't understand. *Nobody* understands. I'm one of the most powerful Jedi alive, but it's not enough. It'll *never* be enough, not until—"

His voice trailed away, and his eyes went distant, and his memory burned with an alien birthing table, and blood, and screams.

"Until what, my love?"

"Until I can *save* you," he murmured.

"Save me?"

"From my nightmares."

She smiled sadly. "Is that what's bothering you?"

"I won't lose you, Padmé. I can't." He sat forward and twisted to take both of her hands, small and soft and deceptively strong and beyond precious, between his own. "I am still learning, Padmé—I have found a key to truths deeper than the Jedi could ever teach me. I will become so powerful that I will keep you *safe*. Forever. I *will*."

"You don't need more power, Anakin." She gently extricated one of her hands and used it to draw him close. "I believe you can save me from anything, just as you are."

She pulled him to her and their lips met, and Anakin gave himself to the kiss, and while it lasted, he believed it, too.

A shroud of twilight lowered upon Galactic City.

Anakin stood at what a clone trooper would have called parade rest—a wide, balanced stance, feet parallel, hands clasped behind his back. He stood one pace behind and to the left of the chair where Palpatine sat, behind his broad desk in the small private office attached to his large public one.

On the other side of the desk stood the Senate delegation.

The way they had looked at him, when they had entered the office—the way their eyes still, even now, flicked to his, then away again before he could fully meet their gaze—the way none of them, not even Padmé, dared to ask why the Supreme Chancellor had a Jedi at his shoulder during what was supposed to be a private meeting . . . it seemed to him that they already guessed why he was here.

They were simply afraid to bring it up.

Now they couldn't be sure where the Jedi stood. The only thing that was clear was where Anakin stood—

Respectfully in attendance upon Supreme Chancellor Palpatine.

Anakin studied the Senators.

Fang Zar: face creased with old laugh lines, dressed in robes so simple they might almost be homespun, unruly brush of hair gathered into a tight topknot, and an even more unruly brush of beard that sprayed uncontrolled around his jaw. He had a gentle, almost simplistic way of speaking that could easily lead one to forget that he was one of the sharpest political minds in the Senate. Also, he was such a close friend of Garm Bel Iblis that the powerful Corellian Senator might as well have been present in person.

Anakin had watched him closely throughout the meeting. Fang Zar had something on his mind, that was certain— something that he did not seem willing to say.

Nee Alavar and Malé-Dee he could dismiss as threats; the two stood together—perhaps needing each other for moral support— and neither had said anything at all. And then, of course, there was Padmé.

Glowing in her Senatorial regalia, the painted perfection of her face luminous as all four of Coruscant's moons together, not a single hair out of place in her elaborate coif—

Speaking in her Politician Voice, and wearing her Politician Look.

Padmé did the talking. Anakin had a sickening suspicion that this was all her idea.

"We are not attempting to delegitimize your government," she was saying. "That's why we're here. If we were trying to organize an opposition—if we sought to impose our requests as demands—we would hardly bring them before you in this fashion. This petition has been signed by two thousand Senators, Chancellor. We ask only that you instruct your governors not to interfere with the legitimate business of the Senate, and that you open peace talks with the Separatists. We seek only to end the war, and bring peace and stability back to our homeworlds. Surely you can understand this."

"I understand a great many things," Palpatine said.

"This system of governors you have created is very troubling—it seems that you are imposing military controls even on loyalist systems."

"Your reservations are noted, Senator Amidala. I assure you that the Republic governors are intended only to make your systems safer—by coordinating planetary defense forces, and ensuring that neighboring systems mesh into cooperative units, and bringing production facilities up to speed in service to the war effort. That's all. They will in no way compete with the duties and prerogatives—with the power—of the Senate."

Something in the odd emphasis he put on the word *power* made Anakin think Palpatine was speaking more for Anakin's benefit than for Padmé's.

All those who gain power are afraid to lose it

"May I take it, then," Padmé said, "that there will be no further amendments to the Constitution?"

"My dear Senator, what has the Constitution to do with this? I thought we were discussing ending the war. Once the Separatists have been defeated, then we can start talking about the Constitution again. Must I remind you that the extraordinary powers granted to my office by the Senate are only in force for the duration of the emergency? Once the war ends, they expire automatically."

"And your governors? Will they 'expire,' too?"

"They are not *my* governors, my lady, they are the Republic's," Palpatine replied imperturbably. "The fate of their positions will be in the hands of the Senate, where it belongs."

Padmé did not seem reassured. "And peace talks? Will you offer a cease-fire? Have you even *tried* a diplomatic resolution to the war?"

"You must trust me to do the right thing," he said. "That is, after all, why I am here."

Fang Zar roused himself. "But surely—"

"I have said I will do what is *right*," Palpatine said, a testy edge sharpening his voice. He rose, drawing himself up to his full height, then inclining his head with an air of finality. "And that should be enough for your . . . committee."

His tone said: *Don't let the door crunch you on the way out.*

Padmé's mouth compressed into a thin, grim line. "On behalf of the Delegation of the Two Thousand," she said with tight-drawn formality, "I thank you, Chancellor."

"And I thank you, Senator Amidala, and your friends—" Palpatine lifted the document reader containing the petition. "—for bringing this to my attention."

The Senators turned reluctantly and began to file out. Padmé paused, just for a second, to meet Anakin's eyes with a gaze as clear as a slap on the mouth.

He stayed expressionless. Because in the end, no matter how much he wanted to, no matter how much it hurt . . . he couldn't quite make himself believe he was on her side.

DEATH ON UTAPAU

When constructing an effective Jedi trap—as opposed to the sort that results in nothing more than an embarrassingly brief entry in the Temple archives—there are several design features that one should include for best results.

The first is an irresistible bait. The commanding general of an outlaw nation, personally responsible for billions of deaths across the galaxy, is ideal.

The second is a remote, nearly inaccessible location, one that is easily taken and easily fortified, with a sharply restricted field of action. It should also, ideally, belong to someone else, preferably an enemy; the locations used for Jedi traps never survive the operation unscathed, and many don't survive it at all. An excellent choice would be an impoverished desert planet in the Outer Rim, with unwarlike natives, whose few cities are built in a cluster of sinkholes on a vast arid plateau. A city in a sinkhole is virtually a giant kill-jar; once a Jedi flies in, all one need do is seal the lid.

Third, since it is always a good idea to remain well out of reach when plotting against a Jedi's life—on the far side of the galaxy is considered best—one should have a reliable proxy to do the actual murder. The exemplar of a reliable proxy would be, for example, the most prolific living Jedi killer, backed up by a squad of advanced combat droids designed, built, and armed specifically to fight Jedi. Making one's proxy double as the bait is an impressively elegant stroke, if it can be managed, since it ensures that the Jedi victim will voluntarily place himself in contact with the Jedi killer—and will continue to do so even *after* he realizes the extent of the trap, out of a combination of devotion to duty and a not-entirely-unjustified arrogance.

The fourth element of an effective Jedi trap is a massively overwhelming force of combat troops who are willing to burn the whole planet, including themselves if necessary, to ensure that the Jedi in question does not escape.

A textbook example of the ideal Jedi trap is the one that waited on Utapau for Obi-Wan Kenobi.

As Obi-Wan sent his starfighter spiraling in toward a landing deck that protruded from the sheer sandstone wall of the biggest of Utapau's sinkhole-cities, he reviewed what he knew of the planet and its inhabitants.

There wasn't much.

He knew that despite its outward appearance, Utapau was not a true desert planet; there was water aplenty in an underground ocean that circled its globe. The erosive action of this buried ocean had undermined vast areas of its surface, and frequent groundquakes collapsed them into sinkholes large enough to land a *Victory*-class Star Destroyer, where civilization could thrive below reach of the relentless scouring hyperwinds on the surface. He knew that the planet had little in the way of high technology, and that their energy economy was based on wind power; the planet's limited interstellar trade had begun only a few decades before, when offworld water-mining companies had discovered that the waters of the world-ocean were rich in dissolved trace elements. He knew that the inhabitants were near-human, divided into two distinct species, the tall, lordly, slow-moving Utapauns, nicknamed Ancients for their astonishing longevity, and the stubby Utai, called Shorts, both for their stature and for their brief busy lives.

And he knew that Grievous was here.

How he knew, he could not say; so far as he could tell, his conviction had nothing to do with the Force. But within seconds of the *Vigilance*'s realspace reversion, he was sure. This was it. One way or another, this was the place his hunt for General Grievous would come to a close.

He felt it in his bones: Utapau was a planet for endings.

He was going in alone; Commander Cody and three battalions of troopers waited in rapid-deployment vehicles—LAAT/i's and *Jadthu*-class landers—just over the horizon. Obi-Wan's plan was to pinpoint Grievous's location, then keep the bio-droid general busy until the clones could attack; he would be a one-man diversionary force, holding the attention of what was sure to be thousands or tens of thousands of combat droids directed inward toward him and Grievous, to cover the approach of the clones. Two battalions would strike full-force, with the third in reserve, both to provide reinforcements and to cover possible escape routes.

"I can keep them distracted for quite some time," Obi-Wan had told Cody on the flight deck of *Vigilance*. "Just don't take too long."

"Come on, boss," Cody had said, smiling out of Jango Fett's face, "have I ever let you down?"

"Well—" Obi-Wan had said with a slim answering smile, "Cato Neimoidia, for starters . . ."

"That was Anakin's fault; *he* was the one who was late . . ."

"Oh? And who will you blame it on *this* time?" Obi-Wan had chuckled as he climbed into his starfighter's cockpit and strapped himself in. "Very well, then. I'll try not to destroy all the droids before you get there."

"I'm counting on you, boss. Don't let me down."

"Have I ever?"

"Well," Cody had said with a broad grin, "there *was* Cato Neimoidia . . ."

Obi-Wan's fighter bucked through coils of turbulence; the rim of the sinkhole caught enough of the hyperwinds above that the first few levels of city resided in a semipermanent hurricane. Whirling blades of wind-power turbines stuck out from the sinkhole's sides on generator pods so scoured by the fierce winds that they might themselves have been molded of liquid sandstone. He fought the fighter's controls to bring it down level after level until the wind had become a mere gale; even after reaching the landing deck in the depths of the sinkhole, R4-G9 had to extend the starfighter's docking claws to keep it from being blown, skidding, right off the deck.

A ribbed semitransparent canopy swung out to enfold the landing deck; once it had settled into place around him, the howl of winds dropped to silence and Obi-Wan popped the cockpit.

A pack of Utai was already scampering toward the starfighter, which stood alone on the deck; they carried a variety of tools and dragged equipment behind them, and Obi-Wan assumed they were some sort of ground crew. Behind them glided the stately form of an Utapaun in a heavy deck-length robe of deep scarlet that had a lapel collar so tall it concealed his vestigial ear-disks. The Utapaun's glabrous scalp glistened with a sheen of moisture, and he walked with a staff that reminded Obi-Wan vaguely of Yoda's beloved gimer stick.

That was quick, Obi-Wan thought. *Almost like they've been expecting me.*

"Greetings, young Jedi," the Utapaun said gravely in accented Basic. "I am Tion Medon, master of port administration for this place of peace. What business could bring a Jedi to our remote sanctuary?"

Obi-Wan sensed no malice in this being, and the Utapaun radiated a palpable aura of fear; Obi-Wan decided to tell the truth. "My business is the war," he said.

"There is no war here, unless you have brought it with you," Medon replied, a mask of serenity concealing what the Force told Obi-Wan was anxiety verging on panic.

"Very well, then," Obi-Wan said, playing along. "Please permit me to refuel here, and to use your city as a base to search the surrounding systems."

"For what do you search?"

"Even in the Outer Rim, you must have heard of General Grievous. It is he I seek, and his army of droids."

Tion Medon took another step closer and leaned down to bring his face near Obi-Wan's ear. "He is here!" Medon whispered urgently. "We are hostages—we are being watched!"

Obi-Wan nodded matter-of-factly. "Thank you, Master Medon," he said in a thoroughly ordinary voice. "I am grateful for your hospitality, and will depart as soon as your crew refuels my starfighter."

"Listen to me, young Jedi!" Medon's whisper became even more intense. "You must depart in *truth!* I was *ordered* to reveal their presence—this is a trap!"

"Of course it is," Obi-Wan said equably.

"The tenth level—thousands of war droids—*tens* of thousands!"

"Have your people seek shelter." Obi-Wan turned casually and scanned upward, counting levels. On the tenth, his eye found a spiny spheroid of metal: a Dreadnaught-sized structure that clearly had not been there for long—its gleaming surface had not yet been scoured to matte by the sand in the constant winds. He nodded absently and spoke softly, as though to himself. "Geenine, take my starfighter back to the *Vigilance*. Instruct Commander Cody to inform Jedi Command on Coruscant that

I have made contact with General Grievous. I am engaging now. Cody is to attack in full force, as planned."

The astromech beeped acknowledgment from its forward socket, and Obi-Wan turned once more to Tion Medon. "Tell them I promised to file a report with Republic Intelligence. Tell them I really only wanted fuel enough to leave immediately."

"But—but what will you *do*?"

"If you have warriors," Obi-Wan said gravely, "now is the time."

In the holocomm center of Jedi Command, within the heart of the Temple on Coruscant, Anakin watched a life-sized holoscan of Clone Commander Cody report that Obi-Wan had made contact with General Grievous.

"We are beginning our supporting attack as ordered. And—if I may say so, sirs—from my experience working with General Kenobi, I have a suspicion that Grievous does not have long to live."

If I were there with *him*, Anakin thought, *it'd be more than a suspicion. Obi-Wan, be* careful—

"Thank you, Commander." Mace Windu's face did not betray the slightest hint of the mingled dread and anticipation Anakin was sure he must be feeling; while Anakin himself felt ready to burst, Windu looked calm as a stone. "Keep us apprised of your progress. May the Force be with you, and with Master Kenobi."

"I'm sure it will be, sir. Cody out."

The holoscan flickered to nothingness. Mace Windu turned brief but seemingly significant glances upon the other two Masters in attendance, both holoscans themselves: Ki-Adi-Mundi from the fortified command center on Mygeeto, and from a guerrilla outpost on Kashyyyk, Yoda.

Then he turned to Anakin. "Take this report to the Chancellor."

"Of course I will, Master."

"And take careful note of his reaction. We will need a full account."

"Master?"

"What he says, Anakin. Who he calls. What he does. Everything. Even his facial expressions. It's very important."

"I don't understand—"

"You don't have to. Just do it."

"Master—"

"Anakin, do I have to remind you that you are still a Jedi? You are still subject to the orders of this Council."

"Yes, Master Windu. Yes, I am," he said, and left.

Once Skywalker was gone, Mace Windu found himself in a chair, staring at the doorway through which the young Jedi Knight had left. "Now we shall see," he murmured. "At last. The waters will begin to clear."

Though he shared the command center with the holoscans of two other Jedi Masters, Mace wasn't talking to them. He spoke to the grim, clouded future inside his head.

"Have you considered," Ki-Adi-Mundi said carefully, from faraway Mygeeto, *"that if Palpatine refuses to surrender power, removing him is only a first step?"*

Mace looked at the blue ghost of the Cerean Master. "I am not a politician. Removing a tyrant is enough for me."

"But it will not be enough for the Republic," Ki-Adi-Mundi countered sadly. *"Palpatine's dictatorship has been legitimized—and can be legalized, even enshrined in a revised Constitution—by the supermajority he controls in the Senate."*

The grim future inside Mace's head turned even darker. The Cerean was right.

"Filled with corruption, the Senate is," Yoda agreed from Kashyyyk. *"Controlled, they must be, until replaced the corrupted Senators can be, with Senators honest and—"*

"Do you *hear* us?" Mace lowered his head into his hands. "How have we come to this? Arresting a Chancellor. Taking over the *Senate*—! It's as though Dooku was *right*—to save the Republic, we'll have to destroy it . . ."

Yoda lifted his head, and his eyes slitted as though he struggled with some inner pain. *"Hold on to hope we must; our true enemy, Palpatine is not, nor the Senate; the true enemy is instead the Sith Lord Sidious, who controls them both. Once destroyed Sidious is . . . all these other concerns, less dire they will instantly become."*

"Yes." Mace Windu rose, and moved to the window, hands folded behind his back. "Yes, that is true."

Indigo gloom gathered among the towers outside.

"And we have put the chosen one in play against the last Lord of the Sith," he said. "In that, we must place our faith, and our hopes for the future of the Republic."

The landing deck canopy parted, and the blue-and-white Jedi starfighter blasted upward into the gale. From deep shadows at the rear of the deck, Obi-Wan watched it go.

"I suppose I am committed, now," he murmured.

Through electrobinoculars produced from his equipment belt, he examined that suspiciously shiny spheroid high above on the tenth level. The spray of spines had to be droid-control antennas. That's where Grievous would be: at the nerve center of his army.

"Then that's where I should be, too." He looked around, frowning. "Never an air taxi when you need one . . ."

The reclosing of the deck canopy quieted the howl of the wind outside, and now from deeper within the city Obi-Wan could hear a ragged choir of hoarsely bellowing cries that had the resonance of large animals—they reminded him of something . . .

Suubatars, that was it—they sounded vaguely like the calls of the suubatars he and Anakin had ridden on one of their last missions before the war, back when the biggest worry Obi-Wan had was how to keep his promise to Qui-Gon . . .

But he had no time for nostalgia. He could practically hear Qui-Gon reminding him to focus on the now, and give himself over to the living Force.

So he did.

Mere moments of following the cries through the shadows of deserted hallways carved into the sandstone brought Obi-Wan in sight of an immense, circular arena-like area, where a ring of balcony was joined to a flat lower level by spokes of broad, corrugated ramps; the ceiling above was hung with yellowish lamp-rods that cast a light the same color as the sunbeams striking through an arc of wide oval archways open to the interior of the sinkhole outside. The winds that whistled through those wide archways also went a long way toward cutting the eye-watering reptile-den stench down from overpowering to merely nauseating.

Squatting, lying, and milling aimlessly about the lower level were a dozen or so large lizard-like beasts that looked like the product of some mad geneticist's cross of Tatooine krayt dragons with Haruun Kal ankkoxen: four meters tall at the shoulder, long crooked legs that ended in five-clawed feet clearly designed for scaling rocky cliffs, ten meters of powerful tail ridged with spines and tipped with a horn-bladed mace, a flexible neck leading up to an armor-plated head that sported an impressive cowl of spines of its own—they looked fearsome enough that Obi-Wan might have thought them some sort of dangerous wild predators or vicious watchbeasts, were it not for the docile way they tolerated the team of Utai wranglers who walked among them, hosing them down, scraping muck from their scales, and letting them take bundles of greens from their hands.

Not far from where Obi-Wan stood, several large racks were hung with an array of high-backed saddles in various styles and degrees of ornamentation, very much indeed like those the Al-wari of Ansion had strapped to their suubatars.

Now he *really* missed Anakin . . .

Anakin disliked living mounts almost as much as Obi-Wan hated to fly. Obi-Wan had long suspected that it was Anakin's gift with machines that worked against him with suubatar or dew-back or bantha; he could never get entirely comfortable riding anything with a mind of its own. He could vividly imagine Anakin's complaints as he climbed into one of these saddles.

It seemed an awfully long time since Obi-Wan had had an opportunity to tease Anakin a bit.

With a sigh, he brought himself back to business. Moving out of the shadows, he walked down one of the corrugated ramps and made a slight, almost imperceptible hand gesture in the direction of the nearest of the Utai dragonmount wranglers. "I need transportation."

The Short's bulging eyes went distant and a bit glassy, and he responded with a string of burbling glottal hoots that had a decidedly affirmative tone.

Obi-Wan made another gesture. "Get me a saddle."

With another string of affirmative burbles, the Short wad-dled off.

While he waited for his saddle, Obi-Wan examined the drag-onmounts. He passed up the largest, and the one most heavily muscled; he skipped over the leanest built-for-speed beast, and didn't even approach the one with the fiercest gleam in its eye. He didn't actually pay attention to outward signs of strength or health or personality; he was using his hands and eyes and ears purely as focusing channels for the Force. He didn't know what he was looking for, but he trusted that he would recognize it when he found it.

Qui-Gon, he reflected with an inward smile, would approve.

Finally he came to a dragonmount with a clear, steady gleam in its round yellow eyes, and small, close-set scales that felt warm and dry. It neither shied back from his hand nor bent submissively to his touch, but only returned his searching gaze with calm, thoughtful intelligence. Through the Force, he felt in the beast an unshakable commitment to obedience and care for its rider: an almost Jedi-like devotion to service as the ultimate duty.

This was why Obi-Wan would always prefer a living mount. A speeder is incapable of caring if it crashes.

"This one," he said. "I'll take this one."

The Short had returned with a plain, sturdily functional saddle; as he and the other wranglers undertook the complicated task of tacking up the dragonmount, he nodded at the beast and said, "Boga."

"Ah," Obi-Wan said. "Thank you."

He took a sheaf of greens from a nearby bin and offered them to the dragonmount. The great beast bent its head, its wickedly hooked beak delicately withdrew the greens from Obi-Wan's hand, and it chewed them with fastidious thoroughness.

"Good girl, Boga. Erm—" Obi-Wan frowned at the Short. "—she *is* a *she,* isn't she?"

The wrangler frowned back. "Warool noggaggllo?" he said, shrugging, which Obi-Wan took to mean *I have no idea what you're saying to me.*

"Very well, then," Obi-Wan said with an answering shrug. "*She* you will have to be, then, Boga. Unless you care to tell me otherwise."

Boga made no objection.

He swung himself up into the saddle and the dragonmount rose, arching her powerful back in a feline stretch that lifted Obi-Wan more than four meters off the floor. Obi-Wan looked down at the Utai wranglers. "I cannot pay you. As compensation, I can only offer the freedom of your planet; I hope that will suffice."

Without waiting for a reply that he would not have understood anyway, Obi-Wan touched Boga on the neck. Boga reared straight up and raked the air with her hooked foreclaws as though she were shredding an imaginary hailfire droid, then gathered herself and leapt to the ring-balcony in a single bound. Obi-Wan didn't need to use the long, hook-tipped goad strapped in a holster alongside the saddle; nor did he do more than lightly hold the reins in one hand. Boga seemed to understand exactly where he wanted to go.

The dragonmount slipped sinuously through one of the wide oval apertures into the open air of the sinkhole, then turned and seized the sandstone with those hooked claws to carry Obi-Wan straight up the sheer wall.

Level after level they climbed. The city looked and felt deserted. Nothing moved save the shadows of clouds crossing the sinkhole's mouth far, far above; even the wind-power turbines had been locked down.

The first sign of life he saw came on the tenth level itself; a handful of other dragonmounts lay basking in the midday sun, not far from the durasteel barnacle of the droid-control center. Obi-Wan rode Boga right up to the control center's open archway, then jumped down from the saddle.

The archway led into a towering vaulted hall, its durasteel decking bare of furnishing. Deep within the shadows that gathered in the hall stood a cluster of five figures. Their faces were the color of bleached bone. Or ivory armorplast.

They looked like they might, just possibly, be waiting for him.

Obi-Wan nodded to himself.

"You'd best find your way home, girl," he said, patting Boga's scaled neck. "One way or another, I doubt I'll have further need of your assistance."

Boga gave a soft, almost regretful honk of acknowledgment, then bent a sharper curve into her long flexible neck to place her beak gently against Obi-Wan's chest.

"It's all right, Boga. I thank you for your help, but to stay here will be dangerous. This area is about to become a free-fire zone. Please. Go home."

The dragonmount honked again and moved back, and Obi-Wan stepped from the sun into the shadow.

A wave-front of cool passed over him with the shade's embrace. He walked without haste, without urgency. The Force layered connections upon connections, and brought them all to life within him: the chill deck plates beneath his boots, and the stone beneath those, and far below that the smooth lightless currents of the world-ocean. He became the turbulent swirl of wind whistling through the towering vaulted hall; he became the sunlight outside and the shadow within. His human heart in its cage of bone echoed the beat of an alien one in a casket of armorplast, and his mind whirred with the electronic signal cascades that passed for thought in Jedi-killer droids.

And when the Force layered into his consciousness the awareness of the structure of the great hall itself, he became aware, without surprise and without distress, that the entire expanse of vaulted ceiling above his head was actually a storage hive.

Filled with combat droids.

Which made him also aware, again without surprise and without distress, that he would very likely die here.

Contemplation of death brought only one slight sting of regret, and more than a bit of puzzlement. Until this very moment, he had never realized he'd always expected, for no discernible reason—

That when he died, Anakin would be with him.

How curious, he thought, and then he turned his mind to business.

Anakin had a feeling Master Windu was going to be disappointed.

Palpatine had hardly reacted at all.

The Supreme Chancellor of the Republic sat at the small desk in his private office, staring distractedly at an abstract twist of neuranium that Anakin had always assumed was supposed to be some kind of sculpture, and merely sighed, as though he had matters of much greater importance on his mind.

"I'm sorry, sir," Anakin said, shifting his weight in front of Palpatine's desk. "Perhaps you didn't hear me. Obi-Wan has made contact with General Grievous. His attack is already under way—they're fighting *right now*, sir!"

"Yes, yes, of course, Anakin. Yes, quite." Palpatine still looked as if he was barely paying attention. "I entirely understand your concern for your friend. Let us hope he is up to the task."

"It's not just concern for Obi-Wan, sir; taking General Grievous will be the final victory for the Republic—!"

"Will it?" He turned to Anakin, and a distinctly troubled frown chased the distraction from his face. "I'm afraid, my boy, that our situation is a great deal more grave than even I had feared. Perhaps you should sit down."

Anakin didn't move. "What do you mean?"

"Grievous is no longer the real enemy. Even the Clone Wars themselves are now only . . . a distraction."

"What?"

"The Council is about to make its move," Palpatine said, grim and certain. "If we don't stop them, by this time tomorrow the Jedi may very well have taken over the Republic."

Anakin burst into astonished laughter. "But sir—please, you can't possibly *believe* that—"

"Anakin, I *know*. I will be the first to be arrested—the first to be *executed*—but I will be far from the last."

Anakin could only shake his head in disbelief. "Sir, I know that the Council and you have . . . disagreements, but—"

"This is far beyond any personal dispute between me and the members of the Council. This is a plot *generations* in the making—a plot to take over the Republic itself. Anakin, *think*—you know they don't trust you. They never have. You know they have been keeping things from you. You know they have made plans behind your back—you know that even your great friend *Obi-Wan* has not told you what their true intentions are . . . It's because you're not *like* them, Anakin—you're a *man*, not just a Jedi."

Anakin's head drew down toward his shoulders as though he found himself under enemy fire. "I don't—they wouldn't—"

"Ask yourself: why did they send you to me with this news? *Why?* Why not simply notify me through normal channels?"

And take careful note of his reaction. We will need a full account

"Sir, I—ah—"

"No need to fumble for an explanation," he said gently. "You've already as much as admitted they've ordered you to spy upon me. Don't you understand that anything you tell them tonight—whatever it may be—will be used as an excuse to order my execution?"

"That's impossible—" Anakin sought desperately for an argument. "The Senate—the Senate would never allow it—"

"The Senate will be powerless to stop it. I told you this is bigger than any personal dislike between the Council and myself. I am only one man, Anakin. My authority is granted by the Senate; it is the Senate that is the true government of the Republic. Killing me is nothing; to control the Republic, the Jedi will have to take over the Senate *first*."

"But the Jedi—the Jedi *serve* the Senate—!"

"Do they?" Palpatine asked mildly. "Or do they serve certain *Senators*?"

"This is all—I'm sorry, Chancellor, please, you have to understand how this *sounds* . . ."

"Here—" The Chancellor rummaged around within his desk

for a moment, then brought forth a document reader. "Do you know what this is?"

Anakin recognized the seal Padmé had placed on it. "Yes, sir—that's the Petition of the Two Thousand—"

"*No*, Anakin! No!" Palpatine slammed the document reader on his desktop hard enough to make Anakin jump. "It is a roll of *traitors*."

Anakin went absolutely still. "What?"

"There are, now, only two kinds of Senators in our government, Anakin. Those whose names are on this so-called *petition*," Palpatine said, "and those whom the Jedi are about to *arrest*."

Anakin could only stare.

He couldn't argue. He couldn't even make himself disbelieve.

He had only one thought.

Padmé . . . ?

How much trouble was she in?

"Didn't I *warn* you, Anakin? Didn't I tell you what Obi-Wan was up to? Why do you think he was meeting with the leaders of this . . . delegation . . . behind your *back*?"

"But—but, sir, please, surely, all they asked for is an end to the war. It's what the Jedi want, too. I mean, it's what we *all* want, isn't it? Isn't it?"

"Perhaps. Though *how* that end comes about may be the single most important thing about the war. More important, even, than who wins."

Oh, Padmé, Anakin moaned inside his head. *Padmé, what have you gotten yourself into?*

"Their . . . sincerity . . . may be much to be admired," Palpatine said. "Or it would be, were it not that there was much more to that meeting than met the eye."

Anakin frowned. "What do you mean?"

"Their . . . petition . . . was nothing of the sort. It was, in fact, a not-so-veiled *threat*." Palpatine sighed regretfully. "It was a show of force, Anakin. A demonstration of the political power the Jedi will be able to muster in support of their rebellion."

Anakin blinked. "But—but surely—" he stammered, rounding Palpatine's desk, "surely Senator *Amidala,* at least, can be trusted . . ."

"I understand how badly you need to believe that," the Chancellor said. "But Senator Amidala is hiding something. Surely you sensed it."

"If she is—" Anakin swayed; the floor seemed to be tilting under his feet like the deck of *Invisible Hand.* "Even if she *is*," he said, his voice flat, overcontrolled, "it doesn't mean that what she is hiding is treason."

Palpatine's brows drew together. "I'm surprised your Jedi insights are not more sensitive to such things."

"I simply don't sense betrayal in Senator Amidala," Anakin insisted.

Palpatine leaned back in his chair, steepling his fingers, studying Anakin skeptically. "Yes, you do," he said after a moment. "Though you don't want to admit it. Perhaps it is because neither you nor she yet understands that by betraying me, she is also betraying *you*."

"She couldn't—" Anakin pressed a hand to his forehead; his dizziness was getting worse. When had he last eaten? He couldn't remember. It might have been before the last time he'd slept. "She could *never* . . ."

"Of course she could," Palpatine said. "That is the nature of politics, my boy. Don't take it too personally. It doesn't mean the two of you can't be happy together."

"What—?" The room seemed to darken around him. "What do you mean?"

"Please, Anakin. Are we not past the point of playing childish games with one another? I *know,* do you understand? I have *always* known. I have pretended ignorance only to spare you discomfort."

Anakin had to lean on the desk. "What—what do you know?"

"Anakin, Padmé was my Queen; I was her ambassador to the Senate. Naboo is my *home*. You of all people know how I value loyalty and friendship; do you think I have no friends among the civil clergy in Theed? Your secret ceremony has never *been* secret. Not from me, at any rate. I have always been very happy for you both."

"You—" Words whirled through Anakin's mind, and none of them made sense. "But if she's going to *betray* us—"

"*That,* my boy," Palpatine said, "is entirely up to *you*."

The fog inside Anakin's head seemed to solidify into a long, dark tunnel. The point of light at the end was Palpatine's face. "I don't—I don't understand . . ."

"Oh yes, that's very clear." The Chancellor's voice seemed to be coming from very far away. "Please sit, my boy. You're looking rather unwell. May I offer you something to drink?"

"I—no. No, I'm all right." Anakin sank gratefully into a dangerously comfortable chair. "I'm just—a little tired, that's all."

"Not sleeping well?"

"No." Anakin offered an exhausted chuckle. "I haven't been sleeping well for a few years, now."

"I quite understand, my boy. Quite." Palpatine rose and rounded his desk, sitting casually on its front edge. "Anakin, we must stop pretending. The final crisis is approaching, and our only hope to survive it is to be completely, absolutely, ruthlessly honest with each other. And with ourselves. You must understand that what is at stake here is nothing less than the fate of the galaxy."

"I don't know—"

"Don't be afraid, Anakin. What is said between us here need never pass beyond these walls. Anakin, *think:* think how hard it has been to hold all your secrets inside. Have you ever needed to keep a secret from *me*?"

He ticked his fingers one by one. "I have kept the secret of your marriage all these years. The slaughter at the Tusken camp, you shared with me. I was there when you executed Count Dooku. And I know where you got the power to defeat him. You see? You have never needed to *pretend* with me, the way you must with your Jedi comrades. Do you understand that you need never hide *anything* from me? That I accept you exactly as you are?"

He spread his hands as though offering a hug. "Share with me the truth. Your absolute truth. Let yourself *out*, Anakin."

"I—" Anakin shook his head. How many times had he dreamed of not having to pretend to be the perfect Jedi? But what else could he be? "I wouldn't even know how to begin."

"It's quite simple, in the end: tell me what you want."

Anakin squinted up at him. "I don't understand."

"Of course you don't." The last of the sunset haloed his ice-white hair and threw his face into shadow. "You've been trained to never think about that. The Jedi never ask what *you* want. They simply *tell* you what you're *supposed* to want. They never give you a choice at all. That's why they take their students—their *victims*—at an age so young that choice is meaningless. By the time a Padawan is old enough to *choose*, he has been so indoctrinated—so *brainwashed*—that he is incapable of even considering the question. But you're different, Anakin. You had a real life, outside the Jedi Temple. You can break through the fog of lies the Jedi have pumped into your brain. I ask you again: what do you want?"

"I still don't understand."

"I am offering you . . . anything," Palpatine said. "Ask, and it is yours. A glass of water? It's yours. A bag full of Corusca gems? Yours. Look out the window behind me, Anakin. Pick something, and it's yours."

"Is this some kind of joke?"

"The time for jokes is past, Anakin. I have never been more serious." Within the shadow that cloaked Palpatine's face, Anakin could only just see the twin gleams of the Chancellor's eyes. "Pick something. Anything."

"All right . . ." Shrugging, frowning, still not understanding, Anakin looked out the window, looking for the most ridiculously expensive thing he could spot. "How about one of those new SoroSuub custom speeders—"

"Done."

"Are you serious? You know how much one of those costs? You could practically outfit a *battle* cruiser—"

"Would you prefer a battle cruiser?"

Anakin went still. A cold void opened in his chest. In a small, cautious voice, he said, "How about the Senatorial Apartments?"

"A private apartment?"

Anakin shook his head, staring up at the twin gleams in the darkness on Palpatine's face. "The whole building."

Palpatine did not so much as blink. "Done."

"It's privately owned—"

"Not anymore."

"You can't just—"

"Yes, I can. It's yours. Is there anything else? Name it."

Anakin gazed blankly out into the gathering darkness. Stars began to shimmer through the haze of twilight. A constellation he recognized hung above the spires of the Jedi Temple.

"All right," Anakin said softly. "Corellia. I'll take Corellia."

"The planet, or the whole system?"

Anakin stared.

"Anakin?"

"I just—" He shook his head blankly. "I can't figure out if you're kidding, or completely insane."

"I am neither, Anakin. I am trying to impress upon you a fundamental truth of our relationship. A fundamental truth of *yourself*."

"What if I really *wanted* the Corellian system? The whole Five Brothers—*all* of it?"

"Then it would be yours. You can have the whole sector, if you like." The twin gleams within the shadow sharpened. "Do you understand, now? I will give you *anything you want.*"

The concept left him dizzy. "What if I wanted—what if I went along with Padmé and her friends? What if I want the *war* to *end*?"

"Would tomorrow be too soon?"

"How—" Anakin couldn't seem to get his breath. "How can you do that?"

"Right now, we are only discussing *what*. *How* is a different issue; we'll come to that presently."

Anakin sank deeper into the chair while he let everything sink deeper into his brain. If only his head would stop spinning—why did Palpatine have to start all this *now*?

This would all be easier to comprehend if the nightmares of Padmé didn't keep screaming inside his head.

"And in exchange?" he asked, finally. "What do *I* have to do?"

"You have to do what you *want*."

"What I want?"

"Yes, Anakin. Yes. Exactly that. Only that. Do the one thing that the Jedi fear most: make up your *own* mind. Follow your own *conscience*. Do what *you* think is right. I know that you have been longing for a life greater than that of an ordinary Jedi. *Commit* to that life. I know you burn for greater power than any Jedi can wield; give yourself *permission* to *gain* that power, and allow yourself license to *use* it. You have dreamed of leaving the Jedi Order, having a family of your own—one that is based on *love*, not on enforced rules of self-denial."

"I—can't . . . I can't just . . . *leave* . . ."

"But you can."

Anakin couldn't breathe.

He couldn't blink.

He sat frozen. Even thought was impossible.

"You can have every one of your dreams. Turn aside from the lies of the Jedi, and follow the truth of yourself. Leave them. Join me on the path of true power. Be my friend, Anakin. Be my student. My apprentice."

Anakin's vision tunneled again, but this time there was no light at the far end. He pulled back his hand, and it was shaking as he brought it up to support his face.

"I'm sorry," he said. "I'm sorry, but—but as much as I want those things—as much as I care for you, sir—I can't. I just can't. Not yet. Because there's only one thing I *really* want, right now. Everything else will just have to wait."

"I know what you truly want," the shadow said. "I have only been waiting for you to admit it to yourself." A hand—a human hand, warm with compassion—settled onto his shoulder. "Listen to me: *I can help you save her.*"

"You—"

Anakin blinked blindly.

"How can *you* help?"

"Do you remember that myth I told you of, *The Tragedy of Darth Plagueis the Wise?*" the shadow whispered.

The myth—

. . . directly influence the midi-chlorians to create life; with such knowledge, to maintain life in someone already living would seem a small matter . . .

"Yes," Anakin said. "Yes, I remember."

The shadow leaned so close that it seemed to fill the world.

"Anakin, it's no mere myth."

Anakin swallowed.

"Darth Plagueis was real."

Anakin could force out only a strangled whisper. "*Real . . . ?*"

"Darth Plagueis was my Master. He taught me the key to his power," the shadow said, dryly matter-of-fact, "before I killed him."

Without understanding how he had moved, without even intending to move, without any transition of realization or dawning understanding, Anakin found himself on his feet. A blue bar of sizzling energy terminated a centimeter from Palpatine's chin, its glow casting red-edged shadows up his face and across the ceiling.

Only gradually did Anakin come to understand that this was his lightsaber, and that it was in his hand.

"You," he said. Suddenly he was neither dizzy nor tired.

Suddenly everything made sense.

"It's *you*. It's *been* you all *along*!"

In the clean blue light of his blade he stared into the face of a man whose features were as familiar to him as his own, but now seemed as alien as an extragalactic comet—because now he finally understood that those familiar features were only a mask.

He had never seen this man's real face.

"I should *kill* you," he said. "I *will* kill you!"

Palpatine gave him that wise, kindly-uncle smile Anakin had been seeing since the age of nine. "For what?"

"You're a *Sith Lord*!"

"I am," he said simply. "I am also your friend."

The blue bar of energy wavered, just a bit.

"I am also the man who has always been here for you. I am the man you have never needed to lie to. I am the man who wants nothing from you but that you follow your conscience. If that conscience requires you to commit murder, simply over a . . . philosophical difference . . . I will not resist."

His hands opened, still at his sides. "Anakin, when I told you that you can have anything you want, did you think I was excluding my life?"

The floor seemed to soften beneath Anakin's feet, and the room started to swirl darkness and ooze confusion. "You—you won't even *fight*—?"

"Fight you?" In the blue glow that cast shadows up from Palpatine's chin, the Chancellor looked astonished that he would suggest such a thing. "But what will happen when you kill me? What will happen to the Republic?" His tone was gently reasonable. "What will happen to Padmé?"

"*Padmé . . .*"

Her name was a gasp of anguish.

"When I die," Palpatine said with the air of a man reminding a child of something he ought to already know, "my knowledge dies with me."

The sizzling blade trembled.

"Unless, that is, I have the opportunity to teach it . . . to my apprentice . . ."

His vision swam.

"I . . ." A whisper of naked pain, and despair. "I don't know what to *do . . .*"

Palpatine gazed upon him, loving and gentle as he had ever been, though only a whisker shy of a lightsaber's terminal curve.

And what if this face was *not* a mask? What if the true face of the Sith was exactly what he saw before him: a man who had cared for him, had helped him, had been his loyal friend when he'd thought he had no other?

What *then*?

"Anakin," Palpatine said kindly, "let's talk."

The four bodyguard droids spread out in a shallow arc between Obi-Wan and Grievous, raising their electrostaffs. Obi-Wan stopped a respectful distance away; he still carried bruises from one of those electrostaffs, and he felt no particular urge to add to his collection.

"General Grievous," he said, "you're under arrest."

The bio-droid general stalked toward him, passing through his screen of bodyguards without the slightest hint of reluctance. "Kenobi. Don't tell me, let me guess: this is the part where you give me the chance to surrender."

"It can be," Obi-Wan allowed equably. "Or, if you like, it can be the part where I dismantle your exoskeleton and ship you back to Coruscant in a cargo hopper."

"I'll take option three." Grievous lifted his hand, and the bodyguards moved to box Obi-Wan between them. "That's the one where I watch you die."

Another gesture, and the droids in the ceiling hive came to life.

They uncoiled from their sockets heads-downward, with a rising chorus of whirring and buzzing and clicking that thickened until Obi-Wan might as well have stumbled into a colony of Corellian raptor-wasps. They began to drop free of the ceiling, first only a few, then many, like the opening drops of a summer cloudburst; finally they fell in a downpour that shook the stone-mounted durasteel of the deck and left Obi-Wan's ears ringing. Hundreds of them landed and rolled to standing; as many more stayed attached to the overhead hive, hanging upside down by their magnapeds, weapons trained so that Obi-Wan now stood at the focus of a dome of blasters.

Through it all, Obi-Wan never moved.

"I'm sorry, was I not clear?" he said. "There is no *option three*."

Grievous shook his head. "Do you never tire of this pathetic banter?"

"I rarely tire at all," Obi-Wan said mildly, "and I have no better way to pass the time while I wait for you to either decide to surrender, or choose to die."

"That choice was made long before I ever met *you*." Grievous turned away. "Kill him."

Instantly the box of bodyguards around Obi-Wan filled with crackling electrostaffs whipping faster than the human eye could see—which was less troublesome than it might have been, for that box was already empty of Jedi.

The Force had let him collapse as though he'd suddenly fainted, then it brought his lightsaber from his belt to his hand and ignited it while he turned his fall into a roll; that roll carried his lightsaber through a crisp arc that severed the leg of one of the bodyguards, and as the Force brought Obi-Wan back to his feet, the Force also nudged the crippled bodyguard to topple sideways into the path of the blade and sent it clanging to the floor in two smoking, sparking pieces.

One down.

The remaining three pressed the attack, but more cautiously; their weapons were longer than his, and they struck from beyond the reach of his blade. He gave way before them, his defensive velocities barely keeping their crackling discharge blades at bay.

Three MagnaGuards, each with a double-ended weapon that generated an energy field impervious to lightsabers, each with reflexes that operated near lightspeed, each with hypersophisticated heuristic combat algorithms that enabled it to learn from experience and adapt its tactics instantly to any situation, were certainly beyond Obi-Wan's ability to defeat, but it was not Obi-Wan who would defeat them; Obi-Wan wasn't even fighting. He was only a vessel, emptied of self. The Force, shaped by his skill and guided by his clarity of mind, fought through him.

In the Force, he felt their destruction: it was somewhere above and behind him, and only seconds away.

He went to meet it with a backflipping leap that the Force used to lift him neatly to an empty droid socket in the ceiling hive. The MagnaGuards sprang after him but he was gone by the time they arrived, leaping higher into the maze of girders and cables and room-sized cargo containers that was the control center's superstructure.

Here, said the Force within him, and Obi-Wan stopped, balancing on a girder, frowning back at the oncoming killer droids that leapt from beam to beam below him like malevolent durasteel primates. Though he could feel its close approach, he had no idea from where their destruction might come . . . until the Force showed him a support beam within reach of his blade and whispered, *Now.*

His blade flicked out and the durasteel beam parted, fresh-cut edges glowing white hot, and a great hulk of ship-sized cargo container that the beam had been supporting tore free of its other supports with shrieks of anguished metal and crashed down upon all three MagnaGuards with the finality of a meteor strike.

Two, three, and four.

Oh, thought Obi-Wan with detached approval. *That worked out rather well.*

Only ten thousand to go. Give or take.

An instant later the Force had him hurtling through a storm of blasterfire as every combat droid in the control center opened up on him at once.

Letting go of intention, letting go of desire, letting go of life, Obi-Wan fixed his entire attention on a thread of the Force that pulled him toward Grievous: not where Grievous was, but where Grievous would be when Obi-Wan got there . . .

Leaping girder to girder, slashing cables on which to swing through swarms of ricocheting particle beams, blade flickering so fast it became a deflector shield that splattered blaster bolts in all directions, his presence alone became a weapon: as he spun and whirled through the control center's superstructure, the blasts of particle cannons from power droids destroyed equipment and shattered girders and unleashed a torrent of red-hot debris that crashed to the deck, crushing droids on all sides. By the time he flipped down through the air to land catfooted on the deck once more, nearly half the droids between him and Grievous had been destroyed by their own not-so-friendly fire.

He cut his way into the mob of remaining troops as smoothly as if it were no more than a canebrake near some sunlit beach; his steady pace left behind a trail of smoking slices of droid.

"Keep *firing*!" Grievous roared to the spider droids that flanked him. *"Blast him!"*

Obi-Wan felt the massive shoulder cannon of a spider droid track him, and he felt it fire a bolt as powerful as a proton grenade, and he let the Force nudge him into a leap that carried him just far enough toward the fringe of the bolt's blast radius so that instead of shattering his bones it merely gave him a very strong, very hot *push*—

—that sent him whirling over the rest of the droids to land directly in front of Grievous.

A single slash of his lightsaber amputated the shoulder cannon of one power droid and continued into a spinning Force-assisted kick that brought his boot heel to the point of the other power droid's duranium chin, snapping the droid's head back hard enough to sever its cervical sensor cables. Blind and deaf, the power droid could only continue to obey its last order; it staggered in a wild circle, its convulsively firing cannon blasting random holes in droids and walls alike, until Obi-Wan deactivated it with a precise thrust that burned a thumb-sized hole through its thoracic braincase.

"General," Obi-Wan said with a blandly polite smile as though unexpectedly greeting, on the street, someone he privately disliked. "My offer is still open."

Droid guns throughout the control center fell silent; Obi-Wan stood so close to Grievous that the general was in the line of fire.

Grievous threw back his cloak imperiously. "Do you believe that I would surrender to you *now*?"

"I am still willing to take you alive." Obi-Wan's nod took in the smoking, sparking wreckage that filled the control center. "So far, no one has been hurt."

Grievous tilted his head so that he could squint down into Obi-Wan's face. "I have *thousands* of troops. You cannot defeat them all."

"I don't have to."

"This is *your* chance to surrender, General Kenobi." Grievous swept a duranium hand toward the sinkhole-city behind him. "Pau City is in my grip; lay down your blade, or I will *squeeze* . . . until this entire sinkhole brims over with innocent blood."

"That's not what it's about to brim with," Obi-Wan said. "You should pay more attention to the weather."

Yellow eyes narrowed behind a mask of armorplast. "What?"

"Have a look outside." He pointed his lightsaber toward the archway. "It's about to start raining clones."

Grievous said again, turning to look, "What?"

A shadow had passed over the sun as though one of the towering thunderheads on the horizon had caught a stray current in the hyperwinds and settled above Pau City. But it wasn't a cloud.

It was the *Vigilance.*

While twilight enfolded the sinkhole, over the bright desert above assault craft skimmed the dunes in a tightening ring centered on the city. Hailfire droids rolled out from caves in the wind-scoured mesas, unleashing firestorms of missiles toward the oncoming craft for exactly 2.5 seconds apiece, which was how long it took for the *Vigilance*'s sensor operators to transfer data to its turbolaser batteries.

Thunderbolts roared down through the atmosphere, and hailfire droids disintegrated. Pinpoint counterfire from the bubble turrets of LAAT/i's met missiles in blossoming fireballs that were ripped to shreds of smoke as the oncoming craft blasted through them.

LAAT/i's streaked over the rim of the sinkhole and spiraled

downward with all guns blazing, crabbing outward to keep their forward batteries raking on the sinkhole's wall, while at the rim above, *Jadthu*-class armored landers hovered with bay doors wide, trailing sprays of polyplast cables like immense ice-white tassels that looped all the way to the ocean mouths that gaped at the lowest level of the city. Down those tassels, rappelling so fast they seemed to be simply falling, came endless streams of armored troopers, already firing on the combat droids that marched out to meet them.

Streamers of cables brushed the outer balcony of the control center, and down them slid white-armored troopers, each with one hand on his mechanized line-brake and the other full of DC-15 blaster rifle on full auto, spraying continuous chains of packeted particle beams. Droids wheeled and dropped and leapt into the air and burst to fragments. Surviving droids opened up on the clones as though grateful for something to shoot at, blasting holes in armor, cooking flesh with superheated steam from deep-tissue hits, blowing some troopers entirely off their cables to tumble toward a messy final landing ten levels below.

When the survivors of the first wave of clones hit the deck, the next wave was right behind them.

Grievous turned back to Obi-Wan. He lowered his head like an angry bantha, yellow glare fixed on the Jedi Master. "To the death, then."

Obi-Wan sighed. "If you insist."

The bio-droid general cast back his cloak, revealing the four lightsabers pocketed there. He stepped back, spreading wide his duranium arms. "You will not be the first Jedi I have killed, nor will you be the last."

Obi-Wan's only reply was to subtly shift the angle of his lightsaber up and forward.

The general's wide-spread arms now *split* along their lengths, dividing in half—even his *hands* split in half—

Now he had *four* arms. And four hands.

And each hand took a lightsaber as his cloak dropped to the floor.

They snarled to life and Grievous spun all four of them in a flourishing velocity so fast and so seamlessly integrated that he seemed to stand within a pulsing sphere of blue and green energy.

"Come on, then, Kenobi! Come for me!" he said. "I have been trained in your Jedi arts by Lord Tyranus himself!"

"Do you mean Count Dooku? What a curious coincidence," Obi-Wan said with a deceptively pleasant smile. "I trained the man who killed him."

With a convulsive snarl, Grievous lunged.

The sphere of blue lightsaber energy around him bulged toward Obi-Wan and opened like a mouth to bite him in half. Obi-Wan stood his ground, his blade still.

Chain-lightning teeth closed upon him.

This is how it feels to be Anakin Skywalker, right now:

You don't remember putting away your lightsaber.

You don't remember moving from Palpatine's private office to his larger public one; you don't remember collapsing in the chair where you now sit, nor do you remember drinking water from the half-empty glass that you find in your mechanical hand.

You remember only that the last man in the galaxy you still thought you could trust has been lying to you since the day you met.

And you're not even angry about it.

Only stunned.

"After all, Anakin, you are the last man who has a right to be angry at someone for keeping a secret. What else was I to do?"

Palpatine sits in his familiar tall oval chair behind his familiar desk; the lampdisks are full on, the office eerily bright.

Ordinary.

As though this is merely another one of your friendly conversations, the casual evening chats you've enjoyed together for so many years.

As though nothing has happened.

As though nothing has changed.

"Corruption had made the Republic a cancer in the body of the galaxy, and no one could burn it out; not the judicials, not the Senate, not even the Jedi Order itself. I was the only man strong and skilled enough for this task; I was the only man who dared even *attempt* it. Without my small deception, how should I have cured the Republic? Had I revealed myself to you, or to anyone else, the Jedi would have hunted me down and murdered me without trial—very much as you nearly did, only a moment ago."

You can't argue. Words are beyond you.

He rises, moving around his desk, taking one of the small chairs and drawing it close to yours.

"If only you could know how I have longed to tell you, Anakin. All these years—since the very day we met, my boy. I have watched over you, waiting as you grew in strength and wisdom, biding my time until now, today, when you are finally ready to understand who you truly are, and your true place in the history of the galaxy."

Numb words blur from your numb lips. "The chosen one . . ."

"Exactly, my boy. *Exactly.* You *are* the chosen one." He leans toward you, eyes clear. Steady. Utterly honest. "Chosen by *me.*"

He turns a hand toward the panorama of light-sprayed cityscape through the window behind his desk. "Look out there, Anakin. A trillion beings on this planet alone—in the galaxy as a whole, uncounted quadrillions—and of them all, I have chosen *you*, Anakin Skywalker, to be the heir to my power. To all that I am."

"But that's not . . . that's not the prophecy. That's not the prophecy of the chosen one . . ."

"Is this such a problem for you? Is not your quest to find a way to *overturn* prophecy?" Palpatine leaned close, smiling, warm and kindly. "Anakin, do you think the Sith did not know of this prophecy? Do you think we would simply sleep while it came to *pass*?"

"You mean—"

"This is what you must understand. This Jedi submission to fate . . . this is not the way of the Sith, Anakin. This is not my way. This is not your way. It has never been. It need never be."

You're drowning.

"I am not . . . ," you hear yourself say, ". . . on your side. I am not *evil*."

"Who said anything about evil? I am bringing peace to the galaxy. Is that evil? I am offering you the power to save Padmé. Is that evil? Have I attacked you? Drugged you? Are you being tortured? My boy, I am *asking* you. I am asking you to *do the right thing*. Turn your back on treason. On all those who would harm the Republic. I'm asking you to do exactly what you have sworn to do: bring peace and justice to the galaxy. And save Padmé, of course—haven't you sworn to protect *her*, too . . . ?"

"I—but—I—" Words will not fit themselves into the answers you need. If only Obi-Wan were here—Obi-Wan would know what to say. What to do.

Obi-Wan could handle this.

Rght now, you know you can't.

"I—I'll turn you over to the Jedi Council—*they'll* know what to do—"

"I'm sure they will. They are already planning to overthrow the Republic; you'll give them exactly the excuse they're looking for. And when they come to execute me, will that be justice? Will they be bringing *peace*?"

"They won't—they *wouldn't*—!"

"Well, of course I hope you're correct, Anakin. You'll forgive me if I don't share your blind loyalty to your comrades. I suppose it does indeed come down, in the end, to a question of loyalty," he said thoughtfully. "That's what you must ask yourself, my boy. Whether your loyalty is to the Jedi, or to the Republic."

"It's not—it's not *like* that—"

Palpatine lifted his shoulders. "Perhaps not. Perhaps it's simply a question of whether you love Obi-Wan Kenobi more than you love your wife."

There is no more searching for words.

There are no longer words at all.

"Take your time. Meditate on it. I will still be here when you decide."

Inside your head, there is only fire. Around your heart, the dragon whispers that all things die.

This is how it feels to be Anakin Skywalker, right now.

There is an understated elegance in Obi-Wan Kenobi's lightsaber technique, one that is quite unlike the feel one might get from the other great swordsbeings of the Jedi Order. He lacks entirely the flash, the pure bold *élan* of an Anakin Skywalker; there is nowhere in him the penumbral ferocity of a Mace Windu or a Depa Billaba nor the stylish grace of a Shaak Ti or a Dooku, and he is nothing resembling the whirlwind of destruction that Yoda can become.

He is simplicity itself.

That is his power.

Before Obi-Wan had left Coruscant, Mace Windu had told him of facing Grievous in single combat atop a mag-lev train during the general's daring raid to capture Palpatine. Mace had told him how the computers slaved to Grievous's brain had apparently analyzed even Mace's unconventionally lethal Vaapad and had been able to respond in kind after a single exchange.

"He must have been trained by Count Dooku," Mace had said, "so you can expect Makashi as well; given the number of Jedi he has fought and slain, you must expect that he can attack in any style, or all of them. In fact, Obi-Wan, I believe that of all living Jedi, you have the best chance to defeat him."

This pronouncement had startled Obi-Wan, and he had protested. After all, the only form in which he was truly even proficient was Soresu, which was the most common lightsaber form in the Jedi Order. Founded upon the basic deflection principles all Padawans were taught—to enable them to protect themselves from blaster bolts—Soresu was very simple, and so restrained and defense-oriented that it was very nearly downright passive.

"But surely, Master Windu," Obi-Wan had said, "you, with the power of Vaapad—or Yoda's mastery of Ataro—"

Mace Windu had almost smiled. "I created Vaapad to answer my weakness: it channels my own darkness into a weapon of the light. Master Yoda's Ataro is also an answer to weakness: the limitations of reach and mobility imposed by his stature and his age. But for you? What weakness does Soresu answer?"

Blinking, Obi-Wan had been forced to admit he'd never actually thought of it that way.

"That is so like you, Master Kenobi," the Korun Master had said, shaking his head. "I am called a great swordsman because I invented a lethal style; but who is greater, the creator of a killing form—or the master of the classic form?"

"I'm very flattered that you would consider me a master, but really—"

"Not a master. *The* master," Mace had said. "Be who you are, and Grievous will never defeat you."

So now, facing the tornado of annihilating energy that is Grievous's attack, Obi-Wan simply is who he is.

The electrodrivers powering Grievous's mechanical arms let each of the four attack thrice in a single second; integrated by combat algorithms in the bio-droid's electronic network of peripheral processors, each of the twelve strikes per second came from a different angle with different speed and intensity, an unpredictably broken rhythm of slashes, chops, and stabs of which every single one could take Obi-Wan's life.

Not one touched him.

After all, he had often walked unscathed through hornet-swarms of blasterfire, defended only by the Force's direction of his blade; countering twelve blows per second was only difficult, not impossible. His blade wove an intricate web of angles and curves, never truly fast but always just fast enough, each motion of his lightsaber subtly interfering with three or four or eight of the general's strikes, the rest sizzling past him, his precise, minimal shifts of weight and stance slipping them by centimeters.

Grievous, snarling fury, ramped up the intensity and velocity of his attacks—sixteen per second, eighteen—until finally, at twenty strikes per second, he overloaded Obi-Wan's defense.

So Obi-Wan used his defense to attack.

A subtle shift in the angle of a single parry brought Obi-Wan's blade in contact not with the blade of the oncoming lightsaber, but with the handgrip.

—*slice*—

The blade winked out of existence a hairbreadth before it would have burned through Obi-Wan's forehead. Half the severed lightsaber skittered away, along with the duranium thumb and first finger of the hand that had held it.

Grievous paused, eyes pulsing wide, then drawing narrow. He lifted his maimed hand and stared at the white-hot stumps that held now only half a useless lightsaber.

Obi-Wan smiled at him.

Grievous lunged.

Obi-Wan parried.

Pieces of lightsabers bounced on the durasteel deck.

Grievous looked down at the blade-sliced hunks of metal that were all he had left in his hands, then up at Obi-Wan's shining sky-colored blade, then down at his hands again, and then he seemed to suddenly remember that he had an urgent appointment somewhere else.

Anywhere else.

Obi-Wan stepped toward him, but a shock from the Force made him leap back just as a scarlet HE bolt struck the floor right where he'd been about to place his foot. Obi-Wan rode the explosion, flipping in the air to land upright between a pair of super battle droids that were busily firing upon the flank of a squad of clone troopers, which they continued to do until they found themselves falling in pieces to the deck.

Obi-Wan spun.

In the chaos of exploding droids and dying men, Grievous was nowhere to be seen.

Obi-Wan waved his lightsaber at the clones. "The general!" he shouted. "Which way?"

One trooper circled his arm as though throwing a proton grenade back toward the archway where Obi-Wan had first entered. He followed the gesture and saw, for an instant in the sunshadow of the *Vigilance* outside, the back curves of twin bladed rings—ganged together to make a wheel the size of a starfighter—rolling swiftly off along the sinkhole rim.

General Grievous was very good at running away.

"Not this time," Obi-Wan muttered, and cut a path through

the tangled mob of droids all the way to the arch in a single sustained surge, reaching the open air just in time to see the blade-wheeler turn; it was an open ring with a pilot's chair inside, and in the pilot's chair sat Grievous, who lifted one of his bodyguards' electrostaffs in a sardonic wave as he took the scooter straight out over the edge. Four claw-footed arms deployed, digging into the rock to carry him down the side of the sinkhole, angling away at a steep slant.

"Blast." Obi-Wan looked around. Still no air taxis. Not that he had any real interest in flying through the storm of battle that raged throughout the interior of the sinkhole, but there was certainly no way he could catch Grievous on foot . . .

From around the corner of an interior tunnel, he heard a resonant *honnnnk!* as though a nearby bantha had swallowed an air horn.

He said, "Boga?"

The beaked face of the dragonmount slowly extended around the interior angle of the tunnel.

"Boga! Come here, girl! We have a general to catch."

Boga fixed him with a reproachful glare. *"Honnnnnk."*

"Oh, very well." Obi-Wan rolled his eyes. "I was wrong; you were right. Can we please *go* now?"

The remaining fifteen meters of dragonmount hove into view and came trotting out to meet him. Obi-Wan sprang to the saddle, and Boga leapt to the sinkhole's rim in a single bound. Her huge head swung low, searching, until Obi-Wan spotted Grievous's blade-wheeler racing away toward the landing decks below.

"There, girl—that's him! Go!"

Boga gathered herself and sprang to the rim of the next level down, poised for an instant to get her bearings, then leapt again down into the firestorm that Pau City had become. Obi-Wan spun his blade in a continuous whirl to either side of the dragonmount's back, disintegrating shrapnel and slapping away stray blasterfire. They plummeted through the sinkhole-city, gaining tens of meters on Grievous with every leap.

On one of the landing decks, the canopy was lifting and parting to show a small, ultrafast armored shuttle of the type favored by the famously nervous Neimoidian executives of the Trade Federation. Grievous's wheeler sprayed a fan of white-hot sparks as it tore across the landing deck; the bio-droid whipped the wheeler sideways, laying it down for a skidding halt that showered the shuttle with molten durasteel.

But before he could clamber out of the pilot's chair, several metric tons of Jedi-bearing dragonmount landed on the shuttle's roof, crouched and threatening and hissing venomously down at him.

"I hope you have another vehicle, General!" Obi-Wan waved his lightsaber toward the shuttle's twin rear thrusters. "I believe there's some damage to your sublights!"

"You're insane! There's no—"

Obi-Wan shrugged. "Show him, Boga."

The dragonmount dutifully pointed out the damage with two whistling strikes of her massive tail-mace—*wham* and *wham* again—which crumpled the shuttle's thruster tubes into crimped-shut knots of metal.

Obi-Wan beckoned. "Let's settle this, shall we?"

Grievous's answer was a shriek of tortured gyros that wrenched the wheeler upright, and a metal-on-metal scream of blades ripping into deck plates that sent it shooting straight toward the sinkhole wall—and, with the claw-arms to help, straight *up* it.

Obi-Wan sighed. "Didn't we just *come* from there?"

Boga coiled herself and sprang for the wall, and the chase was on once more.

They raced through the battle, clawing up walls, shooting through tunnels, skidding and leaping, sprinting where the way was clear and screeching into high-powered serpentines where it was not, whipping around knots of droids and bounding over troopers. Boga ran straight up the side of a clone hovertank and sprang from its turret directly between the high-slanting ring-wheels of a hailfire, and a swipe of Obi-Wan's blade left the droid crippled behind them. Native troops had taken the field: Uta-paun dragonriders armed with sparking power lances charged along causeways, spearing droids on every side. Grievous ran right over anything in his path, the blades of his wheeler shred-ding droid and trooper and dragon alike; behind him, Obi-Wan's lightsaber caught and returned blaster bolts in a spray that shat-tered any droid unwise enough to fire on him. A few stray bolts he batted into the speeding wheeler ahead, but without visible effect.

"Fine," he muttered. "Let's try this from a little *closer.*"

Boga gained steadily. Grievous's vehicle had the edge in raw speed, but Boga could out-turn it and could make instant leaps at astonishing angles; the dragonmount also had an uncanny in-stinct for where the general might be heading, as well as a seem-ingly infinite knowledge of useful shortcuts through side tunnels, along sheer walls, and over chasms studded with locked-down wind turbines. Grievous tried once to block Obi-Wan's pursuit by screeching out onto a huge pod that held a whole bank of wind turbines and knocking the blade-brakes off them with quick blows of the electrostaff, letting the razor-edged blades spin freely in the constant gale, but Obi-Wan merely brought Boga alongside the turbines and stuck his lightsaber into their whirl. Sliced-free chunks of carboceramic blade shrieked through the air and shattered on the stone on all sides, and with a curse Grievous kicked his vehicle into motion again.

The wheeler roared into a tunnel that seemed to lead straight into the rock of the plateau. The tunnel was jammed with groundcars and dragonmounts and wheelers and jetsters and all manner of other vehicles and every kind of beast that might bear or draw the vast numbers of Utapauns and Utai fleeing the battle. Grievous blasted right into them, blade-wheel chewing through groundcars and splashing the tunnel walls with chunks of shredded lizard; Boga raced along the walls above the traffic, sometimes even galloping on the ceiling with claws gouging chunks from the rock.

With a burst of sustained effort that strangled her *honnnk*ing to thin gasps for air, Boga finally pulled alongside Grievous. Obi-Wan leaned forward, stretching out with his lightsaber, barely able to reach the wheeler's back curve, and carved away an arc of the wheeler's blade-tread, making the vehicle buck and skid; Grievous answered with a thrust of his electrostaff that crackled lightning against Boga's extended neck. The great beast jerked sideways, honking fearfully and whipping her head as though the burn was a biting creature she could shake off her flank.

"One more leap, Boga!" Obi-Wan shouted, pressing himself along the dragonmount's shoulder. "Bring me even with him!"

The dragonmount complied without hesitation, and when Grievous thrust again, Obi-Wan's free hand flashed out and seized the staff below its discharge blade, holding it clear of Boga's vulnerable flesh. Grievous yanked on the staff, nearly pulling Obi-Wan out of the saddle, then jabbed it back at him, discharge blade sparking in his face—

With a sigh, Obi-Wan realized he needed both hands.

He dropped his lightsaber.

As his deactivated handgrip skittered and bounced along the tunnel behind him, he reflected that it was just as well Anakin wasn't there after all; he'd have never heard the end of it.

He got his other hand on the staff just as Grievous jerked the wheeler sideways, half laying it down to angle for a small side tunnel just ahead. Obi-Wan hung on grimly. Through the Force he could feel Boga's exhaustion, the buildup of anaerobic breakdown products turning the dragonmount's mighty legs to cloth. An open archway showed daylight ahead. Boga barely made the turn, and they raced side by side along the empty darkened way, joined by the spark-spitting rod of the electrostaff.

As they cleared the archway to a small, concealed landing deck deep in a private sinkhole, Obi-Wan leapt from the saddle, yanking on the staff to swing both his boots hard into the side of Grievous's duranium skull. The wheeler's internal gyros screamed at the sudden impact and shift of balance. Their shrieks cycled up to bursts of smoke and fragments of metal as their catastrophic failure sent the wheeler tumbling in a white-hot cascade of sparks.

Dropping the staff, Obi-Wan leapt again, the Force lifting him free of the crash.

Grievous's electronic reflexes sent him out of the pilot's chair in the opposite direction.

The wheeler flipped over the edge of the landing deck and into the shadowy abyss of the sinkhole. It trailed smoke all the way down to a distant, delayed, and very final crash.

The electrostaff had rolled away, coming to rest against the landing jack of a small Techno Union starfighter that stood on the deck a few meters behind Obi-Wan. Behind Grievous, the archway back into the tunnel system was filled with a panting, exhausted, but still dangerously angry dragonmount.

Obi-Wan looked at Grievous.

Grievous looked at Obi-Wan.

There was no longer any need for words between them.

Obi-Wan simply stood, centered in the Force, waiting for Grievous to make his move.

A concealed compartment in the general's right thigh sprang open, and a mechanical arm delivered a slim hold-out blaster to his hand. He brought it up and fired so fast that his arm blurred to invisiblity.

Obi-Wan . . . reached.

The electrostaff flipped into the air between them, one discharge blade catching the bolt. The impact sent the staff whirling—

Right into Obi-Wan's hand.

There came one instant's pause, while they looked into each other's eyes and shared an intimate understanding that their relationship had reached its end.

Obi-Wan charged.

Grievous backed away, unleashing a stream of blaster bolts as fast as his half a forefinger could pull the trigger.

Obi-Wan spun the staff, catching every bolt, not even slowing down, and when he reached Grievous he slapped the blaster out of his hand with a crack of the staff that sent blue lightning scaling up the general's arm.

His following strike was a stiff stab into Grievous's jointed stomach armor that sent the general staggering back. Obi-Wan hit him again in the same place, denting the armorplast plate, cracking the joint where it met the larger, thicker plates of his chest as Grievous flailed for balance, but when he spun the staff for his next strike the general's flailing arm flailed itself against the middle of the staff and his other hand found it as well and he seized it, yanking himself upright against Obi-Wan's grip, his metal skull-face coming within a centimeter of the Jedi Master's nose.

He snarled, "Do you think I am foolish enough to arm my bodyguards with weapons that can actually *hurt* me?"

Instead of waiting for an answer he spun, heaving Obi-Wan right off the deck with effortless strength, whipping up him over his head to slam him to the deck with killing power; Obi-Wan could only let go of the staff and allow the Force to angle his fall into a stumbling roll. Grievous sprang after him, swinging the electrostaff and slamming it across Obi-Wan's flank before the Jedi Master could recover his balance. The impact sent Obi-Wan tumbling sideways and the electroburst discharge set his robe on fire. Grievous stayed right with him, attacking before Obi-Wan could even realize exactly what was happening, attacking faster than thought—

But Obi-Wan didn't need to think. The Force was with him, and he *knew*.

When Grievous spun the staff overhand, discharge blade sizzling down at Obi-Wan's head for the killing blow, Obi-Wan went to the inside.

He met Grievous chest-to-chest, his upraised hand blocking the general's wrist; Grievous snarled something incoherent and bore down on the Jedi Master's block with all his weight, driving the blade closer and closer to Obi-Wan's face—

But Obi-Wan's arm had the Force to give it strength, and the general's arm only had the innate crystalline intermolecular structure of duranium alloy.

Grievous's forearm bent like a cheap spoon.

While the general stared in disbelief at his mangled arm, Obi-Wan had been working the fingers of his free hand around the lower edge of Grievous's dented, joint-loose stomach plate.

Grievous looked down. "What?"

Obi-Wan slammed the elbow of his blocking arm into the general's clavicle while he yanked as hard as he could on the stomach plate, and it ripped free in his hand. Behind it hung a translucent sac of synthskin containing a tangle of green and gray organs.

The true body of the alien inside the droid.

Grievous howled and dropped the staff to seize Obi-Wan with his three remaining arms. He lifted the Jedi Master over his head again and hurled him tumbling over the landing deck toward the precipice above the gloom-shrouded drop. Reaching into the Force, Obi-Wan was able to connect with the stone itself as if he were anchored to it with a cable tether; instead of hurtling over the edge he slammed down onto the rock hard enough to crush all breath from his lungs.

Grievous picked up the staff again and charged.

Obi-Wan still couldn't breathe. He had no hope of rising to meet the general's attack.

All he could do was extend a hand.

As the bio-droid loomed over him, electrostaff raised for the kill, the hold-out blaster flipped from the deck into Obi-Wan's palm, and with no hesitation, no second thoughts, not even the faintest pause to savor his victory, he pulled the trigger.

The bolt ripped into the synthskin sac.

Grievous's guts exploded in a foul-smelling shower the color of a dead swamp. Energy chained up his spine and a mist of vaporized brain burst out both sides of his skull and sent his face spinning off the precipice.

The electrostaff hit the deck, followed shortly by the general's knees.

Then by what was left of his head.

Obi-Wan lay on his back, staring at the circle of cloudless sky above the sinkhole while he gasped air back into into his spasming lungs. He barely managed to roll over far enough to smother the flames on his robe, then fell back.

And simply enjoyed being alive.

Much too short a time later—long before he was actually ready to get up—a shadow fell across him, accompanied by the smell of overheated lizard and an admonitory *honnnk*.

"Yes, Boga, you're right," Obi-Wan agreed reluctantly. Slowly, painfully, he pushed himself to his feet.

He picked up the electrostaff, and paused for one last glance at the remains of the bio-droid general.

"So . . ." He summoned a condemnation among the most offensive in his vocabulary. ". . . *uncivilized*."

He triggered his comlink, and directed Cody to report to Jedi Command on Coruscant that Grievous had been destroyed.

"Will do, General," said the tiny holoscan of the clone commander. *"And congratulations. I knew you could do it."*

Apparently everyone did, Obi-Wan thought, *except Grievous, and me . . .*

"*General? We do still have a little problem out here. About ten thousand heavily armed little problems, actually.*"

"On my way. Kenobi out."

Obi-Wan sighed and clambered painfully onto the dragon-mount's saddle.

"All right, girl," he said. "Let's go win *that* battle, too."

As has been said, the textbook example of a Jedi trap is the one that was set on Utapau, for Obi-Wan Kenobi.

It worked perfectly.

The final element essential to the creation of a truly effective Jedi trap is a certain coldness of mind—a detachment, if you will, from any desire for a particular outcome.

The best way to arrange matters is to create a win–win situation.

For example, one might use as one's proxy a creature that not only is expendable, but would eventually have to be killed anyway. Thus, if one's proxy fails and is destroyed, it's no loss—in fact, the targeted Jedi has actually done one a favor, by taking care of a bit of dirty work one would otherwise have to do oneself.

And the final stroke of perfection is to organize the Jedi trap so that by walking into it at all, the Jedi has already lost.

That is to say, a Jedi trap works best when one's true goal is merely to make sure that the Jedi in question spends some hours or days off somewhere on the far side of the galaxy. So that he won't be around to interfere with one's *real* plans.

So that by the time he can return, it will be already too late.

REVELATION

Mace Windu stood in the darkened comm center of Jedi Command, facing a life-sized holoscan of Yoda, projected from a concealed Wookiee comm center in the heart of a wroshyr tree on Kashyyyk.

"Minutes ago," Mace said, "we received confirmation from Utapau: Kenobi was successful. Grievous is dead."

"Time it is to execute our plan."

"I will personally deliver the news of Grievous's death." Mace flexed his hands. "It will be up to the Chancellor to cede his emergency powers back over to the Senate."

"Forget not the existence of Sidious. Anticipate your action, he may. Masters will be necessary, if the Lord of the Sith you must face."

"I have chosen four of our best. Master Tiin, Master Kolar, and Master Fisto are all here, in the Temple. They are preparing already."

"What about Skywalker? The chosen one."

"Too much of a risk," Mace replied. "I am the fourth."

With a slow purse of the lips and an even slower nod, Yoda

said, *"On watch you have been too long, my Padawan. Rest you must."*

"I will, Master. When the Republic is safe once more." Mace straightened. "We are waiting only for your vote."

"Very well, then. Have my vote, you do. May the Force be with you."

"And with you, Master."

But he spoke to empty air; the holoscan had already flickered to nonexistence.

Mace lowered his head and stood in the darkness and the silence.

The door of the comm center shot open, spilling yellow glare into the gloom and limning the silhouette of a man half collapsed against the frame.

"Master . . ." The voice was a hoarse half whisper. "Master Windu . . . ?"

"Skywalker?" Mace was at his side in an instant. "What's wrong? Are you hurt?"

Anakin took Mace's arm in a grip of desperate strength, and used it like a crutch to haul himself upright.

"Obi-Wan . . . ," he said faintly. "I need to talk to *Obi-Wan*—!"

"Obi-Wan is operational on Utapau; he has destroyed General Grievous. We are leaving now to tell the Chancellor, and to see to it that he steps down as he has promised—"

"Steps—steps *down*—" Anakin's voice had a sharply bitter edge. "You have no *idea* . . ."

"Anakin—? What's wrong?"

"Listen to me—*you have to listen to me*—" Anakin sagged against him, shaking; Mace wrapped his arms around the young Jedi and guided him into the nearest chair. "You can't—please, Master Windu, give me your word, promise me it'll be an *arrest*, promise you're not going to *hurt* him—"

"Skywalker—Anakin. You must try to answer. Have you been attacked? Are you injured? You have to tell me what's wrong!"

Anakin collapsed forward, face into his hands.

Mace reached into the Force, opening the eye of his special gift of perception—

What he found there froze his blood.

The tangled web of fault lines in the Force he had seen connecting Anakin to Obi-Wan and to Palpatine was no more; in their place was a single spider-knot that sang with power enough to crack the planet. Anakin Skywalker no longer had shatterpoints. He *was* a shatterpoint.

The shatterpoint.

Everything depended on him.

Everything.

Mace said slowly, with the same sort of deliberate care he would use in examining an unknown type of bomb that might have the power to destroy the universe itself, "Anakin, look at me."

Skywalker raised his head.

"Are you hurt? Do you need—"

Mace frowned. Anakin's eyes were raw, and red, and his face looked swollen. For a long time he didn't know if Anakin would answer, if he *could* answer, if he could even speak at all; the young Jedi seemed to be struggling with something inside himself, as though he fought desperately against the birth of a monster hatching within his chest.

But in the Force, there was no *as though;* there was no *seemed to be.* In the Force, Mace could feel the monster inside Anakin Skywalker, a *real* monster, *too* real, one that was eating him alive from the inside out.

Fear.

This was the wound Anakin had taken. This was the hurt that had him shaking and stammering and too weak to stand. Some black fear had hatched like fever wasps inside the young Knight's brain, and it was killing him.

Finally, after what seemed forever, Anakin opened his blood-raw eyes.

"Master Windu . . ." He spoke slowly, painfully, as though each word ripped away a raw hunk of his own flesh. "I have . . . bad news."

Mace stared at him.

"Bad news?" he repeated blankly.

What news could be bad enough to make a Jedi like Anakin Skywalker collapse? What *news* could make Anakin Skywalker look like the stars had gone out?

Then, in nine simple words, Anakin told him.

———

This is the moment that defines Mace Windu.

Not his countless victories in battle, nor the numberless battles his diplomacy has avoided. Not his penetrating intellect, or his talents with the Force, or his unmatched skills with the lightsaber. Not his dedication to the Jedi Order, or his devotion to the Republic that he serves.

But this.

Right here.

Right now.

Because Mace, too, has an *attachment*. Mace has a secret love.

Mace Windu loves the Republic.

Many of his students quote him to students of their own: *"Jedi do not fight for peace. That's only a slogan, and is as misleading as slogans always are. Jedi fight for* civilization, *because only* civilization *creates* peace.*"*

For Mace Windu, for all his life, for all the lives of a thousand years of Jedi before him, true civilization has had only one true name: the Republic.

He has given his life in the service of his love. He has taken lives in its service, and lost the lives of innocents. He has seen beings that he cares for maimed, and killed, and sometimes worse: sometimes so broken by the horror of the struggle that their only answer was to commit horrors greater still.

And because of that love now, here, in this instant, Anakin Skywalker has nine words for him that shred his heart, burn its pieces, and feed him its smoking ashes.

Palpatine is Sidious. The Chancellor is the Sith Lord.

He doesn't even hear the words, not really; their true meaning is too large for his mind to gather in all at once.

They mean that all he's done, and all that has been done to him—

That all the Order has accomplished, all it has suffered—

All the Galaxy *itself* has gone through, all the years of suffering and slaughter, the death of entire *planets*—

Has all been for nothing.

Because it was all done to save the Republic.

Which was already gone.

Which had already fallen.

The corpse of which had been defended only by a Jedi Order that was now under the command of a Dark Lord of the Sith.

Mace Windu's entire existence has become crystal so shot-through with flaws that the hammer of those nine words has crushed him to sand.

But because he is Mace Windu, he takes this blow without a change of expression.

Because he is Mace Windu, within a second the man of sand is stone once more: pure Jedi Master, weighing coldly the risk of facing the last Dark Lord of the Sith without the chosen one—

Against the risk of facing the last Dark Lord of the Sith with a chosen one eaten alive by fear.

And because he is Mace Windu, the choice is no choice at all.

"Anakin, wait in the Council Chamber until we get back."

"Wh—what? Master—"

"That's an *order*, Anakin."

"But—but—but the *Chancellor*—" Anakin says desperately, clutching at the Jedi Master's hand. "What are you going to *do*?"

And it is the true measure of Mace Windu that, even now, he still is telling the truth when he says, "Only as much as I have to."

In the virtual nonspace of the HoloNet, two Jedi Masters meet.

One is ancient, tiny, with skin of green leather and old wisdom in his eyes, standing in a Kashyyyk cave hollowed from the trunk of a vast wroshyr tree; the other is tall and fierce, seated before a holodisk in Coruscant's Jedi Temple.

To each other, they are blue ghosts, given existence by scanning lasers. Though they are light-years apart, they are of one mind; it hardly matters who says what.

Now they know the truth.

For more than a decade, the Republic has been in the hands of the Sith.

Now, together, blue ghost to blue ghost, they decide to take it back.

PART THREE

APOCALYPSE

The dark is generous, and it is patient, and it always wins.

It always wins because it is everywhere.

It is in the wood that burns in your hearth, and in the kettle on the fire; it is under your chair and under your table and under the sheets on your bed. Walk in the midday sun and the dark is with you, attached to the soles of your feet.

The brightest light casts the darkest shadow.

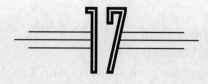

THE FACE OF THE DARK

Depowered lampdisks were rings of ghostly gray floating in the gloom. The shimmering jewelscape of Coruscant haloed the knife-edged shadow of the chair.

This was the office of the Chancellor.

Within the chair's shadow sat another shadow: deeper, darker, formless and impenetrable, an abyssal umbra so profound that it drained light from the room around it.

And from the city. And the planet.

And the galaxy.

The shadow waited. It had told the boy it would. It was looking forward to keeping its word.

For a change.

Night held the Jedi Temple.

On its rooftop landing deck, thin yellow light spilled in a stretching rectangle through a shuttle's hatchway, reflecting upward onto the faces of three Jedi Masters.

"I'd feel better if Yoda were here." This Master was a Nautiloid, tall and broad-shouldered, his glabrous scalp-tentacles restrained by loops of embossed leather. "Or even Kenobi. On Ord Cestus, Obi-Wan and I—"

"Yoda is pinned down on Kashyyyk, and Kenobi is out of contact on Utapau. The Dark Lord has revealed himself, and we dare not hesitate. Think not of *if,* Master Fisto; this duty has fallen to us. We will suffice." This Master was an Iktotchi, shorter and slimmer than the first. Two long horns curved downward from his forehead to below his chin. One had been amputated after being shattered in battle a few months before. Bacta had accelereated its regrowth, and the once maimed horn was now a match to the other. "We will suffice," he repeated. "We will have to."

"Peace," said the third Master, a Zabrak. Dew had gathered on his array of blunt vestigial skull-spines, glistening very like sweat. He gestured toward a Temple door that had cycled open. "Windu is coming."

Clouds had swept in with the twilight, and now a thin drizzling rain began to fall. The approaching Master walked with his shaven head lowered, his hands tucked within his sleeves.

"Master Ti and Gate Master Jurokk will direct the Temple's defense," he said as he reached the others. "We are shutting down all nav beacons and signal lights, we have armed the older Padawans, and all blast doors are sealed and code-locked." His gaze swept the Masters. "It's time to go."

"And Skywalker?" The Zabrak Master cocked his head as though he felt a distant disturbance in the Force. "What of the chosen one?"

"I have sent him to the Council Chamber until our return." Mace Windu turned a grim stare upon the High Council Tower, squinting against the thickening rain. His hands withdrew from his sleeves. One of them held his lightsaber.

"He has done his duty, Masters. Now we shall do ours."

He walked between them into the shuttle.

The other three Masters shared a significant silence, then

Agen Kolar nodded to himself and entered; Saesee Tiin stroked his regrown horn, and followed.

"I'd *still* feel better if Yoda were here . . . ," Kit Fisto muttered, and then went in as well.

Once the hatch had sealed behind him, the Jedi Temple belonged entirely to the night.

Alone in the Chamber of the Jedi Council, Anakin Skywalker wrestled with his dragon.

He was losing.

He paced the Chamber in blind arcs, stumbling among the chairs. He could not feel currents of the Force around him; he could not feel echoes of Jedi Masters in these ancient seats.

He had never dreamed there was this much pain in the universe.

Physical pain he could have handled even without his Jedi mental skills; he'd always been tough. At four years old he'd been able to take the worst beating Watto would deliver without so much as making a sound.

Nothing had prepared him for this.

He wanted to rip open his chest with his bare hands and claw out his heart.

"What have I *done*?" The question started as a low moan but grew to a howl he could no longer lock behind his teeth. *"What have I done?"*

He knew the answer: he had done his duty.

And now he couldn't imagine why.

When I die, Palpatine had said, so calmly, so warmly, so reasonably, *my knowledge dies with me . . .*

Everywhere he looked, he saw only the face of the woman he loved beyond love: the woman for whom he channeled through his body all the love that had ever existed in the galaxy. In the universe.

He didn't care what she had done. He didn't care about con-spiracies or cabals or secret pacts. Treason meant nothing to him now. She was everything that had ever been loved by anyone, and he was watching her die.

His agony somehow became an invisible hand, stretching out through the Force, a hand that found her, far away, alone in her apartment in the dark, a hand that felt the silken softness of her skin and the sleek coils of her hair, a hand that dissolved into a field of pure energy, of pure *feeling* that reached *inside* her—

And now he felt her, really *felt* her in the Force, as though she could have been some kind of Jedi, too, but more than that: he felt a bond, a connection, deeper and more intimate than he'd ever had before with anyone, even Obi-Wan; for a precious eter-nal instant he *was* her . . . he was the beat of her heart and he was the motion of her lips and he was her soft words as though she spoke a prayer to the stars—

I love you, Anakin. I am yours, in life, and in death, wherever you go, whatever you do, we will always be one. Never doubt me, my love. I am yours.

—and her purity and her passion and the truth of her love flowed into him and through him and every atom of him screamed to the Force *how can I let her die?*

The Force had no answer for him.

The dragon, on the other hand, did.

All things die, Anakin Skywalker. Even stars burn out.

And no matter how hard he tried to summon it, no wisdom of Yoda's, no teaching of Obi-Wan's, not one scrap of Jedi lore came to him that could choke the dragon down.

But there *was* an answer; he'd heard it just the other night.

With such knowledge, to maintain life in someone already liv-ing would seem a small matter, don't you agree?

Anakin stopped. His agony evaporated.

Palpatine was right.

It *was* simple.

All he had to do was decide what he wanted.

The Coruscant nightfall was spreading through the galaxy.

The darkness in the Force was no hindrance to the shadow in the Chancellor's office; it *was* the darkness. Wherever darkness dwelled, the shadow could send perception.

In the night, the shadow felt the boy's anguish, and it was good. The shadow felt the grim determination of four Jedi Masters approaching by air.

This, too, was good.

As a Jedi shuttle settled to the landing deck outside, the shadow sent its mind into the far deeper night within one of the several pieces of sculpture that graced the office: an abstract twist of solid neuranium, so heavy that the office floor had been specially reinforced to bear its weight, so dense that more sensitive species might, from very close range, actually perceive the tiny warping of the fabric of space–time that was its gravitation.

Neuranium of more than roughly a millimeter thick is impervious to sensors; the standard security scans undergone by all equipment and furniture to enter the Senate Office Building had shown nothing at all. If anyone had thought to use an advanced gravimetric detector, however, they might have discovered that one smallish section of the sculpture massed slightly less than it should have, given that the manifest that had accompanied it, when it was brought from Naboo among the then-ambassador's personal effects, clearly stated that it was a single piece of solid-forged neuranium.

The manifest was a lie. The sculpture was not entirely solid, and not all of it was neuranium.

Within a long, slim, rod-shaped cavity around which the sculpture had been forged rested a device that had lain, waiting, in absolute darkness—darkness beyond darkness—for decades.

Waiting for night to fall on the Republic.

The shadow felt Jedi Masters stride the vast echoic emptiness of the vaulted halls outside. It could practically hear the cadence of their boot heels on the Alderaanian marble.

The darkness within the sculpture whispered of the shape and the feel and every intimate resonance of the device it cradled. With a twist of its will, the shadow triggered the device.

The neuranium got warm.

A small round spot, smaller than the circle a human child might make of thumb and forefinger, turned the color of old blood.

Then fresh blood.

Then open flame.

Finally a spear of scarlet energy lanced free, painting the office with the color of stars seen through the smoke of burning planets.

The spear of energy lengthened, drawing with it out from the darkness the device, then the scarlet blade shrank away and the device slid itself within the softer darkness of a sleeve.

As shouts of the Force scattered Redrobes beyond the office's outer doors, the shadow gestured and lampdisks ignited. Another shout of the Force burst open the inner door to the private office. As Jedi stormed in, a final flick of the shadow's will triggered a recording device concealed within the desk.

Audio only.

"Why, Master Windu," said the shadow. "What a pleasant surprise."

Shaak Ti felt him coming before she could see him. The infra- and ultrasound-sensitive cavities in the tall, curving montrals to either side of her head gave her a sense analogous to touch: the texture of his approaching footsteps was ragged as old sacking. As he rounded the corner to the landing deck door, his breathing felt like a pile of gravel and his heartbeat was spiking like a Zabrak's head.

He didn't look good, either; he was deathly pale, even for a human, and his eyes were raw.

"Anakin," she said warmly. Perhaps a friendly word was what he needed; she doubted he'd gotten many from Mace Windu. "Thank you for what you have done. The Jedi Order is in your debt—the whole galaxy, as well."

"Shaak Ti. Get out of my way."

Shaky as he looked, there was nothing unsteady in his voice: it was deeper than she remembered, more mature, and it carried undertones of authority that she had never heard before.

And she was not blind to the fact he had neglected to call her *Master.*

She put forth a hand, offering calming energies through the Force. "The Temple is sealed, Anakin. The door is code-locked."

"And you're in the way of the pad."

She stepped aside, allowing him to the pad; she had no reason to keep him here against his will. He punched the code hungrily. "If Palpatine retaliates," she said reasonably, "is not your place here, to help with our defense?"

"I'm the *chosen one*. My place is *there*." His breathing roughened, and he looked as if he was getting even sicker. "I have to be there. That's the prophecy, isn't it? *I have to be there—*"

"Anakin, why? The Masters are the best of the Order. What can you possibly do?"

The door slid open.

"I'm the chosen one," he repeated. "Prophecy can't be changed. I'll do—"

He looked at her with eyes that were dying, and a spasm of unendurable pain passed over his face. Shaak Ti reached for him— he should be in the infirmary, not heading toward what might be a savage battle—but he lurched away from her hand.

"I'll do what I'm *supposed* to do," he said, and sprinted into the night and the rain.

[the following is a transcript of an audio recording presented before the Galactic Senate on the afternoon of the

*first Empire Day; identities of all speakers verified and con-
firmed by voiceprint analysis*]

PALPATINE: Why, Master Windu. What a pleasant surprise.

MACE WINDU: Hardly a surprise, Chancellor. And it
will be pleasant for neither of us.

PALPATINE: I'm sorry? Master Fisto, hello. Master
Kolar, greetings. I trust you are well. Master Tiin—I see
your horn has regrown; I'm very glad. What brings four
Jedi Masters to my office at this hour?

MACE WINDU: We know who you are. What you are.
We are here to take you into custody.

PALPATINE: I beg your pardon? What I am? When last
I checked, I was Supreme Chancellor of the Republic you
are sworn to serve. I hope I misunderstand what you
mean by *custody*, Master Windu. It smacks of treason.

MACE WINDU: You're under arrest.

PALPATINE: Really, Master Windu, you cannot be serious. On what charge?

MACE WINDU: You're a Sith Lord!

PALPATINE: Am I? Even if true, that's hardly a crime.
My philosophical outlook is a personal matter. In fact—
the last time I read the Constitution, anyway—we have
very strict laws against this type of persecution. So I ask
you again: what is my alleged crime? How do you expect
to justify your mutiny before the Senate? Or do you intend to arrest the Senate as well?

MACE WINDU: We're not here to argue with you.

PALPATINE: No, you're here to imprison me without trial. Without even the pretense of legality. So this is the plan, at last: the Jedi are taking over the Republic.

MACE WINDU: Come with us. Now.

PALPATINE: I shall do no such thing. If you intend to murder me, you can do so right here.

MACE WINDU: Don't try to resist.

[*sounds that have been identified by frequency resonances to be the ignition of several lightsabers*]

PALPATINE: Resist? How could I possibly resist? This is *murder*, you Jedi traitors! How can *I* be any threat to you? Master Tiin—you're the telepath. What am I thinking right now?

[*sounds of scuffle*]

KIT FISTO: Saesee—

AGEN KOLAR: [*garbled; possibly "It doesn't hurt"(?)*]

[*sounds of scuffle*]

PALPATINE: Help! Help! Security—*someone*! Help me! *Murder! Treason!*

[*recording ends*]

A fountain of amethyst energy burst from Mace Windu's fist. "Don't try to resist."

The song of his blade was echoed by green fire from the hands of Kit Fisto, Agen Kolar, and Saesee Tiin. Kolar and Tiin closed on Palpatine, blocking the path to the door. Shadows dripped and oozed color, weaving and coiling up office walls, slipping over chairs, spreading along the floor.

"Resist? How could I possibly resist?" Still seated at the desk, Palpatine shook an empty fist helplessly, the perfect image of a tired, frightened old man. "This is *murder*, you Jedi traitors! How can *I* be any threat to you?"

He turned desperately to Saesee Tiin. "Master Tiin—you're the telepath. What am I thinking right now?"

Tiin frowned and cocked his head. His blade dipped. A smear of red-flashing darkness hurtled from behind the desk.

Saesee Tiin's head bounced when it hit the floor.

Smoke curled from the neck, and from the twin stumps of the horns, severed just below the chin.

Kit Fisto gasped, "Saesee!"

The headless corpse, still standing, twisted as its knees buckled, and a thin sigh escaped from its trachea as it folded to the floor.

"It doesn't . . ." Agen Kolar swayed.

His emerald blade shrank away, and the handgrip tumbled from his opening fingers. A small, neat hole in the middle of his forehead leaked smoke, showing light from the back of his head.

". . . hurt . . ."

He pitched forward onto his face, and lay still.

Palpatine stood at the doorway, but the door stayed shut. From his right hand extended a blade the color of fire.

The door locked itself at his back.

"Help! Help!" Palpatine cried like a man in desperate fear for his life. "Security—*someone*! Help me! *Murder! Treason!*"

Then he smiled.

He held one finger to his lips, and, astonishingly, he winked.

In the blank second that followed, while Mace Windu and Kit Fisto could do no more than angle their lightsabers to guard, Palpatine swiftly stepped over the bodies back toward his desk, reversed his blade, and drove it in a swift, surgically precise stab down through his desktop.

"That's enough of *that*."

He let it burn its way free through the front, then he turned, lifting his weapon, appearing to study it as one might study the face of a beloved friend one has long thought dead. Power gathered around him until the Force shimmered with darkness.

"If you only knew," he said softly, perhaps speaking to the Jedi Masters, or perhaps to himself, or perhaps even to the scarlet blade lifted now as though in mocking salute, "how long I have been waiting for this . . ."

Anakin's speeder shrieked through the rain, dodging forked bolts of lightning that shot up from towers into the clouds, slicing across traffic lanes, screaming past spacescrapers so fast that his shock-wake cracked windows as he passed.

He didn't understand why people didn't just get out of his way. He didn't understand how the trillion beings who jammed Galactic City could go about their trivial business as though the universe hadn't changed. How could they think they counted for anything, compared with him?

How could they think they still mattered?

Their blind lives meant nothing now. None of them. Because ahead, on the vast cliff face of the Senate Office Building, one window spat lightning into the rain to echo the lightning of the storm outside—but this lightning was the color of clashing lightsabers.

Green fans, sheets of purple—

And crimson flame.

He was too late.

The green fire faded and winked out; now the lightning was only purple and red.

His repulsorlifts howled as he heeled the speeder up onto its side, skidding through wind-shear turbulence to bring it to a bobbing halt outside the window of Palpatine's private office. A blast of lightning hit the spire of 500 Republica, only a kilometer away, and its white burst flared off the window, flash-blinding him; he blinked furiously, slapping at his eyes in frustration.

The colorless glare inside his eyes faded slowly, bringing into focus a jumble of bodies on the floor of Palpatine's private office.

Bodies in Jedi robes.

On Palpatine's desk lay the head of Kit Fisto, faceup, scalp-tentacles unbound in a squid-tangle across the ebonite. His lidless eyes stared blindly at the ceiling. Anakin remembered him in the arena at Geonosis, effortlessly carving his way through wave after wave of combat droids, on his lips a gently humorous smile as though the horrific battle were only some friendly jest. His severed head wore that same smile.

Maybe he thought death was funny, too.

Anakin's own blade sang blue as it slashed through the window and he dived through the gap. He rolled to his feet among a litter of bodies and sprinted through a shattered door along the small private corridor and through a doorway that flashed and flared with energy-scatter.

Anakin skidded to a stop.

Within the public office of the Supreme Chancellor of the Galactic Republic, a last Jedi Master battled alone, blade-to-blade, against a living shadow.

Sinking into Vaapad, Mace Windu fought for his life.

More than his life: each whirl of blade and whipcrack of lightning was a strike in defense of democracy, of justice and peace, of the rights of ordinary beings to live their own lives in their own ways.

He was fighting for the Republic that he loved.

Vaapad, the seventh form of lightsaber combat, takes its name from a notoriously dangerous predator native to the moons of Sarapin: a vaapad attacks its prey with whipping strikes of its blindingly fast tentacles. Most have at least seven. It is not uncommon for them to have as many as twelve; the largest ever killed had twenty-three. With a vaapad, one never knew how many tentacles it had until it was dead: they move too fast to count. Almost too fast to see.

So did Mace's blade.

Vaapad is as aggressive and powerful as its namesake, but its power comes at great risk: immersion in Vaapad opens the gates that restrain one's inner darkness. To use Vaapad, a Jedi must allow himself to *enjoy* the fight; he must give himself over to the thrill of battle. The rush of *winning*. Vaapad is a path that leads through the penumbra of the dark side.

Mace Windu created this style, and he was its only living master.

This was Vaapad's ultimate test.

Anakin blinked and rubbed his eyes again. Maybe he was still a bit flash-blind—the Korun Master seemed to be fading in and out of existence, half swallowed by a thickening black haze in which danced a meter-long bar of sunfire. Mace pressed back the darkness with a relentless straight-ahead march; his own blade, that distinctive amethyst blaze that had been the final sight of so many evil beings across the galaxy, made a haze of its own: an oblate sphere of purple fire within which there seemed to be dozens of swords slashing in all directions at once.

The shadow he fought, that blur of speed—could that be *Palpatine*?

Their blades flared and flashed, crashing together with bursts of fire, weaving nets of killing energy in exchanges so fast that Anakin could not truly see them—

But he could feel them in the Force.

The Force itself roiled and burst and crashed around them, boiling with power and lightspeed ricochets of lethal intent.

And it was darkening.

Anakin could feel how the Force fed upon the shadow's murderous exaltation; he could feel fury spray into the Force though some poisonous abscess had crested in both their hearts.

There was no Jedi restraint here.

Mace Windu was cutting loose.

Mace was deep in it now: submerged in Vaapad, swallowed by it, he no longer truly existed as an independent being.

Vaapad is a channel for darkness, and that darkness flowed both ways. He accepted the furious speed of the Sith Lord, drew the shadow's rage and power into his inmost center—

And let it fountain out again.

He reflected the fury upon its source as a lightsaber redirects a blaster bolt.

There was a time when Mace Windu had feared the power of the dark; there was a time when he had feared the darkness in himself. But the Clone Wars had given him a gift of understanding: on a world called Haruun Kal, he had faced his darkness and had learned that the power of darkness is not to be feared.

He had learned that it is fear that gives the darkness power.

He was not afraid. The darkness had no power over him. But—

Neither did he have power over it.

Vaapad made him an open channel, half of a superconducting loop completed by the shadow; they became a standing wave of battle that expanded into every cubic centimeter of the Chancellor's office. There was no scrap of carpet nor shred of chair that might not at any second disintegrate in flares of red or purple; lampstands became brief shields, sliced into segments that whirled through the air; couches became terrain to be climbed for advantage or overleapt in retreat. But there was still only the cycle of power, the endless loop, no wound taken on either side, not even the possibility of fatigue.

Impasse.

Which might have gone on forever, if Vaapad were Mace's only gift.

The fighting was effortless for him now; he let his body handle it without the intervention of his mind. While his blade spun and crackled, while his feet slid and his weight shifted and his shoulders turned in precise curves of their own direction, his mind slid along the circuit of dark power, tracing it back to its limitless source.

Feeling for its shatterpoint.

He found a knot of fault lines in the shadow's future; he chose the largest fracture and followed it back to the here and the now—

And it led him, astonishingly, to a man standing frozen in the slashed-open doorway. Mace had no need to look; the presence in the Force was familiar, and was as uplifting as sunlight breaking through a thunderhead.

The chosen one was here.

Mace disengaged from the shadow's blade and leapt for the window; he slashed away the transparisteel with a single flourish.

His instant's distraction cost him: a dark surge of the Force nearly blew him right out of the gap he had just cut. Only a desperate Force-push of his own altered his path enough that he slammed into a stanchion instead of plunging half a kilometer from the ledge outside. He bounced off and the Force cleared his head and once again he gave himself to Vaapad.

He could feel the end of this battle approaching, and so could the blur of Sith he faced; in the Force, the shadow had become a pulsar of fear. Easily, almost effortlessly, he turned the shadow's fear into a weapon: he angled the battle to bring them both out onto the window ledge.

Out in the wind. Out with the lightning. Out on a rain-slicked ledge above a half-kilometer drop.

Out where the shadow's fear made it hesitate. Out where the shadow's fear turned some of its Force-powered speed into a Force-powered grip on the slippery permacrete.

Out where Mace could flick his blade in one precise arc and slash the shadow's lightsaber in half.

One piece flipped back in through the cut-open window. The other tumbled from opening fingers, bounced on the ledge, and fell through the rain toward the distant alleys below.

Now the shadow was only Palpatine: old and shrunken, thinning hair bleached white by time and care, face lined with exhaustion.

"For all your power, you are no Jedi. All you are, my lord," Mace said evenly, staring past his blade, "is under arrest."

"Do you see, Anakin? Do you?" Palpatine's voice once again had the broken cadence of a frightened old man's. "Didn't I warn you of the Jedi and their treason?"

"Save your twisted words, my lord. There are no politicians here. The Sith will never regain control of the Republic. It's over. You've lost." Mace leveled his blade. "You lost for the same reason the Sith always lose: defeated by your own fear."

Palpatine lifted his head.

His eyes smoked with hate.

"Fool," he said.

He lifted his arms, his robes of office spreading wide into raptor's wings, his hands hooking into talons.

"Fool!" His voice was a shout of thunder. "Do you think the fear you feel is *mine*?"

Lighting blasted the clouds above, and lightning blasted from Palpatine's hands, and Mace didn't have time to comprehend what Palpatine was talking about; he had time only to slip back into Vaapad and angle his blade to catch the forking arcs of pure, dazzling hatred that clawed toward him.

Because Vaapad is more than a fighting style. It is a state of mind: a channel for darkness. Power passed into him and out again without touching him.

And the circuit completed itself: the lightning reflected back to its source.

Palpatine staggered, snarling, but the blistering energy that poured from his hands only intensified.

He fed the power with his pain.

"Anakin!" Mace called. His voice sounded distant, blurred, as if it came from the bottom of a well. "Anakin, help me! This is your chance!"

He felt Anakin's leap from the office floor to the ledge, felt his approach behind—

And Palpatine was not afraid.

Mace could feel it: he wasn't worried at all.

"Destroy this traitor," the Chancellor said, his voice raised over the howl of writhing energy that joined his hands to Mace's blade. "This was never an arrest. It's an *assassination*!"

That was when Mace finally understood. He had it. The key to final victory. Palpatine's shatterpoint. The absolute shatterpoint of the Sith.

The shatterpoint of the dark side itself.

Mace thought, blankly astonished, *Palpatine trusts Anakin Skywalker* . . .

Now Anakin was at Mace's shoulder. Palpatine still made no move to defend himself from Skywalker; instead he ramped up the lightning bursting from his hands, bending the fountain of Mace's blade back toward the Korun Master's face.

Palpatine's eyes glowed with power, casting a yellow glare that burned back the rain from around them. "He is a traitor, Anakin. Destroy him."

"You're the chosen one, Anakin," Mace said, his voice going thin with strain. This was beyond Vaapad; he had no strength left to fight against his own blade. "Take him. It's your *destiny*."

Skywalker echoed him faintly. "Destiny . . ."

"Help me! I can't hold on any longer!" The yellow glare from Palpatine's eyes spread outward through his flesh. His skin flowed like oil, as though the muscle beneath was burning away, as though even the bones of his skull were softening, were bending and bulging, deforming from the heat and pressure of his electric hatred. "He is *killing* me, Anakin—! Please, Anaa*ahhh*—"

Mace's blade bent so close to his face that he was choking on ozone. "Anakin, he's too *strong* for me—"

"*Ahhh*—" Palpatine's roar above the endless blast of lightning became a fading moan of despair.

The lightning swallowed itself, leaving only the night and the rain, and an old man crumpled to his knees on a slippery ledge.

"I . . . can't. I give up. I . . . I am too weak, in the end. Too old, and too weak. Don't kill me, Master Jedi. Please. I surrender."

Victory flooded through Mace's aching body. He lifted his blade. "You Sith *disease*—"

"*Wait*—" Skywalker seized his lightsaber arm with desperate strength. "Don't kill him—you can't just *kill* him, Master—"

"Yes, I can," Mace said, grim and certain. "I have to."

"You came to *arrest* him. He has to stand *trial*—"

"A trial would be a joke. He controls the courts. He controls the Senate—"

"So are you going to kill all *them*, too? Like he *said* you would?"

Mace yanked his arm free. "He's too dangerous to be left alive. If you could have taken *Dooku* alive, would you have?"

Skywalker's face swept itself clean of emotion. "That was *different*—"

Mace turned toward the cringing, beaten Sith Lord. "You can explain the difference after he's dead."

He raised his lightsaber.

"*I* need him *alive!*" Skywalker shouted. "I need him to save *Padmé!*"

Mace thought blankly, *Why?* And moved his lightsaber toward the fallen Chancellor.

Before he could follow through on his stroke, a sudden arc of blue plasma sheared through his wrist and his hand tumbled away with his lightsaber still in it and Palpatine roared back to his feet and lightning speared from the Sith Lord's hands and without his blade to catch it, the power of Palpatine's hate struck him full-on.

He had been so intent on Palpatine's shatterpoint that he'd never thought to look for Anakin's.

Dark lightning blasted away his universe.

He fell forever.

Anakin Skywalker knelt in the rain.

He was looking at a hand. The hand had brown skin. The hand held a lightsaber. The hand had a charred oval of tissue where it should have been attached to an arm.

"What have I done?"

Was it his voice? It must have been. Because it was his question.

"What have I done?"

Another hand, a warm and human hand, laid itself softly on his shoulder.

"You're following your destiny, Anakin," said a familiar gentle voice. "The Jedi are traitors. You saved the Republic from their treachery. You can see that, can't you?"

"You were right," Anakin heard himself saying. "Why didn't I know?"

"You couldn't have. They cloaked themselves in deception, my boy. Because they feared your power, they could never trust you."

Anakin stared at the hand, but he no longer saw it. "Obi-Wan—Obi-Wan trusts me . . ."

"Not enough to tell you of their plot."

Treason echoed in his memory.

. . . this is not an assignment for the record . . .

That warm and human hand gave his shoulder a warm and human squeeze. "I do not fear your power, Anakin, I *embrace* it. You are the greatest of the Jedi. You can be the greatest of the Sith. I believe that, Anakin. I believe in *you. I* trust you. I *trust* you. I trust *you.*"

Anakin looked from the dead hand on the ledge to the living one on his shoulder, then up to the face of the man who stood above him, and what he saw there choked him like an invisible fist crushing his throat.

The hand on his shoulder was human.

The face . . . wasn't.

The eyes were a cold and feral yellow, and they gleamed like those of a predator lurking beyond a fringe of firelight; the bone around those feral eyes had swollen and melted and flowed like durasteel spilled from a fusion smelter, and the flesh that blanketed it had gone corpse-gray and coarse as rotten synthplast.

Stunned with horror, stunned with revulsion, Anakin could only stare at the creature. At the shadow.

Looking into the face of the darkness, he saw his future.

"Now come inside," the darkness said.

After a moment, he did.

Anakin stood just within the office. Motionless.

Palpatine examined the damage to his face in a broad expanse of wall mirror. Anakin couldn't tell if his expression might be revulsion, or if this were merely the new shape of his features. Palpatine lifted one tentative hand to the misshapen horror that he now saw in the mirror, then simply shrugged.

"And so the mask becomes the man," he sighed with a hint of philosophical melancholy. "I shall miss the face of Palpatine, I think; but for our purpose, the face of Sidious will serve. Yes, it will serve."

He gestured, and a hidden compartment opened in the office's ceiling above his desk. A voluminous robe of heavy black-on-black brocade floated downward from it; Anakin felt the current in the Force that carried the robe to Palpatine's hand.

He remembered playing a Force game with a shuura fruit, sitting across a long table from Padmé in the retreat by the lake on Naboo. He remembered telling her how grumpy Obi-Wan would be to see him use the Force so casually.

Palaptine seemed to catch his thought; he gave a yellow sidelong glance as the robe settled onto his shoulders.

"You must learn to cast off the petty restraints that the Jedi have tried to place upon your power," he said. "Anakin, it's time. I need you to help me restore order to the galaxy."

Anakin didn't respond.

Sidious said, "Join me. Pledge yourself to the Sith. Become my apprentice."

A wave of tingling started at the base of Anakin's skull and spread over his whole body in a slow-motion shockwave.

"I—I can't."

"Of course you can."

Anakin shook his head and found that the rest of him threatened to begin shaking as well. "I—came to save your life, sir. Not to betray my friends—"

Sidious snorted. "*What* friends?"

Anakin could find no answer.

"And do you think that task is finished, my boy?" Sidious seated himself on the corner of the desk, hands folded in his lap, the way he always had when offering Anakin fatherly advice; the misshapen mask of his face made the familiarity of his posture into something horrible. "Do you think that killing one traitor will end treason? Do you think the Jedi will ever stop until I am dead?"

Anakin stared at his hands. The left one was shaking. He hid it behind him.

"It's them or me, Anakin. Or perhaps I should put it more plainly: It's them or *Padmé*."

Anakin made his right hand—his black-gloved hand of durasteel and electrodrivers—into a fist.

"It's just—it's not . . . easy, that's all. I have—I've been a Jedi for so long—"

Sidious offered an appalling smile. "There is a place within you, my boy, a place as briskly clean as ice on a mountaintop, cool and remote. Find that high place, and look down within yourself; breathe that clean, icy air as you regard your guilt and shame. Do not deny them; observe them. Take your horror in your hands and look at it. Examine it as a phenomenon. Smell it. Taste it. Come to know it as only you can, for it is yours, and it is precious."

As the shadow beside him spoke, its words became true. From a remote, frozen distance that was at the same time more extravagantly, hotly intimate than he could have ever dreamed, Anakin handled his emotions. He dissected them. He reassembled them and pulled them apart again. He still felt them—if anything, they burned hotter than before—but they no longer had the power to cloud his mind.

"You have found it, my boy: I can feel you there. That cold distance—that mountaintop within yourself—that is the first key to the power of the Sith."

Anakin opened his eyes and turned his gaze fully upon the grotesque features of Darth Sidious.

He didn't even blink.

As he looked upon that mask of corruption, the revulsion he felt was real, and it was powerful, and it was—

Interesting.

Anakin lifted his hand of durasteel and electrodrivers and cupped it, staring into its palm as though he held there the fear that had haunted his dreams for his whole life, and it was no larger than the piece of shuura he'd once stolen from Padmé's plate.

On the mountain peak within himself, he weighed Padmé's life against the Jedi Order.

It was no contest.

He said, "Yes."

"Yes to what, my boy?"

"Yes, I want your knowledge."

"Good. Good!"

"I want your power. I want the power to stop death."

"That power only my Master truly achieved, but together we will find it. The Force is strong with you, my boy. You can do *anything*."

"The Jedi betrayed you," Anakin said. "The Jedi betrayed both of us."

"As you say. Are you ready?"

"I am," he said, and meant it. "I give myself to you. I pledge myself to the ways of the Sith. Take me as your apprentice. Teach me. Lead me. Be my Master."

Sidious raised the hood of his robe and draped it to shadow the ruin of his face.

"Kneel before me, Anakin Skywalker."

Anakin dropped to one knee. He lowered his head.

"It is your will to join your destiny forever with the Order of the Sith Lords?"

There was no hesitation. "Yes."

Darth Sidious laid a pale hand on Anakin's brow. "Then it is done. You are now one with the Order of the Dark Lords of the Sith. From this day forward, the truth of you, my apprentice, now and forevermore, will be Darth . . ."

A pause; a questioning in the Force—

An answer, dark as the gap between galaxies—

He heard Sidious say it: his new name.

Vader.

A pair of syllables that meant *him*.

Vader, he said to himself. *Vader.*

"Thank you, my Master."

"Every single Jedi, including your friend Obi-Wan Kenobi, have been revealed as enemies of the Republic now. You understand that, don't you?"

"Yes, my Master."

"The Jedi are relentless. If they are not destroyed to the last being, there will be civil war without end. To sterilize the Jedi Temple will be your first task. Do what must be done, Lord Vader."

"I always have, my Master."

"Do not hesitate. Show no mercy. Leave no living creature behind. Only then will you be strong enough with the dark side to save Padmé."

"What of the other Jedi?"

"Leave them to me. After you have finished at the Temple, your second task will be the Separatist leadership, in their 'secret bunker' on Mustafar. When you have killed them all, the Sith will rule the galaxy once more, and we shall have peace. Forever.

"Rise, Darth Vader."

The Sith Lord who once had been a Jedi hero called Anakin Skywalker stood, drawing himself up to his full height, but he looked not outward upon his new Master, nor upon the planet-city beyond, nor out into the galaxy that they would soon rule. He instead turned his gaze inward: he unlocked the furnace gate within his heart and stepped forth to regard with new eyes the cold freezing dread of the dead-star dragon that had haunted his life.

I am Darth Vader, he said within himself.

The dragon tried again to whisper of failure, and weakness, and inevitable death, but with one hand the Sith Lord caught it, crushed away its voice; it tried to rise then, to coil and rear and strike, but the Sith Lord laid his other hand upon it and broke its power with a single effortless twist.

I am Darth Vader, he repeated as he ground the dragon's corpse to dust beneath his mental heel, as he watched the dragon's dust and ashes scatter before the blast from his furnace heart, *and you—*

You are nothing at all.

He had become, finally, what they all called him.

The Hero With No Fear.

Gate Master Jurokk sprinted through the empty vaulted hallway, clattering echoes of his footsteps making him sound like a platoon. The main doors of the Temple were slowly swinging inward in answer to the code key punched into the outside lockpad.

The Gate Master had seen him on the monitor.

Anakin Skywalker.

Alone.

The huge doors creaked inward; as soon as they were wide enough for the Gate Master to pass, he slipped through.

Anakin stood in the night outside, shoulders hunched, head down against the rain.

"Anakin!" he gasped, running up to the young man. "Anakin, what happened? Where are the Masters?"

Anakin looked at him as though he wasn't sure who the Gate Master was. "Where is Shaak Ti?"

"In the meditation chambers—we felt something happen in the Force, something awful. She's searching the Force in deep meditation, trying to get some feel for what's going on . . ."

His words trailed away. Anakin didn't seem to be listening.

"Something *has* happened, hasn't it?"

Jurokk looked past him now. The night beyond the Temple was full of clones. Battalions of them. Brigades.

Thousands.

"Anakin," he said slowly, "what's going on? Something's happened. Something horrible. How bad *is* it—?"

The last thing Jurokk felt was the emitter of a lightsaber

against the soft flesh beneath his jaw; the last thing he heard, as blue plasma chewed upward through his head and burst from the top of his skull and burned away his life, was Anakin Skywalker's melancholy reply.

"You have no idea . . ."

ORDER SIXTY-SIX

Pau City was a cauldron of battle.

From his observation post just off the landing ramp of the command lander on the tenth level, Clone Commander Cody swept the sinkhole with his electrobinoculars. The droid-control center lay in ruins only a few meters away, but the Separatists had learned the lesson of Naboo; their next-generation combat droids were equipped with sophisticated self-motivators that kicked in automatically when control signals were cut off, delivering a program of standing orders.

Standing Order Number One was, apparently, Kill Everything That Moves.

And they were doing a good job of it, too.

Half the city was rubble, and the rest was a firestorm of droids and clones and Utapaun dragon cavalry, and just when Commander Cody was thinking how he really wished they had a Jedi or two around right now, several metric tons of dragon-mount hurtled from the sky and hit the roof of the command lander hard enough to buckle the deck beneath it.

Not that it did the ship any harm; *Jadthu*-class landers are basically flying bunkers, and this particular one was triple-armored and equipped with internal shock buffers and inertial dampeners powerful enough for a fleet corvette, to protect the sophisticated command-and-control equipment inside.

Cody looked up at the dragonmount, and at its rider. "General Kenobi," he said. "Glad you could join us."

"Commander Cody," the Jedi Master said with a nod. He was still scanning the battle around them. "Did you contact Coruscant with the news of the general's death?"

The clone commander snapped to attention and delivered a crisp salute. "As ordered, sir. Erm, sir?"

Kenobi looked down at him.

"Are you all right, sir? You're a bit of a mess."

The Jedi Master wiped away some of the dust and gore that smeared his face with the sleeve of his robe—which was charred, and only left a blacker smear across his cheek. "Ah. Well, yes. It has been a . . . stressful day." He waved out at Pau City. "But we still have a battle to win."

"Then I suppose you'll be wanting this," Cody said, holding up the lightsaber his men had recovered from a traffic tunnel. "I believe you dropped it, sir."

"Ah. Ah, yes."

The weapon floated gently up to Kenobi's hand, and when he smiled down at the clone commander again, Cody could swear the Jedi Master was blushing, just a bit. "No, ah, need to mention this to, erm, Anakin, is there, Cody?"

Cody grinned. "Is that an order, sir?"

Kenobi shook his head, chuckling tiredly. "Let's go. You'll have noticed I *did* manage to leave a few droids for you . . ."

"Yes, sir." A silent buzzing vibration came from a compartment concealed within his armor. Cody frowned. "Go on ahead, General. We'll be right behind you."

That concealed compartment held a secure comlink, which was frequency-locked to a channel reserved for the commander in chief.

Kenobi nodded and spoke to his mount, and the great beast overleapt the clone commander on its way down into the battle.

Cody withdrew the comlink from his armor and triggered it.

A holoscan appeared on the palm of his gauntlet: a hooded man.

"It is time," the holoscan said. *"Execute Order Sixty-Six."*

Cody responded as he had been trained since before he'd even awakened in his crèche-school. "It will be done, my lord."

The holoscan vanished. Cody stuck the comlink back into its concealed recess and frowned down toward where Kenobi rode his dragonmount into selflessly heroic battle.

Cody was a clone. He would execute the order faithfully, without hesitation or regret. But he was also human enough to mutter glumly, "Would it have been too much to ask for the order to have come through *before* I gave him back the bloody *lightsaber* . . . ?"

The order is given once. Its wave-front spreads to clone commanders on Kashyyyk and Felucia, Mygeeto and Tellanroaeg and every battlefront, every military installation, every hospital and rehab center and spaceport cantina in the galaxy.

Except for Coruscant.

On Coruscant, Order Sixty-Six is already being executed.

Dawn crept across Galactic City. Fingers of morning brought a rose-colored glow to the wind-smeared upper reach of a vast twisting cone of smoke.

Bail Organa was a man not given to profanity, but when he caught a glimpse of the source of that smoke from the pilot's chair of his speeder, the curse it brought to his lips would have made a Corellian dockhand blush.

He stabbed a code that canceled his speeder's programmed route toward the Senate Office Building, then grabbed the yoke and kicked the craft into a twisting dive that shot him through half a dozen crisscrossing streams of air traffic.

He triggered his speeder's comm. "Antilles!"

The answer from the captain of his personal crew was instant. *"Yes, my lord?"*

"Route an alert to SER," he ordered. "The Jedi Temple is on fire!"

"Yes, sir. We know. Senate Emergency Response has announced a state of martial law, and the Temple is under lockdown. There's been some kind of Jedi rebellion."

"What are you talking about? That's impossible. Why aren't there fireships onstation?"

"I don't have any details, my lord; we only know what SER is telling us."

"Look, I'm right on top of it. I'm going down there to find out what's happening."

"My lord, I wouldn't recommend it—"

"I won't take any chances." Bail hauled the control yoke to slew the speeder toward the broad landing deck on the roof of the Temple ziggurat. "Speaking of not taking chances, Captain: order the duty crew onto the *Tantive* and get her engines warm. I've got a bad feeling about this."

"Sir?"

"Just do it."

Bail set the speeder down only a few meters from the deck entrance and hopped out. A squad of clone troopers stood in the open doorway. Smoke billowed out from the hallway behind them.

One of the troopers lifted a hand as Bail approached. "Don't worry, sir, everything is under control here."

"Under control? Where are the SER teams? What is the *army* doing here?"

"I'm sorry, I can't talk about that, sir."

"Has there been some kind of attack on the Temple?"

"I'm sorry, I can't talk about that, sir."

"Listen to me, Sergeant, I am a Senator of the Galactic Republic," Bail said, improvising, "and I am late for a meeting with the Jedi Council—"

"The Jedi Council is not in session, sir."

"Maybe you should let me see for myself."

The four clones moved together to block his path. "I'm sorry, sir. Entry is forbidden."

"I am a *Senator*—"

"Yes, sir." The clone sergeant snapped his DC-15 to his shoulder, and Bail, blinking, found himself staring into its blackened muzzle from close enough to kiss it. "And it is time for you to leave, sir."

"When you put it that way . . ." Bail backed off, lifting his hands. "Yes, all right, I'm going."

A burst of blasterfire ripped through the smoke and scattered into the dawn outside. Bail stared with an open mouth as a Jedi flashed out of nowhere and started cutting down clones. No: not a Jedi.

A boy.

A child, no more than ten years old, swinging a lightsaber whose blade was almost as long as he was tall. More blasterfire came from inside, and a whole platoon of clones came pelting toward the landing deck, and the ten-year-old was hit, and hit again, and then just shot to rags among the bodies of the troopers he'd killed, and Bail started backing away, faster now, and in the middle of it all, a clone wearing the colors of a commander came out of the smoke and pointed at Bail Organa.

"No witnesses," the commmander said. "Kill him."

Bail ran.

He dived through a hail of blasterfire, hit the deck, and rolled under his speeder to the opposite side. He grabbed on to its pilot's-side door and swung his leg onto a tail fin, using the vehicle's body as cover while he stabbed the keys to reinitialize its autorouter. Clones charged toward him, firing as they came.

His speeder heeled over and blasted away.

Bail pulled himself inside as the speeder curved up into the congested traffic lanes. He was white as flimsiplast, and his hands were shaking so badly he could barely activate his comm.

"Antilles! Organa to Antilles. Come in, Captain!"

"Antilles here, my lord."

"It's worse than I thought. Far worse than you've heard. Send someone to Chance Palp—no, strike that. Go yourself. Take five men and go to the spaceport. I know at least one Jedi ship is on the ground there; Saesee Tiin brought in *Sharp Spiral* late last night. I need you to steal his homing beacon."

"What? His beacon? Why?"

"No time to explain. Get the beacon and meet me at the *Tantive*. We're leaving the planet."

He stared back at the vast column of smoke that boiled from the Jedi Temple.

"While we still can."

———

Order Sixty-Six is the climax of the Clone Wars.

Not the end—the Clone Wars will end some few hours from now, when a coded signal, sent by Nute Gunray from the secret Separatist bunker on Mustafar, deactivates every combat droid in the galaxy at once—but the climax.

It's not a thrilling climax; it's not the culmination of an epic struggle. Just the opposite, in fact. The Clone Wars were never an epic struggle. They were never intended to be.

What is happening right now is why the Clone Wars were fought in the first place. It is their reason for existence. The

Clone Wars have always been, in and of themselves, from their very inception, the revenge of the Sith.

They were irresistible bait. They took place in remote locations, on planets that belonged, primarily, to "somebody else." They were fought by expendable proxies. And they were constructed as a win–win situation.

The Clone Wars were the perfect Jedi trap.

By fighting at all, the Jedi lost.

With the Jedi Order overextended, spread thin across the galaxy, each Jedi is alone, surrounded only by whatever clone troops he, she, or it commands. War itself pours darkness into the Force, deepening the cloud that limits Jedi perception. And the clones have no malice, no hatred, not the slightest ill intent that might give warning. They are only following orders.

In this case, Order Sixty-Six.

Hold-out blasters appear in clone hands. ARC-170s drop back onto the tails of Jedi starfighters. AT-STs swivel their guns. Turrets on hovertanks swung silently.

Clones open fire, and Jedi die.

All across the galaxy. All at once.

Jedi die.

Kenobi never saw it coming.

Cody had coordinated the heavy-weapons operators from five different companies spread over an arc of three different levels of the sinkhole-city. He'd served under Kenobi in more than a dozen operations since the beginning of the Outer Rim sieges, and he had a very clear and unsentimental estimate of just how hard to kill the unassuming Jedi Master was. He wasn't taking any chances.

He raised his comlink. "Execute."

On that order, T-21 muzzles swung, shoulder-fired torps locked on, and proton grenade launchers angled to precisely calibrated elevations.

"Fire."

They did.

Kenobi, his dragonmount, and all five of the destroyer droids he'd been fighting vanished in a fireball that for an instant outshone Utapau's sun.

Visual polarizers in Cody's helmet cut the glare by 78 percent; his vision cleared in plenty of time to see shreds of dragonmount and twisted hunks of droid raining into the ocean mouth at the bottom of the sinkhole.

Cody scowled and keyed his comlink. "Looks like the lizard took the worst of it. Deploy the seekers. All of them."

He stared down into the boil of the ocean mouth.

"I want to see the body."

C-3PO paused in the midst of dusting the Tarka-Null original on its display pedestal near his mistress's bedroom view wall, and used the electrostatic tissue to briefly polish his own photoreceptors. The astromech in the green Jedi starfighter docking with the veranda below—could that be R2-D2?

Well, this should be interesting.

Senator Amidala had spent the better part of these predawn hours simply staring over the city, toward the plume of smoke that rose from the Jedi Temple; now, at last, she might get some answers.

He might, too. R2-D2 was far from the sort of sparkling conversationalist with whom C-3PO preferred to associate, but the little astromech had a positive gift for jacking himself into the motherboards of the most volatile situations . . .

The cockpit popped open, and inevitably the Jedi within was revealed to be Anakin Skywalker. In watching Master Anakin climb down from the starfighter's cockpit, 3PO's photoreceptors captured data that unexpectedly activated his threat-aversion subroutines. "Oh," he said faintly, clutching at his power core. "Oh, I don't like the looks of *this* at all . . ."

He dropped the electrostatic tissue and shuffled as quickly as he could to the bedroom door. "My lady," he called to Senator Amidala, where she stood by the broad window. "On the veranda. A Jedi starfighter," he forced out. "Has docked, my lady."

She blinked, then rushed toward the bedroom door.

C-3PO shuffled along behind her and slipped out through the open door, making a wide circle around the humans, who were engaged in one of those inexplicable embraces they seemed so fond of.

Reaching the starfighter, he said, "Artoo, are you all right? What is going on?"

The astromech squeaked and beeped; C-3PO's autotranslator interpreted: NOBODY TELLS ME ANYTHING.

"Of course not. You don't keep up your end of the conversation."

A whirring squeal: SOMETHING'S WRONG. THE FACTORS DON'T BALANCE.

"You can't possibly be more confused than I am."

YOU'RE RIGHT. *NOBODY* CAN BE MORE CONFUSED THAN YOU ARE.

"Oh, very funny. Hush now—what was that?"

The Senator was sitting now, leaning distractedly on one of the tasteful, elegant bistro tables that dotted the veranda, while Master Anakin stood above her. "I think—he's saying something about a *rebellion*—that the Jedi have tried to overthrow the Republic! And—oh, my goodness. Mace Windu has tried to assassinate Chancellor Palpatine! Can he be *serious?*"

I DON'T KNOW. ANAKIN DOESN'T TALK TO ME ANYMORE.

C-3PO shook his cranial assembly helplessly. "How can Master Windu be an assassin? He has such impeccable manners."

LIKE I TOLD YOU: THE FACTORS DON'T ADD UP.

"I've been hearing the most awful rumors—they're saying the government is going to *banish* us—banish *droids,* can you imagine?"

DON'T BELIEVE EVERYTHING YOU HEAR.

"Shh. Not so loud!"

I'M ONLY SAYING THAT WE DON'T KNOW THE TRUTH.

"Of course we don't." C-3PO sighed. "And we likely never will."

"What about Obi-Wan?"

She looked stricken. Pale and terrified.

It made him love her more.

He shook his head. "Many of the Jedi have been killed."

"But . . ." She stared out at the rivers of traffic crosshatching the sky. "Are you *sure?* It seems so . . . *unbelievable* . . ."

"I was there, Padmé. It's all true."

"But . . . but how could *Obi-Wan* be involved in something like that?"

He said, "We may never know."

"Outlawed . . . ," she murmured. "What happens now?"

"All Jedi are required to surrender themselves immediately," he said. "Those who resist . . . are being dealt with."

"Anakin—they're your *family*—"

"They're traitors. *You're* my family. You and the baby."

"How can *all* of them be traitors—?"

"They're not the only ones. There were Senators in this as well."

Now, finally, she looked at him, and fear shone from her eyes.

He smiled.

"Don't worry. I won't let anything happen to you."

"To *me*?"

"You need to distance yourself from your . . . friends . . . in the Senate, Padmé. It's very important to avoid even the appearance of disloyalty."

"Anakin—you sound like you're *threatening* me . . ."

"This is a dangerous time," he said. "We are all judged by the company we keep."

"But—I've opposed the war, I opposed Palpatine's emergency powers—I publicly called him a *threat to democracy*!"

"That's all behind us now."

"*What* is? What I've done? Or democracy?"

"Padmé—"

Her chin came up, and her eyes hardened. "Am I under suspicion?"

"Palpatine and I have discussed you already. You're in the clear, so long as you avoid . . . inappropriate associations."

"How am I *in the clear*?"

"Because you're with *me*. Because I *say* you are."

She stared at him as if she'd never seen him before. "You told him."

"He knew."

"Anakin—"

"There's no more need for secrets, Padmé. Don't you see? *I'm not a Jedi anymore*. There *aren't* any Jedi. There's just *me*."

He reached for her hand. She let him take it. "And you, and our child."

"Then we can *go*, can't we?" Her hard stare melted to naked appeal. "We can leave this planet. Go somewhere we can be *together*—somewhere *safe*."

"We'll be together *here*," he said. "You *are* safe. I have *made* you safe."

"Safe," she echoed bitterly, pulling her hand away. "As long as Palpatine doesn't change his mind."

The hand she had pulled from his grasp was trembling.

"The Separatist leadership is in hiding on Mustafar. I'm on my way to deal with them right now."

"*Deal* with them?" The corners of her mouth drew down. "Like the Jedi are being *dealt with*?"

"This is an important mission. I'm going to end the war."

She looked away. "You're going alone?"

"Have faith, my love," he said.

She shook her head helplessly, and a pair of tears spilled from her eyes. He touched them with his mechanical hand; the fingertips of his black glove glistened in the dawn.

Two liquid gems, indescribably precious—because they were *his*. He had earned them. As he had earned *her;* as he had earned the child she bore.

He had paid for them with innocent blood.

"I love you," he said. "This won't take long. Wait for me."

Fresh tears streamed onto her ivory cheeks, and she threw herself into his arms. "Always, Anakin. Forever. Come back to me, my love—my *life*. Come back to me."

He smiled down on her. "You say that like I'm already gone."

Icy salt water shocked Obi-Wan back to full consciousness. He hung in absolute blackness; there was no telling how far underwater he might be, nor even which direction might be up. His lungs were choked, half full of water, but he didn't panic or even particularly worry; mostly, he was vaguely pleased to discover that even in his semiconscious fall, he'd managed to hang on to his lightsaber.

He clipped it back to his belt by feel, and—using only a minor exercise of Jedi discipline to suppress convulsive coughing—he contracted his diaphragm, forcing as much water from his lungs as he could. He took from his equipment belt his rebreather, and a small compressed-air canister intended for use in an emergency, when the breathable environment was not adequate to sustain his life.

Obi-Wan was fairly certain that his current situation qualified as an emergency.

He remembered . . .

Boga's wrenching leap, twisting in the air, the shock of impacts, multiple detonations blasting both of them farther and farther out from the sinkhole wall . . .

Using her massive body to shield Obi-Wan from his own troops.

Boga had *known*, somehow . . . the dragonmount had known what Obi-Wan had been incapable of even suspecting, and without hesitation she'd given her life to save her rider.

I suppose that makes me more than her rider, Obi-Wan thought as he discarded the canister and got his rebreather snugged into place. *I suppose that makes me her friend.*

It certainly made her mine.

He let grief take him for a moment; grief not for the death of a noble beast, but for how little time Obi-Wan had had to appreciate the gift of his friend's service.

But even grief is an attachment, and Obi-Wan let it flow out of his life.

Good-bye, my friend.

He didn't try to swim; he seemed to be hanging motionless, suspended in infinite night. He relaxed, regulated his breathing, and let the water take him whither it would.

C-3PO barely had time to wish his little friend good luck and remind him to stay alert as Master Anakin brushed past him and climbed into the starfighter's cockpit, then fired the engine and blasted off, taking R2-D2 goodness knows where—probably to some preposterously horrible alien planet and into a perfectly ridiculous amount of danger—with never a thought how his loyal *droid* might feel about being *dragged* across the galaxy without so much as a by-your-leave . . .

Really, what *had* happened to that young man's manners?

He turned to Senator Amidala and saw that she was crying.

"Is there anything I can do, my lady?"

She didn't even turn his way. "No, thank you, Threepio."

"A snack, perhaps?"

She shook her head.

"A glass of water?"

"No."

All he could do was stand there. "I feel so *helpless* . . ."

She nodded, looking away again, up at the fading spark of her husband's starfighter.

"I know, Threepio," she said. "We all do."

In the underground shiplift beneath the Senate Office Building, Bail Organa was scowling as he boarded *Tantive IV*. When Captain Antilles met him at the top of the landing ramp, Bail nodded backward at the scarlet-clad figures posted around the accessways. "Since when do Redrobes guard Senate ships?"

Antilles shook his head. "I don't know, sir. I have a feeling there are some Senators whom Palpatine doesn't want leaving the planet."

Bail nodded. "Thank the Force I'm not one of them. Yet. Did you get the beacon?"

"Yes, sir. No one even tried to stop us. The clones at Chance Palp seemed confused—like they're not quite sure who's in charge."

"That'll change soon. Too soon. We'll *all* know who's in charge," Bail said grimly. "Prepare to raise ship."

"Back to Alderaan, sir?"

Bail shook his head. "Kashyyyk. There's no way to know if any Jedi have lived through this—but if I had to bet on one, my money'd be on Yoda."

Some undefinable time later, Obi-Wan felt his head and shoulders breach the surface of the lightless ocean. He unclipped his lightsaber and raised it over his head. In its blue glow he could see that he had come up in a large grotto; holding the lightsaber high, he tucked away his rebreather and sidestroked across the current to a rock outcropping that was rugged enough to offer handholds. He pulled himself out of the water.

The walls of the grotto above the waterline were pocked with openings; after inspecting the mouths of several caves, Obi-Wan came upon one where he felt a faint breath of moving air. It had a distinctly unpleasant smell—it reminded him more than a bit of the dragonmount pen—but when he doused his lightsaber for a moment and listened very closely, he could hear a faint rumble that might have been distant wheels and repulsorlifts passing over sandstone—and what was that? An air horn? Or possibly a very disturbed dragon . . . at any rate, this seemed to be the appropriate path.

He had walked only a few hundred meters before the gloom ahead of him was pierced by the white glare of high-intensity searchlights. He let his blade shrink away and pressed himself into a deep, narrow crack as a pair of seeker droids floated past.

Apparently Cody hadn't given up yet.

Their searchlights illuminated—and, apparently, awakened— some sort of immense amphibian cousin of a dragonmount; it blinked sleepily at them as it lifted its slickly glistening starfighter-sized head.

Oh, Obi-Wan thought. *That explains the smell.*

He breathed into the Force a suggestion that these small bobbing spheroids of circuitry and durasteel were actually, contrary to smell and appearance, some unexpected variety of immortally delicious confection sent down from the heavens by the kindly gods of Huge Slimy Cave-Monsters.

The Huge Slimy Cave-Monster in question promptly opened jaws that could engulf a bantha and snapped one of the seekers from the air, chewing it to slivers with every evidence of satisfaction. The second seeker emitted a startled and thoroughly alarmed *wheeepwheepwheep* and shot away into the darkness, with the creature in hot pursuit.

Reigniting his lightsaber and moving cautiously back out into the cavern, Obi-Wan came upon a nest of what must have been infant Huge Slimy Cave-Monsters; picking his way around it as they lunged and snapped and squalled at him, he reflected absently that people who thought all babies were cute should really get out more.

Obi-Wan walked, and occasionally climbed or slid or had to leap, and walked some more.

Soon the darkness in the cavern gave way to the pale glow of Utapaun traffic lighting, and Obi-Wan found himself standing in a smallish side tunnel off a major thoroughfare. This was clearly little traveled, though; the sandy dust on its floor was so thick it was practically a beach. In fact, he could clearly see the tracks of the last vehicle to pass this way.

Broad parallel tracks pocked with divots: a blade-wheeler.

And beside them stretched long splay-clawed prints of a running dragon.

Obi-Wan blinked in mild astonishment. He had never entirely grown accustomed to the way the Force always came through for him—but neither was he reluctant to accept its gifts. Frowning thoughtfully, he followed the tracks a short distance around a curve, until the tunnel gave way to the small landing platform.

Grievous's starfighter was still there. As were the remains of Grievous.

Apparently not even the local rock-vultures could stomach him.

Tantive IV swept through the Kashyyyk system on silent running; this was still a combat zone. Captain Antilles wouldn't even risk standard scans, because they could so easily be detected and backtraced by Separatist forces.

And the Separatists weren't the only ones Antilles was worried about.

"There's the signal again, sir. Whoops. Wait, I'll get it back." Antilles fiddled some more with the controls on the beacon. "Blasted thing," he muttered. "What, you can't calibrate it without using the Force?"

Bail stared through the forward view wall. Kashyyyk was only a tiny green disk two hundred thousand kilometers away. "Do you have a vector?"

"Roughly, sir. It seems to be on an orbital tangent, headed outsystem."

"I think we can risk a scan. Tight beam."

"Very well, sir."

Antilles gave the necessary orders, and moments later the scan tech reported that the object they'd picked up seemed to be some sort of escape pod. "It's not a Republic model, sir—wait, here comes the database—"

The scan tech frowned at his screen. "It's . . . Wookiee, sir. That doesn't make any sense. Why would a Wookiee escape pod be *outbound* from *Kashyyyk*?"

"Interesting." Bail didn't yet allow himself to hope. "Lifesigns?"

"Yes—well, maybe . . . this reading doesn't make any . . ." The scan tech could only shrug. "I'm not sure, sir. Whatever it is, it's no Wookiee, that's for sure . . ."

For the first time all day, Bail Organa allowed himself to smile. "Captain Antilles?"

The captain saluted crisply. "On our way, sir."

Obi-Wan took General Grievous's starfighter screaming out of the atmosphere so fast he popped the gravity well and made jump before the *Vigilance* could even scramble its fighters. He reverted to realspace well beyond the system, kicked the starfighter to a new vector, and jumped again. A few more jumps of random direction and duration left him deep in interstellar space.

"You know," he said to himself, "integral hyperspace capability is rather useful in a starfighter; why don't *we* have it yet?"

While the starfighter's nav system whirred and chunked its way through recalculating his position, he punched codes to gang his Jedi comlink into the starfighter's system.

Instead of a holoscan, the comlink generated an audio signal—an accelerating series of beeps.

Obi-Wan knew that signal. Every Jedi did. It was the recall code.

It was being broadcast on every channel by every HoloNet repeater. It was supposed to mean that the war was over. It was supposed to mean that the Council had ordered all Jedi to return to the Temple immediately.

Obi-Wan suspected it actually meant what had happened on Utapau was far from an isolated incident.

He keyed the comlink for audio. He took a deep breath.

"Emergency Code Nine Thirteen," he said, and waited.

The starfighter's comm system cycled through every response frequency.

He waited some more.

"Emergency Code Nine Thirteen. This is Obi-Wan Kenobi. Repeat: Emergency Code Nine Thirteen. Are there any Jedi out there?"

He waited. His heart thumped heavily.

"Any Jedi, please respond. This is Obi-Wan Kenobi declaring a Nine Thirteen Emergency."

He tried to ignore the small, still voice inside his head that whispered he might just be the only one out here.

He might just be the only one, period.

He started punching coordinates for a single jump that would bring him close enough to pick up a signal directly from Coruscant when a burst of fuzz came over his comlink. A quick glance confirmed the frequency: a Jedi channel.

"Please repeat," Obi-Wan said. "I'm locking onto your signal. Please repeat."

The fuzz became a spray of blue laser, which gradually resolved into a fuzzy figure of a tall, slim human with dark hair and an elegant goatee. *"Master Kenobi? Are you all right? Have you been wounded?"*

"Senator Organa!" Obi-Wan exclaimed with profound relief. "No, I'm not wounded—but I'm certainly *not* all right. I need help. My clones turned on me. I barely escaped with my life!"

"There have been ambushes all over the galaxy."

Obi-Wan lowered his head, offering a silent wish to the Force that the victims might find peace within it.

"Have you had contact with any other survivors?"

"Only one," the Alderaanian Senator said grimly. *"Lock onto my coordinates. He's waiting for you."*

A curve of knuckle, skinned, black scab corrugated with dirt and leaking red—

The fringe of fray at the cuff of a beige sleeve, dark, crusted with splatter from the death of a general—

The tawny swirl of grain in wine-dark tabletop of polished Alderaanian kriin—

These were what Obi-Wan Kenobi could look at without starting to shake.

The walls of the small conference room on *Tantive IV* were too featureless to hold his attention; to look at a wall allowed his mind to wander . . .

And the shaking began.

The shaking got worse when he met the ancient green stare of the tiny alien seated across the table from him, for that wrinkled leather skin and those tufts of withered hair were his earliest memory, and they reminded Obi-Wan of the friends who had died today.

The shaking got worse still when he turned to the other being in the room, because he wore politician's robes that reminded Obi-Wan of the enemy who yet lived.

The deception. The death of Jedi Masters he had admired, of Jedi Knights who had been his friends. The death of his oath to Qui-Gon.

The death of Anakin.

Anakin must have fallen along with Mace and Agen, Saesee and Kit; fallen along with the Temple.

Along with the Order itself.

Ashes.

Ashes and dust.

Twenty-five thousand years wiped from existence in a single day.

All the dreams. All the promises.

All the *children* . . .

"We took them from their *homes*." Obi-Wan fought to stay in his chair; the pain inside him demanded motion. It became wave after wave of tremors. "We *promised* their *families*—"

"Control yourself, you must; still Jedi, you are!"

"Yes, Master Yoda." That scab on his knuckle—focused on that, he could suppress the shaking. "Yes, we are Jedi. But what if we're the *last*?"

"If the last we are, unchanged our duty is." Yoda settled his chin onto hands folded over the head of his gimer stick. He looked every day of his nearly nine hundred years. "While one Jedi lives, survive the Order does. Resist the darkness with every breath, we must."

He lifted his head and the stick angled to poke Obi-Wan in the shin. "Especially the darkness in *ourselves,* young one. Of the dark side, despair is."

The simple truth of this called to him. Even despair is attachment: it is a grip clenched upon pain.

Slowly, very slowly, Obi-Wan Kenobi remembered what it was to be a Jedi.

He leaned back in his chair and covered his face with both hands, inhaling a thin stream of air between his palms; into himself with the air he brought pain and guilt and remorse, and as he exhaled, they trailed away and vanished in the air.

He breathed out his whole life.

Everything he had done, everything he had been, friends and enemies, dreams and hopes and fears.

Empty, he found clarity. Scrubbed clean, the Force shone through him. He sat up and nodded to Yoda.

"Yes," he said. "We may be the last. But what if we're *not?*"

Green leather brows drew together over lambent eyes. "The Temple beacon."

"Yes. Any surviving Jedi might still obey the recall, and be killed."

Bail Organa looked from one Jedi to the other, frowning. "What are you saying?"

"I'm saying," Obi-Wan replied, "that we have to go back to Coruscant."

"It's too dangerous," the Senator said instantly. "The whole planet is a *trap*—"

"Yes. We have a—ah . . ."

The loss of Anakin stabbed him.

Then he let that go, too.

"*I* have," he corrected himself, "a policy on traps . . ."

THE FACE OF THE SITH

Mustafar burned with lava streaming from volcanoes of glittering obsidian.

At the fringe of its gravity well, a spray of prismatic starlight warped a starfighter into existence. Declamping from its hyperdrive ring, the starfighter streaked into an atmosphere choked with dense smoke and cinders.

The starfighter followed a preprogrammed course toward the planet's lone installation, an automated lava mine built originally by the Techno Union to draw precious metals from the continuous rivers of burning stone. Upgraded with the finest mechanized defenses that money could buy, the settlement had become the final redoubt of the leaders of the Confederacy of Independent Systems. It was absolutely impenetrable.

Unless one had its deactivation codes.

Which was how the starfighter could land without causing the installation's defenses to so much as stir.

The habitable areas of the settlement were spread among towers that looked like poisonous toadstools sprung from the bank of a river of fire. The main control center squatted atop the largest, beside the small landing deck where the starfighter had alit. It was from this control center, less than an hour before, that a coded command had been transmitted over every HoloNet repeater in the galaxy.

At that signal, every combat droid in every army on every planet marched back to its transport, resocketed itself, and turned itself off. The Clone Wars were over.

Almost.

There was a final detail.

A dark-cloaked figure swung down from the cockpit of the starfighter.

Bail Organa strode onto the *Tantive*'s shuttle deck to find Obi-Wan and Yoda gazing dubiously at the tiny cockpit of Obi-Wan's starfighter. "I suppose," Obi-Wan was saying reluctantly, "if you don't mind riding on my lap . . ."

"That may not be necessary," Bail said. "I've just been summoned back to Coruscant by Mas Amedda; Palpatine has called the Senate into Extraordinary Session. Attendance is required."

"Ah." Obi-Wan's mouth turned downward. "It's clear what this will be about."

"I am," Bail said slowly, "concerned it might be a trap."

"Unlikely this is." Yoda hobbled toward him. "Unknown, is the purpose of your sudden departure from the capital; dead, young Obi-Wan and I are both presumed to be."

"And Palpatine won't be moving against the Senate as a whole," Obi-Wan added. "At least, not yet; he'll need the illusion of democracy to keep the individual star systems in line. He won't risk a general uprising."

Bail nodded. "In that case—" He took a deep breath. "—perhaps I can offer Your Graces a lift?"

Inside the control center of the Separatist bunker on Mustafar . . .

Wat Tambor was adjusting the gas mix inside his armor—

Poggle the Lesser was massaging his fleshy lip-tendrils—

Shu Mai was fiddling with the brass binding that restrained her hair into the stylish curving horn that rose behind her head—

San Hill was stretching his bodystocking, which had begun to ride up in the crotch—

Rune Haako was shifting his weight nervously from foot to foot—

While Nute Gunray spoke to the holopresence of Darth Sidious.

"The plan has gone exactly as you promised, my lord," Gunray said. "This is a glorious day for the galaxy!"

"Yes, indeed. Thanks, in great part, to you, Viceroy, and to your associates of the Techno Union and the IBC. And, of course, Archduke Poggle. You have all performed magnificently. Have your droid armies completed shutdown?"

"Yes, my lord. Nearly an hour ago."

"Excellent! You will be handsomely rewarded. Has my new apprentice, Darth Vader, arrived?"

"His ship touched down only a moment ago."

"Good, good," the holoscan of the cloaked man said pleasantly. *"I have left your reward in his hands. He will take care of you."*

The door cycled open.

A tall cloaked figure, slim but broad-shouldered, face shadowed by a heavy hood, stood in the doorway.

San Hill beat the others to the greeting. "Welcome, Lord Vader!" His elongated legs almost tangled with each other in his rush to shake the hand of the Sith Lord. "On behalf of the leadership of the Confederacy of Independent Systems, let me be the first to—"

"Very well. You will be the first."

The cloaked figure stepped inside and made a gesture with a

black-gloved hand. Blast doors slammed across every exit. The control panel exploded in a shower of sparking wires.

The cloaked figure threw back its hood.

San Hill recoiled, hands flapping like panicked birds sewn to his wrists.

He had time to gasp, "You're—you're *Anakin Skywalker!*" before a fountain of blue-white plasma burned into his chest, curving through a loop that charred all three of his hearts.

The Separatist leadership watched in frozen horror as the corpse of the head of the InterGalactic Banking Clan collapsed like a depowered protocol droid.

"The resemblance," Darth Vader said, "is deceptive."

The Senate Guard blinked, then straightened and smoothed the drape of his robe. He risked a glance at his partner, who flanked the opposite side of the door.

Had they really just gotten as lucky as he thought they had?

Were this Senator and his aides really walking right out of the turbolift with a couple of as-yet-uncaptured *Jedi?*

Wow. Promotions all around.

The guard tried not to stare at the two Jedi, and did his best to sound professional. "Welcome back, Senator. May I see your clearance?"

An identichip was produced without hesitation: Bail Organa, senior Senator from Alderaan.

"Thank you. You may proceed." The guard handed back the identichip. He was rather pleased with how steady and business-like he sounded. "We will take custody of the Jedi."

Then the taller of the two Jedi murmured gently that it would be better if he and his counterpart were to stay with the Senator, and really, he seemed like such a reasonable fellow, and it was such a good idea—after all, the Grand Convocation Chamber of the Galactic Senate was so secure there was really no way for a Jedi to cause any trouble for anyone and they could just as easily be apprehended on their way out, and the guard didn't want to seem like an unreasonable fellow himself, and so he found himself nodding and agreeing that yes, indeed, it would be better if the Jedi stayed with the Senator.

And everyone was so reasonable and agreeable that it seemed perfectly reasonable and agreeable to the guard that the Jedi and the Senator, instead of staying together as they'd said, made low-voiced *Force-be-with-you* farewells; it never occurred to the guard to object even when the Senator entered the Convocation Chamber and the two Jedi headed off for . . . well, apparently, somewhere else.

All eight members of Decoy Squad Five were deployed at a downlevel loading dock, where supplies that Jedi could not grow in their own Temple gardens had been delivered daily.

Not anymore.

This deep in Coruscant's downlevels, the sun never shone; the only illumination came from antiquated glow globes, their faded light yellow as ancient parchment, that only darkened the shadows around. In those shadows lived the dregs of the galaxy, squatters and scavengers, madmen and fugitives from the justice above. Parts of Coruscant's downlevels could be worse than Nar Shaddaa.

The men of Decoy Squad Five would have been alert on any post. They were bred to be. Here, though, they were in a combat zone, where their lives and their missions depended on their perceptions, and on how fast their blasters could come out from inside those Jedi-style robes.

So when a ragged, drooling hunchback lurched out of the gloom nearby, a bundle cradled in his arms, Decoy Squad Five took it for granted that he was a threat. Blasters appeared with miraculous speed. "Halt. Identify yourself."

"No, no, no, Yer Graces, oh, no, I'm bein' here to *help,* y'see,

I'm on *yerr* side!" The hunchback slurped drool back into his slack lips as he lurched toward them. "Lookit I got here, I mean, *lookit*—'sa Jedi *babby*, ennit?"

The sergeant of the squad squinted at the bundle in the hunchback's arms. "A Jedi baby?"

"Oooh, sher. Sher, Yer Grace. Jedi babby, sher azzell iddiz! Come from outcher Temple, dinnit? Lookit!"

The hunchback was now close enough that the sergeant could see what he carried in his filthy bundle. It *was* a baby. Sort of. It was the ugliest baby the sergeant had ever seen, alien or not, wizened and shriveled like a worn-out purse of moldly leather, with great pop eyes and a toothless idiot's grin.

The sergeant frowned skeptically. "Anyone could grab some deformed kid and claim it's anything they want. How do you know it's a Jedi?"

The baby said, "My lightsaber, the first clue would be, hmm?"

A burning blade of green slanted across the sergeant's face so close he could smell the ozone, and the hunchback wasn't a hunchback anymore: he now held a lightsaber the color of a summmer sky, and he said in a clipped, educated Coruscanti accent, "Please don't try to resist. No one has to get hurt."

The men of Decoy Squad Five disagreed.

Six seconds later, all eight of them were dead.

Yoda looked up at Obi-Wan. "To hide the bodies, no point there is."

Obi-Wan nodded agreement. "These are clones; an abandoned post is as much a giveaway as a pile of corpses. Let's get to that beacon."

Bail slipped into the rear of the Naboo delegation's Senate pod as Palpatine thundered from the podium, "These Jedi murderers left me *scarred*, left me *deformed*, but they could not scar my *integrity*! They could not deform my *resolve*! The remaining traitors will be hunted down, rooted out wherever they may hide, and brought to justice, dead or alive! All collaborators will suffer the same fate. Those who protect the enemy *are* the enemy! Now is the time! Now we will strike back! Now we will *destroy* the *destroyers*! *Death to the enemies of democracy!*"

The Senate roared.

Amidala didn't even glance at Bail as he slid into a seat beside her. On the opposite side, Representative Binks nodded at him, but said nothing, blinking solemnly. Bail frowned; if even the irrepressible Jar Jar was worried, this looked to be even worse than he'd expected. And he had expected it to be very, very bad.

He touched Amidala's arm softly. "It's all a lie. You know that, don't you?"

She stared frozenly toward the podium. Her eyes glistened with unshed tears. "I don't know *what* I know. Not anymore. Where have you been?"

"I was . . . held up." As she once had told him, some things were better left unsaid.

"He's been presenting evidence all afternoon," she said in a flat, affectless monotone. "Not just the assassination attempt. The Jedi were about to overthrow the Senate."

"It's a lie," he said again.

In the center of the Grand Convocation Chamber, Palpatine leaned upon the Chancellor's Podium as though he drew strength from the Great Seal on its front. "This has been the most trying of times, but we have passed the test. The war is *over*!"

The Senate roared.

"The Separatists have been utterly defeated, and the *Republic will stand*! United! United and *free*!"

The Senate roared.

"The Jedi Rebellion was our final test—it was the last gasp of the forces of darkness! Now we have left that darkness behind us forever, and a new day has begun! It is *morning* in the Republic!"

The Senate roared.

Padmé stared without blinking. "Here it comes," she said numbly.

Bail shook his head. "Here what comes?"

"You'll see."

"Never again will we be divided! Never again will sector turn against sector, planet turn against planet, *sibling* turn against *sibling*! We are one nation, *indivisible*!"

The Senate roared.

"To ensure that we will always stand together, that we will always speak with a single voice and act with a single hand, the Republic must change. We must *evolve*. We must *grow*. We have become an empire in fact; let us become an Empire in name as well! We *are* the first *Galactic Empire*!"

The Senate went wild.

"What are they doing?" Bail said. "Do they understand what they're *cheering* for?"

Padmé shook her head.

"We are an Empire," Palpatine went on, "that will continue to be ruled by this august body! We are an Empire that will never return to the political maneuvering and corruption that have wounded us so deeply; we are an Empire that will be directed by a *single* sovereign, chosen for *life*!"

The Senate went wilder.

"We are an Empire ruled by the *majority*! An Empire ruled by a new Constitution! An Empire of *laws*, not of politicians! An Empire devoted to the preservation of a just society. Of a *safe* and *secure* society! We are an Empire that will *stand ten thousand years*!"

The roar of the Senate took on a continuous boiling roll like the inside of a permanent thunderstorm.

"We will celebrate the anniversary of this day as *Empire Day*. For the sake of our *children*. For our children's children! For the next ten thousand years! Safety! Security! Justice and peace!"

The Senate went berserk.

"Say it with me! Safety, Security, Justice, and Peace! Safety, Security, Justice, and Peace!"

The Senate took up the chant, louder and louder until it seemed the whole galaxy roared along.

Bail couldn't hear Padmé over the din, but he could read her lips.

So this is how liberty dies, she was saying to herself. *With cheering, and applause.*

"We can't let this happen!" Bail lurched to his feet. "I have to get to my pod—we can still enter a motion—"

"No." Her hand seized his arm with astonishing strength, and for the first time since he'd arrived, she looked straight into his eyes. "No, Bail, you can't enter a motion. You *can't*. Fang Zar has already been arrested, and Tundra Dowmeia, and it won't be long until the entire Delegation of the Two Thousand are declared enemies of the state. You stayed off that list for good reason; don't add your name by what you do today."

"But I can't just stand by and *watch*—"

"You're right. You can't just watch. You have to vote *for* him."

"What?"

"Bail, it's the only way. It's the only hope you have of remaining in a position to do *anyone* any good. Vote for Palpatine. Vote for the Empire. Make Mon Mothma vote for him, too. Be good little Senators. Mind your manners and keep your heads down. And keep doing . . . all those things we can't talk about. All those things I can't know. *Promise* me, Bail."

"Padmé, what you're talking about—what we're *not* talking about—it could take *twenty years*! Are you under suspicion? What are you going to do?"

"Don't worry about me," she said distantly. "I don't know I'll live that long."

Within the Separatist leadership bunker's control center were dozens of combat droids. There were armed and armored guards. There were automated defense systems.

There were screams, and tears, and pleas for mercy.

None of them mattered.

The Sith had come to Mustafar.

Poggle the Lesser, Archduke of Geonosis, scrambled like an animal through a litter of severed arms and legs and heads, both metal and flesh, whimpering, fluttering his ancient gauzy wings until a bar of lightning flash-burned his own head free of his neck.

Shu Mai, president and CEO of the Commerce Guild, looked up from her knees, hands clasped before her, tears streaming down her shriveled cheeks. "We were promised a *reward*," she gasped. "A h—h—*handsome* reward—"

"I am your reward," the Sith Lord said. "You don't find me handsome?"

"Please!" she screeched through her sobbing. *"Pleee—"*

The blue-white blade cut into and out from her skull, and her corpse swayed. A negligent flip of the wrist slashed through her column of neck rings. Her brain-burned head tumbled to the floor.

The only sound, then, was a panicky stutter of footfalls as Wat Tambor and the two Neimoidians scampered along a hallway toward a nearby conference room.

The Sith Lord was in no hurry to pursue. All the exits from the control center were blast-shielded, and they were sealed, and he had destroyed the controls.

The conference room was, as the expression goes, a dead end.

Thousands of clone troops swarmed the Jedi Temple.

Multiple battalions on each level were not just an occupying force, but engaged in the long, painstaking process of preparing dead bodies for positive identification. The Jedi dead were to be tallied against the rolls maintained in the Temple archives; the clone dead would be cross-checked with regimental rosters. All the dead had to be accounted for.

This was turning out to be somewhat more complicated than the clone officers had expected. Though the fighting had ended hours ago, troopers kept turning up missing. Usually small patrolling squads—five troopers or less—that still made random sweeps through the Temple hallways, checking every door and window, every desk and every closet.

Sometimes when those closets were opened, what was found inside was five dead clones.

And there were disturbing reports as well; officers coordinating the sweeps recorded a string of sightings of movement—usually a flash of robe disappearing around a corner, caught in a trooper's peripheral vision—that on investigation seemed to have been only imagination, or hallucination. There were also multiple reports of inexplicable sounds coming from out-of-the-way areas that turned out to be deserted.

Though clone troopers were schooled from even before awakening in their Kaminoan crèche-schools to be ruthlessly pragmatic, materialistic, and completely impervious to superstition, some of them began to suspect that the Temple might be haunted.

In the vast misty gloom of the Room of a Thousand Fountains, one of the clones on the cleanup squad caught a glimpse of someone moving beyond a stand of Hylaian marsh bamboo. "Halt!" he shouted. "You there! Don't move!"

The shadowy figure darted off into the gloom, and the clone turned to his squad brothers. "Come on! Whatever that was, we can't let it get away!"

Clones pelted off into the mist. Behind them, at the spill of bodies they'd been working on, fog and gloom gave birth to a pair of Jedi Masters.

Obi-Wan stepped over white-armored bodies to kneel beside blaster-burned corpses of children. Tears flowed freely down tracks that hadn't had a chance to dry since he'd first entered the Temple. "Not even the younglings survived. It looks like they made a stand here."

Yoda's face creased with ancient sadness. "Or trying to flee they were, with some turning back to slow the pursuit."

Obi-Wan turned to another body, an older one, a Jedi fully mature and beyond. Grief punched a gasp from his chest. "Master Yoda—it's the *Troll* . . ."

Yoda looked over and nodded bleakly. "Abandon his young students, Cin Drallig would not."

Obi-Wan sank to his knees beside the fallen Jedi. "He was my lightsaber instructor . . ."

"And his, was I," Yoda said. "Cripple us, grief will, if let it we do."

"I know. But . . . it's one thing to know a friend is dead, Master Yoda. It's another to find his *body* . . ."

"Yes." Yoda moved closer. With his gimer stick, he pointed at a bloodless gash in Drallig's shoulder that had cloven deep into his chest. "Yes, it is. See this, do you? This wound, no blaster could make."

An icy void opened in Obi-Wan's heart. It swallowed his pain and his grief, leaving behind a precariously empty calm.

He whispered, "A *lightsaber*?"

"Business with the recall beacon, have we still." Yoda pointed with his stick at figures winding toward them among the trees and pools. "Returning, the clones are."

Obi-Wan rose. "I will learn who did this."

"Learn?"

Yoda shook his head sadly.

"Know already, you do," he said, and hobbled off into the gloom.

Darth Vader left nothing living behind when he walked from the main room of the control center.

Casually, carelessly, he strolled along the hallway, scoring the durasteel wall with the tip of his blade, enjoying the sizzle of disintegrating metal as he had savored the smoke of charred alien flesh.

The conference room door was closed. A barrier so paltry would be an insult to the blade; a black-gloved hand made a fist. The door crumpled and fell.

The Sith Lord stepped over it.

The conference room was walled with transparisteel. Beyond, obsidian mountains rained fire upon the land. Rivers of lava embraced the settlement.

Rune Haako, aide and confidential secretary to the viceroy of the Trade Federation, tripped over a chair as he stumbled back. He fell to the floor, shaking like a grub in a frying pan, trying to scrabble beneath the table.

"Stop!" he cried. "Enough! We *surrender,* do you understand? You can't just *kill* us—"

The Sith Lord smiled. "Can't I?"

"We're unarmed! We surrender! Please—please, you're a *Jedi!*"

"You fought a war to destroy the Jedi." Vader stood above the shivering Neimoidian, smiling down upon him, then fed him half a meter of plasma. "Congratulations on your success."

The Sith Lord stepped over Haako's corpse to where Wat Tambor clawed uselessly at the transparisteel wall with his armored gauntlets. The head of the Techno Union turned at his approach, cringing, arms lifted to shield his faceplate from the flames in the dragon's eyes. "Please, I'll give you *anything. Anything you want!*"

The blade flashed twice; Tambor's arms fell to the floor, followed by his head.

"Thank you."

Darth Vader turned to the last living leader of the Confederacy of Independent Systems.

Nute Gunray, viceroy of the Trade Federation, stood trembling in an alcove, blood-tinged tears streaming down his green-mottled cheeks. "The war . . . ," he whimpered. "The war is *over*—Lord Sidious *promised*—he promised we would be left in *peace* . . ."

"His transmission was garbled." The blade came up. "He promised you would be left in *pieces*."

In the main holocomm center of the Jedi Temple, high atop the central spire, Obi-Wan used the Force to reach deep within the shell of the recall beacon's mechanism, subtly altering the pulse calibration to flip the signal from *come home* to *run and hide*. Done without any visible alteration, it would take the troopers quite a while to detect the recalibration, and longer still to reset it. This was all that could be done for any surviving Jedi: a warning, to give them a fighting chance.

Obi-Wan turned from the recall beacon to the internal security scans. He had to find out exactly what he was warning them against.

"Do this not," Yoda said. "Leave we must, before discovered we are."

"I have to *see* it," Obi-Wan said grimly. "Like I said downstairs: knowing is one thing. Seeing is another."

"Seeing will only cause you pain."

"Then it is pain that I have earned. I won't hide from it." He keyed a code that brought up a holoscan of the Room of a Thousand Fountains. "I am not afraid."

Yoda's eyes narrowed to green-gold slits. "You should be."

Stone-faced, Obi-Wan watched younglings run into the

room, fleeing a storm of blasterfire; he watched Cin Drallig and a pair of teenage Padawans—was that Whie, the boy Yoda had brought to Vjun?—backing into the scene, blades whirling, cutting down the advancing clone troopers with deflected bolts.

He watched a lightsaber blade flick into the shot, cutting down first one Padawan, then the other. He watched the brisk stride of a caped figure who hacked through Drallig's shoulder, then stood aside as the old Troll fell dying to let the rest of the clones blast the children to shreds.

Obi-Wan's expression never flickered.

He opened himself to what he was about to see; he was prepared, and centered, and trusting in the Force, and yet . . .

Then the caped man turned to meet a cloaked figure behind him, and he was—

He was—

Obi-Wan, staring, wished that he had the strength to rip his eyes out of his head.

But even blind, he would see this forever.

He would see his friend, his student, his brother, turn and kneel in front of a black-cloaked Lord of the Sith.

His head rang with a silent scream.

"The traitors have been destroyed, Lord Sidious. And the archives are secured. Our ancient holocrons are again in the hands of the Sith."

"Good . . . good . . . Together, we shall master every secret of the Force." The Sith Lord purred like a contented rancor. *"You have done well, my new apprentice. Do you feel your power growing?"*

"Yes, my Master."

"Lord Vader, your skills are unmatched by any Sith before you. Go forth, my boy. Go forth, and bring peace to our Empire."

Fumbling nervelessly, Obi-Wan somehow managed to shut down the holoscan. He leaned on the console, but his arms would not support him; they buckled and he twisted to the floor.

He huddled against the console, blind with pain.

Yoda was as sympathetic as the root of a wroshyr tree. "Warned, you were."

Obi-Wan said, "I should have let them *shoot* me . . ."

"What?"

"No. That was already too late—it was already too late at Geonosis. The Zabrak, on Naboo—I should have died *there* . . . before I ever *brought* him here—"

"*Stop* this, you will!" Yoda gave him a stick-jab in the ribs sharp enough to straighten him up. "*Make* a Jedi fall, one cannot; beyond even Lord Sidious, this is. *Chose* this, Skywalker did."

Obi-Wan lowered his head. "And I'm afraid I might know why."

"Why? *Why* matters not. There is no *why*. There is only a Lord of the Sith, and his apprentice. Two Sith." Yoda leaned close. "And two Jedi."

Obi-Wan nodded, but he still couldn't meet the gaze of the ancient Master. "I'll take Palpatine."

"Strong enough to face Lord Sidious, you will never be. Die you will, and painfully."

"Don't make me kill Anakin," he said. "He's like my *brother*, Master."

"The boy you trained, gone he is—twisted by the dark side. Consumed by Darth Vader. Out of this misery, you must put him. To visit our new Emperor, *my* job will be."

Now Obi-Wan did face him. "Palpatine faced Mace and Agen and Kit and Saesee—four of the greatest swordsmen our Order has ever produced. By *himself*. Even both of us together wouldn't have a chance."

"True," Yoda said. "But both of us apart, a chance we might *create* . . ."

CHIAROSCURO

C-3PO identified the craft docking on the veranda as a DC0052 Intergalactic Speeder; to be on the safe side, he left the security curtain engaged.

In these troubled times, safety outweighed courtesy, even for him.

A cloaked and hooded human male emerged from the DC0052 and approached the veil of energy. C-3PO moved to meet him. "Hello, may I help you?"

The human lifted his hands to his hood; instead of taking it down, he folded it back far enough that C-3PO could register the distinctive relationship of eyes, nose, mouth, and beard.

"Master Kenobi!" C-3PO had long ago been given detailed and quite specific instructions on the procedure for dealing with the unexpected arrival of furtive Jedi.

He instantly deactivated the security curtain and beckoned. "Come inside, quickly. You may be seen."

As C-3PO swiftly ushered him into the sitting room, Master Kenobi asked, "Has Anakin been here?"

"Yes," C-3PO said reluctantly. "He arrived shortly after he and the army saved the Republic from the Jedi Rebellion—"

He cut himself off when he noticed that Master Kenobi suddenly looked fully prepared to dismantle him bolt by bolt. Perhaps he should not have been so quick to let the Jedi in.

Wasn't he some sort of outlaw, now?

"I, ah, I should—" C-3PO stammered, backing away. "I'll just go get the Senator, shall I? She's been lying down—after the Grand Convocation this morning, she didn't feel entirely well, and so—"

The Senator appeared at the top of the curving stairway, belting a soft robe over her dressing gown, and C-3PO decided his most appropriate course of action would be to discreetly withdraw.

But not too far; if Master Kenobi was up to mischief, C-3PO had to be in a position to alert Captain Typho and the security staff on the spot.

Senator Amidala certainly didn't seem inclined to *treat* Master Kenobi as a dangerous outlaw . . .

Quite the contrary, in fact: she seemed to have fallen into his arms, and her voice was thoroughly choked with emotion as she expressed a possibly inappropriate level of joy at finding the Jedi still alive.

There followed some discussion that C-3PO didn't entirely understand; it was political information entirely outside his programming, having to do with Master Anakin, and the Republic having fallen, whatever that meant, and with something called a Sith Lord, and Chancellor Palpatine, and the dark side of the Force, and really, he couldn't make sense of any of it. The only parts he clearly understood had to do with the Jedi Order being outlawed and all but wiped out (that news had been all over the Lipartian Way this morning) and the not-altogether-unexpected revelation that Master Kenobi had come here seeking Master Anakin. They *were* partners, after all (though despite all their years together, Master Anakin's recent behavior made it sadly clear that Master Kenobi's lovely manners had entirely failed to rub off).

"When was the last time you saw him? Do you know where he is?"

C-3PO's photoreceptors registered the Senator's flush as she lowered her eyes and said, "No."

Three years running the household of a career politician stopped C-3PO from popping back out and reminding the Senator that Master Anakin had told her just yesterday he was on his way to Mustafar; he knew very well that the Senator's memory failed only when she decided it should.

"Padmé, you must help me," Master Kenobi said. "Anakin must be found. He must be stopped."

"How can you *say* that?" She pulled back from him and turned away, folding her arms over the curve of her belly. "He's just won the war!"

"The war was never the Republic against the Separatists. It was Palpatine against the Jedi. We lost. The rest of it was just play-acting."

"It was real enough for everyone who *died!*"

"Yes." Now it was Master Kenobi's turn to lower his eyes. "Including the children at the Temple."

"What?"

"They were *murdered,* Padmé. I saw it." He took her shoulders and turned her back to face him. "They were murdered by *Anakin.*"

"It's a *lie*—" She pushed him away forcefully enough that C-3PO nearly triggered the security alert then and there, but Master Kenobi only regarded her with an expression that matched C-3PO's internal recognition files of sadness and pity. "He could *never* . . . he could never . . . not my Anakin . . ."

Master Kenobi's voice was soft and slow. "He must be found."

Her reply was even softer; C-3PO's aural sensor barely recorded it at all.

"You've decided to kill him."

Master Kenobi said gravely, "He has become a very great threat."

At this, the Senator's medical condition seemed to finally overcome her; her knees buckled, and Master Kenobi was forced to catch her and help her onto the sofa. Apparently Master Kenobi knew somewhat more about human physiology than did C-3PO; though his photoreceptors hadn't been dark to the on-going changes in Senator Amidala's contour, C-3PO had no idea what they might signify.

At any rate, Master Kenobi seemed to comprehend the situation instantly. He settled her comfortably onto the sofa and stood frowning down at her.

"Anakin is the father, isn't he?"

The Senator looked away. Her eyes were leaking again.

The Jedi Master said, hushed, "I'm very sorry, Padmé. If it could be different . . ."

"Go away, Obi-Wan. I won't help you. I can't." She turned her face away. "I won't help you kill him."

Master Kenobi said again, "I'm very sorry," and left.

C-3PO tentatively returned to the sitting room, intending to inquire after the Senator's health, but before he could access a sufficiently delicate phrase to open the discussion, the Senator said softly, "Threepio? Do you know what this is?"

She lifted toward him the pendant that hung from the cord of jerba leather she always wore around her neck.

"Why, yes, my lady," the protocol droid replied, bemused but happy, as always, to be of service. "It's a snippet of japor. Younglings on Tatooine carve tribal runes into them to make amulets; they are supposed by superstitious folk to bring good fortune and protect one from harm, and sometimes are thought to be love charms. I must say, my lady, I'm quite surprised *you've* forgotten, seeing as how you've worn that one ever since it was given to you so many years ago by Master An—"

"I hadn't forgotten what it was, Threepio," she said distantly.

"Thank you. I was . . . reminding myself of the boy who gave it to me."

"My lady?" If she hadn't forgotten, why would she ask? Before C-3PO could phrase a properly courteous interrogative, she said, "Contact Captain Typho. Have him ready my skiff."

"My lady? Are you going somewhere?"

"*We* are," she said. "We're going to Mustafar."

From the shadows beneath the mirror-polished skiff's landing ramp, Obi-Wan Kenobi watched Captain Typho try to talk her out of it.

"My lady," the Naboo security chief protested, "at least let me come *with* you—"

"Thank you, Captain, but there's no need," Padmé said distantly. "The war's over, and . . . this is a *personal* errand. And, Captain? It must *remain* personal, do you understand? You know nothing of my leaving, nor where I am bound, nor when I can be expected to return."

"As you wish, my lady," Typho said with a reluctant bow. "But I *strongly* disagree with this decision."

"I'll be fine, Captain. After all, I have Threepio to look after me."

Obi-Wan could clearly hear the droid's murmured "Oh, dear."

After Typho finally climbed into his speeder and took off, Padmé and her droid boarded the skiff. She wasted no time at all; the skiff's repulsorlifts engaged before the landing ramp had even retracted.

Obi-Wan had to jump for it.

He swung inside just as the hatch sealed itself and the gleaming starship leapt for the sky.

Darth Vader stood on the command bridge of the Mustafar control center, hand of durasteel clasping hand of flesh behind him, and gazed up through the transparisteel view wall at the galaxy he would one day rule.

He paid no attention to the litter of corpses around his feet.

He could feel his power growing, indeed. He had the measure of his "Master" already; not long after Palpatine shared the secret of Darth Plagueis's discovery, their relationship would undergo a sudden . . . transformation.

A fatal transformation.

Everything was proceeding according to plan.

And yet . . .

He couldn't shake a certain creeping sensation . . . a kind of cold, slimy ooze that slithered up the veins of his legs and spread clammy tendrils through his guts . . .

Almost as though he was still *afraid* . . .

She will die, you know, the dragon whispered.

He shook himself, scowling. Impossible. He was Darth Vader. Fear had no power over him. He had destroyed his fear.

All things die.

Yet it was as though when he had crushed the dragon under his boot, the dragon had sunk venomed fangs into his heel.

Now its poison chilled him to the bone.

Even stars burn out.

He shook himself again and strode toward the holocomm. He would talk to his Master.

Palpatine had always helped him keep the dragon down.

A comlink chimed.

Yoda opened his eyes in the darkness.

"Yes, Master Kenobi?"

"We're landing now. Are you in position?"

"I am."

A moment of silence.

"Master Yoda . . . if we don't see each other again—"

"Think not of *after*, Obi-Wan. Always now, even eternity will be."

Another moment of silence.

Longer.

"May the Force be with you."

"It is. And may the Force be with you, young Obi-Wan."

The transmission ended.

Yoda rose.

A gesture opened the grating of the vent shaft where he had waited in meditation, revealing the vast conic well that was the Grand Convocation Chamber of the Galactic Senate. It was sometimes called the Senate Arena.

Today, this nickname would be particularly apt.

Yoda stretched blood back into his green flesh.

This was his time.

Nine hundred years of study and training, of teaching and of meditation, all now focused, and refined, and resolved into this single moment; the sole purpose of his vast span of existence had been to prepare him to enter the heart of night and bring his light against the darkness.

He adjusted the angle of his blade against his belt.

He draped his robe across his shoulders.

With reverence, with gratitude, without fear, and without anger, Yoda went forth to war.

A silvery flash outside caught Darth Vader's eye, as though an elegantly curved mirror swung through the smoke and cinders, picking up the shine of white-hot lava. From one knee, he could look right through the holoscan of his Master while he continued his report.

He was no longer afraid; he was too busy pretending to be respectful.

"The Separatist leadership is no more, my Master."

"It is finished, then." The image offered a translucent mock-

ery of a smile. *"You have restored peace and justice to the galaxy, Lord Vader."*

"That is my sole ambition. Master."

The image tilted its head, its smile twisting without transition to a scowl. *"Lord Vader—I sense a disturbance in the Force. You may be in danger."*

He glanced at the mirror flash outside; he knew that ship. *In danger of being kissed to death, perhaps . . .*

"How should I be in danger, Master?"

"I cannot say. But the danger is real; be mindful."

Be mindful, be mindful, he thought with a mental sneer. *Is that the best you can do? I could get that much from Obi-Wan . . .*

"I will, my Master. Thank you."

The image faded.

He got to his feet, and now the sneer was on his lips and in his eyes. "You're the one who should be *mindful,* my 'Master.' I *am* a disturbance in the Force."

Outside, the sleek skiff settled to the deck. He spent a moment reassembling his Anakin Skywalker face: he let Anakin Skywalker's love flow through him, let Anakin Skywalker's glad smile come to his lips, let Anakin Skywalker's youthful energy bring a joyous bounce to his step as he trotted to the entrance over the mess of corpses and severed body parts.

He'd meet her outside, and he'd keep her outside. He had a feeling she wouldn't approve of the way he had . . . redecorated . . . the control center.

And after all, he thought with a mental shrug, *there's no arguing taste . . .*

The holding office of the Supreme Chancellor of the Republic comprised the nether vertex of the Senate Arena; it was little more than a circular preparations area, a green room, where guests of the Chancellor might be entertained before entering the Senate Podium—the circular pod on its immense hydraulic pillar, which contained controls that coordinated the movement of floating Senate delegation pods—and rising into the focal point of the chamber above.

Above that podium, the vast holopresence of a kneeling Sith bowed before a shadow that stood below. Guards in scarlet flanked the shadow; a Chagrian toady cringed nearby.

"But the danger is real; be mindful."

"I will, my Master. Thank you."

The holopresence faded, and where its huge translucency had knelt was now revealed another presence, a physical presence, tiny and aged, clad in robes and leaning on a twist of wood. But his physical presence was an illusion; the truth of him could be seen only in the Force.

In the Force, he was a fountain of light.

"Pity your new disciple I do; so lately an apprentice, so soon without a Master."

"Why, Master Yoda, what a delightful surprise! Welcome!" The voice of the shadow hummed with anticipation. "Let me be the first to wish you Happy Empire Day!"

"Find it happy, you will not. Nor will the murderer you call Vader."

"Ah." The shadow stepped closer to the light. "So *that* is the threat I felt. Who is it, if I may ask? Who have you sent to kill him?"

"Enough it is that you know your *own* destroyer."

"Oh, pish, Master Yoda. It wouldn't be Kenobi, would it? *Please* say it's Kenobi—Lord Vader gets such a thrill from killing people who care for him . . ."

Behind the shadow, some meters away, Mas Amedda—the Chagrian toady who was Speaker of the Galactic Senate—heard a whisper in Palpatine's voice. *Flee.*

He did.

Neither light nor shadow gave his exit a glance.

"So easily slain, Obi-Wan is not."

"Neither are you, apparently; but that is about to change." The shadow took another step, and another.

A lightsaber appeared, green as sunlight in a forest. "The test of that, today will be."

"Even a fraction of the dark side is more power than your Jedi arrogance can conceive; living in the light, you have never seen the depth of the darkness."

The shadow spread arms that made its sleeves into black wings.

"Until now."

Lightning speared from outstretched hands, and the battle was on.

Padmé stumbled down the landing ramp into Anakin's arms.

Her eyes were raw and numb; once inside the ship, her emotional control had finally shattered and she had sobbed the whole way there, crying from relentless mind-shredding dread, and so her lips were swollen and her whole body shook and she was just so *grateful,* so incredibly grateful, that again she flooded with fresh tears: grateful that he was alive, grateful that he'd come bounding across the landing deck to meet her, that he was still strong and beautiful, that his arms still were warm around her and his lips were soft against her hair.

"Anakin, my *Anakin* . . ." She shivered against his chest. "I've been so *frightened . . .*"

"Shh. Shh, it's all right." He stroked her hair until her trembling began to fade, then he cupped her chin and gently raised her face to look into his eyes. "You never need to worry about me. Didn't you understand? No one can hurt me. No one will ever hurt either of us."

"It wasn't that, my love, it was—oh, Anakin, he said such terrible things about you!"

He smiled down at her. "About me? Who would want to say bad things about me?" He chuckled. "Who would dare?"

"Obi-Wan." She smeared tears from her cheeks. "He said—he told me you turned to the dark side, that you murdered Jedi . . . even *younglings* . . ."

Just having gotten the words out made her feel better; now all she had to do was rest in his arms while he held her and hugged her and promised her he would never do anything like any of that, and she started half a smile aimed up toward his eyes—

But instead of the light of love in his eyes, she saw only reflections of lava.

He didn't say, *I could never turn to the dark side.*

He didn't say, *Murder younglings? Me? That's just crazy.*

He said, "Obi-Wan's *alive?*"

His voice had dropped an octave, and had gone colder than the chills that were spreading from the base of her spine.

"Y-yes—he, he said he was looking for you . . ."

"Did you tell him where I am?"

"*No*, Anakin! He wants to *kill* you. I didn't tell him *anything*—I wouldn't!"

"Too bad."

"Anakin, what—"

"He's a traitor, Padmé. He's an enemy of the state. He has to die."

"Stop it," she said. "Stop *talking* like that . . . you're frightening me!"

"You're not the one who needs to be afraid."

"It's like—it's like—" Tears brimmed again. "I don't even know who you *are* anymore . . ."

"I'm the man who *loves* you," he said, but he said it through clenched teeth. "I'm the man who would do *anything* to protect you. *Everything* I have done, I have done for *you*."

"Anakin . . ." Horror squeezed her voice down to a whisper: small, and fragile, and very young. ". . . what *have* you done?"

And she prayed that he wouldn't actually answer.

"What I have done is bring *peace* to the Republic."

"The Republic is *dead*," she whispered. "You killed it. You and Palpatine."

"It needed to die."

New tears started, but they didn't matter; she'd never have enough tears for this. "Anakin, can't we just . . . *go*? Please. Let's leave. Together. Today. Now. Before you—before something happens—"

"Nothing will happen. Nothing *can* happen. *Let* Palpatine call himself Emperor. Let him. He can do the dirty work, all the messy, brutal oppression it'll take to unite the galaxy forever— unite it *against* him. He'll make himself into the most hated man in history. And when the time is right, we'll throw him *down*—"

"Anakin, stop—"

"Don't you see? We'll be *heroes*. The whole galaxy will *love* us, and we will *rule. Together*."

"Please stop—Anakin, please, stop, I can't *stand* it . . ."

He wasn't listening to her. He wasn't looking at her. He was looking past her shoulder.

Feral joy burned from his eyes, and his face was no longer human.

"You . . ."

From behind her, calmly precise, with that clipped Coruscanti accent: "Padmé. Move away from him."

"Obi-Wan?" She whirled, and he was on the landing ramp, still and sad. *"No!"*

"You," growled a voice that should have been her love's. "You *brought* him here . . ."

She turned back, and now he *was* looking at her.

His eyes were full of flame.

"Anakin?"

"Padmé, move *away*." There was an urgency in Obi-Wan's voice that sounded closer to fear than Padmé had ever heard from him. "He's not who you think he is. He *will* harm you."

Anakin's lips peeled off his teeth. "I would thank you for this, if it were a gift of love."

Trembling, shaking her head, she began to back away. "No, Anakin—no . . ."

"Palpatine was right. Sometimes it is the closest who cannot see. I loved you too much, Padmé."

He made a fist, and she couldn't breathe.

"I loved you too much to *see* you! To see what you *are*!"

A veil of red descended on the world. She clawed at her throat, but there was nothing there her hands could touch.

"Let her go, Anakin."

His answer was a predator's snarl, over the body of its prey. "You will not take her from me!"

She wanted to scream, to beg, to howl, *No, Anakin, I'm sorry! I'm sorry . . . I love you . . .*, but her locked throat strangled the truth inside her head, and the world-veil of red smoked toward black.

"Let her go!"

"Never!"

The ground fell away beneath her, and then a white flash of impact blasted her into night.

In the Senate Arena, lightning forked from the hands of a Sith, and bent away from the gesture of a Jedi to shock Redrobes into unconsciousness.

Then there were only the two of them.

Their clash transcended the personal; when new lightning blazed, it was not Palpatine burning Yoda with his hate, it was the Lord of all Sith scorching the Master of all Jedi into a smoldering huddle of clothing and green flesh.

A thousand years of hidden Sith exulted in their victory.

"Your time is *over*! The *Sith* rule the galaxy! Now and *forever*!"

And it was the whole of the Jedi Order that rocketed from its huddle, making of its own body a weapon to blast the Sith to the ground.

"At an end your rule is, and not short enough it was, I must say."

There appeared a blade the color of life.

From the shadow of a black wing, a small weapon—a hold-out, an easily concealed backup, a tiny bit of treachery expressing the core of Sith mastery—slid into a withered hand and spat a flame-colored blade of its own.

When those blades met, it was more than Yoda against Palpatine, more the millennia of Sith against the legions of Jedi; this was the expression of the fundamental conflict of the universe itself.

Light against dark.

Winner take all.

Obi-Wan knelt beside Padmé's unconscious body, where she lay limp and broken in the smoky dusk. He felt for a pulse. It was thin, and erratic. "Anakin—Anakin, what have you *done*?"

In the Force, Anakin burned like a fusion torch. "You turned her against me."

Obi-Wan looked at the best friend he had ever had. "You did that yourself," he said sadly.

"I'll give you a chance, Obi-Wan. For old times' sake. Walk away."

"If only I could."

"Go some place out of the way. Retire. Meditate. That's what you like, isn't it? You don't have to fight for peace anymore. Peace is *here*. My Empire *is* peace."

"*Your* Empire? It will *never* have peace. It was founded on treachery and innocent blood."

"Don't make me kill you, Obi-Wan. If you are not with me, you are against me."

"Only Sith deal in absolutes, Anakin. The truth is never black and white." He rose, spreading empty hands. "Let me take Padmé to a medcenter. She's hurt, Anakin. She needs medical attention."

"She stays."

"Anakin—"

"*You* don't get to take her *anywhere*. You don't get to *touch* her. She's *mine*, do you understand? It's *your* fault, *all* of it—you made her *betray me*!"

"Anakin—"

Anakin's hand sprouted a bar of blue plasma.

Obi-Wan sighed.

He brought out his own lighstaber and angled it before him. "Then I will do what I must."

"You'll try," Anakin said, and leapt.

Obi-Wan met him in the air.

Blue blades crossed, and the volcano above echoed their lightning with a shout of fire.

C-3PO cautiously poked his head around the rim of the skiff's hatch.

Though his threat-avoidance subroutines were in full screaming overload, and all he really wanted to be doing was finding some nice dark closet in which to fold himself and power down until this was all over—preferably an *armored* closet, with a door that locked from the inside, or could be welded shut (he wasn't particular on that point)—he found himself nonetheless creeping down the skiff's landing ramp into what appeared to be a perfectly appalling rain of molten *lava* and burning *cinders* . . .

Which was an entirely ridiculous thing for any sensible droid to be doing, but he kept going because he hadn't liked the sound of those conversations at all.

Not one little bit.

He couldn't be entirely certain what the disagreement

among the humans was concerned with, but one element had been entirely clear.

She's hurt, Anakin . . . she needs medical attention . . .

He shuffled out into the swirling smoke. Burning rocks clattered around him. The Senator was nowhere to be seen, and even if he could find her, he had no idea how he could get her back to her ship—he certainly had not been designed for transporting anything heavier than a tray of cocktails; after all, weight-bearing capability was what *cargo* droids were for—but through the volcano's roar and the gusts of wind, his sonoreceptors picked up a familiar *ferooo-wheep peroo,* which his autotranslation protocol converted to DON'T WORRY. YOU'LL BE ALL RIGHT.

"Artoo?" C-3PO called. "Artoo, are you out here?"

A few steps more and C-3PO could see the little astromech: he'd tangled his manipulator arm in the Senator's clothing and was dragging her across the landing deck. "Artoo! Stop that this instant! You'll damage her!"

R2-D2's dome swiveled to bring his photoreceptor to bear on the nervous protocol droid. WHAT EXACTLY DO YOU SUGGEST? it whistled.

"Well . . . oh, all right. We'll do it together."

There came a turning point in the clash of the light against the dark.

It did not come from a flash of lightning or slash of energy blade, though there were these in plenty; it did not come from a flying kick or a surgically precise punch, though these were traded, too.

It came as the battle shifted from the holding office to the great Chancellor's Podium; it came as the hydraulic lift beneath the Podium raised it on its tower of durasteel a hundred meters and more, so that it became a laserpoint of battle flaring at the focus of the vast emptiness of the Senate Arena; it came as the

Force and the podium's controls ripped delegation pods free of the curving walls and made of them hammers, battering rams, catapult stones crashing and crushing against each other in a rolling thunder-roar that echoed the Senate's cheers for the galaxy's new Emperor.

It came when the avatar of light resolved into the lineage of the Jedi; when the lineage of the Jedi refined into one single Jedi.

It came when Yoda found himself alone against the dark.

In that lightning-speared tornado of feet and fists and blades and bashing machines, his vision finally pierced the darkness that had clouded the Force.

Finally, he saw the truth.

This truth: that he, the avatar of light, Supreme Master of the Jedi Order, the fiercest, most implacable, most devastatingly powerful foe the darkness had ever known . . .

just—

didn't—

have it.

He'd never had it. He had lost before he started.

He had lost before he was born.

The Sith had changed. The Sith had grown, had adapted, had invested a thousand years' intensive study into every aspect of not only the Force but Jedi lore itself, in preparation for exactly this day. The Sith had remade themselves.

They had become *new.*

While the Jedi—

The Jedi had spent that same millennium training to refight the *last* war.

The new Sith could not be destroyed with a lightsaber; they could not be burned away by any torch of the Force. The brighter his light, the darker their shadow. How could one win a war against the dark, when war itself had become the dark's own weapon?

He knew, at that instant, that this insight held the hope of the galaxy. But if he fell here, that hope would die with him.

Hmmm, Yoda thought. *A problem this is . . .*

Blade-to-blade, they were identical. After thousands of hours in lightsaber sparring, they knew each other better than brothers, more intimately than lovers; they were complementary halves of a single warrior.

In every exchange, Obi-Wan gave ground. It was his way. And he knew that to strike Anakin down would burn his own heart to ash.

Exchanges flashed. Leaps were sideslipped or met with flying kicks; ankle sweeps skipped over and punches parried. The door of the control center fell in pieces, and then they were inside among the bodies. Consoles exploded in fountains of white-hot sparks as they ripped free of their moorings and hurtled through the air. Dead hands spasmed on triggers and blaster bolts sizzled through impossibly intricate lattices of ricochet.

Obi-Wan barely caught some and flipped them at Anakin: a desperation move. Anything to distract him; anything to slow him down. Easily, contemptuously, Anakin sent them back, and the bolts flared between their blades until their galvening faded and the particles of the packeted beams dispersed into radioactive fog.

"Don't make me destroy you, Obi-Wan." Anakin's voice had gone deeper than a well and bleak as the obsidian cliffs. "You're no match for the power of the dark side."

"I've heard that before," Obi-Wan said through his teeth, parrying madly, "but I never thought I'd hear it from *you.*"

A roar of the Force blasted Obi-Wan back into a wall, smashing breath from his lungs, leaving him swaying, half stunned. Anakin stepped over bodies and lifted his blade for the kill.

Obi-Wan had only one trick left, one that wouldn't work twice—

But it was a very good trick.

It had, after all, worked rather splendidly on Grievous . . .

He twitched one finger, reaching through the Force to reverse the polarity of the electrodrivers in Anakin's mechanical hand.

Durasteel fingers sprang open, and a lightsaber tumbled free.

Obi-Wan reached. Anakin's lightsaber twisted in the air and flipped into his hand. He poised both blades in a cross before him. "The flaw of power is arrogance."

"You hesitate," Anakin said. "The flaw of *compassion*—"

"It's not compassion," Obi-Wan said sadly. "It's reverence for life. Even yours. It's respect for the man you were."

He sighed. "It's regret for the man you should have been."

Anakin roared and flew at him, using both the Force and his body to crash Obi-Wan back into the wall once more. His hands seized Obi-Wan's wrists with impossible strength, forcing his arms wide. "I am so *sick* of your *lectures*!"

Dark power bore down with his grip.

Obi-Wan felt the bones of his forearms bending, beginning to feather toward the greenstick fractures that would come before the final breaks.

Oh, he thought. *Oh, this is bad.*

The end came with astonishing suddenness.

The shadow could feel how much it cost the little green freak to bend back his lightnings into the cage of energy that enclosed them both; the creature had reached the limits of his strength. The shadow released its power for an instant, long enough only to whirl away through the air and alight upon one of the delegation pods as it flew past, and the creature leapt to follow—

Half a second too slow.

The shadow unleashed its lightning while the creature was still in the air, and the little green freak took its full power. The shock blasted him backward to crash against the podium, and he fell.

He fell a long way.

The base of the Arena was a hundred meters below, littered with twisted scraps and jags of metal from the pods destroyed in the battle, and as the little green freak fell, finally, above, the victorious shadow became once again only Palpatine: a very old, very tired man, gasping for air as he leaned on the pod's rail.

Old he might have been, but there was nothing wrong with his eyesight; he scanned the wreckage below, and he did not see a body.

He flicked a finger, and in the Chancellor's Podium a dozen meters away, a switch tripped and sirens sounded throughout the enormous building; another surge of the Force sent his pod streaking in a downward spiral to the holding office at the base of the Podium tower. Clone troops were already swarming into it.

"It was Yoda," he said as he swung out of the pod. "Another assassination attempt. Find him and kill him. If you have to, blow up the building."

He didn't have time to direct the search personally. The Force hummed a warning in his bones: Lord Vader was in danger.

Mortal danger.

Clones scattered. He stopped one officer. "You. Call the shuttle dock and tell them I'm on my way. Have my ship warmed and ready."

The officer saluted, and Palpatine, with vigor that surprised even himself, ran.

With the help of the Force, Yoda sprinted along the service accessway below the Arena faster than a human being could run; he sliced conduits as he passed, filling the accessway behind him with coils of high-voltage cables, twisting and spitting lightning. Every few dozen meters, he paused just long enough to slash a hole in the accessway's wall; once his pursuers got past the cables, they would have to divide their forces to search each of his possible exits.

But he knew they could afford to; there were thousands of them.

He pulled his comlink from inside his robe without slowing down; the Force whispered a set of coordinates and he spoke them into the link. "Delay not," he added. "Swiftly closing is the pursuit. Failed I have, and kill me they will."

The Convocation Center of the Galactic Senate was a drum-mounted dome more than a kilometer in diameter; even with the aid of the Force, Yoda was breathing hard by the time he reached its edge. He cut through the floor beneath him and dropped down into another accessway, this one used for maintenance on the huge lighting system that shone downward onto Republic Plaza through transparisteel panels that floored the underside of the huge dome's rim. He cut into the lightwell; the reflected wattage nearly blinded him to the vertiginous drop below the transparisteel on which he stood.

Without hesitation he cut through that as well and dived headlong into the night.

Catching the nether edges of his long cloak to use as an improvised airfoil, he let the Force guide him in a soaring free fall away from the Convocation Center; he was too small to trigger its automated defense perimeter, but the open-cockpit speeder toward which he fell would get blasted from the sky if it deviated one meter inward from its curving course.

He released his robe so that it flapped upward, making a sort of drogue that righted him in the air so that he fell feetfirst into the speeder's passenger seat beside Bail Organa.

While Yoda strapped himself in, the Senator from Alderaan pulled the rented speeder through a turn that would have impressed Anakin Skywalker, and shot away toward the nearest intersection of Coruscant's congested skyways.

Yoda's eyes squeezed closed.

"Master Yoda? Are you wounded?"

"Only my pride," Yoda said, and meant it, though Bail could not possibly understand how deep that wound went, nor how it bled. "Only my pride."

With Anakin's grip on his wrists bending his arms near to breaking, forcing both their lightsabers down in a slow but un-stoppable arc, Obi-Wan let go.

Of everything.

His hopes. His fears. His obligation to the Jedi, his promise to Qui-Gon, his failure with Anakin.

And their lightsabers.

Startled, Anakin instinctively shifted his Force grip, releasing one wrist to reach for his blade; in that instant Obi-Wan twisted free of his other hand and with the Force caught up his own blade, reversing it along his forearm so that his swift parry of Anakin's thundering overhand not only blocked the strike but directed both blades to slice through the wall against which he stood. He slid Anakin's following thrust through the wall on the opposite side, guiding both blades again up and over his head in a circular sweep so that he could use the power of Anakin's next chop to drive himself backward through the wall, outside into the smoke and the falling cinders.

Anakin followed, constantly attacking; Obi-Wan again gave ground, retreating along a narrow balcony high above the black-sand shoreline of a lake of fire.

Mustafar hummed with death behind his back, only a mo-ment away, somewhere out there among the rivers of molten rock. Obi-Wan let Anakin drive him toward it.

It was a place, he decided, they should reach together.

Anakin forced him back and back, slamming his blade down with strength that seemed to flow from the volcano overhead. He spun and whirled and sliced razor-sharp shards of steel from the wall and shot them at Obi-Wan with the full heat of his fury. He slashed through a control panel along the walkway, and the ray shield that had held back the lava storm vanished.

Fire rained around them.

Obi-Wan backed to the end of the balcony; behind him was only a power conduit no thicker than his arm, connecting it to the main collection plant of the old lava mine, over a riverbed that flowed with white-hot molten stone. Obi-Wan stepped backward onto the conduit without hesitation, his balance flaw-less as he parried chop after chop.

Anakin came on.

Out on the tightrope of power conduit, their blades blurred even faster than before. They chopped and slashed and parried and blocked. Lava bombs thundered to the ground below, shed-ding drops of burning stone that scorched their robes. Smoke shrouded the planet's star, and now the only light came from the hell-glow of the lava below them and from their blades them-selves. Flares of energy crackled and spat.

This was not Sith against Jedi. This was not light against dark or good against evil; it had nothing to do with duty or philoso-phy, religion or morals.

It was Anakin against Obi-Wan.

Personally.

Just the two of them, and the damage they had done to each other.

Obi-Wan backflipped from the conduit to a coupling nexus of the main collection plant; when Anakin flew in pursuit, Obi-Wan leapt again. They spun and whirled throughout its levels, up its stairs, and across its platforms; they battled out onto the col-lection panels over which the cascades of lava poured, and Obi-Wan, out on the edge of the collection panel, hunching under a curve of durasteel that splashed aside gouts of lava, deflecting Force blasts and countering strikes from this creature of rage that had been his best friend, suddenly comprehended an unexpectedly profound truth.

The man he faced was everything Obi-Wan had devoted his life to destroying: Murderer. Traitor. Fallen Jedi. Lord of the Sith. And here, and now, despite it all . . .

Obi-Wan still loved him.

Yoda had said it, flat-out: *Allow such attachments to pass out of one's life, a Jedi must,* but Obi-Wan had never let himself understand. He had argued for Anakin, made excuses, covered for him again and again and again; all the while this attachment he denied even feeling had blinded him to the dark path his best friend walked.

Obi-Wan knew there was, in the end, only one answer for attachment . . .

He let it go.

The lake of fire, no longer held back by the ray shield, chewed away the shore on which the plant stood, and the whole massive structure broke loose, sending both warriors skidding, scrabbling desperately for handholds down tilting durasteel slopes that were rapidly becoming cliffs; they hung from scraps of cable as the plant's superstructure floated out into the lava, sinking slowly as its lower levels melted and burned away.

Anakin kicked off from the toppling superstructure, swinging through a wide arc over the lava's boil. Obi-Wan shoved out and met him there, holding the cable with one hand and the Force, angling his blade high. Anakin flicked a Shien whipcrack at his knees. Obi-Wan yanked his legs high and slashed through the cable above Anakin's hand, and Anakin fell.

Pockets of gas boiled to the surface of the lava, gouting flame like arms reaching to gather him in.

But Anakin's momentum had already swung back toward the dissolving wreck of the collection plant, and the Force carried him within reach of another cable. Obi-Wan whipped his legs around his cable, altering its arc to bring him within reach of the one from which Anakin now dangled, but Anakin was on to this game now, and he swung cable-to-cable ahead of Obi-Wan's advance, using the Force to carry himself higher and higher, forcing Obi-Wan to counter by doing the same; on this terrain, altitude was everything.

Simultaneous surges of the Force carried them both spinning up off the cables to the slant of the toppling superstructure's crane deck. Obi-Wan barely got his feet on the metal before Anakin pounced on him and they stood almost toe-to-toe, blades whirling and crashing on all sides, while around them the collection plant's maintenance droids still tinkered mindlessly away at the doomed machinery, as they would continue to do until lava closed over them and they melted to their constituent molecules and dissolved into the flow.

A roar louder even than the volcano's eruption came from the river ahead; metal began to shriek and stretch. The river dropped away in a vertical sheet of fire that vanished into boiling clouds of smoke and gases.

The whole collection plant was being carried, inexorably, out over a vast lava-fall.

Obi-Wan decided he didn't really want to see what was at the bottom.

He turned Anakin's blade aside with a two-handed block and landed a solid kick that knocked the two apart. Before Anakin could recover his balance, Obi-Wan took a running leap that became a graceful dive headlong off the crane deck. He hurtled down past level after level, and only a few tens of meters above the lava itself the Force called a dangling cable to his hand, turning his dive into a swing that carried him high and far, to the very limit of the cable.

And he let it go.

As though jumping from a swing in the Temple playrooms,

his velocity sent him flying up and out over a catenary arc that shot him toward the river's shore.

Toward. Not quite *to*.

But the Force had led him here, and again it had not betrayed him: below, humming along a few meters above the lava river, came a big, slow old repulsorlift platform, carrying droids and equipment out toward a collection plant that its programming was not sophisticated enough to realize was about to be destroyed.

Obi-Wan flipped in the air and let the Force bring him to a catfooted landing. An adder-quick stab of his lightsaber disabled the platform's guidance system, and Obi-Wan was able to direct it back toward the shore with a simple shift of his weight.

He turned to watch as the collection plant shrieked like the damned in a Corellian hell, crumbling over the brink of the falls until it vanished into invisible destruction.

Obi-Wan lowered his head. "Good-bye, old friend."

But the Force whispered a warning, and Obi-Wan lifted his head in time to see Anakin come hurtling toward him out from the boil of smoke above the falls, perched on a tiny repulsorlift droid. The little droid was vastly swifter than Obi-Wan's logy old cargo platform, and Anakin was easily able to swing around Obi-Wan and cut him off from the shore. Obi-Wan shifted weight one way, then another, but Anakin's droid was nimble as a sand panther; there was no way around, and this close to the lava, the heat was intense enough to crisp Obi-Wan's hair.

"This is the end for you, Master," he said. "I wish it were otherwise."

"Yes, Anakin, so do I," Obi-Wan said as he sprinted into a leaping dive, making a spear of his blade.

Anakin leaned aside and deflected the thrust almost contemptuously; he missed a cut at Obi-Wan's legs as the Jedi Master flew past him.

Obi-Wan turned his dive into a forward roll that left him barely teetering on the rim of a low cliff, just above the soft black sand of the riverbank. Anakin snarled a curse as he realized he'd been suckered, and leapt off his droid at Obi-Wan's back—

Half a second too slow.

Obi-Wan's whirl to parry didn't meet Anakin's blade. It met his knee. Then his other knee.

And while Anakin was still in the air, burned-off lower legs only starting their topple down the cliff, Obi-Wan's recovery to guard brought his blade through Anakin's left arm above the elbow. He stepped back as Anakin fell.

Anakin dropped his lightsaber, clawing at the edge of the cliff with his mechanical hand, but his grip was too powerful for the lava bank and it crumbled, and he slid down onto the black sand. His severed legs and his severed arm rolled into the lava below him and burned to ash in sudden bursts of scarlet flame.

The same color, Obi-Wan observed distantly, as a Sith blade.

Anakin scrabbled at the soft black sand, but struggling only made him slip farther. The sand itself was hot enough that digging his durasteel fingers into it burned off his glove, and his robes began to smolder.

Obi-Wan picked up Anakin's lightsaber. He lifted his own as well, weighing them in his hands. Anakin had based his design upon Obi-Wan's. So similar they were.

So differently they had been used.

"Obi-Wan . . . ?"

He looked down. Flame licked the fringes of Anakin's robe, and his long hair had blackened, and was beginning to char.

"You were the chosen one! It was said you would destroy the Sith, not join them. It was you who would bring balance to the Force, not leave it in darkness. You were my brother, Anakin," said Obi-Wan Kenobi. "I loved you, but I could not save you."

A flash of metal through the sky, and Obi-Wan felt the darkness closing in around them both. He knew that ship: the Chancellor's shuttle. Now, he supposed, the *Emperor*'s shuttle.

Yoda had failed. He might have died.

He might have left Obi-Wan alone: the last Jedi.

Below his feet, Darth Vader burst into flame.

"I *hate* you," he screamed.

Obi-Wan looked down. It would be a mercy to kill him.

He was not feeling merciful.

He was feeling calm, and clear, and he knew that to climb down to that black beach might cost him more time than he had.

Another Sith Lord approached.

In the end, there was only one choice. It was a choice he had made many years before, when he had passed his trials of Jedi Knighthood, and sworn himself to the Jedi forever. In the end, he was still Obi-Wan Kenobi, and he was still a Jedi, and he would not murder a helpless man.

He would leave it to the will of the Force.

He turned and walked away.

After a moment, he began to run.

He began to run because he realized, if he was fast enough, there was one thing he still could do for Anakin. He still could do honor to the memory of the man he had loved, and to the vanished Order they both had served.

At the landing deck, C-3PO stood on the skiff's landing ramp, waving frantically. "Master Kenobi! Please hurry!"

"Where's Padmé?"

"Already inside, sir, but she is badly hurt."

Obi-Wan ran up the ramp to the skiff's cockpit and fired the engines. As the Chancellor's shuttle curved in toward the landing deck, the sleek mirror-finished skiff streaked for the stars.

Obi-Wan never looked back.

A NEW JEDI ORDER

A Naboo skiff reverted to realspace and flashed toward an alien medical installation in the asteroid belt of Polis Massa.

Tantive IV reentered reality only moments behind.

And on Mustafar, below the red thunder of a volcano, a Sith Lord had already snatched from sand of black glass the charred torso and head of what once had been a man, and had already leapt for the cliffbank above with effortless strength, and had already roared to his clones to *bring the medical capsule immediately!*

The Sith Lord lowered the limbless man tenderly to the cool ground above, and laid his hand across the cracked and blackened mess that once had been his brow, and he set his will upon him.

Live, Lord Vader. Live, my apprentice.

Live.

Beyond the transparent crystal of the observation dome on the airless crags of Polis Massa, the galaxy wheeled in a spray of hard, cold pinpricks through the veil of infinite night.

Beneath that dome sat Yoda. He did not look at the stars.

He sat a very long time.

Even after nearly nine hundred years, the road to self-knowledge was rugged enough to leave him bruised and bleeding.

He spoke softly, but not to himself.

Though no one was with him, he was not alone.

"My failure, this was. Failed the Jedi, I did."

He spoke to the Force.

And the Force answered him. *Do not blame yourself, my old friend.*

As it sometimes had these past thirteen years, when the Force spoke to him, it spoke in the voice of Qui-Gon Jinn.

"Too old I was," Yoda said. "Too rigid. Too arrogant to see that the old way is not the *only* way. These Jedi, I trained to become the Jedi who had trained me, long centuries ago—but those ancient Jedi, of a different time they were. Changed, has the galaxy. Changed, the Order did not—because *let* it change, *I* did not."

More easily said than done, my friend.

"An infinite mystery is the Force." Yoda lifted his head and turned his gaze out into the wheel of stars. "Much to learn, there still is."

And you will have time to learn it.

"Infinite knowledge . . ." Yoda shook his head. "Infinite time, does that require."

With my help, you can learn to join with the Force, yet retain consciousness. You can join your light to it forever. Perhaps, in time, even your physical self.

Yoda did not move. "Eternal life . . ."

The ultimate goal of the Sith, yet they can never achieve it; it comes only by the release of self, not the exaltation of self. It comes through compassion, not greed. Love is the answer to the darkness.

"Become one with the Force, yet influence still to have . . ." Yoda mused. "A power greater than all, it is."

It cannot be granted; it can only be taught. It is yours to learn, if you wish it.

Slowly, Yoda nodded. "A very great Jedi Master you have become, Qui-Gon Jinn. A very great Jedi Master you always were, but too blind I was to see it."

He rose, and folded his hands before him, and inclined his head in the Jedi bow of respect.

The bow of the student, in the presence of the Master.

"Your apprentice, I gratefully become."

He was well into his first lesson when the hatch cycled open behind him. He turned.

In the corridor beyond stood Bail Organa. He looked stricken.

"Obi-Wan is asking for you at the surgical theater," he said. "It's Padmé. She's dying."

Obi-Wan sat beside her, holding one cold, still hand in both of his. "Don't give up, Padmé."

"Is it . . ." Her eyes rolled blindly. "It's a girl. Anakin thinks it's a girl."

"We don't know yet. In a minute . . . you have to stay *with* us."

Below the opaque tent that shrouded her from chest down, a pair of surgical droids assisted with her labor. A general medical droid fussed and tinkered among the clutter of scanners and equipment.

"If it's . . . a girl—oh, oh, oh *no* . . ."

Obi-Wan cast an appeal toward the medical droid. "Can't you do something?"

"All organic damage has been repaired." The droid checked another readout. "This systemic failure cannot be explained."

Not physically, Obi-Wan thought. He squeezed her hand as though he could keep life within her body by simple pressure. "Padmé, you *have* to hold on."

"If it's a girl . . . ," she gasped, "name her Leia . . ."

One of the surgical droids circled out from behind the tent, cradling in its padded arms a tiny infant, already swabbed clean and breathing, but without even the hint of tears.

The droid announced softly, "It's a boy."

Padmé reached for him with her trembling free hand, but she had no strength to take him; she could only touch her fingers to the baby's forehead.

She smiled weakly. *"Luke . . ."*

The other droid now rounded the tent as well, with another clean, quietly solemn infant. ". . . and a girl."

But she had already fallen back against her pillow.

"Padmé, you have twins," Obi-Wan said desperately. "They *need* you—please hang on . . ."

"Anakin . . ."

"Anakin . . . isn't here, Padmé," he said, though he didn't think she could hear.

"Anakin, I'm sorry. I'm so sorry . . . Anakin, please, I *love* you . . ."

In the Force, Obi-Wan felt Yoda's approach, and he looked up to see the ancient Master beside Bail Organa, both staring the same grave question down through the surgical theater's observation panel.

The only answer Obi-Wan had was a helpless shake of his head.

Padmé reached across with her free hand, with the hand she had laid upon the brow of her firstborn son, and pressed something into Obi-Wan's palm.

For a moment, her eyes cleared, and she knew him.

"Obi-Wan . . . there . . . is still good in him. I know there is . . . still . . ."

Her voice faded to an empty sigh, and she sagged back against the pillow. Half a dozen different scanners buzzed with conflicting alarm tones, and the medical droids shooed him from the room.

He stood in the hall outside, looking down at what she had pressed into his hand. It was a pendant of some kind, an amulet, unfamiliar sigils carved into some sort of organic material, strung on a loop of leather. In the Force, he could feel traces of the touch of her skin.

When Yoda and Bail came for him, he was still standing there, staring at it.

"She put this in my hand—" For what seemed the dozenth time this day, he found himself blinking back tears. "—and I don't even know what it is."

"Precious to her, it must have been," Yoda said slowly. "Buried with her, perhaps it should be."

Obi-Wan looked down at the simple, child-like symbols carved into it, and felt from it in the Force soaring echoes of transcendent love, and the bleak, black despair of unendurable heartbreak.

"Yes," he said. "Yes. Perhaps that would be best."

Around a conference table on *Tantive IV,* Bail Organa, Obi-Wan Kenobi, and Yoda met to decide the fate of the galaxy.

"To Naboo, send her body . . ." Yoda stretched his head high, as though tasting a current in the Force. "Pregnant, she must still appear. Hidden, safe, the children must be kept. Foundation of the new Jedi Order, they will be."

"We should split them up," Obi-Wan said. "Even if the Sith find one, the other may survive. I can take the boy, Master Yoda, and you take the girl. We can hide them away, keep them safe— train them as Anakin *should* have been trained—"

"No." The ancient Master lowered his head again, closing his eyes, resting his chin on his hands that were folded over the head of his stick.

Obi-Wan looked uncertain. "But how are they to learn the self-discipline a Jedi needs? How are they to master skills of the Force?"

"Jedi training, the sole source of self-discipline is not. When right is the time for skills to be taught, to us the living Force will bring them. Until then, wait we will, and watch, and learn."

"I can . . ." Bail Organa stopped, flushing slightly. "I'm sorry to interrupt, Masters; I know little about the Force, but I do know something of love. The Queen and I—well, we've always talked of adopting a girl. If you have no objection, I would like to take Leia to Alderaan, and raise her as our daughter. She would be loved with us."

Yoda and Obi-Wan exchanged a look. Yoda tilted his head. "No happier fate could any child ask for. With our blessing, and that of the Force, let Leia be your child."

Bail stood, a little jerkily, as though he simply could no longer keep his seat. His flush had turned from embarrassment to pure uncomplicated joy. "Thank you, Masters—I don't know what else to say. Thank you, that's all. What of the boy?"

"Cliegg Lars still lives on Tatooine, I think—and Anakin's stepbrother . . . Owen, that's it, and his wife, Beru, still work the moisture farm outside Mos Eisley . . ."

"As close to kinfolk as the boy can come," Yoda said approvingly. "But Tatooine, not like Alderaan it is—deep in the Outer Rim, a wild and dangerous planet."

"Anakin survived it," Obi-Wan said. "Luke can, too. And I can—well, I could take him there, and watch over him. Protect him from the worst of the planet's dangers, until he can learn to protect himself."

"Like a father you wish to be, young Obi-Wan?"

"More an . . . eccentric old uncle, I think. It is a part I can play very well. To keep watch over Anakin's son—" Obi-Wan sighed, finally allowing his face to register a suggestion of his old gentle smile. "I can't imagine a better way to spend the rest of my life."

"Settled it is, then. To Tatooine, you will take him."

Bail moved toward the door. "If you'll excuse me, Masters, I have to call the Queen . . ." He stopped in the doorway, looking back. "Master Yoda, do you think Padmé's twins will be able to defeat Palpatine?"

"Strong the Force runs, in the Skywalker line. Only hope, we can. Until the time is right, disappear we will."

Bail nodded. "And I must do the same—metaphorically, at least. You may hear . . . disturbing things . . . about what I do in the Senate. I must appear to support the new Empire, and my comrades with me. It was . . . Padmé's wish, and she was a shrewder political mind than I'll ever be. Please trust that what we do is only a cover for our true task. We will never betray the legacy of the Jedi. I will never surrender the Republic to the Sith."

"Trust in this, we always will. Go now; for happy news, your Queen is waiting."

Bail Organa bowed, and vanished into the corridor.

When Obi-Wan moved to follow, Yoda's gimer stick barred his way. "A moment, Master Kenobi. In your solitude on Tatooine, training I have for you. I and my new Master."

Obi-Wan blinked. "Your new Master?"

"Yes." Yoda smiled up at him. "And your *old* one . . ."

C-3PO shuffled along the starship's hallway beside R2-D2, following Senator Organa who had, by all accounts, inherited them both. "I'm certain I can't say why she malfunctioned," he was telling the little astromech. "Organics are so terribly complicated, you know."

Ahead, the Senator was met by a man whose uniform, C-3PO's conformation-recognition algorithm informed him, indicated he was a captain in the Royal Alderaan Civil Fleet.

"I'm placing these droids in your care," the Senator said. "Have them cleaned, polished, and refitted with the best of everything; they will belong to my new daughter."

"How lovely!" C-3PO exclaimed. "His daughter is the child of Master Anakin and Senator Amidala," he explained to R2-D2. "I can hardly wait to tell her all about her parents! I'm sure she will be *very* proud—"

"Oh, and the protocol droid?" Senator Organa said thoughtfully. "Have its mind wiped."

The captain saluted.

"Oh," said C-3PO. "Oh, dear."

In the newly renamed Emperor Palpatine Surgical Recon-
struction Center on Coruscant, a hypersophisticated prototype
Ubrikkian DD-13 surgical droid moved away from the project
that it and an enhanced FX-6 medical droid had spent many days
rebuilding.

It beckoned to a dark-robed shadow that stood at the edge
of the pool of high-intensity light. "My lord, the construction is
finished. He lives."

"Good. Good."

The shadow flowed into the pool of light as though the overhead illuminators had malfunctioned.

Droids stepped back as it came to the rim of the surgical
table.

On the table was strapped the very first patient of the EmPal
SuRecon Center.

To some eyes, it might have been a pieced-together hybrid of
droid and human, encased in a life-support shell of gleaming
black, managed by a thoracic processor that winked pale color
against the shadow's cloak. To some eyes, its jointed limbs might
have looked ungainly, clumsy, even monstrous; the featureless
curves of black that served it for eyes might have appeared inhu-
man, and the underthrust grillwork of its vocabulator might have
suggested the jaws of a saurian predator built of polished blast
armor, but to the shadow—

It was *glorious*.

A magnificent jewel box, created both to protect and to ex-
hibit the greatest treasure of the Sith.

Terrifying.

Mesmerizing.

Perfect.

The table slowly rotated to vertical, and the shadow leaned close.

"Lord Vader? Lord Vader, can you hear me?"

This is how it feels to be Anakin Skywalker, forever:

The first dawn of light in your universe brings pain.

The light burns you. It will always burn you. Part of you will always lie upon black glass sand beside a lake of fire while flames chew upon your flesh.

You can hear yourself breathing. It comes hard, and harsh, and it scrapes nerves already raw, but you cannot stop it. You can never stop it. You cannot even slow it down.

You don't even have lungs anymore.

Mechanisms hardwired into your chest breathe for you. They will pump oxygen into your bloodstream forever.

Lord Vader? Lord Vader, can you hear me?

And you can't, not in the way you once did. Sensors in the shell that prisons your head trickle meaning directly into your brain.

You open your scorched-pale eyes; optical sensors integrate light and shadow into a hideous simulacrum of the world around you.

Or perhaps the simulacrum is perfect, and it is the world that is hideous.

Padmé? Are you here? Are you all right? you try to say, but another voice speaks for you, out from the vocabulator that serves you for burned-away lips and tongue and throat.

"Padmé? Are you here? Are you all right?"

I'm very sorry, Lord Vader. I'm afraid she died. It seems in your anger, you killed her.

This burns hotter than the lava had.

"No . . . no, it is not *possible*!"

You loved her. You will always love her. You could never will her death.

Never.

But you remember . . .

You remember *all* of it.

You remember the dragon that you brought Vader forth from your heart to slay. You remember the cold venom in Vader's blood. You remember the furnace of Vader's fury, and the black hatred of seizing her throat to silence her lying mouth—

And there is one blazing moment in which you finally understand that there was no dragon. That there was no Vader. That there was only you. Only Anakin Skywalker.

That it was all you. Is you.

Only you.

You did it.

You killed her.

You killed her because, finally, when you *could* have saved her, when you could have gone *away* with her, when you could have been thinking about *her*, you were thinking about *yourself* . . .

It is in this blazing moment that you finally understand the trap of the dark side, the final cruelty of the Sith—

Because now your *self* is all you will ever have.

And you rage and scream and reach through the Force to crush the shadow who has destroyed you, but you are so far less now than what you were, you are more than half machine, you are like a painter gone blind, a composer gone deaf, you can remember where the power was but the power you can touch is only a memory, and so with all your world-destroying fury it is only droids around you that implode, and equipment, and the table on which you were strapped shatters, and in the end, you cannot touch the shadow.

In the end, you do not even want to.

In the end, the shadow is all you have left.

Because the shadow understands you, the shadow forgives you, the shadow gathers you unto itself—

And within your furnace heart, you burn in your own flame.

This is how it feels to be Anakin Skywalker.

Forever . . .

The long night has begun.

Huge solemn crowds line Palace Plaza in Theed, the capital of Naboo, as six beautiful white gualaars draw a flower-draped open casket bearing the remains of a beloved Senator through the Triumphal Arch, her fingers finally and forever clasping a snippet of japor, one that had been carved long ago by the hand of a nine-year-old boy from an obscure desert planet in the far Outer Rim . . .

On the jungle planet of Dagobah, a Jedi Master inspects the unfamiliar swamp of his exile . . .

From the bridge of a Star Destroyer, two Sith Lords stand with a sector governor named Tarkin, and survey the growing skeleton of a spherical battle station the size of a moon . . .

But even in the deepest night, there are some who dream of dawn.

On Alderaan, the Prince Consort delivers a baby girl into the loving arms of his Queen.

And on Tatooine, a Jedi Master brings an infant boy to the homestead of Owen and Beru Lars—

Then he rides his eopie off into the Jundland Wastes, toward the setting suns.

The dark is generous, and it is patient, and it always wins—but in the heart of its strength lies weakness: one lone candle is enough to hold it back.

Love is more than a candle.

Love can ignite the stars.

LEGENDS

STAR WARS

DARK LORD

THE RISE OF DARTH VADER

JAMES LUCENO

For Abel Lucero Lima, ace guide at Tikal
(aka Yavin 4), with whom I've left bootprints
throughout the Mundo Maya

Acknowledgments

Sincere thanks to Shelly Shapiro, Sue Rostoni, Howard Roffman, Amy Gary, Leland Chee, Pablo Hidalgo, Matt Stover, Troy Denning, and Karen Traviss. Special thanks to Ryan Kaufman, formerly of LucasArts, who described what it felt like to wear the Suit.

PART I
THE OUTER RIM SIEGES

Dropping into swirling clouds conjured by Murkhana's weather stations, Roan Shryne was reminded of meditation sessions his former Master had guided him through. No matter how fixed Shryne had been on touching the Force, his mind's eye had offered little more than an eddying whiteness. Years later, when he had become more adept at silencing thought and immersing himself in the light, visual fragments would emerge from that colorless void—pieces to a puzzle that would gradually assemble themselves and resolve. Not in any conscious way, though frequently assuring him that his actions in the world were in accord with the will of the Force.

Frequently but not always.

When he veered from the course on which the Force had set him, the familiar white would once again be stirred by powerful currents; sometimes shot through with red, as if he were lifting his closed eyes to the glare of a midday sun.

Red-mottled white was what he saw as he fell deeper into Murkhana's atmosphere. Scored to reverberating thunder; the rush of the wind; a welter of muffled voices . . .

He was standing closest to the sliding door that normally sealed the troop bay of a Republic gunship, launched moments earlier from the forward hold of the *Gallant*—a *Victory*-class Star Destroyer, harried by vulture and droid tri-fighters and awaiting High Command's word to commence its own descent through Murkhana's artificial ceiling. Beside and behind Shryne stood a platoon of clone troopers, helmets fitting snugly over their heads, blasters cradled in their arms, utility belts slung with ammo magazines, talking among themselves the way seasoned warriors often did before battle. Alleviating misgivings with inside jokes; references Shryne couldn't begin to understand, beyond the fact that they were grim.

The gunship's inertial compensators allowed them to stand in the bay without being jolted by flaring anti-aircraft explosions or jostled by the gunship pilots' evasive maneuvering through corkscrewing missiles and storms of white-hot shrapnel. Missiles, because the same Separatists who had manufactured the clouds had misted Murkhana's air with anti-laser aerosols.

Acrid odors infiltrated the cramped space, along with the roar of the aft engines, the starboard one stuttering somewhat, the gunship as battered as the troopers and crew it carried into conflict.

Even at an altitude of only four hundred meters above sea level the cloud cover remained dense. The fact that Shryne could barely see his hand in front of his face didn't surprise him. This was still the war, after all, and he had grown accustomed these past three years to not seeing where he was going.

Nat-Sem, his former Master, used to tell him that the goal of the meditative exercises was to see clear through the swirling whiteness to the other side; that what Shryne saw was only the shadowy expanse separating him from full contact with the Force. Shryne had to learn to ignore the clouds, as it were. When he had learned to do that, to look through them to the radiant expanse beyond, he would be a Master.

Pessimistic by nature, Shryne's reaction had been: *Not in this lifetime.*

Though he had never said as much to Nat-Sem, the Jedi Master had seen through him as easily as he saw through the clouds.

Shryne felt that the clone troopers had a better view of the war than he had, and that the view had little to do with their helmet imaging systems, the filters that muted the sharp scent of the air, the earphones that dampened the sounds of explosions. Grown for warfare, they probably thought the Jedi were mad to go into battle as they did, attired in tunics and hooded robes, a lightsaber their only weapon. Many of them were astute enough to see comparisons between the Force and their own white plastoid shells; but few of them could discern between armored and unarmored Jedi—those who were allied with the Force, and those who for one reason or another had slipped from its sustaining embrace.

Murkhana's lathered clouds finally began to thin, until they merely veiled the planet's wrinkled landscape and frothing sea. A sudden burst of brilliant light drew Shryne's attention to the sky. What he took for an exploding gunship might have been a newborn star; and for a moment the world tipped out of balance, then righted itself just as abruptly. A circle of clarity opened in the clouds, a perforation in the veil, and Shryne gazed on verdant forest so profoundly green he could almost taste it. Valiant combatants scurried through the underbrush and sleek ships soared through the canopy. In the midst of it all a lone figure stretched out his hand, tearing aside a curtain black as night . . .

Shryne knew he had stepped out of time, into some truth beyond reckoning.

A vision of the end of the war, perhaps, or of time itself.

Whichever, the effect of it comforted him that he was indeed where he was supposed to be. That despite the depth to which the war had caused him to become fixed on death and destruction, he was still tethered to the Force, and serving it in his own limited way.

Then, as if intent on foiling him, the thin clouds quickly conspired to conceal what had been revealed, closing the portal an errant current had opened. And Shryne was back where he started, with gusts of superheated air tugging at the sleeves and cowl of his brown robe.

"The Koorivar have done a good job with their weather machines," a speaker-enhanced voice said into his left ear. "Whipped up one brute of a sky. We used the same tactic on Paarin Minor. Drew the Seps into fabricated clouds and blew them to the back of beyond."

Shryne laughed without merriment. "Good to see you can still appreciate the little things, Commander."

"What else is there, General?"

Shryne couldn't make out the expression on the face behind the tinted T-visor, but he knew that shared face as well as anyone else who fought in the war. Commander of the Thirty-second air combat wing, the clone officer had somewhere along the line acquired the name Salvo, and the sobriquet fit him like a gauntlet.

The high-traction soles of his jump boots gave him just enough added height to stand shoulder-to-shoulder with Shryne, and where his armor wasn't dinged and scored it was emblazoned with rust-brown markings. On his hips he wore holstered hand blasters and, for reasons Shryne couldn't fathom, a version of the capelike command skirt that had become all the rage in the war's third year. The left side of his shrapnel-pitted helmet was laser-etched with the motto LIVE TO SERVE!

Torso markings attested to Salvo's participation in campaigns on many worlds, and while he wasn't an ARC—an Advanced Reconnaissance Commando—he had the rough edges of an ARC, and of their clone template, Jango Fett, whose headless body Shryne had seen in a Geonosian arena shortly before Master Nat-Sem had fallen to enemy fire.

"Alliance weapons should have us in target lock by now," Salvo said as the gunship continued to descend.

Other assault ships were also punching through the cloud cover, only to be greeted by flocks of incoming missiles. Struck by direct hits, two, four, then five craft were blown apart, flaming fuselages and mangled troopers plummeting into the churning scarlet waves of Murkhana Bay. From the nose of one gunship flew a bang-out capsule that carried the pilot and co-pilot to within meters of the water before it was ripped open by a resolute heat seeker.

In one of the fifty-odd gunships that were racing down the well, three other Jedi were going into battle, Master Saras Loorne among them. Stretching out with the Force, Shryne found them, faint echoes confirming that all three were still alive.

He clamped his right hand on one of the slide door's view slots as the pilots threw their unwieldy charge into a hard bank, narrowly evading a pair of hailfire missiles. Gunners ensconced in the gunship's armature-mounted turrets opened up with blasters as flights of Mankvim Interceptors swarmed up to engage the Republic force. The anti-laser aerosols scattered the blaster beams, but dozens of the Separatist craft succumbed to missiles spewed from the gunships' top-mounted mass-drive launchers.

"High Command should have granted our request to bombard from orbit," Salvo said in an amplified voice.

"The idea is to *take* the city, Commander, not vaporize it," Shryne said loudly. Murkhana had already been granted weeks to surrender, but the Republic ultimatum had expired. "Palpatine's policy for winning the hearts and minds of Separatist populations might not make good military sense, but it makes good political sense."

Salvo stared at him from behind his visor. "We're not interested in politics."

Shryne laughed shortly. "Neither were the Jedi."

"Why fight if you weren't bred for it?"

"To serve what remains of the Republic." Shryne's brief green vision of the war's end returned, and he adopted a rueful grin. "Dooku's dead. Grievous is being hunted down. If it means anything, I suspect it'll be over soon."

"The war, or our standing shoulder-to-shoulder?"

"The war, Commander."

"What becomes of the Jedi then?"

"We'll do what we have always done: follow the Force."

"And the Grand Army?"

Shryne regarded him. "Help us preserve the peace."

Murkhana City was visible now, climbing into steep hills that rose from a long crescent of shoreline, the sheen of overlapping particle shields dulled by the gray underbelly of the clouds. Shryne caught a fleeting glimpse of the Argente Tower before the gunship dropped to the crests of the frothing waves and altered course, pointing its blunt nose toward the stacked skyline and slaloming through warheads fired from weapons emplacements that lined the shore.

In a class with Mygeeto, Muunilinst, and Neimoidia, Murkhana was not a conquered planet but a host world—home to former Senator and Separatist Council member Passel Argente, and headquarters of the Corporate Alliance. Murkhana's deal makers and litigators, tended to by armies of household droids and private security guards, had fashioned a hedonistic domain of towering office buildings, luxurious apartment complexes, exclusive medcenters, and swank shopping malls, casinos, and nightclubs. Only the most expensive speeders negotiated a vertical cityscape of graceful, spiraling structures that looked as if they had been grown of ocean coral rather than constructed.

Murkhana also housed the finest communications facility in that part of the Outer Rim, and was a primary source of the "shadowfeeds" that spread Separatist propaganda among Republic and Confederacy worlds.

Arranged like the spokes of a wheel, four ten-kilometer-long bridges linked the city to an enormous offshore landing platform. Hexagonal in shape and supported on thick columns anchored in the seabed, the platform was the prize the Republic needed to secure before a full assault could be mounted. For that to happen, the Grand Army needed to penetrate the defensive umbrellas and take out the generators that sustained them. But with nearly all rooftop and repulsorlift landing platforms shielded, Murkhana's arc of black-sand beach was the only place where the gunships could insert their payloads of clone troopers and Jedi.

Shryne was gazing at the landing platform when he felt someone begin to edge between him and Commander Salvo, set on getting a better look through the open hatch. Even before he saw the headful of long black curls, he knew it was Olee Starstone. Planting his left hand firmly on the top of her head, he propelled her back into the troop bay.

"If you're determined to make yourself a target, Padawan, at least wait until we hit the beach."

Rubbing her head, the petite, blue-eyed young woman glanced over her shoulder at the tall female Jedi standing behind her. "You see, Master. He does care."

"Despite all evidence to the contrary," the female Jedi said.

"I only meant that it'll be easier for me to bury you in the sand," Shryne said.

Starstone scowled, folded her arms across her chest, and swung away from both of them.

Bol Chatak threw Shryne a look of mild reprimand. The raised cowl of her black robe hid her short vestigial horns. An Iridonian Zabrak, she was nothing if not tolerant, and had never taken Shryne to task for his irascible behavior or interfered with his teasing relationship with her Padawan, who had joined Chatak in the Murkhana system only a standard week earlier, arriving with Master Loorne and two Jedi Knights. The demands of the Outer Rim Sieges had drawn so many Jedi from Coruscant that the Temple was practically deserted.

Until recently, Shryne, too, had had a Padawan learner . . .

For the Jedi's benefit, the gunship pilot announced that they were closing on the jump site.

"Weapons check!" Salvo said to the platoon. "Gas and packs!"

As the troop bay filled with the sound of activating weapons, Chatak placed her hand on Starstone's quivering shoulder.

"Use your unease to sharpen your senses, Padawan."

"I will, Master."

"The Force will be with you."

"We're all dying," Salvo told the troopers. "Promise yourselves you'll be the last to go!"

Access panels opened in the ceiling, dropping more than a dozen polyplast cables to within reach of the troopers.

"Secure to lines!" Salvo said. "Room for three more, General," he added while armored, body-gloved hands took tight hold of the cables.

Calculating that the jump wouldn't exceed ten meters, Shryne shook his head at Salvo. "No need. We'll see you below."

Unexpectedly, the gunship gained altitude as it approached the shoreline, then pulled up short of the beach, as if being reined in. Repulsorlifts engaged, the gunship hovered. At the same time, hundreds of Separatist battle droids marched onto the beach, firing their blasters in unison.

The intercom squawked, and the pilot said, "Droid buster away!"

A concussion-feedback weapon, the droid buster detonated

at five meters above ground zero, flattening every droid within a radius of fifty meters. Similar explosions underscored the ingress of a dozen other gunships.

"Where were these weapons three years ago?" one of the troopers asked Salvo.

"Progress," the commander said. "All of a sudden we're winning the war in a week."

The gunship hovered lower, and Shryne leapt into the air. Using the Force to oversee his fall, he landed in a crouch on the compacted sand, as did Chatak and Starstone, if less expertly.

Salvo and the clone troopers followed, descending one-handed on individual cables, triggering their rifles as they slid to the beach. When the final trooper was on the ground, the gunship lifted its nose and began to veer away from shore. Up and down the beach the same scenario was playing out. Several gunships failed to escape artillery fire and crashed in flames before they had turned about.

Others were blown apart before they had even off-loaded.

With projectiles and blaster bolts whizzing past their heads, the Jedi and troopers scurried forward, hunkering down behind a bulkhead that braced a ribbon of highway coursing between the beach and the near-vertical cliffs beyond. Salvo's communications specialist comlinked for aerial support against the batteries responsible for the worst of the fire.

Through an opening in the bulkhead hastened the four members of a commando team, with a captive in tow. Unlike the troopers, the commandos wore gray shells of *Katarn*-class armor and carried heftier weapons. Hardened against magnetic pulses, their suits allowed them to penetrate defensive shields.

The enemy combatant they had captured wore a long robe and tasseled headcloth but lacked the sallow complexion, horizontal facial markings, and cranial horns characteristic of the Koorivar. Like their fellow Separatists the Neimoidians, Passel

Argente's species had no taste for warfare, but felt no compunction about employing the best mercenaries credits could buy.

The burly commando squad leader went immediately to Salvo.

"Ion Team, Commander, attached to the Twenty-second out of Boz Pity." Turning slightly in Shryne's direction, the commando nodded his helmeted head.

"Welcome to Murkhana, General Shryne."

Shryne's dark brows beetled. "The voice is familiar . . . ," he began.

"The face even more so," the commando completed.

The joke was almost three years old but still in use among the clone troopers, and between them and the Jedi.

"Climber," the commando said, providing his sobriquet. "We fought together on Deko Neimoidia."

Shryne clapped the commando on the shoulder. "Good to see you again, Climber—even here."

"As I told you," Chatak said to Starstone, "Master Shryne has friends all over."

"Perhaps they don't know him as well as I do, Master," Starstone grumbled.

Climber lifted his helmet faceplate to the gray sky. "A good day for fighting, General."

"I'll take your word for it," Shryne said.

"Make your report, squad leader," Salvo interrupted.

Climber turned to the commander. "The Koorivarr are evacuating the city, but taking their sweet time about it. They've a lot more faith in these energy shields than they should have." He beckoned the captive forward and spun him roughly to face Salvo. "Meet Idis—human under the Koorivar trappings. Distinguished member of the Vibroblade Brigade."

"A mercenary band," Bol Chatak explained to Starstone.

"We caught him . . . with his trousers down," Climber continued, "and persuaded him to share what he knows about the shoreline defenses. He was kind enough to provide the location of the landing platform shield generator." The commando indicated a tall, tapered edifice farther down the beach. "Just north of the first bridge, near the marina. The generator's installed two floors below ground level. We may have to take out the whole building to get to it."

Salvo signaled to his comlink specialist. "Relay the building coordinates to *Gallant* gunnery—"

"Wait on that," Shryne said quickly. "Targeting the building poses too great a risk to the bridges. We need them intact if we're going to move vehicles into the city."

Salvo considered it briefly. "A surgical strike, then."

Shryne shook his head no. "There's another reason for discretion. That building is a medcenter. Or at least it was the last time I was here."

Salvo looked to Climber for confirmation.

"The general's correct, Commander. It's still a medcenter."

Salvo shifted his gaze to Shryne. "An *enemy* medcenter, General."

Shryne compressed his lips and nodded. "Even at this point in the war, patients are considered noncombatants. Remember what I said about hearts and minds, Commander." He glanced at the mercenary. "Is the shield generator accessible from street level?"

"Depends on how skilled you are."

Shryne looked at Climber.

"Not a problem," the commando said.

Salvo made a sound of distaste. "You'd trust the word of a merc?"

Climber pressed the muzzle of his DC-17 rifle into the small of the mercenary's back. "Idis is on our side now, aren't you?"

The mercenary's head bobbed. "Free of charge."

Shryne looked at Climber again. "Is your team carrying enough thermal detonators to do the job?"

"Yes, sir."

Salvo still didn't like it. "I strongly recommend that we leave this to the *Gallant*."

Shryne regarded him. "What's the matter, Commander, we're not killing the Separatists in sufficient numbers?"

"In sufficient numbers, General. Just not quickly enough."

"The *Gallant* is still holding at fifty kilometers," Chatak said in a conciliatory tone. "There's time to recon the building."

Salvo demonstrated his displeasure with a shrug of indifference. "It's your funeral if you're wrong."

"That's neither here nor there," Shryne said. "We'll rendezvous with you at rally point Aurek-Bacta. If we don't turn up by the time the *Gallant* arrives, feed them the building's coordinates."

"You can count on it, sir."

Murkhana had been a dangerous world long before it had become a treacherous one. Magistrate Passel Argente had been content to allow crime to flourish, under the condition that the Corporate Alliance and its principal subsidiary, Lethe Merchandising, received their fair share of the action. By the time Argente had joined Count Dooku's secessionist movement and drawn Murkhana into the Confederacy of Independent Systems there was almost no distinguishing the Corporate Alliance's thug tactics from those of Black Sun and similar gangster syndicates, save for the fact that the Alliance was more interested in corporate acquisitions than it was in gambling, racketeering, and the trade in illegal spice.

Where persuasion failed, the Corporate Alliance relied on the tank droid to convince company owners of the wisdom of acceding to offers of corporate takeover, and scores of those treaded war machines had taken up positions on the steep streets of Murkhana City to thwart Republic occupation.

Shryne knew the place about as well as anyone, but he let the commandos take the point. Dodging blasterfire from battle droids and roving bands of mercenaries, and trusting that the captive fighter had known better than to steer them wrong, the three Jedi followed the four special ops troopers on a circuitous course through the switchbacked streets. High overhead, laser and ion bolts splashed against the convex energy shields, along with droid craft and starfighters crippled in the furious dogfights taking place in the clouds.

Shortly the allied team reached the approach avenues of the southernmost of the quartet of bridges that joined the city and the landing platform. Encountering no resistance at the med-center, they infiltrated the building's soaring atrium. Wan light streamed through tall permaplex windows; dust and debris wafted down to a mosaic floor as the building trembled in concert with the intensifying Republic bombardment.

The particle-filled air buzzed with current from the shield generator, raising the hairs on the back of Shryne's neck. The place looked and felt deserted, but Shryne sent Chatak, Star-stone, and two of the commandos to reconnoiter the upper floors, just in case. Still trusting to the captive's intelligence, Shryne, Climber, and Ion Team's explosives specialist negotiated a warren of faintly lighted corridors that led to a turbolift the captive had promised would drop them into the shield generator room.

"Sir, I didn't want to say anything in front of General Chatak," Climber said as they were descending, "but it's not often you find a Jedi and a commander at odds about tactics."

Shryne knew that to be true. "Commander Salvo has good instincts. What he lacks is patience." He turned fully to the hel-meted commando. "The war's changed some of us, Climber. But the Jedi mandate has always been to keep the peace without killing everyone who stands in the way."

Climber nodded in understanding. "I know of a few com-manders who were returned to Kamino for remedial training."

"And I know a few Jedi who could use as much," Shryne said. "Because all of us want this war over and done with." He touched Climber on the arm as the turbolift was coming to a halt. "Apologies up front if this mission turns out to be a waste of time."

"Not a problem, sir. We'll consider it leave."

Outside the antigrav shaft, the deafening hum of the generator made it almost impossible to communicate without relying on comlinks. Prizing his from a pouch on his utility belt, Shryne set it to the frequency Climber and his spec-three used to communicate with each other through their helmet links.

Warily, the three of them made their way down an unlighted hallway and ultimately onto a shaky gantry that overlooked the generator room. Most of the cavernous space was occupied by the truncated durasteel pyramid that fed power to the landing platform's veritable forest of dish-shaped shield projectors.

Macrobinoculars lowered over his tinted visor, Climber scanned the area.

"I count twelve sentries," he told Shryne through the comlink.

"Add three Koorivar technicians on the far side of the generator," the spec-three said from his position.

Even without macrobinoculars, Shryne could see that the majority of the guards were mercenaries, humans and humanoids, armed with blaster rifles and vibroblades, the brigade's signature weapon. Cranial horns—a symbol of status, especially among members of Murkhana's elite—identified the Koorivar among the group. Three Trade Federation battle droids completed the contingent.

"Generator's too well protected for us to be covert," Climber said. "Excuse me for saying so, but maybe Commander Salvo was right about letting the *Gallant* handle this."

"As I said, he has good instincts."

"Sir, just because the guards aren't here for medical care doesn't mean we can't make patients of them."

"Good thinking," Shryne said. "But we're three against twelve."

"You're good for at least six of them, aren't you, sir?"

Shryne showed the commando a narrow-eyed grin. "On a good day."

"In the end you and Salvo both get to be right. Even better, we'll be saving the *Gallant* a couple of laser bolts."

Shryne snorted a laugh. "Since you put it that way, Climber."

Climber flashed a series of hand gestures at his munitions expert; then the three of them began to work their way down to the greasy floor.

Surrendering thought and emotion, Shryne settled into the Force. He trusted that the Force would oversee his actions so long as he executed them with determination rather than in anger.

Taking out the guards was merely something that needed to be done.

At Climber's signal he and the spec-three dropped four of the sentries with precisely aimed blaster bolts, then juked into return fire to deal with those who were still standing.

As tenuous as his contact with the Force sometimes was, Shryne was still a master with a sword, and almost thirty years of training had honed his instincts and turned his body into an instrument of tremendous speed and power. The Force guided him to areas of greatest threat, the blue blade of his lightsaber cleaving the thick air, deflecting fire, severing limbs. Moments expanded, allowing him to perceive each individual energy bolt, each flick of a vibroblade. Unfaltering intention gave him ample time to see to every danger, and to carry out his task.

His opponents fell to his clean slashes, even one of the droids, whose melted circuitry raised an ozone reek. One mercenary whimpered as he fell backward, air rasping through a hole in his chest, blood leaking from vessels that hadn't been cauterized by the blade's passing.

Another, Shryne was forced to decapitate.

He sensed Climber and the spec-three to either side of him, meeting with similar success, the sibilant sound of their weapons punctuating the shield generator's ceaseless hum.

A droid burst apart, flinging shrapnel.

Shryne evaded a whirling storm of hot alloy that caught a Koorivar full-on, peppering his sallow face and robed torso.

Tumbling out of the reach of a tossed vibroblade, he noticed two of the technicians fleeing for their lives. He was willing to let them go, but the spec-three saw them, as well, and showed them no quarter, cutting both of them down before they had reached the safety of the room's primary turbolift.

With that, the fight began to wind down.

Shryne's breathing and heartbeat were loud in his ears but under control. Thought, however, intruded on his vigilance, and he lowered his guard before he should have.

The shivering blade of a mercenary's knife barely missed him. Spinning on his heel, he swept his attacker's feet out from under him, and in so doing rid the human of his left foot. The merc howled, his eyes going wide at the sight, and he lashed out with both hands, inadvertently knocking the lightsaber from Shryne's grip and sending it skittering across the floor.

Some distance away, Climber had been set upon by a battle droid and two mercenaries. The droid had been taken out, but its sparking shell had collapsed on top of Climber, pinning his right hand and blaster rifle, and the pair of mercs were preparing to finish him off.

Climber managed to hold one of his would-be killers at bay with well-placed kicks, even while he dodged a blaster bolt that ricocheted from the floor and the canted face of the shield generator. Rushing onto the scene, the spec-three went hand-to-hand with the merc Climber had booted aside, but Climber was out of tricks for dealing with his second assailant.

Vibroblade clasped in two hands, the enemy fighter leapt.

Shryne moved in a blur—not for Climber, because he knew that he could never reach him in time—but for the still-spinning lightsaber hilt, which he toed directly into Climber's gloved and outstretched left hand. In the same instant the merc was leaning over Climber to deliver what would have been a fatal blow, the commando's thumb hit the lightsaber's activation stud. A column of blue energy surged from the hilt, and through the Separatist's chest, impaling him.

Shryne hurried to Climber's side while the spec-three was moving through the room, making certain no further surprises awaited them.

Yoda or just about any other Jedi Master would have been able to rid Climber of the battle droid with a Force push, but Shryne needed Climber's help to move the sparking carcass aside. Years back, he would have been able to manage it alone, but no longer. He wasn't sure if the weakness was in him or if, with the death of every Jedi, the war was leaching some of the Force out the universe.

Climber rolled the mercenary's body to one side and sat up. "Thanks for the save, General."

"Just didn't want you to end up like your template."

Climber stared at him.

"Headless, I mean."

Climber nodded. "I thought you meant killed by a Jedi."

Shryne held out his hand for the lightsaber, which Climber was regarding as if noticing it for the first time. Then, feeling Shryne's gaze on him, he said, "Sorry, sir," and slapped the hilt into Shryne's hand.

Shryne hooked the lightsaber to his belt and yanked Climber

to his feet, his eyes falling on Chatak, Starstone, and Ion Team's other two commandos, who had rushed into the room with weapons drawn.

Shryne gestured to them that everything was under control.

"Find any patients?" he asked Chatak when she was within earshot.

"None," she said. "But we hadn't checked out the entire building when we heard the blasterfire."

Shryne turned to Climber. "Set your thermal charges. Then contact Commander Salvo. Tell him to alert airborne command that the landing platform energy shield will be dropping, but that someone is still going to have to take out the shore batteries on the bridge approaches before troops and artillery can be inserted. General Chatak and I will finish sweeping the building and catch up with you at the rally point."

"Affirmative, sir."

Shryne started off, then stopped in his tracks. "Climber."

"General?"

"Tell Commander Salvo for me that we probably could have done things his way."

"You certain you want me to do that?"

"Why not?"

"For one thing, sir, it's only going to encourage him."

Ras says you made a kill with General Shryne's lightsaber," one of the commandos who had accompanied Bol Chatak said to Climber while all four members of Ion Team were slaving thermal detonators to the shield generator's control panels.

"That's right. And knowing that you'd want to see it, I had my helmet cam snap a holo."

Climber's sarcasm was lost on the small-arms expert, a spec-two who went by the name Trace.

"How'd it handle?"

Climber sat still for a moment. "More like a tool than a weapon."

"Good tool for opening up mercenaries," Ras said from nearby.

Climber nodded. "No argument. But give me a seventeen any day."

"Shryne's all right," Trace said after they had gone back to placing the charges.

"I'll take him over Salvo in a firefight," Climber said, "but not on a battlefield. Shryne's too concerned about collateral damage."

Completing his task, he walked with purpose through the control room, assessing everyone's work. Ion Team's comlink specialist hurried over while Climber was adjusting the placement of one of the detonators.

"Has Commander Salvo been updated?" Climber asked.

"The commander is on the freq now," the spec-one said. "Wants to speak to you personally."

Climber distanced himself from the rest of the team and chinned the helmet comlink stud to an encrypted frequency. "Spec-zero Climber secure, Commander."

"Are the Jedi with you?" Salvo said abruptly.

"No, sir. They're sweeping the rest of the building in case we overlooked anyone."

"What's your situation, squad leader?"

"We're out of here as soon as the rest of the thermals are set. T-five, at most."

"Retain a couple of those thermals. Your team is to rejoin us soonest. We have a revised priority."

"Revised, how?"

"The Jedi are to be killed."

Climber fell silent for a long moment. "Say again, Commander."

"We're taking out the Jedi."

"On whose orders?"

"Are you questioning my authority?"

"No, sir. Just doing my job."

"Your job is to obey your superiors."

Climber recalled Shryne's actions in the generator room; his speed and accuracy, his skill with the lightsaber.

"Yes, sir. I'm just not too keen about going up against three Jedi."

"None of us is, Climber. That's why we need your team here. I want to set up an ambush short of the rally point."

"Understood, Commander. Will comply. Out."

Climber rejoined his three teammates, all of whom were watching him closely.

"What was all that about?" Trace asked.

Climber sat on his haunches. "We've been ordered to spring an ambush on the Jedi."

Ras grunted. "Odd time for a live-fire exercise, isn't it?"

Climber turned to him. "It's not an exercise."

Ras didn't move a muscle. "I thought the Jedi were on our side."

Climber nodded. "So did I."

"So what'd they do?" Trace asked.

Climber shook his head. "Salvo didn't say. And it's not a question we're supposed to ask, are we clear on that?"

The three specs regarded one another.

"How do you want to handle it?" Ras said finally.

"The commander wants us to blow an ambush," Climber said in a determined voice. "I say we give him what he wants."

From the sheer heights above the medcenter, Shryne, Chatak, and Starstone watched the towering building tremble as the shield generator buried at its base exploded. Clouds of smoke billowed into the chaotic sky, and the structure swayed precariously. Fortunately it didn't collapse, as Shryne feared it might, so the bridges that spanned the bay suffered no damage. Ten kilometers away, the shimmering energy shield that umbrellaed the landing platform winked out and failed, leaving the huge hexagon open to attack.

Not a moment passed before squadrons of Republic V-wing starfighters and ARC-170 bombers fell from the scudding clouds, cannons blazing. In defense, anti-aircraft batteries on the landing field and bridges opened up, filling the sky with hyphens of raw energy.

Far to the south the *Gallant* hung motionless, five hundred meters above the turbulent waters of the bay. Completing quick-turn burns, Republic gunships were streaking from the Star Destroyer's docking bays and racing shoreward through storms of intense fire.

"Now it begins in earnest," Shryne said.

The three Jedi struck west, moving deeper into the city, then south, angling for the rendezvous point. They avoided engagements with battle droids and mercenaries when they could, and won their skirmishes when evasion wasn't an option. Shryne was relieved to see that Chatak's curly-haired Padawan demonstrated remarkable courage, and was as deft at handling a lightsaber as many full-fledged Jedi Knights. He suspected that she had a stronger connection with the Force than he had had even during his most stalwart years as an eager learner.

When he wasn't seeking ways to avoid confrontation, Shryne was obsessing over his wrong call regarding the medcenter.

"A surgical strike would have been preferable," he confessed to Chatak as they were hurrying through a gloomy alley Shryne knew from previous visits to Murkhana.

"Ease up on yourself, Roan," she told him. "The generator was there precisely because the Corporate Alliance knew that we would show the medcenter mercy. What's more, Commander Salvo's opinion of you hardly matters in the scheme of things. If both of you weren't so hooked on military strategy, you could be off somewhere sharing shots of brandy."

"If either of us drank."

"Never too late to start, Roan."

Starstone loosed a loud sigh. "This is the wisdom you impart to your Padawan—that it's never too late to start drinking?"

"Did I hear a voice?" Shryne said, glancing around in theatrical concern.

"Not an important one," Chatak assured him.

Starstone was shaking her head back and forth. "This is not the apprenticeship I expected."

Shryne threw her a look. "When we get back to Coruscant, I'll be sure to slip a note into the Temple's suggestion box that

Olee Starstone has expressed disappointment with the way she's being trained."

Starstone grimaced. "I was at least under the impression that the hazing would stop once I became a Padawan."

"That's when the hazing *begins*," Chatak said, suppressing a smile. "Wait till you see what you have to endure at the trials."

"I didn't realize the trials would include psychological torture."

Chatak glanced at her. "In the end, Padawan, it all comes down to that."

"The war is trial enough for anyone," Shryne said over his shoulder. "I say that all Padawans automatically be promoted to Jedi Knights."

"You won't mind if I quote you to Yoda?" Starstone said.

"That's *Master* Yoda to you, Padawan," Chatak admonished.

"I apologize, Master."

"Even if Yoda and the rest of the High Council members have their heads in the clouds," Shryne muttered.

Starstone bit her lip. "I'll pretend I'm not hearing this."

"You'd better hear it," Shryne said, turning to her.

They held to their southwesterly course.

The fighting along the shoreline was becoming ferocious. Starfighters and droid craft flying well below optimum altitudes were disappearing in balls of flame. Overwhelmed by ranged ion cannon fire from the *Gallant,* energy shields throughout the city were beginning to fail and a mass exodus was under way, with panicked crowds of Koorivar fleeing shelters, homes, and places of business. Mercenary brigades, reinforced by battle droids and tanks, were fortifying their positions in the hills. Shryne surmised that the fight to occupy Murkhana was going to be long and brutal, perhaps at an unprecedented cost in lives.

Two hundred meters shy of the rendezvous, he was shaken by a sudden restiveness that had nothing to do with the overarching battle. Feeling as if he had unwittingly led his fellow Jedi into the sights of enemy snipers, he motioned Chatak and Starstone to a halt, then guided them without explanation to the refuge of a deserted storefront.

"I thought I was the only one sensing it," Chatak said quietly.

Shryne wasn't surprised. Like Starstone, the Zabrak Jedi had a deep and abiding connection to the Force.

"Can you get to the heart of it?" he asked.

She shook her head no. "Not with any clarity."

Starstone cut her eyes from one Jedi to the other. "What's wrong? I don't sense anything."

"Exactly," Shryne said.

"We're close to the rendezvous, Padawan," Chatak said in her best mentor's voice. "So where is everyone? Why haven't the troopers set up a perimeter?"

Starstone mulled it over. "Maybe they're just waiting for us to arrive."

The young woman's offhand remark went to the core of what Shryne and Chatak were feeling. Trading alert glances, they unclipped their lightsabers and activated the blades.

"Be mindful, Padawan," Chatak cautioned as they were leaving the shelter of the storefront. "Stretch out with your feelings."

Farther on, at a confluence of twisting streets, Shryne perceived Commander Salvo and a platoon of troopers dispersed in a tight semicircle. Not, however, to provide the Jedi with cover fire in case they were being pursued. Shryne's earlier sense of misgiving blossomed into alarm, and he shouted for Chatak and Starstone to drop to the ground.

They no sooner did when a series of concussive detonations shook the street. But the blasts had been shaped to blow at Salvo's position rather than at the Jedi.

Shryne grasped instantly that the flameless explosions had

been produced by ECDs—electrostatic charge detonators. Used to disable droids, an ECD was a tactical version of the magnetic-pulse weapon the gunships had released on reaching the beach. Caught in the detonators' indiscriminate blast radius, Salvo and his troopers yelled in surprise as their helmet imaging systems and weapons responded to the surge by going offline. Momentarily blinded by light-flare from heads-up displays, the troopers struggled to remove their helmets and simultaneously reach for the combat knives strapped to their belts.

By then, though, Captain Climber and the rest of Ion Team had rushed into the open from where they had been hiding, two of the commandos already racing toward the temporarily blinded troopers.

"Gather weapons!" Climber instructed. "No firing!"

Blaster in hand and helmet under one arm, Climber advanced slowly on the three Jedi. "No mind tricks, General," he warned.

Shryne wasn't certain that the Jedi technique was even included in his repertoire any longer, but he kept that to himself.

"My specs have their white-noise hardware enabled," Climber went on. "If they hear me repeat so much as a phrase of what you say to me, they have orders to waste you. Understood?"

Shryne didn't deactivate his lightsaber, but allowed it to drop from his right shoulder to point at the ground. Chatak and Starstone followed suit, but remained in defensive stances.

"What's this about, Climber?"

"We received orders to kill you."

Shryne stared at him in disbelief. "Who issued the order?"

Climber gave his jaw a flick, as if to indicate something behind him. "You'll have to ask Commander Salvo, sir."

"Climber, where are you?" Salvo shouted as Climber's spec-two was escorting the commander forward. The commander's helmet was off and he had his gloved hands pressed to his eyes. "You blew those ECDs?"

"We did, sir. To get to the bottom of this."

Sensing Shryne's approach, Salvo raised his armored fists.

"At ease, Commander," Shryne told him.

Salvo relaxed somewhat. "Are we your prisoners, then?"

"You gave the order to kill us?"

"I won't answer that," Salvo said.

"Commander, if this has anything to do with our earlier head-butting—"

"Don't flatter yourself, General. This is beyond both of us."

Shryne was confused. "Then the order didn't originate with you. Did you ask for verification?"

Salvo shook his head no. "That wasn't necessary."

"Climber?" Shryne said.

"I don't know any more than you know, General. And I doubt that Commander Salvo will be as easily persuaded to part with information as our captive merc was."

"General Shryne," the spec-one interrupted, tapping his forefinger against the side of his helmet. "Comlink from forward operations. Additional platoons are on their way to Aurek-Bacta to reinforce."

Climber looked Shryne in the eye. "Sir, we're not going to be able to stop all of them, and if it comes to a fight, we're not going to be able to help you any more than we have. We don't kill our own."

"I understand, Climber."

"This has to be a mistake, sir."

"I agree."

"For old times' sake, I'm giving you a chance to escape. But orders are orders. If we find you, we will engage." Climber held Shryne's gaze. "Of course, sir, you could kill all of us now, and increase your odds of surviving."

Salvo and the spec-two made nervous movements.

"As you put it," Shryne said, "we don't fire on our own."

Climber nodded in relief. "Exactly what I would have expected you to say, General. Makes me feel all right about disobeying a direct order, and accepting whatever flak flies our way as a result."

"Let's hope it doesn't come to that, Climber."

"Hope is not something we store in our kit, General."

Shryne touched him on the upper arm. "One day you may have to."

"Yes, sir. Now get a move on before you're forced to put those lightsabers to the test."

A chorus of ready tones announced that helmet imaging systems, heads-up displays, and weapons had recovered from the magnetic-pulse effects of the ECDs and were back online.

The troopers, also recovered, didn't waste a moment in arming their rifles and leveling them at the four commandos, who had their DC-17s raised in anticipation of just such a standoff.

Arms outstretched, Commander Salvo rushed to position himself between the two groups before a blaster bolt could be fired.

"Stand down, all of you!" he snapped. "That's an order!" He glanced menacingly at Climber. "You had better comply this time."

While weapons were being lowered all around and the first of the reinforcement platoons was arriving—the troopers plainly confused by the scene unfolding in front of them—Salvo motioned the squad leader off to one side.

"Has your programming been wiped?" Salvo asked. "Our orders came down from the top of the command chain."

"I thought the Jedi were the top of the chain."

"From the Commander in Chief, Climber. Do you copy?"

"Supreme Chancellor Palpatine?"

Salvo nodded. "Evidently you and your team need reminding that we serve the Chancellor, not the Jedi."

Climber considered it. "Were you apprised of what the Jedi have done to prompt an order of execution?"

Salvo's upper lip curled. "That doesn't concern me, Climber, and it shouldn't concern you."

"You're right, Commander. I must have been misprogrammed. All this time I've accepted that the Grand Army and the Jedi Knights served the *Republic*. No one said anything to me about serving Palpatine first and foremost."

"Palpatine *is* the Republic, Climber."

"Palpatine issued the orders personally?"

"His command was to execute an order that has been in place since before the start of the war."

Climber took a moment to consider it. "Here's my take on it, Commander. It all comes down to serving the ones who are fighting alongside you, watching your back, putting a weapon in your hand when you need it most."

Salvo sharpened his tone. "We're not going to argue this now. But I promise you this much: if we don't catch them, you'll pay for your treason—you and your entire team."

Climber nodded. "We knew that going in."

Salvo took a breath and gave his head a rueful shake. "You shouldn't be thinking for yourself, brother. It's more dangerous than you know."

He swung to the members of his platoon and the recent arrivals.

"Platoon leaders, switch your comlinks to encrypted command frequency zero-zero-four. Have your troopers fan out. Grid search. Every building, every nook and cranny. You know what you're up against, so keep your wits about you."

"Ever see a Jedi run, Commander?" a platoon leader asked. "My guess is they're already ten klicks from here."

Salvo turned to his comlink specialist. "Contact the *Gallant*. Inform command that we have a situation, and that we're going to need whatever seeker droids and BARC detachments can be spared."

"Commander," the same platoon leader said, "unless the Seps are in on this hunt, we're going to have our hands full. Are we here to take Murkhana or the Jedi?"

Climber smirked. "Don't make matters worse by trying to confuse him, Lieutenant."

Gesturing with his forefinger, Salvo said: "Worse for you if they escape."

Shryne knew Murkhana City by heart.

"This way . . . Down here . . . Up there," he instructed as they made their escape, using the speed granted by the Force to put kilometers between themselves and their new enemy.

The city was wide open to bombardment now. The energy shields were down and the anti-laser aerosols had diffused. Two additional Star Destroyers hung over the bay, but Republic forces were continuing to show restraint. Most of the intense fighting was still occurring around the landing platform, although the hexagonal field itself was not being targeted, as it and the three bridges that remained were essential for moving troopers and matériel into the city. Shryne figured that once the landing plat-form was taken, the Separatists would probably blow the rest of the bridges, if only to slow the inevitable occupation, while resi-dents continued to flee for their lives.

In the streets, firefights were undergoing a conspicuous change now that the clone troopers had been issued a new priority. Separatist mercenaries and battle droids were making the most of the confusion. Shryne, Chatak, and Starstone had witnessed several instances when platoons of clones disengaged from fighting, presumably to continue the hunt for the Jedi.

When Shryne felt that the three of them had a moment to spare he led them into a deserted building and pulled his comlink from his belt.

"The troopers have changed frequencies to prevent our eavesdropping on them," he said.

"That doesn't affect our knowing their methods for conducting a search," Chatak said.

"We can avoid them for however long it takes to clear this up. If it comes down to worst cases, I have contacts in the city who might be able to help us escape."

"Whose lives are we protecting here," Starstone asked in an edgy voice, "ours or the troopers'? I mean, aren't we the ones who had them grown?"

Shryne and Chatak traded secret glances.

"I'm not going to start killing troopers," Shryne said emphatically.

Chatak glanced at her Padawan. "That's what battle droids were created for."

Starstone gnawed at her lower lip. "What about Master Loorne and the others?"

Shryne made adjustments to his comlink. "Still no response from any of them. And not because of signal jamming."

Knowing that Chatak was doing the same, he stretched out with the Force, but no reverberations attended his call.

Chatak's shoulders slumped. "They've been killed."

Starstone sighed and hung her head.

"Draw on your training, Padawan," Chatak said quickly. "They're with the Force."

They're dead, Shryne thought.

Starstone looked up at him. "Why have they turned on us?"

"Salvo implied that the order came from high up."

"That can only mean the Office of the Supreme Chancellor," Chatak said.

Shryne shook his head. "That doesn't make sense. Palpatine owes his life to Skywalker and Master Kenobi."

"Then this has to be a miscommunication," Starstone chimed in. "For all we know, the Corporate Alliance broke the High Command code and issued counterfeit orders to our company commanders."

"Right about now that would be a *best*-case scenario," Shryne said. "If our comlinks were powerful enough to contact the Temple . . ."

"But the Temple can contact us," Starstone said.

"And it might yet," Chatak said.

"Maybe Passel Argente cut a deal with the Supreme Chancellor to spare Murkhana," Starstone said.

Shryne glanced at her. "How many more theories are you planning to offer?" he said, more harshly than he meant to.

"I'm sorry, Master."

"Patience, Padawan," Chatak said in a comforting voice.

Shryne slipped the comlink back into its pouch. "We need to avoid further engagements with droids or mercenaries. Lightsaber wounds are easy to identify. We don't want to leave a trail."

Exiting the building, they resumed their careful climb into the hills.

Everywhere they turned, the streets were crowded with clone troopers, battle droids, and masses of fleeing Koorivar. Before they had gone even a kilometer, Shryne brought them to a halt once more.

"We're getting nowhere fast. If we ditch our robes, we might have better luck at blending in."

Chatak regarded him dubiously. "What do you have in mind, Roan?"

"We find a couple of mercenaries and take their robes and headcloths." He gazed at Chatak and Starstone in turn. "If the troopers can switch sides, then so can we."

Salvo ended his helmet comlink communication with Murkhana's theater commanders and joined Climber at what had
become the troopers' forward command base. The other three
commandos were searching for the escaped Jedi, but Salvo didn't
want the squad leader out of his sight.

"General Loorne and the two Jedi Knights he arrived with
were ambushed and killed," Salvo shared with Climber. "Apparently no troopers among the Twenty-second staked a claim to
the moral high ground."

Climber let the remark go. "Did you report our actions to
High Command?"

Salvo shook his head. "But don't think I won't. Like I told
you, it depends on whether we're able to kill them. Just now I
don't want your actions reflecting negatively on my command."

"Did you learn anything about what prompted the execution
order?"

Salvo spent a moment arguing with himself about what he
should and should not reveal. "Theater command reports that
four Jedi Masters attempted to assassinate Supreme Chancellor

Palpatine in his chambers on Coruscant. The reason is unclear, but it appears that the Jedi have been angling from the start to assume control of the Republic, and that the war may have been engineered to help bring that about."

Climber was stunned. "So Palpatine's order was put in place because he anticipated that the Jedi might try something?"

"It's not unusual to have a contingency plan, Climber. You should know that better than anyone."

Climber thought hard about it. "How does it make you feel, Commander—about what the Jedi did, I mean?"

Salvo took a moment to respond. "As far as I'm concerned, their treachery just adds more enemies to the list. Other than that, I don't feel one way or another about it."

Climber studied Salvo. "You know, word among some of the troopers is that the Jedi had a hand in ordering the creation of the Grand Army. Were they figuring we'd side with them when they grabbed control, or would they have turned on us eventually?"

"No way to know."

"Except they made their move too soon."

Salvo nodded. "Even now, troopers and Jedi are battling it out inside the Temple on Coruscant. Thousands are believed dead."

"I've never been to Coruscant," Climber said, breaking a brief silence. "Closest I ever came was training on one of the inner worlds of that system. You've been there?"

"Once. Before the start of the Outer Rim Sieges."

"Who would you rather be serving, Commander—Palpatine or the Jedi?"

"That's outside the scope of the part we were created to play, Climber. When this war ends, we'll be sitting pretty. I wouldn't have thought so even twelve hours ago, but now, with the Jedi out of the picture, I suspect we're in for a promotion."

Climber glanced at the sky. "Going to be dark soon. Puts our search teams at high risk of being ambushed by Seps."

Salvo shrugged. "More than a hundred seeker droids have been deployed. Shouldn't be hard to find three Jedi."

Climber blew his breath out in derision. "You know as well as I do that they're too smart to be caught."

"Granted," Salvo said. "By now, they're probably wearing bodysuits and armor."

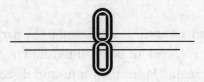

Eat," Shryne said, forcing some of the rations he had taken from his utility belt on a distracted Olee Starstone. "We don't know when we'll have another chance."

Several hours had passed since they had fled the ambush site, and they'd traveled clear across the city to an empty warehouse close to the access ramps of the northernmost of the landing platform bridges. It was midnight, and they were attired in the garb of three mercenaries they had taken by surprise behind the Argente Tower.

Shryne continued. "There may come a point when we'll have to get rid of our comlinks, beacon transceivers, and lightsabers. Being taken prisoner could be our way off Murkhana."

"Should we use Force influence?" Starstone said.

"That might work on a couple of troopers at a time," Shryne said, "but not an entire platoon, much less a full company."

Chatak eyed her Padawan with clear intent. "It's a matter of surviving until the Republic is victorious."

Shryne had a ration pack lifted to his mouth when his beacon transceiver began to vibrate. He fished the device from the deep pocket of the Koorivar robe and regarded it in silence.

"Could be troopers, tapping into our frequencies," Chatak said.

Shryne studied the beacon's small display screen. "It's a coded burst-transmission from the Temple."

Chatak hurried to his side to peer over his shoulder. "Can you decipher it?"

"It's not a simple Nine Thirteen," Shryne said, referring to the code the Jedi used to locate one another in emergency situations. "Give me a moment." When the burst-transmission began to recycle, he turned to Chatak in stark incredulity. "The High Council is ordering all Jedi back to Coruscant."

Chatak was dumbfounded.

"No explanation," Shryne said.

Chatak stood up and paced away from him. "What could have happened?"

He thought about it. "A follow-up attack on Coruscant by Grievous?"

"Perhaps," Chatak said. "But that doesn't account for the clone troopers' disloyalty."

"Maybe there's been a universal clone trooper revolt," Starstone suggested. "The Kaminoans could have betrayed us. All these years, they could have been in league with Count Dooku. They could have programmed the troopers to revolt at a predetermined time."

Shryne was glancing at Chatak. "Does she ever stop?"

"I haven't been able to find the off switch."

Shryne moved to the nearest window and watched the night sky.

"Republic starfighters will be setting down on the landing platform by late morning," he said.

Chatak joined him at the window. "Then Murkhana is won."

Shryne turned to face her. "We have to reach the platform. The troopers have their orders, and now we have ours. If we can seize a transport or starfighters, we may yet be able to return to Coruscant."

Throughout the long night and morning, explosive light strobed through the warehouse's arched windows as Republic and Separatist forces clashed at sea and in the air. The battle for the landing platform raged well into the afternoon. But now the Separatist forces were in full retreat, streaming across the two intact bridges, leaving the platform's defense to homing spider droids, hailfire weapons platforms, and tanks.

By the time the Jedi managed to reach the more northern of the pair of bridges, the wide avenue was so closely packed with fleeing mercenaries and other Separatist fighters they could scarcely make any headway against the flow. A crossing that should have taken an hour required more than three, and the sun was low on the horizon when they reached the end of the bridge.

They were just short of the platform itself when a succession of powerful explosions took out the final hundred meters of the span and split the massive hexagon into thirds, sending hundreds of clone troopers, mercenaries, and Separatist droids plummeting into the churning water.

Shryne knew that the Separatists were responsible for the explosions. Before too long, munitions planted under the final bridge would be detonated, as well. By then, though, there would be no stopping the Republic onslaught.

While mercenaries shouldered past him in a frenzy, Shryne surveyed the forest of bridge pylons left exposed by the explosions, calculating their distance from one another and the odds of accomplishing what he had in mind.

Finally he said: "Either we frog-leap for the platform or we head back into the city." He looked at Starstone. "You decide."

Her blue eyes sparkled and she put on a brave face. "Not a problem, Master. We leap for it."

Shryne almost grinned. "Right. One at a time."

Chatak put her arm around her Padawan's shoulder. "Let's just hope no clone troopers are watching."

Shryne gestured to his pilfered outfit of robe and head-cloth. "We're just a bunch of very agile mercs."

Chatak took the lead, with Starstone right on her heels. Shryne waited until they were halfway along before following. The first few leaps were easy, but the closer he got to the platform, the greater the distance between the pylons, many of which had been left with jagged tops. On his penultimate jump, he nearly lost his balance, and on his final leap for the edge of the platform his hands arrived well in front of his feet.

A last-moment grab from Starstone was all that saved him from a plunge into the waves.

"Remind me to mention this to the Council, Padawan," he told her.

The platform was being hammered, but not past the point of utility. On one fractured section gunships were beginning to land, along with a vanguard flight of troop transports. Elsewhere, battle droids were being flattened by magpulse busters, then picked off before they had a chance to reactivate by V-wings and ARC-170s performing lightning-fast strafing runs.

With night falling, the Jedi wove through firefights and foun-taining explosions, using their captured blasters rather than their lightsabers to defend themselves against teams of clone troopers and commandos, though without killing any.

They came to a halt at a ruined stretch of permacrete, at the far end of which a squadron of starfighters was touching down.

"Can you pilot a ship?" Shryne asked Starstone in a rush.

"Only an interceptor, Master. But without an astromech droid I doubt I could fly one to Coruscant. And I've never even seen the cockpit of a V-wing."

Shryne considered it. "Then it'll have to be an ARC-one-seventy." He pointed to a bomber that was just landing, probably to refuel. "That's our ship. It's our best bet, anyway. Enough chairs for the three of us, and hyperspace-capable."

Chatak watched the crew for a moment. "We may have to stun the copilot and tail gunner."

Shryne was on the verge of moving when he felt the beacon transceiver vibrate again, and he pawed it from the deep pocket of the robe.

"What is it, Roan?" Chatak asked while he was staring in stupefaction at the device. *"What?"* she repeated.

"Another coded burst from the beacon," he said without moving his gaze from the screen.

"Same order?"

"The opposite." Eyes wide, he looked up at Chatak and Starstone. "All Jedi are ordered to avoid Coruscant at all costs. We're to abandon whatever missions we're involved in, and go into hiding."

Chatak's mouth fell open.

Shryne made his lips a thin line. "We still need to get off Murkhana."

They double-checked their blasters and again were on the verge of setting out for the starfighter when every Separatist droid and war machine on the landing platform abruptly began to power down. At first Shryne thought that another droid buster had been delivered without his being aware of it. Then he realized his mistake.

This was something different.

The droids hadn't simply been dazzled. They had been deactivated, even the hailfires and tanks. Red photoreceptors lost their glow, alloy limbs and antennas relaxed, every soldier and war machine stood motionless.

At once, a full wing of gunships dropped out of the noon sky, releasing almost a thousand clone troopers, riding polyplast cables to the platform's ruined surface.

Shryne, Chatak, and Starstone watched helplessly as they were almost instantly surrounded.

"Capture is infinitely preferable to execution," Shryne said. "It could still be our way out."

Closest to the ragged edge of the platform, he allowed his blaster, comlink, beacon transceiver, and lightsaber to slip from his hands into the dark waters far below.

PART II

THE EMPEROR'S EMISSARY

The Star Destroyer *Exactor*, second in a line of newly minted
Imperator-class naval vessels, emerged from hyperspace and inserted into orbit, its spiked bow aimed at the former Separatist
world of Murkhana. At sixteen hundred meters in length, the
Exactor, unlike its *Venator*-class predecessors, was a product of
Kuat Drive Yards, and featured gaping ventral launching bays
rather than a dorsal flight deck.

Moved by gravity rather than by their ion drives, the car-
casses of Banking Clan and Commerce Guild warships were grim
reminders of the Republic invasion that had been launched in the
concluding weeks of the war. Murkhana, however, had fared far
better than some contested worlds, and the Corporate Alliance
elite had decamped for remote systems in the galaxy's Tingel
Arm, taking much of the planet's wealth with it.

In his quarters aboard the capital ship now under his personal
command, Darth Vader, gloved and artificial right hand clamped
on the hilt of his new lightsaber, knelt before a larger-than-life
hologram of Emperor Palpatine. Only four standard weeks had
elapsed since the war had ended and Palpatine had proclaimed

himself Emperor of the former Republic, to the adulation of the leaders of countless worlds that had been drawn into the protracted conflict, and to the sustained acclaim of nearly the entire Senate.

Palpatine wore a voluminous embroidered robe of rich weave, the cowl of which was raised, concealing in shadow the scars he had suffered at the hands of the four treasonous Jedi Masters who had attempted to arrest him in his chambers in the Senate Office Building, as well as other deformations resulting from his fierce battle with Master Yoda in the Rotunda of the Senate itself.

"This is an important time for you, Lord Vader," Palpatine was saying. "You are finally free to make *full* use of your powers. If not for us, the galaxy would never have been restored to order. Now you must embrace the sacrifices you made to bring this about, and revel in the fact that you have fulfilled your destiny. It can all be yours, my young apprentice, anything you wish. You need only have the determination to *take it,* at whatever cost to those who stand in your way."

Palpatine's disfigurements were really nothing new; nor was his deliberate, vaguely contemptuous voice. The Emperor had used the same voice to procure his first apprentice; to ensnare Trade Federation Viceroy Nute Gunray in facilitating his dark designs; to persuade Count Dooku to unleash a war; and finally to seduce Vader—former Jedi Knight Anakin Skywalker—to the dark side, with the promise that he could keep Anakin's wife from dying.

Few among the galaxy's trillions were aware that Palpatine was also a Sith Lord, known by the title Darth Sidious, or that he had manipulated the war in order to bring down the Republic, crush the Jedi, and place the entire galaxy under his full control. Fewer still knew of the crucial role Sidious's current apprentice had played in those events, having helped Sidious defend himself against the Jedi who had sought his arrest; having led the assault on the Jedi Temple on Coruscant; having killed in cold blood the half dozen members of the Separatist Council in their hidden fortress on volcanic Mustafar.

And who there had suffered even more gravely than Palpatine.

Down on one knee, his black-masked face raised to the hologram, tall, fearsome Vader was wearing the bodysuit and armor, helmet, boots, and cloak that both camouflaged the evidence of his transformation and sustained his life.

Without revealing his distress at being unable to maintain the kneeling posture, Vader said: "What are your orders, Master?"

And asked himself: *Is this poorly designed suit the source of my distress, or is something else at work?*

"Do you recall what I told you about the relationship between power and understanding, Lord Vader?"

"Yes, Master. Where the Jedi gained power through understanding, the Sith gain understanding through power."

Palpatine smiled faintly. "This will become clearer to you as you continue your training, Lord Vader. And to that end I will provide you with the means to increase your *power*, and broaden your *understanding*. In due time, power will fill the vacuum created by the decisions you made, the acts you carried out. Married to the order of the Sith, you will need no other companion than the dark side of the Force . . ."

The remark stirred something within Vader, but he was unable to make full sense of the feelings that washed through him: a commingling of anger and disappointment, of grief and regret . . .

The events of Anakin Skywalker's life might have occurred a lifetime ago, or to someone else entirely, and yet some residue of Anakin continued to plague Vader, like pain from a phantom limb.

"Word has reached me," Palpatine was saying, "that a group of clone troopers on Murkhana may have deliberately refused to comply with Order Sixty-Six."

Vader tightened his hold on the lightsaber. "I had not heard, Master."

He knew that Order Sixty-Six had not been hardwired into the clones by the Kaminoans who had grown them. Rather, the troopers—the commanders, especially—had been programmed to demonstrate unfailing loyalty to the Supreme Chancellor, in his role as Commander in Chief of the Grand Army of the Republic. And so when the Jedi had revealed their seditious plans, they had become a threat to Palpatine, and had been sentenced to death.

On myriad worlds Order 66 had been executed without misfortune—on Mygeeto, Saleucami, Felucia, and many others. Taken by surprise, thousands of Jedi had been assassinated by troopers who had for three years answered almost exclusively to them. A few Jedi were known to have escaped death by dint of superior skill or accident. But on Murkhana, apparently unique events had played out; events that were potentially more dangerous to the Empire than the few Jedi who had survived.

"What was the cause of the troopers' insubordination, Master?" Vader asked.

"Contagion." Palpatine sneered. "Contagion brought about by fighting alongside the *Jedi* for so many years. Clone or otherwise, there is only so much a being can be programmed to do. Sooner or later even a lowly trooper will become the sum of his experiences."

Light-years distant in his inner sanctum, Palpatine leaned toward the holotransceiver's cam.

"But you will demonstrate to them the peril of independent thinking, Lord Vader, the refusal to obey orders."

"To obey you, Master."

"To obey *us,* my apprentice. Remember that."

"Yes, my Master." Vader paused with purpose. "It's possible, then, that some Jedi may have survived?"

Palpatine adopted a look of consummate displeasure. "I am not worried about your pathetic former *friends,* Lord Vader. I want those clone troopers punished, as a reminder to all of them that for the rest of their abbreviated lives they would do well to understand whom they truly serve." Retracting his face into the hood of his robe, he said in a seething tone: "It is time that you were revealed as my authority. I leave it to you to drive the point home."

"And the escaped Jedi, Master?"

Palpatine fell silent for a moment, as if choosing his words carefully. "The escaped Jedi . . . yes. You may kill any you come across during the course of your mission."

Vader didn't rise until the Emperor's holoimage had de-rezzed entirely. Then he stood for a long moment with his sheathed arms dangling at his sides, his head mournfully bowed. Finally he turned and moved for the hatch that opened onto the *Exactor*'s ready room.

To the galaxy at large, Jedi Knight Anakin Skywalker—poster boy for the war effort, the "Hero with No Fear," the *Chosen One*—had died on Coruscant during the siege of the Jedi Temple.

And to some extent that was true.

Anakin is dead, Vader told himself.

And yet, if not for events on Mustafar, Anakin would sit now on the Coruscant throne, his wife by his side, their child in her arms . . . Instead, Palpatine's plan could not have been more flawlessly executed. He had won it all: the war, the Republic, the fealty of the one Jedi Knight in whom the entire Jedi order had placed its hope. The revenge of the self-exiled Sith had been complete, and Darth Vader was merely a minion, an errand boy, allegedly an apprentice, the public face of the dark side of the Force.

While he retained his knowledge of the Jedi arts, he felt uncertain about his place in the Force; and while he had taken his first steps toward awakening the power of the dark side, he felt uncertain about his ability to sustain that power. How far he might have been now had fate not intervened to strip him of almost everything he possessed, as a means of remaking him!

Or of humbling him, as Darths Maul and Tyranus had been humbled before him; as indeed the Jedi order itself had been humbled.

Where Darth Sidious had gained everything, Vader had lost everything, including—for the moment, at least—the self-confidence and unbridled skill he had demonstrated as Anakin Skywalker.

Vader turned and moved for the hatch.

But this is not walking, he thought.

Long accustomed to building and rebuilding droids, super-charging the engines of landspeeders and starfighters, upgrading the mechanisms that controlled the first of his artificial limbs, he was dismayed by the incompetence of the medical droids responsible for his resurrection in Sidious's lofty laboratory on Coruscant.

His alloy lower legs were bulked by strips of armor similar to those that filled and gave form to the long glove Anakin had worn over his right-arm prosthesis. What remained of his real limbs ended in bulbs of grafted flesh, inserted into machines that triggered movement through the use of modules that interfaced with his damaged nerve endings. But instead of using durasteel, the medical droids had substituted an inferior alloy, and had failed to inspect the strips that protected the electromotive lines. As a result, the inner lining of the pressurized bodysuit was continually snagging on places where the strips were anchored to knee and ankle joints.

The tall boots were a poor fit for his artificial feet, whose claw-like toes lacked the electrostatic sensitivity of his equally false fingertips. Raised in the heel, the cumbersome footgear canted him slightly forward, forcing him to move with exaggerated caution lest he stumble or topple over. Worse, they were so heavy that he often felt rooted to the ground, or as if he were moving in high gravity.

What good was motion of this sort, if he was going to have to call on the Force even to walk from place to place! He may as well have resigned himself to using a repulsor chair and abandoned *any* hope of movement.

The defects in his prosthetic arms mirrored those of his legs.

Only the right one felt *natural* to him—though it, too, was artificial—and the pneumatic mechanisms that supplied articulation and support were sometimes slow to respond. The weighty cloak and pectoral plating so restricted his movement that he could scarcely lift his arms over his head, and he had already been forced to adapt his lightsaber technique to compensate.

He could probably adjust the servodrivers and pistons in his forearms to provide his hands with strength enough to crush the hilt of his new lightsaber. With the power of his arms alone, he had the ability to lift an adult being off the ground. But the Force had always given him the ability to do that, especially in moments of rage, as he had demonstrated on Tatooine and elsewhere. What's more, the sleeves of the bodysuit didn't hug the prostheses as they should, and the elbow-length gloves sagged and bunched at his wrists.

Gazing at the gloves now, he thought: *This is not seeing.*

The pressurized mask was goggle-eyed, fish-mouthed, short-snouted, and needlessly angular over the cheekbones. Coupled with a flaring dome of helmet, the mask gave him the forbidding appearance of an ancient Sith war droid. The dark hemispheres that covered his eyes filtered out light that might have caused further injury to his damaged corneas and retinas, but in enhanced mode the half globes reddened the light and prevented him from being able to see the toes of his boots without inclining his head almost ninety degrees.

Listening to the servomotors that drove his limbs, he thought: *This is not hearing*.

The med droids rebuilt the cartilage of his outer ears, but his eardrums, having melted in Mustafar's heat, had been beyond repair. Sound waves now had to be transmitted directly to implants in his inner ear, and sounds registered as if issuing from underwater. Worse, the implanted sensors lacked sufficient discrimination, so that too many ambient sounds were picked up, and their distance and direction were difficult to determine. Sometimes the sensors needled him with feedback, or attached echo or vibrato effects to even the faintest noise.

Allowing his lungs to fill with air, he thought: *This is not breathing*.

Here the med droids had truly failed him.

From a control box he wore strapped to his chest, a thick cable entered his torso, linked to a breathing apparatus and heartbeat regulator. The ventilator was implanted in his hideously scarred chest, along with tubes that ran directly into his damaged lungs, and others that entered his throat, so that should the chest plate or belt control panels develop a glitch, he could breathe unassisted *for a limited time*.

But the monitoring panel beeped frequently and for no reason, and the constellation of lights served only as steady reminders of his vulnerability.

The incessant rasp of his breathing interfered with his ability to rest, let alone sleep. And sleep, in the rare moments it came to him, was a nightmarish jumble of twisted, recurrent memories that unfolded to excruciating sounds.

The med droids had at least inserted the redundant breathing tubes low enough so that, with the aid of an enunciator, his scorched vocal cords could still form sounds and words. But absent the enunciator, which imparted a synthetic bass tone, his own voice was little more than a whisper.

He could take food through his mouth, as well, but only when he was inside a hyperbaric chamber, since he had to remove the triangular respiratory vent that was the mask's prominent feature. So it was easier to receive nourishment through liquids, intravenous and otherwise, and to rely on catheters, collection pouches, and recyclers to deal with liquid and solid waste.

But all those devices made it even more difficult for him to move with ease, much less with any *grace*. The pectoral armor that protected the artificial lung weighed him down, as did the electrode-studded collar that supported the outsize helmet, necessary to safeguard the cybernetic devices that replaced the uppermost of his vertebrae, the delicate systems of the mask, and the ragged scars in his hairless head, which owed as much to what he had endured on Mustafar as to attempts at emergency trephination during the trip back to Coruscant aboard Sidious's shuttle.

The synthskin that substituted for what was seared from his bones itched incessantly, and his body needed to be periodically cleansed and scrubbed of necrotic flesh.

Already he had experienced moments of claustrophobia—moments of desperation to be rid of the suit, to emerge from the shell. He needed to build, or have built, a chamber in which he could feel human again . . .

If possible.

All in all, he thought: *This is not living*.

This was solitary confinement. Prison of the worst sort. Continual torture. He was nothing more than wreckage. Power without clear purpose . . .

A melancholy sigh escaped the mouth grille.

Collecting himself, he stepped through the hatch.

*   *   *

Commander Appo was waiting in the ready room, the special ops officer who had led the 501st Legion against the Jedi Temple.

"Your shuttle is prepared, Lord Vader," Appo said.

For reasons that went beyond the armor and helmets, the imaging systems and boots, Vader felt more at home among the troopers than he did around other flesh-and-bloods.

And Appo and the rest of Vader's cadre of stormtroopers seemed to be at ease with their new superior. To them it was only reasonable that Vader wore a bodysuit and armor. Some had always wondered why the Jedi left themselves exposed, as if they had had something to prove by it.

Vader looked down at Appo and nodded. "Come with me, Commander. The Emperor has business for us on Murkhana."

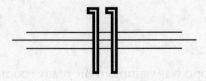

Shryne squinted against the golden wash of Murkhana's primary, which had just climbed from behind the thickly forested hills that walled Murkhana City to the east. By his reckoning he had spent close to four weeks confined with hundreds of other captives to a windowless warehouse somewhere in the city. Hours earlier all of them had been marched through the dark to a red-clay landing field that had been notched into one of the hills and was currently swarming with Republic troops.

On its hardstand sat a military transport Shryne surmised would deliver everyone to a proper prison on or in orbit around some forlorn Outer Rim world. Thus far, though, none of the prisoners had been ordered to board the transport. Instead, a head count was being conducted. More important, the clone troopers were obviously waiting for someone or something to arrive.

When his eyes had adjusted fully to the light, Shryne scanned the prisoners to all sides of him, relieved to find Bol Chatak and her Padawan standing some fifty meters away, among a mixed group of indigenous Koorivar fighters and an assortment of

Separatist mercenaries. He called to them through the Force, figuring that Chatak would be first to respond, but it was Starstone who turned slightly in his direction and smiled faintly. Then Chatak looked his way, offering a quick nod.

On their capture at the landing platform, the three of them had been separated. The fact that Chatak had managed to retain her headcloth perhaps explained why her short cranial horns hadn't singled her out as Zabrak and raised an alert among her captors.

Assuming that the conditions of her captivity had been similar to his, Chatak's being overlooked made perfect sense to Shryne. Rounded up with hundreds of enemy fighters following the still-puzzling deactivation of Murkhana's battle droids and other war machines, Shryne had been searched, roughed up, and marched into the dark building that would become his home for the next four weeks—a special torment reserved for mercenaries. Any who hadn't willingly surrendered their weapons had been executed, and dozens more had died in fierce fights that had broken out for the few scraps of food that had been provided.

It hadn't taken long for Shryne to grasp that winning the hearts and minds of Separatist fighters was no longer tops on Chancellor Palpatine's list.

It also hadn't taken long for him to give up worrying about being found out, since he had been placed in the custody of low-ranking clone troopers whose armor blazes identified them as members of companies other than Commander Salvo's. The troopers had rarely spoken to any of the prisoners, so there had been no news of the war or of events that might have prompted the High Council to order the Jedi to go into hiding. Shryne knew only that the fighting on Murkhana had stopped, and that the Republic had triumphed.

He was considering the advantage of edging himself closer to where Chatak and Starstone stood when a convoy of military speeders and big-wheeled juggernauts arrived on the scene. Commander Salvo and some of his chief officers stepped from one of the landspeeders; from the hatch of one of the juggernauts emerged commando squad leader Climber, and the rest of Ion Team.

Shryne wondered about the timing of the commander's arrival. Perhaps Salvo was determined to have a close look at each and every prisoner before any were loaded into the transport. That Shryne was farther back from the leading edge of the crowd than Chatak and Starstone were meant nothing. Given the amount of time they had spent with Salvo, he would have no trouble identifying all of them.

Oddly, though, the commander wasn't paying much attention to the prisoners. His T-visor gaze was fixed instead on a Republic shuttle that was descending toward the landing field.

"*Theta*-class," one of the prisoners said quietly to the mercenary standing alongside him.

"You don't see many of those," the second human said.

"Must be one of Palpatine's regional governors."

The first man sniffed. "When they care enough to send the very best . . ."

The shuttle had commenced its landing sequence. With ion drive powering down and repulsorlift engaged, the craft folded its long wings upward to provide access to the main hold, then settled gently to the ground. No sooner had the boarding ramp extended than a squad of elite troopers filed out, the red markings on their armor identifying them as Coruscant shock troopers.

A much taller figure followed, attired head-to-foot in black.

"What in the moons of Bogden—"

"New breed of trooper?"

"Only if someone furnished the cloners with a donor a lot taller than the original."

Salvo and his officers hastened over to the figure in black.

"Welcome, Lord Vader."

"Vader?" the merc closest to Shryne said.

Lord, Shryne thought.

"That's no clone," the first human said.

Shryne didn't know what to make of Vader, although it was evident from the reaction of Salvo and his officers that they had been told to expect someone of high rank. With his large helmet and flowing black cape, Vader looked like something borrowed from the Separatists—a grotesque, Grievous-like marriage of humanoid and machine.

"Lord Vader," Shryne repeated under his breath.

Like Count Dooku?

Salvo was gesturing to Climber and the other commandos, who had remained at the juggernaut. From inside the enormous vehicle floated a large antigrav capsule with a transparent lid, which two of the commandos began to guide toward Vader's shuttle. As the capsule passed close to Shryne, he caught a glimpse of brown robes, and his stomach lurched into his throat.

When the capsule finally reached Salvo, the commander opened an access panel in its base and removed three gleaming cylinders, which he proffered to Vader.

Lightsabers.

Vader nodded for the commander of his shock troopers to accept them, then, in a deep, synthesized voice, said to Salvo: "What were you saving the bodies for, Commander—posterity?"

Salvo shook his head. "We weren't issued any instructions—"

Vader's gloved right hand waved him silent. "Dispose of them in any fashion you see fit."

Salvo was motioning Climber to remove the antigrav coffin when Vader stopped him.

"Have you forgotten anyone, Commander?" Vader asked.

Salvo regarded him. "Forgotten, Lord Vader?"

Vader folded his arms across his massive chest. "*Six* Jedi were assigned to Murkhana, not three."

Shryne traded brief glances with Chatak, who was also close enough to Vader to hear the remark.

"I'm sorry to report, Lord Vader, that the other three evaded capture," Salvo said.

Vader nodded. "I already know that, Commander. And I haven't come halfway across the galaxy to chase them down." He drew himself erect with a haughty air. "I've come to deal with the ones who allowed them to escape."

Climber immediately stepped forward. "That would be me."

"And us," the rest of Ion Team announced in unison.

Vader stared down at the commandos. "You disobeyed a direct order from High Command."

"The order made no sense at the time," Climber answered for everyone. "We thought it might be a Separatist trick."

"What you 'thought' has no bearing on this," Vader said, pointing at Climber. "You are expected to follow orders."

"And we follow any reasonable ones. Killing our own didn't qualify."

Vader continued to point his forefinger at Climber's chest. "They weren't your allies, squad leader. They were traitors, and you sided with them."

Climber stood his ground. "Traitors how? Because a few of them tried to arrest Palpatine? I still don't see how that warrants a death penalty for the lot of them."

"I'll be sure to notify the Emperor of your concerns," Vader said.

"You do that."

Shryne closed his mouth and swallowed hard. *Jedi had tried to arrest Palpatine.* The Republic now had an *Emperor*!

"Unfortunately," Vader was saying, "you won't be alive to learn of his response."

In one swift motion he drew aside his cloak and pulled a lightsaber from his belt. Igniting with a *snap-hiss,* the hilt projected a crimson blade.

If Shryne had been confused earlier, he was now overwhelmed.

A Sith blade?

The four commandos fell back, raising their weapons.

"We'll accept execution for our actions," Climber said. "But not from some lapdog of the Emperor."

Quickly Salvo and his officers stepped forward, but Vader only showed them the palm of his hand. "No, Commander. Leave this to me."

With that he moved on the commandos.

Spreading out, they fired, but not a single bolt made it past Vader's blade. Deflected bolts went straight through the helmet visors of two of the commandos, and in two furious sweeps Vader opened the pair from shoulder to hip, as if they were flimsy ration containers. Climber and the third commando took advantage of the moment to break for the nearby tree line, firing as they fled. A deflection shot from Vader caught Climber in the left leg, but the bolt didn't so much as slow him down.

Vader tracked them, then motioned to his cadre of troopers. "I want them *alive,* Commander Appo."

"Yes, Lord Vader."

Appo's shock troopers raced off in pursuit of the commandos. Not one of Salvo's officers had fired a weapon, but now all of them were regarding Vader with vigilant uncertainty, their rifles half raised.

"Don't let my weapon fool you," Vader told them, as if reading their thoughts. "I am not a Jedi."

From off to Shryne's left, a familiar voice shouted. "But *I* am!"

Bol Chatak had unwound her headcloth, revealing her vestigial horns, and had ignited the lightsaber Shryne thought she'd had sense enough to ditch when they were captured.

Vader whirled, watching Chatak as she began to stalk him, prisoners and troopers alike giving her wide berth.

"So much the better that one of you survived," he said, waving his lightsaber back and forth in front of him. "The commandos saved your life, and now you hope to save theirs, is that it?"

Chatak held her blue blade at shoulder height. "My only intent is to take you out of the hunt."

Vader's angled his blade to point toward the ground. "You won't be the first Jedi I've killed."

Their blades met with an explosion of light.

Fearing that the prisoners would use the distraction to scatter, Salvo's men hurried in to form a cordon around them. Pressed in among everyone, Shryne lost sight of Chatak and Vader, but he could tell from the angry clashes of their blades that the duel was fast and furious. Momentarily immobilized, he allowed himself to be swept up in the surge of the crowd, so that he might be raised up over the heads of those in front of him.

For a moment he was.

Just long enough to glimpse Chatak, all grace and speed, working her way into her opponent's space. Her moves were broad and circular, and the lightsaber seemed an extension of her. Vader, by contrast, was clumsy, and his strikes were mostly vertical. He was, however, a full head taller than Chatak and incredibly powerful. At various times his stances and techniques mimicked those of Ataro and Soresu, but Vader appeared to lack a style of his own, and executed his moves stiffly.

With a whirling motion Chatak got far enough inside Vader's long reach to inflict a forearm wound. But Vader scarcely reacted to the hit, and instead of seeing cauterized flesh

Shryne saw sparks and smoke fountain through Vader's slashed glove.

Then he lost sight of them again.

Wedged into the crowd, he wondered if he could use the Force to call one of the trooper's blaster rifles into his grip. At the same time he hoped that Starstone had abandoned her lightsaber at the landing platform, and wouldn't attempt to join her Master against Vader.

We need to learn what happened to the Jedi, he tried to send to her. *Our time for dealing with Vader will come. Be patient.*

He wondered if he was right. Maybe he should attempt to reach Chatak, weapon or no. Maybe his life was meant to end here, on Murkhana.

He looked to the Force for guidance, and the Force restrained him.

A pained cry cut through the chaos, and the crowd of prisoners parted just long enough for Shryne to see Chatak down on her knees in front of Vader, her sword arm amputated at the elbow. Vader had simply beaten her into submission, and now, with a flick of his bloodshine blade, he decapitated her.

Sorrow lanced Shryne's heart.

Unreadable behind his mask, Vader gazed down at Chatak's slack body.

The clone troopers relaxed the cordon somewhat, allowing the prisoners to spread out. And the moment they did, Vader began to scan faces in the crowd.

There were techniques for concealing one's Force abilities, and Shryne employed them. He also prepared for the possibility that he could be found out. But Vader's black gaze moved right past him. Instead, it appeared to focus on Olee Starstone.

Vader took a step in her direction.

Now I have no choice, Shryne thought.

He was ready to lunge when a shock trooper called to Vader,

reporting that the commandos had been captured. Vader stopped in his tracks, glancing in Starstone's direction before turning to Salvo.

"Commander, see to it that the prisoners are loaded into the transport." Again, Vader scanned the crowd. "A less accommodating dungeon awaits them on Agon Nine."

Vader had no sooner turned his back to the prisoners than Shryne was in motion, edging, elbowing, shouldering his way through the crowd to Starstone, whose narrow shoulders heaved as she attempted to suppress her grief at her Master's death. Realizing Shryne was at her side, she turned into his comforting but brief embrace.

"Your Master is with the Force," he told her. "Rejoice for that."

She narrowed her eyes at him. "Why didn't you help her?"

"I thought we'd agreed to abandon our lightsabers."

She nodded. "I abandoned mine. But you could have done *something*."

"You're right. Maybe I should have challenged 'Lord Vader' to a fistfight." Shryne's nostrils flared. "Your Master reacted in anger and in vengeance. She would have been more use to us alive."

Starstone reacted as if she had been slapped. "That's a heartless remark."

"Don't confuse emotion with truth. Even if Bol Chatak had defeated Vader, she would have been killed."

Starstone gestured vaguely in Vader's direction. "But that monster would be *dead*."

Shryne held her accusing gaze. "Vengeance isn't becoming in a Jedi, Padawan. Your Master died for nothing."

The prisoners were on the move now, troopers herding them toward the boarding ramp of the military transport.

"Fall back," Shryne said into Starstone's ear.

The two of them slowed down, allowing other captives to maneuver around them.

"Who is Vader?" Starstone asked after a moment.

Shryne shook his head in ignorance. "That's something we might be able to learn if we can remain alive."

Starstone took her lower lip between her teeth. "I'm sorry about what I said, Master."

"Don't worry about that. Tell me how Bol Chatak was able to keep the lightsaber hidden from the guards."

"Force persuasion," Starstone said quietly. "At first we thought we might be able to escape, but my Master wanted to wait until she knew what had happened to you. We were locked away in a building and left to fend for ourselves. Very little food, and troopers everywhere. Even if my Master had used her lightsaber then, I don't know how far we would have gotten before troopers were all over us."

"Did you use Force persuasion at any time?"

She nodded. "That's how I was able to hold on to my Master's beacon transceiver."

Shryne eyed her in surprise. "You have it with you?"

"Master Chatak told me to keep it."

"Foolish," he said, then asked: "Were you able to learn anything about the war?"

"Nothing." Starstone let her misgiving show. "Did you hear Vader say that he would tell the 'Emperor'?"

"I heard him."

"Could the Senate have named Palpatine Emperor?"

"Seems like something the Senate would do."

"But Emperor of what Empire?"

"I've been asking myself that." He glanced at her. "I think the war has ended."

She thought about it for a moment. "Then why were the troopers ordered to kill us?"

"Jedi on Coruscant may have attempted to arrest Palpatine *before* he was promoted—or crowned, I suppose I should say."

"That's why we were ordered into hiding."

"Good theory—for a change."

They were closing on the lip of the boarding ramp now, almost at the end of the line. Accepting of the inevitable, most of the prisoners were demonstrating remarkable discipline, and many of the troopers were drifting away as a result. Two troopers were stationed at the top of the ramp, one to either side of the rectangular hatch, and three more were moving more or less alongside the two Jedi.

"Vader is a *Sith*, Master," Starstone said.

Shryne showed her a long-suffering look. "What do you know of the Sith?"

"Before Master Chatak chose me as her Padawan, I trained under Master Jocasta Nu in the Temple archives. For my review, I elected to be tested in Sith history."

"Congratulations. Then I don't need to remind you that a crimson blade doesn't guarantee that the wielder is a Sith, any more than every person strong in the Force is a Jedi. Asajj Ventress was a mere apprentice to Dooku, not a true Sith. A crimson blade can owe to nothing more than a synthetic power crystal. Then crimson is simply a color, like Master Windu's amethyst blade."

"Yes, but Jedi normally don't wield crimson blades," Starstone argued, "if only because of their *association* with the Sith. So even if Vader was nothing more than another apprentice of Count Dooku, why is he now serving Palpatine—*Emperor* Palpatine—as an executioner?"

"You're assuming too much," Shryne said. "Even if you're right, why is that so hard to believe, when Dooku did just the opposite—went from serving the Jedi order to serving the Sith?"

Starstone shook her head. "I suppose it shouldn't be hard to believe, Master. But it is."

He looked at her. "Here is what matters: Vader suspects that two Jedi are going to be aboard the prison transport. Eventually he'll identify us and we'll be killed, unless we take our chances, here and now."

"How, Master?"

"Drop back with me to the end of the line. I'm going to try something, and I hope the Force is with me. If I fail, we board as instructed. Understood?"

"Understood."

The last of the captive mercenaries and Koorivar moved past the two reluctant Jedi, up the ship's ramp and through the hatch. At the top Shryne made a passing motion with his hand to one of the troopers.

"There's no reason to detain us," he said.

The trooper gazed at him from inside the helmet. "There's no reason to detain them," he told his comrades.

"We're free to return to our homes."

"They're free to return to their homes."

"Everything's fine. It's time for you to board the ship."

"Everything's fine. It's time for us to board the ship."

Shryne and Starstone waited until the final trooper had filed inside; then they leapt from the ramp onto the clay field and concealed themselves behind one of the landing gear pods.

When an opportunity presented itself, they hurried from beneath the ship and escaped into the thick vegetation, heading for what remained of Murkhana City.

In his personal quarters aboard the *Exactor*, Vader examined the damage the Zabrak Jedi's lightsaber had done to his left forearm. After assuring himself that the pressure suit had self-sealed above the burn, he had peeled off the long glove and used a fine-point laser cutter to remove flaps of armorweave fabric that had been fused to the alloy beneath. The Jedi's lightsaber had sliced through the shielding that bulked the glove and had melted some of the artificial ligaments that allowed the hand to pronate. Permanent repairs would have to wait until he returned to Coruscant. In the meantime he would have to entrust his arm to the care of one of the Star Destroyer's med droids.

His own lightsaber rested within reach, but the longer he gazed at it, and at the blackened furrow in the alloy, the more disheartened he became. Had the hand been flesh and blood it would be shaking now. Only Dooku, Asajj Ventress, and Obi-Wan had been good enough with a blade to injure him, so how had an undistinguished Jedi Knight been able to do so?

With the loss of my limbs, have I also lost strength in the Force?

Vader recognized the voice of the one who posed the question as the specter of Anakin. Anakin telling him that he was not as powerful as he thought he was. The little slave boy, cowering because he was not the master of his fate. A mere accessory in the world, owned by another, passed over.

And now newly enslaved!

He lifted his masked face to the cabin's ceiling and growled in torment. Sidious's inept med droids had done this to him! Slowed his reflexes, burdened him with armor and padding. He relished having destroyed them.

Or . . . had Sidious deliberately engineered this prison?

Again, it was Anakin who asked, that small node of fear in Vader's heart.

Was this punishment for having failed at Mustafar? Or had Mustafar merely provided Sidious with an excuse to weaken him? Perhaps all along the promise of apprenticeship had been nothing more than a ploy, when, in fact, Sidious merely needed someone to command his army of stormtroopers.

Another *Grievous,* while Sidious reaped the real rewards of power, confident that his newest minion posed no threat to his rule.

Vader dwelled on it, fearing he would drive himself mad, and at last reached an even more disheartening conclusion. Grievous was *duped* into serving the Sith. But Sidious had sent Anakin to Mustafar for one reason only: to kill the members of the Separatist Council.

Padmé and Obi-Wan were the ones who had sentenced him to his black-suit prison.

Sentenced by his wife and his alleged best friend, their love for him warped by what they had perceived as betrayal. Obi-Wan, too brainwashed by the Jedi to recognize the power of the dark side; and Padmé, too enslaved to the Republic to understand that Palpatine's machinations and Anakin's defection to the Sith had been essential to bringing peace to the galaxy! Essential to placing power in the hands of those resourceful enough to use it properly, in order to save the galaxy's myriad species from themselves; to end the incompetence of the Senate; to dissolve the bloated, entitled Jedi order, whose Masters were blind to the decay they had fostered.

And yet their Chosen One had seen it; so why hadn't they followed his lead by embracing the dark side?

Because they were too set in their ways; too inflexible to adapt.

Vader mused.

Anakin Skywalker had died on Coruscant.

But the Chosen One had died on Mustafar.

Blistering rage, as seething as Mustafar's lava flows, welled up in him, liquefying self-pity. This was what he saw behind the mask's visual enhancers: bubbling lava, red heat, scorched flesh—

He had only wanted to save them! Padmé, from death; Obi-Wan, from ignorance. And in the end they had failed to recognize his power; to simply accede to him; to accept on faith that he knew what was best for them, for *everyone*!

Instead Padmé was dead and Obi-Wan was running for his life, as stripped of everything as Vader was. Without friends, family, purpose . . .

Clenching his right hand, he cursed the Force. What had it ever provided him but pain? Torturing him with foresight, with visions he was unable to prevent. Leading him to believe that he had great power when he was little more than its *servant*.

But no longer, Vader promised himself. The power of the dark side would render the *Force* subservient, minion rather than ally.

Extending his right arm, he took hold of the lightsaber and turned it about in his hand. Just three standard weeks old, assembled—as Sidious had wished—in the shadow of the moonlet-size terror weapon he was having constructed, it had now tasted first blood.

Sidious had provided the synthcrystal responsible for the crimson blade, along with his own lightsaber to serve as a model. Vader, though, had no fondness for antiques, and while he could appreciate the handiwork that had gone into fashioning the inlaid, gently curved hilt of Sidious's lightsaber, he prefered a weapon with more ballast. Determined to please his Master, he had tried to create something novel, but had ended up fashioning a black version of the lightsaber he had wielded for more than a decade, with a thick, ridged handgrip, high-output diatium power cell, dual-phase focusing crystal, and forward-mounted adjustment knobs. Down to the beveled emitter shroud, the hilt mimicked Anakin's.

But there was a problem.

His new hands were too large to duplicate the loose grip Anakin had favored, right hand wrapped not on the grip but around the crystal-housing cylinder, close to the blade itself. Vader's hands required that the grip be thicker and longer, and the result was an inelegant weapon, verging on ungainly.

Another cause of the injury to his left arm.

The Sith grew past the use of lightsabers, Sidious had told him. *But we continue to use them, if only to humiliate the Jedi.*

Vader yearned for the time when memories of Anakin would fade, like light absorbed by a black hole. Until that happened, his life-sustaining suit would be an ill fit. Even if it was well suited to the darkness in his invulnerable heart . . .

The comlink chimed.

"What is it, Commander Appo?"

"Lord Vader, I've been informed of a discrepancy in the prisoner count. Allowing for the Jedi you killed on Murkhana, two prisoners are unaccounted for."

"The others who survived Order Sixty-Six," Vader said.

"Shall I instruct Commander Salvo to initiate a search?"

"Not this time, Commander. I will handle it myself."

"Down there?" Starstone said, halting at the head of a creepy stairway Shryne was already descending. The stairs led to the basement of a rambling building that had been left unscathed by the battle, and was typical of those that crowned the verdant hills south of Murkhana City. But she had a bad feeling about the stairway.

"Don't worry. This is only Cash's way of keeping out the riffraff."

"Doesn't appear to be slowing you down any," she said, following him into the stairway's dark well.

"Glad to see that your sense of humor has returned. You must have been the life of the dungeon."

And Shryne meant it, because he didn't want her dwelling on Bol Chatak's death. In the long hours it had taken them to get from the landing field to Cash Garrulan's headquarters Starstone seemed to have made peace with what had happened.

"How is it you know this person?" she asked over his shoulder.

"Garrulan's the reason the Council first sent me to Murkhana. He's a former Black Sun vigo. I came here to put him out of business, but he turned out to be one of our best sources of intelligence on Separatist activities in this quadrant. Years before Geonosis, Garrulan was warning us about the extent of Dooku's military buildup, but no one on the Council or in the Senate seemed to take the threat seriously."

"And in return for the intelligence you allowed Garrulan to remain in business."

"He's not a Hutt. He deals in, well, wholesale commodities."

"So not only are we on the run, we're turning to gangsters for help."

"Maybe you have a better idea?"

"No, Master, I don't."

"I didn't think so. And stop calling me 'Master.' Someone will either make the Jedi connection or get the impression you're my servant."

"Force forbid," Starstone muttered.

"I'm Roan. Plain and simple."

"I'll try to remember that—*Roan*." She laughed at the sound of it. "I'm sorry, it just doesn't ring true."

"You'll get used to it."

At the foot of the stairs was an unadorned door. Shryne rapped his knuckles on the jamb, and to the droid eyeball that poked through a circular portal in response said something in what Starstone surmised was Koorivar. A moment later the door slid into its housing to reveal a muscular and extensively tattooed human male, cradling a DC-17 blaster rifle. Smiling at Shryne, he ushered them into a surprisingly opulent foyer.

"Still sneaking up on people, huh, Shryne?"

"Old habits."

The man nodded sagely, then gave Shryne and Starstone the once-over. "What's with the getups? You look like you've spent a month in a trash compactor."

"That would have been a step up," Starstone said.

Shryne peered into the back room. "Is he here, Jally?"

"He's here, but not for long. Just packing up what we couldn't move before the invasion. I'll tell him—"

"Let's make it a surprise."

Jally laughed shortly. "Oh, he'll be surprised, all right."

Shryne motioned for Starstone to follow him. On the far side of a beaded-curtain entryway a mixed group of humans, aliens, and labor droids were hauling packing crates into a spacious turbolift. Even more well appointed than the foyer, the room was cluttered with furniture, infostorage and communications devices, weapons, and more. The humanoid standing in the midst of it and dispensing orders to his underlings was a Twi'lek with fatty lekku and a prominent paunch. Sensing someone behind him, he turned and stared openmouthed at Shryne.

"I heard you'd been killed."

"Wishful thinking," Shryne said.

Cash Garrulan moved his head from side to side. "Perhaps." He extended his fat arms and shook both of Shryne's hands, then gestured to Shryne's filthy robe. "I love the new look."

"I got tired of wearing brown."

His gazed shifted. "Who's your new friend, Roan?"

"Olee," Shryne said without elaboration. He aimed a glance at the packing crates. "Clearance sale, Cash?"

"Let's just say that peace has been bad for business."

"Then it is over?" Shryne asked solemnly.

Garrulan inclined his large head. "You hadn't heard? It was all over the HoloNet, Roan."

"Olee and I have been out of touch."

"Apparently so." The Twi'lek turned to bark instructions at two of his employees, then motioned Shryne and Starstone into a small and tidy office, where Garrulan and Shryne sat down.

"Are you two in the market for blasters?" Garrulan asked. "I've got BlasTechs, Merr-Sonns, Tenloss DXs, you name it. And

I'll let you have them cheap." When Shryne shook his head no, Garrulan said: "What about comlinks? Vibroblades? Tatooine handwoven carpets—"

"Fill us in on how the war ended."

"How it ended?" Garrulan snapped his fat fingers. "Just like that. One moment Chancellor Palpatine has been kidnapped by General Grievous; the next, Dooku and Grievous are dead, the Jedi are traitors, the battle droids shut down, and we're one big happy galaxy again, more united than before—an Empire, no less. No formal surrender by the Confederacy of Independent Systems, no bogged-down Senate, no trade embargoes. And whatever the Emperor wants, the Emperor gets."

"Any comments from the members of the Separatist Council?"

"Not a peep. Although rumors abound. The Emperor had them put to death. They're still on the run. They're holed up in the Tingel Arm, in the company of Passel Argente's cronies . . ."

Shryne extended his arm to prevent Starstone from pacing. "Sit down," he said. "And stop chewing on your lip."

"Yes, Mas—Roan."

"I have to say," Garrulan went on, "I never would have guessed that the Jedi would be held accountable."

"For attempting to arrest Palpatine, you mean," Shryne said.

"No—for the *war*." Garrulan stared at Shryne for a long moment. "You really don't know what's happened, do you? Maybe you two should have a drink."

Garrulan was halfway to his feet when Shryne said: "No drinks. Just tell us."

The Twi'lek looked genuinely dismayed. "I hate to be the bearer of bad news, Roan—especially to you, of all people—but the war has been laid at the feet of the Jedi. You manipulated the whole charade: vat-grown troopers on one side, Master Dooku on the other, all in an attempt to overthrow the Republic and place yourselves in charge. That's why Palpatine ordered your execution, and why the Jedi Temple was sacked."

Shryne and Starstone traded looks of dread.

Reading their expressions, the crime boss adopted a somber tone. "From what I understand, nearly all of the Jedi were killed—in the Temple, or on one world or another."

Shryne put his arm around Starstone's quaking shoulders. "Steady, kid," he said, as much to himself as to Olee.

The second beacon transmission, ordering all Jedi to go to ground, suddenly made sense. The Temple, defenseless in the absence of so many Jedi Knights, had been attacked and plundered; teachers and younglings slaughtered by Coruscant's shock troopers—stormtroopers, as they were now being called. How many Jedi had returned to the Core, Shryne wondered, only to be killed on arrival?

The order was finished. Not only was there nothing for Shryne and Starstone on Coruscant, there was nothing for them *anywhere*.

"For what it's worth," Garrulan said, "I don't believe a word of it. Palpatine is behind this. He has been from the start."

Starstone was shaking her head back and forth in disbelief. "It's not possible that every Jedi has been killed." She turned to Shryne. "Some Jedi weren't even with clone troopers, Master. Other commanders may have refused to obey High Command's execution orders."

"You're right," Shryne said, trying to sound comforting.

"We'll find other survivors."

"Sure we will."

"The order will rebuild itself."

"Absolutely."

Garrulan waited for them to fall silent before saying: "A lot of others have had the carpet yanked out from under them— even those of us at the bottom of the food chain." He laughed regretfully. "War has always been better for us than peace. At least the Corporate Alliance was willing to tolerate us for a share of the profits. But the regional governors the Emperor installed are out to cast us as the new enemy. And between you and me, I'd sooner deal with the Hutts."

Shryne studied him. "Where's that leave you, Cash?"

"Not on Murkhana, that much is certain. My Koorivar competitors in crime have my blessings, and my sympathy." Garrulan returned Shryne's look. "What about you, Roan? Any ideas?"

"Not right now," Shryne said.

"Perhaps you should consider working for me. I could use people with your special talents, especially now. I owe you a favor, in any case."

Starstone glared at him. "We haven't fallen so low as to—" she started to say when Shryne clamped his hand over her mouth.

"Maybe I will consider it. But first you've got to get us off Murkhana."

Garrulan showed Shryne the palms of his hands. "I don't owe you *that* much."

"Make it happen, and I'll owe *you*."

Starstone looked from Shryne to Garrulan and back again. "Is this the way you were before the war? Cutting deals with anyone you pleased?"

"Don't mind her," Shryne said. "What about it, Cash?"

Garrulan sat back in his oversize chair. "Shouldn't be too hard to equip you with false identities and outwit the local garrison troopers."

"Normally, I'd agree," Shryne cut in. "But someone new has been added to the mix. A Lord Vader." When Garrulan didn't react to the name, he continued. "A sort of black-armored version of Grievous, only more dangerous, and apparently in charge of doing Palpatine's dirty work."

"Really," Garrulan said, clearly interested. "I haven't heard anything about him."

"You will," Shryne said. "And he could present a problem to our getting off this rock."

Garrulan stroked his lekku. "Well, then, I may have to rethink my offer—in the interest of avoiding Imperial complications. Or we may simply need to take additional precautions."

Black armorweave and feats of strength weren't the only things that distinguished Darth Vader from Anakin Skywalker. Where Anakin had had limited access to the Jedi Temple data room, Vader—even light-years from Coruscant—could peruse any data he wished, including archival records, ancient texts, and holocrons fashioned by past Masters. Thus was he able to learn the identities of the six Jedi who had been assigned to Murkhana at the end of the war; the four who had been killed—Masters Loorne and Bol Chatak, and two Jedi Knights—and the two who remained at large: Roan Shryne and Chatak's Padawan, Olee Starstone, now presumably in the care of the older and more experienced Shryne.

A petite young woman with dark curly hair and an engaging smile, Starstone until recently had seemed destined to become a Temple acolyte, having been selected by Master Joscasta Nu to serve as her apprentice in the archives room. Shortly before the start of the war, and in the interest of broadening her understanding of the rest of the galaxy, Starstone had asked to be allowed to do fieldwork, and it was during a brief visit to Eriadu that she had attracted the attention of Bol Chatak.

Chatak hadn't accepted her as a learner, however, until the war's second year, and only then at the behest of the High Council. With so many Jedi Knights participating in military campaigns on far-flung worlds, the Temple was no place for an able-bodied young Jedi who could be of greater service to the Republic as a warrior than as a librarian.

By all accounts Starstone had shown great promise. Candid, smart as a vibro-whip, and a brilliant researcher, she should probably have never been allowed to leave the Temple. Although she would have died there, a victim of Darth Vader's blade or the blaster bolts of Commander Appo's shock troopers.

Roan Shryne was another matter, and it was Shryne's holo-image Vader was circling, as data about the long-haired rogue Jedi Knight scrolled in a separate holoprojector field.

Shryne had originally been encountered on the Outer Rim world of Weytta, which happened to be in the same galactic neighborhood as Murkhana. His file contained passing references to an "incident" that had attended his procurement, but Vader hadn't been able to locate a detailed account of what had occurred.

At the Temple he had demonstrated an early talent for being able to sense the presence of the Force in others, and so had been encouraged to pursue a course that would have landed him in the Temple's Acquisition Division. When he was old enough to understand what acquisition entailed, however, he had stead-fastly refused further tutelage, for reasons the records also didn't make clear.

The matter was brought before the High Council, which ultimately decided that Shryne should be allowed to find his own path rather than be pressed into service. The path Shryne eventually followed was the study of weapons of war, both ancient and modern, from which had grown an interest in the role played by crime syndicates in the spread of illegal arms.

Shryne's condemnation of the loopholes in Republic laws that had allowed the Trade Federation and similar groups to amass droid armies was what had brought him initially to Murkhana, shortly before the outbreak of the war. There he had had dealings with a crime boss of local repute, who had gradually become Shryne's informant on the Separatist military buildup. As a result, Shryne had made frequent journeys to Murkhana, even during the war, both as an undercover singleton and with a Padawan learner.

A couple of years older than Obi-Wan Kenobi, Shryne, like Obi-Wan, had been a peripheral member of what some Jedi had referred to as the "Old Guard"—a select group that had included Dooku, Qui-Gon Jinn, Sifo-Dyas, Mace Windu, and others, many of whom had been or would be named to sit on the High Council. But unlike Obi-Wan, Shryne had never been privy to Council discussions or decisions.

Interestingly, Shryne had been among those Jedi sent to Geonosis on the rescue mission that had wound up becoming the spark that ignited the war. During the battle there, his former Master, Nat-Sem, had been killed, along with Shryne's first Padawan.

Then, two and a half years into the war, Shryne lost a *second* learner at the Battle of Manari.

It was noted in the records that Shryne's fellow Jedi began to see a change in him after Manari, not only with regard to the war, but also with regard to the role the Jedi had been constrained to play—*manipulated* to play, Vader now understood—and many Jedi had expected him to leave the order, as several other Jedi Knights had done, either finding their way to the Separatist side or simply vanishing from sight.

Continuing to study the ghostly image of Shryne, Vader activated the cabin comm.

"What have you learned?" he asked.

"Still no sign of either Jedi, Lord Vader," Appo said. "But the Twi'lek crime boss has been located."

"Good work, Commander. He will prove to be all the lead we need."

Cash Garrulan was trying to figure out how he could unload eight hundred pairs of knockoff Neuro-Saav electrobinoculars in a hurry when Jally burst into his office to draw his attention to the security monitors.

In mounting annoyance, Garrulan watched twenty clone troopers climb from a wheeled transport and take up positions around the aged, sprawling structure that was his headquarters.

"Stormtroopers, no less," Garrulan said. "Probably sent by the regional governor to grab whatever they can before we depart." Pushing himself upright, he swept a stack of data cards from his desk into an open attaché case. "Give the troopers our munitions overstock. Don't make a stand, whatever you do. If things get rough, offer them more—the electrobinoculars, for instance." He grabbed his cloak and threw it over his shoulders. "I, however, am not about to suffer the indignity of an arrest. I'll take the back stairs and meet you at the docking bay."

"Good choice. We'll handle the clones."

Hurrying out of his office and through the stockroom, he pressed the release for the back door, only to find a towering figure filling the entryway. Dressed in black from outsize helmet to knee-high boots, the masked figure had his gloved fists planted on his hips in a way that spread his cloak wide.

"Going somewhere, *Vigo*?"

The slightly bass voice was enhanced by a vocoder of some sort and underscored by deep, rhythmical breathing, obviously regulated by the control box strapped to the figure's broad and armored chest.

Vader, Garrulan told himself. The Grievous-like monstrosity Shryne said had been "added to the mix."

"May I inquire who wishes to know?"

"You're free to ask," Vader said, but left it at that.

Garrulan tried to compose his thoughts. Vader and his stormtroopers hadn't come for handouts. They were hot on Shryne's trail. Still, he thought there might be a way to win Vader over.

"I'm not and never have been a Separatist. I just happen to be living on a Sep world."

"Your former allegiances don't concern me," Vader said.

Stretching out his right hand, Vader yanked Garrulan off his feet and carried him through the foyer and into the office, where he deposited him in a castered chair, which rolled backward and struck the wall.

"Make yourself comfortable," Vader said.

Garrulan rubbed the back of his head. "It's going to be like that, is it?"

"Yes. Like that."

Garrulan forced a breath. "Well, I'd offer you a chair, as well, but I don't think I have another one large enough."

The commander of Vader's troopers entered from the front room while Vader was taking in the office's lavish appointments.

"You've done well for yourself, Vigo."

"I get by," Garrulan said.

Vader stood over him. "I'm searching for two Jedi who escaped a transport that was to have delivered them to Agon Nine."

"Enchanting spot. But what makes you think—"

"Before you say another word," Vader cut him off, "be advised that I know that you and one of the Jedi go back a long way."

Garrulan immediately revised his plans. "You're talking about Roan Shryne and the girl."

"Then they did come here."

Garrulan nodded. "They asked for my help in leaving Murkhana."

"What arrangements did you make?"

"Arrangements?" Garrulan gestured broadly to the room. "I didn't come by all this by accident. I was surprised even to see Shryne alive. I told them that I don't help traitors. In fact, I reported their visit to local authorities."

Vader turned to the stormtrooper commander, who nodded his head and moved into the packing room.

"You wouldn't lie to me, Vigo." Vader didn't make it a question.

"Not until I get to know you better."

The commander returned. "He did contact the local garrison commander, Lord Vader."

It was impossible to determine if Vader was at all satisfied. At last, Vader said: "Do you know where Shryne was headed from here?"

Garrulan shook his head. "He didn't say. But he knows Murkhana well, and I'm only one of his local contacts. But, of course, you already know that."

"I wanted to hear it from you," Vader said.

Garrulan smiled to himself. Vader had taken the bait. "Happy to oblige . . . Lord Vader."

"If you were Shryne, what would be your next move?"

"Well, now we're speculating, aren't we," Garrulan said, relaxing somewhat. "I mean, you appear to be asking my professional opinion on the matter."

"And if I am?"

"I only thought there might be something in it for me."

"What is it you want, Vigo? You already appear to have more than you need."

Garrulan adopted a more serious tone. "Material things," he

said in a dismissive manner. "I need you to put in a good word for me with the regional governor."

Vader nodded. "That can be arranged—providing that your professional opinion amounts to anything."

Garrulan leaned forward. "There's this Koorivar by the name of Bioto. Dabbles in smuggling and other ventures. Owns a very fast ship called the *Dead Ringer*." He paused while the commander disappeared once more, undoubtedly to communicate with Space Traffic Control. "If *I* were in a hurry to get offworld with the least amount of problems, Bioto's the one I'd turn to."

"Lord Vader," the commander said suddenly, "STC reports that the *Dead Ringer* recently launched from Murkhana Landing. We have the projected flight path."

Vader turned, his cloak swirling. "Contact the *Exactor*, Commander. Order that the ship be moved into a position to intercept." Without further word he moved into the front room, only to stop short after a few long strides. "You're very clever, Vigo," he said, turning partway to Garrulan. "I won't forget this."

Garrulan inclined his head in a bow of respect. "Nor will I, Lord Vader."

A moment after Vader exited, Jally returned, blowing out his breath in relief.

"Not someone I'd feel good about crossing, boss."

"He does have a way," Garrulan said, getting to his feet. "Forget the rest of this junk. Have our ship readied for launch. We're done with Murkhana."

Wings folded above its fuselage and running lights powering down, Vader's shuttle entered the *Exactor*'s main docking bay and alighted on the lustrous deck. Nearby, and surrounded by clone troopers, sat the *Dead Ringer*, a somewhat boxy cargo transport, heavily armed with turbolaser cannons and outfitted with a state-of-the-art hyperdrive. Also under guard, the transport's mostly Koorivar crew of seven stood with their hands clasped atop their horned heads while troopers completed a search of the ship. Already off-loaded cargo containers were stacked outside the *Dead Ringer*'s starboard docking ring, awaiting scans.

Vader and Appo descended the shuttle's boarding ramp and strode over to where the crew had been gathered. A trooper indicated the captain, and Vader approached him.

"What is your cargo, Captain?"

The Koorivar glowered up at him. "I demand to speak to the officer in charge."

"You are speaking to him."

The captain blinked in surprise, but managed to hold on to

his angry tone. "I don't know who you are, but be forewarned that if my ship suffered any damage as a result of being targeted by your tractor beam, I will lodge a formal complaint with the regional governor."

"Duly noted, Captain," Vader said. "And I'm certain that the regional governor will take a keen interest in you once he learns that you are transporting proscribed weapons." He swung to the officer in charge of the troopers. "Escort them to the brig!"

"Lord Vader," Appo said while the crew was being whisked away, "security reports that two humans have been found in a secret compartment beneath the ship's galley."

Vader turned in the direction of the transport. "Interesting. Let's see what security has uncovered."

By the time Vader and Appo had moved around to the transport's port side, a detail of troopers was emerging from the ship, with two humans in custody. The man was tall and long-haired, and very protective of the young woman by his side. The pair were dressed alike in robes and headcloths typical of the mercenary brigade that had fought for the Separatists on Murkhana.

Their eyes widened on seeing Vader.

"They are unarmed, Lord Vader," one of the troopers announced.

"We stowed away without the captain's knowledge," the man said. "We're only trying to get to Ord Mantell."

"You're not stowaways," Vader said. "The captain was well paid to take you aboard his ship, and you have been promised payment, as well."

The girl began to quake in fear. "We didn't know we were doing anything illegal! We're not smugglers or criminals. I'm telling you the truth. We did it only for the credits!"

Vader appraised her. "I will consider sparing your lives if you tell me who hired you to carry out this deception."

The man firmed his lips, then swallowed hard and spoke. "Some of Cash Garrulan's goons."

Vader nodded. "Just as I suspected." He swung to Appo. "Commander, have the *Exactor*'s scanners detected anything yet?"

"Nothing yet."

"They will, soon enough."

Vader turned to the head of the trooper detail. "Lock these two away with the crew."

All color drained from the girl's face. "But you said—"

"That I would *consider* sparing you," Vader cut her off.

"Lord Vader, our sensors may have found something," Appo said suddenly. "The craft is only a CloakShape that launched from the outskirts of Murkhana City. But it is pursuing a course that will take it close to the *Exactor*'s previous position, and it is attempting to evade our scans."

"The Jedi are aboard that craft. Can we interdict from our present position, Commander?"

"No. The CloakShape is out of the range of our tractor beam."

Vader growled in displeasure. "We will need to remedy that. Is my starfighter prepared?"

"It's waiting in launching bay three."

"Assign two pilots to serve as my wingmates. Tell them to rendezvous with me in the launching bay." Vader shrugged his cloak behind his shoulders. "And, Commander, the vigo will be attempting to flee Murkhana. Don't bother capturing him. Target his vessel, and make certain that everyone on board is killed."

The CloakShape, a broad-winged craft with a transverse maneuvering fin, had been modified for spaceflight. The cockpit had been enlarged to accommodate pilot and copilot, and a rear-facing gunner's chair had been installed in the tail section. Shryne was forward; Starstone, aft; and in the pilot's seat was Brudi Gayn, a freelancer who made occasional runs for Cash Garrulan. A rangy, dark-haired human a few years older than Shryne, he spoke Basic with a strong Outer Rim accent.

Shryne had already decided that Gayn was the most casual pilot he had ever flown with. Any farther from the instrument panel and his chair would have been adjacent to Starstone's. His hold on the yoke was negligent. Yet he handled the craft masterfully, and didn't miss a trick.

"Well, they've got a good fix on us," he told Shryne and Starstone through their helmet comlinks. "Definitely going to have to upgrade our countermeasures at some point."

Hanging far to starboard, Vader's massive warship was just visible through the CloakShape's triangle of transparisteel viewport.

"I hate the look of these new mass-produced *Imperator*-class Destroyers," Gayn continued. "None of the artistry that went into the old Acclamators and Venators—even the Victory Twos." He shook his head in disappointment. "So goes elegance."

"Wars'll do that," Shryne said into his helmet comm.

The console issued an alert chime, and Gayn leaned forward a bit to study one of the display screens.

"Three bandits closing on our tail. Signatures ID them as two V-wings and what might be a modified Jedi Interceptor. This Vader character?"

"Good bet."

"Guess the Empire isn't any more choosy about commandeering Jedi hardware than it is Sep gear."

"Obviously, we're still serving Palpatine in our own way."

"Are you two aware that three starfighters are chasing us?" Starstone broke in.

"Thanks for the heads-up, sweetheart, but we're on it," Gayn said.

"Here's another heads-up for you, *flyboy*. They're gaining on us. Can't you coax any more speed out of this junker? It's about as lethargic as you are."

Gayn laughed shortly. "I suppose I could try jettisoning the tail gunner. That ought to lighten us up."

"First you might try letting some of the hot air out of yourself," Starstone fired back.

"Ouch," Gayn said. "Is she always like this, Shryne?"

"She was a librarian. You know how they can be."

"A librarian with the Force . . . Very dangerous combination." He chuckled to himself, then asked: "What happens to the Force now? Without the Jedi order, I mean?"

"I don't know," Shryne said. "Maybe it goes into hibernation."

Gayn rocked his head from side to side. "Well, here's a little something to show you that the Force isn't the only game in town."

Gazing in the direction indicated by Brudi Gayn's gloved right hand, Shryne saw a swift space skiff approaching the Cloak-Shape on an intercept course.

"Hope it's on our side."

Gayn laughed again. "It's our ticket out of here."

All but wedged into the cockpit of his black interceptor, Vader was in full command of the situation. He had the starfighter's inertial compensator dialed down, and felt revitalized by the experience of near weightlessness. In another life he had flown without helmet or flight suit, but those necessary accoutrements notwithstanding, he felt unburdened, released from gravity's reign.

This was not the craft Anakin Skywalker had piloted to

Mustafar, and the starfighter's socketed astromech droid had a black dome. Nor was this the craft he would have chosen to fly. But the interceptor would do, at least until Sienar Fleet Systems completed the starfighter that was being built to his specifications.

After all, despite the manifold losses he had endured, he remained the galaxy's best pilot.

The CloakShape's lead evaporated as he made adjustments and poured on speed. The Jedi's choice of escape vehicles was a reflection of their desperation, since the CloakShape lacked a hyperdrive of any sort. But Vader saw what they had in mind. They hoped to rendezvous with the Sorosuub skiff that even now was angling toward them. The plan would have worked, however, only if Vader had taken the Twi'lek crime boss at his word. And because he hadn't, the Jedi wouldn't have enough time to transfer to the larger ship. By then both the CloakShape and the skiff would be in proton torpedo range.

"Form up on me," he told the clone pilots in the escort V-wings, "and fire on my command. There's no need to take them alive."

"Lord Vader, we have identified the Sorosuub," one of the pilots returned. "The registry is Murkhana. The owner is Cash Garrulan."

"So," Vader said, mostly to himself. "It all ends here."

"But there is something else, Lord Vader. The CloakShape appears to be fitted with external booster-ring adapters."

Glancing at the display screen in which the CloakShape was centered, Vader issued a command to the astromech droid to display the skiff on a secondary screen.

Instantly he understood.

"All speed," he ordered the clone pilots. "This is not a rendezvous. Fire proton torpedoes the moment our targets are in range."

It was going to be close, Vader realized.

He enabled the interceptor's laser cannon. The CloakShape, too, was traveling flat-out, and was faster than he would have thought possible. The pilot was skilled and artful. At this distance it would be difficult to keep him in laser lock.

The astromech sent an update to the cockpit data screen, and at the same time the voice of one of the escort pilots issued through the console comlink.

"Lord Vader, the skiff is positioning a hyperdrive booster in the CloakShape's flight path."

The vision enhancers built into Vader's mask delivered a close-up of the red-and-white hypermatter ring. Quickly he thumbed the triggers on the steering yoke, and a hail of crimson bolts streaked from the interceptor's long-barreled laser cannons. But it was unlikely that the bolts would ever reach their targets, because the targets would be long gone.

Still calling all power from the ion drive, Vader watched the CloakShape slip neatly into the precisely positioned booster ring and make the jump to lightspeed. A split second later Cash Garrulan's skiff engaged its hyperdrive and disappeared.

Allowing the interceptor to power down, Vader gazed in defeat at the distant starfield.

He had much to do to make himself whole once more.

One of the V-wing pilots hailed him. "Escape vectors are being plotted, Lord Vader."

"Delete the calculations, pilot," he said. "If the Jedi are so determined to disappear, then let them."

PART III

IMPERIAL CENTER

You have my full assurance that I will not disband the Senate," the Emperor told the small audience he had summoned to his new chambers. "Furthermore, I don't want you to think of yourselves as mere accessories, ratifying legislation and facilitating the business of governing. I will seek your counsel in enacting laws that will serve the growth and integrity of our Empire."

He fell silent for a moment, then delivered his bombshell.

"The difference now is that when I have taken into account your contributions and those of my advisers, my judgment will be *final*. There will be no debates, no citations of constitutional precedent, no power of veto, no court proceedings or deferrals. My decrees will be issued simultaneously to our constituent worlds, and they will take effect immediately."

The Emperor leaned forward in the high-backed chair that was his temporary throne, but not so far forward that his disfigured face was placed in the light.

"Understand this: you no longer represent your homeworlds solely. Coruscant, Alderaan, Chandrila . . . All these and tens of thousands of worlds far removed from the Core are cells of the

Empire, and what affects one, affects us all. No disturbances will be tolerated. Interplanetary squabbles or threats of secession will meet with harsh reprisals. I have not led us through three years of galactic warfare to allow a resurgence of the old ways. The Republic is *extinct*."

Bail Organa barely managed to keep from squirming in his chair, as some of the Emperor's other invited guests were doing—Senators Mon Mothma and Garm Bel Iblis especially, in what almost amounted to overt defiance. But if the Emperor was taking notes, he was doing so without most of his guests being aware of it.

The Emperor's new chambers—the throne room, for all intents and purposes—occupied an upper floor of Coruscant's tallest building and, in design, more closely resembled what had been Palpatine's holding office below the Senate Rotunda than his former quarters in the Senate Office Building.

Divided into two levels by a short but wide staircase, the sanitized room was longer than it was wide, with large permaplas windows surrounding the upper tier. Flanking the burnished staircase were a pair of cup-shaped duty stations, in each of which stood a Red Guard—an Imperial Guard—with the Emperor's advisers seated behind them. The center of the gleaming dais was occupied by the throne, the back of which arched over Palpatine's head, placing him in perpetual shadow, as the cowl of his cloak did his sallow and deeply lined face. Recessed into the wide arms of the chair were modest control pads into which his slender fingers would enter occasional input.

The corridors of the Senate were rife with rumors that the Emperor had a second and more private suite, along with some sort of medical facility, in the very crown of the building.

"Your Majesty, if I may," the human Senator from Commenor said in a suitably deferential tone. "Perhaps you could shed some light on the matter of why the Jedi betrayed us. As you are undoubtedly aware, the HoloNet seems reluctant to provide details."

Well beyond the need to employ diplomacy or deception to achieve his ends, the Emperor made a derisive sound.

"The Order deserved all that it received for deluding us into believing that they served *me* in serving you. The complexity of their nefarious plan continues to astound me. Why they didn't attempt to kill me three years ago is something I will never understand. As if I could have stood against them. If it were not for the recent actions of my guards and our troopers, I would be dead."

Palpatine's off-color eyes clouded with hatred.

"In fact, the Jedi believed that they could oversee the galaxy better than we could, and they were willing to perpetuate a war simply to leave us defenseless and susceptible to their treason. Their vaunted Temple was a fort, their base of operations. They came to me with tales of having killed General Grievous—a *cyborg,* no less—and sought to arrest me because I refused to take them at their word that the fighting was suddenly over, the Separatists defeated.

"When I dispatched a legion of troopers to reason with them, they drew their lightsabers and the battle was met. We have the Grand Army to thank for our victory. Our noble commanders recognized the truth of the Jedi's treachery, and they executed my commands with vigor. The very fact that they did so, without question, without hesitation, suggests to me that our troopers had some inkling all along that the Jedi were manipulating events.

"After all these weeks, we still lack confirmation that Viceroy Gunray and his powerful allies are dead. That their battle droids and war machines stand motionless on hundreds of worlds we can take as a sign of their surrender. At the same time, however, we must focus our attention on solidifying the Empire world by world."

Palpatine sat back in his chair.

"The Jedi order is a lesson to us that we cannot permit any agency to become powerful enough to pose a threat to our designs, or to the freedoms we enjoy. That is why it is essential we increase and centralize our military, both to preserve the peace and to protect the Empire against inevitable attempts at insurrection. To that end I have already ordered the production of new classes of capital ships and starfighters, suitable for command by nonclone officers and crew, who themselves will be the product of Imperial academies, made up of candidates drawn from existing star system flight schools.

"No less important, our present army of clone troopers is aging at an accelerated rate, and will need to be supplemented, gradually replaced, by new batches of clones. I suspect that the Jedi had a hand in creating a short-lived army in full confidence that there would be no need for troopers once they had overthrown the Republic and instituted their theocracy based on the Force.

"But that is no longer a concern.

"By bringing the known worlds of the galaxy under one law, one language, the enlightened guidance of *one* individual, corruption of the sort that plagued the former Republic will never be able to take root, and the regional governors I have installed will prevent the growth of another Separatist movement."

When everyone in the room was satisfied that Palpatine was finished, the Senator from Rodia said: "Then species other than human need not fear discrimination or partiality?"

Palpatine spread his crooked, long-nailed hands in a placating gesture. "When have I ever shown myself to be intolerant of species differences? Yes, our army is human, I am human, and most of my advisers and military officers are human. But that is merely the result of circumstance."

*   *   *

"The war continues," Mon Mothma said to Bail.

Confident that they were beyond the reach of the building's assortment of eavesdropping devices and far enough from anyone who might be an Internal Security Bureau spy, Bail said: "Palpatine will use his disfigurement to distance himself further from the Senate. We may never get that close to him again."

Mon Mothma lowered her head in sadness as they continued to walk.

Coruscant was already beginning to adapt to its new title of Imperial Center. Red-patched stormtroopers were more present than they had been at the height of the war, and unfamiliar faces and uniformed personnel crowded the corridors of the building. Military officers, regional governors, security agents . . . the Emperor's new minions.

"When I look at that hideous face or survey the damage done to the Rotunda, I can't help thinking, *this* is what's become of the Republic and the Constitution," Mon Mothma said.

"He maintains he has no plans for disbanding the Senate or punishing the various hive species that supported the Confederacy—" Bail started.

"For the moment," Mon Mothma interrupted. "Besides, the homeworlds of those species have already been punished. They are disaster areas."

"He can't afford to move against anyone just now," Bail went on. "Too many worlds are still too well armed. Yes, new clone troopers are being grown and new capital ships are coming off the line, but not fast enough for him to risk becoming enmeshed in another war."

She looked at him skeptically. "You're very confident all of a sudden, Bail. Or is that circumspection I hear?"

Bail asked himself the same question.

In the throne room, he had tried to puzzle out which among the Emperor's cabal of advisers, human or otherwise, were aware that Palpatine was a Sith Lord who had manipulated the entire war and eradicated his sworn enemies, the Jedi, as part of a plan to assume absolute power over the galaxy.

Certainly Mas Amedda knew, along with Sate Pestage, and possibly Sly Moore. Bail doubted that Armand Isard or any of Palpatine's military advisers knew. How would their knowing change things, in any case? To the few beings who knew or cared, the Sith were nothing more than a quasi-religious sect that had disappeared a millennium ago. What mattered was that Palpatine was now *Emperor* Palpatine, and that he enjoyed the staunch support of most of the Senate and the unwavering allegiance of the Grand Army.

Only Palpatine knew the full story of the war and its abrupt conclusion. But Bail knew a few things that Palpatine didn't; primarily, that Anakin Skywalker and Padmé Amidala's twin children had not died with her on the asteroid known as Polis Massa; and that in the twins Jedi Masters Obi-Wan Kenobi and Yoda were placing their trust for the eventual defeat of the dark side. Even now infant Luke was on Tatooine, in the care of his aunt and uncle, and being watched over by Obi-Wan. And infant Leia—Bail grinned just thinking about her—infant Leia was on Alderaan, probably in the arms of Bail's wife, Breha.

During Palpatine's brief abduction by General Grievous, Bail had promised Padmé that should anything untoward happen to her, he would do all he could to protect those close to her. The fact that Padmé was pregnant had been something of an open secret, but at the time Bail had been referring to Anakin, never realizing that events would draw him into a conspiracy with Obi-Wan and Yoda that would end with his assuming custody of Leia.

It had taken only days for Bail and Breha to come to love the child, though initially Bail had worried that they may have been entrusted with too great a challenge. Given their parentage, chances were high that the Skywalker twins would be powerful in the Force. What if Leia should show early signs of following in the dark footsteps of her father? Bail had wondered.

Yoda had eased his mind.

Anakin hadn't been *born* to the dark side, but had arrived there because of what he had experienced in his short life, instances of suffering, fear, anger, and hatred. Had Anakin been discovered early enough by the Jedi, those emotional states would never have surfaced. More important, Yoda appeared to have had a change of heart regarding the Temple as providing the best crucible for Force-sensitive beings. The steadfast embrace of a loving family would prove as good, if not better.

But the adoption of Leia was only one of Bail's concerns.

For weeks following Palpatine's decree that the Republic would henceforth be an Empire, he had been concerned for his—indeed, Alderaan's—safety. His name was prominent on the Petition of the Two Thousand, which had called for Palpatine to abrogate some of the emergency powers the Senate had granted him. Worse, Bail had been the first to arrive at the Jedi Temple after the slaughter there; and he had rescued Yoda from the Senate following the Jedi Master's fierce battle with Sidious in the Rotunda.

Holocams at the Temple or in the former Republic Plaza might easily have captured his speeder, and those images could have found their way to Palpatine or his security advisers. Word might have leaked that Bail was the person who had arranged for Padmé to be delivered to Naboo for the funeral. If Palpatine had been apprised of that fact, he might begin to wonder if Obi-Wan, having carried Padmé from distant Mustafar, had informed Bail about Palpatine's secret identity, or about the horrors committed on Coruscant by Anakin, renamed Darth Vader by the Sith Lord, whom Obi-Wan had left for dead on the volcanic world.

And then Palpatine might begin to wonder if Padmé's child, or children, had in fact died with her . . .

Bail and Mon Mothma hadn't seen each other since Padmé's funeral, and Mon Mothma knew nothing of the role Bail had played in the final days of the war. However, she had heard that

Bail and Breha had adopted a baby girl, and was eager to meet baby Leia.

The problem was, Mon Mothma was also eager to continue efforts to undermine Palpatine.

"There's talk in the Senate about building a palace to house Palpatine, his advisers, and the Imperial Guard," she said as they were nearing one of the repulsorlift landing platforms attached to what had become Palpatine's building.

Bail had heard the talk. "And statues," he said.

"Bail, the fact that Palpatine doesn't have full faith in his New Order makes him all the more dangerous." She came to a sudden halt when they reached the walkway to the landing platform and turned to him. "Every signatory of the Petition of the Two Thousand is suspect. Do you know that Fang Zar has fled Coruscant?"

"I do," Bail said, just managing to hold Mon Mothma's gaze.

"Clone army or no, Bail, I'm not going to abandon the fight. We have to act while we still can—while Sern Prime, Enisca, Kashyyyk, and other worlds are prepared to join us."

Bail worked his jaw. "It's *too* soon to act. We have to bide our time," he said, repeating what Padmé had told him in the Senate Rotunda on the day of Palpatine's historical announcement. "We have to place our trust in the future, and in the Force."

Mon Mothma adopted a skeptical look. "Right now there are members of the military who will side with us, who know that the Jedi *never* betrayed the Republic."

"What counts is that the clone troopers believe that the Jedi did betray the Republic," Bail said; then he lowered his voice to add: "We risk everything by placing ourselves in Palpatine's sights just now."

He kept to himself his concerns for Leia.

Mon Mothma didn't say another word until they stepped

onto the landing platform, where stormtroopers and a tall, startling figure in black were striding down the boarding ramp of a *Theta*-class shuttle that had just set down.

"Some Jedi must have survived the execution order," Mon Mothma said at last.

For reasons he couldn't fully understand, Bail's attention was riveted on the masked figure, who appeared to be in command of the clones, and who also appeared to glance with clear purpose in Bail's direction. The group passed close enough to Bail for him to hear one of the stormtroopers say: "The Emperor is waiting for you in the facility, Lord Vader."

Bail felt as if someone had let the air out of him.

His legs began to shake and he grabbed hold of the platform railing for support, somehow managing to keep apprehension from his voice when he said to Mon Mothma: "You're right. Some Jedi did survive."

In the capable hands of gangly Brudi Gayn, the modified CloakShape and the booster ring that had allowed it to enter hyperspace completed three short jumps in as many hours, emerging in a remote area of the Tion Cluster, far from any inhabited worlds. Waiting there, however, was a twenty-year-old Corellian freighter as large as a *Tantive*-class corvette, but with a circular command module.

Shryne counted five gun turrets; he already knew from Brudi that the *Drunk Dancer* boasted sublights and a hyperdrive better suited to a ship twice its size.

Brudi disengaged from the booster ring while they were still some distance from the freighter, then in his own good time maneuvered the CloakShape through a magnetic containment shield in the *Drunk Dancer*'s starboard side, and into a spacious docking bay. On their landing disks sat a small drop ship and a swift, split-winged Incom Relay, not much bigger than the CloakShape.

Brudi popped the canopy, and Shryne and Starstone climbed down to the deck, slipping out of their helmets and flight suits at the bottom of the ladder. The two Jedi were wearing the simple spacer garments that Cash Garrulan had provided. Long accustomed to executing undercover missions, Shryne didn't feel out of place without a tunic and robe, even without a lightsaber. He knew better than to convince himself that, having escaped Murkhana, they were suddenly in the clear. Before and during the war he had had his share of close calls and times when he had been chased, but going into *hiding* was entirely new.

Even newer to Olee Starstone, who looked as if the events of the past couple of weeks, the past thirty-six hours especially, were finally beginning to catch up to her. He could tell from her uncertain gestures that Starstone, who had probably never worn anything but Temple robes or field outfits, was still adjusting to their new circumstances.

Shryne resisted the temptation to console her. Their future was cloudier than the gunship drop into Murkhana City had been, and the sooner Starstone learned to take responsibility for herself, the better.

Alerted to the CloakShape's arrival, several members of the *Drunk Dancer*'s crew were waiting in the docking bay. Shryne had encountered their type before, primarily in those outlying systems that had drifted into Count Dooku's embrace before the Separatist movement had been formalized as the Confederacy of Independent Systems. Just from the look of them Shryne could see that they lacked the discipline of crews belonging to Black Sun or the Hutt syndicates, despite Brudi's disclosure that the *Drunk Dancer* accepted occasional contracts from a variety of crime cartels.

Dressed in bits and pieces of apparel they had obviously obtained on dozens of worlds, they were a ragtag band of freelance smugglers, without star system or political affiliation, or bones to pick with anyone. Determined to maintain their autonomy, they had learned that smugglers didn't get rich by working for others.

In the docking bay Shryne and Starstone were introduced to

the *Drunk Dancer*'s first mate, Skeck Draggle, and the freighter's security chief, Archyr Beil. Both were humanoids as long-limbed as Brudi Gayn, with six-fingered hands and severe facial features that belied cheerful dispositions.

In the ship's main cabin space the two Jedi met Filli Bitters, a towheaded human slicer who took an immediate interest in Starstone, and the *Drunk Dancer*'s communications expert, Eyl Dix, whose hairless dark green head hosted two pair of curling antennae, in addition to a pair of sharp-tipped ears.

Before long everyone, including a couple of inquisitive droids, had gathered in the main cabin to hear Shryne and Starstone's account of their narrow escape from Murkhana. The fact that no one mentioned anything about the hunt for Jedi made Shryne uneasy, but not uneasy enough to pursue the point—at least not until he had a clearer sense of just where he and Starstone stood in the eyes of the smugglers.

"Cash asked that we bring you to Mossak," Skeck Draggle said after the Jedi had entertained everyone with details of the daring flight. "Mossak's just the other side of Felucia, and a decent hub for jumps into the Tingel Arm or just about anywhere up and down the Perlemian Trade Route." He looked directly at Shryne. "We, ah, normally don't offer free transport. But seeing how it was Cash who asked, and, uh, knowing what you folk have had to endure, we'll cover the costs."

"We appreciate that," Shryne said, sensing the sharp-featured Skeck had left something unstated.

"The Twi'lek fix you with new identichips?" Archyr asked, in what seemed to be actual concern.

Shryne nodded. "Good enough to fool agents at Murkhana STC, anyway."

"Then they'll pass muster on Mossak, as well," the lanky security chief said. "You shouldn't have too much trouble finding temporary work, if that's your plan." Archyr regarded Shryne. "You have any contacts you can trust?"

Shryne's eyebrows bobbed. "Good question."

When the assembled crew members fell into a separate conversation, Starstone moved close to Shryne. "Just what is our plan, Mas—"

Shryne's lifted finger stopped her midsentence. "No order; no ranks."

"You don't know that," she said, echoing his quiet tone. "You agreed that other Jedi probably survived."

"Listen, kid," he said, gazing at her for emphasis, "the Climbers of this galaxy are few and far between."

"Jedi could have survived by other means. It's our duty to locate them."

"Our *duty*?"

"To ourselves. To the Force."

Shryne took a deep breath. "How do you propose we do that?"

She gnawed at her lower lip while she considered it, then looked at him pointedly. "We have Master Chatak's beacon transceiver. If we could patch it into the *Drunk Dancer*'s communications suite, we could issue a Nine Thirteen code on encrypted frequencies."

Shryne laughed in spite of himself. "You know, that could actually work." He glanced at the crew members. "Still, I wouldn't get my hopes up if I were you."

She returned the smile. "But you're not me."

When Shryne turned back to the crew, he found Skeck gazing at him. "So I guess your scheme failed, huh?"

"Which scheme would that be, chief?"

Skeck glanced at his crewmates before answering. "Knocking Palpatine off his perch. Fighting the war the way it probably should have been fought all along."

"You've been misinformed," Shryne said flatly.

Skeck sat back in feigned nonchalance. "Really? We've all heard the recordings of what went on in Palpatine's chambers."

The other crew members nodded somberly.

"Don't get me wrong," the first mate continued before Shryne could respond. "I've nothing against any of you personally. But you have to admit, the way some of your people conducted themselves when Republic interests were at stake . . . The prestige you enjoyed. The wealth you amassed."

"I give the Jedi credit for trying," the slicer, Filli Bitters, chimed in. "But you should never have left yourselves so short-handed on Coruscant. Not with so many troopers garrisoned there."

Shryne laughed cheerlessly. "We were needed in the Outer Rim Sieges, you see."

"Don't you get it?" Eyl Dix said. "The Jedi were played." When she shrugged her narrow shoulders, her twin antennae bobbed. "That's what Cash thinks, anyway."

Skeck laughed in derision. "From where I sit, getting played is worse than losing."

"You'll be safe from Imperial reach on Mossak," Bitters said quickly, in an obvious attempt to be cheerful.

Sudden silence told Shryne that none of the *Drunk Dancer*'s crew was buying the slicer's optimism.

"I realize that we're already in your debt," he said at last, "but we've a proposition for you."

Skeck's green eyes widened in interest. "Lay it out. Let's see how it looks."

Shryne turned to Starstone. "Tell them."

She gestured to herself. "Me?"

"It was your idea, kid."

"Okay," Starstone began uncertainly. "Sure." She cleared her voice. "We're hoping to make contact with other Jedi who survived Palpatine's execution orders. We have a transceiver capable of transmitting on encrypted frequencies. Any Jedi who survived will be doing the same thing, or listening for special transmissions. The thing is, we'd need to use the *Drunk Dancer*'s communications suite."

"That's a little like whistling in the stellar wind, isn't it?" Dix said. "From what we hear, the clones got the drop on all of you."

"*Almost* all of us," Starstone said.

Bitters was rocking his head back and forth in uncertainty, but Shryne could tell that the white-haired computer expert was excited by the idea—and perhaps grateful for a chance to win points with Olee. Regardless, Filli said: "Could be dangerous. The Empire might be on to those frequencies by now."

"Not if as many of us are dead as all of you seem to think," Shryne countered.

Bitters, Dix, and Archyr waited for Skeck to speak.

"Well, of course, we'd have to get the captain to agree," he said at last. "Anyway, I'm still waiting to hear the rest of the proposition—the part that makes it worth *our* while."

Everyone looked at Shryne.

"The Jedi have means of accessing emergency funds," he said, with a covert motion of his hand. "You don't have to worry about being paid for your services."

Skeck nodded, satisfied. "Then we don't have to worry about being paid for our services."

While Starstone was staring at Shryne in appalled disbelief and the crew members were talking among themselves about how best to slave the Jedi beacon transceiver to the communications suite, Brudi Gayn and a tall human woman entered the cabin space from the direction of the *Drunk Dancer*'s bulbous cockpit. The woman's black hair was shot through with gray, and her age showed there and in her face more than in the way she moved.

"Captain," Skeck said, coming to his feet, but she ignored him, her gray eyes fixed on Shryne.

"*Roan* Shryne?" she said.

Shryne looked up at her. "Last time I checked."

She forced an exhale and shook her head in incredulity. "Stars' end, it really is you." She sat down opposite Shryne, without once taking her eyes off him. "You're the image of Jen."

Baffled, Shryne said: "Do I know you?"

She nodded and laughed. "On a cellular level, at any rate." She touched herself on the chest. "I gave birth to you. I'm your *mother*, Jedi."

The Emperor's medical rehabilitation laboratory occupied the crown of Coruscant's tallest building. A room of modest size, the laboratory's antechamber closely resembled his former chambers in the Senate Office Building, and featured a semicircle of padded couch, three swivel chairs with shell-shaped backs, and a trio of squat holoprojectors shaped like truncated cones.

Palpatine sat in the center chair, his hands on his knees, the lights of Coruscant blazing behind him through a long arc of fixed windows. The cowl of his heavy robe was lowered, and the blinking telltales of an array of devices and control panels lit his deeply creased face, the face he kept concealed from his advisers and Senatorial guests.

For here he was not simply Emperor Palpatine, he was Darth Sidious, Dark Lord of the Sith.

On the far side of thick panels of transparisteel that separated the antechamber from a rib-walled operating theater, Vader sat on the edge of the surgical table on which he had been recalled to life and transformed. His flaring black helmet had been lifted from his head by servos that extended from the laboratory's ceiling, revealing the pasty complexion of his synthflesh face and the raised wounds on his head that might never fully heal.

The medical droids responsible for repairing what had remained of Vader's amputated limbs and incinerated body, some of which had observed and participated in the cyborg transformation of General Grievous on Geonosis a decade earlier, had been reduced to scrap by a scream that had torn from Vader's scorched throat on his learning of his wife's death. Now a 2-1B droid responding to Vader's voiced instruction was tending to an injury to Vader's left-arm prosthesis, the cause of which he had yet to explain.

"The last time you were in this facility, you were in no condition to supervise your own convalescence, Lord Vader," Sidious said, his words transmitted to the pressurized laboratory by the antechamber's sensitive enunciators.

"And I will remain ward of myself from this point forward," Vader said through the intercom system.

"Ward of yourself," Sidious repeated in an exacting tone.

"When it comes to overseeing modifications of this . . . shell, Master," Vader clarified.

"Ah. As it should be."

The humaniform 2-1B was in the midst of executing Vader's instructions when sparks geysered from Vader's left forearm, and blue electricity began to gambol across his chest. With an infuriated growl, Vader lifted the injured arm, hurling the med droid halfway across the laboratory.

"Useless machine!" he shouted. "Useless! Useless!"

Sidious watched his apprentice with rising concern.

"What is troubling you, my son? I'm aware of the suit's limitations, and of the exasperation you must be experiencing. But anger is wasted on the droid. You must reserve your rage for times when you can profit from it." He appraised Vader again. "I think I begin to understand the cause of your frustration . . .

Your rage owes little to the suit or the droid's ineptitude. Something disturbing occurred on Murkhana. Some occurrence you have elected to keep from me. For your good or mine? I wonder."

Vader took a long moment to reply. "Master, I found the three Jedi who escaped Order Sixty-Six."

"What of it?"

"The damage to my arm was done by one of them, though she is now dead, by my blade."

"And the other two?"

"They eluded me." Vader lifted his scarred face to regard Sidious. "But they wouldn't have if this suit didn't restrict me to the point of immobility! If the Star Destroyer you placed at my command was properly equipped! If Sienar had completed work on the starfighter I designed!"

Sidious waited until Vader was finished, then stood up and walked to within a meter of the room's transparent panels. "So, my young apprentice, two Jedi slip through your grasp and you scatter the blame like leaves blown about by a storm."

"Master, if you had been there—"

"Keep still," Sidious interrupted, "before you damage yourself all the more." He gave Vader a moment to compose himself. "First, let me reiterate that the Jedi mean *nothing* to us. In having survived, Yoda and Obi-Wan aren't exceptions to the rule. I'm certain that dozens of Jedi escaped with their lives, and in due time you will have the pleasure of killing many of them. But of greater import is the fact that their order has been crushed. *Finished,* Lord Vader. Do I make myself clear?"

"Yes, Master," Vader muttered.

"In burying their heads in the sands and snows of remote worlds, the surviving Jedi *humble* themselves before the Sith. So let them: let them atone for one thousand years of arrogance and self-absorption."

Sidious watched Vader, displeased.

"Once more your thoughts betray you. I see that you are not yet fully convinced."

Glancing at him, Vader gestured to his face and black-cloaked body, then gestured in similar fashion to Sidious. "Look at us. Are these the faces of victory?"

Sidious was careful to keep himself from becoming too angry, or too sickened by his pupil's self-pity.

"We are not this crude stuff, Lord Vader. Have you not heard that before?"

"Yes," Vader said. "Yes, I've heard it before. Too often."

"But from me you will learn the *truth* of it."

Vader lifted his face. "In the same way you told me the truth about being able to save Padmé?"

Sidious was not taken aback. For the past month he had been expecting to hear just such an accusation from Vader. "I had nothing to do with Padmé Amidala's death. She died as a result of your anger at her betrayal, my young apprentice."

Vader looked at the floor. "You're right, Master. I brought about the very thing I feared for her. I'm to blame."

Sidious adopted a more compassionate tone. "Sometimes the Force has other plans for us, my son. Fortunately I arrived at Mustafar in time to save you."

"Save me," Vader said without emotion. "Yes, yes, of course you did, Master. And I suppose I should be grateful." He got up from the table and walked to the panel to place himself opposite Sidious. "But what good is power without reward? What good is power without joy?"

Sidious didn't move. "Eventually you will come to see that power *is* joy. The path to the dark side is not without terrible risk, but it is the only path worth following. It matters not how we *appear*, in any case, or who is sacrificed along the way. We have won, and the galaxy is ours."

Vader's eyes searched Sidious's face. "Did you promise as much to Count Dooku?"

Sidious bared his teeth, but only briefly. "Darth Tyranus knew what he risked, Lord Vader. If he had been stronger in the dark side, *you* would be dead, and he would be my right hand."

"And if you should encounter someone stronger than I am?"

Sidious almost smiled. "There is none, my son, even though your body has been crippled. This is your *destiny*. We have seen to that. Together we are unconquerable."

"I wasn't strong enough to defeat Obi-Wan," Vader said.

Sidious had had enough.

"No, you weren't," he said. "So just imagine what Yoda might have done to you." He flung his words with brutal honesty. "Obi-Wan triumphed because he went to Mustafar with a single intention in mind: to kill Darth Vader. If the Jedi order had showed such resolute intention, if it had remained focused on what needed to be done rather than on fears of the dark side, it might have proved more difficult to topple and eradicate. You and I might have lost *everything*. Do you understand?"

Vader looked at him, breathing deeply. "Then I suppose I should be grateful for what little I have been able to hold on to."

"Yes," Sidious said curtly. "You should."

20

The crew of the *Drunk Dancer* was every bit as surprised by their captain's revelations as Shryne was. For most of them, though, the disclosure only explained why they had come to place so much trust in Jula's judgment and intuition.

Shryne and the woman who claimed to be his mother were sitting in a dark alcove off the main cabin, untouched meals between them and blue-tinted holoimages to one side, allegedly showing a nine-month-old Roan taking his first steps outside the modest dwelling that had been his home for just over three years. He had never enjoyed seeing likenesses of himself, and the images merely served to increase his embarrassment over the entire situation.

Master Nat-Sem had once told him that vanity was the cause of such uneasiness, and had ordered Shryne to spend a full week staring at his own reflection in a mirror, in an effort to teach Shryne that what he saw was no more who he was than a map of a place could be considered the territory itself.

Clear across the cabin, Eyl Dix, Filli Bitters, and Starstone were huddled around the ship's communications suite, into which Filli had managed to patch Bol Chatak's beacon transceiver, and the *Drunk Dancer* was now transmitting on frequencies Jedi would scan in case of trouble, or if attempting to establish contact with other Jedi. The talented young slicer, whose face was nearly as colorless as his short spiked hair, was still trying his best to engage Starstone's interest, but she was either ignoring his attempts or simply too focused on awaiting a return signal to be aware of them.

With her dark complexion and black curls, and Bitters's towheaded brilliance, they made for an interesting-looking couple, and Shryne wondered if perhaps Starstone hadn't unwittingly stumbled on a new path to follow.

Elsewhere in the main cabin, Brudi, Archyr, and Skeck were playing cards at a circular table, labor droids whirring in to clean up their dropped snacks and spilled drinks. All in all it was a pleasant setup, Shryne decided. Almost like a family living room, with the kids playing games, the adults watching competition sports on the HoloNet, and the hired help in the kitchen preparing a big lunch for everyone.

As a Jedi, he had scant familiarity with any of it. The Temple had been more like a huge dormitory, and one was constantly aware of being in service to a cause greater than one's family or oneself. Frequently there were classes or briefings to attend, chores that needed completing as part of one's training, and long meditative or lightsaber combat sessions with Masters or peers, except for those rare days when one was allowed to wander about Coruscant, sampling bits of a different reality.

In some ways the Jedi *had* led a life of royalty.

The order had been wealthy, privileged, entitled.

And that was why we didn't see it coming, Shryne thought.

Why so many of the Jedi had turned a blind eye to the trap Palpatine had been setting. Because they had refused to accept that such entitlement could ever come to an end—could all come crashing down around them. And yet even those who hadn't denied the possibility would never have believed that thousands of Jedi could be killed in one fell swoop, or that the order could be ended with one bold stroke, as if pierced through the heart.

We were played, he told himself.

And Skeck was right: knowing that you had been played was worse than losing.

But Roan Shryne—by a quirk of fate, circumstance, the will of the Force—had survived, been brought face-to-face with his mother, and was now at a loss as to what to make of it.

He had seen his share of mothers interacting with their children, and he understood what a child was *supposed* to feel, how he or she was *supposed* to behave. But all he felt toward the woman opposite him was an unspecific connection in the Force.

Shryne wasn't the first Jedi to have inadvertently encountered a blood relative. Over the years he had heard stories about Padawans, Jedi Knights, even Masters running into parents, siblings, cousins . . .

Unfortunately, he had never heard how any of the stories ended.

"I never wanted you to be found," Jula said when she had deactivated the holoprojector. "To this day I don't understand how your father could hand you over to the Jedi. When I learned he had contacted the Temple, and that Jedi agents were coming for you, I tried to talk your father into hiding you."

"That rarely happens," Shryne said. "Most Force-sensitive infants were voluntarily surrendered to the Temple."

"Really? Well, it happened to me."

Shryne regarded her with his eyes, and through the Force.

"Who do you think you inherited your abilities from?" Jula asked.

"Awareness does not always run in families." He smiled

lightly. "But I sensed the Force in you the moment you entered the cabin."

"And I knew you did."

Shryne exhaled and sat back in the chair. "So your own parents chose to keep you from joining the order."

She nodded. "And I'm grateful they did. I would never have been able to abide by the rules. And I never wanted you to have to abide by them, Roan." She considered something. "I have a confession to make: all my life I've known that I would meet you somewhere along the way. I think that's partly the reason I took up piloting after your father and I separated. In the hope of, well, bumping into you. It's because of our Force connection that I brought the *Dancer* to this sector. I *sensed* you, Roan."

For many Jedi, luck and coincidence didn't exist, but Shryne wasn't one of them. "What happened between you and your husband?" he asked finally.

Jula laughed shortly. "*You,* really. Jen, your father, simply didn't agree with me about the need to protect you—to hide you, I mean. We argued bitterly about it, but he was a true believer. He felt that I should never have been hidden; that I'd basically turned my back on what would ultimately have been a more fulfilling life. And, of course, that you would profit from being raised in the Temple.

"Jen had the strength—I guess you could call it strength—to forget about you after he handed you over to the Jedi. No, that's too harsh. He had confidence enough in his decision to believe that he had made the right choice, and that you were doing well." Jula shook her head. "I could never get there. I missed you. It broke my heart to see you leave, and know that I might never see you again. That's what eventually ruined us."

Shryne mulled it over. "Jen sounds like he was Jedi without the title."

"How so?"

"Because he understood that you have to accept what destiny sets in front of you. That you have to pick and choose your battles."

Her gray eyes searched his face. "What does that make me, Roan?"

"A victim of attachment."

She smiled weakly. "You know what? I can live with that."

Shryne glanced away, catching Starstone's look before she quickly turned back to the communications console. She was eavesdropping on their conversation, worrying that the efforts she had made to keep Shryne on the proper path were suddenly being undermined. Shryne could feel her wanting to tear herself away from the communications suite before it was too late, and Shryne was lost to the cause.

He looked at Jula once more. "I'll provide a confession in exchange for yours: I refused an assignment in the Temple's Acquisition Division. I'm still not sure why, except that I'd persuaded myself on some level that I didn't like the idea of kids being separated from their families." He paused briefly. "But that was a long time ago."

She took his meaning. "Long ago in years, maybe. But I'm guessing you still feel like you missed out."

"On what?"

"*Life*, Roan. Desire, romance, love, laughter, *fun*—all the things you've been denied. And children. How about that? A Force-sensitive child you could nurture and learn from."

He made his eyes dull. "I'm not sure how Force-sensitive a child of mine would be."

"Why is that?"

He gave his head a sharp shake. "Nothing."

Jula was willing to let the point drop, but she had more to say.

"Roan, just hear me out. From everything I've heard, the

Jedi order has been vanquished. Probably ninety-nine percent of the Jedi are dead. So it's not like you have a choice. Like it or not, you're in the real world. Which means you could get to meet and know your father, your uncles and aunts. All of them still talk about you. Having a Jedi in the family is a pretty big deal in some places. Or at least it was." She fell briefly silent. "When I heard what happened, I thought for a moment . . ." She laughed to push some memory aside. "I don't want to get into all that. Someday you can tell me the truth about what happened on Coruscant, and why Palpatine betrayed you."

Shryne narrowed his eyes. "If we ever learn the truth."

From the comm suite came a cheer of excitement, and a moment later Starstone was hurrying across the cabin toward them.

"Roan, we got a hit! From a group of Jedi on the run." She turned to Jula. "Captain, with your permission we'd like to arrange a rendezvous with their ship."

Filli appeared at Starstone's side to elaborate. "We'd have to divert from our course to Mossak. But the rendezvous wouldn't take us too far out of the way."

Shryne felt Jula's eyes on him. "I won't try to convince you," he said. "It's your ship, and I'm sure you have important business elsewhere."

Jula took a long moment to respond. "I'll tell you why I'm going to do it: just to have more time with you. With luck, enough time to persuade you to get to know us, and ultimately to stay with us." She cut her eyes to Starstone. "There's room for you, too, Olee."

Starstone blinked in indignation. "Room for me? I'm not about to abandon my Jedi oath to go gallivanting around the galaxy with a band of smugglers. Especially now that I know that other Jedi survived." She looked hard at Shryne. "We have contact, Roan. You can't be taking her offer seriously?"

Shryne laughed out loud. "Normally Padawans don't talk

like this to Masters," he said to Jula. "You can see how fast things have changed."

Starstone folded her arms across her chest. "You said I shouldn't call you 'Master.' "

"That doesn't mean you shouldn't respect your elders."

"I do respect you," she said. "It's your decisions I don't respect."

"Many Jedi have left the Temple to lead regular lives," Jula thought to point out. "Some have gotten married and had children."

"No," Starstone said, shaking her head back and forth. "Maybe apprentices, but not Jedi Knights."

"That can't be true," Jula said.

"It is true," Starstone said firmly, before Shryne could say a word. "Only twenty Jedi have ever left the order."

"Don't try to argue with her," Shryne advised Jula. "She spent half her life in the Temple library polishing the busts of those Lost Twenty."

Starstone shot him a gimlet look. "Don't even think about being number twenty-one."

Shryne let his sudden seriousness show. "Despite your claims for me, I'm not a Master, and there is no order. How many times are you going to have to hear it before you accept the truth?"

She compressed her lips. "That has no bearing on being a *Jedi*. And you can't be a Jedi and serve the Force if your attention is divided or if you're emotionally involved with others. Love leads to attachment; attachment to greed."

So much for Olee and Filli Bitters, Shryne thought.

At the same time, Jula was regarding Starstone as if the young Jedi had lost her mind. "They certainly did a bang-up job on you, didn't they." She held Starstone's gaze. "Olee, love is about all we have left."

Instead of reacting to the remark, Starstone said: "Are you going to help us or not?"

"I already said I would." Standing up, Jula gave Shryne a look. "But just so we understand each other, Roan? You and I both know that you don't have access to any 'secret funds.' You make one more attempt at using Force persuasion on any members of my crew, and I may forget that I'm your mother."

Darth Sidious had had most of his beloved Sith statues and ancient bas-reliefs removed from his ruined chambers in the Senate Office Building, where four Jedi had lost their lives and one had been converted to the dark side. Relocated to the throne room, the statues had been placed on the dais, the scuptures mounted on the long walls.

Swiveling his throne, Sidious gazed at them now.

As some Jedi had feared from the start, Anakin had been ripe for conversion when Qui-Gon Jinn had first brought him to the Temple, and for well over a decade all of Sidious's plans for the boy had unfolded without incident. But even Sidious hadn't foreseen Anakin's defeat by Obi-Wan Kenobi on Mustafar. Anakin had still been between worlds then, and vulnerable. The failure to defeat his former Master had worked to prolong that vulnerability.

Sidious recalled the desperate return trip to Coruscant; recalled using all his powers, and all the potions and devices contained in his medkit, to minister to Anakin's hopelessly blistered body and truncated limbs.

He recalled thinking: *What if Anakin should die?*

How many years would he have had to search for an apprentice even half as powerful in the Force, let alone one created by the Force itself to restore balance, by allowing the dark side to percolate fully to the surface after a millennium of being stifled?

None would be found.

Sidious would have had to discover a way to compel midichlorians to do his bidding, and bring into being one as powerful as Anakin. As it was, Sidious and a host of medical droids had merely restored Anakin to life, which—while no small feat—was a far cry from returning someone from death. For thousands of years, the ability to survive death had been pursued by Sith and Jedi alike, and no one had been successful at discovering the secret. Beings had been saved from dying, but no one had cheated death. The most powerful of the ancient Sith Lords had known the secret, but it had been lost or, rather, misplaced. Now that the galaxy was his to rule, there was nothing to prevent Sidious, too, from unlocking that mystery.

Then he and his crippled apprentice might hold sway over the galaxy for ten thousand years, and live *eternally.*

If they didn't kill each other first.

In large part because Padmé Amidala had died.

Sidious had deliberately brought her and Anakin together three years earlier, both to rid the Senate of her vote against the Military Creation Act and to put temptation in Anakin's path. Following the murder of Anakin's mother, Anakin had secretly married Padmé. When he had learned of the marriage, Sidious knew for certain that Anakin's pathological attachment to her would eventually supply the means for completing his conversion to the dark side.

Anakin's fears for her, in actuality and in visions—and especially after Padmé had become pregnant—had been heightened by keeping him far from her. Then it simply had been a matter of unmasking the Jedi for the hypocrites that they were, sacrificing Dooku to Anakin's rage, and promising Anakin that Padmé could be saved from death . . .

The latter, an exaggeration necessary for Anakin's turn from what the Jedi called right thinking; for opening his eyes to his true calling. But such was the way of the Force. It provided opportunities, and one needed only to be ready to seize them.

Not for the first time Sidious wondered what might have happened had Anakin not killed Padmé on Mustafar. For all she loved him, she never would have understood or forgiven Anakin's action at the Jedi Temple. In fact, that was one of the reasons Sidious had sent him there. Clone troopers could have dealt with the instructors and younglings, but Anakin's presence was essential in order to cement his allegiance to the Sith, and, more important, to seal Padmé's fate. Even if she had survived Mustafar, their love would have died—Padmé might even have lost the will to live—and their child would have become Sidious's and Vader's to raise.

Might that child have been the first member of a new Sith order of thousands or millions? Hardly. The idea of a Sith order was a corruption of the intent of the ancient Dark Lords. Fortunately, Darth Bane had understood that, and had insisted that only in rare instances should there exist more than two lords, Master and apprentice, at any given time.

But *two* were necessary for the perpetuation of the Sith order.

And so it fell to Sidious to *complete* Vader's convalescence.

As Emperor Palpatine, he had no need to reveal his Sith training and mastery to anyone, and for the moment Vader was his crimson blade. Let the galaxy think what it would of Vader: fallen Jedi, surfaced Sith, political enforcer . . . It scarcely mattered, since *fear* would ultimately bring and keep everyone in line.

Yes, Vader was not precisely what he had bargained for.

Vader's legs and arms were artificial, and he would never be able to summon lightning or leap about like the Jedi had been fond of doing. His dark side training was just beginning. But Sith power resided not in the flesh but in the *will*. Self-restraint was praised by the Jedi only because they didn't know the power of the dark side. Vader's real weaknesses were psychological rather than physical, and for Vader to overcome them he would need to be driven deeper into himself, to confront all his choices and his disappointments.

Powered by treachery, the Sith Master–apprentice relationship was always a dangerous game. Trust was encouraged even while being sabotaged; loyalty was demanded even while betrayal was prized; suspicion was nourished even while honesty was praised.

In some sense, it was survival of the fittest.

Fundamental to Vader's growth was the desire to overthrow his Master.

Had Vader killed Obi-Wan on Mustafar, he might have attempted to kill Sidious, as well. In fact, Sidious would have been surprised if Anakin *hadn't* made an attempt. Now, however, incapable of so much as breathing on his own, Vader could not rise to the challenge, and Sidious understood that he would need to do everything in his power to shake Vader out of his despair, and reawaken the incredible power within him.

Even at Sidious's own peril . . .

Alert to a mild disturbance in the Force, he swung toward the throne room holoprojector a moment before a half-life-size image of Mas Amedda resolved from thin air.

"My lord, I apologize for intruding on your meditation," the Chagrian said, "but an encrypted Jedi code transmission has been picked up and is being monitored in the Tion Cluster."

"More survivors of Order Sixty-Six," Sidious said.

"Apparently so, my Lord. Shall I summon Lord Vader?"

Sidious considered it. Would additional Jedi deaths be enough to heal Vader's wounds? Perhaps, perhaps not.

But not yet, in any case.

"No," he said finally. "I have need of Lord Vader on Coruscant."

Right . . . *now,*" Shryne overheard Filli tell Starstone.

The communications suite chimed and Filli, Starstone, and Eyl Dix leaned in to study a display screen. "The Jedi ship has reverted to realspace," Dix said, almost in awe, antennae twitching.

Filli stood to his full height, stretching his arms over his head in theatrical nonchalance and beaming. "I love it when I'm right."

Starstone glanced up at him. "I can tell that about you."

His frowned dramatically. "No put-downs in the main cabin."

"It's not a criticism," Starstone was quick to explain. "What I mean is that I was the same way at the Jedi Temple library. Someone would come in looking for data, and I would almost always be able to direct them right to the files they needed. I just had a sense for it." Her voice broke momentarily; then she continued in a confident tone. "I think you should be proud of doing what you do best, instead of hiding behind false humility, or"—she gave Shryne a furtive glance—"letting disillusion convince you that you need a new life."

Shryne got out of his seat. "I'll take that as my cue to leave."

A droid directed him to the corridor that led to the *Drunk Dancer*'s ample cockpit, where Jula and Brudi Gayn sat in adjacent chairs behind a shimmering sweep of instrument console. A crescent of red planet hung in the forward viewport, and local space was strewn with battle debris.

Shryne rapped his knuckles against the cockpit's retracted hatch. "Permission to enter, Captain?"

Jula glanced at him over her shoulder. "Only if you promise not to tell me how to pilot."

"I'll keep my mouth shut."

She patted the cushion of the acceleration chair behind hers. "Then take a load off."

Brudi gestured to a point of reflected light far to port. "That's them. On schedule."

Shryne studied the console's friend-or-foe display screen, in which a schematic of a sharp-nosed, broad-winged ship was rotating. "Republic SX troop transport," he said. "Wonder how they got ahold of that."

"I'm sure there's a story," Brudi said.

Shryne lifted his eyes to the viewports, and to the wreckage beyond. "What happened here?"

"Seps used this system as a staging area for reinforcing Felucia," Jula said. "Republic caught them napping and dusted them." She gestured to what Shryne had initially taken for marker buoys. "Mines. Command-detonated, but still a potential hazard. Better warn the transport to steer clear of them, Brudi."

He swiveled his chair to the comm unit. "I'm on it."

Shryne continued to gaze at the debris. "That's a docking arm of a TradeFed Lucrehulk. What's left of it, anyway."

When Jula finally spoke, she said: "Something's not right."

Brudi turned slightly in her direction. "Transport's registering the signature they transmitted before rendezvous."

She shook her head in uncertainty. "I know, but . . ."

"There are Jedi aboard the transport," Shryne said.

She glanced at him out of the corner of her eye. "Even I know that much. No, it's something else—"

A tone from the threat board cut her off, and Brudi swiveled again.

"Count six, make that eight bandits emerging from hyperspace," he said tersely. "Dead on the transport's vector."

Shryne watched the IFF transponder. "ARC-one-seventies."

"Affirmative," Brudi said. "Aggressive ReConnaissance starfighters."

Visual scanners caught the craft as their transverse wings were unfolding, splaying for battle and increased thermal stability. Jula's left hand made adjustments to the instruments while her right held tight to the yoke.

"Is the transport aware of them?"

"I'd say so," Shryne said. "It's going evasive."

Brudi pressed his headset tighter to his ear. "The transport's warning us away."

"Makes me like them already," Jula said. "Scramble our signature before the ARCs can get a lock on us."

"You may not be able to jam them," Shryne said. "They're not like V-wings. And they punch harder, too."

"Try anyway, Brudi," Jula said. "Last thing I want is the Empire chasing us all over the galaxy. And I am not about to get a new ship." She flipped an intercom switch. "Skeck, Archyr, are you there?"

Skeck's voice issued through the cockpit speaker. "Weapons are powering up, Captain. Just say when."

Jula looked at Shryne. "Any ideas, Jedi?"

Shryne swept his eyes over the display screens. "The ARCs are maintaining a wedge formation. They'll wait until they're within firing range of the transport, then they'll break formation and attempt to outflank it."

"Skeck," Jula said toward the audio pickup, "do you copy?"

"Loud and clear."

"Are the ARCs within range of your turbolasers?" Shryne asked.

"Almost," Skeck said.

"Anticipate the formation break. Lead them, and open up."

Brudi ran a fast calculation on the rate at which the Imperial starfighters were gaining on the transport. "You're good to go," he said.

"Firing!" Skeck announced.

Dense packets of scarlet light tore from the *Drunk Dancer*'s forward batteries, converging on their distant targets. A quartet of fiery blossoms lighted local space.

Archyr whooped. "Pursuit squadron reduced by half!"

"Nice," Jula said, grinning at Shryne. "What other tricks do you have up your sleeve?"

Shryne didn't answer her. On Murkhana, and despite everything that had happened, he had tried to avoid killing any clone troopers. Now here he was, lining them up to be blown to pieces.

"Roan," Jula said sharply.

"The remaining ARCs will regroup, forming up behind the squadron leader," he said at last. Tapping Brudi on the shoulder, he added: "Instruct the transport to nose up over the ecliptic. When the ARCs follow suit, Skeck and Archyr should have a clear shot at their bellies."

"Copy that," Brudi said.

Jula was studying one of the display screens. "Transport is outward bound. ARCs are up and away."

"Firing!" Skeck reported.

A fifth explosion blossomed over the red planet's north pole. Other laser beams went wide of their marks.

"They've figured us out," Shryne said. "They'll scatter now."

"Transport is angling for the mines," Brudi updated.

"Just what I'd do," Jula said.

The threat board loosed another alert tone.

Brudi tapped his finger on the long-distance scanner array screen. "Six more starfighters have emerged from hyperspace."

Jula forced a short exhale. "Tell whoever's piloting the transport to go to full throttle. He may not even be aware of the new players."

"He won't miss this," Brudi said somberly.

Shryne eased out of his seat to peer over Brudi's shoulder. "What?"

"Republic light cruiser," Jula said. "But don't worry, we can outrun it."

On the console's central screen, the scanners assembled a facsimile of the hourglass-shaped warship, highlighting its dozens of turbolaser and ion cannons.

"You won't outrun those guns," Shryne said.

Jula considered it. "Brudi, divert power to the forward deflectors. I'm going to try to take us behind that Lucrehulk arm." She took a moment to glance at Shryne. "Guess the Jedi are more important than I thought, if the Empire's sending cruisers after you."

"Cruiser's turbos are firing," Skeck said over the speaker.

"Hold tight," Jula warned.

Blinding light splashed against the viewports. Jolted, the *Drunk Dancer* lost power momentarily, then returned to life.

"We're okay," Brudi confirmed, "but the transport's in trouble."

"Instruct them to raise their aft shields and rendezvous with us behind the Lucrehulk arm," Jula said. "Tell them we'll hold off the cruiser and ARCs while they make a run for it."

Brudi relayed the instructions and waited for a response. "They'll try. But the transport's shields are heavily damaged. One more hit from the cruiser and they're dead in space."

Jula muttered a curse. The *Drunk Dancer* was just dropping behind the curved fragment of docking arm when she said: "I'm going to bring us back in the open. Rig for ion cannon fire. Let's see if we can surprise them."

The smugglers' ship sustained two powerful strikes as it was emerging from cover, but not enough to incapacitate it.

"Ion surprise," Archyr said.

"Laser chaser," Skeck chimed in.

White light flared in the distance, and blue current coruscated over the cruiser's dark hull.

Brudi bent to one of the screens. "Solid hit. And they definitely didn't see it coming. Their shields are dazed."

"Taking us back into cover," Jula said. "Where's the transport?"

Brudi spoke to it. "Weaving through the last of the mines."

"Archyr, get those ARCs off the transport's tail!"

"Will do, Captain."

Pulsed light streaked from the ship once more, and Shryne watched another starfighter come apart. But the remaining ARCs were gaining rapidly on the transport.

"Projected rendezvous in five-point-five," Brudi said. "Cruiser has come to, and is returning fire."

Jula firmed her lips. "We're not deep enough into cover. This is going to be a bad one."

Shryne hung on to the arms of the chair. Taking the brunt of the capital ship's enfilade, the docking arm vaporized. Tossed back by the blast, the *Drunk Dancer* lived up to its name. Klaxons blared deep within the ship, and the instrument console howled in alarm.

"Shuttle is still closing," Brudi said when he could.

Jula slammed her hand down on the intercom stud. "Prep the bay for emergency docking!" She swiveled to face Brudi. "Tell the transport we're done swapping punches with that

cruiser. Either they make their move now, or we're bowing out."
To Skeck, she said: "All power to the forward batteries. Fire at
will."

The ship rumbled as coherent light raced from the cannon
turrets.

"Transport is lined up for its approach," Brudi said.

Jula's right hand entered data into the navicomputer. "Calculating the jump to lightspeed."

Explosive light flashed outside the viewports, the *Drunk
Dancer* quaking as enemy fire ranged closer.

Brudi sighed in disappointment. "The transport fumbled its
first approach. They're reorienting for another try."

"Coordinates for the jump are in," Jula told him. "Countdown commencing." She swung around to face Shryne. "I'm
sorry, Roan."

He nodded in understanding. "You did what you could."

The ship shook again.

"Transport is aboard," Brudi said suddenly.

Jula clamped her hands on the yoke. "Divert power to the
sublights. Give us all the distance you can."

"We're going to get our stern burned," Brudi warned.

"Small price to pay."

"Hyperspace engines engaged."

Jula reached for the control stick. "Now!"

And the distant stars became streaks of light.

Brudi hadn't said that the transport was *safely* aboard, and Shryne knew why the moment he and Starstone reached the docking bay. The wedge-shaped ship had skidded in on its port side, gouging the deck, destroying arrays of landing lights, reducing two labor droids to spare parts, and ultimately flattening its pointed bow against an interior bulkhead.

No one inside was injured in the crash, however.

Any more than they were already injured.

The six bedraggled Jedi who literally staggered down the transport's crumpled boarding ramp were a mix of alien, human, and humanoid. Neither Shryne nor Starstone knew any of them by sight, name, or reputation. Face and arms burned by blaster-fire, Siadem Forte was a short, thick-bodied human, older than Shryne but still a Knight. His Padawan was a young Togruta named Deran Nalual, who had been blinded during the same firefight in which Forte had been wounded. Klossi Anno, a Chalactan, was also a learner, her Master having died saving her life; where exactly the opposite had happened to Iwo Kulka, a bruised and limping Ho'Din Knight. Unranked human Jedi Jambe Lu and Nam Poorf were agricultural specialists who had been returning to Coruscant from a mission on Bonadan.

On board was a seventh Jedi, who had died during the transport's hyperspace jump to the rendezvous.

Med droids tended to the wounds of new arrivals. Then, after the Jedi had rested and been fed, everyone gathered in the main cabin, where Shryne, Starstone, and a few of the smugglers listened to accounts of savage engagements and close escapes on half a dozen worlds.

As Shryne had guessed, no other clone troopers were known to have refused to obey the Jedi execution order Palpatine was believed to have issued. Two of the Jedi had managed to kill the troopers who had turned on them. Another had escaped and survived by donning clone armor. The pair of Jedi from the Agricultural Corps hadn't been in the company of troopers, but had been fired on and pursued when a shuttle they were aboard had arrived at a Republic orbital facility.

Originally ten in number, they had gathered on Dellalt after receiving a 913 code transmitted by Forte, the eldest among them. It was on Dellalt that they had commandeered the transport, during a battle in which two of the Jedi had been killed and many of the others wounded—and seemingly from Dellalt that the light cruiser and ARC-170s had pursued them.

By the time all the stories had been told and endlessly discussed, the *Drunk Dancer* had emerged from hyperspace in a remote system of barren planets that had long served Jula and her crew as a hideout of sorts. Relieved of her pilot duties, she entered the main cabin and sat down next to Shryne just as talk was turning to HoloNet accounts of what had occurred on Coruscant following Palpatine's decree that the Grand Army had been victorious, and that the Republic was now an Empire.

"Some of the information released has to be false or exaggerated," the agronomist Jambe Lu said. "Holoimages we've seen thus far show that the Temple was certainly attacked. But I refuse to accept that *everyone* was killed. Surely Palpatine would have ordered the troopers to spare the younglings. Perhaps some instructors and administrators, as well."

"I agree," Lu's partner, Nam Poorf, said. "If Emperor Palpatine had wanted for some reason to exterminate the entire Jedi order, he could have done so at the start of the war."

Forte ridiculed the idea. "And who would have led the Grand Army—*Senators*? What's more, even if you're correct about the Temple, the best we can hope is that an untold number of Jedi are imprisoned somewhere. What we know to be true is that Masters Windu, Tiin, Fisto, and Kolar died in the attempt to arrest Palpatine; and that Ki-Adi-Mundi, Plo Koon, and other High Council members are reported to have been assassinated on Separatist worlds."

"Any word on Yoda or Obi-Wan?" Shryne asked Forte.

"Nothing more than HoloNet speculation."

"About Skywalker, as well," Nam Poorf said. "Although we heard rumors on Dellalt that he died on Coruscant."

The Ho'Din Jedi Knight glanced meaningfully at Shryne. "If Skywalker is dead, does that mean that the prophecy died with him?"

"What prophecy?" Forte's sightless Togruta Padawan asked.

Again, Iwo Kulka looked at Shryne. "I see no reason for secrecy now, Roan Shryne."

"An ancient prophecy," Shryne explained for the benefit of Nalual, Klossi Anno, and the two agronomists, "that a Chosen One would be born in the dark times to restore balance to the Force."

"And Anakin Skywalker was thought to have been this Chosen One?" Lu said in astonishment.

"Some members of the High Council believed there was justification for thinking so." Shryne looked at Iwo Kulka. "So in answer to your question, I don't know where the prophecy fits into all that's happened. Foretelling was never my area of expertise."

It came out more bluntly than Shryne had intended. But he was exasperated by the fact that everyone was talking around the real issues: that the Jedi were suddenly homeless and rudderless, and that important decisions had to made.

"What matters," he said into the silence that followed his sarcasm, "is that we—that *all* Jedi—are prey. Palpatine's initial actions might not have been premeditated. We'll leave that for the historians to determine. But he's intent on eliminating us now, and we're probably placing ourselves at greater risk by grouping together."

"But that's exactly what we have to do," Starstone argued. "Everything that has just been said is reason enough to remain together. Jedi being held prisoner. The younglings. The unknown fates of Masters Yoda and Kenobi . . ."

"To what end, Padawan?" Forte said.

"If nothing else, to prevent the Jedi flame from being extinguished." Starstone glanced around, in search of a sympathetic face. That she couldn't find one didn't prevent her from continuing. "This isn't the first time the Jedi order has been brought to the brink of extinction. Five thousand years ago the Sith thought that they could destroy the Jedi, but all their attempts failed, and the Sith Lords only ended up destroying one another. Palpatine might not be a Sith, but, in time, his greed and lust for power will be his undoing."

"That's a very hopeful attitude to take," Forte said. "But I don't see how it helps us now."

"Your best chance of surviving is in the Tingel Arm," Jula said suddenly, "while Palpatine's full control is still limited to the inner systems."

"Suppose we do go there," Starstone said while separate discussions were breaking out. "Sure, we can assume new identities and find remote worlds to hide on. We can mask our Force abilities from others, even from other Forceful individuals. But is that what you want to do? Is that what the *Force* wants for us?"

While the Jedi were considering it, Shryne said: "Have any of you heard the name *Lord Vader*?"

"Who is Vader?" Lu asked for all of them.

"The Sith who killed my Master on Murkhana," Starstone said before Shryne could speak.

Iwo Kulka looked hard at Shryne. "A Sith?"

Shryne lifted his eyes to the ceiling, then looked at Starstone. "I thought we agreed—"

"Vader fought with a crimson lightsaber," she interrupted.

Shryne took a calming breath and began again. "Vader assured the troopers on Murkhana that he wasn't a Jedi. And I'm not sure what he is. Possibly humanoid, but not fully organic."

"Like Grievous," Forte assumed.

"Again—possible. The black suit he wears appears to keep him alive. Beyond that, I don't know how much of Vader is cyborg."

Poorf was shaking his head in confusion. "I don't understand. Is this Vader an Imperial commander?"

"He's superior to the commanders. The troopers showed him the sort of respect they'd reserve for someone of very high rank or status. My guess is that he answers directly to Palpatine." Shryne felt exasperation surfacing once more. "What I'm getting at is that Vader is the one we need to worry about. He *will* track us down."

"What if we get to him first?" Forte said.

Shryne gestured broadly. "We're eight against someone who may be Sith, and one of the largest armies ever amassed. What does that tell you?"

"We wouldn't go after him immediately," Starstone said,

quickly picking up on Forte's question. "Palpatine isn't embraced by everyone." She looked at Jula. "You yourself said that his reach is limited to the inner systems. Which means we could work covertly to persuade Outer Rim Senators and military leaders to join our cause."

"You're neglecting the fact that most species are now convinced that we had a hand in starting and perpetuating the war," Shryne said strongly. "Even those who aren't convinced would risk too much by helping us, even by providing sanctuary."

Starstone was not deterred. "We were two yesterday, and we're eight today. Tomorrow we could be twenty or even fifty. We can keep transmitting—"

"I can't allow that," Jula cut her off. "Not from my ship, anyway." She looked at Forte and the others. "You say you were tracked from Dellalt. But just suppose the Empire is also monitoring Jedi frequencies for Nine Thirteen transmissions? All Palpatine would have to do is wait until you were all in one place, then send in the clones. Or this Vader character."

Starstone's silence lasted only a moment. "There's another way. If we could learn which worlds Jedi were assigned to, we could actively search for survivors."

Lu thought about it for a moment. "The only way to learn that would be by accessing the Temple's data banks."

"Not from the *Drunk Dancer,* you won't," Jula said.

"Couldn't happen anyway, Captain," Eyl Dix said. "Accessing the data banks would require a much more powerful hyperwave transceiver than we have, and one that would be very hard to come by."

Dix glanced at Filli for corroboration.

"Eyl's right," Filli said. Then, around a forming grin, he added: "But I know just where we can find one."

Rain was rare on weather-controlled Coruscant, but every so often microclimatic storms would build in the bustling sky and sweep across the technoscape. Today's had blown in from The Works and moved east with great speed, lashing the abandoned Jedi Temple with unprecedented force.

Vader's enhanced hearing could pick up the sound of fat, wind-driven raindrops spattering against the Temple's elegant spires and flat roof, an eerie counterpoint to the sound of his boot heels striking the adamantine floor and echoing in the darkened, deserted corridors. Sidious had sent him here on a mission, ostensibly to search the archives for certain Sith holocrons long rumored to have been brought to the Temple centuries earlier.

But Vader knew the truth.

Sidious wants to rub my masked face in the aftermath of the slaughter I spearheaded.

Though the corpses had been removed by stormtroopers and droids, most of the spilled blood washed away, scorch marks on the walls and ceiling attested to the surprise attack. Columns lay toppled, heritage tapestries hung in shreds, rooms reeked of carnage.

But evidence of a less tangible sort also existed.

The Temple teemed with ghosts.

What might have been the wind wending into holed hallways never before penetrated sounded like the funereal keening of spirits waiting to be avenged. What might have been the resonance of the footfalls of Commander Appo's stormtroopers sounded like the beat of distant war drums. What might have been smoke from fires that should have gone out weeks earlier seemed more like wraiths writhing in torment.

Emperor Palpatine had yet to announce his plans for that sad shell of a place. Whether it was to be razed, converted into his palace, deeded to Vader as some sort of cruel joke, or perhaps left as a mausoleum for all of Coruscant to gaze on, a reminder of what would befall those who kindled Palpatine's disfavor.

Most of Vader's Anakin memories grew fainter by the day, but not Anakin's memories of what had happened here. They were as fresh as this morning's sunrise, glimpsed from the rooftop chamber in which Vader rested. True sleep continued to lie just out of reach, an object pursued in vain in an unsettling dream. He no longer had visions, either. That ability, that double-edged ability, seemingly had been burned out of him on Mustafar.

But Vader remembered.

Remembered being in thrall of what he had done in Palpatine's office. Watching the old man plead for his life; listening to the old man promising that only he had the power to save Padmé; rushing to his defense. Sith lightning hurling an astonished Mace Windu through what had been a window . . .

Anakin kneeling before Sidious and being dubbed Vader.

Go to the Jedi Temple, Sidious had said. *We will catch them off balance. Do what must be done, Lord Vader. Do not hesitate. Show no mercy. Only then will you be strong enough with the dark side to save Padmé.*

And so he had gone to the Temple.

Instrument of the same resolute intent that had carried Obi-Wan to Mustafar with one goal in mind: death to the enemy.

In his mind's eye Vader saw his and the 501st's march to the Temple gates, their wrathful attack, the mad moments of blood-lust, the dark side unleashed in all its crimson fury. Some moments he remembered more clearly than others: pitting his blade against that of swordmaster Cin Drallig, beheading some of the very Masters who had instructed him in the ways of the Force, and, of course, his cold extermination of the younglings, and with them the future of the Jedi order.

He had wondered beforehand: could he do it? Still new to the dark side, would he be able to call on its power to guide his hand and lightsaber? In answer, the dark side had whispered: *They are orphans. They are without family or friends. There is nothing that can be done with them. They are better off dead.*

But this recalling, weeks later, curdled his blood.

This place should never have been built!

In fact, he hadn't killed the Jedi to serve Sidious, though Sidious was meant to believe just that. In his arrogance Sidious was unaware that Anakin had seen through him. Had the Sith Lord thought he would simply shrug off the fact that, from the start, Sidious had been manipulating Anakin *and* the war?

No, he hadn't killed the Jedi in service to Sidious, or, for that matter, to demonstrate his allegiance to the order of the Sith.

He had executed Sidious's command because the Jedi would never have understood Anakin's decision to sacrifice Mace and the rest in order that Padmé might survive the tragic death she suffered in Anakin's visions. More important, the Jedi would have attempted to stand in the way of the decisions he and Padmé would have needed to make regarding the fate of the galaxy.

Beginning with the assassination of Sidious.

Oh, but on Mustafar she had worked herself into a state over what he had done at the Temple, so much so that she hadn't heard a word he was saying. Instead she had made up her mind that he had come to care more about power than he cared for her.

As if one matters without the other!

And then cursed Obi-Wan had shown himself, interrupting before Anakin could explain fully that everything he had done, in Palpatine's office and at the Temple, had all been for *her* sake, and for the sake of their unborn child. Had Obi-Wan not arrived he would have persuaded her to understand—he would have *made* her understand—and, together, they would have moved against the Sith Lord . . .

The rasp of Vader's breathing became more audible.

Flexing his artificial hands did nothing to waylay his rage, so he hunched his broad shoulders under the armor pectoral and heavy cloak, shuddering.

Why didn't she listen to me? Why didn't any of them listen to me?

His anger continued to build as he neared the Temple's archives room, where he parted company with Commander Appo and his stormtroopers, as well as with the members of the Internal Security Bureau who, Vader was given to understand, had their separate mission to perform.

He paused at the entrance to the library's vast and towering main hall, shaken not by memory but by memory's effect on his still-healing heart and lungs. The mask's optical hemispheres imparted a murkiness to the normally well-lighted hall, which had once boasted row after row of neatly arranged and cataloged holobooks and storage disks.

Blood let here still showed in maroon constellations that marred large areas of the floor and speckled some of the few still-standing sculpture-topped plinths that lined both sides of the long hallway.

Even if he had killed Sidious, even if he had won the war single-handedly for the Republic, the Jedi would have fought him to the bitter end. They might even have insisted on taking custody of his and Padmé's child, for their offspring would have been powerful in the Force indeed. Perhaps beyond measure! If only the High Council Masters hadn't been so set in their ways, so deceived by their own pride, they would have grasped that the Jedi *needed* to be brought down. Like the Republic itself, their order had grown stale, self-serving, corrupt.

And yet, if the High Council had seen fit to recognize his power, had granted him the status of Master, perhaps he could have abided their continued existence. But to call him the Chosen One only to hold him back; to lie to him and expect him to lie for them . . . What had they imagined the outcome would be? *Old fools.*

He understood now why they had discouraged use of the dark side. Because they had feared losing the power base they enjoyed, even though enslavement to attachment was what had helped pull down the Sith! The Jedi had been conspirators in their own downfall, complicit in the reemergence of the dark side, and as important to its victory as Sidious had been.

Sidious—their *ally.*

Attachment to power was the downfall of all orders, because most beings were incapable of controlling power, and power ended up controlling them. That, too, had been the cause of the galaxy's tip into disorder; the reason for Sidious's effortless rise to the top.

Vader's heart pounded in his chest, and the respirator fed his heart's needs with rapid breaths. For his own health and sanity, he realized that he would have to avoid places that whipped his anger into such a frenzy.

The recognition that he would probably never be able to set foot on Naboo or Tatooine tore an anguished moan from him that toppled the rest of the plinths as if they were dominoes, leaving their crowning bronzium busts sliding and spinning across the polished, blood-flecked floor.

Hollowed by the mournful outpouring, he supported himself against a broken column for what seemed an eternity.

The chirping of the comlink on his belt returned him to the present, and after a long moment he activated it.

From the device's small speaker issued the urgent voice of the Internal Security Bureau chief, Armand Isard, communicating from the Temple's data room.

Someone, Isard reported, was attempting remote access of the Jedi beacon databanks.

I n the dimly lighted corridor of a forlorn Separatist facility far across the stars, Shryne stopped to gaze at one of the niched statues that lined both walls.

Six meters high and exquisitely carved in the round, the statue was equal parts humanoid and winged beast. While it might have been modeled on an actual creature, the deliberate vagueness of its facial features suggested some mythical creature from antiquity. The indistinct visage was partly concealed by a hooded robe that fell to taloned feet. Identical statues stood in identical recesses for as far as Shryne could see in the wan light.

The complex of ancient, geometric structures the Separatists had converted into a communications facility had certainly stood on Jaguada's moon for thousands of standard years; perhaps tens of thousands of years. Scanners classified the metal used in the construction as "unidentifiable," and lightning fissures in the foundations of the largest buildings indicated that the complex had suffered the effect of the small satellite's every tectonic shift and meteor impact.

The light of Shryne's luma revealed details of the statue's intricately rendered wings. Locally quarried, the worked stone matched the striated rock of the sheer cliffs that walled the complex on two sides, from which had been carved statues thirty meters tall, the gaze of their time-dimpled faces directed not down the narrow valley over which they stood silent guard, but toward the moon's eastern horizon.

Based on similarities to holoimages she had seen of statuary on Ziost and Korriban, Starstone believed that the site could date to the time of the ancient Sith, and that the Separatists' reoccupation of the complex was in keeping with the fact that Count Dooku had become a Sith Lord.

The moon was arid Jaguada's sole companion in a desolate system slaved to a dying star, far from major hyperlanes. The fact that remote Jaguada should host a garrison of clone troopers in the desert planet's modest population center struck Shryne as something of a mystery. But the troopers' presence could owe to plans to salvage the Separatist war machines that had been left abandoned on the moon, as troopers were known to be doing in numerous Outer Rim systems.

This wasn't the first time Jula and her band of smugglers had visited the moon, but the secrecy that had attended the recent arrival had less to do with prior knowledge of the terrain than to the *Drunk Dancer*'s jamming capabilities. The ship had inserted into stationary orbit on the moon's far side without being detected by the Imperial troops on Jaguada, leaving Shryne, Starstone, and Jula, along with some of the crew members and Jedi, to ride down the well in the drop ship, slipping into the moon's thin atmosphere like a sabacc card up a gambler's sleeve.

Heaped with windblown sand, the facility's retrofitted landing platform appeared not to have seen use in several years. Shryne's estimate was borne out by the fact that the hundreds of deactivated droids that welcomed the drop ship party were early-generation Trade Federation infantry droids, of the sort controlled by centralized computers rather than super battle droids equipped with autonomous droid brains. As if the surfeit of silent war machines didn't render the place ghostly enough, there were the fanged carvings affixed to each doorway lintel, and the kilometers of parched corridors studded with gruesome statuary.

Access to the structure that housed the communications center hadn't been a problem, since whatever remote transmissions deactivated the droids had silenced the facility, as well. The power generators, however, were still functional, and Filli Bitters and Eyl Dix had been able to override the deactivation codes and bring some of the internal illuminators to life, along with the hyperwave transceiver the Jedi were intent on using to slice into the Temple beacon database.

Shryne had left the slicers, Starstone, and some of the other Jedi to what he regarded as their business, and had been wandering the aged corridors ever since, thinking through his dilemma.

Even this deep into the complex, the ceramacrete floors were covered with sand and bits of other inorganic debris carried in by the moon's constant, nerve-racking winds. To Shryne, the combination of wind and gloom couldn't have been more apropos to puzzling out whether his coming to Jaguada was in accord with the will of the Force, or merely symptomatic of a deep denial of the truth. Yet another attempt to convince himself that his actions had some import.

Perhaps if he hadn't recognized in Starstone and the other Jedi a powerful need to *believe*—a need to hold on to something in the wake of all that had been snatched from them—he might have tried harder to discourage them. But their need wasn't enough to keep him from asking himself whether this was the way he wanted to spend the rest of his days, hanging on to a dream that the Jedi order could be reassembled; that a handful of Jedi could mount an insurgency against as formidable an enemy as Emperor Palpatine. He couldn't escape the feeling that the Force had thrown him a curious curve once again. Just when he thought he was through with Jedi business, and that the Force had deserted him, he was in deeper than ever.

Roan Shryne, who had lost not one but *two* learners to the war.

Jula's words about reconnecting with family kept replaying themselves. Perhaps he wasn't so far gone that he couldn't actually benefit from attachment, if only as a means of making himself more human. But never to use the Force again . . . that was the bigger issue. His ability to sense the Force in others was so much a part of his nature that he doubted he would simply be able to set it aside, along with his robes and lightsaber.

He suspected that he would always feel like a freak among normal humans, and the idea of exiling himself among aliens with similar talents for telepathy held little appeal.

For the time being he was willing to remain with Starstone, if not mentor her. That was an entirely different problem: Starstone and the others were looking to him for leadership he simply couldn't provide, in part because leadership had never been his strength, but more because the war had eroded whatever measure of self-confidence he had once possessed. With any luck the attempts at locating surviving Jedi would lead eventually to a Jedi of greater Mastery than Shryne, to whom he could surrender the lead and gracefully bow out.

Or perhaps there would be no returns from the Temple beacon database.

Archived HoloNet images he had accessed while aboard the *Drunk Dancer* had showed smoke pouring from the Jedi Temple in the aftermath of the troopers' attack. So it was certainly conceivable that the beacon had been damaged or destroyed, or that the databases had been hopelessly corrupted.

Which would cause an abrupt end to the search.

And to the dreaming, as well.

He had begun to move deeper into the corridor when Jula appeared out of the gloom, a luma in hand, and fell into step beside him.

"Where are the guides when you need them?" she said.

"Just what I was thinking."

She had her jacket folded over her arm, a blaster holstered on her hip. Shryne wondered for a moment what her life might have been like had he remained in her care. Would her marriage to Shryne's father have endured, or would what seemed an unquenchable thirst for adventure have placed Jula just where she was now? Save with Roan at her side, part of her crew, her partner in crime.

"How are they doing back there?" he asked, nodding with his chin toward the communications room.

"Well, Filli's already sliced into the beacon. No surprises there. Now I suppose it's a matter of worming into the database itself." She regarded Shryne while they walked. "You're not interested in being there when they start downloading the names and possible whereabouts of your scattered confederates?"

Shryne shook his head. "Starstone and Forte can see to that. My credits aren't on their succeeding, anyway."

Jula laughed. "Then you won't get any side action from me." She looked at him askance. "Olee and Filli are two of a kind, don't you think?"

"I did for a while. But I figure she's already found her life partner."

"The Force, you mean." Jula forced an exhale. "That's dedication of a scary sort."

Shryne stopped walking and turned to her. "Why'd you say yes to taking us here, Jula?"

She smiled lightly. "I thought I'd made myself clear. I'm still hoping to convince you to join us." Scanning his face for clues, she asked: "Any movement at all on that front?"

"I don't know what I'm thinking."

"But you'll keep me updated?"

"Sure I will."

Shortly they reached the end of the corridor of winged statues and turned the corner into an intersecting corridor lined with smaller carvings.

In the bobbing light of the lumas, Shryne said: "How did Filli know about this place?"

"We made a couple of runs here six or so years back. Communications hardware for the hyperwave transceiver. And before you go all patriotic on me, Roan, we didn't realize that the facility would eventually be used to eavesdrop on Republic transmissions."

"That would have stopped you—knowing that a war against the Republic was brewing?"

"It might have. But you have to understand, we were hungry, like a lot of other freelancers in the outlying systems. It still amazes me that Coruscant remained in the dark about what was going on out here after Dooku formed the Separatist movement. Weapons buildup, Baktoid Armor Workshop installing foundries on dozens of worlds . . . Back then, there was a lot to be said for free and unrestricted trade."

"I would have figured that would be bad for business."

"Yes and no. Free trade invited competition, but it also meant we didn't have to worry about being chased by local system defense forces or Jedi Knights."

"Who hired you to bring in the comm hardware?"

"Someone named Tyranus, although none of us ever met him face-to-face."

"Tyranus," Shryne repeated, in uncertain recollection.

"Ring a bell?"

"Maybe. I'll have to run it by the librarian—Olee. So when did the Separatists pull up stakes?"

"Shortly after the Battle of Geonosis—"

Shryne came to a sudden halt in front of a tall, cloaked statue wearing a goggle-eyed mask.

"Gruesome," Jula started; then the corridor's regularly placed illuminators suddenly flooded the area with light. Squinting, she said, "I thought the idea was to avoid drawing too much attention to ourselves."

Distant rumblings overpowered Shryne's response. In one swift action, he drew and ignited the lightsaber clipped to his belt.

Jula raised her brows in surprise. "Where'd you come by that?"

"It belonged to the Master of one of the Padawans." Spinning on his heel, he began to race back toward the communications control room, Jula right behind him.

Shryne realized that the rumbling sounds were being made by doors and hatchways opening and closing. He hastened his pace, weaving through stands of deactivated battle droids.

In the control room Filli, his spiked hair matted to his skull, was doing furious input at a console, while Eyl Dix and Starstone paced behind him, Olee gnawing away at her lower lip. A few meters away Jedi Knights Forte and Iwo Kulka looked as if they were having second thoughts about what they had set in motion.

"Filli, what's going on?" Jula shouted.

The slicer's right hand pointed to Starstone, while his left continued to fly across the keys of a control pad. "She told me to do it!"

"Do what?" Shryne said, looking from Starstone to Filli and back again.

"Boost the transceiver with a burst from the power generator," Dix answered for Filli.

"We didn't have enough juice to download from the database," Starstone said. "I thought it would be fine."

Shryne's forehead wrinkled in confusion. "So what's the problem?"

"The generator wants to reactivate the entire facility," Filli said in a rush of words. "I can't get it to shut down!"

Slamming, hissing sounds began to replace the rumble of sliding doors.

Jula looked sharply at Shryne. "This entire place is sealing up."

A series of determined clicks and ready tones punctuated the din raised by descending hatches. All at once every battle droid in the control room powered up.

Swinging its thin head toward him and raising its blaster rifle, the battle droid standing closest to Shryne said: *"Intruders."*

26

Behind Armand Isard and the two Internal Security Bureau technicians seated at the Temple beacon control console, Vader stood with his arms folded across his chest, Commander Appo at his right hand.

"I want to know how the beacon was accessed," Vader said.

"By means of a Jedi transceiver, Lord Vader," the tech closest to Armand said.

"Cross-check the transceiver code with the identity database," the ISB chief said, anticipating Vader.

"The name should be coming up in a moment," the other tech said, eyes glued to rapidly scrolling text on one of the display screens. "Chatak," he added a moment later. "Bol Chatak."

The sound of Vader's breathing filled the ensuing silence.

Shryne and Starstone, he thought. Obviously they had been in possession of Chatak's beacon transceiver when they had evaded him at Murkhana. Now they were attempting to determine the location of other Jedi when Order Sixty-Six had been issued. Certainly they were hoping to establish contact with survivors, hoping to pick up the pieces of their shattered order.

And . . . what?

Devise their revenge? Unlikely, since that would entail calling on the dark side. Formulate a plan to kill the Emperor? Perhaps. Although, ignorant of the fact that Palpatine was a Sith, they would not plot an assassination. So perhaps they were contemplating an attack on the Emperor's enforcer?

Vader considered reaching out to Shryne through the Force, but rejected the idea.

"What is the source of the transmission?" he asked finally.

"The Jaguada system, Lord Vader," the first technician said. "More precisely, the moon of the system's only inhabited world."

A large holomap of the galaxy emerged from the console's holoprojector. Linked to myriad databases throughout the Temple, the map made use of a palette of colors to indicate trouble spots. Just now, in preservation of the moment Order Sixty-Six had been executed, more than two hundred worlds glowed blood red.

Perhaps this explained why Sidious hadn't had the Temple dismantled, Vader thought. So he could regard it from his lofty new throne room and *gloat*.

The holomap began to close tighter and tighter on a remote area of the Outer Rim. When, finally, the Jaguada system hung in midair, Vader strode into its midst.

"This moon," he said, gesturing with the forefinger of his black-gloved hand.

"Yes, Lord Vader," the tech said.

Vader glanced at Appo, who had already comlinked Central Operations on Coruscant.

"The moon is the site of an abandoned Separatist communications facility," Appo said. "Whoever is in possession of the Jedi transceiver must have brought the facility's hyperspace communications network online."

"Do we have any vessels in that sector, Commander?"

"No vessels, Lord Vader," Appo said. "But there is a small Imperial garrison on Jaguada."

"Instruct the garrison commander to scramble his troopers immediately."

"Capture or kill, Lord Vader?"

"Either would please me."

"I understand."

Vader cupped the holoimage of the tiny moon in his hand. "I have you now," he said quietly, and made a fist.

The lightsaber Klossi Anno had given Shryne felt foreign in his hand, but it was finely wrought, and its dense blue blade was perfect for deflecting the hail of blaster bolts the battle droids had unleashed. Beside him Jula was firing steadily and with impressive accuracy, dropping those droids Shryne's parried bolts didn't. Crouched behind the control console, Filli and Dyx were somehow managing to continue entering commands on the keyboards while the flashing lightsabers of Starstone, Forte, and Kulka provided cover.

In the control room and elsewhere in the facility, alert sirens were warbling, lights were flashing, and hatchways were sealing.

"Whatever you did, undo it!" Shryne said to Filli without missing a blaster bolt. "Deactivate the droids!"

A glance at display screens that had been sleeping moments earlier showed that scores of infantry droids and droidekas were hurrying toward the control center from all areas of the complex.

"Filli, hurry!" Jula added for emphasis. "More are headed this way!"

Shryne took a moment to look around the control room. The doorway through which he and Jula had entered was one of three, positioned 120 degrees from one another.

"Filli, can you seal us in here?" he shouted.

"Probably," the slicer yelled back. "But we may have bigger troubles."

"We can handle the droidekas," Forte assured him.

Filli raised his head above the console and shook it negatively. "Someone at the Temple knows that we've sliced in!"

Starstone whirled on him. "How do you—"

"We're getting an echo from the beacon," Eyl Dix explained.

Redirecting a flurry of bolts, Shryne reduced six droids to shrapnel. "How long before the Temple ascertains our location?"

"Depends on who's at the other end," Filli said.

"Then cancel the link!" Jula said.

"We're still downloading," Starstone said. "We need all the data we can get."

Shryne glowered at her. "What good is all the data in the Temple if we're not around to put it to use?"

She narrowed her eyes. "I knew you'd say that. Do it, Filli," she said over her shoulder. "Zero the link." Glancing apologetically at Forte and Kulka, she added: "We'll make the best of what we have."

"Done," Filli announced.

Shryne's deflection shot dismantled another droid. "Now shut the power down before we're shot to death or entombed in here!"

A moment later the droids returned to their inert status, and the control room was plunged into darkness. Five lumas provided just enough light to see by.

"I trust that someone knows the way out of here," Forte said.

"I do," Dix said, her antennae standing straight up.

"Then let's hope the exit's still open," Shryne said.

Filli nodded. "It is. I got a look at the security screen before we cut the power."

"Good job," Shryne started to say, when blasterfire erupted from somewhere outside the control room.

"You said you zeroed it, Filli," Jula snapped.

He spread his hands in confusion. "I did!"

Shryne listened closely to the distant discharges. "Those aren't droid blasters," he said after a moment. "Those are DC-fifteens."

Starstone stared at him. "Stormtroopers? Here?"

Jula's comlink chimed and she grabbed for it. "Archyr," she said for everyone's benefit.

"Captain, we've got company," Archyr said from the drop ship. "Troopers from the Jaguada garrison."

Shryne traded looks with Starstone.

"Whoever's at the Temple didn't waste any time," she said.

Shryne nodded. "They must have been monitoring us from the start."

"How many troopers?" Jula was asking Archyr.

"A couple of squads," he said. "Skeck and I are pinned down on the landing platform. But most of the troopers have headed inside."

"I can try to seal the entrances . . ." Filli said.

"No, don't," Shryne cut him off. "You think you can you rig a delay to the power generator?"

His luma grasped in his teeth, Filli began to riffle through his tool kit. "I'm sure I can cobble something together," he said.

Shryne turned to Jula. "How long will it take us to reach the front entrance, closest to the cliffs?"

She threw him a questioning look. "That'll dump us way downvalley, Roan. A good kilometer from the drop ship."

He nodded. "But we avoid engaging troopers on the way out."

Her brow continued to furrow. "Then why do you want Filli to—" She grinned in sudden revelation and turned to Filli. "Set it to power up in a standard quarter, Filli."

"That's cutting things pretty close, Captain."

"The closer, the better," she said.

By the time a holotransmission from the commander of the Jaguada garrison reached the Temple beacon room, Vader already knew that something had gone wrong.

"I'm sorry, Lord Vader," the helmeted stormtrooper was saying, "but we're trapped inside the facility with several hundred reactivated infantry and destroyer droids." The commander dodged blaster bolts and returned fire at something distant from the holocam's transmission grid. "All accesses sealed when the facility powered up."

"Where are the Jedi?" Vader asked.

"They left before the facility went online. We're trapped in here until we find a way to blow one of the doors."

"Did you destroy the ship the Jedi arrived in?"

"Negative," the commander said as bolts lanced the air around him. "The smugglers detonated a magpulse while the second squad was advancing. My troopers were expecting it, but in the time it took our hardware to reboot, the Jedi got their ship airborne."

Off cam a trooper said: "Fallback positions two and three have been overrun, Commander. We'll have to make a stand here."

"There's just too many of them!" the commander said as diagonal lines of noise began to interfere with the transmission.

Abruptly, it derezzed completely.

Armand Isard and the ISB technicians busied themselves at the beacon controls, if only to avoid having to look at Vader.

"Lord Vader," Appo said, "Jaguada base reports that jump points are limited in that system, and that they are scanning for vagrant traces of the Jedi ship. They may be able to calculate possible escape vectors."

Vader nodded.

Infuriated, he turned and stormed from the beacon room, wishing he had the power to simply reach out and pluck the Jedi from the sky.

Conclude their extermination.

Sidious was wrong, he told himself as he hurried through the empty hallways.

They are a threat.

The *Drunk Dancer* tore through mottled hyperspace, leaving desolate Jaguada light-years behind. Skeck had sustained a nasty blaster burn to his right arm during the troopers' attempt to disable the drop ship, but no one else had been hurt. Emerging from the facility moments before Filli's time delay initiated the power generator, Shryne and the others had raced upvalley to the landing platform and had arrived in time to catch a squad of Imperials in a crossfire.

Sealed inside the facility, the remaining squads were up to their T-visors in reactivated battle droids.

After Skeck's wound had been bandaged, Shryne had retired to the dormitory cabin space Jula had provided for the Jedi. He had always had a fondness for hyperspace travel—more, the sense of being outside time—and was kneeling in meditation when he sensed Starstone approaching the cabin. Simultaneous with her excited entry he rose to his feet, eyes on the sheaf of flimsiplast printouts she was holding.

"We have data on hundreds of Jedi," she said, rattling the printouts. "We know where more than seventy Masters were at the end of the war—when the clone commanders received their orders."

Accepting the proffered flimsies, Shryne thumbed through them, then glanced at Starstone. "How many of these hundreds do you think might actually have survived the attacks?"

She gave her head a quick shake. "I'm not even going to try to guess. We can begin our search with systems closest to Mossak, and fan out from there toward Mygeeto, Saleucami, and Kashyyyk."

Shryne shook the flimsies. "Has it occurred to you that if *we* have this information, then so does the Empire? What do you think our adversaries were doing in the Temple beacon room, playing hide-and-seek?"

Starstone winced at the harshness of his tone, but only briefly. "Has it occurred to you that our adversaries, as you call them, were there precisely because a good many Jedi survived? It's crucial that we reach those survivors before they're hunted down. Or are you proposing that we leave them to the Empire— to Vader and his stormtroopers?"

Shryne made a start at replying, then bit back his words and motioned to the edge of the nearest cot. "Sit down, and try for a moment to stop thinking like a HoloNet hero."

When Starstone ultimately lowered herself to the cot, Shryne sat opposite her.

"Don't misunderstand me," he began. "Your goal couldn't be more noble. And for all I know there are five hundred Jedi scattered throughout the Rim in need of rescue. *My* point is, I don't want to see your name added to the casualty list. What happened at Jaguada is only a foretaste of what's in store for us if we continue to band together."

"I—"

Shryne stopped her before she could go on. "Think about the final beacon message we received at Murkhana. The message didn't tell us to gather together and coordinate a strike on Coruscant, or on Palpatine, or even on the troopers. It instructed us, each of us who received it, to *hide*. Yoda or whoever ordered the transmission knew that the Jedi were in a fight we couldn't win. The message was a way of saying just that—that the order is over and done with. That the Jedi are finished."

He hid his ruefulness. "Does that mean that you have to stop honoring the Force? Of course not. All of us will live out our lives honoring the Force. But not with lightsabers in hand, Olee. With right action, and right thinking."

"I'd rather die honoring the Force with my lightsaber," she said.

He had expected as much. "How is dying honoring the Force, when you could be out doing good works, passing on to others all that you've learned about the Force?"

"Is that what you plan to do—devote yourself to good works?"

Shryne smiled. "Right now I only know what I'm *not* going to do, and that's help rush you into a grave on some remote world." He held her gaze. "I'm sorry. But I've already lost two Padawans to this rotten war, and I don't want to lose you to it."

"Even though I'm not your learner?"

He nodded. "Even though."

She sighed with purpose. "I appreciate your concern for me, Master—and I *will* call you that because right now you're the only Master we have. But the Force tells me that we can make a difference, and I can't turn my back on that. Master Chatak instilled in me every day that I should follow the Force's lead, and that's exactly what I'm going to do."

She adopted an even more serious look. "Jula believes that you *can* turn your back. The Force is with her, but she's not a Jedi, Master. You can't unlearn overnight the teachings and practices of decades. Even if you should succeed, you'll regret it."

Shryne firmed his lips and nodded again. "Then you and I will be parting ways at Mossak."

Sadness pulled down the corners of her mouth. "I wish it didn't have to be this way, Master."

"That doesn't begin to say how I feel about it."

They stood, and he hugged her tenderly.

"You'll tell the others?" he said while she was gathering up the flimsies.

"They already know."

Shryne didn't watch her leave. But no sooner did she exit the cabin than Jula entered.

"Jedi business?"

Shryne looked at her. "You can probably figure it out."

Jula averted her gaze. "Olee's a fine young woman—they're all decent beings. But they're deluded, Roan. It's over. They have to realize that and get on with their lives. You told me that attachment is the root of many of our problems. Well, that includes being so attached to the Jedi order that you can't leave it behind. If being a Jedi means being able to accept what has happened and move on, then they honor the order best by letting go."

She looked at him now. "For some of them it's all about the loss of prestige, and the power to decide what's right or wrong. To believe that everything you do is motivated by the Force, and that you always have the Force on your side. But that's not always the way it works. I've no love for the order, you know that. Sometimes the Jedi caused as many problems as they solved. Now, for whatever reason, whether it's Palpatine or the fact that the Jedi couldn't accept the idea of taking second place to the Republic—the Force isn't necessarily your best ally."

She reached for his hands. "They took you from me once, Roan. I won't let you go a second time without a fight." She laughed lightly. "And that, ladies and gentlemen, concludes my little speech." Gazing at him, she said: "Join us."

"In crime, you mean."

A fire came into her eyes. "We're not criminals. All right, we've done some questionable things, but so have you, and that was in the past. If you come aboard, I promise we'll stick to taking contracts that will allow you to keep on doing good deeds, if that's what it's going to take."

"Such as?" Shryne said.

"Well, we already happen to have a good deed on deck. A contract to transport a former Senator from the Core to his home system."

Shryne allowed his skepticism to show. "Why would a former Senator have to be smuggled to his home system?"

"I don't have all the details. But my guess? The Senator doesn't share the ideals of the new regime."

"Is this a Cash Garrulan contract?"

Jula nodded. "And maybe that's another reason for you to say yes to accepting the offer. Because you owe him for arranging for your escape from Murkhana."

Shryne pretended scorn. "I don't owe Cash any favors."

"Okay. Then you'll do it to honor his memory."

Shryne stared at her.

"Imperial troopers caught up with him soon after all of you left Murkhana. Cash is dead."

From the high-backed chair that was his seat of power, Sidious watched Darth Vader turn and march from the throne room, long black cloak whooshing, black helmet burnished by the lights, anger palpable.

Atop a pedestal alongside the chair sat the holocrons Sidious had asked his apprentice to search out and retrieve from the Jedi archives room. Pyramidal in shape, as opposed to the geodesic Jedi version, the holocrons were repositories of recorded knowledge, accessible only to those who were highly evolved in the use of the Force. Arcane writing inscribed on the holocrons Vader had fetched told Sidious that they had been recorded by Sith during the era of Darth Bane, some one thousand standard years earlier. Sidious didn't have to imagine the content of the devices, because his own Master, Darth Plagueis, had once allowed him access to the *actual* holocrons. The ones stored in the Temple archives room were nothing more than clever forgeries—Sith disinformation of a sort.

Vader didn't realize that they were forgeries, of course, although he was certainly smart enough to have puzzled out that the holocrons were hardly the reason Sidious had ordered him to return to the Temple. But Vader's obvious anger hinted that something unexpected had occurred. Instead of helping Vader come to terms with his choices, the specious mission had muddled his emotions, and perhaps made matters worse.

What is to be done with him? Sidious thought.

Perhaps I will have to send him back to Mustafar, as well.

He mused on a strategy for a moment; then, depressing a button on the control panel set into the arm of the chair, he summoned Mas Amedda into the room.

The tall-horned Chagrian, now the Emperor's interface with sundry utterly dispensable Senatorial groups, moved cautiously between the Imperial Guards who flanked the door, inclining his head in a bow of respect as he approached Sidious.

Through the open door to the waiting room, Sidious glimpsed a familiar face. "Is that Isard outside?"

"Yes, my lord."

"Why is he here?"

"He asked that I inform you of an incident that occurred while he and Lord Vader were in the Temple."

"Indeed?"

"I'm given to understand that unknown parties accessed certain databases, by means of the beacon."

"Jedi," Sidious said, drawing out the word.

"None other, my lord."

"And Lord Vader was on hand to witness this remote infiltration?"

"He was, my lord. Once the source of the transmission was located, Lord Vader ordered a local garrison of troopers to descend on the Jedi responsible."

"The troopers *failed*," Sidious said, leaning forward in interest.

Mas Amedda nodded gravely.

More of his fugitive Jedi, Sidious thought. *He has not allowed himself to be done with them.*

"No matter," he said at last. "What business originally brought you here?"

"Senator Fang Zar, my lord."

Sidious interlocked the fingers of his fat hands and sat back in the chair. "One of the more vocal of the illustrious two thousand who wished to see me removed from office. Has he had a sudden change of heart?"

"Of a sort. You will recall, my lord, that following your announcement that the war had been won, Fang Zar and several other signatories of the Petition of the Two Thousand were briefly detained for questioning by Internal Security Bureau officers."

"Come to the point," Sidious snapped.

"Fang Zar was instructed not to leave Coruscant, and yet he did, managing to reach Alderaan, where he has been in residence at the Aldera Palace ever since. Now, however, the conflict that engulfed his home system has come to an end, and Fang Zar is apparently determined to return to Sern Prime without attracting the notice of the ISB or anyone else."

Sidious considered it. "Continue."

Mas Amedda spread his huge blue hands. "Our only concern is that his sudden return to Sern Prime might prompt dissension in certain outlying systems."

Sidious smiled tolerantly. "Some dissension should be encouraged. Better they rant and rave in the open than plot behind my back. But tell me, does Senator Organa know that Zar was questioned before he fled Coruscant?"

"Perhaps he does now, though it is unlikely he knew when he granted refugee status to Fang Zar."

Sidious grew interested once more. "How is Zar planning to reach Sern Prime without, as you say, attracting attention?"

"We know that he made contact wtih a crime lord on Murkhana—"

"Murkhana?"

"Yes, my lord. Perhaps he wishes to avoid involving Senator Organa in his predicament."

Sidious fell silent for a long moment, attuned to the currents of the Force. Currents linking Vader and Murkhana, and now Zar and Murkhana. And perhaps fugitive Jedi and Murkhana . . .

Into his thoughts came the words of Darth Plagueis.

Tell me what you regard as your greatest strength, so I will know how best to undermine you; tell me of your greatest fear, so I will know which I must force you to face; tell me what you cherish most, so I will know what to take from you; and tell me what you crave, so that I might deny you . . .

"Perhaps it would be more prudent for Fang Zar to remain on Alderaan awhile longer," he said finally.

Mas Amedda bowed his head. "Shall I inform Senator Organa of your wish?"

"No. Lord Vader should deal with the situation."

"To deflect his hunger for the Jedi," the Chagrian risked saying.

Sidious shot him a look. "To *sharpen* it."

29

Perhaps it was because Alderaan presented such a pleasant picture from deep space that it had enjoyed such a long history of peace, prosperity, and tolerance.

Even deeper into its intoxicating atmosphere, closer to its montage of alabaster clouds, blue seas, and green plains, the picture held. Coruscant's neighbor in the Core was a gem of a world.

The pacific impression didn't begin to diminish until one reached street level on the island-city of Aldera, and only then as a result of the day's activities, which demonstrated that for tolerance to endure, voice had to be granted to all, even when free expression challenged the perpetuation of peace.

Bail Organa understood this, as had his predecessors in the Galactic Senate. But Bail's compassion for those who had taken to Aldera's narrow streets was not a case of noblesse oblige, for he shared the concerns of the demonstrators and had deep sympathy for their cause. As many said of Bail, were it not for genetics, he might have been a Jedi. And indeed for most of his adult life he had been a valued friend of the order.

He stood in plain sight of the crowds, on a balcony of the

Royal Palace, in the heart of Aldera, which itself lay in the embrace of green mountains, their gentle summits sparkling with freshly fallen snow. Below him marched hundreds of thousands of demonstrators—refugees representing scores of species displaced by the war, bundled up in colorful clothing against the mountains' frigid downdrafts. Many of the refugees had been on Alderaan since the earliest days of the Separatist movement, living in housing Alderaan had provided; many more were recently arrived onplanet, to show their support. Now that the war had ended, almost all of them were eager to return to their home systems, pick up the pieces of their shattered lives, and reunite with members of their widely dispersed families.

But the Empire was attempting to thwart them.

Placards flashed and holoimages sprang from hand- and flipper- and tentacle-held devices as the throng moved past Bail's lofty perch in the north tower, behind the palace's high white walls and the arcs of reflecting pools that had long ago served as defensive moats.

PALPATINE'S PUPPET! one of the holoslogans read.

REPEAL THE TAX! read another.

RESIST IMPERIALIZATION! a third.

The first was a reference to the regional governor Emperor Palpatine had installed in that part of the Core, who had decreed that all refugees of former Confederacy worlds were required to submit to rigorous identity checks before being issued documents of transit.

The "tax" referred to the toll that had been levied on anyone seeking travel to outlying systems.

Already a catchphrase, the third slogan was aimed at any who feared the Emperor's attempts to bind all planetary systems, autonomous or otherwise, to Coruscant's rule.

While little of the angry chanting was directed at Alderaan's government or Queen Breha—Bail's wife—many in the crowd

were looking to Bail to intercede with Palpatine on their behalf.
Alderaan was merely their gathering place, after the demonstration's organizers had decided against holding the march on Coruscant, under the watchful gaze of stormtroopers, and with the
memory of what had happened at the Jedi Temple fresh in everyone's mind.

Demonstrations were nothing new, in any case. Alderaanians
were known throughout the galaxy for their missions of mercy
and their unstinting support of oppressed groups. More important, Alderaan had been a hotbed of political dissent throughout
the war, with Aldera University's Students of Collus—named for
a celebrated Alderaanian philosopher—leading the movement.

With his homeworld thoroughly politicized, Bail had been
forced to play a careful game in the galactic capital, where he was
at once an advocate for refugee populations and a principal member of the Loyalist Committee; that is, loyal to the Constitution,
and to the Republic for which it stood.

A reasonable man, one of a handful of rankled delegates who
had found themselves caught between support for Palpatine and
outright contention, Bail had understood that political wran-
gling was the only way to introduce change. As a result, he and
Palpatine had engaged in numerous disputes, openly in the Rotunda as well as in private, on issues relating to Palpatine's rapid
rise to incontestable power, and the subsequent slow but steady
erosion of personal liberties.

Only with the war's sudden and shocking end had Bail come
to understand that what had seemed political maneuvering on Palpatine's part had been nothing less than inspired machination—
the unfolding of a diabolical scheme to prolong the war, and to
so frustrate the Jedi that when they finally sought to hold him accountable for refusing to proclaim the war concluded with the
deaths of Count Dooku and General Grievous, Palpatine could
not only declare them traitors to the Republic, but also pro-

nounce them guilty of having fomented the war to serve their own ends, and therefore deserving of execution.

Ever since, Bail had been forced to play an even more treacherous game on Coruscant—Imperial Center—for he now knew Palpatine to be a more dangerous opponent than anyone suspected; indeed a more dangerous foe than most could even begin to guess. While Senators such as Mon Mothma and Garm Bel Iblis were expecting Bail to join in their attempts to mount a secret rebellion, circumstance compelled him to maintain a low profile, and to demonstrate greater allegiance to Palpatine than he ever had.

That circumstance was Leia. And Bail's fears for her safety had only increased since his close encounter with Darth Vader on Coruscant.

He had spoken of the encounter only to Raymus Antilles, captain of the consular ship *Tantive IV.* Antilles had been given custody of Anakin's protocol and astromech droids, C-3PO and R2-D2. The former had undergone a memory wipe to safeguard the truth for as long as necessary, and to assure the continued protection of the Skywalker twins.

Could Vader actually be Anakin Skywalker? the two men wondered.

Based on Obi-Wan's account of what had occurred on Mustafar, Anakin's survival didn't seem possible. But perhaps Obi-Wan had underestimated Anakin. Perhaps Anakin's peerless strength in the Force had allowed him to survive.

Was Bail, then, raising the child of a man who was still alive?

What alternative was there? That Palpatine—that *Sidious*—had dubbed some other apprentice Darth Vader? That the black monstrosity Bail had seen on the landing platform was merely a droid version of Anakin, as General Grievous had been a cyborg version of his former self?

If that was true, would stormtroopers like Appo allow themselves to be commanded by a such a being, even if ordered to by Sidious?

The questions had gnawed at Bail without answer, and events such as the refugee march only served to place him at greater risk on Coruscant and heighten his concerns for Leia.

Unaided, Palpatine was capable of crushing any who opposed him. And yet he continued to allow others to do his dirty work, to preserve his image as a benevolent dictator. Palpatine used his regional governors to issue the harshest of his decrees, and his stormtroopers to enforce them.

The march's organizers had promised Bail that it would be a peaceful demonstration, but Bail suspected that Palpatine had infiltrated spies and professional agitators into the crowds. Riots could be used as an excuse by the regional governor to arrest dissidents and perceived troublemakers, and to announce new edicts that would make travel even more difficult and expensive for the refugees.

With so many ships arriving from nearby worlds, it had been impossible to screen for Imperial agents or saboteurs. Even if there had been some way to identify them, Bail would only have played into Palpatine's hands by issuing restrictions, thus alienating refugees and their ardent supporters alike, who viewed Alderaan as one of the last bastions of freedom.

Thus far, Alderaanian law enforcement units were doing a good job of confining the marchers to their preassigned circuit of the Royal Palace. Contingents of Royal Guards surrounded the palace, and the sky was filled with police skimmers and surveillance craft to ensure that the situation remained under control. On Bail's orders, active measures could only be used as a last resort.

Standing at the edge of the balcony, the object of shouts, appeals, chants, and flurries of raised fists, Bail ran his hand over his mouth, hoping that the Force was with him.

"Senator!" someone called from behind him.

Bail turned and saw Captain Antilles hurrying toward him from the direction of the palace's Grand Reception Room. Accompanying Antilles were two of Bail's aides, Sheltray Retrac and Celana Aldrete.

Antilles directed Bail's attention to a nearby holoprojector.

"You're not going to be pleased," the starship captain said by way of warning.

The holoimage of an enormous warship resolved in the projector's blue field.

Bail's brow wrinkled in confoundment.

"*Imperator*-class Star Destroyer," Antilles explained. "Hot off the line. And now parked in stationary orbit above Aldera."

"This is outrageous," Celana Aldrete said. "Even Palpatine wouldn't be so bold as to interfere in our affairs."

"Don't fool yourself," Bail said. "He would and he has." He swung to Antilles. "Comm the vessel," he ordered as Aldera's vizier and other advisers were hastening onto the balcony to gawk at the projected holoimage.

Before Antilles could activate his comlink, the holoprojector image faded and was replaced by the pinched, clean-shaven face of Palpatine's chief henchman, Sate Pestage.

"Senator Organa," Pestage said. "I trust you are receiving me."

Of all of Palpatine's advisers, Pestage came closest to being Bail's archnemesis. A thug, with no understanding of the legislative process, Pestage had no business being in a position of authority. But he had been one of Palpatine's chief advisers since Palpatine's arrival on Coruscant from Naboo, as that world's Senator.

Bail positioned himself on the projector's transmission grid and signaled for Antilles to open a link to Pestage.

"There you are," Pestage said after a moment. "Will you grant permission for our shuttle to land, Senator?"

"How unlike you to extend us the courtesy of a warning, Sate. What brings you to this part of the Core, in a Star Destroyer, no less?"

Pestage smiled without showing his teeth. "I'm merely a passenger aboard the *Exactor*, Senator. As to our business here . . . Well, let me say first how much I've enjoyed watching HoloNet feeds of your . . . political rally."

"It's a peaceful gathering, Sate," Bail fired back. "And it's likely to remain so unless your agitators succeed in doing what they do best."

Pestage adopted a surprised look. "My agitators? You can't be serious."

"I'm very serious. But suppose you get back to telling me why you are here."

Pestage tugged at his lower lip. "Now that I think about it, Senator, it might be more prudent for me to leave the explanation to the Emperor's emissary."

Bail stood akimbo. "That has always been your position, Sate."

"No longer, Senator," Pestage said. "I now answer to a superior."

"Who are you talking about?"

"Someone you've not yet had the pleasure of meeting. Darth Vader."

Bail froze, but only on the inside. He managed to keep from glancing at Antilles, and his voice belied none of his sudden dread when he said: "Darth Vader? What sort of name is that?"

Pestage smiled again. "Well, actually it's something of a title *and* a name." The smile collapsed. "But make no mistake, Senator, Lord Vader speaks for the Emperor. You would do well to bear that in mind."

"And this *Darth* Vader is coming here?" Bail said in a composed voice.

"Our shuttle should be setting down momentarily, assuming, of course, that we have your permission to land."

Bail nodded for the holocam. "I'll see to it that you receive approach and landing coordinates."

Pestage's holoimage had no sooner deresolved than Bail snatched his comlink from his belt and tapped a code into the keypad. To the female voice that answered, he said, "Where are Breha and Leia?"

"I believe they're already on their way to join you, sir," the Queen's attendant said.

"Do you know if Breha has her comlink with her?"

"I don't believe she does, sir."

"Thank you." Bail silenced the comlink and turned to his aides. "Find the Queen. She must be somewhere in the main residence. Tell her that she is not to leave the residence under any circumstances, and that she is to contact me as soon as possible. Is that understood?"

Retrac and Aldrete nodded, spun on their heels, and hurried off.

Bail swung to Antilles, eyes bulging in concern. "Are the droids on the *Tantive IV* or downside?"

"Here," Antilles said, exhaling. "Somewhere in the palace or on the grounds."

Bail tightened his lips. "They have to be located and kept out of sight."

Never was one for crowds, myself," Skeck said as he, Archyr, and Shryne were negotiating Aldera's throng of demonstrators.

"Is that what first took you to the Outer Rim?" Shryne asked.

Skeck mocked the idea with a motion of dismissal. "I just hang there for the food."

In addition to keeping out the cold, their long coats, hats, and high boots supplied hiding places for blasters and other tools of the smuggling trade. Jula, Brudi, and Eyl Dix had remained with the drop ship, which was docked in a circular bay a couple of kilometers west of the palace.

It was Shryne's first visit to Alderaan. From what little he had seen, the planet lived up to its reputation as both a beautiful world and an arena for political dissent, notwithstanding Alderaan's allegedly pacifist views. The mood of the enormous crowd, made up of war refugees and those who had arrived from countless worlds to demonstrate their solidarity, seemed to be in keeping with those views. But Shryne had already zeroed in on scores of beings who clearly hoped to provoke the marchers to violence, perhaps as a means of being assured extensive HoloNet coverage, and thus making their point with Palpatine.

Or maybe, just maybe, Alderaan had the Emperor himself to thank for the rabble-rousers.

Judging by the way in which Aldera's police units were deployed, they had no interest in confrontation, and perhaps had been ordered to exercise restraint at all costs. The mere fact that the marchers were being allowed to voice their protests and display their holoslogans in such close proximity to the Royal Palace, and that Senator Bail Organa himself would occasionally plant himself in full view of the crowd, showed that the restraint was genuine.

Alderaan really did care about the little guy.

For Shryne, the presence of such a huge crowd also suggested that Senator Fang Zar was more than a clever politician. While spiriting him off Alderaan would never have posed an insurmountable challenge, the milling crowds combined with Alderaan's deliberately lax policy toward orbital insertions and exits was going to make the pickup as easy as one, two, three.

Not bad for Shryne's first mission.

There might even be a small amount of good attached to it—particularly if the rumors he had heard about Zar over the years were true.

Now it boiled down to keeping the appointment with him.

Shryne, Skeck, and Archyr had already circled the palace twice, primarily to scope out potential problems at the south gate entrance, where the prearranged meet was supposed to take place. Shryne found it interesting that Zar's ostensible reason for making a low-key departure was to keep from involving

Organa in his problems, but Shryne wasn't clear on just what those problems were. Both Zar and Organa had been outspoken members of the Loyalist Committee, so what could Zar have done to cause problems for himself that didn't already involve Organa?

Was he in a fix with Palpatine?

Shryne tried to convince himself that Zar's troubles were none of his business; that the sooner he accustomed himself to simply executing a job, the better—for him and for Jula. This, as opposed to thinking like a Jedi, which involved looking to the Force as a means of gauging possible repercussions and ramifications of his actions.

In that sense, the Alderaan mission was the first day of the rest of his life.

Olee Starstone was the only other issue he had to clear from his mind. His feelings for her didn't spring from attachment of the sort she would be the first to ridicule. In plain fact, he was worried about her to the point of distraction.

In response to Shryne's decision to follow his own path, she was about as angry as a Jedi was allowed to be, though some of the other Jedi had said that they understood.

All seven had taken the battered transport and gone in search of surviving Jedi. Shryne feared that it would just be a matter of time before they got themselves in serious trouble, but he wasn't about to serve as their watchdog. More to the point, they had seen the risks they were taking as flowing from the will of the Force.

Well, who knew for sure?

Shryne wasn't omniscient. Maybe they would succeed against all odds. Maybe the Jedi, in league with political protestors and sympathetic military commanders, could bring Palpatine to justice for what he had done.

Unlikely. But a possibility, nevertheless.

Jula had been generous enough to loan Filli to the Jedi, out-
wardly to help them sort through the data they had downloaded
from the beacon databases. Shryne suspected, however, that
Jula's real intent was to disable Starstone's reckless determination. The closer Starstone and Filli grew, the more the young
Jedi would be forced to take a hard look at her choices. With
time, Filli might even be able to lure her out of her attachment
to the perished Jedi order, just as Jula had Shryne.

But then, Shryne had been halfway along before his mother
had even entered the picture.

His mother.

He was still getting used to that development: that he was
the son of this particular woman. Perhaps the way some of the
troopers had had to adjust to the fact that they were all clones of
one man.

Through his comlink's wireless earpiece, Shryne heard Jula's
voice.

"I just heard from our bundle," she said. "He's in motion."

"We're working our way around to him now," Shryne said
into the audio pickup fastened to the synthfur collar of his coat.

"You sure you're going to be able to recognize him from the
holoimages?"

"Recognizing him won't be a problem. But finding him in
this crowd could be."

"I'm guessing he didn't expect this big a turnout."

"I'm guessing no one did."

"Does that say something for the Emperor's days being
numbered?"

"Someone's days, anyway." Shryne paused, then said: "Hold
for a moment."

The palace's south gate entrance was within sight now, but
in the time it had taken Shryne, Skeck, and Archyr to complete their third circuit, a mob had formed. Three human

speakers standing atop repulsorlift platforms were urging everyone to press through the tall gates and onto the palace grounds.
Anticipating trouble, a group of forty or so royal troops dressed
in ceremonial armor and slack hats had deployed themselves
outside the gates, armed with an array of nonlethal crowd
control devices, including sonic devices, shock batons, and stun
nets.

"Roan, what's going on?" Jula asked.

"Things are getting rowdy. Everyone's being warned away
from the south gate entrance."

The crowd surged, and Shryne felt himself lifted from his feet
and carried toward the palace. The cordon of troops issued a final
warning. When the crowd surged again, two front-line guards
sporting backpack rigs began to coat the cobblestone plaza with
a thick layer of repellent foam. The crowd surged back in response, but dozens of demonstrators closest to the front failed to
step back in time and were immediately immobilized in the
rapidly spreading goo. A few of them were able to retreat by
surrendering their footgear, but the rest were stuck fast. The
trio of hovering agitators took advantage of the situation, accusing Alderaan's Queen and vizier of attempting to hinder the
marchers' rights to free assembly, and of kowtowing to the Emperor.

The surges grew more powerful, with demonstrators trapped
in the center of the crowd taking the brunt of all the pushing and
shoving. Shryne began to edge toward the perimeter, with Skeck
and Archyr to either side of him. When he could, he enabled his
comlink.

"Jula, we're not going to be able to get to the gate."

"Which also means that our bundle won't be able to exit the
grounds that way."

"Do we have a substitute rendezvous?"

"Roan, I've lost voice contact with him."

"Probably temporary. When you hear from him, just tell him to stay put, wherever he is."

"Where will you be?"

Shryne studied the palace's curved south wall. "Don't worry, we'll find a way in."

T hose poor beings, trapped in that terrible foam," C-3PO said as he and R2-D2 hastened for a narrow access door in the palace's south wall.

Close to the palace's underground droid-maintenance facility, where both droids had enjoyed an oil bath, the door was the same one they had used to exit the palace grounds earlier that day, when the protestors were just beginning their march.

"I think we'll be much better off inside the palace."

R2-D2 chittered a response.

C-3PO tilted his head in bafflement. "What do you mean we've been ordered inside anyway?"

The astromech chirped and fluted.

"Ordered to conceal ourselves?" C-3PO said. "By whom?" He waited for an answer. "Captain Antilles? How thoughtful of him to show concern for our well-being in the midst of this confusion!"

R2-D2 zithered, then buzzed.

"Something else?" C-3PO waited for R2-D2 to finish. "Don't tell me you *can't* say. It's simply that you *refuse* to say. I've every right to know, you secretive little machinist."

C-3PO fell briefly silent as the shadow of a low-flying craft passed over them.

His single photoreceptor tracking the flight of a midnight-black Imperial shuttle, R2-D2 began to whistle and hoot in obvious alarm.

"What is it now?"

The astromech loosed a chorus of warbles and shrill peeps. C-3PO fixed his photoreceptors on him in incredulity.

"Find Queen Breha? What *are* you going on about? A moment ago you said that Captain Antilles had ordered us into hiding!" Arms crooked, almost akimbo, C-3PO couldn't believe what he was hearing.

"*You* changed your mind. Since when do you get to decide what's important and what isn't? Oh, you're intent on getting us in trouble. I know it!"

By then they had reached the access door in the wall. R2-D2 extended a slender interface arm from one of the compartments in his squat, cylindrical torso and was in the process of inserting it into a computer control terminal alongside the doorway when the voice of a flesh-and-blood said: "Misplace your starfighter, droid?"

Turning completely about, C-3PO found himself looking at a human and two six-fingered humanoids wearing long coats and tall boots. The human's left hand was patting R2-D2's dome of a head.

"Oh! Who are you?"

"Never mind that," one of the humanoids said. Parting his coat, he revealed a blaster wedged into the wide belt that cinched his pants. "Do you know what this is?"

R2-D2 mewled in distress.

C-3PO's photoreceptors refocused. "Why, yes, it's a DL-Thirteen ion blaster."

The humanoid smiled nastily. "You're very learned."

"Sir, it is my fondest wish that my master recognize as much. Working with other droids has become so tiresome—"

"Ever see what an ionizer on full power can do to a droid?" the humanoid interrupted.

"No, but I can well imagine."

"Good," the human said. "Then here's the way it's going to work: you're going to lead us into the palace like we're all the best of friends."

While C-3PO was trying to make sense of it, the man added: "Of course, if you have a problem with that, my friend here"— he gestured to the other humanoid—"who happens to be very knowledgeable about droids, will just tap into this one's memory and retrieve the entry code. And then both of you will get to enjoy the effects of an ionizer firsthand."

C-3PO was too stunned to respond, but R2-D2 made up for the sudden silence by filling it with beeps and zithers.

"My counterpart says," C-3PO started to interpret, then stopped himself. "You certainly will *not* do as he says, you coward! These beings are not our masters! You should be willing to be disassembled rather than offer them the slightest help!"

But C-3PO's admonitions fell on deaf auditory sensors. R2-D2 was already unlocking the door.

"This is most unbecoming," C-3PO said sadly. "Most unbecoming."

"Good droid." The long-haired human patted the astromech's dome again, then threw C-3PO a narrow-eyed gaze. "Any attempts to communicate with anyone and you'll wish you'd never been built."

"Sir, you don't know how many times I've already wished that very thing," C-3PO said as he followed R2-D2 and the three armed organics through the door and onto the palace grounds.

Vader stood at the foot of the shuttle's boarding ramp, gazing at the white spires of the Royal Palace. Commander Appo and six of his stormtroopers spread out to flank him as Bail Organa and several others emerged from the ornate building. For a moment neither group moved; then Organa's contingent walked onto the landing platform and approached the shuttle.

"You are Lord Vader?" Organa asked.

"Senator," Vader said, inclining his head slightly.

"I demand to know why you've come to Alderaan."

"Senator, you are in no position to demand anything."

The vocoder built into his mask added menace to the remark. But, in fact, for perhaps the first time Vader felt as if he were wearing a disguise—a macabre costume, as opposed to a suit of life-sustaining devices and durasteel armor.

As Anakin, Vader hadn't known Bail Organa well, even though he had been in his company on numerous occasions, in the Jedi Temple, the corridors of the Senate, and in Palpatine's former office. Padmé had spoken of him highly and often, and Vader suspected that it was Organa, along with Mon Mothma, Fang Zar, and a few others, who had persuaded Padmé to withdraw her support of Palpatine prior to the war's finish. That, however, didn't trouble Vader as much as the fact that Organa, according to stormtroopers of the 501st, had been the first outsider to turn up at the Temple following the massacre, and was lucky to have escaped with his life.

Vader wondered if Organa had had a hand in helping Yoda, and presumably Obi-Wan, recalibrate the Temple beacon to cancel the message Vader had transmitted, which should have called all the Jedi back to Coruscant.

Aristocratic Organa was Anakin's height, dark-haired and handsome, and always meticulously dressed in the style of the Republic's Classic era, like the Naboo, rather than in the ostentatious fashion of Coruscant. But where Padmé had earned her status by being elected Queen, Organa had been born into wealth and privilege, on picture-perfect Alderaan.

Mercy missions or no, Vader wondered whether Organa had

any real sense of what it meant to live in the outlying systems, on worlds like sand-swept Tatooine, plagued by Tusken Raiders and lorded over by Hutts.

He felt a sudden urge to put Organa in his place. Pinch off his breath with a narrowing of his thumb and forefinger; crush him in his fist . . . But the situation didn't call for that—yet. Besides, Vader could see in Organa's nervous gestures that he understood who was in charge.

Power.

He had power over Organa, and over all like him.

And it was Skywalker, not Vader, who had lived on Tatooine.

Vader's life was just beginning.

Organa introduced him to his aides and advisers, as well as to Captain Antilles, who commanded Alderaan's Corellian-made consular ship, and who tried but failed to conceal an expression of profound hostility toward Vader.

If Antilles only knew who he was dealing with . . .

From beyond the palace's walls came the sound of angry voices and chanting. Vader surmised that at least some of the turbulence owed to the presence of an Imperial shuttle on Alderaan. The thought entertained him.

Like the Jedi, the demonstrators were another group of deluded, self-important beings convinced that their petty lives had actual meaning; that their protests, their dreams, their accomplishments amounted to anything. They were ignorant of the fact that the universe was changed not by individuals or by mobs, but by what occurred in the Force. In reality, all else was unimportant. Unless one was in communication with the Force, life was only *existence* in the world of illusion, born as a consequence of the eternal struggle between light and dark.

Vader listened to the sounds of the crowd for a moment more, then turned to regard Organa.

"Why do you permit this?" he asked.

Organa's restless eyes searched for something, perhaps a peek at the man behind the mask. "Are such demonstrations no longer permitted on Coruscant?"

"Harmony is the ideal of the New Order, Senator, not dissension."

"When harmony becomes the standard for all, then protests will cease. What's more, by allowing voices to be heard here, Alderaan saves Coruscant any unmerited embarrassment."

"There may be some truth to that. But in due time, protests will cease, one way or another."

Vader recognized that Organa was in a quandary about something. Clearly he resented being challenged on his own world, but his tone of voice was almost conversational.

"I trust that the Emperor knows better than to end them by fear," he was saying.

Vader had no patience for verbal fencing, and having to match wits with judicious men like Organa only reinforced his growing distaste at being the Emperor's errand boy. When would his actual Sith training finally commence? Try as he might to convince himself, his was not real power, but merely the *execution* of power. He wasn't the swordmaster so much as the weapon; and weapons were easily replaceable.

"The Emperor would not be pleased by your lack of faith, Senator," he said carefully. "Or by your willingness to allow others to display their distrust. But I haven't come to discuss your little march."

Organa fingered his short beard. "What does bring you here?"

"Former Senator Fang Zar."

Organa seemed genuinely surprised. "What of him?"

"Then you don't deny that he's here?"

"Of course not. He has been a guest of the palace for several weeks."

"Are you aware that he fled Coruscant?"

Organa frowned in uncertainty. "It sounds as if you're suggesting that he wasn't permitted to leave of his own free will. Was he under arrest?"

"Not arrest, Senator. Internal Security had questions for him, some of which were left unanswered. ISB requested that he remain in Imperial Center until matters were resolved."

Organa shook his head once. "I knew nothing of this."

"No one is questioning your decision to house him, Senator," Vader said, gazing down at him. "I simply want your assurance that you won't interfere with my escorting him back to Coruscant."

"Back to—" Organa left the rest of it unfinished and began again. "I won't interfere. Except in one instance."

Vader waited.

"If Senator Zar requests diplomatic immunity, Alderaan will grant it."

Vader folded his arms across his chest. "I'm not certain that privilege still exists. Even if it does, you may find that refusing the Emperor's request is hardly in your best interest."

Again, Organa's confliction was obvious. *What is he hiding?*

"Is that a threat, Lord Vader?" he said finally.

"Only a fact. For too long the Senate encouraged political chaos. Those days are ended, and the Emperor will not permit them to resurface."

Organa showed him a skeptical look. "You speak of him as if he is all-powerful, Lord Vader."

"He is more powerful than you know."

"Is that why you've agreed to serve him?"

Vader took a moment to respond. "My decisions are my own. The old system is dead, Senator. You would be wise to subscribe to the new one."

Organa exhaled with purpose. "I'll take my chances that freedom is still alive." He fell silent for a moment, deliberating. "I don't mean to impugn your authority, Lord Vader, but I wish to consult with the Emperor personally on this matter."

Vader could scarcely believe what he was hearing. Was Organa deliberately attempting to obstruct him; to make him appear inept in the eyes of Sidious? Anger welled up in him. Why was he wasting his time chasing fugitive Senators when it was the Jedi who posed a risk to the New Order?

To the balance of the Force.

A nearby holoprojector chimed, and from it emerged the holoimage of a dark-haired woman with an infant in her arms.

"Bail, I'm sorry I've been delayed," the woman said. "I just wanted to let you know that I'll be there shortly."

Organa looked from Vader to the holoimage and back again. As the image faded he said: "Perhaps it's better if you spoke with Senator Zar in person." He gulped and found his voice. "I'll have him escorted to the conference room as soon as possible."

Vader turned and waved a signal to Commander Appo, who nodded. "Who is the woman?" Vader asked Organa.

"My wife," Organa said nervously. "The Queen."

Vader regarded Organa, trying to read him more clearly.

"Inform Senator Zar that I'm waiting," he said at last. "In the meantime, I would enjoy meeting the Queen."

More than seven centuries old, the palace was a rambling and multistoried affair of ramparts and turrets, bedrooms and ballrooms, with as many grand stairways as it had turbolifts. Without a map, its kilometers of winding corridors were nearly impossible to follow. And so where walking from the droid-maintenance room to the hallway that accessed the south gate had seemed a simple matter, it was in fact akin to negotiating a maze.

"The droid's more clever than it looks," Archyr said when it finally dawned on them that the two machine intelligences had been walking them in circles for the past quarter hour. "I think it's leading us on a wild gundark chase."

"Oh, he would never do that," C-3PO said. "Would you, Artoo?" When the astromech didn't answer, C-3PO slammed his hand down on R2-D2's dome. "Don't you even think about giving me the silent treatment!"

Skeck tugged the ion weapon from his belt and brandished it. "Maybe it forgot about this."

"No need to threaten us further," C-3PO said. "I'm certain

that Artoo isn't attempting to mislead you. We don't know the palace very well. You see, we've only been with our present master for two local months, and we're not very well acquainted with the layout."

"Where were you before two months ago?" Skeck asked.

C-3PO fell silent for a long moment. "Artoo, just where were we before that?"

The astromech honked and razzed.

"None of my business? Oh, here we go again. This little droid can be very stubborn sometimes. In any case, as to where we were . . . I think I recall acting as an interface with a group of binary loadlifters."

"Loadlifters?" Archyr said. "But you're programmed for protocol, aren't you?"

C-3PO looked as distressed as a droid could look. "That's true! However, I can't imagine that I'm mistaken! I know I have been programmed for—"

"Get ahold of yourself, droid," Skeck said.

Shryne brought the five of them to an abrupt halt. "This isn't the way to the south entrance. Where are we?"

C-3PO gazed around. "I believe that we have somehow ended up in the royal residence wing."

Archyr's pointed jaw dropped. "What the frizz are we doing here? We're a hundred and eighty degrees from where we want to be!"

Skeck aimed the ionizer at the astromech's photoreceptor. "You can navigate a starfighter through hyperspace and you can't get us to the south gate? Any more tricks and we're going to fry you."

Shryne stepped away from everyone and activated his comlink. "Jula, any word from—"

"Where in the galaxy have you three been? I've been trying to reach you for—"

"We got turned around," Shryne said. "We'll fix it. Any word from our bundle?"

"That's what I wanted to tell you. He *moved*."

"Where to?"

"The east gate."

Shryne blew out his breath. "All right, we'll get there. Just make sure you tell him to remain where he is." Silencing the comlink, he rejoined the others.

"*East* gate?" Skeck said when Shryne relayed the bad news. He turned himself through a circle and pointed. "That way, I think."

The astromech began to chitter. Shryne and the others looked to C-3PO for a translation.

"He says, sirs, that the quickest route to the east gate will involve our ascending one more level—"

"We're supposed to be going *down*!" Archyr said in exasperation.

"That's true," C-3PO continued. "But my counterpart advises that unless we go *up* first, we will be forced to detour around the upper reaches of the Grand Ballroom atrium."

"Enough," Shryne said, ending further argument. "Let's just get this over with."

With the astromech leading, rolling along on its three treads, the five of them filed into a turbolift and rode it up one floor. No sooner had they arrived than R2-D2 made a sudden left into the stately corridor and hurried off.

"What, all of a sudden it's in a rush?" Archyr said.

"Artoo, slow down!" C-3PO called, struggling to keep up.

The astromech disappeared around a bend in the corridor. Skeck muttered a curse and drew the ionizer again.

"I think it's trying to get away!"

The three of them began to race after their quarry, dashing around the same corner only to narrowly avoid colliding with a regally dressed woman cradling a sleeping baby in her arms.

Stopping suddenly, the astromech loosed an ear-piercing screech and extended half a dozen of its interface arms, waving them about like weapons.

Confronted with the sight, the woman pulled the baby closer to her with one hand while the other reached out to slap a security alarm stud set into the wall. Rudely awakened by the astromech's screech and the blare of alarms, the baby took a quick look at the droid and began wailing at the top of its lungs.

Exchanging the briefest of panicked looks, Shryne, Archyr, and Skeck about-faced and ran.

Bail's assured posture in one of the reception room's elegant chairs belied his sense of raw desperation.

A few meters away, standing at one of the tall windows, Darth Vader gazed out on crowds of demonstrators who were becoming more turbulent with every passing moment.

The cadence of his deep breathing filled the room.

This is Leia's father, Bail told himself, certain of it now.

Anakin Skywalker. Rescued somehow on Mustafar, and returned to life, though now confined to a suit that made manifest what Skywalker had become at the end of the war: betrayer, butcher of children, apprentice of Sidious, follower of the dark side of the Force. And soon Leia would be in his presence . . .

When Breha had comlinked him unexpectedly, Bail had come close to telling her to flee, fully prepared to suffer whatever consequences would descend on him. To ensure Leia's safety, he had even been ready to sacrifice Fang Zar.

Would Vader recognize Leia through the Force as his child? What would happen if he did? Would he compel Bail to reveal where Obi-Wan was; where Luke was?

No, Bail would die first.

"What's taking Senator Zar so long?" Vader asked.

Bail had his mouth open to reply that the palace's guest wing was some distance away when Sheltray Retrac entered the reception room, her expression alone making it clear that something was wrong. Approaching Bail, she leaned low to say in a quiet voice, "Fang Zar is not in the residence. We don't know where he is."

Before Bail could reply Vader swung to the two of them.

"Was Zar alerted of my coming?"

Bail came to his feet quickly. "No one was apprised beforehand of the reason for your visit."

Vader glanced at Commander Appo. "Find him, Commander, and bring him to me."

The words had scarcely left the black grille that concealed Vader's mouth than security alarms began to sound throughout the palace. Captain Antilles immediately moved into the transmission field of the reception room's holoprojector, where a half-life-size image of a security officer was already resolving.

"Sir, three unidentified beings have gained access to the palace. Their motive is unknown, but they are armed and were last seen in the residential wing, in the company of two droids."

Two droids! Bail thought, rushing across the room in an effort to beat Vader to the holoprojector.

"Do we have images of the intruders?" Retrac asked before Bail could silence her.

Bail's heart skipped a beat. If it was C-3PO and R2-D2—

"Only of the intruders," the security officer said.

"Show them," Antilles ordered.

The security cam image showed three males, one human and two humanoids, dashing down one of the corridors.

"Freeze the image!" Vader said from alongside the holoprojector. "Close in on the human."

Bail was as confused as everyone else. Did Vader know the intruders? Were they agitators dispatched by Coruscant to work the protestors into a frenzy?

"Jedi," Vader said, mostly to himself.

Bail wasn't sure he had heard Vader correctly.

"Jedi? That can't be possible—"

Vader whirled on him. "They've come for Fang Zar." He stared at Bail from inside the mask. "Zar is attempting to return to Sern Prime. Apparently he hoped to keep from implicating you in his flight."

The reception room fell silent, but only for a moment. From the holoprojector appeared an image of Breha, holding a distraught Leia in her arms.

"Bail, I won't be joining you, after all," she said, loud enough to be heard over the infant's crying. "We had a disturbing encounter with three trespassers and a couple of droids, who nearly frightened the baby to death. She's in no condition to be introduced to company. I'm trying to calm her—"

"That's probably best," Bail said in a rush. "I'll check back with you in a moment." Deactivating the holoprojector, he turned slowly to Vader, arranging his features to suggest a mix of mild disappointment at his wife's message, and deep concern for just about everything else that had occurred.

"I'm certain there'll be another time, Lord Vader."

"I look forward to it," Vader said.

With that, he turned and marched away.

Bail nearly collapsed. Exhaling in guarded relief, he dropped back into his chair.

"Jedi?" Antilles said, in obvious bewilderment.

Bail shook his head from side to side. "I don't understand, either. But that *is* Skywalker." Abruptly, he stood up. "We have to find Zar before he does."

If I ever run into that astromech again . . . ," Skeck said as he, Archyr, and Shryne were racing for the palace's east entrance.

Archyr nodded in agreement. "Never a good feeling when you're tricked by an appliance."

His comlink enabled, Shryne was speaking with Jula.

"We're almost there. But that's no guarantee we can make it outside without being arrested."

"Roan, I'm going to reposition the ship. Close to our rendezvous there's a landing platform reserved for HoloNet correspondents."

"What makes you think you'll be allowed to set down?"

"No one's going be happy about it. But the good thing about Alderaan is that no one's going to blast us out of the sky, either."

"Parking ticket, huh?"

"Maybe not even."

"Then we'll see you there," Shryne said. "Out."

With the ornate east entrance in sight, the three of them slowed down to survey the situation. A pair of enormous doors opened on a broad staircase; from the last step, a paved footpath led to an arched bridge that spanned a crescent of reflecting pool. On the far side of the pool, the path led directly to a gated access in the high rampart. Perhaps a hundred meters beyond the wall was the media landing platform Jula had mentioned.

Shryne scanned the beings assembled on the narrow bridge and the green lawn between it and the rampart. Ultimately his gaze found a short, dark-complectioned man with a shock of long, white beard.

"That's Zar," he said, pointing out the Senator to Skeck and Archyr.

"And here comes trouble," Skeck said, indicating four Royal Guards who were hurrying for the gate, rifles slung over their shoulders.

"We need to make our move," Archyr said. "Before any more of them show up."

Skeck parted his long coat, reached around to the small of his back, and drew a blaster. "So much for pulling this off without a hitch."

Shryne placed his right hand on the weapon while Skeck was checking the power level. "You might not have to use it. Those long rifles are no match for even a hand blaster, and the guards know it. Besides, they probably haven't fired a round since the last royal funeral."

"Yeah, but can I quote you on that?" Skeck said.

Shryne took a step toward the doors, froze, then retreated, pressing himself to the wall.

Archyr regarded him in bafflement. "What—"

"Vader," Shryne managed.

Archyr's eyes widened. "The black stormtrooper? Let me see—"

Shryne restrained him from moving. "He's no storm-trooper."

Skeck was staring at Shryne, openmouthed. "Why's he here? For you?"

Shryne shook his head to clear it. "I don't know. He answers directly to the Emperor." He looked at Skeck. "He could be here for Zar."

"Doesn't really matter, does it," Archyr said. "Point being, he's *here*."

Shryne reached under his coat for his blaster. "If he is here for Zar, he's going to forget all about him when he sees me."

Skeck planted his hands on Shryne's shoulders. "You want to think this through?"

Shryne vouchsafed a thin smile. "I just did."

Vader hunted the hallways of the palace, the suit's array of sensors enhancing every sound and smell, every stray movement, his heavy cloak hooked around the hilt of his lightsaber.

The Emperor foresaw that this would happen, he told himself. *That is why he sent me. Despite what he says, he is concerned about the Jedi.*

Outside the palace, marchers continued to chant and circulate; inside, guards and others scurried about, stopping only to stare and move out of his path. Half of them were certainly in search of Fang Zar, and all of them were off course. But then, they lacked Vader's *sympathy* for those who were pushed and pulled and otherwise manipulated by the Force.

There was also the fact that Vader knew how Jedi *thought*.

Sensing a subtle presence, he stopped. At the same time, someone behind him shouted:

"Vader!"

Igniting his lightsaber, Vader turned completely around.

Hands by his sides, Shryne stood at the intersection of two corridors, one of which led to the palace's east portal, the other to the ballroom. Clearly, Zar had been found, was perhaps being moved out of the palace even then, or Shryne would not have shown himself.

"So you're the bait," Vader said after a moment. "It's an old ploy, Shryne. A ploy I've used. And it won't work this time."

"I have a backup plan."

Shryne flourished the blaster.

Vader focused on the weapon. "I see that you've abandoned your lightsaber."

"But not my commitment to justice." Shryne took a moment to glance down the hallway that led out of the palace. "You know how it is, Vader. Once a good guy, always a good guy. Then again, you probably don't know anything about that."

Vader advanced on him. "Don't be too sure of yourself."

"We're just trying to help Zar get home," Shryne said, retreating into the corridor. "Suppose we leave it at that."

"The Emperor has his reasons for recalling Zar to Coruscant."

"And you do whatever the Emperor tells you to do?"

In the intersection now, Vader could discern that Shryne was merely waiting for a chance to bolt through the doors. Well behind Shryne, on the far side of a footbridge that crossed a gentle curve of reflecting pool, one of Shryne's armed accomplices was holding four Royal Guards at bay while the other was all but dragging Fang Zar toward a gated breach in the palace's defensive wall, beyond which the conspirators surely had a getaway craft waiting.

Shryne fired a quick burst, then sprinted for the doorway. Behind him, his humanoid accomplices were also in motion, stunning the guards to unconsciousness and racing for the open gate.

Angling his blade, Vader deflected the bolts with intent, but by jinking and jagging Shryne managed to evade each parry.

Vader leapt, his powerful prosthetic legs carrying him to the top of a broad but short flight of steps in time to see Shryne sprint across the bridge at Jedi speed, motioning to his accomplices to move Zar through the gate.

Vader leapt again, this time to the bridge, and to within only a few meters of Shryne, who spun about, dropping to one knee and firing repeatedly. This time Vader decided to show Shryne whom he was dealing with. Holding his lightsaber to one side, he raised his right hand to turn the blaster bolts.

Clearly astonished, Shryne remained on one knee, but only briefly. In an instant he had passed through the gate and was shouldering his way through the crowd outside the wall.

Vader's final leap landed him just short of the rampart. Over the heads of the milling beings, at the forward edge of a landing platform, a woman with gray-laced black hair was gesturing frantically to Shryne and his cohorts, who were already hauling Fang Zar up the platform steps.

All too easy, Vader told himself.

Time to end it.

Bail and his two aides stood by the reception room holoprojector, awaiting some word of Fang Zar's whereabouts. From
the direction of the residence wing came Antilles and the droids.

"Go ahead, Threepio, tell him," Antilles said when the three
of them were within earshot of Bail.

"Master Organa, I hardly know where to begin," C-3PO
said. "You see, sir, my counterpart and I were about to enter the
palace grounds—"

"Threepio," Antilles said sharply. "Save the long story for another occasion."

R2-D2 communicated something in bleating tones.

C-3PO turned to the astromech. "Verbose? Tiresome? Just
you mind your enunciator, you—"

"See-Threepio!" Antilles repeated.

The protocol droid fell silent. "I'm very sorry, sirs. I'm simply unaccustomed to so much excitement."

"That's all right, See-Threepio," Bail said. "Take your time."

"Thank you, Master Organa. I only wanted to report that
the three intruders who held us captive were apparently intent on

collecting some sort of 'bundle'—that was the word they used—at the palace's east gate."

"Quickly!" Bail said to his aides.

Aldrete bent to adjust the holoprojector's controls. An instant later an east gate security cam captured a holoimage of Fang Zar, seized in the grip of two humanoids who were running him toward a landing platform that had been designated for HoloNet personnel.

A second cam found Vader, crimson-bladed lightsaber in hand, fending off blasterfire from a long-haired human male who was also racing for the east gate.

"Sir," Sheltray Retrac said suddenly.

Following Asta's worried gaze, Bail saw Sate Pestage striding into the reception room.

"Senator, I have just learned that Senator Zar is at this moment being conducted from the palace," Pestage said, in what Bail sensed was almost theatrical spleen. "If this is your way of providing immunity—"

"We've only just discovered his whereabouts," Bail cut him off, motioning to the holoimages. "In any case, it looks as if the Emperor's 'emissary' has the situation well in hand."

Pestage dismissed Bail's anger with a superfluous wave of his hand. "Through no help of yours, Senator. I demand that you secure the palace before it's too late!"

Bail glanced at the holoimages of Vader, the long-haired man, Fang Zar . . .

"Seal it, I tell you!"

Bail took a final glance at the images, then complied.

Firing on the run, Shryne made a mad dash for the rampart gate. If his retreat struck Skeck, or Archyr, or even Fang Zar, as cowardly, then so be it. For it was clear that Vader wasn't going to be stopped by blaster bolts, and Shryne was a long way from the nearest lightsaber.

Shryne wasn't surprised that Vader knew him by name; that he did only reinforced the fact that Vader and the Emperor had full access to the Jedi Temple databases. For all Shryne knew, Vader had been at the Temple when Filli Bitters had sliced into the beacon.

Outside the gate now, he began to zigzag through the densely packed crowd. Catching sight of his weapon, many of the marchers hastened to open a path for him—an obvious berserker in their midst. Through gaps in the throng, Shryne could see Skeck, Archyr, Jula, and Zar on the landing platform, surrounded by what Shryne took to be irate HoloNet correspondents, yelling at them and gesticulating to the drop ship that had set down without permission.

Judging by her gestures, Jula was attempting to placate everyone, or at least assure them that the ship would soon be on its way—assuming that Vader didn't scuttle their plans with a single leap.

Midway up the stairway that led to the landing platform, Shryne came to a halt, to take what he hoped would be a last look at Vader, who was still on the palace grounds, a couple of meters shy of the rampart gate. Of greater interest to Shryne, however, was the fact that an alloy curtain, thick as a blast shield, was descending rapidly from the head jamb of the arched entrance.

The palace was being sealed shut, and Vader was in risk of not making it through the gate in time!

Understanding as much, the Emperor's executioner was moving faster now. A jump carried him to the rampart, just short of the lowering shield, where he did something so unexpected that it took Shryne a moment to make sense of what was happening.

Vader hurled his ignited lightsaber through the air.

For a split second Shryne thought that he had done so in anger. Then, in awe, he grasped that Vader had *aimed*.

Spinning out from under the lowering security grate, the crimson blade sailed high over the crowd, following a trajectory that took it north of the landing platform; then, on reaching the distal end of its arc, it began to boomerang back.

Shryne flew for the top of the stairway, his gaze fully engaged on the twirling blade, his heart hammering in his chest. Calling on the Force, he tried to influence the course of the lightsaber, but either the Force wasn't with him or Vader's Force abilities were overpowering his.

The blade was whipping toward the landing platform now, close enough for Shryne to hear it whine through the air, and spinning so swiftly it might have been a blood-red disk.

Passing within a meter of Shryne's outstretched hands, the lightsaber struck Fang Zar first, ripping a deep gouge across his upper chest and nearly decapitating him; then, continuing on, it struck an unsuspecting Jula across the back before completing its swift and lethal circle and slamming into the upper reaches of the fully lowered rampart gate, where it switched off and plummeted to the paving stones with a metallic clangor.

On the landing platform, Skeck was bent low over Fang Zar; Archyr, over Jula.

Rooted in place Shryne could sense Vader on the far side of the gate, a black hole of rage.

Shryne commenced a stiff-legged descent of the stairway, deaf to all sound, blind to color, scarcely in possession of his self.

He didn't come to his senses until he reached the foot of the stairs, where he turned and ran to help get his mother and Zar aboard the drop ship.

One by one Palpatine's military advisers appeared before him, standing in postures of obeisance below the throne room's dais, their eyes narrowed against the orange blaze of Coruscant's setting sun, delivering their reports and appraisals, their expert assessments of the state of his Empire.

Royal Guards stood to both sides of the high-backed chair; behind them sat Mas Amedda, Sly Moore, and other members of Palpatine's inner circle.

He listened to everyone without comment.

In some outlying systems, arsenals of Separatist weapons, in some cases entire flotillas of droid-piloted warships, had been commandeered by rogue paramilitary groups before Imperial forces could reach them.

In Hutt space, smugglers, pirates, and other scoundrels were taking advantage of the Emperor's need to consolidate power by blazing new routes for the movement of spice and other pro-scribed goods.

On many former CIS worlds, bounty hunters were tracking down former Separatist colluders.

In the Mid Rim, Imperial academies were filling with recruits obtained from flight schools throughout the galaxy.

In the Outer Rim, three new batches of stormtroopers were being grown.

Closer to the Core, capital ships were being turned out by Sienar, Kuat Drive, and other yards.

And yet at present there were simply too few battle groups or stormtroopers to deploy at every potential trouble spot.

Massive protests had been held on Alderaan, Corellia, and Commenor.

Progress was lagging on several of the Emperor's most cherished projects, owing to a lack of construction workers . . .

When the last of his advisers had come and gone, Palpatine dismissed everyone, including the members of his inner circle, and sat gazing over the western cityscape as it came to brilliant light in the deepening dusk.

Under the rule of the ancient Sith, the future of the galaxy had been in the able hands of many dark sovereigns. Now responsibility for maintaining order rested only with Darth Sidious.

For the moment it was enough that his advisers and minions respected him—for reestablishing peace, for eliminating the group that had posed the greatest threat to continued stability—but eventually those same advisers would need to fear him. To understand the great power he wielded, as both Emperor and Dark Lord of the Sith. And to that end, Sidious needed Vader.

For if someone as potent as Vader answered to the Emperor, then how powerful must the Emperor be!

After he had spent several hours drifting on the currents of possible futures, Palpatine summoned Sate Pestage. Swiveling his chair from the view of Coruscant when the most trusted of his advisers entered the throne room, Palpatine ordered Pestage to take a seat and appraised him.

"Events unfolded as you assured they would," Pestage said when Palpatine nodded for him to speak. "Organa was very predictable. My intervention was minimal."

"Senator Organa was willing to allow Fang Zar to escape, you mean."

"It certainly seemed that way."

Palpatine considered it. "He may bear watching in the future. But at present we won't make an issue of it. And Senator Zar?"

Pestage sighed with meaning. "Gravely wounded. Perhaps dead."

"Pity. Does Organa know?"

"Yes. He was very troubled by the outcome."

"And Lord Vader?"

"Even more troubled by the outcome."

Palpatine allowed a grin of satisfaction. "Even better."

Returned to its astral sanctuary, the *Drunk Dancer* drifted in space.

From the hatch to medbay, a 2-1B droid hovered out to report that it had been able to save Jula, but that Fang Zar had died on the operating table.

"Damage sustained by major vessels that supply the heart was too extensive to repair, sir," the droid told Shryne. "Everything that could be done, was done."

Shryne looked in on Jula, who was heavily sedated.

"I dragged you right back into it," she said weakly.

He pushed her hair off her forehead. "There might have been other forces at work."

"Don't say that, Roan. We just need to get farther away."

He smiled with effort. "I'll ask Archyr about outfitting the ship with an intergalactic drive."

He let her drift into sleep and went to his bunk. Whenever he shut his eyes, he would see the trajectory of Vader's blade; would see it slicing through Zar, through Jula . . . He didn't need to shut his eyes to recall how it had felt to be overwhelmed by Vader's ability to use the Force.

To use the power of the dark side.

A Sith.

Shryne was certain now.

A Sith in service to Emperor Palpatine.

That was the revelation he couldn't banish.

Count Dooku might as well have won the war, save for the fact that in place of independent systems, free trade, and the rest, the galaxy answered to the exclusive rule of Palpatine.

But how? Shryne asked himself. How had it happened?

Had Palpatine's alliance with Vader been brought about by the death of the Chosen One? Had Vader—*Darth* Vader—killed Anakin Skywalker? Had he struck a deal with Palpatine beforehand, promising Palpatine unlimited power in exchange for sanctioning Vader's murder of the Chosen One and the elimination of the Jedi, thus tipping the galaxy fully to the dark side?

Was it any wonder, then, that beings were fleeing for the far-flung reaches of known space?

And was it any wonder that Shryne had lacked the strength to alter the course of Vader's lightsaber? He had thought of his diminished abilities as a personal failure—owing to the fact that he had lost his faith in the Jedi order, allowed his two Padawans to die, grown thought-bound—when, in fact, it was the Force as the Jedi had known it that had been defeated.

The flame extinguished.

On the one hand, it meant that Shryne's transition into regular life could probably proceed more smoothly than he had thought; by contrast, that regular life meant existing in a world where evil had triumphed and ruled.

*   *   *

In the antechamber of his private retreat, Sidious, dressed in a dark blue cowled robe, paced in front of the curved window wall. Vader stood rigidly at the center of the room, his gloved hands crossed in front of him.

"It appears you attended to our little problem on Alderaan, Lord Vader," Sidious said.

"Yes, Master. Fang Zar need no longer concern you."

"I know I should feel some sense of relief. But in fact, I'm not entirely pleased with the outcome. Zar's death could arouse sympathy in the Senate."

Vader stirred. "He left me no recourse."

Sidious came to a halt and turned toward Vader. "No recourse? Why didn't you simply apprehend him, as I asked?"

"He made the mistake of attempting to flee."

"But *you* against someone like Fang Zar? It hardly seems an equitable match, Lord Vader."

"Zar was not alone," Vader said with venom. "What's more, if you don't like the way . . ."

Suddenly intrigued, Sidious moved closer. "Ah, what's this? Allowing your words to trail off—as if I can't see their destination." Anger showed in his yellow eyes. "As if I can't see the *thought* behind them!"

Vader said nothing.

"Perhaps you're not enjoying your new station in life, is that it? Perhaps you tire already of executing my commands." Sidious stared at him. "Perhaps you think you're better suited to occupy the throne than I am. Is that it, Lord Vader? If so, then admit as much!"

Breathing deeply, Vader remained silent for a moment more. "I am but an apprentice. *You* are the Master."

"Interesting that you refrain from calling me *your* Master."

Vader inclined his head to Sidious. "I meant nothing by it, my Master."

Sidious sneered. "Perhaps you wish you could strike me down, is that it?"

"No, Master."

"What stops you from doing so? Obi-Wan was once your Master, and you were certainly prepared to kill him. Even if you *failed*."

Vader clenched his right hand. "Obi-Wan did not understand the power of the dark side."

"And you do?"

"No, Master. Not yet. Not fully."

"And that's why you don't try to strike me down? Because I possess powers you lack?" Sidious lifted his arms, hands deployed like claws, as if to summon and hurl Sith lightning. "Because you know that I could easily overwhelm the delicate electrical systems of your suit."

Vader stood his ground. "I don't fear death, Master."

Sidious grinned maliciously. "Then why go on living, my young apprentice?"

Vader looked down at him. "To learn to become more powerful."

Sidious lowered his hands. "Then I ask you one final time, Lord Vader. Why not strike me down?"

"Because you are my path to power, Master," Vader said. "Because I need you."

Sidious narrowed his eyes and nodded. "Just like I needed my Master—for a time."

"Yes, Master," Vader said finally. "For a time."

"Good. Very good." Sidious smiled in satisfaction. "And *now* you are ready to release your anger."

Vader evinced confusion.

"Your fugitive Jedi, my apprentice," Sidious said. "They are traveling to Kashyyyk." He tipped his head to one side. "Perhaps, Lord Vader, they hope to lay a trap for you."

Vader clenched his hands. "That would be my most fervent wish, my Master."

Sidious clamped his hands on Vader's upper arms. "Then go to them, Lord Vader. Make them sorry they didn't hide while they had the chance!"

PART IV
KASHYYYK

Inside the battered transport that had once belonged to an Imperial garrison on Dellalt, Olee Starstone and the six Jedi who had joined her crusade waited to be granted clearance to continue on to Kashyyyk space. The commanders of the half dozen Imperial corvettes that made up the inspection-point picket answered not to distant Coruscant but to the regional governor, headquartered on Bimmisaari.

The Jedi had done all they could to make the ship look the part of a military-surplus transport. Thanks mostly to Jula's crew, the drives had been tweaked to produce a new signature, the ship's profile had been altered, the defensive shields and countermeasures suite repaired. To ensure that what remained conformed to Imperial standards, many of the advanced sensors and scanners had been eliminated, along with most of the laser cannons. The *Drunk Dancer*'s maintenance droids had given the ship a quick paint job and had helped remove some of the seats amidships, to create a common cabin space.

To Starstone, the vessel's fresh look matched the false identities the Jedi had adopted, as well as the clothes that made them look like a motley crew of struggling space merchants.

The transport's cockpit was spacious enough to accommodate Starstone and Filli Bitters, in addition to Jambe Lu and Nam Poorf, late of the Temple's Agricultural Corps, who were doing the piloting, and still-sightless Deran Nalual, who was tucked into the cramped communications duty station.

No one had said a word since Nalual had transmitted the ship's authorization key to the picket array's cardinal corvette. Filli was confident that the transport's altered drive signature would pass muster, but—new to forging Imperial code—he was less certain about the authorization key.

Starstone placed her hand on Jambe's shoulder, as a way of saying: *Be ready to make a run for it.*

Jambe was centering himself behind the steering yoke when an officious voice issued from the cockpit speakers.

"*Vagabond Trader*, you are cleared for approach to Kashyyyk. Commerce Control will provide you with vector coordinates for atmospheric entry and landing."

"Understood," Deran said into the mouthpiece of her headset.

Engaging the transport's sublight drive, Jambe and Nam began to edge the transport through the cordon.

Starstone heard Filli's eased exhalation and turned to him.

"You all right?"

"I am now," he said. "I was flying blind with that code."

"I guess we're both that good," Deran said from behind him.

Starstone touched Deran on the arm and smiled at Filli.

He smiled back. "Glad to help."

Starstone was still getting used to Filli's frequently awkward attempts at flirtation. But then, she wasn't even ranked a beginner. The idea that the towheaded slicer was on temporary loan from the *Drunk Dancer* was absurd. Shryne was merely using Filli as a means of keeping tabs on the Jedi, but she refused to let that bother her. If Filli's slicing skills could help locate fugitive

Jedi, so much the better, even if she did have to pretend to be flattered by his attention, as opposed to being embarrassed by it. She liked him more and more, but she had her priorities straight, and involvement wasn't among them.

She wasn't Shryne.

Initially she had been angry at him and at his ever-persuasive mother, but in the end she had realized that her anger was rooted more in attachment than anything else. Shryne had his own path to follow in the Force, despite his beliefs to the contrary, and despite the fact that she missed him.

The worst part about it was that she had somehow assumed the mantle of leader. Notwithstanding that both Siadem Forte and the Ho'Din, Iwo Kulka, were Jedi Knights, they had relinquished their due as higher-ranking Jedi without the issue ever being raised. For that matter, even Jambe and Nam outranked her. But because the search had been her idea, everyone had essentially granted her tacit approval to do most of the thinking.

Clear evidence of everyone's sense of dispossession, she thought.

On a mission that wasn't a Jedi mission, but was all about being a Jedi.

And thus far the crusade had come to nothing.

On every world they had visited between Felucia and Saleucami it had been the same: the Jedi had been revealed as traitors to the Republic and had been killed by the clone troopers they had commanded. None had survived, Starstone and the others had been told. And pity any who had survived, for anti-Jedi sentiment was widespread, especially in the Outer Rim, among populations that had been drawn into the war and now saw themselves as having been mere performers in a game the Jedi had been playing to assume control of the Republic.

Justification for Shryne to say *I told you so* when they next met.

Even in the few standard weeks since the war's end, a dramatic change had taken place. With the rapid diffusion of the symbols of the Empire, *fear* was radiating from the Core. On worlds where peace should have brought relief, distrust and suspicion prevailed. The war was over, and yet brigades of stormtroopers remained garrisoned on hundreds of worlds, formerly Separatist and Republic alike. The war was over, and yet Imperial inspection points dotted the major hyperlanes and sector jump points. The war was over, and yet the call was out for recruits to serve in the Imperial armed forces.

The war was over, and yet the HoloNet addressed little else.

Starstone believed she understood why: because in the depths of his black heart, the Emperor knew that the next war wouldn't be fought from the outside in, but rather from the inside out. That not a generation would pass, much less the ten thousand *years* Palpatine had predicted the Empire to endure, before the disease that had now taken root on Coruscant would infect every system in the galaxy.

Even so, as desperate as the quest seemed, she was still counting on the Wookiees to provide the Jedi with the hope they needed to carry on. From information gleaned from the Temple beacon database, they knew that three Jedi had been dispatched to Kashyyyk: Quinlan Vos, Luminara Unduli, and Master Yoda himself, who, according to Forte and Kulka, had enjoyed a longstanding relationship with the Wookiees.

If there was a planet where Jedi could have survived Palpatine's execution order, Kashyyyk would be it.

"Wookiee World," Nam said as he dropped the bow of the transport.

The planet rose into view, whitecapped, otherwise green and blue. Dozens of huge vessels hung in orbit, including the perforated hulks of several Separatist warships. Ferries and drop ships could be seen emerging from and disappearing into Kashyyyk's high-stacked clouds.

Jambe indicated a Separatist ship, tipped over on its starboard side, its underbelly heavily punctured by turbolaser bolts. Umbilicaled to it were a pair of craft that looked more like musical horns than space vessels.

"Wookiee ships," Jambe said. "They're probably cannibalizing whatever's useful."

Filli leaned toward the viewports for a better look. "They take immigrant technology and make it all their own. For enough credits, they could probably build us a wooden starship."

Starstone had heard as much. Inventive handiwork was the primary reason Wookiees frequently fell prey to slave traders, especially Trandoshans, their reptilian planetary neighbors. Skill, however, hadn't brought the Separatists to Kashyyyk, or the Trade Federation before them. The system was not only close to several major hyperlanes, but also an entry point for an entire quadrant of space. A Wookiee guild of cartographers known as the Claatuvac were said to have mapped star routes that didn't even appear on Republic or Separatist charts.

The communications console chimed a repeating series of tones.

"Vector routing from Commerce Control," Deran said.

"Make sure they understand we want to set down near Kachirho," Starstone said.

Deran nodded. "Transmitting our request. Relaying course coordinates to navigation."

Nam threw an excited look over his shoulder. "I've wanted to visit Kashyyyk for ten years."

"Half the Core would like to visit Kashyyyk," Filli said. "But the Wookiees don't cater to tourists."

"What, no luxury accommodations?" Jambe said.

Filli shook his head. "They *might* be willing to provide a tent."

"How many times have you been here?" Starstone asked him.

He thought about it, then shrugged. "Ten, twelve. In between regular jobs, we'd sometimes run scrap technology here."

"Can you speak the language?" Nam asked.

Filli laughed. "I once met a human who could bark a couple of useful phrases, but the best I could ever manage was a 'thank you,' and that worked only one out of ten times."

Starstone frowned. "Do we have a translator droid or some sort of emulator?"

"We won't need one," Filli said. "The Wookiees employ a mixed-species staff of go-betweens to help out with sales and trades."

"Who do we ask for?" Starstone said.

Filli took a moment. "Last time I was here, there was a guy named Cudgel . . ."

The *Vagabond Trader* began its descent into Kashyyyk's aromatic atmosphere, light fading as the ship dropped below the canopy of the planet's three-hundred-meter-tall wroshyr trees into an area of majestic cliffs crowned with vegetation. Adjusting course, Jambe and Nam guided the transport to a lakeshore landing platform made of wood. Towering majestically over the platform and the aquamarine lake rose the city of Kachirho, which consisted of a cluster of giant, tiered wroshyrs.

In his eagerness to fulfill a ten-year dream, Nam nearly botched the landing, but no one was hurt, despite being tossed about. As soon as everyone had exited the ship, Filli disappeared to find Cudgel.

Starstone gazed at the trees and sheer cliffs in wonderment. Her hopes for finding Yoda notwithstanding, the Wookiee world rendered other planets she had visited prosaic by comparison.

The scene at the exotic landing platform alone was impressive, with ships coming and going, and groups of Wookiees and their liaison crews haggling with beings representing dozens of different species. Outsize logs and slabs of fine-grained hardwoods were heaped about, and the air was rich with the heady smell of tree sap, and loud with the drone of nearby lumber mills. Protocol and labor droids supervised the loading and off-loading of cargo, which was moved by teams of hornless banthas or exquisitely crafted hoversleds. All of the activity shaded and dwarfed by trees that seemed to reach to the very edge of space . . .

Starstone had to catch her breath. The gargantuan size of everything made her feel like an insect. She was still gaping like a tourist when Filli returned, accompanied by a thickset male human dressed in short trousers and a sleeveless shirt. If he wasn't quite as hairy as a Wookiee, it was not for want of trying.

"Cudgel," Filli said, by way of introduction.

Cudgel smiled at everyone in turn, jocular but clearly dubious, and Starstone immediately saw why. While she and her band of fugitive Jedi could dress the part of merchants, even talk the part, they couldn't *stand* the part.

Literally.

Straight-backed, silent, hands clasped in front of them, they looked more like a group of vacationing meditators, which was not far from the truth.

"First time to Kashyyyk?" Cudgel said.

"Yes," Starstone answered for everyone. "Hopefully not our last."

"Welcome, then." Forcing a smile, he eyed the transport. "This is an L two hundred, isn't it?"

"Military surplus," Filli said quickly.

Cudgel cocked a flaring eyebrow. "Already? I was under the impression there wasn't any surplus." Before Filli could respond, he continued: "Can't be carrying much in the way of trade goods. Are you off a freighter up top?"

"We're not here to trade, exactly," Filli said. "More in the way of a fact-finding mission."

"We're in the market for an Oevvaor catamaran," Starstone explained.

Cudgel blinked in surprise. "Then your ship had better be filled with aurodium credits."

"Our client is prepared to pay a fair price," Starstone said.

Cudgel stroked his chest-length beard. "Not a question of price. More of availability."

"How bad were things here?" Forte asked abruptly. "The battle, I mean?"

Cudgel followed the Jedi's gaze to the tree-city. "Bad enough. The Wookiees are still cleaning up."

"Many killed?" Nam asked.

"Even one's too many."

"Were any Jedi involved?"

Jambe's question seemed to stop Cudgel cold. "Why do you ask?"

"We just came from Saleucami," Starstone said, hoping to put Cudgel at ease. "We heard that several Jedi were killed by clone troopers during the battle."

Cudgel appraised her. "I wouldn't know about that. I was in Rwookrrorro during most of it." He pointed. "Other side of the escarpment."

A short silence fell over everyone.

"Well, let's see if I can't find someone who knows catamarans," Cudgel said at last.

Starstone kept quiet until the hirsute middleman had moved off. "I don't think that went so well," she said to Forte and the others.

"Shouldn't matter," Iwo Kulka said. "Kashyyyk isn't Saleucami or Felucia. We're in Jedi-friendly territory."

"That's what you said on Boz Pity—" Starstone started to say when Filli cut her off.

"Cudgel's back."

With four rangy Wookiees in tow, Starstone saw.

"These are the folk I told you about," Cudgel was telling the Wookiees, in Basic.

Before Starstone could open her mouth to speak, the Wookiees bared their fangs and brandished the most bizarre-looking hand blasters she had ever seen.

The Star Destroyer *Exactor* and its older sibling, *Executrix*, drifted side by side, bow-to-stern, forming a parallelogram of armor and armament.

Vader's black shuttle navigated the short distance between them.

He sat in the passenger hold's forward row of seats, his cadre of stormtroopers behind him, and his thoughts focused on what awaited him on Kashyyyk, rather than on the imminent meeting, which he suspected was little more than a formality.

His last conversation with Sidious, weeks earlier but as if only yesterday, had made it clear that his Master was manipulating him now as much as he had before he had turned. Before and during the war Sidious's intention had been to entice him into joining the Sith; since, the goal was to transform him into a Sith. That was, to impress upon Vader that the power of the dark side did not flow from understanding but from appetite, rivalry, avarice, and malice. The very qualities the Jedi considered base and corrupt.

As a means of keeping their plucked pupils from exploring the deeper sides of their nature; as a means of reining them, lest they discovered for themselves the real power of the Force.

Anger leads to fear; fear to hatred; hatred to the dark side . . .

Precisely, Vader thought.

At Sidious's insistence, he had spent the recent weeks sharpening his ability to summon and make use of his rage, and felt poised at the edge of a significant increase in his abilities.

Deep space was appropriate to such feelings, he told himself as he gazed out the cabin's viewport. Space was more appropriate for the Sith than for the Jedi. The invisible enslavement to gravity, the contained power of the stars, the utter insignificance of life . . . Hyperspace, by contrast, was more suitable to the Jedi: nebulous, neither here nor there, incoherent.

When the shuttle had docked in the *Executor*'s hold, Vader led his contingent of stormtroopers out of the vessel, only to find that his host hadn't shown him the courtesy of being on hand to greet him. Waiting, instead, was his host's contingent of gray-uniformed crew members, commanded by a human officer named Darcc.

The games begin, Vader thought, as he allowed Captain Darcc to escort him deeper into the ship.

The cabin to which he was ultimately led was in the uppermost reaches of the Star Destroyer's conning tower. On entering, Vader found his host sitting behind a gleaming slab of desk, plainly debating whether to remain seated or to stand; whether to place himself on equal footing with Vader, or, by appearance, to continue to suggest superiority. Knowing, in any case, that Vader preferred to remain on his feet, his host was not likely to gesture him to a chair. Knowing, too, that Vader was capable of strangling him from clear across the cabin might also figure into his decision.

What to do? his host must have been thinking.

And then he stood, a slender, sharp-featured man, coming around from behind the desk with his hands clasped behind his back.

"Thank you for detouring from your course," Wilhuff Tarkin said.

The expression of gratitude was unexpected. But if Tarkin was intent on prolonging the game, then Vader would humor him, since in the end it amounted to nothing more than establishing status.

This was what the Empire would be, he thought. A contest among men intent on clawing their way to the top, to sit at Sidious's feet.

"The Emperor requested it," Vader said finally.

Tarkin pursed his thin lips. "I suppose we can attribute that to the Emperor's astute ability to bring like-minded beings together."

"Or pit them against one another."

Tarkin adopted a more sober look. "That, too, Lord Vader."

With a mind as sharp as his cheekbones, Tarkin had risen quickly through the ranks of Palpatine's newly formed staff of political and military elite, among whom naked ambition was highly prized. So much so that a new honorific had been created for Tarkin and ambitious men like him: *Moff*.

Vader had met him once before, aboard a *Venator*-class Star Destroyer, at the remote location where the Emperor's secret weapon was under construction. Vader, still new to his suit then; awkward, uncertain, between worlds.

Tarkin perched himself on the edge of his desk and smiled thinly. "Perhaps between the two of us, we can determine the reason the Emperor arranged this rendezvous."

Vader crossed his gloved hands in front of him. "I suspect that you know more about the purpose of this meeting than I do, Moff Tarkin."

Tarkin's smile disappeared, and in its place came a look of sharp attentiveness. "Surely you can guess, my friend."

"Kashyyyk."

"Bravo."

Tarkin activated a holoplate that sat atop his desk. In the cone of blue light that rose from it, a bruised transport of military design could be seen moving through a cordon of Imperial corvettes.

"This was recorded approximately ten hours ago, local, at the Kashyyyk system checkpoint. As you may have already guessed, the transport belongs to the Jedi. It appears to be a civilian model, but it isn't. It was hijacked on Dellalt some weeks ago, and was the object of a pursuit that ended in the destruction of several Imperial starfighters. We have, however, been successful at tracking its movements ever since."

"You've been tracking them," Vader said in genuine surprise. "Was the Emperor apprised of this?"

Tarkin smiled again. "Lord Vader, the Emperor is apprised of *everything.*"

But his apprentice isn't, Vader thought.

"I ordered our checkpoint personnel to ignore the obvious fact that the transport's signature has been altered," Tarkin continued, "and to ignore, as well, the fact that whatever codes the transport furnished were likely to be counterfeit."

"Why weren't the Jedi simply taken into custody at the checkpoint?"

"We had our reasons, Lord Vader. Or perhaps I should say that the Emperor had his."

"They are on Kashyyyk now?"

Tarkin stopped the holoimage and nodded. "We thought they might be refused entry. Apparently, however, someone aboard the ship is familiar with Kashyyyk's trading protocols."

Vader considered it for a moment. "You said that you

had your reasons for clearing the transport through the check-point."

"Yes, I'm coming to that," Tarkin said, standing to his full height and beginning to pace in front of the desk. "I realize that you of all people require no assistance in . . . bringing the fugitive Jedi to justice. But I want to lay out a somewhat broader plan for your consideration. Should you accept the proposition, I'm in a position to provide you with whatever ships, personnel, and matériel you think necessary."

"What is the proposition, Moff Tarkin?"

Tarkin came to a stop and turned fully to Vader. "Simply this. The Jedi are your priority, as they should be. Certainly the Empire can't permit potential insurgents to run around loose. But—" He raised a bony forefinger. "—my plan allows for the Empire to profit even more substantially from your under-taking."

Reactivating the holoprojector, Tarkin turned his attention to an image of the Emperor's moonlet-size secret project, or-bitally anchored at its deep-space retreat. Vader had learned that the Emperor had placed Tarkin in charge of supervising certain aspects of construction.

Clearly, though, Tarkin was angling for more.

"How does my hunt for a few rogue Jedi figure into your scheme regarding the Emperor's weapon?" Vader asked.

"My 'scheme,' " Tarkin said, with a short laugh. "All right, then. Here's the truth of it. The project is already far behind schedule. It has been beset with engineering problems, delays in shipments, the unreliability of contractors, and, most important, a shortage of skilled laborers." He stared at Vader. "You must understand, Lord Vader, I wish nothing more than to please the Emperor."

This is Sidious's real power, Vader thought. *The ability to make others wish nothing more than to please him.*

"I accept that at face value," he said at last.

Tarkin studied him. "You would be willing to help me achieve this goal?"

"I see a possibility."

Narrowing his eyes, Tarkin nodded in a way that came close to being a bow of respect. "Then, my friend, our real partnership is just beginning."

They're interested in knowing why you're so interested in knowing whether any Jedi were here during the battle," Cudgel explained to Starstone and the others while the quartet of armed Wookiees glared down at them.

"Idle curiosity," Filli said, which only succeeded in eliciting rumbling growls from the four.

"They're not buying it," Cudgel said needlessly.

Starstone gazed up into the wide bronzium muzzles of weapons she suspected she would need the Force to heft, let alone fire. Peripherally she was aware that the confrontation had begun to draw the attention of other landing parties. Humans and aliens alike were suddenly interrupting their transactions with liaison staffers and Wookiees, and turning toward the transport.

Quickly she made up her mind to risk everything by simply telling the truth.

"We're Jedi," she said just loud enough to be heard.

From the way the Wookiees tilted their enormous shaggy heads, she grasped instantly that they had understood her. They kept their exotic weapons enabled and raised, but at the same time their expressions of wariness softened somewhat.

One of them brayed a remark to Cudgel.

Cudgel stroked his long beard. "Now, that's even harder to swallow than the idle-curiosity explanation, don't you think? I mean, considering the fact that the Jedi were wiped out."

The same Wookiee lowed and gobbled, and, again, Cudgel nodded, then centered his gaze on Starstone.

"Maybe if you'd said that *you* were a Jedi, then all of us on the happy side of these blasters would be convinced. But—" He counted heads. "—you can't be telling me all eight of you are Jedi. Seven anyway, 'cause I know Filli's almost as far from being a Jedi as it gets."

"I meant *me*," Starstone said. "I'm a Jedi."

"So it's just you, then?"

"She's lying," Siadem Forte said before she could respond.

Two of the Wookiees snarled in plain displeasure.

Cudgel looked from Forte to Starstone. "Lying? See, now you have everyone really confused, 'cause we always thought of the Jedi as truth tellers."

The Wookiees spoke among themselves, then one of them barked an outpouring at Cudgel.

"Guania, here, points out that you arrive in a military transport. You look as though you can handle yourselves. You start asking questions about Jedi . . . He's thinking that you might be bounty hunters."

Starstone shook her head back and forth. "Check the transport. Under the navicomputer console, you'll find six lightsabers—"

"Means nothing," Cudgel cut in. "You could have taken them off your quarries, just the way General Grievous did."

"Then how do we prove it?" Starstone said. "What do you want us to do, perform Force tricks?"

The Wookiees issued a yodeling warning.

Cudgel lowered his voice to say: "In the unlikely event that you are Jedi, that might not be such a good idea out here in the open."

Starstone forced an exhale, and looked up at the Wookiees. "We know that Masters Yoda, Luminara Unduli, and Quinlan Vos were here with brigades of troopers." When she saw in their deep brown eyes that she had their full attention, she continued. "We've risked a lot to come here. But we know that Master Yoda had good relations with you, and we're hoping that still counts for something."

The Wookiees didn't actually lower their weapons, but they did disable them. One of them lowed to Cudgel, who said: "Lachichuk suggests we continue this conversation in Kachirho."

Starstone asked Filli and Deran to remain with the ship; then she, Forte, Kulka, and the others began to follow Cudgel and the Wookiees toward the gargantuan wroshyr that stood at the center of Kachirho tree-city. No sooner had they left the landing platform than Cudgel's attitude changed.

"I heard that *none* of you survived," he said to Starstone as they walked.

"It's beginning to look like we're the only ones," she said sadly. Putting the edge of her hand to her brow, she gazed up at the huge balconies that tiered the tree, some of which showed evidence of recent damage.

"Do you know if any Jedi died here?"

Cudgel shook his head. "The Wookiees haven't told me anything. For a while it looked like Kashyyyk was going to have its own garrison of clone troopers, but after the Sep droids and war machines shut down, the troopers decamped. Ever since, the

Wookiees have been making good use of everything that was left behind."

"For weapons?"

"You bet, for weapons. Seps or no, they've still got enemies— species that want to exploit them."

Cudgel led everyone into the hollowed base of the tree, and finally to a turbolift that accessed Kachirho's upper levels.

Similar to everything she had seen since leaving the land-ing platform, the turbolift was an ingenious blend of wood and alloy, the technology that drove it artfully concealed. And at each tier, her astonishment only increased. In addition to the exterior platforms that grew like burls from the bole, the tree contained vast interior rooms, with shimmering parquet floors and curved walls inset with wooden and alloy mosaics. There didn't seem to be a straight line anywhere, and everywhere Star-stone looked she saw Wookiees engaged in building, carving, sanding . . . as devoted to their work as Jedi had been in fashion-ing the Temple. Except the Wookiees hadn't enslaved themselves to symmetry or order; rather, they allowed their creations to emerge naturally from the wood. In fact, they seemed to invite a certain kind of imperfection—some detail to which the eye would be drawn, setting off an entire wall panel, or an expanse of floor.

Covered walkways and bridges crisscrossed the tree's interior shaft, and irregular openings brought verdant Kashyyyk *inside*. At every turn, every staircase spiral or turbolift stop, exterior views of the lake, the forest, and the sheer cliffs were framed by finely worked apertures and clefts. What Kachirho lacked in color, it made up for in luster and deep patina.

Fifty or so meters above the lake, the Jedi were ushered into a kind of central control room, which looked out over the glint-ing water and was perhaps the purest example yet of the Wook-iees' ability to combine organic and high-tech elements. Console display screens and holoprojectors showed views of the landing platform, as well as loading operations in orbit.

There, their escorts exchanged muted growls and snorts, snuffs and rumbles, with two others, one of whom was certainly the tallest Wookiee Starstone had seen.

"This is Chewbacca," Cudgel said, introducing the shorter of the pair, "and this is one of Kachirho's war chiefs, Tarfful."

Starstone introduced herself and the rest of the Jedi, then lowered herself onto a beautifully carved stool built for human-size beings. Similar stools were rushed into the room, along with soft seat cushions and plates of food.

While all this was going on, Tarfful and Chewbacca were being briefed by Lachichuk. Bronzium bands gathered the chieftain's long hair into rope-thick tassels that fell to his belted waist. The shoulder straps of his baldric joined at an ornate pectoral. Chewbacca, whose black fur was cinnamon-tipped and nowhere near as long as Tarfful's, wore a simple baldric Starstone thought might double as an ammunition bandolier.

When everyone was seated and the Wookiees had finished conversing, Cudgel said: "Chieftain Tarfful understands and applauds the courage you've shown in coming to Kashyyyk, but it grieves him to report that he has nothing but sad tidings for you."

"They're . . . dead?" Starstone asked.

"Master Vos was presumed killed by fire from a tank," Cudgel explained, "Master Unduli by blasterfire."

"And Master Yoda?" she asked quietly.

Tarfful and Chewbacca fell into a long conversation—almost a debate—before expressing themselves to Cudgel, whose eyebrows shot up in surprise.

"Apparently, Yoda escaped Kashyyyk in an evacuation pod. Chewbacca, here, says he carried Yoda on his shoulders to the pod."

Starstone came to her feet, nearly tipping over a platter of food. "He's alive?"

"He could be," Cudgel said after a moment. "After the last of the clone troopers left, the Wookiees searched local space for the pod, but no distress-beacon transmissions were picked up."

"Was the pod hyperspace-capable?"

Cudgel shook his head.

"But it could have been retrieved by a passing ship."

The Wookiees conversed.

Cudgel listened attentively. "There's a chance it was."

Starstone looked at Tarfful. "What makes you think so?"

Cudgel ran his hand over his mouth. "Wookiee Senator Yarua reported that rumors circulating in the Senate claim Yoda led an attack on Emperor Palpatine in the Senate Rotunda itself."

"And?"

"Same rumor has it he was killed."

"Master Yoda doesn't lose," Siadem Forte said from his stool.

Cudgel returned a sympathetic nod. "Lots of us used to say that about the Jedi."

Starstone broke the silence that descended on the control room. "If Master Yoda *is* alive, then there's hope for all of us. He'll find us before we find him."

She felt renewed; hopeful once more.

"Tarfful asks what you plan to do now," Cudgel said.

"I suppose we'll continue our search," Starstone said. "Master Kenobi was on Utapau, and has yet to be heard from."

Tarfful issued what sounded like a sustained groan.

"He is honored to offer you safe haven on Kashyyyk, if you wish. The Wookiees can make it appear that you are valued customers."

"You would do that for us?" Starstone asked Tarfful.

His response was plaintive.

"The Wookiees owe the Jedi a great debt," Cudgel translated. "And debts are always honored."

A signal sounded from one of the consoles, and Cudgel and the Wookiees gathered around an inset screen. The human's expression was grave when he swung to the Jedi.

"An Imperial troop carrier is descending to the Kachirho platform."

Starstone's face lost color. "We shouldn't have come here," she said suddenly. "We've endangered all of you!"

By the time Cudgel returned to the landing platform the situation was already veering out of control. Blaster rifles raised and faced off with more than one hundred very indignant Wookiees, two squads of stormtroopers were deployed around the carrier that had delivered them to Kachirho, perhaps half a kilometer from where the Jedi transport was parked.

"Or are you going to tell us that your weapons are all the permission you need?" a human liaison staffer was saying to the troopers' commander as Cudgel hurried in.

The officer's armor was marked with green, and he wore a short campaign skirt. His sidearm was still holstered, but his enhanced voice was filled with menace. "Authorization was granted by Sector Three Command and Control. If you have any complaints, take them up with the regional governor."

"Commander," Cudgel said in a deferential tone, "how may I be of service?"

The officer gestured broadly to the gathered Wookiees. "Only if you can get these beasts to answer my questions."

High-decibel snarls and furious roars rose from the crowd.

"You might want to find a more politic way to refer to Kashyyyk's indigenes, Commander."

From behind the T-visored helmet, the trooper said: "I'm not here to be diplomatic. Let them howl all they want." He gazed at Cudgel. "Identify yourself."

"I'm known as Cudgel, far and wide."

"What are your duties here?"

"I assist with commerce. I can probably set you up with a nice selection of product, if you're interested."

"What would we want with wood?"

"What, you don't have campfires?"

The crowd woofed with laughter.

The commander put his gloved right hand on his blaster. "There'll be fires soon enough—*Cudgel*. Right where you can see them."

"I'm not sure I take your meaning, Commander."

The officer adjusted his stance, readying himself for action. "Kashyyyk is harboring enemies of the Empire."

Cudgel shook his head. "If there are enemies of the Empire here, the Wookiees are unaware of them."

"There are *Jedi* here."

"You mean you actually missed a few?"

The commander raised his left hand and poked Cudgel hard in the chest. "Either they are surrendered to us immediately, or we take this place apart, beginning with you." At the commander's wave, the stormtroopers began to spread out. "Search the landing area and the tree-city! All non-indigenes are to be seized and brought here!"

The Wookiees loosed a chorus of earsplitting yowls.

Cudgel backed out of range of the commander's armored fist. "They don't like it when people track dirt in."

Drawing his sidearm, the commander said: "I'm done with you."

But the words had scarcely left the officer's helmet enunciator when a Wookiee raced forward, knocking the blaster from his hand and hurling him into the troop carrier with such force that the commander's forearm and elbow armor remained in the Wookiee's grip.

At the same time, several Wookiee clarions roared in the distance.

The troopers turned, covering one another as the gathered crowd began to advance on them.

A ratcheting noise filled the western sky. Two gunships dropped from the treetops to reinforce the advance squads, stormtroopers descending from the open bay on rappel ribbons.

Rushing onto the landing platform, the new arrivals stopped short on hearing the familiar *snap-hiss* of igniting lightsabers.

Central to half a dozen blade-wielding Jedi stood a young raven-haired woman, with her weapon poised over her right shoulder.

"We hear you're looking for us," she said.

Standing on the bridge of the *Exactor,* Vader regarded distant Kashyyyk through the forward viewports. Commander Appo approached from one of the duty stations.

"Lord Vader, the conflict has begun. Theater commanders await your orders."

"Raise them, Commander, and join me in the situation room."

Leaving the bridge, Vader entered an adjacent cabin space just as holoimages were resolving above a ring of several holoprojectors. Appo came through the hatch behind him, waiting at the perimeter of the ring.

Members of the Emperor's new admiralty, the commanders were human, attired in formfitting jackets and trousers. Certainly each of them had been informed that Vader was to be treated with the same respect they showed the Emperor, but Vader could see in their ghostly faces that they had yet to make up their minds about him. Was he man, machine, something in between? Was he clone, apostate Jedi, *Sith*?

Kashyyyk would tell them all they needed to know, Vader thought.

I am something to be feared.

"Commanders, I want you to position your task forces to cover all major population centers." A holomap eddied from a holoprojector outside the ring, detailing Kashyyyk and the tree-cites of Kachirho, Rwookrrorro, Kepitenochan, Okikuti, Chena-chochan, and others. "Furthermore, I want Interdictor cruisers deployed to prevent any ships from jumping to hyperspace."

"Admiral Vader," one of the men said. "The Wookiees have no ranged weapons or planetary defense shields. Orbital bombardment would simplify matters greatly."

Vader decided not to make an issue of the misplaced honorific. "Perhaps, Commander," he said, "if this were an exercise in obliteration. But since it isn't, we'll adhere to my plan."

"I've had some experience with the Wookiees," another said. "They won't be taken into captivity without a fight."

"I fully expect a fight, Commander," Vader said. "But I want as many as possible taken *alive*—males, females, and younglings. Order your troops to drive them from their tree-cities into open spaces. Then use whatever means are at our disposal to disarm and subdue them."

"Kashyyyk hosts many merchants," a third said, leadingly.

"Casualties of war, Commander."

"Do you intend to occupy the planet?" the same asked.

"That is not my intention."

"Excuse me, sir, but what, then, are we supposed to do with tens of thousands of Wookiee captives?"

Vader faced the one who had challenged him. "Herd them into containment and keep them contained until they have accepted their defeat. You will then receive further orders."

"From whom?" the challenger said.

"From *me*, Commander."

The officer folded his arms in mild defiance. "From you."

"You seem to have a problem with that. Perhaps you wish to speak with the Emperor?"

The officer was quick to adopt a more military pose. "No, of course not . . . Lord Vader."

Better and better, Vader thought.

"Where will you be, Lord Vader?" the first asked.

Vader looked at all of them before answering. "My task needn't concern you. You have your orders. Now carry them out."

Try as she might to convince herself that her actions were justified, that the clone army had become the enemy not only of the Jedi but also of democracy and freedom, Starstone couldn't surrender herself fully to combat. Brought into being to serve the Republic, the troopers, like the Jedi, had fallen victim to Palpatine's treachery. And now they were dying at the hands of those who had helped create them.

This is wrong, all wrong, she told herself.

And yet, clearly, the notion of tragic irony hadn't been incorporated into the clones' programming. The troopers were out to kill her. Only the flashing blue blade of her lightsaber stood between her and certain death.

The stormtroopers who had been the first to land were already dead, from blaster rounds, bowcaster quarrels, lightsaber slashes, blows from war clubs and the occasional giant, shaggy fist. But more and more Imperial craft were dropping from the wan sky—gunships, troop carriers, scores of two-person infantry support platforms. Worse, word had it that the incursion wasn't confined to Kachirho, but was being repeated in tree-cites world-wide.

If the hearsay was true, then the Jedi weren't the priority. The Empire was merely using their presence to justify a full-scale invasion. And the fact that Imperial forces were refraining from launching orbital bombardments told Starstone that the ultimate goal was something other than speciecide.

The troopers had been ordered not to amass high body counts, but to return with prisoners.

Starstone held herself accountable. Inevitable or not, she had furnished the Empire with grounds to invade. Forte and Kulka were wrong to have deferred to her lead. She was not a Master. She should have listened to Shryne.

The surround of towering cliffs and trees made it difficult for large vessels to hover or land outside the perimeter of the landing platform. The lake that fronted Kachirho was expansive enough to accommodate a *Victory*-class Star Destroyer, but a subsequent offensive would entail storming the shoreline, as the Separatists had attempted to do, and Kachirho, at almost four hundred meters in height, presented a formidable battlement.

Natural fortresses, wroshyr trees not only deflected ordinary blaster bolts but also provided hundreds of defensive platforms. More important, trees that had endured for thousands of years were not easily burned, let alone uprooted or felled. Without employing turbolasers and resigning themselves to massive death tolls, Imperial forces faced a grueling battle.

Judging by the manner in which they had deployed the gun-ships and troop carriers, Kashyyyk's theater commanders were relying on the fact that the Wookiees had no ranged weapons and little in the way of anti-aircraft defense. But the Imperials had failed to take into account the thousands of war machines that had been abandoned by Separatist and Republic forces alike following the fierce engagement on the Wawaatt Archipelago—tank droids, missile platforms, spider and crab droids, All Terrain Walkers and juggernauts. And just now the Wookiees were putting all that they had salvaged to good use.

Imperial gunships were unable to descend below treetop level without the risk of being blown from the sky by commandeered artillery that had been moved to Kachirho's loftiest platforms, or by fluttercraft retrofitted with laser cannons. Closer to the ground, those gunships that succeeded in evading the fire and flak found themselves set upon by flights of catamarans mounted with rocket launchers and repeating blasters.

Troopers attempting to rappel from incapacitated ships were picked off by hails of bowcaster quarrels, blaster bolts fired from rifles taller than Starstone, sometimes bands of Wookiees swinging out from the tree-city platforms on braided vines. The few troopers who survived the airborne barrages and reached the ground faced focused fire from blaster nests high in the trees, volleys of grenades, and showers of red-hot debris sizzling down through the leafy canopy.

Fighting alongside Tarfful, Chewbacca, and hundreds of Wookiee warriors, Starstone and the other Jedi were still involved in the chaotic fray on the landing platform. Employing carved shields and eccentric blasters, Wookiee females fought as ferociously as the males, and many of the offworld merchants were pitching in, recognizing that the Empire had no intention of sparing them. Weapons cleverly concealed in drop ships and transports were targeting anything the Wookiees missed, and many ferries were racing up the well, intent on carrying entire Wookiee families to safety.

In areas where there were lulls in the fighting, many Wookiee females and younglings were falling back toward the tree-city, or evacuating Kachirho's lower levels for the refuge of the high forest.

Starstone wondered just how much the Empire was willing

to risk at Kashyyyk. Had Palpatine's minions considered that, faced with captivity, the Wookiees might flee their arboreal cities and become a rebel force the likes of which the Grand Army had yet to confront?

The thought provided her with a moment of solace.

Then she glimpsed something that sent her heart racing.

Sensing her sudden distraction, Forte and Kulka followed her gaze to midlevel Kachirho, where a black Imperial shuttle was drifting in for a landing on one of the tree-city's enormous balconies.

"It's Vader," Starstone said when the two Jedi Knights asked.

"Are you certain?" Forte said.

At Starstone's nod, Kulka gestured broadly to the ongoing fight. "This is more about us than the Wookiees even know."

Starstone shut her eyes briefly and forced a determined exhalation. "Then it's up to us to make this about *Vader*."

Leading an exodus of women and younglings from Kachirho's lowest levels, Chewbacca thought about his own family in distant Rwookrrorro, which apparently was also under siege. Rwookrrorro was days away on foot, but only minutes by ship. He would get there one way or another.

Off to his left, the six Jedi who had been fighting alongside him for the better part of a local hour were suddenly racing back toward Kachirho's central wroshyr. Lifting his eyes, Chewbacca saw no significant threat, save for a *Theta*-class shuttle that was taking heavy fire as it attempted to fold its wings and settle on one of the tree-city balconies.

Higher up, the sky was crisscrossed by laserfire and contrails, and still filling with gunships, eerily reminiscent of what had happened only weeks earlier, when the Separatists had launched their invasion. Wookiee fluttercraft and an assortment of traders' vessels were engaging the Imperial ships, but the outcome was clear.

The sheer number of descending gunships gave evidence of a sizable flotilla of capital ships in orbit. For all the Wookiees' success in repelling the first wave, it was surely only a matter of time before the Star Destroyers would open fire. And then only a matter of time until Kashyyyk fell.

Anyone who thought that the Jedi were responsible for having brought the Empire down on Kashyyyk had no understanding of the nature of power. From the moment the troopers of Commander Gree's brigade had turned on Yoda, Unduli, and Vos, Chewbacca, Tarfful, and the elders of Kachirho had grasped the truth: that despite all the rhetoric about taxation, free trade, and decentralization, there was no real difference between the Confederacy and the Republic. The war was nothing more than a struggle between two evils, with the Jedi caught in the middle, all because of their misplaced loyalty to a government they should have abandoned, and to a pledge that had superseded their oath to serve the Force above all.

If there was any difference between the Separatists and the newly born Imperialists, it was that the latter needed to *legitimize* their invasion and occupation, lest other threatened species rebel while they stood a fighting chance.

But a planet could fall without its species being defeated; a planet could be occupied without its species being imprisoned.

That was what separated Kashyyyk from the rest.

Back- and hip-packs bulging with survival food and rations, Wookiees were streaming down the city staircases, racing across the footbridges, and disappearing into the thick vegetation that surrounded the lake. Blazed as a defense against sneak attacks by Trandoshan slavers, hundreds of well-maintained evacuation routes cached with arms and supplies radiated from Kachirho and wove through the isolated rock outcroppings to the high forest beyond.

More to the point, Wookiees even as young as twelve, fresh from their coming-of-age hrrtayyk ceremonies, knew how to construct shelters from saplings, how to fashion implements from the stalks of giant leaves, and how to make rope. They knew which plants and insects were edible; the location of freshwater springs; the areas where dangerous reptiles or predatory felines lurked.

Despite all the elements of high technology they had incorporated into their lives, Wookiees never considered themselves separate from Kashyyyk's grand forest, which on its own could provide them everything they needed to survive, for as long as necessary.

Targeted by unexpected anti-aircraft fire, Vader's shuttle jinked for the largest of the Kachirho's arboreal balconies, its powerful defensive shields raised and its quad lasers spewing unrelenting fire at a pair of hailfire droids the Wookiees had hoisted into their massive tree-fortress. Bolts from the shuttle's forward weapons reduced the missile platforms to slagged heaps and chewed into the balcony's wooden columns and beams, filling the air with splinters hard as nails. The explosions flung the bodies of Kachirho's furry defenders far and wide. Hurled clear off the tier, some plummeted to the ground a hundred meters below.

In the cabin space of the shaken shuttle, Vader was being addressed by the holoimage of one of the task force commanders.

"Our circumspect attacks are being repulsed planetwide, Lord Vader. As I thought I made clear, Wookiees do not take lightly to the threat of captivity. Already they're abandoning the tree-cities for the high forests. If they penetrate deeply enough, we will need months, perhaps years to find and root them out. Even then, the cost to us will be great, in terms of matériel and lives."

Vader muted the holoprojector's audio pickup and glanced across the aisle to Commander Appo. "Do you concur, Commander?"

"As it is we're losing too many troopers," Appo said without hesitation. "Grant permission to the naval commanders to initiate surgical bombardment from orbit."

Vader mulled it over for a moment. He didn't like being wrong, much less admitting that he had been wrong, but he saw no way out. "You may commence bombardment, Commander, but make certain you save Kachirho for last. I have business to finish up here."

As the holoimage faded, Vader turned to the cabin's small porthole, meditating on the whereabouts of his Jedi quarries, and what nature of trap they had set for him. The thought of confronting them stirred his impatience and his anger.

Wings uplifted, the shuttle made a rough landing on the tier, bolts from Wookiee blasters careening from the fuselage. When the boarding ramp had extended, Appo and his stormtroopers hurried outside, Vader right behind him, his ignited blade deflecting fire from all sides.

Three troopers fell before they made it two meters from the ramp.

The Wookiees were dug in, shooting from behind makeshift barricades and from crossbeams high above the balcony. Raising the shuttle on repulsorlift power, the clone pilot took the craft through a 180-degree sweep, drenching the area with laserfire. At the same time, two Wookiees with satchel charges slung over their shoulders rushed from cover and managed to hurl the explosives through the shuttle's open hatch. A deafening explosion blew off one of the wings and sent the craft spinning and skidding to the very rim of the tier.

Counterattacking, Vader strode through fountaining flames to take the fight to the Wookiees. Crimson blade slashing left and right, he parried blaster bolts and amputated limbs and heads. Caterwauling and howling, showing their fangs and waving their long arms about, the Wookiees tried to hold their positions, but they had never faced anything like him, even in the darkest depths of Kashyyyk's primeval forest.

As tall as some of them, Vader waded in, his lightsaber cleaving intricately carved war shields, sending blasters and bowcasters flying, setting fire to shaggy coats, leaving more than a score of bodies in his wake.

He was waving Appo and the other troopers forward when flashes of refulgent blue light caught his eye, and he swung to the source.

Emerging from a covered bridge anchored distally to the bole of the giant tree rushed six Jedi, deflecting blaster bolts from the stormtroopers as they attacked, doing to Appo's cadre just what Vader had done to the Wookiees.

Forging through the offensive, three Jedi raced in to square off with Vader.

He recognized the petite, black-haired female among them, and tipped his blade in salute.

"You've saved me the trouble of looking for you, Padawan Starstone. These others must be the ones you gathered by accessing the Temple beacon."

Starstone's dark eyes bored into him. "You defiled the Temple by setting foot in it."

"More than you know," he told her.

"Then you'll pay for that, as well."

He angled the lightsaber in front of him, tip pointed slightly downward. "You're very much mistaken, Padawan. It is you who will pay."

Before Starstone could make a move, Siadem Forte and Iwo Kulka stepped in front of her and attacked Vader.

As was the case with many Jedi Knights, the two were familiar with accounts of what had happened on Geonosis when Obi-Wan Kenobi and Anakin Skywalker had gone after the Sith Lord, Count Dooku. And so Forte and Kulka went in as a team, each of them employing a radically different lightsaber style, determined to off-balance Vader.

But Vader merely stood like a statue, his blade angled toward the ground until the very instant the two Jedi unleashed their assault.

Then, as the three blades joined in scatterings of dazzling light and grating static sounds, he moved.

Forte and Kulka were skilled duelists, but Vader was not only faster than Starstone remembered him being on Murkhana against Master Chatak, but also more agile. He employed his awesome power to put a quick end to the fancy twirling of his opponents, who fell back against the hammering blows of Vader's bloodshine blade.

Time and again the two Jedi Knights attempted to alter their style, but Vader had an answer for every lunge, parry, and riposte. His style borrowed elements from all techniques of combat, even from the highest, most dangerous levels, and his moves were crisp and unpredictable. In addition, his remarkable foresight allowed him to anticipate Forte's and Kulka's strategies and maneuvers, his blade always one step ahead of theirs, notwithstanding the two-handed grip he employed.

Toying with the Jedi, he grazed Forte on the left shoulder, then on the right thigh; Kulka, he pierced lightly in the abdomen, then shaved away the flesh on the right side of the Ho'Din's face.

Seeing the two Jedi Knights drop to their knees, wincing in pain, Padawan Klossi Anno broke from where she was helping Jambe and Nam engage the stormtroopers and got to Vader one step ahead of Starstone.

Sidestepping, Vader slashed her across the back, sending her sprawling across the balcony; then he whirled on Forte and Kulka just as they were clambering to their feet and decapitated them. From behind Vader came Jambe and Nam, neither of whom was an experienced fighter and both of whom Vader immediately eliminated from the fight, amputating Jambe's right arm, and Nam's right leg.

To her horror, Starstone realized she was suddenly alone with Vader, who immediately signaled his stormtroopers to leave her to him, and to devote themselves to slaughtering the few Wookiees who remained on the tier.

"Now you, Padawan," he said, as he began to circle her.

Calling on the Force, Starstone fell on him in a fury, striking wildly and repeatedly, *and with anger.* Moments into her attack she understood that Vader was merely allowing her to vent, as the Temple's swordmaster had often done with students, allowing them to believe that they were driving him back, when in fact he was simply encouraging them to wear themselves out before disarming them in one rapid motion.

So she retreated, altering her strategy and calming herself.

Vader is so tall, so imposing . . . But perhaps I can get under or inside his guard as Master Chatak did—

"Your thoughts give you away, Padawan," he said in a flash. "You mustn't take the time to *think*. You must act on impulse. Instead of repressing your anger, *call on it!* Make use of it to defeat me."

Starstone feigned an attack, then sidestepped and slashed at him.

Shifting to a one-handed hold on his lightsaber, he parried her blade and lunged forward. She snapped aside in the nick of time, but he kept coming at her, answering her increasingly frantic strikes with harsher ones and driving her inexorably toward the rim of the balcony.

He flicked his blade, precisely, economically, forcing her back and back . . .

She felt as if she were fighting a droid, although a droid programmed to counter all her best stratagems. Ducking out from under a broad sweep of the crimson blade, she somersaulted to safety.

But only for a moment.

"You're skittish, Padawan."

Sweat dripped into her eyes. She tried to center herself in the Force. At the same time she was vaguely aware of a new sound in the air, cutting through the chaos of the battle below. And just then a familiar ship slammed down on the tier alongside the crippled shuttle, two equally familiar figures leaping from the hatch even while the ship was still in motion.

At once, and seemingly of its own accord, the blood-smeared hilt of Master Forte's lightsaber shot from the balcony floor, whizzing past Vader's masked face to snap into the hand of one

of the figures and ignite. A gurgled sound issued from somewhere close to the newly arrived ship and something metallic hit
the floor and began to roll forward.

His black cloak unfurling, Vader spun around to find the helmeted head of Commander Appo coming to a rocky rest at his
feet.

A few meters away Roan Shryne stood with his legs spread to
shoulder width, Forte's blue blade angled high and to one side.
Alongside him, blasters in both six-fingered hands, Archyr was
dropping every stormtrooper who approached.

"Get away from him!" Shryne yelled at Starstone.

She gaped at him. "How did you—"

"Filli was keeping us updated. Now move away—hurry!"

Vader made no effort to prevent her from slinking past him.
"Very touching, Shryne," he said after a moment. "Treating her
like your personal learner."

Shryne gestured broadly. "Olee, get the wounded into the
drop ship!" Advancing on Vader, he said: "I'm the one you want,
Vader. So here's your chance. Me for them."

"Shryne, no—" Starstone started.

"Take the wounded!" he cut her off. "Jula's waiting."

"I'm not leaving you!"

"I'll catch up with you when I'm done with him."

Vader looked from Shryne to Starstone. "Listen to your Master, Padawan. He has already lost two learners. I'm certain he
doesn't want to lose a third."

Coming back to herself, Starstone hurried to help Lambe,
Klossi, Nam, and some of the Wookiees get aboard the drop
ship. Determined to quiet her fears for Shryne, she forced herself
not to look at him, but she could feel him reaching out to her.

He is a Jedi again.

With gunships circling Kachirho like insects spilled from an aggravated nest, Skeck powered the drop ship over the edge of the balcony and dived for the beleaguered landing platform. Airbursts from Imperial artillery crawlers raked and scorched the ship, inside which Starstone sat slumped on her knees with her arm around Klossi Anno, who was going in and out of consciousness, the wound on her back like a blackened trench. Across the cramped passenger bay Lambe and Nam, white-faced with fear, were nursing their amputated limbs and calling on the Force to keep from going into shock.

Wookiees huddled, braying in anger or whimpering in pain. Two of those Starstone and Archyr had helped carry aboard were dead.

Who was Vader? she asked herself. *What* was he?

She looked again at Klossi's wound, then at the one in her upper arm she hadn't even felt herself sustain. Vader's way of marking them with a Sith brand.

Could even Shryne defeat him?

"Hold tight!" Archyr yelled from the drop ship's copilot's seat. "This'll be one to remember!"

Skeck was taking the ship in *fast*. While the impaired repulsors were managing to keep it airborne, the ship was tipped acutely to one side. As a result, the wing on that side made first contact with the platform, gouging a ragged furrow in the wooden surface and whipping the ship into a spin that sent it crashing into a parked ferry in even sorrier condition.

Starstone's head slammed against the bulkhead with such force that she saw stars. Setting Klossi down gently, she checked on Lambe and Nam. Then she stumbled through the drop ship hatch, with Archyr trailing while Skeck remained at the controls.

Daylight was fading and the air was filled with the smoke and grit of battle.

The sky wailed with ships and pulsed with strobing explosions. Wookiees and other beings were running every which way across the landing platform. Elsewhere, bands of Wookiees, including some of those the Jedi had met, were carrying the wounded to shelter. Many of the traders' ships had lifted off, but just as many had been savaged by gunship fire or were buried under debris that had fallen from Kachirho's uppermost limbs and branches.

Principal fighting had moved east of the platform, closer to the lake. There, several crashed gunships were in flames, and the ground was piled high with the bodies of dead Wookiees and clone troopers. Imperial forces were storming the tree-city from all sides, even from the far shore of the lake, arriving on swamp-speeders and other watercraft. Searing hyphens of blasterfire were streaming from fortified positions high up the trunk, but what with the circling gunships and mobile artillery, the Wookiees were slowly being driven toward the ground.

Her head swimming, Starstone steadied herself against the drop ship's tipped fin.

Out of billowing smoke came Filli, running in a crouch and leading Deran Nalual by her left hand. Converging on Starstone from another direction appeared Cudgel and a dozen or so

Wookiees, Chewbacca among them, some of them limping, some with blood-matted fur.

"Where are the others?" Filli asked her, loud enough to be heard above the maelstrom of smoke and fire.

She motioned to the drop ship. "Skeck, Lambe, Nam, and Klossi are inside."

"Forte?" Filli said. "Kulka . . . ?"

"Dead."

Deran Nalual hung her head and clutched on to Filli's arm.

"Shryne?"

Wide-eyed she gazed up at the balcony, as if just recalling him. "Up there."

Filli's eyes remained on her. "The *Drunk Dancer*'s upside. You ready to leave?"

She stared at him. "Leave?"

He nodded. "Try to, anyway."

She looked around in naked dread. "We can't leave them to this! We brought this on!"

Filli firmed his lips. "What happened to your idea of perpetuating the Jedi order?" He reached for her hands, but she backed away. "If you want to die a hero here, then I'll stay and die with you," he said flatly. "But only if I'm convinced that you know our deaths aren't going to affect the outcome."

"Filli's right," Archyr said from behind her, shouting to be heard. "Punish yourself later, Olee. If we're gonna survive this, the sooner we're airborne, the better."

Starstone swept her eyes over the ruined landing platform. "We take as many as we can with us."

Overhearing her, Cudgel began gesticulating to the Wookiees with whom he had arrived. "Chewbacca, pack the drop ship and the transport! Get everyone you can inside."

Others heard her, as well, and it wasn't long before dozens of Wookiees began to press forward. Shortly the area was crowded with more Wookiees and traders than the two ships could possibly accommodate. But in the midst of the mad crush for space aboard the craft, Imperial gunships abruptly began to break off their attack on Kachirho.

The reason for the sudden withdrawal was soon made clear, as colossal turbolaser beams lanced from the sky, scorching areas of the surrounding forests into which thousands of Wookiees had fled. With great booming sounds, giant limbs broke from the wroshyrs, and hot wind and flames swept over the landing platform, setting fire to nearly everything flammable.

With explosive sounds rumbling, Wookiees ran screaming from the forest, fur singed, blackened, or ablaze.

It took Starstone a moment to realize that she was flat on her back on the landing platform. Picking herself up, hair blowing in a hot, foul-smelling wind, she struggled to her feet in time to hear Cudgel say: "Orbital barrage—"

The rest of his words were subsumed in a thunderous noise that commenced in the upper reaches of Kachirho as dozens of huge limbs fractured and fell, plummeting into the lake and flattening acres of shoreline vegetation.

Suddenly Archyr was tapping her on the shoulder.

"Olee, we're as full as we can be and still be able to lift off."

She nodded by rote.

Filli turned and started back toward the transport, only to stop, swing around, and show her an alarmed look. "Wait! Who's going to fly that thing?"

She gaped at him. "I thought—"

"I'm no pilot! What about Lambe or Nam?"

She shook her head back and forth. "They're in no shape." Scanning everyone, her gaze fell on Cudgel. "Can you pilot the transport?"

He gestured to himself in incredulity. "Sure. Providing you don't care about being shot out of the air as soon as we launch."

Her dread mounted, the rush of blood pounding in her ears. *I can't leave everyone here!* All at once Cudgel was calling to her and motioning Chewbacca forward.

"Chewbacca can pilot the transport!"

She shot the Wookiee a dubious glance, then looked to Cudgel for assurance. "Can he even *fit?*"

Chewbacca barked and brayed to Cudgel.

"He'll do the piloting in return for your allowing him to take the transport back down the well to Rwookrrorro," Cudgel explained. "His home village. He has family there."

Starstone was already nodding. "Of course he can."

"Everyone on board," Archyr yelled. "Seal 'em up!" Swinging to Starstone, he said: "Which one are you going up in?"

She shook her head. "I'm not. I'm waiting here for Shryne."

"Oh, no, you're not," he said.

"Archyr, you saw Vader!"

"And so did Roan."

"But—"

"We'll try to grab him on the way up." Archyr gestured to the transport. "Now get aboard, and tell Chewbacca to stick close. Skeck and I will provide cover fire."

"I was rather fond of Commander Appo," Vader said, toeing the amputated head of the clone officer out of his path as he moved closer to Shryne.

Shryne tightened his grip on the hilt of Forte's lightsaber and sidestepped cautiously to the left, forcing Vader to adjust his course. "I felt the same about Bol Chatak."

"Tell me, Shryne, are *you* the trap the others hoped to spring on me?"

Shryne continued to circle Vader. "I wasn't even part of their plan. In fact, I tried to talk them out of doing something like this."

"But in the end you just couldn't stay away. Even if it meant abandoning what might have been a lucrative career as a smuggler."

"Losing Senator Fang Zar was a blow to our reputation. I figured I'd better eliminate the competition."

"Yes," Vader said, raising his blade somewhat, "I am your worst rival."

Lightsaber grasped in both hands, Vader took a single forward step and performed a lightning-fast underhand sweep that almost knocked Forte's lightsaber from Shryne's grip. Spinning, Shryne regained his balance and raced forward, feinting a diagonal slash from the left, then twisting the blade around to the right and surging forward. The blade might have gotten past Vader's guard, but instead it glanced off the back of his upraised left hand, smoke curling from the black glove. Shryne countered quickly with an upsweep to Vader's neck, but Vader spun to the right, his blade held straight out in front of him as he completed a circle, nearly cutting Shryne in half.

Folding himself at the waist, Shryne skittered backward, parrying a rapid series of curt but powerful slashes. Backflipping out of range, he twisted his body to the right, set the blade over his right shoulder, and rushed forward, hammering away. Vader deflected the blows without altering his stance or giving ground, but in the process left his lower trunk and legs unprotected.

In a blink Shryne dropped into a crouch and pivoted through a turn.

For an instant it seemed that the blade was going to pass clear through Vader's knees, but Vader leapt high, half twisting in midair and coming down behind Shryne. Shryne rolled as Vader's crimson shaft struck the floor at the spot he had just vacated. Scrambling to his feet, Shryne hurled himself forward, catching Vader in the right forearm.

Snarling, Vader took his left hand from the lightsaber hilt to dampen sparking at the site of what should have been a wound.

Astonishment eclipsed Shryne's follow-up attack.

"I know you don't have a heart," he said, taking stalking steps, "but I didn't realize that you're *all* droid."

Vader may have been about to reply when packets of blinding light speared through the balcony, opening holes ten meters across. The great wroshyr shook as if struck by the full force of a lightning storm, and branches and leaves rained down on what was left of the deck. With a loud splitting sound, a large section of the rim broke away, taking Vader's shuttle with it.

"There goes your ride home," Shryne said when he could. "Guess you're stuck here with me."

Vader was a good distance away, one hand and one knee pressed to the floor, his blade angled away from him. Slowly he stood to his full height, leaves falling around him, black cloak flapping in the downdrafts. Then, with determined strides, he advanced on Shryne, sweeping his blade from side to side.

"I wouldn't have it any other way."

Shryne took a quick look around.

With most of the tier behind him blown away, and gaping holes elsewhere, he began to back toward the hollowed trunk of the tree.

"Almost seems like your own people are trying to kill you, Vader," he said. "Maybe they don't like the idea of a Sith influencing the Emperor."

Vader continued his resolute march. "Trust me, Shryne, the Emperor couldn't be more pleased."

Shryne cast a quick glance over his shoulder. They were entering an enormous interior space of wooden ramps, walkways, bridges, and concourses. "He doesn't have enough experience with your kind."

"And you do?"

"Enough to know that you'll turn on him eventually."

Vader loosed what could have been a laugh. "What makes you think the Emperor won't turn on me first?"

"Like he turned on the Jedi," Shryne said. "Although I suspect that was mostly your doing."

Five meters away, Vader stopped short. "Mine?"

"You convinced him that with you by his side, he could get away with just about anything."

Again, Vader's exhalation approximated a laugh. "It's thinking like that that blinded the Jedi to their fate." He raised his sword. "Now it's time for you to join them."

Vader closed the distance between them in a heartbeat, slashing left and right with potent vertical strokes, narrowly missing Shryne time and again, but destroying everything touched by the blade. No whirling now; no windmilling or deft lunges. He simply used his bulk and size to remain wedded to the floor. It was an old style, the very opposite of what was said to have been Dooku's style, and Shryne had no defense against it.

If I could see his face, his eyes, Shryne found time to think.

If he could knock that outsize helmet from Vader's head.

If he could lance his lightsaber through the control panel on Vader's chest—

That was the key! That was the reason for Vader's antique style—to protect his center, as Grievous had been forced to do.

If he could only get to that control panel . . .

The two craft lifted off into smoke and withering night, spiraling up through resuming enemy fire toward Kachirho's mid-level balconies. In the transport's cramped cockpit with Cudgel, Filli, and Chewbacca—wedged into his seat, his head grazing the ceiling—Starstone clenched her white-knuckled hands on the shaking arms of the acceleration chair.

She couldn't bring herself to lift her gaze to the viewports, for fear of what sights might greet her.

As if reading her mind, Cudgel said: "You can't save an entire planet, kid. And it's not like you didn't try."

Chewbacca reinforced the remark with a gutsy bass rumble, repeatedly slamming his huge hands down on the transport's control yoke for emphasis.

"The Wookiees knew that their days of freedom were numbered," Cudgel translated. "Kashyyyk will only be the first non-human world to be enslaved."

Chewbacca threw the weary transport through a sudden evasive turn, nearly spilling everyone from their chairs. Through the viewport, Starstone caught a glimpse of Vader's black shuttle, tumbling toward the ground. Firewalling the throttle, Chewbacca clawed for altitude, barely escaping the flames of the crashed shuttle's mushrooming fireball.

Archyr's voice issued through the cockpit enunciators as the drop ship appeared in the starboard panel of the viewport. "Close call!"

Growling irritably, Chewbacca ran a fast systems check.

"Tail singed," Cudgel told Archyr through the comlink. "But everything else is intact."

The drop ship remained in view to starboard.

"Half the balcony fell with the shuttle," Archyr continued. "There isn't much room to put down, even if you're still fool enough to risk it. Whatever Olee has in mind, she'd better be quick about it."

Cudgel swiveled to her. "You got that?"

She nodded as the ravaged balcony came into view, in worse shape than she had feared. Most of the rim was gone, and the few areas that still clung to the trunk of the wroshyr had been holed and crisped by turbolaser bolts. The bodies of Wookiees and stormtroopers sprawled in the spreading flames.

"I don't see any sign of Shryne *or* Vader," Archyr said over the comlink.

"Turbos could have killed them—" Cudgel started when Starstone cut him off.

"No. I would know."

Chewbacca directed a yodeling bray at her.

"He believes you," Cudgel translated.

Starstone leaned toward Chewbacca. "You think you can set us down?"

Chewbacca lowed dubiously, then nodded. Feathering the repulsorlift lever, he began to cheat the transport closer to the wroshyr. The craft was meters from landing when, without warning, what remained of the wooden tier sheared away from the massive trunk, taking several lower tiers with it as it disintegrated and fell.

Starstone sucked in her breath as Chewbacca pulled the ship sharply away from the bole. Half out of her chair, she focused her gaze on the cave-like opening to the tree's dimly lighted interior and stretched out with the Force.

"They're inside! I can feel them."

Filli pulled her back into her chair. "There's nothing we can do."

Archyr's voiced barked through the enunciator. "Gunships approaching."

Cudgel forced her to look at him. "What would Shryne want you to do?"

She didn't have to think about it. Blowing out her breath, she said: "Chewbacca, get us out of this."

Relieved sighs came from Filli and Cudgel, a melancholy rumble from the Wookiee, who lifted the transport's nose and accelerated.

"Steer clear of the lake," Archyr warned. Again the drop ship came alongside, warding off strikes from inrushing Imperial gunships. "We've only got a narrow escape vector, north-northwest."

Dodging fire, the two ships raced into a burnt-orange sunset and climbed for the stars, mingling with scores of escaping ferries and cargo haulers. Turbolaser bolts rained down from ships in orbit, and across the darkening curve of the planet, fires raged.

Lowing in anguish and pounding one giant fist on the instrument panel, Chewbacca pointed to a bright burning in the canopy.

"Rwookrrorro," Cudgel said. "Chewbacca's tree-village."

The stars were just losing their shimmer when the communications suite toned. Filli routed the transmission through the cockpit speakers.

"Glad to see you've come to your senses," Jula said. "Is Roan with either of you?"

"Negative, Jula," Filli said sadly.

Save for bursts of static, the enunciator remained silent for a long moment; then Jula's voice returned. "After Alderaan, there was nothing I could say . . ." Her words trailed off, but she wasn't finished. "None of us is out of this yet, anyway. Vader or whoever's in charge has Interdictor cruisers parked in orbit. No ships have been able to jump to hyperspace."

"Does the *Drunk Dancer* have enough firepower to take on the cruiser?" Cudgel asked.

"Filli," Jula said, "inform whoever asked that question that I'm not about to go to guns with a Detainer CC-twenty-two-hundred."

As the transport reached the edge of Kashyyyk's envelope, magnified views of local space showed hundreds of ships trapped in the artificial gravity well generated by the Interdictor's powerful projectors. Interspersed among the ensnared vessels drifted the blackened husks of Separatist warships that had been there since the end of the war.

"Too bad we can't start up one of those Sep destroyers," Cudgel lamented. "They have guns enough to deal with that cruiser."

Starstone and Filli looked at each other.

"We might know a way," he said.

On Kashyyyk, rapacious fires held night at bay. The shadows of running figures crisscrossed the ground. Spilled blood shone glossy black, as black as the charred bark of the wroshyr trees.

Safe inside their plastoid shells an occupying force of stormtroopers rappelled into the burning forests, flushing fleeing Wookiees back into the open, out onto the debris-strewn landing platform, the shore of the lake, the public spaces between the tree clusters that made up Kachirho.

Imperial war machines closed in from all sides; speeders and swift boats roaring up onto the sandy banks, gunships coiling down from the treetops, *Victory*-class Destroyers descending from the stars, their wedge-shaped armored hulls outlined by bright running lights.

Driven from tree-city and forest, the Wookiees found themselves surrounded by companies of troopers. Male and female alike, the largest were stunned into submission or killed. And yet the Wookiees continued to fight, even the youngest among them, and often with only tooth and nail, tearing scores of troopers limb from limb before succumbing to blasterfire.

Not all of Kachirho's tens of thousands were rounded up, but more than enough to satisfy the Empire's current needs. Should more be needed, the troopers would know where to look for them.

Herded to the center of the landing platform with countless others, Tarfful raised his long arms above his head and loosed a mournful, stentorian roar at the heavens.

Kashyyyk had fallen.

Shryne's slashing strike to Vader's lower left leg, owing as much to luck as to skill, released another shower of sparks.

Vader's enraged response was Shryne's only assurance that he was fighting a living being. Whatever had happened to Vader, by accident or volition, he had to be more flesh-and-blood than cyborg, or he wouldn't have raged or been able to call on the Force with such intensity.

High up in the smoke-filled latticelike room, they stood facing each other on a suspension bridge that linked two fully enclosed walkways, the gloom cut by shafts of explosive light from the continuing attack on Kachirho.

Shryne's determination to thrust his lightsaber into the control box Vader wore on his chest had forced the Sith to adopt a more defensive style that had left his limbs vulnerable. Throughout the fight that had taken them up the room's wooden ramps, Vader had kept his crimson blade straight out in front of him, manipulating it deftly with wrists only, elbows pressed tightly to his sides. Only when Shryne left him no choice did he shuffle his feet or leap.

"Artificial limbs and body armor seem a curious choice for a Sith," Shryne said, poised for Vader's riposte to his lucky strike. "Belittling to the dark side."

Vader adjusted his grip on the sword and advanced. "No more than throwing in with smugglers denigrates the Force, Shryne."

"Ah, but I saw the light. Maybe it's time you did."

"You have it backward."

Shryne was steeling himself for a lunging attack when, abruptly, Vader halted and withdrew the blade into the lightsaber's hilt.

Before Shryne could begin to make sense of it, he heard a creaking sound from below, and something flew at him from one of the ramps. Only a last-instant turn of his sword kept the object from striking him in the head.

It was a plank—ripped from a ramp they had taken to the bridge.

Shryne gazed in awe at unreadable Vader, then began to race toward him, blade held high over his right shoulder.

He didn't make half the distance when a storm of similar planks and lengths of handrail came whirling at him. Vader was using his dark side abilities to dismantle the ramps!

Surrendering to the guidance of the Force, Shryne swung his lightsaber in a flurry of deflecting maneuvers—side-to-side, overhead, low down, behind his back—but the floorboards were coming in larger and larger pieces, from all directions, and faster than he could parry them.

The butt end of a board struck him on the outer left thigh.

The face of a wide plank slammed him across the shoulders.

Wooden pegs flew at his face; other speared into his arms.

Then a short support post hit him squarely in the forehead, knocking the wind out of him and dropping him to his knees.

Blood running into his eyes, he fought to remain conscious,

extending the lightsaber in one shaking hand while clamping the other on the bridge's handrail. Five meters away Vader stood, his hands crossed in front of him, lightsaber hanging on his belt.

Shryne tried to keep him in focus.

Another board, whirling end-over-end, came out of nowhere, hitting him in the kidneys.

Reflexively the hand that was grasping the railing went to the small of his back, and he lost balance. Trying but failing to catch himself, he fell through space.

Give in the wooden floor saved his life, but at the expense of all the bones in his left arm and shoulder.

Above him Vader jumped from the bridge, dropping to the floor with a grace he hadn't displayed before and alighting just meters away.

Ignoring the pain in his shattered limb, Shryne began to propel himself in a backward crawl toward the opening through which he and Vader had entered the wroshyr's trunk, a hot wind howling at him, whipping his long hair about.

The balcony was gone. Fallen.

There was nothing between Shryne and the ground but gritty air filled with burning leaves. Far below, Wookiees were being herded onto the landing platform. The forests were in flames . . .

Vader approached, drawing and igniting his Sith blade.

Shryne blinked blood from his eyes; lifted his lightsaber hand only to realize that he had lost the sword during his fall. Slumping back, he loosed a ragged, resigned exhalation.

"I owe you a debt," he told Vader. "It took you to bring me back to the Force."

"And you to firm my faith in the power of the dark side, Master Shryne."

Shryne swallowed hard. "Then tell me. Were you trained by Dooku? By Sidious?"

Vader came to a halt. "Not by Dooku. Not yet by Sidious."

"Not yet," Shryne said, as if to himself. "Then you're his apprentice?" His eyes darted right and left, searching for some means of escape. "Is Sidious also in league with Emperor Palpatine?"

Vader fell silent for a moment, making up his mind about something. "Lord Sidious *is* the Emperor."

Shryne gaped at Vader, trying to make sense of what he had said. "The order to kill the Jedi—"

"Order Sixty-Six," Vader said.

"*Sidious* issued it." Pieces to the puzzle Shryne had been grappling with for weeks assembled themselves. "The military buildup, the war itself . . . It was all part of a plan to eliminate the Jedi order."

Vader nodded. "All about this." He gestured to Shryne. "About you and me, you could say."

Shryne's stomach convulsed, and he coughed blood. The fall hadn't only broken his bones, but ruptured a vital organ. He was dying. Backing farther out the opening, he gazed into the night sky, then at Vader.

"Did Sidious turn you into the monstrosity you've become?"

"No, Shryne," Vader said in a flat voice. "I did this to myself—with some help from Obi-Wan Kenobi."

Shryne stared. "You knew Obi-Wan?"

Vader regarded him. "Haven't you guessed by now? I was a Jedi for a time."

Shryne let his bafflement show. "You're one of the Lost Twenty. Like Dooku."

"I am the twenty-first, Master Shryne. Surely you've heard of Anakin Skywalker. The Chosen One."

The Commerce Guild ship Starstone and the others had chosen to infiltrate grew larger in the transport's cockpit viewports. Just over a thousand meters in length and bristling with electromagnetic sensor antennas and point-defense laser cannons, the *Recusant*-class support destroyer had taken a turbolaser bruising during the Battle of Kashyyyk, but its principal cannons and trio of aft thrust nozzles appeared to be undamaged.

Elsewhere local space was dotted with Imperial landers and troop transports, along with hundreds of freighters that had fled the surface of the tormented planet. Central to the latter craft, and a good distance from the support destroyer, floated the Interdictor cruiser that was preventing the traders' ships from jumping to hyperspace.

Those trapped ships are the reason I was spared, Starstone thought.

The reason she had been rescued by Shryne . . .

"Any response from the droid brain?" she asked over Filli's shoulder.

"Well, we're chatting," the slicer said from the cockpit's

comm suite. "It recognized the code we used to activate the facility at Jaguada, but it refuses to accept any remote commands. My guess is that it was rudely shut down during the battle, and wants to run a systems check before bringing the destroyer fully online."

"Be best if we can keep from announcing ourselves," Cudgel said from the copilot's chair. "You think you can keep the brain from lighting up the entire ship?"

Chewbacca woofed in agreement.

"Not initially," Filli said. "The brain will probably restore universal power gradually as part of its diagnostic analysis. Once that's over and done with, I can task it to kill all the running lights, except for those around the forward docking bay."

A sudden growl from Chewbacca called Starstone's attention to the forward viewports.

Fore-to-aft, the pod-like warship was coming to life.

Cudgel muttered a curse. "The Interdictor's scanners are bound to pick that up."

"Just a couple of moments more," Filli said.

Everyone waited.

"Done!" Filli announced.

In reverse order the destroyer's running lights began to blink out, save for an array of illuminators that defined the rectangular entrance to the docking bay.

Filli flashed Starstone a grin. "The brain's being very cooperative. We're good to dock."

Chewbacca brayed an interrogative.

"Any atmosphere?" Cudgel translated.

Filli did rapid input at the keyboard.

"The ship originally carried several squadrons of vulture and droid tri-fighters," he said. "But unless the Gossams converted it fully to droid operation I'd expect there be atmosphere and artificial gravity in some areas . . ." His eyes darted to the display screen. "Looks like a bit of both: Gossam and droid crew."

"Battle droids?" Starstone said.

Filli nodded. " 'Fraid so."

"You can't shut them down?"

"Not without shutting down the command bridge."

Starstone frowned and turned to Cudgel. "Gather up as many blasters as we've got aboard. And while you're at it, you'll find some rebreathers in the main cabin—just in case there's no atmosphere."

"You want a blaster," he asked as he stood up, "or are you sticking with a lightsaber?"

"This is an occasion that calls for both," she said.

"Archyr, Skeck, are you copying all this?" Filli said toward the audio pickup.

"Affirmative," Archyr responded from the drop ship. "But we'll precede you into the docking bay. We're better armed and better shielded. After that there's nothing to do but fight our way to the command bridge."

Filli displayed a schematic of the destroyer on one of the suite's monitor screens. "Most of the habitable areas are amidships, but the command bridge is in the outrigger superstructure above the bow."

"Lucky break for us," Archyr said. "It's closer to the bay."

Starstone was studying the destroyer when the drop ship came alongside the transport. Without having to be told, Chewbacca decelerated and fell in behind the smaller craft.

Starstone slipped into the vacant copilot's chair to watch the drop ship glide into the bay. Almost immediately blaster bolts crisscrossed the darkness. By the time the transport nosed through the opening, battle droids were dropping like targets in a shooting gallery, and the deck was strewn with spindly body parts.

Rebreathers strapped to their faces, lumas to their foreheads, Starstone, Cudgel, and Filli were standing at the boarding ramp hatch when Chewbacca set the transport down. Shortly the

Wookiee joined them there, the bowcaster he carried over his shoulder assembled and gripped in his hands.

As the transport's outer hatch slid open, the harsh sibilance of blasterfire infiltrated the ship. Starstone and the others hurried out into the thick of the fighting, their headlamps casting long shadows all over the bay. Archyr and several well-armed Wookiees were off to one side, clearing a path through battle droids toward a hatch in the bay's forward bulkhead.

Firing on the run and hurtling pieces of disintegrated droids, Starstone, Filli, Cudgel, and Chewbacca made a desperate dash for the hatch. The corridor beyond was crowded with battle droids marching in to reinforce those in the docking bay.

Explosive quarrels from Chewbacca's bowcaster combined with blasterfire and deflections from Starstone's lightsaber dropped a dozen droids at a time. But for every dozen destroyed, another dozen appeared. Archyr and some of the Wookiees brought up the rear, ultimately allowing Starstone's contingent to shoot their way into a turbolift that accessed the destroyer's outrigger arm.

Prepared for the worst, the four of them burst onto the command bridge, only to find a group of befuddled humaniform technical droids, outfitted with power studs at the backs of the heads that allowed them to be quickly and methodically shut down.

Realizing that the bridge had oxygen, everyone removed their rebreathers. Chewbacca dogged the hatch to the corridor while Filli centered himself at the ship's control console and activated the bridge's emergency lights.

"Gossams have longer fingers than I have," he said in the scarlet glow of the illuminators. "This could take some time."

"We're running short as it is," Cudgel said. "Just get the main cannons enabled."

Battle droids on the far side of the sealed hatch were already trying to pound their way onto the bridge.

Filli went back to work, but a moment later said: "Uh-oh."

Chewbacca loosed a trolling roar at him.

"Uh-oh, what?" Starstone asked.

Abruptly the destroyer lurched and began to nose about toward Kashyyyk's crescent of bright side.

"The brain wants to complete the task it was in the middle of when the ship was shut down," Filli said.

Starstone turned to him. "What was the task?"

"It thinks that the Separatists are losing Kachirho. It's converting itself into a giant bomb!"

"Can't you retask it?"

"I'm trying. It won't listen!"

Cudgel muttered to himself, and Chewbacca issued a sound that was somewhere between a growl and a groan.

"Filli!" Starstone said sharply. "Let the brain think what it wants. Just assign it a new target."

His blank stare yielded slowly to a grin of comprehension. "Can do."

Starstone returned the smile, then glanced at Cudgel. "Comlink the *Drunk Dancer* to prepare to receive guests."

As soon as Jula received word that the drop ship and transport had exited the Commerce Guild warship, she left the *Drunk Dancer* in the capable hands of Brudi Gayn and Eyl Dix and headed for the docking bay. Her eagerness sabotaged by the lightsaber gash she had suffered on Alderaan, she moved slowly and carefully, arriving just as the two craft were drifting through the hatch. Forewarned that both were carrying injured, she had ordered the ship's med droids to rendezvous with her there.

Forewarned.

But not thoroughly enough to prepare her for the number of wounded evacuees who hobbled from the ships, Wookiees squeezing out like circus performers from an absurdly cramped vehicle, and many of them in grave condition.

As for the Jedi, only five of the original seven had survived, and just barely, from the look of them. Jambe Lu, Nam Poorf, and Klossi Anno especially were in a lot worse shape than when they had first come aboard the *Drunk Dancer,* weeks earlier.

Even the ship's med droids were dismayed. "This may prove overwhelming, Captain," one of them said from behind Jula.

"Do all you can," she told the droid.

It was an unnerving sight, however, and she felt a bit panicked. But the tears she had been holding back since learning of Roan's sacrifice didn't gush forth until she set eyes on Filli and Starstone. Seeing her standing distraught, crying into the palms of her hands, Starstone hurried over to wrap her in a comforting embrace.

Jula allowed herself to be held for a long moment. But when she finally stepped out of the embrace, she saw that Starstone's cheeks were slick with tears, and that only got her crying again. Gently she stroked the young woman's face.

"What happened to avoiding attachment?" Jula said, sniffling.

Starstone backhanded tears from her cheeks. "I've lost the skill. It doesn't seem to fit well with the Emperor's New Order, anyway." She held Jula's searching gaze. "Your son saved our lives. We tried to go back for him, but . . ."

Jula averted her eyes. "Someone had to try to stop Vader."

"I don't know that Vader can be stopped," Starstone said.

Jula nodded. "Maybe if I'd raised Roan, he wouldn't have turned out to be so stubborn." She frowned in distress. "Some people can't be talked out of being a hero."

"Or a Jedi."

Jula nodded. "That's what I meant."

Starstone smiled sadly, then turned to regard a Wookiee and a bearded human who were standing at the foot of the transport's boarding ramp, speaking with Filli, Archyr, and Skeck. Taking Jula by the hand, Starstone led her over to the unlikely pair, whom she introduced as Chewbacca and Cudgel.

Clearly in distress, the Wookiee was leaning against the ship, resting his head on his folded arms, and slamming his paws against the hull.

"We saw Chewbacca's tree-city in flames," Cudgel explained. "There's no way to know whether his family escaped in time."

"I promised him the transport," Starstone told Jula.

Jula looked at Cudgel. "We'll get it refueled as quickly—"

"No need," Cudgel cut her off. "Chewie knows that it's too late. He figures he can do more for his people as a fugitive than he could as a captive."

The Wookiee affirmed it with a melancholy roar.

"You're speaking for all of us, Chewbacca," Starstone said.

"So," Cudgel continued, "we're wondering, Chewie and I, if we could ride out of this with you."

Jula's comlink toned while she was nodding yes.

"Captain, we're T-ten for the jump to hyperspace," Brudi said from the bridge, almost casually. "Assuming everything goes according to plan."

"Have you been able to notify the other ships?" Jula asked.

"As best I could. And I'm trusting that that Interdictor isn't eavesdropping on every comlink frequency."

"See what jump options the navicomputer provides," Jula said. "I'll join you in a moment."

She moved away from Starstone and the others to gaze at Kashyyyk's waning crescent of bright side. Tears streaming down her face, she said in a quiet voice: "I love you, Roan. I thank the Force that I got to know you for a time. But I'll miss you more now than I ever did."

In command of the Detainer parked above Kachirho, Captain Ugan normally refused to allow himself to be disturbed when he was on the bridge. But Ensign Nullip was so insistent about seeing him that he finally granted permission for the young technician to be escorted onto the command deck.

A swarthy man with blunt features, Ugan remained seated in his chair, his dark gaze shifting between projected holoimages of the invasion on Kashyyyk and the viewport panorama of the planet itself.

"Be quick about it," he warned Nullip.

"Yes, sir," the ensign promised. "It's simply that we've been monitoring some unusual readings from one of the Separatist ships that was left in orbit after the battle here. Specifically, a Commerce Guild *Recusant*-class support destroyer. I've tried repeatedly to convince someone in tactical to bring this to your attention, sir, but—"

Ugan cut him off. "What makes these readings 'unusual,' Ensign?"

"They are initiation readings, sir." In response to the captain's dubious look, Nullip continued: "I know, sir. I was puzzled, too. That's why I took it upon myself to check the scanner recordings. Much to my surprise, sir, I learned that the destroyer's central control computer had been remotely enabled to run a diagnostic, and then to bring several of the ship's systems online."

When Ugan's expression of perplexity deepened, Nullip activated a small holoplate he had placed on the palm of his right hand. A grainy recording shone from the device.

"You can see two craft entering the destroyer, just here, at the forwardmost docking bays." Nullip's forefinger fast-forwarded the recording. "Here, you can see the craft leaving. We're still trying to determine their destination."

Ugan glanced from the recording to Nullip. "Salvagers?"

"That was my first thought, sir. But, in fact, when the craft exited, the destroyer itself was in motion."

Ugan stared at him. "In motion? What's its heading?"

"That's just it, sir. It's heading toward us." Turning to the forward viewports, Nullip indicated a dark shape moving through the greater darkness. "Just there, you see?"

Ugan swiveled to an officer at the tactical duty station. "A Separatist ship is approaching our port side. Scan it, immediately!" Rising from his chair, he walked to the viewport, Nullip a step behind him.

"Captain," the tactical officer said, "the ship is a Confederacy droid-piloted support destroyer—"

"I already know that!" Ugan said, whirling around. "Does it pose any risk to us?"

"Checking, sir."

The officer spent a moment studying the duty station's array of display screens, then turned toward Ugan, ashen-faced.

"Captain, the destroyer's main reactor is in critical failure. The ship is effectively a massive bomb!"

Shryne sprawled in the wroshyr's cavernous opening, the wind tugging at his clothing, blood trickling from the corners of his mouth, clearly struggling with the revelation he had been granted.

Vader stood over him, his right hand resting on the hilt of the lightsaber, though he had no intention of drawing it from his belt again. One strong gust could topple Shryne to his final resting place.

It is enough to let him die knowing that the order was betrayed by one of its own.

More important, Vader's bloodlust had been appeased; replaced by self-possession of a sort he had never before experienced. It was as if he had crossed some invisible threshold to a new world. He could feel the power of the dark side surging through him like an icy torrent. He felt invulnerable in a way that had nothing to do with his durasteel prostheses, his suit of armor and gadgets, which now seemed little more than an outfit. And it had taken a Jedi—yet *another* Jedi—to usher him over that threshold.

He gazed down at Shryne, emblematic of the defeated Jedi order, as Obi-Wan should have been. He recalled the way Dooku had gazed down at him on Geonosis, and the way Anakin had gazed down at Dooku in the General's quarters aboard the *Invisible Hand*.

Someday he would gaze down at Sidious in the same way.

After he took an apprentice, perhaps. Someone with the same rebellious spirit that Shryne demonstrated.

Shryne coughed weakly. "What are you waiting for, Skywalker? Strike me down. You're only killing a Jedi."

Vader planted his fists on his hips. "Then you do accept the truth."

"I accept that you and Palpatine are a perfect match—" Shryne began, when without warning an immense explosion turned a small region of the western sky bright as day. Eclipsing stars, a roiling ball of fire blossomed high over Kashyyyk, expanding and expanding until the vacuum of space suffocated it.

When Vader looked at Shryne again, the Jedi appeared to be grinning.

"Would that be one of your ships? Your Interdictor cruiser, maybe?" He coughed blood and a laugh. "They've escaped you again, haven't they."

"If so, they will be found, and killed."

Shryne's expression suddenly changed, from smug to almost rapturous.

"I've seen this," he uttered, mostly to himself. "I envisioned this . . ."

Vader pressed closer to hear him. "Your death, you mean."

"An explosion bright as a star," Shryne said. "A forest world, intrepid defenders, escaping ships, and . . . *you*, I think, somehow at the center of it all." His bloodstained lips formed themselves into a sublime smile, and a tear ran from his right eye. "Skywalker, it won't matter if you find them. It won't matter if you

find and kill every Jedi who survived Order Sixty-Six. I understand now . . . the Force will never die."

Vader was still gazing down at Shryne's inert body when several
stormtroopers emerged from one of the Wookiees' ingenious
turbolifts and hurried over to him.

"Lord Vader," the officer among them said. "The Interdictor
positioned over Kachirho has been destroyed. As a result, hundreds of evacuation ships succeeded in jumping to hyperspace."

Vader nodded. "Inform the group commanders that they are
to continue their orbital bombardment," he said angrily. "I want
every Wookiee flushed out of hiding, even if that means burning
these forests to the ground!"

EPILOGUE

TWO THERE SHOULD BE; NO MORE NO LESS.
ONE TO EMBODY POWER, THE OTHER TO CRAVE IT.

—DARTH BANE

A half-life-size holoimage of Wilhuff Tarkin shone from one of the cone-shaped holoprojectors that studded the lustrous floor of the throne room.

"The planet suffered more damage that I might have anticipated," the Moff was saying, "especially given the military resources I placed at Lord Vader's disposal. Although I suppose I shouldn't be surprised by the Wookiees' intractability."

The Emperor gestured negligently. "What is one world, more or less, when the galaxy is being reordered?"

Tarkin took a moment to reply. "I will bear that in mind, my lord."

"What of the Wookiees themselves?"

"Some two hundred thousand were rounded up and placed in containment camps on the Wawaatt Archipelago."

"Can you accommodate that many?"

"We could accommodate twice that number."

"I see," the Emperor said. "Then you have my permission to transport the slaves to the weapon."

"Thank you, my lord."

"Be certain to inform the regional governor of your activities, but make no mention of the Wookiees' final destination. Oh, and see to it, Moff Tarkin, that you cover your tracks well. Questions are already being asked." The Emperor paused, then leaned forward to add: "I don't want any problems."

Tarkin inclined his head in a bow. "I appreciate the need for utmost secrecy, my lord."

"Good." The Emperor sat back. "And, tell me, what is your opinion of Lord Vader's handling of the occupation of Kashyyyk?"

"He proved very capable, my lord. No one involved in the operation will soon forget his . . . sense of commitment, shall we say?"

"Do the fleet commanders concur with your assessment?"

Tarkin stroked his high-cheekboned face. "May I speak candidly?"

"I suggest you make it a practice, Moff Tarkin."

"The commanders are not pleased. They don't know who Lord Vader is under his mask and armor. They have no inkling of the true extent of his power, or how he came to be your liaison with the regional governors and the fledgling Imperial Navy. There are rumors, my lord."

"Continue to speak freely."

"Some are convinced that Lord Vader is a former Jedi who assisted you in your counterstrike against the order. Others believe that he was an apprentice of the late Count Dooku."

"Who is spreading these rumors?"

"From what I have been able to ascertain, the rumors began among the special ops legions that attacked and secured the Jedi Temple. If you wish, my lord, I could pursue the matter further."

"No, Tarkin," the Emperor said. "Let the rumors persist. And let the regional governors and naval officers think what they will of Lord Vader. His identity shouldn't concern them. I am interested only in their obeying his commands, as they would mine."

"If nothing else, my lord, they understand that much. Word of what happened at Kashyyyk is spreading quickly through the ranks."

"As I knew it would."

Tarkin nodded. "My lord, I wonder if I might call on Lord Vader's . . . expertise from time to time, if only in the interest of enhancing his reputation among the fleet commanders."

"You may, indeed. Both you and Lord Vader will profit from such a partnership. When the battle station is completed, your responsibilities will be manifold. Lord Vader will relieve you of the need to oversee every matter personally."

"I look forward to that day, my lord." Tarkin bowed once more, and the holoimage disappeared.

Sidious was pleased. Vader had done well. He had sensed the change in him, even in the brief conversation they had had following the events on Kashyyyk. Now that Vader had begun to tap deeply into the power of the dark side, his true apprenticeship could begin. The Jedi were incidental to him. He was covetous of the power Sidious wielded, and believed that one day they would be equals.

You must begin by gaining power over yourself; then another; then a group, an order, a world, a species, a group of species . . . finally, the galaxy itself.

Sidious could still hear Darth Plagueis lecturing him.

Envy, hatred, betrayal . . . They were essential to mastering the dark side, but only as a means of distancing oneself from all common notions of morality in the interest of a higher goal. Only when Sidious had understood this fully had he acted on it, killing his Master while he slept.

Unlike Plagueis, Sidious knew better than to sleep.

More important, by the time Vader was capable of becoming

a risk to his Mastery, Sidious would be fully conversant with the secrets Plagueis had spent a lifetime seeking—the power of life over death. There would be no need to fear Vader. No real reason to have an apprentice, except to honor the tradition Darth Bane had resurrected a millennium earlier.

The ancient Sith had been utter fools to believe that power could be shared by thousands.

The power of the dark side should be shared only by two; one to embody it, the other to crave it.

Vader's transformation meant that Sidious, too, was able to focus once more on important matters. With Vader in his place, Sidious could now devote himself to intensifying his authority over the Senate and the outlying star systems, and to rooting out and vanquishing any who posed a threat to the Empire.

He had brought peace to the galaxy. Now he meant to rule it as he saw fit—with a hand as strong and durable as one of Vader's prostheses. Crushing any opponents who rose up. Instilling fear in any who thought to obstruct or thwart him.

Vader would prove to be a powerful apprentice, at least until a more suitable one was found.

And a powerful weapon, as well, at least until a more powerful one was readied . . .

For some time, Sidious sat, musing on the future; then he called for Sate Pestage to join him in the throne room.

The time had come to give the rest of the galaxy a look at Darth Vader.

Oh, Bail, Breha, what a precious child," Mon Mothma said while she rocked Leia in her arms. "And such a feisty one!" she added a moment later as Leia worked one arm, then the other, out from under her swaddlings, curled her hands into tiny fists, and let out a wail that echoed in the palace's great room. "Ah, you want your mom and dad, don't you, Princess Leia?"

Queen Breha was already hurrying over to relieve Mon Mothma of a now gesticulating and kicking Leia.

"That's her *feed-me* cry," Breha said. "If you'll excuse me, Senator . . ."

"Of course, Your Majesty," Mon Mothma said, rising to her feet. She watched Breha leave the room, then swung to Bail, who was seated by the room's gaping fireplace. "I'm so happy for the two of you."

"We couldn't be happier ourselves," Bail said.

He wished he could tell Mon Mothma the truth about the child she had just held in her arms, but he couldn't risk it; not yet, perhaps never. Particularly with "Darth Vader" on the loose.

Picking up on Bail's moment of introspection, Mon Mothma returned to her chair and adopted a more serious look.

"I hope you understand why I couldn't trust this conversation to the usual means, Bail," she said. "Are we secure here?"

"Of course, I understand. And yes, we can speak freely here."

Mon Mothma closed her eyes briefly and shook her head in dismay. "Most of the Senate is actually willing to accept that Fang Zar was under suspicion for committing acts of sedition on Coruscant, and that he came to Alderaan only to rally anti-Imperial sentiment."

Bail nodded. "I've heard the reports. There's no truth to any of them. He was fleeing for his life."

"Has Palpatine remarked on the fact that you granted him refuge?"

"I honestly didn't know that he'd been questioned by Internal Security and ordered to remain on Coruscant. When Palpatine's . . . *agents* told me as much, I said I would grant him diplomatic immunity if he asked for it—though I doubt he would have asked, knowing that Alderaan would suffer the repercussions."

"Even so, Palpatine's silence is curious." She looked hard at Bail. "Perhaps he's trusting that you won't reveal the truth about what went on here."

Bail nodded in agreement. "Something like that. Although it could work to our long-term advantage to have him believe that I'm willing to support even his lies."

Mon Mothma compressed her lips in doubt. "That's probably true. But I'm concerned about the message your silence sends to our allies in the Senate. Sern Prime is in an uproar over this incident. The president-elect has threatened to recall the entire delegation from Coruscant. This could provide just the impetus we need."

Bail stood up and paced away from his chair. "Palpatine wanted to make an example of Fang Zar. He won't hesitate to make an example of Sern Prime itself, if the president-elect isn't careful."

"How did Zar die?" Mon Mothma said, watching him pace.

"Vader," Bail said sharply.

Mon Mothma shook her head in ignorance. "Who is Vader? One of Armand Isard's agents?"

Bail finally sat down, resting his elbows on his knees. "Worse, far worse. He's Palpatine's right hand."

Mon Mothma's expression of uncertainty intensified. "Closer to him than Pestage?"

Bail nodded. "Closer to Palpatine than any of them."

"Out of the blue? I mean, how is it that none of us encountered Vader before now?"

Bail grasped for words that would reveal enough, without revealing too much. "He . . . came to prominence during the war. He wields a lightsaber."

Mon Mothma's eyes widened in surprise.

"No, he's not a Jedi," Bail said, before she could ask. "His blade is crimson."

"What does the color have to do with anything?"

"He's a Sith. A member of the same ancient order to which Dooku swore allegiance."

Mon Mothma loosed a fatigued exhalation. "I've never understood any of this, about the Siths' involvement in the war."

"You only need to understand that Vader is Palpatine's executioner. He's powerful almost beyond belief." Bail studied his hands. "Fang Zar was not the first person to feel the wrath of Vader's blade."

"Then Vader is all the more reason for us to act while there's still time," Mon Mothma said in a forceful voice. "Palpatine's plan to kill a few to instill fear in the rest is already working. Half the signatories of the Petition of the Two Thousand are all but recanting the demands we issued. I understand that you want to honor Padmé Amidala's advice to you about biding our time. But what did she know, really? She supported Palpatine almost to the very end.

"Bail, he's assembling a vast navy. Half the budget is going to the production of these enormous new Star Destroyers. He's having new stormtroopers grown. And that's not the worst of it. The Finance Committee can't even account for some of the spending. Rumor has it that Palpatine has some secret project in the works."

She fell silent, then continued in a quieter tone. "Think back to what happened three years ago. If it wasn't for the secret army the Jedi created, the Republic wouldn't have had a hope of defending itself against Dooku's Confederacy. Granted, Palpatine took advantage of the situation to crown himself Emperor. But consider what's happening now. We don't have an army of insurgents waiting in the wings, and we'll never have one if we don't begin to marshal support. Palpatine's military will rule by the sword. He'll do as he wishes, whatever he wishes, in the name of keeping the Empire intact. Don't you see?"

The question hung in the air, but only for a moment.

Raymus Antilles appeared in the wide doorway to say: "Senators, there's something the two of you need to see."

Antilles hastened to the HoloNet receiver and switched it on.

". . . At this moment, details remain sketchy," a celebrated commentator was saying, "but reliable sources have stated that the Wookiees were allowing a band of rogue Jedi to use Kashyyyk as a base for rebel strikes against the Empire. The police action is believed to have begun with a demand that the Jedi be surrendered. Instead, the Wookiees resisted, and the result was a battle that left tens of thousands dead, including the Jedi insurgents, and perhaps hundreds of thousands imprisoned."

Bail and Mon Mothma traded looks of astonishment.

"On Coruscant," the commentator continued, "Kashyyyk Senator Yarua and the members of his delegation were placed under house arrest before any statements could be issued. But on the minds of many just now is the identity of this person, captured by holocam on a landing platform normally reserved for the Emperor himself."

"Vader," Bail said, on seeing the tall figure in black, leading a cadre of stormtroopers into the Emperor's building.

"HoloNet News has learned that he is known in the highest circles as Lord Vader," the commentator said. "Beyond that, almost nothing is known, save for the fact that he led the action on Kashyyyk.

"Is he human? Clone? The Emperor's own General Grievous? No one seems to know, but everyone wants to—"

"Switch it off," Bail said to Antilles.

"Kashyyyk," Mon Mothma said in incredulity. She ran her hands down her face and stared at Bail. "We're too late. A dark time has begun."

Bail didn't respond immediately. Into the silence stepped Breha, holding Leia against her shoulder, and into Bail's rattled mind came thoughts of Yoda, Obi-Wan, and Leia's twin brother, Luke.

"All the more reason to keep hope hidden," he said softly.

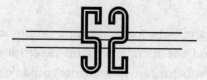

The *Drunk Dancer* was home, parked in the cold gloom, light-years from any inhabited systems. This far from the Core, HoloNet broadcasts were standard days, sometimes weeks, behind and always degraded, but clear enough just now for Starstone, Jula, and everyone else—Jedi and crew members alike—to identify the bodies of Iwo Kulka and Siadem Forte.

". . . All the Jedi who took part in the battle were killed," a correspondent was saying when Starstone asked Filli to mute the recorded feed. Everyone had already seen the original reports, which had since been embellished with exaggerations and out-right lies.

Gazing around the cabin space at Jambe, Nam, Deran Nalual, and Klossi Anno, Starstone couldn't help but think that the five of them made up what could be thought of as the final Jedi Council. With herself having called for the meeting, as master of ceremonies, without ever having passed the trials, let alone been dubbed a teacher.

But she could remember Shryne saying on Murkhana that the war was *trial enough for anyone*.

"What I'm about to say was already said by Master Shryne,"

she began at last. "He warned us that by gathering together we would make ourselves a larger target for the Empire, and that we would end up drawing others into our predicament. We can't risk fomenting another Kashyyyk. The Empire will have to come up with justifications that don't rely on the presence of Jedi.

"Because there are no more Jedi.

"That much is clear to me now, and I'll never forgive myself for not having had sense enough to recognize it sooner. Maybe then I wouldn't have to think of what happened at Kashyyyk as further diminishing the legacy of the Jedi among those who never doubted that Palpatine betrayed us. But if we can't be Jedi, we can at least continue to honor that legacy in our own way."

Starstone looked at Chewbacca. "Just before we jumped from Kashyyyk, Chewbacca said that he believed he could be of greater help to his people from afar. I feel the same, and I know that some of you do, as well."

She took a breath before continuing. "I've decided to remain aboard the *Drunk Dancer* with Jula, Filli, Archyr, and the rest of this mad crew." She smiled weakly. "Chewbacca and Cudgel are also going to remain aboard for a time. Our priority will be to learn where so many of Chewbacca's people were taken, and to help liberate them, if at all possible. I'm hoping that by finding them, we'll also be able to learn why the Empire was so intent on invading Kashyyyk to begin with.

"Along the way . . ." Starstone shrugged. "Along the way we're going to keep our eyes open for any Jedi survivors who surface on their own, or are forced into the open by Imperial spies. Not to repeat the mistakes we made at Kashyyyk, but to get them to safety. Gradually, other smugglers will spread word of what we're doing, and of the safe routes we'll establish, and maybe some Jedi will actually come looking for us.

"Beyond that, we'll undermine the Empire at every opportunity, any way that we can."

"We're going to keep my son's memory alive," Jula said.

The cabin fell silent for a moment.

"I know this may sound like I've gone over to the enemy," Jambe Lu said, "but I plan to sign up with a flight school somewhere, and try to finagle my way into one of the Imperial academies. Once inside, I'm going to foster whatever dissent I can."

"We have something similar in mind," Nam said, speaking for himself, Klossi Anno, and Deran Nalual. "But by getting ourselves attached to Imperial agricultural or construction projects, and engineering what flaws we can into the Empire's designs."

Starstone's eyes brightened.

"I trust that all of you understand there can be no contact among us—ever again. That's going to be the hardest part for me." She sighed deeply. "I guess I've grown attached to all of you. But I'm certain of this much: Palpatine's Empire will rot from the inside out, and eventually someone will cast him from his throne. I only hope that all of us are alive to witness that day."

She drew her lightsaber from her belt. "We need to say good-bye to these, as well." She ignited the blade briefly, then summoned it back into the hilt and placed it at her feet on the deck.

Regarding everyone, she said: "May the Force be with all of us."

ord Vader," the gunnery officer said, nodding his head in salute as Vader passed by his station.

"Lord Vader," the communications officer said, saluting in similar fashion.

"Lord Vader," the *Exactor*'s captain said, in crisp acknowledgment.

Vader continued on to the end of bridge walkway, thinking: *This is how I will be greeted from now on, wherever I set foot.*

Standing at the forward viewports, he scanned the stars with his reconstructed eyes.

He had guardianship of all this, or at least joint custody of it. The Jedi no longer mattered; they were no different from others who would interfere with his and Sidious's realm. Their mission was to maintain order, so that the dark side could continue to reign supreme.

Anakin was gone; a memory so deeply buried he might have dreamed rather than lived it. The Force as Anakin knew it was interred with him, and inseparable from him.

Just as Sidious promised, he was now married to the order of the Sith, and needed no other companion than the dark side of the Force. He embraced all that he had done to bring balance to the Force, by dismantling the corrupt Republic and toppling the Jedi, and he reveled in his power. It could all be his, anything he wished. He needed only the determination to take it, at whatever cost to those who stood in his way.

But . . .

He was also married to Sidious, who doled out precious bits of Sith technique as if merely lending them—just enough to increase his apprentice's power, without making him supremely powerful.

There would come a day, however, when they would be equals.

He scanned the stars, looking forward to a time when he could find an apprentice of his own and, together with that one, topple Darth Sidious from his throne.

It gave him something to live for.

"Another glass, stranger?" the cantina owner asked Obi-Wan Kenobi.

"What will it cost me?"

"Ten credits for refills."

"That's as much as a shot of one of your imported brandies."

"The price of staying hydrated on Tatooine, my friend. Yes or no?"

Obi-Wan nodded. "Fill it."

Gathered by the cantina's single moisture vaporator, the water was somewhat cloudy and had a metallic taste, but it was of a higher quality than that gathered by Obi-Wan's own vaporator. If he was to survive in the hovel he had found, he would need to have the vaporator repaired, or somehow obtain a newer one from the Jawa traders who occasionally passed through the region he now called home.

If it hadn't been for the kindness of the maroon-cloaked creatures, he would still be walking to Anchorhead rather than sitting in the scant shade of the cantina's veranda, sipping water. A wind-scoured settlement close to Tatooine's Western Dune

Sea, Anchorhead was little more than a trading post frequented by the moisture farmers who made up the Great Chott salt flat community, or by merchants traveling between Mos Eisley and Wayfar, in the south. Anchorhead had a small resident population, a dozen or so pourstone stores, and two small cantinas. But it was known mainly for the power generator located at the edge of town.

Named for its owner, Tosche Station supplied energy to the moisture farms and served as a recharge depot for the farmers' landspeeders and other repulsorlift vehicles. The station also boasted a hyperwave repeater, which—when it functioned— received HoloNet feeds relayed from Naboo, Rodia, and, occasionally, Nal Hutta, in Hutt space.

Tosche was working today, and The Weary Traveler's handful of afternoon customers were catching up on news and the outcome of sports events that had taken place standard weeks earlier. Obi-Wan—known locally as Ben—had taken possession of an abandoned home on a bluff in the Jundland Wastes. He glanced at the HoloNet display from time to time, but the focus of his interest was a provisions store across the street from the cantina.

In the months since he had arrived on Tatooine his hair and beard had grown quickly, and his face and hands had turned nut brown. In his soft boots and long robe, its cowl raised over his head, no one would have taken him for a former Jedi, let alone a Master who had sat on the High Council. In any case, Tatooine wasn't a world where questions were asked. Residents wondered, and they gossiped and theorized, but they rarely inquired about the reasons that brought strangers to remote Tatooine. Coupled with the fact that the world was still largely under the sway of the Hutts, the prevailing frontier etiquette had made Tatooine a refuge for criminals, smugglers, and outlaws from star systems galaxywide.

Many of the locals were just learning that the former Republic was now an Empire, and most of them didn't care one way or another. Tatooine was on the fringe, and fringe worlds might as well have been invisible to distant Coruscant.

Months earlier, when he and Anakin had been in pursuit of clues they had hoped would lead them to Darth Sidious, Obi-Wan had told Anakin that he could think of far worse places to live than Tatooine, and he still felt that way. He took in stride the ubiquitous sand that had so rankled Anakin. Tatooine's double-sunset skies were always a marvel to behold.

And the isolation suited him.

All the more because Anakin had been subverted by Palpatine and, for a brief time, had served this new Emperor.

Given everything that had happened since, the one image Obi-Wan knew he would never be able to erase from his memory was that of Anakin—Darth Vader, as Sidious had dubbed him—kneeling in allegiance to the Dark Lord, after having gone on a murderous spree in the Jedi Temple. If there was a second image, it was of Anakin burning on the shore of one of Mustafar's lava flows, cursing him.

Had he been wrong to let Anakin die there? Could he have been redeemed, as Padmé had believed to the last? These were questions that plagued him, and pained him more deeply than he would ever have thought possible.

And now, all these months later, here he was on Tatooine, Anakin's homeworld, watching over Anakin's infant son, Luke.

Obi-Wan's reason for living.

Watching from afar, at any rate. Today was as close as he had come to the child in weeks. Just across the street, Luke sat in a front carrier worn by Beru while she purchased sugar and blue milk; neither she nor her husband, Owen, was aware of Obi-Wan's presence on the cantina veranda, his vigilant though covert gaze.

As Obi-Wan brought the water glass to his mouth and

sipped, a HoloNet news report caught his ear and he swung to the cantina's display, simultaneous with a torrent of static that interrupted the feed.

"What was she saying?" Obi-Wan asked a human seated two tables away.

"Band of Jedi were killed on Kashyyyk," the man said. Close to Obi-Wan's age, he wore utilities of the sort affected by docking bay workers in Mos Eisley spaceport.

Had the HoloNet reporter been referring to Jedi who had been on Kashyyyk with Yoda—

No, Obi-Wan realized when the feed suddenly returned. The reporter was talking about more recent events! About Jedi who had obviously survived Order Sixty-Six and been discovered on Kashyyyk!

He continued to listen, growing colder and colder inside.

The Empire had accused Kashyyyk of plotting rebellion . . . Thousands of Wookiees had died; hundreds of thousands more had been imprisoned . . .

Obi-Wan squeezed his eyes shut in dismay. He and Yoda had recalibrated the Temple beacon to warn surviving Jedi *away* from Coruscant. What could the ones discovered on Kashyyyk have been thinking, banding together like that, drawing attention to themselves instead of going to ground as they had been ordered to do? Did they think they could gather enough strength to go after Palpatine?

Of course they did, Obi-Wan realized.

They hadn't realized that Palpatine had manipulated the war; that a Sith occupied the throne; that like everyone else, the Jedi had failed to grasp a truth that should have been evident years earlier: the Republic had never been worth fighting for.

The ideals of democracy hadn't been stamped out by Palpatine. The Jedi had carried out missions of dubious merit for any number of Supreme Chancellors, but always in the name of safe-guarding peace and justice. What they had failed to understand was that the Senate, the Coruscanti, the citizens of countless world and star systems, grown weary of the old system, had *allowed* democracy to die. And in a galaxy where the goal was single-minded control from the top, and wherein the end justi-fied the means, the Jedi had no place.

That had been the final revenge of the Sith.

When Obi-Wan lifted his gaze, the intermittently garbled HoloNet was displaying an image of someone outfitted in what almost seemed a costume of head-to-toe black. Human or humanoid—the being's species wasn't mentioned—the masked Imperial had apparently played a role in tracking down and exe-cuting the "insurrectionist" Jedi, and enslaving their Wookiee confederates.

The burst of static that accompanied the reporter's mention of the figure's identity might have surged from Obi-Wan's brain. Still chilled by the earlier announcement about the Jedi, he was now paralyzed by sudden dread.

He couldn't have heard what he thought he heard!

He whirled to the spaceport worker. "What did she say? Who is that?"

"Lord Vader," the man said, all but into his glass of brandy.

Obi-Wan shook his head. "No, that's not possible!"

"You didn't ask if I thought it was possible, sand man. You asked me what she said."

Obi-Wan stood up in a daze, knocking over his table.

"Hey, take it easy, friend," the man said, rising.

"Vader," Obi-Wan muttered. "Vader's alive."

The cantina's other customers turned to regard him.

"Get ahold of yourself," the man told Obi-Wan under his breath. He called for the cantina owner. "Pour him a drink—a *real* one. And put it on my tab." Righting the table, he urged

Obi-Wan back into his chair and lowered himself onto an adjoining one.

The cantina owner brought the drink and set it down in front of Obi-Wan. "Is he all right?"

"He's fine," the man from Mos Eisley said. "Aren't you, friend?"

Obi-Wan nodded. "Heatstroke."

The cantina owner seemed satisfied. "I'll bring you some more water."

Obi-Wan's new friend waited until they were alone to say, "You really all right?"

Obi-Wan nodded again. "Really."

The man adopted a conspiratorial voice. "You want to remain all right, you'll keep your voice down about Vader, understand? You'll keep from asking questions about him, too. Even in this Force-forsaken place."

Obi-Wan studied him. "What do you know about him?"

"Just this: I have a friend, a trader in hardwoods, who was on Kashyyyk when the Imperials launched their attack on a place called Kachirho. I guess he was lucky to get his ship raised and jumped. But he claims he got a glimpse of this guy Vader, ripping into Wookiees like they were stuffed toys, and going to lightsabers with the Jedi who were onworld." The spaceport worker glanced furtively around the cantina. "This Vader, he *toasted* Kashyyyk, friend. From what my friend says, it'll be years before a piece of wroshyr goes up the well."

"And the Wookiees?" Obi-Wan said.

The stranger shrugged forlornly. "Anyone's guess." Placing a few credits on the table, he stood up. "Take care of yourself. These desert wastes aren't as remote as you may think they are."

When the water arrived, Obi-Wan downed it in a gulp, shouldered his rucksack, and left the cool shade of the veranda for the harsh light of Anchorhead's principal street. He moved in a daze that had little to do with the glare or the heat.

As impossible as it seemed, Anakin had survived Mustafar and had resumed the Sith title of Darth Vader. How could Obi-Wan have been so foolish as to bring Luke *here,* of all worlds? Anakin's homeworld, the grave of his mother, the home of his only family members . . .

Obi-Wan gripped the lightsaber he carried under his robe.

Had he driven Anakin deeper into the dark side by abandoning him on Mustafar?

Could he face Anakin again?

Could he kill him this time?

From the far side of the street, he shadowed Owen and Beru as they moved from store to store, stocking up on staples. Should he warn them about Vader? Should he take Luke away from them and hide him on an even more remote world in the Outer Rim?

His fear began to mount. His and Yoda's hopes for the future, dashed, just as the Chosen One had dashed the Jedi's hopes of bringing balance to the Force—

Obi-Wan.

He came to an abrupt halt. It was a voice he hadn't heard in years, speaking to him not through his ears, but directly into his thoughts.

"Qui-Gon!" he said. "Master!" Realizing that the locals were quickly going to brand him a madman if they heard him talking to himself, he ducked into the narrow alley between two stores. "Master, is Darth Vader Anakin?" he asked after a moment.

Yes. Although the Anakin you and I knew is imprisoned by the dark side.

"I was wrong to leave him on Mustafar. I should have made *sure* he was dead."

The Force will determine Anakin's future. Obi-Wan: Luke must not be told that Vader is his father until the time is right.

"Should I take further steps to hide Luke?"

The core of Anakin that resides in Vader grasps that Tatooine is the source of nearly everything that causes him pain. Vader will never set foot on Tatooine, if only out of fear of reawakening Anakin.

Obi-Wan exhaled in relief. "Then my obligation is unchanged. But from what Yoda told me, I know that I have much to learn, Master."

You were always that way, Obi-Wan.

Qui-Gon's voice faded, and Obi-Wan's fears began to dissipate, replaced by renewed expectation.

Returning to the dazzling light of Tatooine's twin suns, he caught up with Owen, Beru, and Luke, and kept silent watch over them for what remained of the day.

ABOUT THE AUTHORS

JAMES LUCENO is the *New York Times* bestselling author of *Star Wars: Labyrinth of Evil,* the *Star Wars: The New Jedi Order* novels *Agents of Chaos I: Hero's Trial* and *Agents of Chaos II: Jedi Eclipse,* as well as *Star Wars: The Unifying Force, Star Wars: Cloak of Deception,* and the eBook *Darth Maul: Saboteur.* He lives in Annapolis, Maryland, with his wife and youngest child.

MATTHEW STOVER is the *New York Times* bestselling author of five previous novels, including *Star Wars: Shatterpoint; Star Wars: The New Jedi Order: Traitor; Heroes Die;* and *The Blade of Tyshalle.* He is an expert in several martial arts. Stover lives outside Chicago.